I0606738

THREE PASSAGES OF ONE SOUL

SHEERU SINGH

CONTENTS

ACKNOWLEDGEMENTS

I want to take a moment to thank the friends and family who have stood unwaveringly by my side. Your encouragement, your patience, and your faith in me have been the quiet strength behind every word of this novel. I am especially grateful to **AjayNairBooks** for bringing this new edition of *Three Passages of One Soul* into the world. Their dedication and commitment have allowed this story to live and breathe once more, reaching readers in a way that honors its history, its struggles, and its heart.

As someone whose roots lie in Fiji, I feel a profound connection to the stories of the indentured labourers from India—our *girmityas.* These men and women endured hardships beyond imagination, yet carried with them courage, faith, and culture that would shape generations to come. Often, I felt the story writing itself—through whispers from my elders, through fragments of stories handed down, through the silences of memory that speak louder than words. Their voices, persistent and unyielding, guided me through every chapter.

In preparing Part 2 – *India to Fiji: The Fateful Expedition,* I immersed myself in research. I read countless articles, explored every archive I could find, and studied photographs that captured fleeting glimpses of a history too often forgotten. It saddened me to realize how little is recorded about the indentured labourers of Fiji. Too frequently, Indo-Fijian history has been neglected, brushed aside, or lost. This book is my humble attempt to shine a light on that hidden past—to give voice to the lives, struggles, and resilience of those who crossed oceans and carried hope in their hearts.

Finally, I dedicate this book to my daughter, Jaanvi Singh. She is my life, my strength, and my reason for everything I do. One day, I hope she reads these pages and feels the heartbeat of her ancestors, understands the sacrifices they made, and carries their courage within her own journey. I hope she learns from these characters, embraces their lessons, and feels a deep pride in where she comes from. And when she closes the last page, I hope she looks at me and says, *"Dad, thank you for this book."*

Part 1- Remorseful Soldier

CHAPTER I

The sun was preparing to obscure itself behind the colossal hills. The clouds, persistent in the skies, were motionless. A light breeze whistled by my sensitive ears. My stomach had butterflies swarming around in bunches. Cool perspiration trickled down the side of my face, vanishing as it reached my prickly beard. Planting my right leg on the grass, I attempted to balance the smoothbore flintlock musket on my wearisome shoulder. Only the Lord knew that my hands did not shake from apprehension. Squinting with one of my eyes, I aimed towards the faraway distance.

"Private, are you ready?" whispered a voice.

I did not know if that question was directed at me or another soldier from the battalion, so I chose not to reply. I was too focused on the equilibrium between fear and courage. My focus was destroyed when a soldier nearby began to vomit. It seemed as if nervousness had conquered him. Instead of reviving the stable attention that was needed, I looked towards my left. An expressionless face, creases on the forehead, eyes tightly shut, nose flared, and the movement of the lips uttering verses from the Bible. The soldier was in search of strength. I was surrounded by a sea of land-based soldiers, dressed in navy-blue, prepared to test their fate. Daring not to breathe openly, the soldiers waited for the Captain's signal. It felt close. I locked into focus mode, tallying an impressive dosage of braveness within myself.

"Ready... steady... steady... fire."

I fired. I reloaded, fired, reloaded, and fired again. Gunsmoke blocked my vision. I did not have an aim. I kept reloading and firing. The battlefield was full of painful screams, nasty screeches, awkward weeping, and foul language. My eardrums were aching because of the loud firing of the musket balls. The Captain yelled at the top of his lungs for his team to move forward. My feet easily lifted themselves off the ground and dashed twenty feet ahead. A soldier, following my lead, knocked me down as he fell to the ground. I turned around to witness the disturbing image. Half of the soldier's face was blown off.

His body was quivering as a pool of blood formed. I swallowed hard, feeling dryness in my throat. The vision of human bodies soaring across the field sent a chill down my spine. I quickly gathered myself up and reloaded. In combat position, I gaped past the cloud of smoke. At last, the enemy was spotted. Dressed in green-colored uniforms, the opponents hollered aggressive words in their mother tongue. I scrunched my left eye, chose a target, and pressed the trigger. Down went the enemy with his body cascading onto the earth. It was the first time I had taken someone's life. To step forward, I erased the past ten seconds of my life and reloaded. Not having a clear vision of the enemy, I was still certain that I had terminated close to a dozen lives with my faithful weapon.

No one was conscious of the time. It felt as if time had ceased, as though the only movement taking place in the universe was on this battlefield. Cannonballs were launched from both sides, leaving behind a deafening noise that shook the ground. Explosive bombshells were traded, accounting for a large number of deaths. And then unexpectedly, we encountered dead air. The firing ceased. The painful screams halted. My ears stopped vibrating. The ground stopped trembling. The silence in the air left the soldiers in a disordered state. Various thoughts entered my brain, leading to the most important question: what next? I looked at the skies only to see that the sun had disappeared. Blackness filled the landscape. The visibility of the battlefield was overly poor for soldiers to continue battling.

"Take rest and wait for dawn. But do remain alert," said the Captain.

When the word 'alert' was voiced, every soldier, including myself, resumed the combat position. My eyes wandered across the battlefield. Hundreds of unmoving bodies lay on the jagged terrain. There was an eerie feeling in the air. My brain said ambush. But was the enemy clever or cruel enough to do so?

After a long period of silence, a mysterious sound was heard in the distance. Heads tilted from side to side as thousands of eyes meandered in pursuit of the sound. As the sound got louder and louder, my ears were able to identify that it was not human. My sharp eyes finally captured the appalling sight. Out in the distance, in the middle of the battlefield, amongst the dead, lay the injured beast. The distance between the mammal and me did not allow me to distinguish its injuries. But I was able to see that the horse was having difficulty rising. My belief was that its powerful legs may have been damaged in the crossfire. The beautiful creature wore a snow coat with black spots. Surely, its owner had departed. The animal was moaning in pain. At one point it started kicking wildly. Its hooves pulverized the dirt. The cries sustained for hours. Neither side was able to put the beast out of its misery. A shot fired meant the wrong signal. A shot fired could indicate the reawakening of war. Out of the thousands of brave men on the field, no one had the nerve to release a musket ball to silence the warhorse. I strived to evade the animal's misery by imagining the faces of my parents.

Friends and close family members say that I look very similar to my father. The pointy nose, large ears, and thin, light brown hair came from the old man. I also inherited his anger and braveness. Mother provided her smile; a smile that I was grateful to have. A smile that was most recognizable by the opposite sex. Greeting a stranger with my smile often fetched me a smile back. What my parents have done for me, I will never forget. Living in the valley, I was born into a middle-class family. Father was a full-time steelworker. Within the family, he was given the title of a farmer only because he spent his evenings in the garden planting fruits and vegetables. By laboring day and night, he was able to place food on our table and clothing on our backs. In contrast, mother was a conventional housewife, ensuring that her children were genteel and conscious of their responsibilities. My siblings were both younger than I, ranging from six to twelve years of age. Living with two sisters was an honor. Both of them had an incredible amount of respect for me. If both were faced with a problem, they knew that their elder brother had solutions for their difficulties. Every so often, they'd knock on my room door and enter shyly with their innocent faces. If the younger sister had a problem, the elder sister would speak for the little one. If the elder sister had a problem, the younger sister would speak for her bigger sister. Once the problems were voiced, I would engage by softly lecturing them. I would dissect their problems and provide them with honest answers. I would use the wisest and easiest words possible for them to understand clearly. Their beautiful eyes would stare at me with astonishment. So innocent, so enthusiastic were my beloved sisters. Both of our parents forced us to attend school. If it had not been for the education I received in school, I would have probably not been able to read and write. As for the decision to join the force, I was not interrogated or disapproved of by my parents. The acceptance without objection took me by surprise. However, my mother became fairly hesitant after her initial response. After all, she was a mother and I was her only son. Even with the fear of losing me buried deep within her heart, she never blatantly uttered, "Son, I don't want you to join the military."

On the other hand, my father was proud that his son had chosen to battle for and defend his country. I still remember the night before my departure. Father ordered me to sit at the dining table. While my sisters assisted mother with the daily meal, father looked into my eyes and voiced his knowledge. "Son, listen to me carefully. You are to protect your motherland. You are to defend this country. You are to annihilate your enemy. You are to kill the enemy who may be someone else's son. A son who may have parents just like you, a son who may have siblings just like you. That son could be a husband. That son could be a father. Killing is forgiven in war. A sin that is overlooked by God," said father.

"Why?" I asked.

"Well, if you don't kill, you will be killed. When you enter the battlefield always remember that your bravery is your father, your determination is your mother, your weapon is faith, and the land you are standing on is God Himself. Never fail your country. Never fear death. If you lose your life, God will grant you another. Do me proud, son, do me proud."

Left speechless, it was the first time I beheld tears in my father's eyes.

A hand touched my shoulder. I was amazed to see that my fellow soldier was not in a combat position.

"Listen, the Captain has ordered the battalion to move ahead. As you can see, Private, the sun is faintly peeking over the hills. The enemy will be presented with a surprise. The Captain has sent his lieutenants to notify other members of the battalion. The word is being passed on from soldier to soldier. I need you to assume the military crawl position and move forward. It's time for some hand-to-hand combat. These bastards don't stand a chance."

After my turn was over, similar lines were repeated to the soldiers behind me. I looked around to see that many of the soldiers had already proceeded forward. It was a sight to behold. The massive colony of piranhas was equipped to ambush the prey. I then dropped to the ground and let my sore arms do the work. Maintaining the crawling position with both shoulders and arms lifting a heavy weapon for hours was no easy task. I felt agony whenever my hands dug into the dirt. While moving forward, I came across a dead body. I examined the deceased soldier. He, one of the adversaries, was missing the lower portion of his body. Unluckily, the man had been hit by a powerful cannonball. The torso lay with a huge quantity of buzzing flies and a nauseous pong that had the ability to give the common man a severe headache. His eyes were half-open, his face covered in a mix of dirt and blood, and his uniform was shredded to pieces. The soldier's right hand was clenched. The skin on his hand was peeling due to the extreme burn he had received from the crossfire. A flash of gold hit my eyes. I leaned near the corpse and from its hand grabbed a circular locket. Astoundingly, it was the same kind of locket my parents had gifted me when I was about to begin school. I cherished that jewel. I promised myself that as long as I live, I will never remove the precious jewel from my neck. My parents resided inside the locket. As you open it, on the left, there is a photo of my well-groomed father. On the right, one can see a photo of my ageless mother. It was hard to believe; however, the evidence of the same locket was there in front of me. The only difference was that my locket was silver and his was gold. My fingers shivered as I opened the personal item. "What could be inside the locket?" I asked myself. I struggled to open it with my cold, quivering hands. Fifteen seconds later, my fingers got the job done. Displayed on the right side of the locket was a photo of an elderly man with black greasy hair, lazy eyes, a round nose, and a thick mustache. Revealed on the left side was a photo of a mature woman with beaming eyes, thin lips, perfectly shaped eyebrows, and silky black hair. She was beautiful. Undeniably, they were the departed soldier's parents.

After forty minutes of noiselessly creeping and crawling, my arms finally buckled. I breathed hard, gasping for the moist air that embraced the battlefield. Signs of light peeked in between the trees. The rays of light indicated that the war was about to restart soon. Not too far away we heard the enemy conversing amongst themselves. Then seconds later, we heard the battalion march towards our direction.

"Soldiers... Ready... Steady... Charge," shouted my Captain.

Shotguns and muskets were fired, cannons and canisters were exploding, and bayonets were slicing flesh. Not looking back once, I weaved past the trees at full speed. One of the rivals came running in my direction, releasing a few shots from his weapon. The rage within me unleashed a blatant cry as I fired, hitting the soldier in the chest. While his wounded body collapsed, I reloaded and unleashed another shot directly into his face for assurance. From around the corner, several green-uniformed soldiers charged with bayonets. Swiftly, I took one knee and let go of the musket. Reaching behind, I pulled out my double-barrelled shotgun from the girdle along my waistline. I hoisted the gun above my shoulders and without aiming blasted a few rounds. Behind me, I heard a soldier running. So I rotated and fired a shot directly into his stomach. Clutching his wounded stomach, the enemy fell to the ground. I then bent down on my knees to search for the musket that I had placed on the ground. My hands were cold as I brushed the grass speedily. A soldier came roaring with his sharp bayonet pointed at my chest. I instantly reacted by kicking his right leg with immense force. The soldier's feet gave in and he tumbled on top of me. My next deed created a loud eruption. The blood from his chest oozed, leaving my uniform permanently decorated. "Thank God, I had the shotgun in my left hand," I said under my breath. Pushing the inactive body aside, I started to observe the battlefield. Bodies had fallen at every step of the battlefield. At last, my eyes captured a lonesome musket with a bayonet. I did not know if it was mine. I did not care. Accurately, I inserted the shotgun into my girdle and moved towards the free weapon. As soon as I grabbed the rifle, I noticed that my right thigh was surrendering. Bloodcurdling pain shot up my leg. An opponent stabbed his dagger into my thigh and then forcefully extracted it. With excessive speed, I took control of the bayonet and unleashed it into his throat. From one end to another, wide open, red body fluid gushed out. As the soldier fell backward, not too far in the distance, a cannonball hit the ground. While plunging onto the ground, dirt, stones, and grass flew into my face.

"Don't fear my soldiers... Charge ahead... Charge ahead... Victory is ours," yelled the Captain.

It was hard to believe, with so many deceased soldiers on the battlefield, my Captain was still breathing. As a matter of fact, I was amazed that I was still breathing. Following the Captain's order, I took to my feet and started running. There was no time to stop the blood that dripped from my thigh. Each time I took a stride with my right leg it felt as if someone were rubbing salt into my wound. Yet, I still considered this pain bearable. Soaring over the lifeless bodies, avoiding eye contact with the dismembered body parts, and ignoring the cloud of smoke left by the artillery, I charged with my bayonet slaying soldiers along the way. And then I noticed the ground within my range vibrate. There was no sound in my ears. A burning sensation was felt under my feet. The soles of my boots were seared. I felt my skin rip. A powerful force lifted my body off the ground. My lids closed and my eyes rolled back. And then my body crashed against the surface. My uniform melted from the burning, my helmet cracked from the impact, and my rifle flew out of my hands. The outcome was so powerful that I bounced up and down several times before coming to a full stop. I was unable to move my body. The pain was unimaginable. Pitch black. Vision revived. Sunlight irritated me. Again, pitch black. Again, vision revived. I received a clear vision of the soldiers battling on the terrain. I searched for my heartbeat. A heartbeat was felt. Loud reverberations entered my ears. I struggled to open my eyes. I saw a glimpse of my Captain nearing. Finally, pitch black.

CHAPTER 2

My lids flickered. I slowly opened my eyes. Rays of light peeked through the filthy curtains. The dust in the air sidetracked my vision. I was alive but with pain that was hard to bear. I endured the sense of warmth on my naked back as I lay with my chest on the bed. The stiff mattress did not provide comfort. My thigh, harmed during the battle, still ached. I felt a throbbing sensation bounce up and down against the walls of my brain. Memories of the battle were still intact. Automatically, my eyes shut tightly and my teeth clenched. An odd mechanism to decrease the incredible pain, I thought. But the mechanism did not work. As the muscles in my body tightened, the pain became worse. Sounds from the battlefield echoed in my ears. The cries, the shouts, the explosions, the firings, and the war horse's groaning tortured my soul. I lifted both hands from the mattress to cover my ears. Luckily, the sounds began fading. My brain was calming down. The ultimate rush of pain was more lethal than any injury I sustained during the war. Awkwardly, I reached for my lower back. I then caressed it with the back of my hand. The skin on my back felt leathery. "Hmm, it must be a third-degree burn," I said to myself. Astonishingly, it took close to a minute before I shifted my tense neck to the other side. And when I did, I beheld the unimaginable. My comrades were scattered around the premises. Many of them wounded, some deceased. The military camp was ruled by an unusual aroma; an aroma that signified death. It seemed as if the lifeless bodies were starting to rot. Across from my bed rested a departed soldier. Staring at the man, I noticed that on the left portion of his neck was a deep endless hole. Blood was dripping from the hole. The damage seemed fresh. I closed my eyes and sighed. "I thank you, God, for not letting bullets or balls penetrate my flesh and torment my insides."

My ears overheard the approach of footsteps.

"Good morning," uttered a manly voice.

Deprived of energy, I was unable to face him.

"No use turning around soldier, your lower back still needs to heal. The lower portion of your back is severely burned. Third-degree burn...It will take some time to heal."

"For God's sake," I wanted to say. "Ok sir," I said.

"Private, I was in the battle too. But you see God loves me. I came out of the war without a scrape on my body. No damaged nerves or bones, no fractures, no lost arm, no lost leg, no holes, no scars, no bruises. Thank you, God."

Feelings of jealousy controlled my senses. I tried giving him a disgusted facial expression, but my only audience was the rock-like pillow located close to my face.

"Well sir, I am a combat medic," he said proudly. "Many of us who have survived are now placed on camp to provide treatment for the injured. You see, it is good to help the less fortunate that is what God preaches. Anyways, there is a certain medical ointment that I will be applying to the wound on your right thigh. As well, I will need to clean the burn. And believe me, it will sting."

"Medic, did you say that you need to clean the burn?" Unable to hear properly after the explosion, I had to ask the medic to confirm if what I heard was accurate.

"Yes, I have been doing that for many days. I have been assigned to the southern division of the camp. You fall under this jurisdiction, thus I attend to you."

"Wait! Wait! Wait! Days...What do you mean by days?"

The medic positioned himself in front of my face. He was a young man in his late teenage years. He consisted of hefty broad shoulders, black wavy hair, a circular-shaped face, and a thin trimmed mustache above his upper lip. Seated in a crouched position, he looked directly into my eyes. One could tell he lacked valuable sleep by noticing the redness in his eyes.

"Oh I see," he murmured. "Well, the living soldiers of the battalion transported you and many other injured soldiers to the camp after the battle ended. You would not believe so, but the truth is that you have been unconscious for the past four days. Your injuries were not that severe compared to the others I have treated. Many of our soldiers have departed on these premises. Some even took their last breath as I was administering treatment. But I knew you would come alive, sooner than later."

Darkness possessed the battlefield. There was not a star in the sky to be spotted. My vision was impaired by the clouds of smoke. Roving the grounds helplessly, I felt my boots pulping the mud. Without a helmet to protect my head and ears, I listened to the outlandish sounds of the wounded soldier horse. I was in search of the animal. It needed my help. I was to put the creature out of its misery. One-shot or maybe two would do the trick. I then felt a little trickle from my ears. Coming to a stop, I touched my lobes. Blood! It was blood. Blood was dripping from my ears. My hands were now covered with gore. The wailing got louder and louder. My heart raced, my eyes wept and my ears ached. My feet were prepared to release themselves. One, two, three and I was off speeding through the blackness that was infused with whitish ghosts. I did not know which direction I was headed. I sprinted ahead, not once looking back. And then my speed declined as a result of a collision with a stable object. My body plummeted to the ground, leading my hands to act as protective shields against the wet landscape. A handful of mud washed my face. My eyelids automatically shut down. I lay there immovable for several minutes hoping that no bones were shattered. Silence pacified my eardrums. Was I deaf? I could not hear the animal bawling. Sidetracking the warhorse, I attempted to discover the object I crashed into. My tiresome feet were about to cry as they lifted me from the earth. As I stood, the smog in the air surrounded my figure. A wild stench pestered my nose. With my agitated hands, I removed the mud that covered my face. At last, I achieved cloudless visibility only to witness the most horrific spectacle. There I stood, in the darkness, with hundreds of lifeless warriors. The grounds were overfilled with deceased soldiers from the country I was to protect and the country I was to conquer. This was the aftermath of war. The object that knocked me to the ground lay in front of me, a soldier from my beloved country. His bloodied flesh was revealed through the numerous rips in his uniform. His back displayed long, thin gashes which most likely had been administered by a dagger, sword, or whip. His face was not revealed due to the positioning of his body. I knelt to roll him over. My cold hands pulled on his shredded uniform. Straightaway, my body felt numb, my hands started to quiver, my eyes widened, my stomach grumbled, breathing stalled and my brain stopped processing. I could not believe it. I had to believe it. Was I staring into a mirror? Perplexed, I was. Frightened, I was. The soldier did not resemble me, it was me. I stood there in flesh and blood, looking down at my own still body lying there in the fields of death. The difference being, simple, one is alive, the other dead.

Rapidly, I lifted my body upwards. My arms and knees were planted firmly against the mattress. Perspiration found its trail down my face. Dabbing the fiery sweat from my temple, I positioned myself to sit on the edge of the uncomfortable bed-side. The beats of my heart were loud and speedy. "What just happened? Why did that kind of dream transpire? How do I interpret those images?" So many questions were crisscrossing in my brain. These complex questions and situations placed me in a dilemma. My brain needed peace.

"You should not be sitting up like that, Private." The God-loving combat medic made an entry. "So how are you feeling today?"

"I'd like to say that I am feeling better than the last day, but I am not."

"Time will heal all. Stress is needless."

"Stress," I said in a defensive tone. "What makes you think that I am stressed?"

"I can see it in your face, you seem tense. Don't worry; you will get the opportunity to return home. Judging by your condition, I don't think you will be sent back to the war grounds."

"Are you saying that I am concerned because the force will send me to the battlefields again? Do you think I am some kind of coward?" I asked, feeling as if I had been insulted. At this point, I felt my blood boiling.

"No sir, I think you don't understand my point. I am just trying..." he paused. "Anyways, I will return in the evening to clean the burn and change the bandage. Hope you feel a wee bit better by then," he said with a tight-lipped smile.

I hurriedly replied to his saying with a meaningful apology. "I am sorry medic; forgive me for the rude behavior."

As the medic ambled on, he replied, "No worries."

"Ambiguous response," I said to myself.

During the rest of the night, thoughts loitered in my brain. At times, I felt as if my brain was about to explode. Thoughts of the unexplainable dream, thoughts of the soldiers I brutally murdered in war, thoughts of the explosion that removed me from the battlefield, thoughts of the ill-fated warhorse, and thoughts of my parents who must speculate about my whereabouts kept my brain occupied. The next morning, the sun placed itself above the hills. I noticed that the physical agony, which I have been suffering from, had decreased immensely. But mentally the agony was still present. Not to forget the container beside my bed reeked of bile which caused more of a headache. I vomited whatever food I had consumed several times during the night. Though it was not recommended, I forced myself to sit upon the recovery bed. I placed my feet on the ground, realizing that it had been a while since I properly used my limbs. I felt the urge to take a brisk walk around the camp, but the medic interfered, "Private, don't even think about it."

"Good morning sir," I welcomed him, ignoring the fact that he eradicated my privilege to move about freely.

"Good morning. And how do you feel today?" he replied.

"I feel well, that is why I am eager to take a stroll around the camp. Boredom is more painful than my injuries," I said wisely.

"Sorry, but I don't recommend that. Did you know that you are suffering from a concussion?"

"A concussion," I acted as if I had never heard of that term before.

"Yes, it's an injury to the brain that results from an impact on the head. So in your case, do you remember the cannonball? I am very sure the explosion lifted you into the air and threw you across the field. Your head must have collided against the ground leaving you unconscious." With all that said, the medic shifted to a question inquiring if I had been suffering from headaches and confusion.

I replied with a sincere, "Yes."

"It is unfortunate that you have both symptoms. But not to worry, time is the ultimate healer," he uttered with a smirk on his face. The young man continued with his usual daily routine of inspecting, cleansing and bandaging my severe burns. I noticed that the medic was indeed professional. When it came to applying the principle to practice he did not lose concentration. He kept mum; no question was asked and no comment was passed. After the medic was finished, he reported that my burns were healing fast.

"You will not be here for long. Soon the boredom will end and freedom will begin."

"Isn't that what every soldier on-premises wants to hear? Anyways, can I ask you for a favor?"

"Sure," he replied as if he was keen to assist.

"Sir, can you please lend me the tools required to write a letter," I asked hesitantly. "Ink, pen, and paper are all I need."

"Then ink, pen, and paper will surely be delivered," he replied with a chuckle.

His laughter brought a smile to my face. It had been a while since my lips curved upwards.

Dear Mother and Father,

God is watching over me. I have survived the war. I understand what you have endured for the last couple of months. I truly apologize for not writing often as I promised. I will not bore you with my excuses of why I did not fulfill this promise. There was not a single day where I did not shed tears reminiscing about you both. You both are all I have. Good news mother, I will not be returning home with major injuries. No broken bones. No lethal wounds. No memory loss. But I really do wish my memory was non-existent. The images that dwell in my brain will always remain. The cruel bloodshed that I have witnessed will never disappear. Father, I am very confused. My conscience is talking to me. We both know why I joined the army. It was to protect our motherland from intruders. If the enemy invades our country, we must destroy and eliminate that force. Yet, in this war, our country was the invader. I was the intruder, father. We stepped onto another country and battled to seize their land. I remember those faces whose lives I have taken. Like I, they was brave soldiers ready to fight for the sake of their beloved motherland. The only difference was that they were fighting for the appropriate reasons. They were not the ones with the best weaponry and firepower, they were not the ones who outnumbered us, they were not the ones who ambushed us and they were not the ones to place their feet onto our land. The battle in which your son participated was not fair, was not proper. My guilty conscience tortures me each and every second. Mother, you were right. In war, there is no real winner. The celebrations will never account for the lives that have been lost on the battlefield. As you both read this, you will be able to notice that my feelings are running wild. But I will be fine. I hope. I honestly don't know when I will be coming home. The medic who has been treating me informed me that it will be soon. If you both are wondering why am I being treated, don't worry? I have a few minor injuries which I will tell you about when I come home. Due to these injuries, I don't think I will be permitted to revisit the battlefield any time soon. Life is strange, is it not? There was a time when I dreamt of becoming a soldier. Today I curse myself, "Anything, but not a soldier." Father, don't fret; I will never let you drop your head in shame. As long as this war continues, I will follow my orders. Regardless of knowing that we are fighting for the wrong reasons, I will serve my country. Lastly, I cannot wait to return home. I do realize that harvesting season is around the corner. Father, I am excited to assist you with the reaping. And mother, I am looking forward to your delicious cooking. I look forward to the fried potatoes, roasted yam, tender baked chicken, sweet porridge, tasty sponge cakes, and crisp corn gathered from our very own backyard. Oh heavens, my mouth is watering already. Anyways, I miss you both dearly. Please tell my sisters that I love them. And don't forget to pray for the families who have lost their sons as a result of this war.

Your son,

Richard.

CHAPTER 3

The next morning was shaded by a rare flock of clouds. I looked through the triangular-shaped openings of the tent only to perceive that there was no sign of radiant hues. No one expected such dullness. Was it a sign? Within an hour of my rising, the medic proceeded with his morning routine. The common, "Good morning, how are you?" was exchanged before the washing and changing started. As usual, the medic was in a vibrant mood.

"Medic, it seems like my wounds have healed. I don't feel as much pain as I used to."

"What about your brain?" he questioned. "Sometimes it takes a long time to heal from a concussion. I know you have a minor concussion, but that does not mean you will not experience the regular side effects. These kinds of things should never be rushed."

"I understand. But I do feel that I am ready to move forward. I cannot just lie here on the bed, day and night. I should be assigned to the battlefields or sent home to my family," I replied aggressively.

The medic stood his ground, looking at me with an impassive expression. His face remained unflustered and his eyes were fixed on the letter near my bed.

"Pardon my manners. I forgot to thank you for your kindness."

"What do you mean?" he asked.

"Well, thank you for the writing materials required for the letter."

"Have you completed the letter?"

"Yes, I have."

"Alright then, hand it over."

"Sorry, I don't understand," I said with a confused expression on my face.

"I will take care of it."

"It is sitting on the counter near my bed."

"Is your address on the letter?"

"Yes, but you don't need to undergo all this trouble for me."

"What trouble? I was right, your brain needs more time to heal," he replied with a mocking laugh.

My face lit up with a smile but it was invisible due to the extensive growth of my facial hair, which descended to cover most of my upper lip. "It is definitely time for a shave," I said to myself.

The medic continued, saying that he would ensure that the letter reached my parents in a day or two. I started to feel as if the medic wanted to be my friend. Or was it that I needed a companion? I remember that before starting my journey to become a soldier my father advised me never to make friends within the regiment. Father expressed that the loss of a close mate during the war may result in serious damage to a person, emotionally and mentally. "The brain should be free from all thoughts when in battle," he used to repeat.

I never overlooked my father's words. To this day, I did not share a friendly relationship with any of the soldiers in my battalion. Their names I did not care to know. My name they did not care to ask. I was by myself, with a focused mind, always prepared for battle. But the medic I was indebted to. The soldier did much for me that I could not disregard.

"Please don't mind sir, but what is your name?"

"Given or Surname?"

"Witty response," I said under my breath. "Let's go with your first name."

"You can call me Walter."

I reached out my hand and said, "My name is Richard."

He acknowledged with a firm handshake. "Okay Richard, please hand over the letter."

Dead bodies covering the grounds of the battlefield, bullets piercing the flesh leaving uncountable holes in the body, the painful jolting of the worthless beast, and the spirited warriors uttering prayers flashed like episodes in my brain. I realized that I was conscious when I felt tears seep down my face. It was the middle of the night, pitch dark, not a footstep to be heard, not a word to be spoken. From the wounded, I was the only person alert. Did I just rise from a dream? My brain did not cooperate. I needed answers. "Am I losing my mind?" I asked myself. I lay helpless in bed for hours until sleep took control of my brain and body.

Commotion filled my ears. Loud chanting interfered with my sleep. Carefully, I lifted myself off the bed. All the injured soldiers on the premises were clueless about what was happening around them. There were deafening cheers, energetic clapping, unbearable singing, and endless boasting coming from outside the tent. Many of the soldiers, including me, walked to the opening of the tent to steal a peek at the happenings around us.

"The war is over, we are victorious, we are victorious," cried a proud soldier as he ran into the tent.

An outpour of merriment, followed by strong handshakes and manly hugs, filled the tent.

"We are conquerors. Their country is ours now," said one of the lieutenants.

I soon realized that I was the only emotionless man on the premises. My brain was corrupted with questions, such as: what have we gained? Have we lost more than what we have gained? What about the lives I have taken? How do I get rid of this remorse? Do I still have a soul? If so, how do I redeem my soul? How can I live with such disturbing experiences from the battlefield? Do I deserve to live? Do I deserve happiness? Do I want to face my parents after what I have experienced? Once again, I asked myself, "Am I losing my mind?"

"I promise that this will be short. It is finally time for us men to return home. The war is over, our enemy has fled. The land that we stand on belongs to me, to you, to all of us. I know that we have lost a countless number of men in this war. But if it wasn't for those men who sacrificed their lives, we'd perhaps have lost this war. My fellow soldiers, our country has gotten bigger and stronger. We are the conquerors and forever we'll remain the conquerors." The Captain's speech was received with a booming ovation. "Bear with me now; there is one more task to be completed. In regards to this matter, I will speak to some of you in person," added the Captain. His last couple of lines were either purposely ignored or not heard due to the loud celebrations. The soldiers were becoming crazier by the minute.

After eating the distasteful food offered, I sat in the corner of my bedside. I did not indulge myself in rum drinking, song singing, and boastful talking.

"Sorry, Richard! Sorry, I could not attend to you in the morning. I am sure you know why," Walter spoke busily. "I have so much to do, so many patients to attend to."

"I understood that as soon as you came by my bedside."

"How so?" he asked.

"You did not greet me with your regular, 'How do you feel today?'"

We both shared a laugh as he initiated the medical checkup.

"So did you hear?"

"Hear what?" I asked with interest.

"The ones in command have requested various Captains from the region to assign their soldiers, who are in good condition, for a special task."

"And what may this special task be?"

"Well, as you know the war has come to an end. So who knows how many bodies are to be buried."

"Are you saying that our men will be assigned to bury the corpses of the soldiers who lost their lives in the war?"

"Unfortunately, yes. Dead soldiers from our country will be returned to their families for a proper burial. As for the dead soldiers with green uniforms, they will be placed six feet under the ground."

"What the hell!" I said with anger in my voice. "For the love of God, should they not get the same respect we do? Is this the honor they receive for striving to protect their motherland? How will their family know about their death? How will their souls rest in peace without a proper burial?" My blood was roasting and my mouth was erupting with loud vocals. I became so vociferous that our neighboring soldiers took notice. Walter stood aside. He remained wordless until the Captain stepped in.

"I heard loud noises. Are you both still celebrating over the hellacious victory?" asked the Captain.

Neither Walter nor I replied to his question.

"Here's the ruthless warrior. You're a remarkable soldier, young man. I saw you on the war grounds and I must say that you are impressive. You have executed many of their soldiers. I am very proud of you." The Captain's remarks stabbed at my brain and large portions of remorse gushed out.

"Damn that cannonball, it got the best of you. If it was not for that massive explosion you'd still be dropping countless bodies on the war grounds," said the Captain with no guilt shown.

I found his words to be relentless. But there was very little I could say or do. After all, he was my superior. Whatever he said, I was to obey. That is why, when he ordered that I be prepared for the next morning to bury the bodies which lay on the battlefield, I did not protest. The Captain asked Walter if I was in good condition to fulfill this particular duty. Walter replied in a husky voice, "Yes Captain, he will be able to fulfill the duty."

"Very well then, Private, you will be assigned under Lieutenant Williams," said the Captain as he studied my appearance. "You will meet him at six on the dot tomorrow morning, at the front of your tent. Now please carry on with the celebrations. Good day, gentlemen." The Captain left my area and proceeded to the next soldier who seemed to look durable and in good condition. I was sure that the Captain was set with his dreadful proposal, and like me, one more soldier would not be able to reject the command.

The celebrations persisted all night long. I felt as if I was the lone soul who did not want to participate. Surrounded by evil laughs, wicked grins, clever winks, frequent handshakes, strange dancing, and excessive drinking, I felt completely out of place. The time was ticking and rest was essential. I did not want my brain to focus on the abysmal morning duty. So, I tried forcing myself to sleep.

During the lukewarm night, I tossed and turned in search of a homely resting nest that would suspend my consciousness. "In order to fall asleep, I will have to close my eyes," I said to myself. But whenever I closed my eyes, vivid images of the gruesome slayings appeared. The entire night, I battled a tiresome war with my conscience until the sunlight made its entry past the stale curtains.

Was my head aching from the concussion, or from lack of sleep? I did not know.

"Rise and shine. How are you?"

"Good morning, Walter. Why are you here so early in the morning?"

Walter's eyes dropped to the floor. "I am very sorry about yesterday, Richard."

"What do you mean?" I questioned.

"I could have lied and helped you escape the unpleasant duty assigned by our Captain. I did not need to say that you were in good health. I was not thinking straight at that time. I get very nervous when a higher authority is nearby. You will not believe it, but the Captain inquired about the health of all the soldiers in my unit. For him, as long as the soldier's arms and legs are in working condition there should be no reason for that person not to fulfill the assigned duty."

I beamed at Walter and said, "No need to be sorry. My arms and legs are indeed in working condition. If the superiors want me to bury dead soldiers from another country, then I will bury dead soldiers from another country. But I tell you my friend, every grave that I dig, I will ensure that it is six feet deep.

"How will that make a difference?"

"That is the only form of respect I can provide to the lifeless bodies."

"Then, I will do the same."

I noticed a smirk on the medic's face. "Did the Captain order you to fulfill this duty as well?"

"No," he replied.

I kept silent for a couple of seconds. "Did you volunteer?"

Walter intervened, "I am blameworthy. It is because of me that you and many of the other injured soldiers have to complete this disrespectful task. I am at fault here. The Captain questioned and I answered. It was my answers that led to his decision to assign the soldier. God knows I have sinned, Richard. My penance is to join you and the other soldiers in this dreadful act."

"You talk about sin, then what about the lives you have taken on the battlefield? Will God forgive us or will God punish us? How does God judge us now, knowing that we have killed other human beings?"

The medic was left aghast. Hesitant to open his mouth, Walter replied, "We'll have to suffer for our wrongdoings."

"I already am," I replied.

CHAPTER 4

For those who don't know me, I am Lieutenant Williams. Every soldier in line should know what they are here for today. If you are ignorant of your duties, please step forward. And those who do step forward, listen carefully, because I will not repeat myself."

Not the slightest movement was made. No soldier dared to move forward. We remained idle, our eyes fixed on the lieutenant's mouth, waiting for his next set of lines.

"Good, so that means everyone understands their assignment. We'll have to march to the battlefield where the fallen soldiers are located. It is our responsibility to lay them to rest six feet under the ground. On the way, if you have questions, please don't ask. But I will answer the one question that lingers in the minds of every soldier here: Why have you been chosen? Well, because you were not there during the final battle in which we claimed victory. The soldiers who survived that battle are long gone. Yes, that is right. Those fortunate bastards have already been sent home. I am sure that once we complete our duties today, only then will we be permitted to retreat home to our loving families. With that in mind, let's not waste more time. Please collect your shotguns, spades, and handkerchiefs. Once the items are collected, I need you to line up in front of me, single-file, please. From now on, it is my order that you must follow. If my order is defied, action will be taken," said Lieutenant Williams, his tone threatening.

In single-file order, we marched on the slightly uphill landscape for at least thirty minutes while the beaming sun irritated our eyes. Once we arrived at the peak of the miniature hills, a foul smell assaulted our nostrils. As the smell grew stronger, we heard a buzzing noise. Over the slope was a picture that truly defined calamity. Millions of rotten flies swarmed, thousands of lifeless bodies lay scattered, and hundreds of operative bodies completed their shameful duty. The cold bodies—some whole, some in halves, and some in many pieces—were decorated with tiny black spots whizzing around. Once the active bodies came near the inactive bodies, the tiny black spots hovered off into the distance.

Lieutenant Williams and his soldiers looked on, their jaws dropping. I was the only soldier who was not traumatized by the alarming scene. This specific picture had appeared in my dreams a few times before. Viewing this spectacle, I was not dumbfounded; instead, I felt disheartened. I looked over my left shoulder to see the reaction on Walter's face. His disappointed eyes confronted mine. He said in a whisper, "This is not right; this is not what I had expected."

His words confused me. "What do you mean?"

"Look at the size of those graves. They are close to fifteen feet deep and fifteen feet wide. The bodies are dumped carelessly into the holes. I was expecting each soldier to have a grave of his own." Walter looked very distressed after seeing the wrongful doings.

"At ease, men," said Lieutenant Williams.

For soldiers, the word 'ease' meant that it was time to take the one-knee position.

"I am not happy with what I see," the lieutenant voiced. "It seems like there has been some kind of change that I have not been informed about." Lieutenant Williams pondered for a second and then continued, "I expected the deceased soldiers to receive a proper burial. Anyway, I will get to the bottom of this. Soldiers, cover your nose and mouth with the handkerchiefs provided. And let's proceed to our destination."

As we paraded to the mournful fields, I noticed that the grass bore stains of black and red. The black resulted from all the shelling and bombing, and the red from the blood of the men who lost their lives. Unwanted time was given to observe more of the disaster while the lieutenant inquired about the cruelty taking place on the field. My eyes were fixated on a mutilated head, partially burnt and abundantly torn. Numerous dismembered body parts were scattered across the war grounds. "Perhaps that is one of the reasons why the soldiers dropped so many bodies into those big, deep holes," I said to myself.

Once again, the ruminations hammered on the walls of my brain, shooting pain from various directions. The massive headache lasted a few minutes. Once viewing the uneasiness on my face, Walter asked if I was in good health. Before I could reply, Lieutenant Williams charged in.

"Ok, men, I will say this once because I hate repeating myself. Therefore, listen—and listen well. Many of you, including me, assumed that we'd be burying one corpse at a time. But that is not the case. Yesterday, the higher authorities made the decision that we are to place as many bodies as we can into deep and wide graves. So, I will assign a group of ten soldiers to certain areas on the field. As you can see, we have close to one hundred soldiers involved with the burying. I don't want you to engage with them in any kind of manner. You will be listening and reporting to me. You are my responsibility. I will be checking up on my groups regularly. Remember: the sooner we finish this duty, the sooner we will be home with our families."

Our lieutenant wasted no time in placing his soldiers into groups and assigning them to particular sections. I thanked the Lord for placing Walter and me in the same group. The brief feeling of elation disappeared as I held the spade firmly in my hands. My disposition abruptly changed as I felt sadness rise from the bottom of my feet to the surface of my head. Walter, I, and my fellow soldiers discussed a strategy. Our first assigned section consisted of at least fifty lifeless bodies. Fifty lifeless bodies versus ten spirited bodies—we were surely outnumbered. We divided ourselves into pairs, resulting in five different groups. Each pair was to dig a grave able to fit no fewer than ten bodies. We ten soldiers were assertive that our strategy would help us maintain a stable pace. Besides, with this strategy, the load was equally distributed.

The sound of the spade grinding the soil assaulted my ears. After the first thirty minutes, my arms became numb, and the overflow of perspiration blurred my vision. My facial hair felt moistened. I glared at the sun, endeavoring not to curse it. There was not a cloud in the sky. I was certain that every soldier dressed in a blue uniform wished for the "God of Rain" to bathe them with precipitation. If that were so, the soil would absorb the rain, making it easier to penetrate with our spades. Unfortunately, the chance of rain was very little. I looked over at the medic, who was using his arms less and feet more, kicking the dirt like a wild man.

"I expected this duty to punish me mentally, but I was not expecting it to punish me physically," said Walter.

"Walter, if you don't know, we do have spades," I said jokingly.

Instead of laughing, he shook his head in frustration.

"You know, Richard, these handkerchiefs are not helping either. No matter how tightly I tie it around my face, the smell of rot still enters my nose."

Wanting to evoke confidence in him, I added, "We're almost done with this grave, Walter. Don't quit. Another thirty minutes of labor remain, so you need to stop falling behind."

"You know what, soldier? You will make a good captain one day. Honestly, I can see you as my superior," said Walter in a humorless tone.

"That day will never come."

"Why do you say that?"

"Simple. I will not be a part of the force. This is the last duty I will fulfill, the last command I will obey, and the last day I will be a soldier."

"What will you do in life once you depart?"

"To be honest, I don't know what I will do or where I will go."

"You behave as if your life has ended."

"Perhaps it has. The pain and guilt I have received from this war is all that remains. I hate myself for what I have become—a murderer. You know, Walter, sometimes I feel that I am not worthy of life. Sometimes, I think about why I continue with such a devastating life. Sometimes, I wish that God could hold out His hand and pull me towards Him."

"Wait a minute, Richard! We fought for our country, for our people, for the future of our people. From this battle and our victory, we have gained power. I understand that we have ended the lives of many humans, but that is what is required from us to protect our motherland."

"Are you sure?" I raised my voice. "Were we the ones protecting our land, or were they protecting theirs? We stepped onto their land to defeat and conquer."

"Let's not argue over this, Richard. I will pray for you, for God to show you the correct path."

I knew I should not, but I laughed at his statement.

"Don't laugh; you have a family, Richard. If your family sees you in this condition, they will be unhappy."

The medic's comment hit directly at the heart. As we conversed, the motion of our arms never stopped. We both violently drove our spades into the dirt.

"I sure hope somebody will help us out of the hole we have dug," Walter said.

"Don't worry. I saw the Lieutenant with a large bag containing a rope. I am certain he will put it to use for this situation."

"This seems like it's fifteen feet deep and fifteen feet wide," I said.

"I agree," Walter replied.

Before I could raise my voice, Walter screamed, "Anyone there? Get us out of this hole! Lieutenant, we have completed our first grave. Please drop the rope!"

After five minutes of screaming at the top of our lungs, Lieutenant Williams came to our rescue. The extensive rope was dropped, and Walter and I were pulled to the surface. We then acknowledged our soldiers for their help. I looked around but could not see

Lieutenant Williams; it seemed as if he had left to inspect another team in a different area. Walter counted the number of bodies that had fallen in our assigned section.

"The total count is thirteen," he said.

Now came the difficult part. The dead were dragged by their hands and feet to the burial site. I did not dare to look at their faces as I used my remaining strength to toss them into the grave. Walter bent down to his knees and clasped his stomach. He then forcefully vomited whatever he had digested earlier that morning. The medic stood, uttering in a frail voice,

"God will not forgive me. I can't believe I vomited into the grave where these deceased soldiers will rest."

"You will be fine. Take some water," I replied.

At that moment, it felt as if our roles had swapped. On the campgrounds, Walter was my caretaker, and on the war grounds, it felt like I was his.

"See, Richard, I don't think God will punish me for ending the lives of other soldiers during the battle. But God will not forgive me for what I am doing right now. I don't care if these soldiers were our enemy; these bodies deserve to be sent back home to their families. If that is not possible, at least they should be buried properly. This is not proper."

"Are you not a firm believer of Christianity?" I asked

"Yes, I am, but why do you ask?"

"I think you forgot. Thou shall not kill. Our sins will not be overlooked. We will mourn, if not in this life, then probably in the next life."

"Sorry, Richard, I don't believe in rebirth. Wait... Are you not a Christian?" he asked, scratching his head.

Ignoring his question, I proceeded and explained how rebirth has nothing to do with religion. "Reincarnation is based on karma. It is our good and bad actions that determine our fate."

Walter was taken aback by my outlook. He interrupted, "So, will you be reborn?"

"I think so. This life itself is not enough for what I have done. I am suffering now, and I will suffer then."

"Are you serious?" asked Walter, his face on the verge of erupting into laughter.

"Hmm," I murmured. "I foresee an unjust journey—a journey with trials and tribulations, hardships, and separations."

As the day continued, Walter and I embraced a machinelike rhythm, relentlessly burrowing, developing the grave to our finest ability. Once the grave was complete, we removed ourselves from the deep hole and began gathering the motionless bodies. With the insufficient energy left in our bodies, we rolled the corpses into the hole, not caring in what manner they were placed. The bodies lay one on top of another. Our goal was to fill the grave with as many bodies as we could.

When the dead soldiers were placed to rest, Walter shut his eyes and muttered words to his beloved God. As God blessed the souls of these dead men, we resumed our duty, covering the grave with the heaps of dirt that we had initially dug. This routine repeated as we carried on forming many different burial sites. The exhaustion we suffered turned us into devils. After all, we were only human.

Walter and I were compelled to invent our own shortcut. Whenever our arms became tired of lobbing the dirt above our heads for it to land on the surface, we began to lob it to a selected corner. Unluckily, the plan failed because, when we returned to the land, we did not have a sufficient amount of dirt to cover the bodies. Regrettably, this increased our workload, as we had to dig more dirt from the surface until the grave was entirely covered.

"Are you hungry, Richard?"

"No, but I know you are."

Walter chuckled.

"Do you remember the days and nights spent on the battlegrounds? We went on for several days without a proper meal. Today, I had no breakfast, and still, I don't feel hungry. Even when I rested in bed with my injuries, I ate once a day. That was plenty to keep my stomach content."

Our aimless talks continued until I observed the sun hiding its face behind the oversized hills in a sedative, waning light. Walter gasped for air. "My ears are impatiently waiting for the lieutenant's order to stop. I cannot bear this pain much longer, Richard."

"We are close to sundown. In an hour, we will retire. Finish the grave you are working on. If you are about to begin a new grave, please don't. Instead, you can help other soldiers in the group. I will return soon to gather you men for our departure," said Lieutenant Williams.

Walter and I had just finished a grave, so we tramped forward to see if other soldiers needed help. Dragging our spades across the land, we encountered a group of soldiers from our unit. They were madly hacking the dirt with their spades. The grave looked as if it were twenty-five feet wide and ten feet deep. On the right side lay a pile of at least forty dead bodies. Our comrades were so engrossed in the excavating that none of the four noticed Walter and me approaching.

"Why must we labor for these sons of bitches?" said one of the soldiers. Unexpectedly, his rage took over, and like an untamed beast, he started hitting a dead body. With his massive boots, he repeatedly stomped on the pale face.

"Tame yourself, soldier. Have some decency," I said, frustration in my voice.

The soldier listened. He gave his feet some rest only to look into my eyes and retort. "Who in the hell are you to order me, you bloody arsehole?"

The insult did not affect me. Walter barged in, "We just came to see if you men need help in finishing this grave."

"Sure, the more hands at work, the better," said the other soldier, who appeared humane.

As I put my spade to work, the savage glared and ground his teeth. I kept calm and did not retort. The man had broad shoulders and a massive chest, perceptible whenever he inhaled and exhaled. His forehead was burnt by the frying sun. The soldier had black, piercing eyes, a stubble-like beard, and a distinct jawline. Filled with arrogance and acrimony, he behaved as if he were the ruler of all lands and people. He probably assumed his bold exterior intimidated me, but it did not. I endeavored not to produce feelings of hate and anger—regular feelings expressed by all, which I neither needed nor wanted, feelings that must be controlled. As this savage looked threateningly into my eyes, I felt an urge to release the violent flames burning within me. I was not sure I had the ability to control them.

One by one, we hauled the cold bodies into the grave. A thudding sound emerged as the corpses banged against the earth. The savage had the strength of a bull. He gripped the bodies and launched them into the hole with ease. He did not have a pinch of sorrow in his heart, nor a hint of regret in his mind, for the expired soldiers. After tossing a body into the grave, he made it routine to expel the slimiest spit into the grave. The other soldiers on his team did not pay attention to him. Either they were very involved in their work, or they did not want to converse with the ogre. I was certain that every conversation with him led to a dispute.

During this period, Walter searched for the lieutenant. "He said he will return soon. The sun is beginning to disappear."

"He is a wise man. Lieutenant Williams will surely come before darkness invades the war grounds," I replied. I soon noticed that only a few more bodies remained to be thrown into the grave.

"There is no more room left in the grave," said Walter.

The ogre yelled at him, "What do you mean there is no more room, you twat?"

"Mind your language, soldier," Walter defended himself.

"We'll have to make room for these remaining bodies." The ogre rushed to the grave full of bodies and started assorting. He used his bulging arms to move the deceased, creating plenty of space for the remaining two bodies.

"Wilson, hand me those poor bastards," he demanded.

"As you wish, Brock," replied the trim soldier Wilson as he handed the lifeless bodies to the savage.

"So the brute has a name," I said under my breath.

Brock grabbed, rammed, squeezed, and positioned the dead bodies in order to complete the task. The man beamed with pride as he ordered his team to assist him out of the grave. Within seconds of his exit, we began pouring the soil into the grave.

Seeing this, Brock shouted at the top of his lungs, "Wait... Wait... Wait. I will show these brave warriors some respect," he said, looking directly into my eyes. He stood in front of the burial site, flashing his audacity. The man lowered his arms and, with his fingers, carefully unzipped his pants. By then, all the onlookers were conscious of his insulting action.

An explosion of rage and recklessness dominated my temperament. A volcanic eruption erupted from my heart. My spade dropped, and my fists clenched. I inhaled the raw, misty air and exhaled firestorms. With my eyes bulging from their sockets, I witnessed the diverse reactions of my teammates. One soldier had surprise written all over his face, another displayed a cunning smile, and Walter shook his head in disgust. My feet sprang into a full charge, my voice burst with a forceful cry, my heart pulsated riotously, and my intense eyes were fixed on the depraved man named Brock.

Walter's arms tried to block my path but were instantly rejected. The voices that warned me were now left far behind. The conscience I relied on to guide me had disappeared. Brock did not expect it. I leaped forward and clobbered him with my knuckles. A fracturing sound emerged as my fist collided with his jaw. The sequence continued with my forearm extending from the waistline to the upper chest, allowing my fist to connect with a devastating uppercut to the bottom portion of his jaw. Brock fell backward.

I heard footsteps approaching. Laughter occupied the grounds. I then looked at my right hand. It was smeared with blood. While rubbing the blood on my uniform, I felt numbness in the hand. The hand began to swell, my knuckles turning blue. "Please don't get up, please don't get up," I chanted to myself.

"Finally, he got what he deserved."

"What a blow."

"Get up, Brock. I want to see a good fight."

"Call for the higher authorities; we need to stop this," was one of the various lines uttered by the soldiers on location.

My stomach quivered with fear. How I wished that the devil would not rise. But one thinks of the devil, and the devil rises. Brock swayed his pate. The dizziness from the blow made it challenging for him to stand. Lines of blood dripped from the corner of his mouth.

"You will pay for this, arsehole," he said, nursing his injured jaw. Brock stomped the earth, leaving deep footprints behind, as he dashed toward my stagnant figure. With slightly bent knees, I firmly planted my feet on the earth. It did not work; Brock pounced. His powerful shoulders crashed against my ribs, knocking the wind out of me. Within seconds, he and I were both on the ground wrestling. He behaved like a hungry animal caged for years. He bombarded me with punches—left, right, and center. Most of them were blocked with my forearms, which angered him even more.

A powerful force came over me, and with a burst of energy, I lifted his body off mine. I crawled, as I had on the battlefield, to gain a bit of leeway.

"Richard," cried the medic. "What are you doing? You must stop this." Walter lifted me from the ground, carrying me further away from the dangerous man. At that moment, lethal waves of pain seized my brain. I tightly grasped my forehead, hoping the soreness would diminish.

"Oh no... Please no... Don't, please don't... Lose the weapon," Walter said, fear in his voice.

Not giving much importance to the severe headache, I faced the ogre. Brock managed to form a smile despite his injured jaw. With his right arm, solid as a rock, he aimed the shotgun. I waited as he waited. I waited for my life to flash before my eyes or a dark tunnel to lead me into the sacred light; neither appeared.

"What was he waiting for? Was I to plead for my life? Not a chance," I said under my breath. Perhaps he waited for me to draw my weapon and challenge him so he would have a legitimate excuse to release a bullet into my flesh. The crowd that formed around us went silent. For once, peace had descended upon the battlegrounds.

At that moment, my mind overflowed with memories of bloodshed caused by my own hands during the war. In my heart, my family lived. But the pain and guilt I suffered because of my sins overcrowded my heart, leaving no space for my loved ones. With a combination of repentance and desperation, I stepped forward.

Walter grabbed my uniform and said, "Please stop; the situation can worsen. You can get killed, Richard."

My ears ignored every word; the sense of sound had been deliberately eradicated. Breaking out of Walter's hold, I stepped forward.

"If you come closer, I will shoot you, you bastard," yelled Brock.

I stared at his shotgun, pointed directly at my chest. "I wish he would shoot me right in the heart. That one bullet to the heart would put me out of my misery," I said to myself.

"I am serious, you prick, I will shoot."

I listened to his soaring voice, yet the words were proudly ignored. On the verge of being shot and killed, I was seized with a craze of not retreating. Eventually, my feet came to a halt, and I stood only eight feet apart from the brute. In the minds of others, this was a suicidal move. In my view, it was the proper move. I had no fear of death.

"Shoot right here," I pointed at my heart. Instantly, I noticed panic in his eyes. Thus, in a provoking manner, I said to him, "Are you a coward? Fire your weapon, soldier."

Brock's hand started to tremble.

"What are you waiting for? Ready, steady, fire!" I shouted.

His face expressed awkwardness. He stood there without releasing his weapon. Brock was silent and immobile, the shotgun still targeting my body.

"Don't worry, soldier, I will help you." Without a second thought, I reached behind and withdrew my shotgun. I aligned the weapon with my shoulders, tilted my head slightly to the right, tightly shut my left eye, and aimed with the support of both hands. By extracting my firearm, I was certain he would send me to hell within the next five seconds.

Finally, he regained movement and quickly placed his index finger on the trigger. I was prepared to accept death. I counted in my head. One... Two... Three... Four... Five... Blast!

A shot was fired. A bullet was released. The cool breeze hit my emotionless face. The booming sound echoed in my ears. I waited for my body to develop some kind of numbness. I waited for the pain to rule every inch of me. I waited for my brain to terminate and lead me into a dark tunnel. I waited for the lights to turn off so my conscience would no longer remain. Nothing of that sort occurred.

The shot alarmed Brock, causing his shotgun to drop. As I perceived the weapon descend to the ground, the lieutenant uttered threats from a distance. I hurriedly turned to face Lieutenant Williams. His right hand, holding a shotgun, was pointed to the sky.

"If you don't stop your disgraceful acts, I swear to God, I will shoot you both in the arse." He stomped past me to challenge the ogre. "I have been monitoring your actions since I arrived. I am confident that you are the one who initiated all this trouble."

The once-raging lion stood uselessly like a feeble little mouse while Lieutenant Williams lectured him with precision. The lieutenant's oration ranged from how soldiers on duty should not behave in such an unfitting manner to how, if he were in charge of Brock, he would have court-martialed him.

"Son, tell me the name of your Captain. Where is the negligent person in charge of you?" our lieutenant questioned the brute.

Brock desperately searched for his leader among the crowd of blue uniforms.

Walter whispered in my ear, "I know for sure that whoever is in charge of Brock is hiding behind one of his soldiers. Why bear such an embarrassment?"

"Soldier, your disrespectful act was captured by my sharp eyes. I was distant from this burial site, which is why it took a while to arrive on the scene. If I had been there when you chose to urinate on the dead bodies, I may have castrated you on the spot," said the lieutenant in a threatening manner. "If you show your face again, The Lord knows what I would do to you. Now be gone."

With no time to waste, Brock disappeared into the crowd. That was the last I saw of him.

The diverse feelings that stirred within my heart had no equilibrium. What I had wished for—was that appropriate? Was I being selfish and insensitive? Did God have something else planned? Was it His orders that I must follow? Was my suicidal act a method to evade life itself? Why is it necessary to continue? Should I pull the trigger and unleash a bullet into my head?

Without rest, question after question surged, in search of answers. It felt as if my brain were about to explode.

CHAPTER 5

Blackness eventually prevailed, and it was time for all the soldiers *toiling* on the battlegrounds to leave. Our superior ordered us to huddle so he could voice his instructions.

"Soldiers, as you can see, with your difficult labor we have turned the battlefield into a graveyard. There remains a high count of bodies to be buried, but that shall be left for the next day." Lieutenant Williams paused, *smiling to reveal his teeth*. "Now let us march back to the camp in single file. My stomach is growling," he added, inducing some of the men to chuckle.

How in the world the lieutenant guided us back to the military camp, we did not know. We trekked in the dark, holding onto one another, not knowing what the next step might lead to. But the next step was always correctly predicted by Lieutenant Williams. He helped the team avoid steep holes, long canals, huge boulders, and muddy swamps. By the time we reached our destination, some of the men fell to their knees from exhaustion. Many were prepared to lay flat on their beds, while others were excited to get their hands on some food.

"Before you men carry on, I advise you to bathe first." The lieutenant's advice seemed more like a command. All nine soldiers from my team, including me, returned our shotguns and spades, then hurried to the well. The cold water splashed against my skin, instilling alertness in my body. The chill relaxed my head. I felt renewed. After the short-lived bath, Walter and I decided to connect with our fellow soldiers where food was being served.

"Let there be a change for once," said Lieutenant Williams, sounding dissatisfied. "Stew, stew, stew—that is all we have been receiving since we set foot in the camp. For all the hard work we put in, we at least deserve roast pig and the finest rum. Don't you agree, my comrades?"

Walter added, "Now that would be divine."

Standing in line with a steel plate and spoon in hand, the lieutenant leaned over to whisper *words of reassurance* into my ear. "Not to worry. If questioned about the incident, I will take care of it."

If Lieutenant Williams believed that his words would relieve my anxiety, he was totally wrong. Fear did not exist within me. If I were hauled into court, deprived of my so-called honorable duties, or ousted from the military force, I would have no regrets. At that moment, feelings of cynicism ruled my thoughts. Once supplied with bountiful portions of stew, we seated ourselves to satisfy our empty stomachs. The stew looked gooier than other days. With such a large portion, a soldier might find only two or three pieces of meat, the rest being stale vegetables. At times, I thought the food served was best suited for animals.

At that moment, I created the perfect description for us soldiers in the military: We are animals that kill when threatened. We are animals that kill to protect our territory. We are animals that kill to fulfill our needs. Thus, being served this kind of meal was acceptable.

It was a triumph to locate a seat in the hall during the evening, due to the high volume of soldiers wanting to feed.

"It is either that you are completely mad or extremely brave," said Lieutenant Williams as we sat in the corner of the hall, trying our best to digest the repulsive stew.

Walter added a clever remark, "Perhaps he wanted to get rid of himself."

I gave Walter a menacing stare.

"Hmm, whatever the reason may be, one needed to rise and punish that arse. I am honored to meet such a daring soldier," said the lieutenant as he raised his cup of rum.

I remained silent, concentrating hard on the remaining stew. Keeping in mind how dreadful it tasted, I wondered if I would be able to eat what was left on my plate. In order for my stomach not to cry for nourishment during the night, I had no other choice but to gobble whatever remained on my steel plate.

"So what time are we to rise in the morning, lieutenant?" asked Walter.

Lieutenant Williams burst into laughter, spraying our faces with the rum he was chugging. Walter was not able to interpret the reason behind the laughter. "Will we not leave for the battlegrounds in the morning to bury the remaining bodies?" he asked.

"I believe that tomorrow every soldier in this military camp will have the privilege to return home."

At first, his words flew above our heads. We snubbed his comment, feeling that the lieutenant was fooling us.

"As I entered the hall, I bumped into the Captain. In his very own words, he indicated that the soldiers of this camp will be relieved from their duties soon. As of tomorrow, several other military camps will be assigned to bury the dead soldiers. So our chances of being sent home look promising," said the lieutenant.

Walter's face lit up with joy. I had never seen my friend in such high spirits. "Did you hear that, Richard? We will be sent home. Thank you, Lord, thank you so much," he said with unbounded excitement.

The slightly intoxicated lieutenant hinted with his index finger for Walter to keep quiet. "You must not tell the others. I do not wish to be annoyed or questioned. If you tell one person, that person will tell another, and soon, everyone will know. Then the soldiers will come running to me, with the same excitement and happiness you have, pestering me with questions and demanding explanations. So, please keep mum."

"Not a word from me, sir. I promise," said Walter, sounding very childlike.

Satisfied with Walter's response, the lieutenant turned to me. "What about you?"

As a reply, I nodded, signaling that I would keep mum.

"Will time be able to heal my fresh scars?" I asked myself while resting on the bed, hoping to fall asleep. Concern entered my mind when Walter said, "This night will probably be the last night spent at the military camp. Richard, we will be returning home to our families who have waited for months and months."

Unable to understand my feelings, I felt crippled. I attempted to dig inside my heart to find joy, but I failed. The layers of sorrow and remorse were too dense to attain ecstasy.

There were no lights in the area. All eyes were shut instantly. A few noses began to incessantly snore. My brain slipped into dream mode. After an extensive journey, which involved boarding the train and walking several miles on foot, I finally arrived at the front gates of my house. My sisters began to move their small feet as fast as they could. Their ankles brushed against the well-kept grass. Standing eight feet apart from the gate, I noticed their feathery hair waving back and forth.

"Brother, you have returned," uttered my sisters concurrently.

Placing my knees on the ground, I extended my arms for both sisters to come running into my chest. Once embraced, I was slightly propelled backward by their energy. Their warm hugs illumined my heart. My eyes looked past their shoulders. By the gate stood a proud father with moist eyes, welcoming his son home. My heart was profoundly affected. I realized how much distress my absence had caused him and the others. Those active eyes of mine kept roaming as they searched for my graceful mother. Then, suddenly, the visionary experience began to diminish. The enchanting imagery was left half-finished.

Early in the morning, the Captain dispatched a team of lieutenants to wake the tiresome soldiers up from their sleep. It took some time and effort on behalf of Lieutenant Williams to help me reach the state of alertness. At first, I felt a vibration on my arm which irked my sleep. Then I felt knuckles hit my noggin to revive awareness within my brain.

"Rise and shine! The Captain has a message to announce," said the lieutenant. He leaned over and muttered, "I told you so."

I responded with a phony smile. He then proceeded on to disturb other soldiers who were fast asleep. There were a few light cheers, a few passionate roars and a few thank you Lords that was expressed once a soldier's name had been announced. As the Captain shouted various names, I remained brain-dead. The question of wanting my name to be called or not didn't matter. After some time, not that it mattered, the Captain said, "Richard Foster."

No feeling touched my heart. No thought occupied my brain. No form of speech escaped from my vocal cord. After the names were revealed, the Captain informed us that sometime in the afternoon the selected officers will be guided to the nearest train station. Once we reached the train station, from there onwards, we were to be left unassisted. He ended with an overdramatic speech on how important soldiers are to the country and how much we are appreciated for our services. His final lines were, "Your absence from the force is not permanent. Don't make yourselves comfortable at home. We will need you to return to the battlefields sometime in the near future. The country is not yet satisfied. Our eyes are on several other lands that are destined for us to rule and conquer. And so the day will return for you soldiers to place your lives on the line for our beloved nation."

As I stood near the bedside, which no longer was to support my deteriorated body, an unexpected tap on my shoulder frightened me for a second. It was Walter with both hands in the air expressing his contentment. "I heard your name on the list, Richard. Congratulations."

"Sorry, but did they announce your name?" I asked.

"They sure did. I was the fourth name on the list. Did you not hear me screaming?

"I was not paying attention. Sorry, Walter!"

"Don't worry, Richard. Besides, we should not be astounded that our names were called. The lieutenant had mentioned before that the soldiers who assisted in the burial of the departed were the ones permitted to leave."

By not responding to him, Walter's facial expression changed. The discomfort in his body language was noticeable as he began to leave the scene.

"Walter, where are you going? Tell me the reason behind the smiles, the winks, the cheers, and the excitement. Who is waiting for you at home?" I asked, hoping to lure him back into the conversation. As a friend, the least I could do was to let him express his pleasure.

He waited for a moment and then said, "I don't think I have told you Richard, but I have a family. My wife and son are waiting for my arrival. I am very grateful to you."

"Me?" I asked, pointing to myself with confusion.

"I would have not set foot onto the battlefield if it was not for the guilt I felt after disclosing that you were able-bodied to the Captain. But let me tell you, I was devastated by the incident in which you provoked Brock to execute you."

"Let's not talk about Brock, my friend. It is done and over with. There is no way or how I can go back and change my actions."

After eating the late breakfast meal, I walked down to the nearby sector. It was promoted by many soldiers on the campground that the higher authorities acquired a barber to shave us clean for our departure. By now my facial hair had grown more dense and broad. It descended below my chest. I believed that from all soldiers on-premises it was I who had the heaviest beard. "If I was to return home with this appearance, no one would be able to recognize who I am," I said under my breath.

"Hmm, these hairs are long indeed," said the barber. The barber's hand trembled. He seemed to be roughly sixty years of age; a very lean man with wrinkles on his face, hands, and feet. After visually examining him, I felt nervous. "Was he the correct person for this job? Were his shaky hands able to cut and trim with finesse?" I asked myself.

The old man interpreted the anxious expressions on my face and said, "Son, I have been in this business since the age of thirteen." The barber proved that he is an expert as soon as he took hold of the blade. His hands stopped trembling. He propelled the blade smoothly, trimming the facial hair to a smaller size, leaving a heap of it on the cemented surface. When the cold blade touched my raw skin it left behind a tingly feeling. The barber raised a mirror to unfold his flawless work. My eyes were in awe. The skin no longer felt prickly, it felt smooth. My face no longer felt heavy, it felt delicate.

"A change in appearance does not change who I am. It does not as hide what I have done," I replied.

"Oh my goodness, is that you?"

"Walter, give it a rest. Stop with the nonsense and help me with the bedsheets."

Walter was in shock as his eyes rested on my uncluttered face. The time had arrived for the privileged soldiers, whose names were announced earlier that morning, to depart. The bed was made with Walter's help, the sac was packed with my torn and dirty uniforms, the boots were cleaned to shine and the body was dressed in a fresh coordinated outfit. The new uniform felt extremely relaxing on the body. A reflection of Walter's metal buttons shined in the corner of my eye. A sea of dark blue waves shadowed my body. With not a single crease perceived, the navy blue coat made Walter look enormous.

"Are you going to button up your coat, Walter?"

"This uniform forces me to sweat. I will leave it open for now and button-up later."

"There is no later," I replied energetically. "We are to report to the front of house in the next fifteen minutes."

"I can see it now; the innocent child in his mother's arms. A familiar voice echoes in his ears. His pure eyes search for his father's face. Then, as I appear before him, his mouth curves and he releases a titter a soft giggle. I take him into my arms delicately. Feelings of eternal bliss overcome."

"No need to dream, reality awaits you. Within several hours, all that you have mentioned will actually happen."

"Add a couple of *more* hours. It will take at least four hours to get home by train and foot combined *reach home by train and foot combined* to reach home by train and on foot combined. How far do you live from the campground?" Walter asked.

"I have a long journey ahead of me. Let's hope the journey is kind and greets with open arms and treats me kindly along the way. I will most likely reach home tomorrow afternoon," I replied.

Walter then dug into his bag and took out a small ink bottle, a used ink pen, and a tattered piece of paper. He placed the items on the corroded table near the bed and bent down to pen various numbers and letters. As he wrote, Walter uttered, "This is my home address. Richard, you must write to me. Life is unpredictable. Only God knows whether our paths will cross again. By writing letters to each other, our friendship will live on."

"I will be the first to write to you. You will receive my mailing details when I send you the first letter I'll send you my details with the first letter."

Walter then asked a surprising question, "Are you married?"

"No. And I don't plan to marry."

"Why is that?"

I took a deep breath and said, "I don't think I can ever fall in love with someone anyone again."

"That is rubbish," he said with bitterness.

"To love someone, one must love himself first. I don't love the person I have become. If I don't feel happy, how can I keep her happy bring her happiness? If I am not in peace with myself, how can I provide a peaceful life for her for her to live in peace?"

"Stop it, Richard. You have to overcome this repentance. Please, I ask you to leave all this here. Don't take with you the experiences and memories of this war. Your family does not deserve to see you like this."

Was he correct? Should I forget my past actions? Should I let go of my sorrows? How could I? It was impossible.

Blackness eventually prevailed, and it was time for all the soldiers toiling on the battlefields to leave. Our superior ordered us to huddle so he could give his instructions.

"Soldiers, as you can see, with your difficult labour we have turned the battlefield into a graveyard. There are still many bodies left to bury, but that shall be left for the next day for tomorrow." Lieutenant Williams paused to smile with his teeth. "Now let us march back to the camp in single file. My stomach is growling," he added, drawing a few chuckles from the men.

How in the world the lieutenant guided us back to the military camp, we did not know. We trekked in the dark, holding on to one another, uncertain of what lay ahead. But the next step was always correctly predicted foreseen by Lieutenant Williams. He helped the team avoid steep holes, long canals, huge boulders, and muddy swamps. By the time we reached our destination, some of the men fell to their knees due to exhaustion from sheer exhaustion. Many were prepared to lay flat on their beds. Others were excited to get their hands on some food.

"Before you men carry on *continue*," The Lieutenant's advice seemed more like a command His words felt more like a strict order. All nine soldiers from my team, including me, returned the shotgun and spade and then hurried to the well. The cold water splashed against my skin, instilling alertness within my body. The coldness of the water relaxed my head. I felt renewed. After the short-lived bath, Walter and I decided to connect with our fellow soldiers at the location where food was being served.

"Let there be a change for once," said Lieutenant Williams, sounding dissatisfied. "Stew, stew, stew, that is all we have been receiving since we've set foot on the camp since arriving at camp. For all the hard work we put in, we at least deserve roast pig and the finest rum. Don't you agree, my comrades?"

Walter added, "Now that would be divine."

Standing in line with a steel plate and spoon in hand, the lieutenant leaned over to utter words of remedy into my ear, "Not to worry. If questioned about the incident, I will take care of it deal with it."

If Lieutenant Williams believed that his saying would help relieve my feelings of anxiety, he was totally wrong. That is because fear did not exist within me had disappeared from me. If I was to be hauled into court, if I was to be deprived of my so-called honourable duties *duties*, if I was to be ousted from the military force, I would have no regrets. At the moment, preoccupied feelings of cynicism ruled my views.

Once supplied with bountiful portions of stew, we seated ourselves to satisfy our empty stomachs. The stew looked gooier than other days. With such a large portion offered, a soldier was to find only two or three pieces of meat as the rest were stale vegetables. At times, I thought the food served was best suited for animals. At that moment, I created the perfect description for us soldiers from the military: We are animals that kill when threatened. We are animals that kill to protect our territory. We are animals that kill to fulfill our needs. Thus, to be served this kind of meal is acceptable.

It was a triumph for one to locate a seat in the hall during the evening because of the high volume of soldiers wanting to feed.

"It is either you are completely mad or extremely brave," said Lieutenant Williams as we sat in the corner of the hall, trying our best to digest the repulsive stew.

Walter added a clever remark, "Perhaps, he wanted to get rid of himself."

I gave Walter a menacing stare.

"Hmm, whatever the reason may be, one needed to rise and punish that arse. I am honoured to meet such a daring soldier," said the Lieutenant as he raised his cup of rum.

I remained silent. I concentrated hard on the remaining stew, keeping in mind how dreadful it tasted. Was I able to eat what was left on my plate? In order for my stomach not to cry for nourishment during the night, I had no other choice but to gobble whatever was left on my steel plate.

"So what time are we to rise in the morning, lieutenant?" asked Walter.

Lieutenant Williams burst into laughter, spraying our faces with the rum he was chugging. Walter was not able to interpret the reason behind the laughter.

"Will we not leave for the battlegrounds in the morning to bury the remaining bodies?" he asked.

"I believe that tomorrow every soldier in this military camp will have the privilege to return home."

At first, his saying flew above our heads. We snubbed his comment because we felt that the lieutenant was fooling us.

"As I entered the hall, I bumped into the Captain. In his very own words, he indicated that the soldiers of this camp will be relieved from their duties soon. As of tomorrow, several other military camps will be assigned to bury the dead soldiers. So our chances of being sent home look promising," said the lieutenant.

Walter's face lit up with joy. I had never seen my friend in such high spirits. "Did you hear that, Richard? We will be sent home. Thank you, Lord, thank you so much," he said with unbounded excitement.

The slightly intoxicated lieutenant motioned with his finger for Walter to remain silent. "You must not tell the others. I wish not to be annoyed or questioned. If you tell one person, that person will tell another, and then soon as you know it, everyone will know. Then the soldiers will come running to me, with the same excitement and happiness you have, pestering me with questions and demanding explanations. So, please keep mum."

"Not a word from me, sir, I promise," said Walter, sounding very childlike.

Satisfied with Walter's response, the lieutenant turned to me. "What about you?"

As a reply, I nodded, signaling that I would keep mum.

"Will time be able to heal my fresh scars," I asked myself while resting on the bed, hoping to fall asleep. Concern entered my brain when Walter had said, "This night will probably be the last night spent on the military camp. Richard, we will be returning home to our families who have waited for months and months."

Not able to understand my own feelings, I felt crippled. I attempted to dig inside my heart to find joy, but I failed. The layers of sorrow and remorse were too dense for me to attain ecstasy.

There were no lights in the area. All eyes were shut instantly. A few noses began to incessantly snore. My brain was in dream mode. After an extensive journey, which involved boarding the train and walking several miles on foot, I finally arrived at the front gates of my house.

My sisters began to move their small feet as fast as they could. Their ankles brushed against the well-kept grass. Standing eight feet apart from the gate, I noticed their feathery hair *wave* sway gently in the breeze.

"Brother, you have returned," uttered my sisters concurrently. Placing my knees on the ground, I extended my arms for both sisters to come running into my chest. Once embraced, I was slightly propelled back due to their energy. Their warm hugs filled my heart with light. My eyes looked past their shoulders. By the gate stood a proud father with moist eyes to welcome home his son. My heart was profoundly affected as I realized how much distress my absence brought upon him and the others. Those active eyes of mine kept roaming as it searched for my graceful mother. Then suddenly the visionary experience began to diminish. The enchanting imagery was left half-finished.

Early in the morning, the Captain dispatched a team of lieutenants to wake the tiresome soldiers from their sleep. It took some time and effort on behalf of Lieutenant Williams to help me reach a state of alertness. At first, I felt a vibration on my arm, which irked my sleep. Then I felt knuckles hit my head to revive awareness within my brain.

"Rise and shine! The Captain has a message to announce," said the lieutenant. He leaned over and muttered, "I told you so."

I responded *back* with a phony smile. He then proceeded to disturb other soldiers who were fast asleep. There were a few light cheers, a few passionate roars, and a few "thank you, Lord"s that were expressed once a soldier's name had been announced.

As the Captain shouted various names, I remained brain-dead. The question of wanting my name to be called or not was irrelevant. After some time, not that it mattered, the Captain said, "Richard Foster."

No feeling touched my heart. No thought occupied my brain. No form of speech escaped from my vocal cords.

After the names were revealed, the Captain informed us that sometime in the afternoon, the selected officers will be guided to the nearest train station. Once we reached the train station, from there onwards, we were to be left unassisted. He ended with an overdramatic speech on how important soldiers are to the country and how much we are appreciated for our services. His final lines were, "Your absence from the force is not permanent. Don't make yourselves comfortable at home. We will need you to return to the battlefields sometime in the near future. The country is not yet satisfied. Our eyes are on several other lands that are destined for us to rule and conquer. And so the day will return for you soldiers to place your lives on the line for our beloved nation."

As I stood near the bedside, which no longer was to support my deteriorated body, an unexpected tap on my shoulder frightened me for a second. It was Walter with both hands in the air expressing his contentment. "I heard your name on the list, Richard. Congratulations."

"Sorry, but did they announce your name?" I asked.

"They sure did. I was the fourth name on the list. Did you not hear me screaming?"

"I was not paying attention. Sorry, Walter."

"Don't worry, Richard. Besides, we should not be astounded that our names were called. The lieutenant had mentioned before that the soldiers who assisted in the burial of the departed were the ones permitted to leave."

By not responding to him, Walter's facial expression changed. The discomfort in his body language was noticeable as he began to leave *from the* the area.

"Walter, where are you going? Tell me the reason behind the smiles, the winks, the cheers, and the excitement. Who is waiting for you at home?" I asked, hoping to lure him back into the conversation. As a friend, the least I could do was to let him express his pleasure.

He waited for a moment and then said, "I don't think I have told you, Richard, but I have a family. My wife and son are waiting for my arrival. I am very grateful to you."

"Me?" I asked, pointing to myself with confusion.

"I would have not set foot onto the battlefield if it was not for the guilt I felt after disclosing that you were able-bodied to the Captain. But let me tell you, I was devastated by the incident in which you provoked Brock to execute you."

"Let's not talk about Brock, my friend. It is done and over with. There is no way that I can go back and change my actions."

After eating the late breakfast meal, I walked down to the nearby sector. It was reported by many soldiers on the campground that the higher authorities acquired a barber to shave us clean for our departure. By now, my facial hair had grown more dense and broad. It descended below my chest. I believed that from all soldiers on the premises, it was I who had the heaviest beard.

"If I was to return home with this appearance, no one would be able to recognize who I am," I said under my breath.

"Hmm, these hairs are long indeed," said the barber. The barber's hand trembled. He seemed to be roughly sixty years of age; a very lean man with wrinkles on his face, hands, and feet. After visually examining him, I felt nervous. "Was he the correct person for this job? Were his shaky hands able to cut and trim with finesse?" I asked myself.

The old man interpreted the anxious expressions on my face and said, "Son, I have been in this business since the age of thirteen." The barber proved that he was an expert as soon as he took hold of the blade. His hands stopped trembling. He propelled the blade smoothly, trimming the facial hair to a smaller size, leaving a heap of it on the cemented surface. When the cold blade touched my raw skin, it left behind a tingly feeling. The barber raised a mirror to reveal his flawless work. My eyes were in awe. The skin no longer felt prickly; it felt smooth. My face no longer felt heavy; it felt delicate.

"Never doubt this old man. It is I who can turn the ugly into the handsome. You were the ugliest one from all the soldiers with that disgusting beard of yours. Now look at you — you are clean and cut, which makes you the most handsome among the soldiers," said the barber with a silly laugh.

"A change in appearance does not change who I *really* am. It does not hide what I have done," I replied.

"Oh my goodness, is that you?"

"Walter, give it a rest. Stop with the nonsense and help me with the bedsheets."

Walter was in shock as his eyes rested on my uncluttered face. The time had arrived for the privileged soldiers, whose names were announced earlier that morning, to depart. The bed was made with Walter's help, the bag was packed with my torn and dirty uniforms, the boots were cleaned to shine, and the body was dressed in a fresh coordinated outfit. The new uniform felt extremely relaxing on the body. A reflection of Walter's metal buttons shined in the corner of my eye. A sea of dark blue waves shadowed my body. With not a single crease perceived, the navy blue coat made Walter look enormous.

"Are you going to button up your coat, Walter?"

"This uniform forces me to sweat. I will leave it open for now and button up later."

"There is no later," I replied energetically. "We are to report to the front of the camp in the next fifteen minutes."

"I can see it now: the innocent child in his mother's arms. A familiar voice echoes in his ears. His pure eyes impatiently wait for his father's appearance. Then, as I appear in front of him, his mouth curves and he releases a titter. I take him into my arms delicately. Feelings of eternal bliss overwhelm me."

"No need to dream, reality awaits you. Within several hours, all that you have mentioned will come true."

"Add a couple of more hours. It will take at least four hours to get home by train and on foot. How far do you live from the campground?" Walter asked.

"I have a long journey ahead of me. Let's hope the journey is kind and welcomes me warmly. I will most likely reach home tomorrow afternoon," I replied.

Walter then dug into his bag and took out a small ink bottle, a used ink pen, and a tattered piece of paper. He placed the items on the corroded table near the bed and then bent down to pen various numbers and letters. As he wrote, Walter uttered, "This is my home address. Richard, you must write to me. Life is unpredictable. Only God knows if our paths will ever cross again. By writing letters to each other, our friendship will live on."

"I will be the first to write to you. You will receive my mailing details when I send you the first letter."

Walter then asked a surprising question, "Are you married?"

"No. And I don't plan to marry."

"Why is that?"

I took a deep breath and said, "I don't think I can ever fall in love with someone."

"That is rubbish," he said with bitterness in his voice.

"To love someone, one must love oneself first. I don't love the person I have become. If I don't feel happy, how can I keep her happy? If I am not in peace with myself, how can I provide a peaceful life for her?"

"Stop it, Richard. You have to overcome this repentance. Please, I ask you to leave all this here. Don't take with you the experiences and memories of this war. Your family does not deserve to see you like this."

Was he correct? Should I forget my past actions? Should I let go of my sorrows? How could I? It was impossible.

CHAPTER 6

An army of twelve men hiked beside the railway tracks, enjoying the scenic view. It was a pleasant change. Instead of the bloody battlefields and congested campgrounds, we were exposed to a heavenly spectacle. Far in the distance were mountains enclosed by faded clouds, grassy fields lit by the radiant sunlight, and a gushing river with crystal clear water. We felt like convicts who were finally released from prison. Our eyes revealed expressions of independence. Impressed by the picturesque scenery, we ignored the fact that our trains were departing from the station in exactly twenty-three minutes. Not a word was uttered by any of the soldiers during the short expedition. Out of the twenty names that were announced in the morning, eight had ventured into the woods on foot. For these soldiers, traveling on foot was more appropriate since their homes were located near the campground. From the remaining twelve, seven of us, including me, were to head westbound. The other five, including Walter, were to head eastbound.

"We have arrived," said the veteran soldier who guided us to the station. Within seconds, he bid us farewell and turned around to pace back to the campground.

"From here onwards, we're on our own, comrades," said Walter as he watched the guide turn the corner.

The limited station, made entirely of wood, had a vintage appearance. It had an intelligible arrangement with a platform and railway tracks on opposite sides. "Certainly, no expert was needed to build this station," I presumed. On the far corner of the platform were barrels full of spare wood and coal. Beside the barrels were gallons of oil and water. Several impatient families were waiting on the platform, rotating their necks around to search for the arriving train. A screeching noise in the distance troubled our ears. As my hands instinctively placed themselves over my ears, the station master came running onto the platform to wave down the locomotive. While the first train situated itself beside the platform, another whistle blasted, signifying that the other locomotive was closing in to enter the station.

I had never viewed such a mechanical phenomenon before. My fingers ran lightly across the steel plate until I felt a burn. Automatically, the brain advised my hand to withdraw. The locomotive had two coaches; each coach was placed on a set of four circular wheels. It also had a cart located near the steam engine, on which were barrels containing coal and wood. A couple of workers on site rushed over to collect the gallons of water and oil placed in the corner of the platform. With their muscular arms, the workers loaded the heavy gallons onto the cart. Approaching the steam engine, I noticed that there was a slight change in the air. A flaming sensation hit my face. It was as if the locomotive was saying, "Keep your distance!" The smell of burning coal pestered my nose. A pole-like structure, high in stature, was attached to the front of the train. From the top of this object, heavy clouds of smoke polluted the natural air.

"My father once mentioned that these kinds of inventions were being created around the world. He also said that new means of transportation are being introduced in our country. The old man expressed his desire to travel in one of these superior locomotives," I muttered to Walter despite the vociferous surroundings.

Meanwhile, the well-groomed conductors from both trains stepped down to check passenger tickets. Passengers not in a military uniform had their tickets inspected. We soldiers did not require a ticket. Many of the soldiers did not want to accept the kind gesture, but the conductors at the station rejected the money we had to offer. To take money from a soldier returning home to his family was not acceptable. The reason soldiers were treated differently was that we put our lives on the line for the country and its civilians. We were greeted with warm handshakes, friendly 'good mornings,' pleasant good nights, cheeky winks, wide smiles, and open laughs. For them, we were supreme human beings. Only if they knew how cold our blood turns, how black our hearts turn, how evil our minds turn. These gullible people need to look at our hands that are covered in blood. And this blood cannot be washed away.

"Hmm, goodbyes are hard. I wish you the best. And don't forget to write. I will respond to every letter, Richard."

"Please come to visit with your family sometime. My family and I would love to have you over," I said while shaking his hand.

"I will only visit if you get married, Richard," he said in a jolly tone. "I will be there to attend your marriage."

"Not in this life. Maybe, in the next life," I said as I reached over to embrace him. "Thank you for everything, Walter."

Walter's train was the first to leave the station. My hand waved farewell as my eyes searched for Walter in the distance. When parting from my family, I knew in my heart that I would see them again. But that was not the case with Walter. "Am I ever going to see him again?" I asked myself. Too absorbed in the farewell procedure, I did not notice that the remaining soldiers on the platform had already boarded the coach. Steps were engaged to board the locomotive, but then I was shooed away because the coach was full. There was no room for another body.

"Sorry private, house full," said one of my fellow soldiers in a rueful manner.

Unexpectedly, the conductor grabbed my right arm. "Let's go, soldier, there is room for you in the other coach." Before permitting entry, the obtrusive conductor said, "Surely, you don't mind traveling with the common folk. A well-respected family for your company, sir. Please, advance." The conductor opened the door. The family of four were in a deep conversation that finished immediately once they viewed a glimpse of the remorseful soldier.

"Sir, I hope you don't have an issue. This young lad here is a trustworthy soldier who is returning home. He is to share this coach with you and your admirable family."

"It will be my privilege to share this compartment with a man of his stature," said the elderly passenger.

"Welcome aboard, son. Please make yourself comfortable."

I proceeded to the empty corner, overlooking the bodies present. My sac was placed between the child and me as I strived to attain comfort in the packed compartment. A lie came out of my mouth when the elderly passenger, who was the father of the family, asked if I felt comfortable in my seat. Then surprisingly, I felt a tremble under my feet. The motion of the train wobbled the coach excessively. The irritating whistle squealed again. Before I knew it, the platform had disappeared, the station was imperceptible, and the narrow river had vanished. Half of the upper portion of my body was leaned against the edge of the window. My eyes were so fixed on the wheels that turned in a circular motion that I did not pay attention to the elderly man's words of knowledge. He was going on about something 'life this,' something 'destiny that,' something 'war this,' something 'soldier that.' But I was absorbed by the endless path of the railway tracks. One had to wonder how fast this bull was traveling. In the corner of my eye, I noticed a shadow. Its body, face, and eyes were probably following the same path I was. Inside I felt unusual. Was it a reflection of the past? Was it a reflection of the future? My limbs became unconstrained. My brain felt unperturbed.

"Be careful, soldier," said the elderly man as he viewed me positioning my head out of the window to feel the wind brush against my face.

I closed my eyes and filled my lungs with fresh air. The smell of the country had evoked memories of my farming days. On weekends, father would be happy to see me standing on the porch, eager to give him a hand with the daily farming activities.

"Son...Son...Son..."

Was that my father's voice?

"Soldier, I am talking to you."

I finally took notice; the father of the clan seemed frustrated.

"I have been trying to get your attention for some time now. Are you fine?"

"Sir, I apologize. I am very fine, thank you. How are you today?"

I should not have asked how the elderly man felt today. That one question welcomed a catastrophe. If I asked one question, his response carried on for the next ten minutes. So after the first three questions, I stopped inquiring and started listening. His various questions were met with one-word answers or mechanical nods. If lucky, he would get two or more words from me. "What a chatterbox," I said under my breath. But my parents' upbringing did not teach me to insult or disrespect an elder no matter how annoying the person may be. Any question on the topic of war I avoided subtly. Sometimes, to avoid replying, I would start coughing loudly until he offered me water. Most of the time, I would purposely change the subject. Then, at times, I would start acting playfully with his eight-year-old son. His son, Albert, was a mischievous child. As soon as I placed my sac on the seat, his hands leisurely moved to the bag. The child's action was detected by his mother. Albert's mother roared, "Bad manners, Albert. The next time I catch you moving your hand, I will punish you." She then looked at me and said, "I am sorry. He is always up to no good. Please, do keep an eye on your belongings."

"Madam, there is no need to apologize. He is only a child," I responded in a manner that impressed her. "Children are pure souls. It is hard for them to understand what is right and what is wrong."

"Do you have children of your own?" she asked.

"No, madam, I don't," I replied as my face turned red. "I am not married yet."

"You are of marriageable age, son. Take my advice, marry soon. You are a handsome one. I am sure you will get a beautiful wife."

With my eyes fixed on the wooden floor, I nodded.

When did the sun disappear? When did the moon form its oval shape? When did the stars fill the heavens? When did the locomotive increase speed? When did the child place his head on my lap to fall asleep? So much had occurred while I was unconscious. I did not find myself liable for this. The elderly man's incessant chatter was at fault. His draining conversations led to one of the blackest nights I have ever perceived. While traveling, Albert moaned in his sleep. "Sister...Sister...Stop it...Stop it."

A resonating sound entered my ears. A titter so soothing that it had the capability to relieve a person from all tensions and pressures. Still, I found it useless to glance towards the sound. The father removed pieces of fresh bread from his bag and handed them over to his wife and the anonymous person beside her.

"Thank you, father," said the enchanting person.

"What a delicate and attractive voice," I said to myself.

As the elderly man shoved a piece of bread in his mouth, my stomach growled. I had not eaten since morning. I gently bit my lower lip and relocated my eyes back to its usual place, the wooden floor.

"Father, your manners... Please offer some bread and water to him. I am sure this long journey has made him very hungry."

To whom did these generous words belong? My eyes roamed in the coach until they fell upon the daughter of the family. I searched for her eyes, which she hid behind the tilted bonnet as if I had lost or misplaced a valuable belonging. She raised her hands close to her mouth to nibble on the bread. My vision was blocked by the dim lighting that surrounded the coach. Desperately, I endeavored to see a glimpse of her face but was unable to.

"Son...," echoed the manly voice. "I apologize for my shameful behavior. I should have offered you a piece first," said the father. Without hesitating, the elderly man offered a piece of bread and a cup of water. I thanked him sincerely and quickly swallowed the piece of bread. As I lifted the cup to take a sip, my sly eyes focused on her. It was as if I had no control over them. She was now gazing out the window. Her hair seemed to be neatly tied up, and the white laced bonnet was placed effortlessly on her head. Wrapped around her shoulders was a burgundy-colored scarf made of pure silk. The woman was covered from head to toe. Not revealing any skin meant that she was reserved. Her dressing showed that she came from a well-cultured family. The formation of her slender neck was the only noticeable feature in the blackness.

"When will I see her face?" I asked myself.

CHAPTER 7

Artistic voices, rhythmic jangles from bottles, and clattering sounds from steel pans and spoons came together to produce a beautiful harmony. I was roused by the six melodious voices along with their bumping and thumping. I did not know when my eyes came to rest. "Comrades, thank you for waking me up," I said to myself.

They were singing a fascinating composition about a war hero and his lady love reuniting after many years. Seated in front of me was the elderly man snoring nonstop while his unconscious wife was leaned leaned against him with her head resting on his shoulder. I was surprised to see Albert scrunched in between his parents. The child looked very relaxed as he lay there motionless. I could not restrain my neck from tilting for another glance towards the fair lady. "Where has she gone?" I said under my breath. My heart started racing.

"This boy is so naughty. I will give him a stern lecture when he rises," said the lady as she gathered the scattered uniforms from the floor.

I felt ashamed as her genuine hands touched my soiled clothing. "Excuse me...Ahhh ...You don't need to...Umm...I can." I searched for the proper words but could not find them. She packed my belongings in the sac which had been thrown on the floor on the floor. "I apologize for my brother's impolite act, Richard." At last, she turned around to expose her divine face. I could not move. She had me memorized.

"Please take it. Richard, take your bag please," she implored.

I remained idle, unwilling to remove her from my sight. I waited for her to come closer. But she remained distant with her stunning, round eyes placed on the empty seat beside me.

"Wait, a second!" I said with confusion. "How do you know my name?"

And then our eyes finally met.

"Do I know you? Have I seen you before? Who are you?" I asked.

"Here are your belongings," she said while placing the sac aside. She then took a couple of steps back and placed herself in the empty seat next to her mother. The lady was draped in an off-white dress with floral embroidery running vertically across the front and back.

"She must have stitched those flowers with her delicate fingers," I said to myself.

"I saw your name written on the uniform while collecting it from the floor. Please don't judge me as a wrongful person. I am not the kind to encroach in another's personal or private life. But it was the awful stitching of your name that caught my attention. You see, Richard, stitching and knitting is my hobby."

Whenever she uttered my name, my heart and mind felt lighter. "Since now you know my name, can I ask for yours?" I asked, hoping that she does not decline my request.

"Shush, father, and mother must not be roused by our voices. If they rise, I will not have the fortunate opportunity to speak to you."

I ogled at her flawless lips move moving as she talked. "I think they are very much deep in sleep. All the singing and banging on the pans and bottles have not awakened your parents. So I doubt that our voices will have an impact."

She acknowledged my sureness with an encouraging beam. "My name is Julia."

The night was blossoming with radiant stars exposed in the heavens. Julia viewed the stars while the train sped along. Her left hand was placed under her chin. Her elbow was balanced on the edge of the window. It was as if an angel descended from the heavens and was expecting the gentleman seated nearby to win her attention.

"What was the force that pulled at my heartstrings?" I asked myself.

This vibrant woman seated only three feet apart from me had captivated my thoughts and feelings. The harrowing experiences and memories of war were unexpectedly forgotten. The eyes did not blink once as I watched her deliver words from her tempting lips. I did not blink once as I watched her lips deliver words. The ears were keen to hear the sound of her womanish voice. The nose was filled with her unique scent that eradicated other kinds of fragrances in the air. What shall I say? What shall I do? Shall I touch her? Shall I shake her hand? Shall I ask her to sit beside me? Shall I compliment her? Shall I ask a question? What shall my next step be? I searched for the answers. My fingers desired to caress her perfectly shaped neck. My lips desired to kiss her subtle cheeks. My eyes desired for her eyes to be planted on me. I felt the urge to whisper in her ear, "Julia, I think I am falling for you."

"Richard, are you awake?"

"Yes."

"Oh my goodness, I thought you had fallen asleep," she said from the dimness that overshadowed her face.

"Madam, I am wide-awake."

"Please don't call me madam, call me by my name, Julia."

"Sorry about that. From now on, I will only call you Julia."

Our conversation lasted for an hour until we heard a loud cough from the father. Was he awake or was he woken? Did he listen to our endless conversations that moved from one topic to another? In the dark, I edgily searched for his eyes. "Oh God, I wish the old man is not alert and still unconscious," I said to myself. Though, it did not matter because the cough frightened Julia. The fear of her parents catching her in the middle of a deep conversation with a rather unknown man stopped her from interacting.

With no exchange of dialogues, the coach was brimming with silence. The brain easily replayed the various topics Julia and I had discussed. With pleasure, I reflected upon the disclosing of her everyday life. She begins her day by having a bath in the morning. Then, she proceeds to lend her mother a helping hand in the kitchen. Learning how to clean, chop and cook the food excited her. Once the food was prepared, she was beckoned to wash and dress her brother Albert for school. The family then held hands at the dining table while the father said grace before filling their stomachs. Once the father left for work, the brother left for school and the mother left to fulfill daily house chores, Julia ran to her bedroom to engage herself with stitching and knitting. During the afternoon hours, Julia and her mother took a brief leave from their household chores to relish a sip of tea in the garden. If both mother and daughter were craving sugar, they added sweet biscuits to their afternoon menu. Then, the ladies continued with their selected errands until Albert came home from school. Once Albert was home, the attention had to be focussed focused on him. The little boy longed for attention. If he went unnoticed by his mother or sister, Albert hid in a cupboard or chest within the house until one of them discovered his hiding spot. It was Albert's technique of ensuring that others were aware of his role as the ultimate attention seeker never to be ignored.

Around dusk, the father entered the house with complaints about the environment in which he labored. But when he perceived Julia's heartwarming smile, all his tensions faded. As the father bathed, the women of the house attended to the kitchen to serve food for dinner. Seated at the dining table, the family once again said God's name before consumption. When heading to sleep, Little Al persuaded her sister into telling him a fairy-tale story about heroes and villains, kings and queens, horses and dragons, or angels and demons. The loving sister would recite the same tales over and over again until his brother's eyes were fully shut. She then handled any unfinished stitching or knitting until her eyes became watery and fingers became weary. Lastly, the charming Julia placed herself on the mattress, covered her graceful body with a blanket, and waited for her mind to clear itself from thoughts of the present, past, and future.

The most delightful part about the minutes spent with Julia was that she never referred to wars, soldiers, weapons, causalities casualties, battlegrounds, and graveyards. I was captivated by her words as she resumed talking and told the story of how her grandmother introduced her to stitching and knitting. She was at the tender age of twelve when she invented her first piece of clothing: a woolen sweater for her father. Julia went on talking about how attached she was to him. That her father always chose her over Little Al. Albert became very jealous that his father showered Julia with more love and attention. One day, in a rage, he marched to his elder sister's bedroom and threw her precious belongings on the floor, removed the covers placed on her mattress, emptied her closet full of clothes, but did not dare to touch her sewing kit.

"Even Little Al knew how much that kit meant to me," she said with her eyes glistening.

"What is your age?" I said, interfering in between her words.

At first, she hesitated to answer, but then she blushed and said, "Sixteen...But I am turning seventeen soon."

"That means you have been working your fingers for close to five years now."

"Yes, almost five years now," she replied with excitement in her voice.

"Several years ago, I heard of this invention..."

"What invention?" she asked.

"Well, it is an invention that had been created in order to assist manual laborers in clothing factories. Some type of machine that does the work for you."

Her giggle was so lively that for a moment I believed her folks were awakened.

"If such a machine has been introduced to our country, how is it that I did not hear of it yet?"

"Hmm, perhaps I have heard wrong then," I replied with a puzzled look on my face.

"For a person who has devoted nearly five years of her life to stitching and knitting by hand, it is difficult to believe that such a machine exists. But then again, with the way the world is changing and humans becoming more innovative and intelligent; your saying may be true."

To avoid the brief gaps in between our conversations, I formed a habit to ask her questions about her most admired topic. As soon as her answer to the initial question came to an end, I was prepared to unleash another question on her plate. I did not want her voice to cease. "What is the difference between stitching and knitting? Where to purchase wool or thread? What kind of needles do you prefer to use? What kind of things have you stitched and knitted?" I asked and asked and asked.

"I can stitch shirts, blouses, pants, skirts, frocks. You name it, I will stitch it," she said with immense confidence. "I prefer embroidery stitching the most. If my dress is visible at this moment, you would be able to see my creative work."

"I have already seen the floral embroidery on the dress," I said under my breath. "And what about knitting?"

"Oh, I have knitted mittens, booties, sweaters, blankets, scarves, and hats. Wait, wait, wait, I also make small cats and dogs out of yarn for Little Al."

"Impressive," I said with the most handsome smile displayed.

"I cannot believe this. For the first time, it is I who is talking uncontrollably. Usually, when I am sitting with another, I talk very little. But with you it's different. For some odd reason, I feel as if I have known you for days, months, years, decades."

Those last set of words she uttered had me feeling special. The heart indicated for me to wake up her parents and ask for Julia's hand, right then and there, at that very moment. The brain said, "Are you mad? Get a grip of yourself." I listened to my brain and searched for new questions to ask her.

"Richard, please don't mind, but it's late. I think it's time for me to sleep now. You should as well," said Julia.

Oh no, please don't. Let us talk until sunrise. Let us look at each other. Let us hold hands. Let us dream about a future together. Let us plan a wedding. Let us find a property and construct a brand new house. Let us decide on a name for our first child. Let us...I pondered. I only wished that I had the courage to say all this. "It's just too soon, she barely even knows who I am," I mumbled.

"What did you say?" she asked.

I was not prepared for that question; my brain came to a full stop, my throat felt clogged and my mouth became parched. "Umm...I...Well...Did you know I have two sisters?" God bless them. At the moment, I felt so grateful that I had two sisters.

"That is a blessing. What about parents?" she asked.

"Well, I have one father and one mother, as you do," I answered wittingly wittingly/casually.

She laughed while covering her mouth, hopeful that no sound drifted into her parent's ears. "Stop it! You are forcing me to laugh. I don't want to disturb my parent's parents' sleep.

"Can I ask you something?"

"Ask me anything."

"Why is it that you did not once mention the war? You do know that I am a soldier."

She kept silent for a moment and then said, "Sorry Richard, I got so carried away with threads, yarns, and needles that I forgot to inquire about your life. And to be honest, I don't want to know what happened in the war. I don't want to know how our country achieved victory. I don't want to know how many soldiers have fallen during this war. Everything related to war saddens me."

"Is there something that you would like to know about me?" I asked, feeling disheartened.

The absence of light made it difficult to interpret her unclear facial expressions. I waited impatiently for her to ask a question.

She then whispered, "Why have you not married anyone, Richard?"

Why did she have to ask such a question? Was she as fond of me as I was of her? Did she feel what I felt for her?

"No one wants to marry a soldier."

Her eyes finally connected with mine. "You became a soldier by your own decision, and you became a human by God's decision."

"What is that supposed to mean?" I asked.

"What is wrong in being married to a soldier?" she asked.

Anger surged within me and resulted in fierce words toward an innocent woman. "A soldier's life is shadowed by remorse and tragedy. How would a wife feel knowing that her husband killed a countless number of men? How can a woman live with a man who has sinned? God will punish me. And while God does punish me for my wrongdoings, He will also punish the ones who have a relation with the sinner. I will not see my loved ones suffer due to my immoralities." I should have bit my tongue before voicing, "I don't see myself getting married today, tomorrow, or in the future."

Julia did not talk for a while. I regretted the fact that I compelled her to ask me a question in the first place. What if I scared her? What if she never talks to me again? I felt like slapping myself across the face.

"Richard?"

"Yes Julia," I answered, nearly falling off my seat.

"A person who feels guilt for his wrongdoing is not immoral. You have to forgive yourself, Richard."

Her beneficial words helped regain the romantic state I was in earlier.

"Thank you for the kind words," I said. "So, why have you not married anyone? I know this is a personal question, if you wish not to answer, I will understand."

"Who says that I am not married?" she responded boldly.

My heart cracked as I heard the unbearable reply. The seriousness in her voice disappeared as she uttered, "I am not married."

Hearing those four joyful words lifted my spirits again.

"I am from the countryside, which means, I will be married soon. Most of the girls I went to school with are now married and have kids."

"Do you want to get married?"

"Yes, I do. I will marry a gentleman that my father selects."

"What if you meet someone?"

"Well then, father must approve. I don't believe that father would say no to my choice. He trusts and loves me dearly."

Julia stretched her arms and yawned. The beautiful creature looked tired. I felt as if I was forcing her to keep awake. So I asked her to rest.

"Richard, you need to rest as well. Even a couple of hours of sleep will do just fine," she said.

"No, I am fine. I will stay awake for a little while longer," I replied.

"Can I...If it is okay with you...Will you allow me to stitch back your name on the uniform?" she asked hesitantly. After seeing the bewildered look on my face, she continued, "The person who stitched your name on the uniform did a terrible job. Half of it is coming off. I will first have to remove the remaining letters before stitching new ones. Are you following me, Richard?"

"Yes, yes, I am," I replied with conviction.

"I will then stitch new letters on the uniform. But this time around, the letters will not come loose."

"Which letters?" I questioned with a smirk on my face.

"R I C H A R D," she replied with her ever so delightful giggle.

"That is very generous of you, Julia. But how will you stitch without light?"

"Don't worry about that. As soon as the sun rises, I will begin."

"What about your sleep?" I asked with concern in my voice.

"A few hours of shut-eye are plenty for me."

I felt like I was troubling her. Amazingly, she understood my feelings. How? Only God knew!

"This is no trouble, Richard. It will be my pleasure to do this for you."

"So I assume that you are carrying the proper equipment with you as we travel?"

"Yes, I never leave home without my kit," she replied.

Searching inside my bag, I came across the uniform she was talking about. The letters C H A R D were partially detached from the uniform while the other letters R and I were attached.

"I hope this does not take much of your time, Julia?"

"It will not. I will have it done before my parents rise."

"And when do they rise?"

"A few hours after sunset," she replied. "I promise that your uniform will be in your hands before the last station arrives."

"I hope that station never arrives," I said to myself.

As I reached over to hand the uniform to Julia I asked her, "Are you sure you want to do this? The uniform has a bad smell; it is tarnished and torn in several places."

"Why do you worry so much? When I stitch, all is forgotten. No scent, filth, or holes will distract me," she replied.

I extended my arm. As she leaned over to grasp the uniform, her delicate fingers touched my hand, sending a tingly sensation through my body. "If her touch brought such pleasure, what would a warm hug or long kiss bring?" I asked myself.

Julia began to twist and turn as she adjusted herself in the corner of the seat. She used a fairly large woolen bag, which she had knitted herself, as her pillow. With her eyes closed, she muttered, "Goodnight, Richard!"

"Goodnight!" I replied.

While the early morning hours loomed, I was in a constant battle to stay awake. Short intervals of unconsciousness took full control. Whenever my eyes rolled back and my lids started closing, the brain would send a transmitting signal for my body to jerk. But, in the end, I lost the hard-fought battle and fell asleep.

"I must have passed out for an hour or so," I said to myself while rubbing my eyes. With sleep irritating my eyes, I noticed the first signs of light resting upon Julia's curved body. I pinched my arm to regain full consciousness. Once I was fully alert, I examined her motionless face, feature by feature. My eyes wandered, exploring her beauty until they rested upon her smooth-edged chin. I then noticed that her jawline was knifelike. In the dull compartment, the knifelike formation was still visible. Julia's upper and bottom lips were both thick and wide. But once puckered, they shrank in size. I was surprised to see her nose was similar to mine. It had the same arch, the perfect amount of sharpness and smoothness. I took my time with the eyelashes, noticing their length and the tiny curves at the ends. Her dense eyebrows were perfectly shaped and not connected. The overall shape of her face was oval and graced with high cheekbones. Due to the bonnet, it was difficult to see if Julia's hair was straight, wavy, or curly. Though, by the reflection of the light, I was able to see the rich brown color of her hair. Observing her serene features, I waited for my eyes to close. I did not have the energy to fight another battle with sleep.

CHAPTER 8

I was fortunate to see the expert at work. She was seated on the edge of her seat. Her long fingers moved inwards and outwards constantly. Her brow did not reveal signs of stress or tension, and her face expressed relaxation. Waiting for her eyes to rest upon mine, I noticed that the sun had risen into the sky. I then looked over at Julia's family members to see if they were awake. Astonishingly, they were in the same position as I had seen them the previous night. The only difference was that the elderly man's snoring had grown more obnoxious. However, on the campgrounds, I had trained my brain to ignore such unimportant matters. I then fixed my eyes permanently on Julia. The tranquility she exuded forced me to envy her. It seemed as if her path had no obstacles. It seemed as if she had never faced a problematic situation. It seemed as if she had no remorse or anguish, or a combination of both, tormenting her soul. It seemed as if she never had any pressures or worries lingering in her mind. To live with a person of that sort, a man would slowly come to dismiss the guilt, pain, and hate that once ruled his life. "Was Julia my savior? Had she descended from the skies for me?" I asked myself.

Finally, Julia broke her focus and looked at me. "When did you rouse, Richard?"

"A little while ago," I replied.

"Why did you not say anything?"

"You looked so engaged; I did not want to bother you."

"I am not quite done, Richard. Give me a couple of minutes. I can't wait for you to see it," she said with a smile brighter than the sun itself.

"When did you begin stitching?"

"As soon as the sun peeked out of the horizon, which was about sixty minutes ago."

"So your poor hands have been active with no rest for the last sixty minutes. I feel so terrible, Julia."

"Please don't. There were times when I stitched for my loved ones for more than five hours without rest."

"Then, why are you stitching for me? Am I a loved one?" I said under my breath.

"What?" she asked, unable to comprehend my whispering.

"Don't your eyes hurt after a while?"

"For several hours I can focus on the hand and thread, but after that, my eyes do start to water. I would request Lil Al to wipe my eyes with a dry cloth."

"Can I wipe your eyes?"

"What?" she asked, confusion etched on her face.

"Ahhh...I...I meant...Since your brother is asleep, I don't mind wiping your eyes if water forms."

She responded with a tight-lipped grin and continued with her task of permanently fixing my name to the uniform.

The crack of dawn never looked so exquisite. The sunshine blended fabulously with the idle sky, creating a mixture of gold, red, and purple. Lines of red and purple streaked the heavens, forming glooms amongst the egg-shaped hills. The scenery of the grasslands fascinated my eyes. In the far distance, I beheld flocks of visible dots scattered above the land. When the dispersed herds merged to become a large union, I realized it was the season of migration. The flapping wings and quacking pleased my ears as these creatures zoomed over the train. Several dozen white feathers came twirling down from the sky onto the moving train. It was a delightful scene to view.

"It's done, it's done," said Julia, grasping my attention. She raised the uniform to her mouth before sinking her teeth into it to rip the remaining strand of thread. "Let me know what you think," she said while placing the uniform in my hands. With my fingers, I touched the stitched name, feeling the smoothness of each letter. As I arrived at the letter D, I felt the warmth of her body. She had knelt to her knees and remained only inches apart from my body.

"Please tell me you like it," she said as I felt her breath touch my skin.

"I love it, Julia. It is perfect. The way you have stitched these letters, I am sure it will never tear or rip. Honestly, I was planning to dispose of the uniforms as soon as I reached home. I knew that if I ever came across these uniforms it would prompt memories of the carnage witnessed on the battlefield; memories that I need to abolish from my brain. But since your precious hands have enhanced this particular uniform, instead of getting rid of it, I will cherish it forever. Thank you so much, Julia."

Before my voice came to rest, I had my left palm tucked under her jaw and fingers spread across her cheek. I did not know when or how it happened, but I was glad it did.

She looked deep into my avid eyes, prepared to remove all my distressful miseries. At that moment, I felt as if she understood the pain that resided in my heart. She humbly relocated her face to place a tender kiss on my privileged fingers. As her lips connected with my skin, an indescribable sensation erupted inside my body. "Julia, I…"

A loud yawn alarmed Julia, causing her to push my hand aside. She then quickly leaped back into her seat, ending the brief moment of affection we shared for one another. I watched the elderly man rub the sleep from his eyes. He shook his head wildly to revive alertness. "Wake up! Wake up now! The sun has risen. We will be arriving at the final station soon," said the father as he forcefully nudged his wife.

As Julia's mother arose, she said, "These people should have a morning rooster to wake the passengers on this locomotive. I don't recall the last time I slept this long. I feel so rotten about it."

"How I wish you had slept longer," I said under my breath.

The father looked over at his daughter with his piercing eyes and asked, "Julia, when did you rise?"

With an expression similar to a child, Julia replied, "Only a couple of minutes before you, father."

I let out a sigh of relief, thinking how fortunate Julia and I were for not being caught by the elderly man.

"Good morning, son. Did you sleep well?" asked the father.

"Well, sir, I did not sleep much last night," I replied.

"Why is that?"

"It must have been that annoying noise that comes from your nose, father," mumbled Albert as he rose from his sleep.

"Yes, that must have been the reason why the gentleman could not sleep at night," said the mother with bluntness in her voice.

Julia burst out with laughter as her father sat there with a blank face.

Ignoring the insults, the elderly man asked, "So, I heard that you are returning home. Where do you live?"

"I am from the countryside. We own ten acres of land up north. The land has been passed on from my grandfather to my father."

"Which means, it will be passed on to you," said the elderly man with a clever smirk on his face.

"What do you do with all that land?" questioned Julia's mother.

"A major quantity of our land consists of a maize plantation."

The father barged into the conversation yet again with one of his devious assumptions.

"During harvest season, your father must earn a lot of profit."

"Father," grumbled Julia, peering at him with serious eyes.

"What about the rest of the land?" the elderly man asked, overlooking Julia's demand to stop with the unnecessary questions.

"The rest of the land is used to grow fruits and vegetables."

"What kind of fruits and vegetables do you plant?" asked Julia's mother.

"Carrots, tomatoes, pumpkins, cabbages, turnips, berries, and grapes," I answered.

"I love grapes," added Albert.

Several questions invaded the brain, yet not a single answer came to my rescue. "Are we just two souls who got caught up in the moment, or do we really have strong feelings for one another? Was this love, or was it infatuation? Was this a sign from God? A sign to retrieve from the path I had already set forth on?" I asked myself.

As the speed of the locomotive decreased, we knew that the final station was close. With her mother and father present, I still managed to capture a few glances of Julia. It seemed to me as if she felt timid. "She may have regretted the abrupt release of passion, the kiss," I said to myself.

Julia's eyes were fixed on her knitted bag placed on her thigh. Her fingers kept fiddling with the tender wool. My eyes searched for hers. "Look at me, Julia, look at me," I said continuously, under my breath. Then, on the spur of the moment, the whistle blew, startling everyone in the compartment. Julia's body trembled at the sound of the whistle. At last, her eyes met mine. And then she quickly lowered them.

"She can remove her eyes from mine, but I will not remove mine from hers," I said to myself. I waited patiently for her to face me. But instead, she faced her parents, who appeared to be deeply involved in a conversation.

"This is your chance, Julia. Seize the opportunity. Who knows if we will ever see each other again," I said to myself, wishing that she would deliver the last glance. My wish came true. Julia stole a glance. I observed water in her eyes. A teardrop attempted to balance itself on the edge of her eyelid. Seconds later, the teardrop came rushing down her left cheek. As soon as she felt wetness on her skin, Julia used the back of her arm to dry the tear. My heart felt heavy. Her eyes said it all: that we were probably never going to see each other again.

I turned to Julia's father and asked, "Where do you live, sir?"

"We don't live too far from the station. Our home is four miles away from the sawmill located in the west."

I had no control over time. I knew that, for me, time was about to expire. But what was I to do? Should I ask for her daughter's hand? I thought.

"Sir, I want to know if..."

My voice was drowned by another blow of the whistle. As the noise faded, loud rah-rah and hurrahs derived from the other coach. The soldiers were full of joy. The commotion indicated that the soldiers had set eyes upon their loved ones.

While the train pulled into the station, I strived to gain the elderly man's attention. He was engaged in collecting his personal belongings. I was to ask him a question that could make or break my life. "Sir, can I..."

He did not tilt his head, open his ears, or blink his eyes.

"Son, it was a pleasure to travel with you. It is due to brave soldiers like you that we ordinary civilians can walk with our heads held high," said the elderly man while putting on his bulky coat.

"Do you have any bread left over?" Julia asked her mother.

"Yes, dear, we do. Are you hungry?"

"No, mother. Can you please give my share to..." her voice came to a stop. "Please give my share to the soldier. He must have a long journey ahead of him," she said, her voice quivering.

Without hesitating, Julia's mother dug into her bag and latched onto a piece of bread. She then placed the bread gently into my hands. I accepted the kindness with a sincere "thank you."

The platform consisted of impatient travelers ready to board the locomotive. Behind the large crowd of passengers was a demonstrative woman blowing flying kisses into the coach ahead of us.

"In a matter of seconds, I will be holding you in my arms," shouted one of the young soldiers, leaning dangerously over the window.

"Get inside before you fall over," voiced another soldier in the coach.

The brouhaha on the platform lured Albert close to the window.

"Not too close to the window, Lil Al," said Julia as she grabbed onto the child's dainty arms and pinched him close to her body.

In response to her sister's affection, Albert jumped onto her lap. Julia embraced his little brother and did not let go of him until it was time to evacuate the compartment.

As soon as I set foot on the platform, sounds of whistles, longing voices, clashing bodies, watery eyes, and forceful handshakes engulfed the station. I prayed to God. I needed to be ignorant of my surroundings. All I wanted was for Julia to express or respond. "Utter a few words of love into my ears, place your gentle hand upon mine, look into my eyes for comfort, do something, do anything," I said under my breath.

After exchanging goodbyes with the parents, my unfulfilled train expedition with Julia and her family came to an end. The entire family walked past me as if I had never existed. My damp eyes focused on Julia's lace bonnet, expecting her to turn her face around. "One last glance—that is all I request from you, Julia."

The sunlight displayed a tint of grey in her eyes. Her face revealed signs of emptiness, desperateness, and sadness. As her body faded in the distance, I accepted the fact that she was not meant to be part of my life. I did not know for how long I had stood there, but I stood idle until the platform became empty. When did my fellow soldiers leave? When did the conductor announce boarding? When did the passengers board? When did the whistles blow? When did the trains depart? I did not recall.

While I stood on the platform, I placed my eyes on the two corroded railway paths. There was no end to the paths. There was nothing that could help me turn back from the path I had already taken. The path that I had set forth upon had been shown by God. In other words, it was the path of a sufferer. For my sinful acts, I had to be penitent. In silence, I reflected upon the moments shared with Julia on the train. These were moments that I decided to keep within my heart for the remainder of my life.

My brain was toiling over the calculations of minutes and miles. The distance from the station to my home is about seven miles, which meant I would need to walk for at least an hour and fifteen minutes. I hung my sac over my left shoulder and headed towards the north. By walking along the narrow roadside, crossing the handmade wooden bridges, running at a fast pace across the shallow streams, and treading past the niggling grasslands, I finally reached home.

An unnerving feeling came over me as the light breeze swept across the maize fields. Instead of stepping forward, I took one step back. "Something is wrong," I said to myself. "Look, it's brother, he has come home," said my younger sister as she waved her hands ecstatically.

"Father, father, look," said my elder sister, pointing from a distance.

My sisters began to move their small feet as fast as they could. Their ankles brushed against the well-kept grass. Standing eight feet apart from the gate, I noticed their feathery hair wave back and forth.

"Brother, you have returned," uttered my sisters concurrently. Placing my knees on the ground, I extended my arms for both sisters to come running into my chest. Once embraced, I was slightly propelled backward due to their energy. Their warm hugs illuminated my heart.

My eyes looked past their shoulders. By the gate stood a proud father with moist eyes, ready to welcome home his son. Profoundly affected were my emotions as I realized how much distress my absence brought upon him and the others. Those active eyes of mine kept roaming as they searched for my graceful mother. I gazed at the front porch, expecting to see her with tears of joy seeping down her face. But she was not there; she was nowhere to be seen.

"Where is mother?" I asked the emotionally troubled man.
Father ignored the question and directed me into the house. As I entered the house, my little sister asked me to bend down. I inclined to reach her height. She then positioned her mouth close to my ears and whispered, "Mother is no more."

CHAPTER 9

R ichard Foster Reporting To Duty,

It has been forty years since I dipped my pen into a bottle of ink to write on a sheet of paper. My old, pale hands were busy for the past few days cleaning and clearing shelves, dressers, cabinets, and boxes. For some odd reason, I felt a sudden need to dispose of all unnecessary things from the household. To satisfy this urge, I had to drag my fatigued body around for several endless hours. While cleaning the most ancient piece of furniture in the household, the wooden cabinet, I came upon a stack of papers with my writing on it. I stayed up during the course of the night reading what I had once written. Everything written on the rolls of paper was exactly what I rehearsed in my brain each and every day for the past forty years of my life. The feelings of remorse and distress have not vanished. The experiences faced on the war grounds have not been forgotten. The memories of father, mother, and Julia have not faded. The dreams of lifeless bodies and the suffering of animals have not ceased. The only way out of this struggle is death. And I am pleased to say that death is not too far away. The sheets of paper that were discovered have inspired me to write again. Experiences that I have faced on the battlefield, to the campground, and the train journey, all play a role in my life today. I cannot leave this story unfinished. There is much to say. There is much to write. The only difficulty is where to start.

"Mother is no more," said my little sister. The words she whispered into my ears turned my body numb. Father asked me to be seated in the living room. He scolded my sisters for clinging to me as I walked to the chair for a seat. The girls were ordered to head to their bedroom. My elder sister understood father's demand and escorted her naive sister to their comfy nest. I was unable to express a single word as my father revealed what had occurred in the past week. He tried his best to control his emotions but failed. In the middle of his dialogue, he stopped. He struggled to fight back the tears. If I could, I would have left my seat to comfort him, but the trauma would not allow my legs to budge. I was petrified. My ears did not want to hear what I anticipated my father would declare.

"I did notice her coughing, but I ignored it," he said regretfully. "At first, I thought it was a minor cold and she would recover fast. You know how your mother is; once she falls sick, the next day she would behave as if she had not caught anything in the first place." I nodded in response, still unable to express a word.

"A day later, your mother informed me that she had a fever, which made her feel very chilly. I told her to rest, but she disregarded my advice and continued with her daily activities. By night, she informed me that she had difficulty breathing and suffered from chest pain. The next morning, without her consent, I went to town to fetch remedial medicine at the market. When I arrived home, your sisters, who were by her bedside, told me that she had vomited twice since I was gone. I got very nervous, son. I had never seen your mother in that kind of condition before. After her meals, we fed her medicine, but it was of no use. Whatever she ate or drank did not remain in her stomach and was immediately discharged from her mouth. As the next few days passed, her fever increased. Then, one evening, I noticed that her body was shaking. I panicked. I did not know what to do. I called for your sisters. It looked as if she was suffering from a seizure. As the seizure ended, I consoled her while she dabbed her tears on the sleeves of my shirt. She was in so much pain. Her pain was something I could not bear to see or stand."

Father continued while he shut his eyes to hold back the tears. "I told her that I needed to visit a doctor and tell the expert about your condition. As you know, Richard, your mother was afraid of doctors and hospitals. She kept pleading for me not to visit a doctor and promised that her condition would improve. I did not want to upset her, but I could not let your mother have her way again. The next day, I went back to town, not for medicine, but to fetch a medical practitioner. With much pleading and bribing, I convinced a doctor to accompany me back home. So when the doctor came home to examine your mother, she gave me an evil stare. She was furious inside but did not say a word to me in front of the healer.

'She has a severe case of pneumonia. She has an increased respiratory rate. She is having difficulty with her breathing. She is also suffering from extreme chills and stern chest pain. This is serious. I will return tomorrow morning. In the meantime, the only thing I can suggest is bed rest,' said the doctor.

While I accompanied the doctor to the front gate, he asked me several questions about your mother's general health. He told me to pray to God and that everything would be fine. So that night, I prayed for God to cure her. Unfortunately, my prayer was not answered. The spiritless night turned out to be miserable. She was unable to sleep. Her mind was not stable. Her face became ghostly. The veins under her skin were clearly visible. Sweat was dripping uncontrollably from one side of her temple. Her hands were swaying around recklessly. She knocked over the cup of water I had put aside for her on the table. The liquid rapidly dispersed on the floor. Her screams penetrated through the walls of the house. Your sisters were hiding behind the open door to my bedroom. Both of them were intimidated by your mother's painful reactions. With my hand, I gestured for them to come into the room. But your sisters did not move.

'Where is he? Where is my son?' asked your mother. 'Please, tell me he is alive. Have they killed him? No, he must be alive. He is my son; nothing will happen to him. But why has he not come yet? Does he not know that his mother is sick? Bring him back. Bring him to me,' she said, forcefully pulling my shirt collar. Then, unexpectedly, she burst into tears. I tried soothing her, but she pushed my hands away. 'Get away from me. Don't come near me,' she said. Your mother then wanted to roll out of her bed. I felt irritated by her actions but tried to stay as calm as possible. I reached over to grab her, ensuring that she did not fall onto the floor. Detecting that the situation had become rampant, your sisters rushed in to lend a hand. As soon as your mother placed her eyes on the beautiful girls, her abnormal behavior came to a stop. She calmed down and the raging temper finally disappeared. As I rubbed her forehead with my fingers, she looked at me with her drowsy eyes. It seemed as if she wanted to ask or tell me something.

'Is there anything I could do for you?' I asked her in a gentle tone.
'I am sorry, but I have to leave,' she said, tears rolling down her cheeks.
'Nothing will happen to you, I assure you. You will be fine, my love,' I said to her.

Her breathing got louder. She struggled with her inhales and exhales. Her words were not clear because of the deep gasps of air and heavy breathing. But I do recall her asking where she was and what was happening around her. She was lost. At that moment, your mother was somewhere in between our universe and the unknown universe."

I examined father as he bit his lip, reluctant to proceed. I understood how difficult it was for him to explain the passing of his wife, my mother, but I did not budge. I could have, but I did not ask for him to stop. I may be selfish, but I had to know every detail. Though these details were hard to endure, they were the last minutes of my mother's short life.

"She used most of her remaining energy to lift her right hand, which she used to point towards her children. And then your mother's hand tumbled down to her bedside. I ushered your sisters to step close. During that moment, your mother's eyes revealed how much she wanted to embrace her daughters. Understanding her desire, I voiced to your sisters, 'Don't be afraid. Hug your mother.' Rachel was too innocent to understand the situation and condition your mother was in, so it was not difficult for her to embrace your mother. As for Margaret, she understood that her mother did not have much time left. The image of Margaret's sobbing eyes and trembling body forced me to comfort her. In silence, we sat by your mother. We prayed, begged, and hoped for your mother to recover. I noticed that her body started to turn extremely pale. Her forehead did not produce any more sweat. Her fingers stopped twitching. Her mouth remained slightly open. Her eyes rolled back. Her limbs became rock solid. Her breathing and heartbeat stopped."

The river from my eyes flowed into an ocean of rage; a rage that spread within my body. Father extended his arms to catch my body as he saw it collapse to the floor.

"I did not know that our Heavenly Father above seeks revenge," I said to my father while on my knees. "I have sinned; therefore God takes my mother? I have taken the lives of numerous soldiers; therefore, my family must undergo such calamity? I always believed that God's decisions were fair. But I see no fairness here. It is I who killed my mother. It is I who killed others. I am the one that should be punished."

Mother was buried exactly three days before I arrived home. Her funeral took place at home, with most of the family members and neighbors attending. It was a small gathering of people who were once close to her. I remember when grandfather died; mother ensured that his body was carried out of the house feet first.

"If the tradition of carrying out a corpse feet first is broken and the dead body is carried out head first, then that is said to be a bad omen. So if the deceased person's face is looking back inside the house, that will lead to other deaths in the family," mother used to say.

My father did not believe in such things. He ordered us not to believe in superstitions. "It is a superstition that is engraved in the minds of people today," father used to repeat.

To come face to face with father, after seeing him cry, took a massive amount of courage.

"Was mother's body taken out feet first?" I asked father, without meeting his eyes. "Yes, son, your mother would have preferred that."

Temporary pleasure filled my heart as I heard the answer to my question. "I am sorry, father. I am sorry for not being there..." I was unable to continue. An override of emotions from my heart rushed into the brain, forming a miserable picture on my face. The loud cry went unheard and unobserved as father embraced me with his chest pressed strongly against my face.

As days passed on, I searched for my mother in all areas of the house. During mornings when I ambled into the kitchen to give my father a hand with the early meals, I reflected on how mother used to prepare everything with rapid speed. The kitchen was her domain where she was in charge of everything. She kept her domain neat, tidy, organized, and categorized. Her voice was stern when she called us to take a seat at the dinner table, announcing that food was ready to be served. So much love and care went into her food preparations. And with that same amount of love and care, she would serve the food as well.

As I walked into my bedroom, I remembered how mother used to knock before entering. She had much respect for my privacy. She would only enter the bedroom after hearing, "Come in, mother." When she entered, automatically my ears would prepare themselves for a scolding. Mother detested an untidy room. After the initial scolding, she would move onto her routine discussion about why I should get married, why this was the perfect age for marriage, why I should meet her friend's daughter for marriage, and why I should marry once I returned from the battlefields. Mother knew I had no interest in settling down, but she would not abandon the unwelcome subject.

Whenever I set foot on the front porch, I reminisced how she used to broadcast her voice into the cornfields where father and I worked during the evening. "Dinner is prepared, come on in, you two," shouted mother, outstretching her vocal cords.

As soon as we heard the broadcast, we forgot about our duties and paced back home to satisfy our hungry stomachs.

For the first couple of months, father had risen before Margaret and Rachel to prepare them for school. Father ensured that breakfast and dinner were placed on the table for his children. He did not shy away from his weekly trips to the market to collect the required food items. Whenever the neighbors called for him to visit, he took out at least fifteen minutes from his busy day to attend. What surprised me was that he had also taken out time for the land. After his shift at the steel plant, he would spend a few hours in the cornfields. He went about his duties as if nothing had happened. It seemed as if mother's passing did not affect him. Until one day, I realized how wrong I was.

I rose in the middle of the night after encountering the same torturous dream in which thousands of bodies lay scattered across the battlefield. I lifted my body from my bed and paced back and forth. "When will these dreams stop?" I asked myself. While using a cloth to remove sweat from my face, I heard a peculiar sound from behind the wall. I placed my right ear against the wall to make out the sound. But the wall that separated the room from my father's was too dense to interpret what the sound might be. I decided to further investigate by entering the hallway.

As I walked towards father's bedroom, I noticed that his door was not entirely shut. I reached over to pull the knob but then held back. It was very disturbing to hear my father weep. I slowly poked my head into his room, prepared to withdraw if father were to see me. Father was in a sitting position by his bedside. He had his eyes fixated on mother's picture. Father struggled to control the volume of his crying. My heart crumbled while viewing the iron-willed man in such a dismal condition. I did not have the nerve to intervene, so I acted as if I heard nothing, saw nothing.

CHAPTER 10

As the year came to an end, the Foster family and household transformed drastically. Father started to behave very strangely. He talked less. He ate less. His habits changed. Usually, he asked me for a lending hand and would let me accompany him to the fields. But for some odd reason, he stopped doing that. At times, it seemed like he did not want to be bothered. Rachel, being the closest to father, would seek his attention. Unfortunately, father did not give much importance to her. There were times when he did not even notice her as she pranced around him. Father did not rise early in the mornings anymore. He did not feel the need to prepare his children for school. Due to father's negligence, Margaret was the one bathing, dressing, and packing lunch for Rachel while I ensured breakfast was served before they departed for school. My absent-minded father would sit on the porch for hours without saying a word. I passed by several times a day to see if he would take notice, but father remained lost in his deep thoughts. He did not participate in the traditional Foster dinner sessions. While my sisters and I ate whatever had been left from the last day's meal, he would hide in his shadowy room. The man did not have a soft corner for his neighbors anymore. His old friend cum neighbor Benjamin waited for him on his porch.

Whenever Benjamin spotted father opening the front gate, he would say, "My friend, where have you been hiding? Why don't you come over to my place today?"

Father rejected his offer, entered our home, marched straight to his room, and shut the door behind him.

"What does he do in that room of his?" I asked myself.

A week after Easter, I received my answer. Margaret came across dozens of empty bottles stored under father's bed as she was dusting his room. When my sister told me about father's hidden bottles, at first, I did not believe her statement. I had never seen my father consume alcohol before. We did not smell the stench of alcohol from his mouth. We did not see him stumble and fall. We did not hear a slur in his speech. He did not exhibit any signs of a drinker. When I looked under the bed myself, I viewed the stacks of bottles tossed into a corner. Was this his technique of forgetting his deceased wife? Was this his method of overcoming the misfortune which transpired close to a year ago? Was alcohol the reason behind his lack of commitment towards Margaret and Rachel? Suffering from the ongoing dreams, living with guilt for the sins I committed, dealing with mother's unfortunate passing, and knowing that my father lost his way confirmed that the world around me had disintegrated. I cried myself to sleep that night.

The next morning, while leaving for work, father ordered me to accompany him in the cornfields during the afternoon hours. His unexpected gesture left me speechless.

"Brother, are you in trouble?" asked Margaret.

"I don't know. However, today is my chance to ask him about his bottle addiction."

Since returning from the war, father and I did not have a proper conversation. That is why it was difficult for one of us to break the silence hovering above us. Both of us were comfortably seated on a long, narrow trail in between the massive cornfields, distant from our home, family, and responsibilities. With help from the soothing breeze, the maize plants swayed from side to side. I noticed that the sun and clouds were having a first-class battle to conquer the skies.

"Son, we need to discuss your future. Are you planning to return to the military base? I heard that the country has declared for soldiers to proceed to the nearest base. There is another war on the horizon."

Before I let my father complete his sentence, I expressed, "I am not going. I will not fight for my country any more. I see no gain from it. I am sorry father, but what I have done and seen in the battlegrounds is enough to live with for the rest of my life."

"A surviving war hero does not need to tell his story by mouth; the story is revealed to others through his eyes. I see it in your eyes, the suffering that you have experienced. That is why I never inquired about your experiences in war."

His words made me feel at ease. I was not expecting any sympathy from my father. What I expected was a round of questions such as, what is the matter with you, why is it that you cannot battle for your motherland, do you want to bring shame upon our family name.

"Father, did you receive my letter?"

"Yes, we did. It came to us a day before the first signs of the lethal infection that detached your mother from this world. She forced me to read the letter to her over and over again. Your mother felt as if she was in heaven when she heard that nothing bad happened to you during the war."

"Was mother concerned about my safety?" I asked father while lowering my face to hide my sentimental eyes.

"She was restless. She attempted to keep herself engaged with household chores. But the mind wanders aimlessly. Most of the time, she was absorbed by thoughts that I believe were about you or related to you. Your mother always talked about your homecoming. That once you come back, she will get you married. To be honest, that is the reason why I told you to accompany me to the fields."

"What reason, father?"

"Well son, I received a letter from your mother's childhood friend, Beth. As you must recall, your mother wanted you to meet Beth's daughter," said father with unease detected in his voice. "I will not waste time and come directly to the point. Do you want to marry?"

"No father." To avoid explaining my response, I decided to change the topic. "Father, can I ask you for a favor?"

"Yes son," he replied, ignoring the fact that I disrespectfully changed the subject.

"Do you think you can get me a job at the plant?"

"Hmm," father pondered. "I will see what I can do about it."

As my father ascended to leave, I gathered enough courage to say, "Father, I know about your drinking. I have seen the bottles under your bed."

"Do Margaret and Rachel know about this?" he asked, without making eye contact.

"Margaret knows about it."

Father became agitated and dabbed cold sweat off his forehead.

He started mumbling to himself, "I...I...did not want...but how...it's too hard."

For the first time in life, I ordered my father like a Colonel would order his battalion. "Father, you have to stop."

"Give me some time," he responded nervously.

After the promise was made to Walter, it took me a year and a half to write him a letter. Faced with tragic incidents, unforeseen changes, and heavy responsibilities, I had not found the opportunity to write and mail it. When Margaret completed her studies and began handling most of the household chores, I finally got some time for myself. In the four-page letter, I informed Walter about my mother's passing and father's alcohol addiction. As I wrote, it felt as if Walter were the only person who could truly understand my inner feelings. The loneliness I was experiencing prompted me to wonder how comforting it would have been if Walter and his family had visited. I poured my heart and soul into the letter, telling my friend about the recurring dreams that haunted me every night, how father ignored Rachel, and how disheartening it was to labor at the steel plant with co-workers mocking him as a worthless alcoholic.

Near the end of the letter, I bombarded him with questions: How are you? How are your son and wife? What have you been up to these days? Are you planning to return to the base? Are you upset with me for writing so late? When will you travel to the northwest? If so, will you pay me a visit? On and on I went, asking question after question. After sending the letter, I anxiously waited for a reply. Days passed, yet no reply. Weeks passed, yet no reply. Months passed, yet no reply.

"Why is Walter not replying?" I asked myself.

Perhaps he was too busy. Perhaps he resented me for writing so late. Perhaps he was in some kind of danger or trouble. What if he no longer lived at the address he had provided? Maybe he had moved. By the end of the year, I stopped trying to figure out the whys and what-ifs.

Every time I approached father to question him about the recently purchased alcohol bottles, he would respond with his usual line, "You need to give me some time." Father became a mess. He did not bathe, eat, or sleep properly. There were days when he did not rise in the morning to be at the plant because of his overnight drinking sessions. At times, his impairment was so severe that he would stumble and fall. In those moments, Margaret and I had to help him to his feet and drag him to his bedroom. Father was not even capable of lifting a spoon or fork due to the chronic trembling of his hands. His daily visits to the cornfields stopped, resulting in poor crop development. The once-cultivated fields had begun to turn into a useless wasteland. Rachel, who craved her father's attention, avoided him because of the stench from his breath. It seemed as if father bathed in liquor rather than water, though that could not have been true, since he did not find it necessary to cleanse himself. Whenever he attempted to speak, which was rare, his words were almost incomprehensible due to his severe stutter.

Then one day, the addiction cost father his post at the steel plant—a position he had held for twenty long years. The loss devastated him. He began believing he was useless, unneeded, and unworthy. Before, he drank to ease his pain; now, he drank to escape from the world entirely.

"Father, if you continue like this, you will end up killing yourself," I said angrily.
He responded, "Give me some more time and I will show you..."

"Show me what?"

His slurred reply was impossible to comprehend.

Five months later, more time was not enough. Father was no longer with us, claimed by a disease that consumed the liver. The physician said the fatal illness was a result of excessive alcohol consumption and had no cure.

"Mechanically the world is advancing, so why not medically?" I said to the doctor, leaving him puzzled. While my mother's death was unexpected and unbearable, father's passing, though tragic, was anticipated. The old man had been bedridden for the last two months of his life. His painful cries still echo in my ears today. To see father helplessly lying on the bed, writhing in pain and desperately calling for his wife as if he had lost his mind, remains etched in my memory.

One day, he surprised us by calling Rachel to his bedside. Rachel, scared by his frail appearance, hesitated, but Margaret encouraged her to take a seat on the edge of the bed. Father embraced her, kissed her cheeks, and said, "I am sorry, my child. Please don't hate me. I never stopped loving you."

Rachel then wiped father's tears with her gentle hands. During that night, when my sisters were asleep, father told me the reason he had kept his distance from Rachel.

"She has your mother's face. She has her eyes, nose, and chin. Whenever the little girl appears in front of me, I am involuntarily transported back to memories of your mother. Son, I wanted to move forward in life. I tried hard to forget the tragedy, but I could not. Please forgive me. I was not able to save your mother." Father wanted to say more, but he could not, as a deep, perturbing soreness unexpectedly seized his insides.

When I was told that father did not have much time to live, I sent letters to all his family members across the country. From all the neglectful relatives, only his closest sibling, Aunt Nancy, arrived with her husband a few weeks before father's death. As soon as she set foot in our home, Aunt Nancy took charge. She washed and fed father till his last day. She made Margaret, Rachel, and me feel like insignificant bystanders. Aunt Nancy had been one of the few relatives constantly in touch with father through letters. Father praised his youngest sister endlessly. In front of her, we acted as if we adored her, but in reality, we despised her. What irritated Margaret and me most was that our aunt encouraged father to remarry only four months after mother's death. The letters in which she suggested he remarry were brought to my attention by Margaret. Thank God, father was not interested in marrying again. He would have had no time for a newlywed wife. His addiction to the bottle was his first priority after losing mother. The bottle became his newfound love.

At the funeral, Aunt Nancy stated that father wanted her to take complete responsibility for Rachel. So now Rachel was to live in a different state with Aunt Nancy and her family of six.

"Are you trying to say father believed that Margaret and I were incapable of taking care of Rachel?" I asked, using a revolted tone.

"No son, he did not mean that. He just thought it would be better if Rachel…"

My blood pressure rose. "Letting our sister go, whom we dearly love, to a different state… What is the matter with you?"

"Watch your tone, young man. She is your aunt. You must show her respect," said Aunt Nancy's defending husband.

"If Rachel lives with us, she will be part of a complete family. It is for her own good; that is why your father made this decision before passing away," said Aunt Nancy.

Margaret repeatedly nudged my arm for attention.

"What?" I barked.

"Please, don't send her. We have lost mother and father. We can't lose Rachel."

"You will be married in a couple of years, and then who will be there to take care of Rachel?" said Aunt Nancy, barging into the conversation.

Margaret responded with a threatening look.

"Richard, please obey your father's last request. You do want his soul to rest in peace now, don't you?" asked the witch, confident that her final phrase had won the battle.

She threw a fit, screamed at the top of her lungs, and cried until her departure. "Brother, don't you love me? Why must I go? Will you both visit me? When can I come back? Sister, who will play with me now? What have I done wrong? Why are you letting them take me?" Her every legitimate question pierced my flesh like a sharp dagger. Until this day, I don't know why I let it happen. When my sister was taken from me, I felt helpless. There was no rage or revolt left in me. The sins I had committed were affecting my loved ones. So, letting Rachel depart was unavoidable. I tried explaining to Margaret how my sins had carried over into their lives, but she did not want to hear about it. On the day Rachel departed, I did not lose one sister; I lost both of them.

"You say you were helpless, but you were not. You had the choice to stop Rachel from going, but you did not," Margaret said before slamming her bedroom door on my face.

In the months that followed, a different side of Margaret emerged. She kept silent. When I stepped into the house after a tedious day at work, she would lock herself in her bedroom. At times, we crossed paths within the household, but not a word was exchanged. Most times when I asked her a question, she found it unnecessary to answer. The very few times she did reply, her answers were no more than two words. Not a smile on her face, not a twinkle in her eye; it was difficult to see Margaret live like this. Something had to be done.

I waited a year for Margaret to turn fifteen. The year seemed prolonged. Any year would seem long if you lived with a person who barely speaks. Aunt Nancy returned to her old habits. The matchmaker informed us she had found a fine gentleman for Margaret. He was our uncle's nephew, recently turned the perfect age of twenty. At first, I hesitated, but then I reasoned: Married life might restore Margaret to her old self. With marriage, happiness could return to her life. She would not have to spend nights under the same roof as me, and she would be closer to Rachel, living in the same city as her.

I responded to Aunt Nancy's letters, telling her that as soon as Margaret turned fifteen, the whole family, along with the gentleman, could come for a visit. I also mentioned that I would not talk to Margaret about marriage. It is a mother's duty to inform her daughter about such matters. Since mother was no longer with us, I entrusted this responsibility to Aunt Nancy. She felt honored and looked forward to discussing the proposal with Margaret. I ended the letter with, "The only condition I have is that at no time should Margaret feel as if she is being forced to marry."

A month after my sister's fifteenth birthday, Aunt Nancy and her family visited our home with Rachel in tow. Through letters, Aunt Nancy kept informing us that Rachel was adapting well to her new home and getting along nicely with her cousins. Rachel leapt into my arms as soon as she saw me waiting for her at the front door. She felt heavier than the last time I held her.

"Oh, my sweet little darling has become so chubby! Seems like Aunt Nancy has been feeding you well," I said to her.
She hid her face in my chest as I reached over to pinch her plump cheeks.
"Rachel, I missed you so much," I said, stroking her back gently. Margaret came running down the steps to the front porch, eagerly snatching Rachel away from me. She instantly showered her with love and affection. What joy it was to see my sisters reunite.

With all eyes on the delightful sisters, the presence of the unfamiliar man was ignored. After he entered the house, I managed to divert my eyes from Rachel and introduced myself.
"Nice to meet you, my name is David," he said with a cheerful smile. He was a tall, slender man with auburn hair parted neatly to the side. The chap impressed me with his

politeness, manners, proper choice of words and gestures, and honest responses to my questions. I was grateful to Aunt Nancy for chatting with Margaret about the marriage proposal. I was not surprised when she told me that Margaret did not require much convincing to reach a decision. My only concern was whether she'd agree to marry the candidate introduced.

David and Margaret spent a week in the household, with me keeping a close eye on both of them. It did not take long for Aunt Nancy to tell me that Margaret and David had developed a mutual liking.

"Really! A week was enough for them to understand and accept each other?" I asked Aunt Nancy, stupefied.

David and Margaret kept in touch via secretive love letters. The marriage date was set for mid-year, with both families meeting several times to finalize the details, costs, and venue. I extended my hours at the plant and focused less on the crops in the fields to earn extra money for the wedding. With three months left until the marriage, I was confident I would save enough funds to spend without hesitation. Every day, I rose before the sun and left home without eating. Then I returned as the sun set behind the hills.

Margaret noticed my early departures and late returns. Without saying a word, every night she set the dining table, prepared hot water for my late-night bath, and then locked herself in her bedroom. One night, while arranging the dining table, Margaret broke her silence. With concern in her voice, she asked,

"Brother, are you working these long hours because of the wedding?"

"Yes, Margaret. As you know, father and mother's remaining money went towards their funeral expenses, so I must provide for the marriage ceremony by working long and tough hours."

Her silence expressed what I had longed for: her care for me. Margaret's heart ached for a brother who came home with an empty stomach, hands covered in minor burns and scrapes, every joint and muscle crying for rest.

At the wedding, before walking her down the aisle, Margaret embraced me and whispered in my ear,

"I am very sorry, brother. Please forgive me for everything."

It was not just her apology that warmed my heart; it was the fact that after such a long time, I was being embraced by my beloved sister. And off she went with her newly wedded husband to begin a new chapter in her life.

CHAPTER 11

A new chapter unfolded in my life. With the deaths of mother and father, Rachel living with her aunt, and Margaret happily married, loneliness crept steadily into my life. Countless months had passed, yet I received no letter from Aunt Nancy, Margaret, or Walter.

"Walter, whatever happened to him?" I asked myself continually.

There were times when I stared at the blank wall for hours, hoping it would speak back to me. My ears paid close attention to the pure silence of the house. I longed to hear Rachel's swift footsteps and Margaret's subtle voice. Sometimes, my eyes searched desperately for a familiar shadow to appear in the distance. Some days, I was reluctant to leave the plant after my shift, dreading the silence at home. With time, I trained my brain to comply with the hard life of isolation. "This is what God has planned for me after observing my sinful acts during the war," I whispered.

Then, one lonesome day, I received a letter. With trembling fingers, I tore open the envelope, noticing no indication of the sender's name on the front or back. My eyes glanced at the top of the page. It read: Mary Walter Parker. I did not know a Mary, I did not know a Parker, but I did know a Walter.

"This letter is probably from Walter's spouse," I said to myself, as a gust of wind blew the letter from my hands. Bending to retrieve it from the ground, I realized the letter was brief but heartfelt. Then I began to read as the whooshing winds grew stronger.

Mary Walter Parker

To my husband's dear friend,

First and foremost, I apologize for the late reply. We received your letter almost three years ago. But my child and I had moved from our home after the tragedy, which is why my family did not come across your letter until this month. My family and I have been struggling to stay strong even today. With a heavy heart, I am very sorry to inform you that Walter Parker is no more. My husband passed away during the war that occurred three years ago. As a loving wife, I pleaded with him not to attend. But Walter did not listen. His pride as a soldier and love for his country were of more importance to him than his family.

"Nothing will happen, God will always protect me," he would always say.

Walter had told me that he and you became good friends. He had planned for the entire family to visit you, but another battle arose, and the visit had to be postponed. If there is anything else you would like to know, please don't hesitate to ask. Wherever he may be, I know Walter is looking down on us. Pray for his soul.

The loss of my friend shook me to the core. Sadness welled for his wife and son. I touched my face to feel wetness. But there were no tears. With so much water having flowed from my eyes over the past years, it seemed the well inside my body had dried up. Besides grief, I also felt a pang of jealousy.

"Wherever he may be," his wife had mentioned in the letter.

"I know where he is—by his beloved God, in bliss," I whispered to the walls that never talked back.

What I needed from God was a natural exit from the world. There were times when my mind urged me to consider the path of a trampling horse carriage or a powerful bull cart. There were days when it tempted me to think about the sharp ax I often used to cut wood, which could separate a neck from the torso. Then, there were several occasions when I contemplated the rope in the backyard and how it could fit snugly around my neck. These dreadful thoughts lingered in my mind, but not once did I feel compelled to act on them. From my father's teachings, I knew that suicide was a sin. But what father taught, he did not follow. In a way, it can be said that father's life ended because of his own selfish decisions. His death was essentially suicide. He did not want to live anymore, so he drank himself to death.

During that night, I contemplated: what was father's reason for not wanting to live? That would be mother's death. And why did mother pass away? Purely because of my sins. In the end, all fingers pointed to my misdeeds. No one should be blamed except me. I shall not take my own life and commit another sin. I will wait for the day God grants me death. And then, I will wait to be born again, to endure pain and accept betrayal. I believe I have not suffered enough for my sins, and that is why I will have to suffer more in another body, another life.

At the age of forty-five, I had been dismissed from the steel plant. One day, the manager invited me to his office and said that my work had deteriorated over the past several years.

Due to this, he was forced to hire a younger and more capable person. I did not lose my mind. In all honesty, I often struggled to keep up with the younger men at work. I told the manager that it was probably due to the sharp pains in my back. "It comes and goes. It is not serious," I said, hoping he would change his mind.

The manager said that most of the workers hired at the plant at the same time as me had been released more than five years ago. In that case, I had no choice but to bid farewell to my co-workers at the steel plant.

"The dollars I have saved over the last twenty years will be enough to survive another twenty years," I kept telling myself as I walked back home from my last shift. I did not have much to worry about; it was not like I was a spending man. My clothes were sufficient, the furniture stable, the walls intact, and the garden full of vegetables. I had few expenses.

By leaving the plant, I finally got the opportunity to concentrate on the land. Everything my father had taught me about the cornfields during my early years I had stored carefully in my mind. The whole year I nurtured the fields as if they were my children. During harvest season, many companies from different states offered generous sums for the mouth-watering maize thriving in my fields. My role in the plantation business ended at the age of fifty due to my lower back, which was no longer capable of handling extensive labor.

I was walking fine, sitting fine, eating fine, reading fine, but when it came to sleeping, I was not fine. Whenever my eyes shut, my brain was held captive by harrowing dreams. The war horse's painful screams, ears bleeding uncontrollably, feet moving faster and faster, landscapes filled with deceased soldiers, falling over motionless bodies, inspecting the lifeless forms, and the sight of my own corpse—these were the vivid pictures that unfolded in my head every other night.

The day I turned sixty, I remembered the pleasant and unpleasant memories that had shaped my life over the past ten years. Rachel, who is married and has two daughters and a son, visited with the whole family three years ago. After marrying a businessman who balances his career and family life, Rachel's days have been flooded with happiness. Margaret has three sons and a daughter, who all take good care of her after the tragic loss of David. The last time I saw her was a couple of years ago, when she came over to spend Christmas with her forlorn brother. Margaret has lived her life, while Rachel continues to live hers.

As for Aunt Nancy, she died ten years ago from a disease that has no known name. All we know is that it attacked her blood. When I last saw her, Aunt Nancy looked nothing like herself. Dazed, frail, bony, and in pain, my aunt exhibited all the signs of impending death. Her gums often bled, and she suffered frequent nosebleeds. God bless her soul. Her husband remarried at a very old age and was never heard from or seen again.

As for mother and father, from time to time, my eyes searched for them, hoping that one day they might appear in some corner of the house.

CHAPTER 12

What about Richard Foster? Well, my days are numbered. This morning, after a five-minute dry coughing session, I got out of bed and went straight to the mirror. The formations of my bones were visible as I stared at my skeletal body. The peeling skin on my hands itched relentlessly. The wrinkles and veins revealed themselves on my depressed face. My hairless skull contained a few deep scars earned during the war. The visible bags under my eyes indicated that I was not getting much sleep. As I looked at my stomach, I waited for it to growl.

But no sounds came from my stomach, which left me astounded. I had not eaten a meal since the previous day. The loss of appetite I had experienced for weeks had turned me from bulky to scrawny. Extending my fingers to the mirror, I paid no attention to the deformity. The fingers on my hands were denser than usual. The nails were extra shiny and soft. Nothing looked normal; everything looked odd. For the past couple of weeks, I had been suffering from high fevers and excessive perspiration during sleep. Fatigue had spread throughout my body.

As I write to you now, I feel that death is near. The call has come for me to leave. Somewhere, I had heard that one fears death, but I await it. I welcome death with open arms. With my household cleaned and sorted, I felt relaxed. The idea of dusting and scrubbing the house only occurred to me when I sensed that death was close. What if I were to die in my sleep? Leaving behind a filthy house could only suggest that the man who lived in it was filthy as well. One could call me a sinner, wrongdoer, transgressor, or slayer, but I am not and never was an unhygienic person.

Forty years is a long time, but not long enough to forget the enchanting face, the mesmerizing eyes, the gentle touch, the heartening kiss. Sitting by my bedside, I ran my fingers back and forth across my stitched name, starting with the R and ending with the D. There were days when I would sit on the porch and attempt to imagine how Julia would look at this age. Probably as beautiful as ever, with no aging wrinkles or spots on her face, no dark bags under her eyes, no stutter or slur in her speech, and no weak or broken bones. Her fine hair must have had a few elegant strands of grey; her hearing and sight must be as sharp as ever, and her tender hands must be as steady as before. I'd picture Julia seated in her lit room, knitting and stitching for hours until her fingers became numb.

I wonder how she is doing. Where is she living? Is she married? If so, does she have children? Is she happy with her married life? Does her husband let her stitch and knit? Does she ever think about me? So many questions, yet no answers.

Every inch of my body cried for help when I lifted myself from the bed, seated myself on a chair to write, extended my arm to dip the pen in an ink bottle, walked to the chest to take out my clothes, dressed myself in my precious uniform, observed myself in the mirror, and dragged my insignificant self to the window to view the late evening sun, which used the titan hills as a veil to cover itself.

"What a beautiful portrait. This may be the last time I view the sun," I said, as the incessant coughing worsened. I struggled to grasp the cup of water sitting on the table beside the window. But as soon as I did, my dry throat was temporarily relieved. The empty cup was then placed back on its original spot near the scattered coins and bundle of bills. The dollars on the table were my hard-earned savings. I kept them aside for my funeral expenses. They would be enough for Rachel and Margaret to provide me with a decent burial site next to mother and father.

A superbly detailed painting was revealed through my window. The hypnotic sunset rested between the tall, lanky trees and their drooping branches. The rays of light peered across the majestic hills as they battled with the dim glooms striving to survive. By the front gate were a group of six passenger pigeons, resting upon the steel fence. Their feathers were a mixture of bluish-gray and wine red, with black streaks and a blot of white on the edges. I concentrated on these rare birds, which were not seen as much as before.

"Have they migrated, or have they been hunted down?" I asked myself.

In the far distance, along the dusty trail leading to the house, I observed an indistinct figure. Squinting, I struggled to identify who this person could be. "At this hour, on my property, who could it be?" I whispered.

"An unexpected visitor is not welcome in my house, especially when I am so close to death."

As the feminine figure came to a stop, my feeble eyes were drawn to the pristine white frock with prints on it. With old age came poor eyesight, which was why I could not distinguish the exact patterns on the dress. Peace entered my mind, lightness filled my heart, butterflies tickled my stomach, and my muscles relaxed. I was not certain, but it seemed as if she was staring directly at the window. I felt as though her eyes were placed upon my face. She then turned, revealing her long natural tresses, which swayed back and forth as her feet began to retreat.

As the unknown figure walked further into the distance, my heart started to ache. A feeling of déjà vu knocked on the walls of my brain. "Has this episode of parting occurred before?" I asked myself. I recalled exactly how my heart shattered into diminutive pieces when the woman I had truly loved departed from my life.

Part 2- India to Fiji: The Fateful Expedition

THE 1ST DAY

"Vaazgha, welcome!" said Old Man Thambi. He was pleased to see that not only low-caste, village-dwelling, Tamil-speaking untouchables were venturing on this fateful expedition.

"Baba," said the Indian man as he rubbed his eyes in disbelief. "Is that you? What are you doing here?"

Before receiving a response, his body was shoved by a large ensemble of Indians, forcing him to part from the old man. The youthful Shivaji was dressed in a white kurta and dhoti, along with a blood-red turban placed upon his head. He was covered in attire from head to toe. Shivaji planted his feet firmly on the slippery wooden base, determined not to be knocked over by the clustered bodies that pressed against him. Due to the nuisance, his right arm mechanically acquired the role of defense. As the enormous crowd was ordered to proceed in the direction of the monumental transport, Shivaji battled to create his own path in the midst of hundreds of people. There was a buzzing noise in the air, not from any insect, but from a large assembly of Indians conversing persistently amongst themselves.

"Eh Vajrama, we will receive food, shelter, and money. There is no need to complain about the white folks. They have finally learned to respect and trust us. Now it is our turn to respect and trust them," said an elder woman dressed in a carroty-colored sari, much of her aging skin revealed through the visible tears.

"They have come to us; we have not gone to them. For once they require our assistance. What the white man cannot do, we will do. They can sit back and let us take charge on the islands," said an immature adolescent, swaying his instructive hands and raising his deafening voice.

"We were not given a choice. We have been forced to board this ship. We did not even get a chance to bid farewell to our loved ones."

"Don't weep, Ramchandran; there will come a day when you and I will return to our graceful land," said the optimistic father as he patted his son's back to comfort him.

"Watch your step. I don't want you to touch me."

"I am sorry, Madam, but it is not my fault. I am unable to control the pushing and bumping. Please forgive me if I have touched you."

"You untouchables are full of excuses. I know that by placing your filthy hands on us high-caste Brahmins you achieve immense pleasure," said the dark-skinned, feisty woman in a brusque manner.

"I have left my father, mother, wife, and kids behind for the sake of a better future. The true necessities of life were not provided by the unfaithful Coimbatore. Father and I worked day and night in the ocean as fishermen. But we still required more coinage to purchase sufficient amounts of rice, flour, and vegetables. I will never forget those days when my children went to bed with empty stomachs," said the Muslim gentleman as he revealed his narrative to others from the same religion.

Hundreds of different voices filled the compressed area. Some voices were full of excitement and pleasure, while others were associated with uneasiness and distress. Shivaji was tempted to cover his ears but did not dare to let go of his wife's needful hand. As his right arm thrust and tugged to create space for him to step forward, the left arm was Vyjanti's guide that led her to the current destination. Both husband and wife had jute bags hung over their shoulders, which added to their existing weight, making it difficult for them to balance themselves on the damp surface. Both jute bags were perfectly hand-sewn by Vyjanti and consisted of essential items such as extra pairs of kurtas, dhotis, saris, and undergarments. Then, from deep within her heart, emerged a sudden fear. Unexpectedly, Vyjanti let go of her husband's hand and reached into her jute bag. Her fragile hand searched between the garments until she felt a solid object.

"What is the matter with you? Why have you let go of my hand? What if I lose you in this massive crowd of people?" asked Shivaji as he physically situated himself in front of her.

"Thank you, Deva God. For a second, I thought I had misplaced you," said Vyjanti as she held out a miniature statue of Lord Shiva for her husband to see.

"Please don't let go of my hand again." Shivaji clutched his wife's arm and with force pulled her close while she managed to slip the brass idol back into her jute bag.

"You did not even give me a moment to spend with Deva. I was about to pray for Anna-brother, Anni sister-in-law, and Karthik. I hope they are fine. After being separated in the village, I have worried so much about them."

"Don't worry! Venkatesh is a wise man. If danger arises, he will be there to protect his family. I am sure we'll be reunited once we board the vessel," said Shivaji, hoping to encourage his wife.

"Please watch over them, Deva," whispered Vyjanti.

A British servant rose from the crowd, waving his hands around, gesturing for the Indians to form a single line. The powerfully built servant of Indian descent was dressed in a red coat made of cotton, white pants that gripped his thighs, and black boots that came up to his knees. Unable to grasp the attention of the Indians who were waiting to board the vessel, the servant took charge by utilizing his authoritative voice. "No one will be boarding the ship unless a single line is formed," he said in a commanding manner.

As all the passengers struggled to arrange and then rearrange themselves to form a single line, the servant burst out with laughter. "You people are useless. Why must it take so long to form a single line?"

"You will go to hell, you traitor," said a passenger from the array of bodies.

Soon after, a different voice surfaced, "You should be ashamed of yourself for acting like the white officials."

"Did you look at yourself in the mirror today? Your skin color is not white," said another person from the crowd.

The last comment led to thunderous applause filled with giggles and cackles which disturbed the servant. With a severely bruised ego, no control over his emotions, fire burning in his eyes, and a bulky stick in his hand, the muscular Indian stomped back and forth in search of the culprits who had the nerve to utter such rash words. With his rough-textured fingers, he curled his outgrown bristly whiskers, smiling from one ear to another. "So, I am a traitor? Well, the person who had the nerve to call me a traitor, I dare you to come forward."

The only sounds perceptible were the inharmonious cries of gulls in the distance. Lips were sealed; not a word was uttered.

"Be careful with what you say. Unwise words can lead to regret and agony," said the Indian servant as he beat his stick on the wooden surface, startling the children around him. After the muscular Indian paraded toward the vessel, the passengers were ordered to board without pushing and shoving. One by one, the soon-to-be laborers were granted access by the British officers and directed to one of the three sections onboard. Section A, the forward part of the ship containing the lower deck, was for families of two or more. Section B, the middle portion, with the upper deck, opulent rooms, a mini pool, and a respectable kitchen, was reserved for the men in charge and their crew. Section C, the cramped rear part, was designated for passengers traveling alone.

"What is this?" asked the fair-skinned British officer while inspecting a villager's belonging.

"You are to leave behind your gods, demi-gods, faith, and beliefs once you board this ship. The only God is Jesus and the only faith is Christianity. Do I make myself clear?"

Frightened, the villager's children hid their innocent faces behind their father's dingy kurta. The sari-clad wife stepped forward to claim her idol of Vishnu. She folded her hands, begging the officer to return the statue she worshipped. Without remorse, the officer took a few steps back, extended his powerful arm, and launched the idol into the air. "You want it? Go get it," he said before bursting into laughter.

With still bodies and stunned faces, the villagers watched their God plummet into the sea. Water formed in the helpless husband's eyes as he chose not to retaliate. He clung to his children, unable to meet the officer's gaze. The family was ordered to move forward with their searched belongings to Section A. The sinful act rattled Vyjanti. She whispered into her husband's ear, "What if they find it? Where do I hide the statue? If they find it, I will not stand and watch. I will fight back."

"I told you not to bring anything besides clothing. Hand over the statue. It is small enough to fit into the folds of my turban."

"Are you sure? Won't it be noticeable?"

Shivaji counted the number of heads in front of him, "seven...eight...nine," then placed his wife before him.

"What are you doing?" asked the bewildered Vyjanti.

"I need you to stay still. If I use your body as cover, the British won't see my act."

Shivaji delved into the bottom of Vyjanti's bag. Feeling the rounded curves and smooth edges of the brass idol, he clutched it, pulled it out, and hid it quickly.

"Vyjanti, find a wide fold in my turban and conceal it," he said, bending low to make it easier.

In less than ten seconds, the idol was tucked into the linen fabric. They turned their necks, checking if anyone had noticed.

"I wish I had a looking glass."

"Trust me, it is not visible. No bulge or outline. No one will tell a statue is hidden in your turban."

"Let's hope I'm not forced to remove it or searched," Shivaji whispered as their bodies touched. Suddenly, he felt a heavy object on his shoulder.

"Are you on your honeymoon? Should I ask the Captain to provide a luxurious bedroom?

You can rattle the bed all night long," said the Indian servant with coarseness.

Shivaji brushed the stick off his shoulder with his left hand. The vulgar remark sent flames through his veins. He said sharply, "Sir, please show respect. We are married. We come from respectable families."

"Why should I respect you? I have none for people lip-locking in public. Your parents would hang their heads in shame. Or perhaps you learned it by watching them," sneered the servant, drawing the crowd's attention.

"Don't speak of my appa (father) and amma (mother) with your filthy mouth," said Shivaji, fists clenched, teeth gnashed.

"Please don't retaliate. No need for trouble," murmured Vyjanti, tugging at his kurta, praying he would step back.

When rage closed in on him, Shivaji forced himself to retreat. He knew his temper could be disastrous. He could not let a quarrel spoil his chances of freedom and a prosperous future.

The ferocity in his eyes, the defiance in his voice, the obstinacy in his stance, the no-nonsense personality he inherited, and the threat he posed planted a thought in Brijnath's mind: "A future leader, rebel, or revolutionary—that man could damage colonial rule, Kulumber commander."

Tittering at the servant's assumption, Chief Officer Anderson eyed the would-be insurgent. "Do you think I'm foolish? Look at him! Small frame, short height, weak arms, thin legs—he is no threat to the British."

"But..." Brijnath swallowed his words after Anderson's scowl ended the conversation.

"Damn him! He is nothing but the white man's help. He forgot where he was born and raised. He does not accept the color of his skin or the religion he belongs to," said Shivaji.

Vyjanti's six months of marriage had already given her celestial insight. She knew that if she added even a few words, it would only escalate the conversation until her husband was shouting personal opinions, beliefs, and complaints until his voice became hoarse. The noble wife kept to her husband's side, casting a jealous glare at a female onlooker who showed too much interest in Shivaji's rambling.

"Look! We are close to boarding the ship now. There is only one family ahead of us," said Shivaji.

"We shall remain calm," said Vyjanti, hoping her pleasant advice would not irritate him.

"I am calm," replied Shivaji. "I hope you are not nervous. Don't show them that you are afraid. Once fear is sensed, these Englishmen will pounce."

A family of four was searched from head to toe by the British officers manning the boarding entrance. Barring the turban and slippers, the father was rigorously patted down. Suddenly, an officer unleashed a vicious blow to the emaciated father's skull. The villager staggered while clutching his head. A loud cry broke out from the children. The torn mother did not know who to look after—her husband or children. She went back and forth until the children's weeping grew louder, then finally extended her arms to the kids, offering security and relief. Meanwhile, Shivaji planted his feet firmly, stiffened his body, and whispered under his breath, "Even if I want to, I shall not react to this injustice."

Vyjanti stood behind him, reluctant to peek over his shoulder. Despite closing her eyes, her ears still ached from the shrill wailing. The crowd erupted after hearing the blow. "Hey, what is going on there?" said an Indian man dressed only from the waist down. "Leave them alone," shouted another, vigorously waving his fist.

The British officer, who had searched and then clobbered the villager, could not interpret what the bystanders voiced. "Hmm, seems like you were planning to cut us open with your dagger. Such belongings are not permitted on this ship," said the bloated officer as he pointed the weapon inches from the villager's throat. "Take them away," he ordered Brijnath.

The weapon was dropped into the enormous pile of seized items near the entrance. Many belongings deemed useless were tossed into the ocean, while items considered dangerous—knives, daggers, belts, and steel bracelets—were kept aside in case of future use.

"Next," shouted one of the British officers, eager to confiscate and castigate. Shivaji and his wife stepped forward with impassive faces, showing no sign of fear. "Your rebel has arrived, Brijanth," said Chief Officer Anderson, leaning against the railing.

Before the inspection commenced, Brijnath whispered into Anderson's ear. "Kulumber, please search this man. Trust me, he is a threat. I am sure he has a weapon." The chief officer's eyes widened at the word "threat." "Step aside, boys. I will take care of this coolie," said Anderson, striding forward with dominance.

The last fragments of fear in Shivaji had dissolved. Unlike the others who lowered their heads in submission, he met Anderson's eyes. Shivaji Nair held his head high, showing Indians were not inferior but equal. The officer sweated as he searched Shivaji, desperate to find a weapon. After the pat-down, he ordered the removal of sandals and turban. Shivaji feigned ignorance.

"What are you waiting for, coolie? Remove your sandals and hat."

Shivaji nodded, removed his sandals, and lifted his turban. Vyjanti held her breath.

"Deva, please let us surpass this obstacle. Protect my husband," she prayed silently.

We are destined to board this ship, destined to sail the ocean, destined to land on a fascinating island, destined to labor for a better future, destined to be free and equal, thought Shivaji.

The chief officer flipped the turban, shook it, and then, disappointed, handed it back. As Shivaji placed it on his head, his fingers brushed the hidden statue. How did he not feel it? Shivaji wondered.

Vyjanti was baffled to see an unusual grin on her husband's face.

"He is clean," said Anderson, frustrated the rebel had broken no rules. With nothing removed from their bags and nothing added to the pile, the couple proceeded. Brijnath lowered his eyes in shame, avoiding Anderson's gaze as he led them to Section A.

For the Indians who encountered him, Brijnath was nothing but a traitorous servant working against his own people. No compassion, respect, or trust was shown to him. As Shivaji and his wife followed Brijnath to their assigned section, they discovered how overcrowded the lower deck had become. Close to two hundred Indians were already on board, with another two hundred still boarding. How will everyone fit? Disputes will surely erupt into sheer madness, thought Shivaji.

As if on cue, he overheard a quarrel between two men. Their raised voices, enraged expressions, frantic hand gestures, and abusive language made it clear the matter was serious.

"This area belongs to me," demanded the Hindu.

The Muslim refused. "I don't see your name written here."

"Well, I was here first."

"Don't trouble my family with lies. My wife and kids have placed their belongings here. Find another spot."

"You low-caste scoundrel, how dare you? I'll bring all the Hindus together and teach you a lesson!"

The fight escalated into threats and insults rooted in religion. A crowd gathered, drawing the attention of the British crew. Deckhands garbed in red and white intervened, threatening action if the quarrel didn't end.

"But he—how—why—it's his fault, he started it, he must leave," sputtered the agitated men.

"Shut up! Another word and I'll call the master," barked the deck leader. "Neither you nor your families will get a chance to rest your hinnies here."

At the mention of the captain, both men fell silent. Their defenses collapsed. The leader ordered his men to escort the families elsewhere: the Hindu family moved to the northeast corner of Section A, the Muslim family to the southwest. The ferocious animals who had fought over a patch of floor were now subdued and relocated.

"Brijnath, place those coolies here," said the deck leader, pointing to a coveted spot. "You lovebirds are in for a treat—an ocean view suite. But remember, no hanky-panky," sneered Brijnath, cheap-talking and fast-walking as ever.

Vyjanti placed a calming hand on Shivaji's shoulder, praying he wouldn't retaliate. Shivaji felt her touch and knew he must let the insult pass. Yet the urge to slap Brijnath burned in him. Disappointed by Shivaji's silence, the servant slunk away, leaving the couple to absorb the sight of the ship Elbe.

Shivaji and his wife had been so preoccupied—by the endless queue and chatter, the nerve-wracking concealment of their idol, the British search party's pat-downs, and the quarrels between Hindus and Muslims—that they hadn't yet studied the monumental vessel.

The Elbe stood with three tall wooden masts piercing the clear sky. They loomed like guardians watching the Indians aboard. The front, middle, and rear masts supported pale sails—narrow at the top, broad at the bottom—that dangled like dreadful ghouls poised to devour the passengers. The bow curved smoothly into a lethal point, a sword ready to annihilate anything in its path.

These features sent a chill down Vyjanti's spine. Despite the dryness in her throat, she whispered, her voice heavy with emotion:

"My dear husband, I respect the decision we've made. But my heart is heavy—with fear. A fear that something is not right. Since boarding, I've felt uncertain. I'm scared—scared of losing you."

Her words ended in a fit of coughing. She clutched her throat, desperate for relief.

"What is this? You should have told me your throat was dry. I'll fetch water. Stay here, don't move."

In panic, Vyjanti seized his sleeve, her eyes wide with worry. She looked deep into Shivaji's eyes and pleaded, "Please don't leave me alone."

"But you need—"

Before Shivaji was able to finish, his wife uttered, "Don't worry, the coughing has stopped. I don't require water anymore." She then changed the topic to ease her husband's concern. "Come, let us rest our feet."

By the time the morning sun fastened itself into the halcyon sky, most of the Indian passengers were aboard the vessel, with a few late batches moving past the body and bag search at a hurried pace. Like the other Indian families on board, Shivaji and his wife examined their new home. Ship Elbe was now their stepmother. In her womb, they were to survive for the next month or so, leaving behind their original mother. India, being the original mother, would truly miss her children. But would the children, who chose to abandon their original mother, eventually come to miss her? Time would tell. Vyjanti eyed the limited space that was designated to her and Shivaji. "What is so special about this area? I have no idea why the two men were fighting for this spot. They behaved like two soldiers from different countries battling to occupy precious land," she said with a pleasant giggle.

"Did you not hear that, that, that..." Shivaji stumbled to find the proper word.

"Traitor," said his wife, providing the needed help.

"Perfect. That was the word I was looking for. Anyways, did you not hear what the traitor said?"

"No," Vyjanti replied with a puzzled look on her face.

Shivaji looked beyond the durable wooden railings and said, "This area gives us the chance to enjoy the ocean's view."

"Hmm...I suppose." Vyjanti took a peek through the railings and said, "I heard that the water surrounding the islands is luminous, which means you can see everything underneath the ocean. Though, I wonder how that can be possible? Whenever I look into the nearby ponds, lakes, and rivers, all I see is contaminated grey or muddy brown. Perhaps it is just a myth, tale, or fib."

"Honestly, I don't care if the waters by the islands are fluorescent or filthy," said Shivaji, using a cold tone.

The rays of light irritated Shivaji's eyes as he struggled to obtain a clear vision of his childhood friend amidst the countless roaming bodies.

"What happened?" asked Vyjanti when she discovered a change in her husband's body language.

Shivaji's eyes lit up with joy. With his hands, he formed a circle around his mouth and hollered, "Venkatesh...Venkatesh Swami, over here!"

Seated with her legs curled in, Vyjanti placed her knees on the deck to help lift her torso. Her neck, along with her eyes, veered from side to side in search of Venkatesh and his family. Meanwhile, Shivaji shouted and waved repeatedly, endeavoring to seize his friend's attention. Not a single ounce of importance was given to the staring faces as he called for his friend. Venkatesh, a tall and slender man of dark complexion, wore a beige-colored kurta and pajama with a white turban that seemed too big for his head. He recognized the familiar voice. As soon as he spotted his friend, he rushed his family past the bunched passengers on the lower deck. "Let's go, Lachmaiya. Maybe Shivaji will be able to provide us with a spot of our own in that corner of the deck," he said to his wife, indicating the location with his forefinger.

Lachmaiya was relieved that Shivaji and his wife were found. Immediately, Venkatesh took his wife's hand and advanced into the congested pathway with Karthik riding piggyback on his father's shoulders. As soon as Vyjanti appeared in front of Karthik's button-shaped eyes, the child unlocked his arms and legs from his father's body. When his tiny feet landed on the deck, he ran to his cherished aunt.

"Attai aunt, where were you? I looked all over for you, attai," he said as he soared into Vyjanti's arms.

Vyjanti embraced the hyperactive child, whom she was very fond of since the day she first set eyes on him. "Oh Karthik, I was so concerned. You have no idea how pleased I am to see you," said Vyjanti while swaying the child in her arms.

"I hope you and anni are both fine?" Shivaji asked his friend.

"Other than the fact that we have waited more than three hours to board the ship, got lectured and insulted by the British officers while lining up, were deprived of many of our personal belongings during the bag and body search, and nearly fell into a verbal argument with a Sikh family over occupying a desired spot on the deck, we are fine."

Shivaji's expressionless reaction confused Venkatesh. "Why are you serious? I was being sarcastic," said Venkatesh, expecting his friend to respond with a smile or laugh. He continued, "Anyways, we have been in search of a place where we can rest our tired bodies but have yet to come across a vacant area. How in the world are these white rascals expecting us to cope with so many bodies and such little space?"

Shivaji's face emerged with a smile from ear to ear. "Good old Venkatesh. Don't be upset. The area we have been given has the capacity to shelter five bodies."

"Yes, anna, you must share this area with us. Both families should remain together during this journey," said Vyjanti.

With his childhood friend and beloved sister by his side, it would have been foolish of Venkatesh to not accept the gracious offer. He treated Vyjanti like his very own sister. He did not dare to ever say no to her. Nor did she have the courage to ever say no to him. As a matter of fact, Venkatesh's left wrist bore the sacred thread that Vyjanti tied on him for the ancient bond of protection festival a couple of months ago. Since then, Venkatesh was often reminded of the moment when he said, "As you tie this 'Rakhi' on my wrist, Vyjanti, I promise to always shield you from evil."

Shivaji noticed a fairly large man of English descent wearing a blue frock coat with gold-laced buttons proceeding down the staircase. His knee-high leather boots pressed hard against the staircase, causing it to creak. Shivaji managed to catch a glimpse of the shining armor secured by the holster placed around the Englishman's waist. The vivid reflections coming from the gleaming sword detained the attention of the indentured laborers on board. As for the pocket-sized revolver, it was not hidden but exposed on the right side of the holster. The deliberate exposure of the revolver was a gesture indicating that the Englishman was armed and dangerous. To carry such weaponry, for protection or for resolving disputes, a person had to be of higher position or status. The light breeze hissing in the air manipulated the light strands of hair attached to the Englishman's face. His overall appearance—barbaric beard, emotionless eyes, cracked skin, and matted hair—made the Indians cringe. The stride in his steps, the pride on his chest, and the hardiness of his shoulders exhibited that he was a man of dominance. The moment Chief Officer Anderson saluted the unidentified person, the passengers on board knew that this man was definitely in charge of the ship. The herculean man stood over six feet tall, which made his crew members appear diminutive in front of him.

"Coolies, listen up! The captain wants your attention. He requires every single one of you to congregate in this area immediately," shouted Anderson. Noticing that more than half of the passengers continued their discussions instead of following the order, he motioned for Brijnath to take the stand. Brijnath repeated what the chief officer had said earlier, but this time in Hindi and Tamil. "Good job, Brijnath," said the chief officer as he observed the massive crowd hovering around the selected area. Meanwhile, the passengers assigned to Section C were herded by the deck crew to Section A, where the assembly was soon to begin. Within minutes, Section A was filled with at least four hundred coolies and close to fifty British seafarers who held various positions on the ship.

"What do these Englishmen want from us now? Is this supposed to be a grand festival?" said Old Thambi under his breath as he labored to move his feet across the platform. His lengthy, unkempt, and colorless beard flopped from side to side as he walked into the abundant crowd. He was extremely fragile, with arms and legs that looked like the twiggy branches of a neem tree. So when his shoulders rubbed against other shoulders, his hips crashed against other hips, his feet got stepped on by other feet, and his hands got pushed away by other hands, Thambi faced immense soreness.

"Damn you, inconsiderate people. You have no respect for the elders. Don't you know how fragile my bones are?" said the elderly man when a brawny arm pushed him aside. "Step aside, old man. You should not even be on this ship. What help will you be to the British?" said the rugged villager.

The words of insult pierced Old Man Thambi's heart. "This man just claimed that I am useless. Why? Is it because of the deep circles under my eyes, the creases on my forehead, or the wrinkles on my hands and legs which indicate that I am prehistoric? Is it because of the hunch in my back that compels me to walk awkwardly? Am I too old?" A whirlwind of thoughts floated in and around Thambi's mind. Keeping his thoughts aside, he threatened the villager, "Don't force me to put a curse on you. An old man's curse lasts forever."
"So the ignorant old man believes he has supreme powers. Go ahead. Let's see what your powerful sayings can do to me," replied the villager with an obnoxious cackle.

As soon as Thambi shut his eyelids, he appeared to be in a hypnotic state, mumbling strange words to himself.

"Attention...Attention...Attention! My name is Captain Sanders. From this moment, I talk and you listen. Listen carefully. I am the one in command of this ship. It is I who is in charge of every passenger on board. It is my responsibility to get you to Fiji. And I will fulfill this responsibility. I, as the leader, will lead you to the islands. So how long is this journey? Well, it takes an ordinary Master close to sixty days to sail his ship to the islands. But a wise, experienced, and honored Captain like I will make sure that the beautiful Elbe reaches Fiji in no more than forty-five days. Now let me lay out the rules and policies. First and foremost, this is a British ship controlled and manned by British seafarers. What we say is always right. What we say must always be followed. What we say must never be ignored. What we say will be for your own benefit. If at any time an order is purposely disregarded or an assigned task is not fulfilled, there will be consequences to pay. In other words, punishment will be served."

The Indians of the assembled mass stared at each other with fear running up their spines. Brijnath's translation of the English phrases voiced by the captain echoed in the ears of the Indians on board. Once realizing that his voice was hoarse, Captain Sanders cleared his throat and spat onto the platform. The saliva splattered on the wooden floor in front of the passengers. "You," he pointed to Brijnath. "Get over here and clean this mess."

Brijnath did not decline. "Yes, Captain, I sure will. It will be my pleasure," replied the Indian servant with a candid smile on his face.

The Indian passengers on the deck observed Brijnath's movements with mixed feelings. Brijnath reached into his pocket and extracted a white, crumpled handkerchief. With immense speed, he bent to his knees and wiped the portion of the deck covered with saliva. Hindi, Urdu, Tamil, and Telugu words were discreetly whispered amongst the crowd of Indians. "How could he? This is shameful. Why does he have a smile on his face? This is where we Indians stand. They have us under their feet. They treat us like dogs. We are nothing but their servants."

The murmurs dispersed as Captain Sanders strained his voice to dictate the end of all conversations. "Silence...I am ordering you all to be silent." With his throat cleared, the captain proceeded with his booming voice. "Hmm...Now, where was I? Oh yes...You are to assist with all the duties assigned by the deck crew on this ship. Our Chief Cook will provide you with two meals per day. You will be served at sunrise and before sunset. Chief Officer Anderson, as most of you may know, is second in command. His assistant, Brijnath, is Indian by blood but British by heart. He is the prime example of how all Indians should be and behave. He is the translator on this ship. And last but not least, the only religion to be followed on this ship is that of Christianity. Jesus is our God, so from now on Jesus is your God also. Your religion, culture, traditions, and rituals must all be forgotten on this ship. Now...Let's begin the expedition."

Four different types of paintings were illustrated on the faces of the hundreds of indentured laborers: hostility, apprehension, incredulity, and submission. Shivaji's burning eyes revealed hostility. Vyjanti's soft lips trembled with apprehension. Old Man Thambi's open-mouthed reaction exposed his incredulity. And Venkatesh stood idle with his head lowered, prepared to submit to oppression.

A sudden motion with extreme impact forced Shivaji to lose control of his balance. The movement of the vessel had total control of his feet as he flung backward, colliding against the wooden railing.

"Oh Deva, are you okay?" asked Vyjanti, concerned for her husband.

"Get down, get down," replied Shivaji as he plummeted to the deck, fighting back the pain in his back from colliding with the railing. Vyjanti and the other passengers immediately descended, hands instinctively reaching to protect their exposed heads. Within seconds, the deck was covered with still bodies, some lying on top of one another. Terror gripped the indentured laborers, silencing every voice. Departing Ship Elbe was a brand-new experience for most Indians on deck. As the vessel left the dock, an unfamiliar sensation whirled in their brains, undulated in their stomachs, fluttered in their ears, wavered in their balance, and quivered under their feet.

"Get up, you foolish coolies. There is nothing to be afraid of. It is the ship, it is moving," said Brijnath while curling the ends of his pointed mustache. His words eased some tension. The Indian passengers carefully began to balance themselves on the moving vessel. At first, it seemed impossible, but within minutes, the adults walked with confidence while the children scurried near their loved ones in playful glee. From the four hundred Indians on board, more than half had their eyes fixed on their motherland, which slowly vanished as the vessel moved into the heart of the sea. Old Man Thambi stood motionless, watching the last reflections of his land in the impure waters. Not an inch of his body stirred; only tears trickled down to the start of his long thread-like beard.

"Karthik, do not lean over the edge of the railing," said Lachmaiya, extending her arms to grab her curious son. "What is the matter with you? If you are not careful, you can fall into the ocean."

Karthik resisted his mother's affection as she pulled him close. "I want to see the waves the ship leaves behind, amma. Look, look amma. It is wonderful!"

Venkatesh lifted his son onto his shoulders.

"Wow, from up here I can see the entire ocean, appa."

Karthik's innocent eyes had never beheld such a magical scene. For most Indian passengers, this was the first glimpse of such a vast body of water. Small ponds, narrow rivers, and shallow lakes were known to some, but for villagers deep inland, the only water they had seen was in wells.

Shivaji did not hesitate to remove his kurta, despite dozens of women glancing from the corners of their eyes. He leaned against the railing, exposing his lower back. Vyjanti's fragile hands rubbed smoothly against his reddened skin. She noticed the sensual eyes on Shivaji, bare from the waist up.

"Are you not ashamed? In front of onlookers, you persist with your demonstrative therapy," teased Shivaji.

"Ssshhh...If you bother me with such words, I will stop," Vyjanti replied.

"You certainly have magical hands. The warmth and delicacy of your touch have relieved the pain in my lower back. Thank you, sweetheart."

"Sheesh...My dear husband speaks in such an inappropriate manner."

Vyjanti rolled her eyes, squinted her nose, and teased with her tongue, reminding Shivaji of the childlike innocence he first noticed on their wedding night. Shivaji's thoughts were interrupted as Captain Sanders bellowed an order. Chief Officer Anderson listened carefully; under his supervision, the deck crew took charge, completed their tasks, and ensured the ship traveled efficiently.

Hand in hand, the couple overlooked the blue skies, the pregnant sun, the endless sea, their fellow passengers, and the seafarers in command. With peace in their hearts, Shivaji and Vyjanti sat back-to-back, using each other as pillars of support. Passing Indians supplied derisive glances and chuckles but received no attention from the couple. This position symbolized the essence of marriage: mutual support and equality.

"My goodness, look at them. Everyone is staring. Why don't you advise Shivaji not to act so obscene?" Lachmaiya protested to Venkatesh, using her scarf to conceal her face.

"Hmm...Not bad. We should try that as well," said Venkatesh, pinching his wife's waist.

"Ouch," cried Lachmaiya. "Stop misbehaving. Put your childish manners to rest."

Venkatesh stretched his long fingers until he met a slap.

"Keep your dirty hands away from me."

"That is not what you say at night," Venkatesh replied, laughing.

Struggling to keep her eyes open, Vyjanti asked Shivaji if she could rest until the food was served. Knowing she had not slept the previous night, Shivaji agreed.

"I wish I could kiss your forehead before you sleep. I do it every night. And now I must skip this routine for the next month or so."

Vyjanti responded with silent love. Within seconds, her eyes closed, and her body relaxed.

"Vyjanti...Vyjanti!"

No reply. With his wife asleep, Shivaji directed his gaze toward the stagnant ocean waters, reflecting on events before boarding this predestined expedition.

From the land where the fresh ocean breeze caresses the skin, where hot winds make breathing difficult, where plains rise and fall, where tigers, monkeys, bats, cobras, mongoose, and rats thrive in scrub jungles, and where seasonal cyclones destroy villages, came a fisherman named Shivaji Nair. Purple, red, and orange stretched across the heavens as the skies released nimble specks of water, leaving the soil moist. A brownish-red rooster lifted its neck to cock-a-doodle-do, reviving the laboring villagers. Grey monkeys peeked from the banyan tree branches. Village women prepared for another day, fetching water, bathing, praying, cooking breakfast, washing clothes and utensils, dusting walls and floors, tending gardens, and preparing feasts for the men returning from labor.

Vyjanti, valuing her role as a housewife, fulfilled these duties diligently. She believed marriage demanded devotion to her husband, yet she maintained her identity. She balanced her role as a capable wife and respected daughter-in-law. Her in-laws, seeing no difference between her and their daughters, admired Vyjanti's values and moral ethics.

When a person is tested by the rooster's ear-splitting calls, coconuts thumping against the solid tin roof, early-morning chit-chat from the parents' room, verbal squabbles among siblings, and the wailing of village children, they are bound to awaken. As the bothersome daylight crept into Shivaji's pupils, the various sounds of the household came to life. He could hear everything—except his wife. Vyjanti's movements were ethereal, as if her feet never touched the ground. She floated silently from one end of the house to the other. When she entered the kitchen to fulfill her duties, the crackling of the fire, the splashing of water, and the clatter of pots and pans never disturbed Shivaji's sleep.

When he was fully alert, he would call for her: "Vyjanti...Vyjanti! Can you please attend?" She always dropped what she was doing and rushed to the bedroom. Every day, Shivaji had a different request, from a sweet kiss to start his day to preparing buckets of water for his morning bath. The fact that he was the last to rise did not concern him or his family. By the time Shivaji bathed, his two sisters had left for the Free Church Mission School for girls, his father's hands were already covered with clay, and his mother was in the middle of her weaving.

Once fed, Shivaji gathered his small hand-casting net and walked to the sandy coastlines of Red Lilies District, where his family lived. Some fishermen ventured far into the ocean for large fish, while others stayed nearshore for smaller ones. Shivaji had never been on a boat, so he remained at the shore. Carefully folding his dhoti to his thighs, he entered the knee-high water, knowing Vyjanti would scold him if it became soaked. With the net balanced over his shoulder, Shivaji released it into the water. Half of the day's catch would be salted and dried under the scorching sun, while the other half remained fresh for customers. Unlike other fishermen, Shivaji charged the same price for salted and fresh fish. If a regular customer wanted larger fish, he remembered to provide extra for the next day. Being a competent swimmer, he ventured deeper to find larger fish, and he never returned home empty-handed.

"Shivaji is the only man who goes the extra mile for a customer," a happy buyer would say.

Most of the nine piles of fish disappeared within hours, though sometimes a quarter remained unsold. As a Tamil Brahmin, Shivaji and his family did not consume meat or seafood, so he could not bring the fish home. One evening, he raised the subject of Brahmins and their dietary restrictions with his father.

"Appa, I know we are Brahmins and don't eat meat. But I saw a Bengali Brahmin buy an entire bundle of fish today. He said his wife prepares it in different ways, and it tastes good."

"Was he not an untouchable?" his father asked sharply.

"No, Appa, he behaved and spoke respectfully," Shivaji replied.

Shaking his head, his father said, "Well, fish is meat. We will never eat it. You can sell it, but if I see you taste it, you must leave this house."

Shivaji accepted this silently, promising himself, *I may not be the purest Brahmin, but I will never let my father's honor be compromised by consuming fish or meat.*

When it was time to leave the market, Shivaji packed his materials quickly, ensuring he avoided the congested crowd. A quarter of the fish piles remained unsold, but he had other plans for them. As he passed vegetable, fruit, flour, rice, and salt vendors, he greeted them with smiles, waves, and nods before finally stepping away from the chaos.

"Look who I see! You've escaped the rush," said the bearded Old Man Thambi, tapping Shivaji's shoulder with his stick.

"I was looking for you. I have a decent amount of fish for you today."

"And what do you want in return?" Thambi asked, rubbing his eyes.

"Like every day, your blessings will do just fine."

Thambi extended his hands, not for alms, but to bless Shivaji. With his hands placed upon Shivaji's head, Thambi said, "May the Lord bless you always with happiness and protect you from evil."

After several minutes of conversing, Shivaji emptied the remaining fish into Thambi's sack. With a limp in his walk, the beggar moved eastward. No one knew where he lived, ate, or slept. He was an untouchable wanderer—without a background, a shilling in his pocket, or suitable clothing. In Red Lilies District, no one would share a moment, start a conversation, lend a hand, show respect, or even glance at Thambi—except Shivaji Nair.

"If touched by an untouchable, one is no longer pure? Let me guess, they must walk barefoot to the Ganges to cleanse themselves. To interact with an untouchable makes one unworthy? They must gurgle and spit out the filth from their mouth? It makes no sense. Untouchables are rejected by society and its ignorant people. Why? I don't believe in high or low caste. God made everyone equal. All living souls are born pure. It is the sins we commit that blemish our purity," Shivaji began lecturing his wife as soon as he entered the compound.

Vyjanti listened, then quietly sauntered to the backyard to fetch a pale of water from the drum, vanishing without a sound as she turned the corner.

"For once, can someone please listen to me?" cried Shivaji, wishing his wife had heard his words. His attentive mother rushed to the front of the house.

"What is the matter? Why are you shouting? Don't you know your father is resting at this hour?" She looked at Shivaji with faint eyes, expecting him to show regret. Her heart melted as Shivaji leaned over and touched her feet.

"May you live a prosperous life," said his mother as Shivaji walked past her.

The family seated themselves comfortably on the kitchen floor. The rich aromas of South Indian cuisine teased their empty stomachs. Their tongues craved the flavorful, spicy, sour, and sweet tastes. Healthy green banana leaves were spread in front of each family member. Vyjanti and his eldest sister-in-law served the dishes: curd rice, savory vada, crispy dosas, toor dal, and coconut chutney. Once the first batch was served, Shivaji's father motioned Vyjanti and his eldest daughter to join them for the meal.

"Guess who I met today?" Shivaji asked his father.

His father remained busy, chewing large portions of curd rice.

"Old Man Thambi? Poor fellow...everyone avoids him as if he's contagious."

He stopped chewing, swallowed hard, sipped water from his tin cup, and cleared his throat. "How many times have I told you to stay away from that man? He is dangerous, practices black magic, and is an untouchable. He doesn't belong in our society. No son or daughter of mine shall associate with him."

"But Appa, he harms no one. He blesses me. He is unfortunate, impoverished. I help the man by giving him the fish unsold at the market.

His father's face reddened. He signaled the women to remove leftover food and utensils, then turned to his son. "Be aware. Be afraid. Be careful. He is a man with evil powers. I know him better than you do. I know his stories. Do you know what he did to his enemies?"

"No, Appa."

"About thirty years ago, before you were born, Thambi appeared in our district. He went house to house begging. His appearance, language, and actions showed he was an untouchable. He had no last name. Was he Hindu, Muslim, Sikh, or Christian? No one knew. Whenever he entered a compound seeking food, he was chased with sticks and stones. Men, women, and children tried to beat him. Within weeks, the sticks and stones were replaced by hoes and knives. He scampered wildly through streets like an insane person. Using a belligerent tone, he cursed the residents:

'You are all demons and devils. You have no heart. Today, you do not feed me. You want me to suffer. You want me to die of hunger. You treat me like an animal. You avoid me as if I carry a deadly virus. Mark my words: a day will come when you will be suffocated, deprived of food and water. Others will call you dogs and treat you as their property.'

Shivaji stayed silent, lowering his eyes, absorbing his father's tale about the supposedly deranged wanderer.

"Then came a day when Thambi crossed paths with four young men sitting under a coconut tree. They were high-society Tamil Brahmins in their early twenties, whistling at women, talking to passersby, waving at bullock cart drivers, and sharing their personal lives. The beggar unexpectedly entered the scene.

'Hey, old man, come here,' called one of the men.

Thambi ignored him.

'You bum! Bring your raggedy self over. We will reward you. Charity is what you need; charity is what you'll get.'

Finally seizing Thambi's attention, the men waved him closer. He walked toward them with palms open for alms, feeling his raging hunger, heartbeat drumming against his chest, and weariness in his unstable legs.

'Quick, quick, put it in my hand,' whispered one of the men, waiting for his friend to place the object in his hand.

Thambi was so captivated by the apparent kindness of the young men that he became blind to their intentions. He imagined fresh bread, plump fruits, and sweet desserts filling his sack. Then, a sudden blow to his temple shattered the illusion. Pain exploded across his forehead, and blood gushed down the side of his face. Numbness spread from his face to his legs. His stumbling feet finally gave way as he collapsed to the ground. With their bellies full of laughter and his belly empty, Thambi unleashed a deafening wail.

'Now that is what you deserve,' said the man who had thrown the heavy stone. 'We don't need scum like you in this district.'

The severely injured beggar felt the dent on his forehead as his quivering body lay on the street. After several tries, he managed to sit cross-legged. Laughter erupted from the young men.

'Look at the beggar; he thinks he's a saint. Scram, untouchable, or be stoned to death,' said the friend who had provided the rock.

Thambi bled profusely. His eyelids were covered in gore, and his bare chest was streaked with red. The intense stare from his eyes unsettled the teenagers.

'You have shattered not only my forehead but also my trust. I believed in you. I thought you would give me alms, but instead you gave me pain. The blood from my forehead may one day flow from yours. You have humiliated and tormented me. A day will come when others will repay you in kind.'

The beggar closed his eyes, inhaled deeply, raised his palms above his head, and began chanting. The mysterious incantations he uttered were unknown even to the most learned priests and mullahs.

'This old man believes he has powers. Nothing you do will harm me. Your black magic will fail,' said the culprit.

When the chanting ended, Thambi lifted himself from the pavement with surprising vitality. The young men were astonished to see that the blood from his forehead had stopped.

'It is not my decision to punish you; it is God's. I only provide a warning, a chance to correct yourself. Do not listen to the devil inside you. Do not harm the innocent, who brings no threat or pain. One week from now, same day, same hour, same place. Be wise...'

Thambi's warning had little effect on the egoistic, discriminatory minds of the young men.

One week later, same day, same time, the four friends gathered under the coconut tree again, indulging in crude jokes and lewd talk. Not far away, a stray cat meandered along the pavement, its black fur patchy from illness. With innocent eyes, it studied the men and let out a plaintive meow.

'Shew, shew. What a dreadful-looking animal. Get out of here,' shouted the culprit.

The cat quickly scuttled away.

'Watch this,' said the culprit with a pompous grin. He crouched to grab a fist-sized rock near the tree.

'Leave it alone. It has passed by,' warned one friend.

'That rock can kill it. Don't do it,' said another.

Ignoring them, the young man hurled the rock. In an instant, he collapsed to the pavement, the loud impact startling the cat, which fled. The friends froze in shock and fear as they saw a pool of blood surrounding his head. Beside his body lay a fallen coconut.

'There is no wind. How did the coconut fall?' asked one.

'The beggar must have cursed him,' said another.

Instead of helping, the friends fled, fearing the beggar's unknown powers.

Shivaji's father paused, expecting questions from his son.

"What happened to the culprit?" asked Shivaji.

"He never recovered fully. The blow caused brain injuries," replied his father.

Shivaji sighed. "Coconuts fall from trees all the time. That teenager was just unlucky, at the wrong place at the wrong time."

"What do you mean? You don't believe my story? You are unwise. I only want you to stay away from that man. That is final," said his father, furious.

"I don't believe Thambi has superior powers, Appa. What happened to the teenager was coincidence—a coincidence he deserved," Shivaji replied.

His father rose, voice stern. "I see your respect for me fading."

"That is not true. Appa, I simply have a different opinion. One you refuse to accept."

"Your opinions and decisions will one day bring you serious trouble," said his father, storming out of the kitchen.

Sunday was the day of leisure. On this day, the adults of the Red Lilies district engaged themselves by attending morning prayers at temples, visiting close family or friends for a special meal, heading to the nearest festival, or spending intimate time with loved ones behind closed doors. Vyjanti and her mother-in-law ensured that every Sunday morning they attended the village temple with a handful of flowers, various fruits, a coconut for Lord Ganesha, and rice pudding offered to Lord Shiva.

For a potter, Sunday meant rest from kneading, wedging, shaping, decorating, drying, and firing. Shivaji's father, Muthuraman Nair; grandfather, Munni Ratnam Nair; and great-grandfather, Murga Swami Nair, had all dedicated their lives to pottery. With bare hands, they crafted pots, selling them across the regional district. Designs passed down through generations were still carved by Muthuraman. Despite stiff competition in the last decade, he continued to supply his fine crafts to markets in towns surrounding the village. Muthuraman frequently tried to persuade his only son to join the family business, but Shivaji consistently declined, stating he was uninterested.

"Fishing is for people of lower castes," Muthuraman deliberately insulted Shivaji. "Out there in the ocean, who do you see? Hindus, Muslims, Christians—all with no class. The untouchables with wild hair, heavy beards, grotesque physiques, tattered clothes, and foul odor seem as if they returned from a fourteen-year exile."

The discussion ended when Shivaji retorted, "When Lord Rama returned to Ayodhya after fourteen years of exile, did he have wild hair? A grotesque body? Torn clothes? Reek of foul odor? Did the people call him an untouchable? I don't think so."

To avoid a sixteen-hour argument with his father, Shivaji, accompanied by Vyjanti, strolled through the knee-high dirt covering the village road, eventually reaching the Swami residence. They were greeted by the couple's only child, Karthik. The evening passed swiftly in conversation until Lachmaiya, Venkatesh's unpretentious wife, served a luscious meal. For the Swami and Nair families, spending quality time together on Sundays was a cherished routine.

Childhood friends Shivaji and Venkatesh shared a bond of unshakable trust. Raised practically together, Shivaji was mischievous, prone to verbal and physical altercations, and often damaged objects or teased others. Venkatesh was curious, always asking why, when, where, and how. During school, both liked the same girl but turned their rivalry into a playful contest: the first to approach her was the winner. Weeks passed with tentative steps, but both ultimately lost interest, as adolescence and school pressures took over.

Belonging to middle-class families with limited income, neither could pursue further studies, which promised government jobs under the English.

"If we educate ourselves, we will have to serve the English," Shivaji said on their final school day.

"Explain," Venkatesh asked.

"If we gain credentials, the English will make us follow their ways—talk, walk, dress, and eat like them. We'd be used to control our own people. Even if my parents could afford further studies, I would refuse. No certificate is worth obeying the British."

Venkatesh understood. "One day, British rule will end. India will be free. How and when—that's what I want to see."

Using his schooling, Venkatesh operated a successful produce business. His family grew and harvested fruits and vegetables while he sold them at his central market stall.

Shivaji usually avoided it, but when helping customers carry large sacs of fish, he occasionally passed by. Venkatesh would greet him warmly: "What will you have today? Try the mangos. Extra ripe, extra sweet—you'll enjoy them."

"No, thank you," Shivaji replied.

"Shivaji, don't say no. What should I pack for you? Carrots, cucumbers, onions? Or tamarind for Vyjanti, so she can make her famous tamarind chutney?"

"Venkatesh, thank you, but I don't want anything from your stall."

"Why not?" asked Venkatesh, a shadow of displeasure on his face.

"Because you don't let me pay. You know me, Venkatesh. I don't want anything free. Accepting it makes me feel I'm taking advantage of a friend."

"Are you serious? I've known you since childhood. It's not right to accept money from you."

"Well, if you came to my stall, I'd charge you for the fish," Shivaji said, laughing.

"I cannot charge you. I don't care what you think. Take some sweet potatoes. From my garden, plucked by my own hands, just for you. No fee accepted." While bagging the sweet potatoes, Venkatesh focused on his hands, unaware that Shivaji had slipped away at the words, "no fee accepted".

At times, Shivaji marveled at how far they had come: playmates, classmates, now workmates at the Red Lilies market. Both were Hindu Brahmins with faith in God—one worshipping at home and in temples, the other carrying God in his heart.

On Karthik's birthday, the Swami family hosted a small gathering. Shivaji and Vyjanti participated, sending heartfelt wishes. The women chatted indoors while the men snacked on crisp murukku and discussed village rumors.

"I overheard the Englishmen talking about a cyclone heading our way," said a villager.

"We had torrential rain all week. I wouldn't be surprised," said Muthuraman.

"We haven't had a major storm in years. Why do you think we'll face one now?" Venkatesh asked.

"I'm just repeating what the British men said. Often, what they say proves true," the villager replied.

Shivaji's stomach churned. Gratitude or admiration toward the British was hard to swallow.

"Were they speaking English or Hindi?" he asked.

"English, obviously," came the reply.

Shivaji grinned. "So you claim to know their words when you cannot understand a word?" Venkatesh and others laughed. Three days later, Shivaji regretted insulting the villager; Venkatesh regretted laughing.

But Almighty could not stop Mother Nature. An implacable cyclone swept across Red Lilies in the early morning. Stray dogs barked nonstop, horses paced anxiously, birds vanished. Torrential rain crashed on tin roofs, waves struck the coast, trees were stripped bare, and straw, stick, and tin houses were destroyed. Only brick and cement walls remained. Farm animals were scattered across debris-filled fields. The siblings of disaster—wind and rain—had struck with ruthless efficiency.

As the storm subsided, Shivaji opened his front door. Dark gray clouds still loomed. His feet sank into filthy ankle-deep water, floating with leaves, twigs, and debris. Knee-deep, he folded his dhoti and moved carefully. He touched his father's pottery wheel, relieved it remained intact, though smeared with grey clay.

"The cyclone has swallowed the pots. The clay dissolves in water. The loss of appa's intricately designed crafts will crush him," Shivaji muttered.

A sudden crash made him leap. The prized jasmine tree lay uprooted, petals floating on the floodwaters. "The sight of these scattered petals will devastate her," he whispered. Vyjanti had cherished the tree since her first day in the house. Amid the stench of water and carcasses, the jasmine scent lingered, an intoxicating mix of disgust and serenity. Shivaji waded with all his strength to the edge of the compound.

Across the street, neighbors struggled to salvage possessions. The Reddy family retrieved undamaged cooking pots. On a field nearby, a family of twelve surveyed ruined crops. "Our bread and butter came from these crops. Why must God be so cruel?" the father lamented.

"Why must you always blame God whenever something bad happens?" his wife replied.

"The crops have been destroyed by the storm, not by God."

"You are naïve. All that happens in this world is controlled by God." After a pause, he murmured, "I wish I knew the answer."

"The answer to what?" asked his wife.

"Why has God chosen our district? Why this ruination?"

The village path was layered with fallen trees, bloodless cattle, crocks, dogs and cats, tin, wood, fruits, vegetables, and hay. The devastation troubled Shivaji. He saw neighbors with homes demolished, fields ruined, garments drifting in floodwaters, and utensils submerged. Walking through the debris, Shivaji noticed a young boy, Velu, known for mischievous antics. On top of a sun-heated tin roof, Velu beat a pot with spoons, singing:

"When I grow up, what shall I be? A farmer, barber, doctor, teacher? First, I must be bigger, smarter, and powerful."

With moist eyes, Shivaji watched Velu search the floodwaters for his belongings. "Velu, the waters can swallow you. Stop," his mother urged. He ignored her, persistent in retrieving his cherished items.

That night, villagers prayed, searched for food, and remained alert. Shivaji and Vyjanti, backs against each other on their mattress, reflected:

"Many have lost everything. Our tomorrow is better. We have shelter, food, clothes. But the ocean's erosion will reduce fish tomorrow. All villagers must unite to restore Red Lilies."

"How?" asked Vyjanti.

"Our district has been invaded and crippled. Help is needed, or it will never recover," Shivaji said.

Vyjanti admired his resolve. "We are fortunate our house stands. Let us help the unfortunate. Venkatesh's house is badly damaged; Karthik showed me the flooded rooms."

Shivaji ran to his father. "Appa, they need our help. Karthik cannot live like this." Muthuraman, recalling the birthday scene with Karthik, agreed reluctantly: "Yes, they may stay. But keep your promise—no more than three days."

Morning brought villagers smiling at the chance to repair and reform. Shivaji and Vyjanti visited Venkatesh. "I don't want to burden you," Venkatesh said.

"You are not a burden. If I cannot help a friend, what use am I?" Shivaji replied, frustration rising. Vyjanti intervened, emphasizing the health risks and moral duty, convincing Venkatesh to accept their hospitality.

By afternoon, friends labored together, emptying water and fixing the roof. Shivaji, scarf covering his face from the malodorous air, reassured: "No human casualties. Our village may suffer, but we survive. That is something to be thankful for."

Venkatesh, however, argued: "Survival is not enough. My crops are ruined, my stall closed. I fear for my family, our income, and our future."

"Don't misunderstand me, Venkatesh. I am just trying to say that the outcome of the cyclone could have been worse. Houses can be rebuilt, crops can be regrown, overflow of water can be removed, but the loss of a loved one can never be replaced."

Venkatesh kept silent, his mind weighed down by overthinking.

"Don't worry, nanban. Everything will work out just fine. Time will heal everything. Look at me—I am jobless. There is no fish for me to catch. Either the fish have washed up near the shore, which means they are dead, or they've been carried further into the sea, making it impossible to trap them."

The childhood friends watched the darkness envelop the village. Except for their somber conversation, both made use of every second, determined to finish the labor. Both were pleased to know that by the next day, the strenuous work would be nearly done.

"Seems like the repairs will be completed by tomorrow," said Venkatesh.

"Yes, it will. Your house will look just like it did before. No one will be able to tell it was damaged," replied Shivaji with a chortle.

"If we do complete the work tomorrow, will you let my family and me leave?"

"No," Shivaji answered brusquely.

"Please, your majesty," said Venkatesh.

"No, nanban. You can leave the day after. I don't want Anni and Karthik walking at night."

"What do you mean?"

"By the time we finish tomorrow, the skies will be black."

"What kind of excuse is that, Shivaji?"

"Please don't argue. It's not often we share the same house, Venkatesh. Let's spend some quality time together. Your house will not run away," Shivaji said, adding a touch of humor.

Near the Nair residence, Venkatesh stopped. "Wait a minute. All day you've been repairing my house. What about yours? I saw the front gates—they're badly damaged. And the compound? Who will clear the debris?"

"I am not worried. I'll repair the gates after helping you. As for the compound, Vyjanti and Amma said they'd handle the debris today. My real concern is the jasmine tree and its flowers. I must plant another for my wife. You should have seen her face, Venkatesh—so pale, tears rolling down. The winds destroyed the branches, scattering every flower. Not a single bloom remained intact."

Venkatesh and his family moved back into their rebuilt home. The family of three labored in the fields, knowing it would take months to recover. Shivaji encouraged Venkatesh to take a loan from a friend who had not suffered much in the cyclone.

"I have to do these degrading jobs, Shivaji. My grandfather taught me never to borrow money. We must earn it ourselves, with sweat, blood, and tears. And I follow his teachings today."

"Yes, it's those teachings that make you so obstinate," Shivaji said, smiling to lighten the mood. Work was work to him, no matter how humble, as long as it was honest and fair.

At home, Shivaji endured thirty minutes of his father's lectures each evening. Muthuraman's words were like a cobra's bite, precise and cutting.

"Why did you reject the job at the cigar factory?"

Shivaji remained silent.

"Are you deaf or mute? Why are you not answering?"

Shivaji kept his eyes on the banana in front of him as his sisters and wife tiptoed to the kitchen.

"Do you know the trouble I faced arranging this interview? Where were you? Why didn't you attend? Answer me."

"I was at the seashore."

"There are no fish in the shallow waters anymore. There won't be fish for months. A good job is at your doorstep, so why close it? Don't you think Vyjanti wants you to have a proper job?"

"Yes, Appa. I will support my family, but not at the cigar factory."

Enraged, Muthuraman lashed out. "You are useless. I feel sorry for your mother, sisters, wife. Your sisters are nearing marriage—who will handle the dowry? Vyjanti has endured your meager earnings as a fisherman. She can't even ask for a sari or necklace."

Muthuraman's words pierced Shivaji, yet he restrained his anger. Like father, like son—both struggled to control resentment. Shivaji's mother intervened, but Muthuraman silenced her.

"Appa, think what you will. I will not work for a British-owned company where employees are treated like slaves. I've heard their stories."

"You need to get your head out of the shithole. People always tell stories, and fools like you believe them."

"I don't want to be a slave."

"You are a slave," Muthuraman snapped. "The British rule the country. We live in theirs now."

"I am no slave, and I refuse to become one."

"I will take no more of this. You have until the end of this month to find a job, or leave."

Vyjanti and her sisters-in-law rushed in.

"Appa, if my husband insulted you, I apologize. But is it fair that he must leave if he finds no work?"

"Vyjanti, don't take his words to heart. He is not in his senses. No one will leave," Shivaji's mother said.

"Yes, Amma. Let's forgive and forget. I hope Appa will too," Vyjanti said, her smile calming the room.

Dinner passed in silence.

Night fell, dark and unnerving. Mango trees along the path hosted bats, chirping bizarrely overhead. Shivaji's mind churned over his father's harsh words. Were they true? Was he useless? Did he care only for himself? Was refusing the factory job a mistake? His questions repeated, yet a small feeling urged him to wait, as if something would save him from this dilemma.

"Aye, are you awake, Vyjanti?" Shivaji tapped her shoulder.

"Yes...waiting for you to fall asleep."

"How did you know?"

"I can sense your brain working overtime," she giggled.

"You too? First Appa insults me, now my wife laughs at me," Shivaji said, misunderstanding her amusement.

"I am not laughing at you, my dear husband. All I want is to see a smile on your face. I know you are stressed. And when you are stressed, how can I sleep? That is why I am awake."

Shivaji felt the urge to vent but subsided as soon as he looked into Vyjanti's enticing eyes. The endless love she had for him was visible in her perfectly shaped eyes. She gazed deep into her husband's eyes, feeling the confusion that clouded his mind.

"Whatever happened today, let us forget it," she said gently.

"Even if I wanted to, I cannot forget those words. Appa's lecture has scarred me. He has no love or compassion for his son. For him, life is all about status and reputation. What matters to him is how much a person earns."

Vyjanti caressed Shivaji's arm with her tender fingers. Her warmth and kindness radiated through her touch.

"I don't want to sell myself to the British. I don't want to become one of their servants. By joining the factory, I will be selling my soul to the demons. That is something I cannot do, I will not do. Why can't Appa understand this?"

Vyjanti replied immediately, "Appa and you come from different generations. When people from different generations collide, conflicts arise. Appa's beliefs, views, likes, and dislikes are different from yours. I believe it is hard for him to understand what you want and don't want in life. At the end of the day, he is trying to protect you. He loves you. After all, you are his only son. He wants the best for you."

"Do you think I should comply with Appa's decision?"

"No. Even if you did not work for the finest company in the district, I'd still love you. Even if you did not earn more than others in the village, I'd still love you. All I want is for you to be happy. I am sure God will help you, me, and the entire family. Belief and patience are all we need."

"Is it true, Vyjanti?"

"What?"

"That I don't care for you? That I only care for myself? Was the amount I earned as a fisherman not enough? Maybe I am useless."

"Please, don't talk like that. It hurts me here," Vyjanti said, pointing to her heart. "I don't want fancy clothes or luxurious jewelry. Even if I have one pair of clothes, one meal a day, a small home with soiled floors, shattered windows, and damaged furniture, I'd still choose to live my life with you. And that is without complaints or concerns."

Shivaji attempted to resist the tears forming in the corners of his eyes. "Thank you, Vyjanti. Your words have lifted my spirit. I was lost, lost in a maze, not knowing which path to take. Then you came, took me by the hand, and steered me in the proper direction. What would I do without you?"

"Don't say that. I will always be here with you...Till the end. Sorry, there is no end. I have lived with you for six months now. I plan to live with you for another six hundred years."

Shivaji traveled by foot every day, rain or shine, walking long distances in search of a suitable job. If there is such a thing as luck in this world, it was surely not on his side. "No, not now, not you, sorry, go away, too bad, keep looking, my good wishes are with you, goodbye," were the common responses to his inquiries about job openings.

Shivaji returned home unsuccessful, with painful blisters on his feet from the endless walking, only to be berated by his father. Though severely bruised by his father's comments, Shivaji did not let it affect his confidence and perseverance. With Vyjanti's support and advice, he truly believed that good things would come.

One bright morning, exactly fifteen days after Muthuraman challenged him to find a job, Shivaji encountered the district's most troublesome beggar. Shivaji's sandals offered no protection against the dirt along the trail into the village. Grime covered his feet, even inside his toenails. As he entered the village, Shivaji heard an eccentric voice from behind the ancient tamarind trees. Ignoring it, he continued along the one-way road.

"The overflow of sins resulted in the overflow of wind and water," the voice repeated firmly.

What did the phrase mean? Shivaji was confounded. As he approached the tree, he saw a man in rags sitting cross-legged with his back against the trunk. Both hands moved in rhythm with the words he repeated. Shivaji's next step felt like an intrusion.

"Who is there? Why are you hiding? Come forward."

Shivaji did not hear the sounds beneath his feet. "How did this unknown individual know I was here?" he wondered.

"Please, son, show me your face."

"Aye baba, it's you," Shivaji said excitedly as he recognized the sullen face of the beggar.

"Kaalai Vanakkam! Good morning! Welcome to my new home. It shelters me from the flaming sun, cold winds, and wet rain. From time to time, my new home feeds me. During the charitable season, nothing beats the sweet and sour taste of ripened fruit. You will not believe it; it also provides me with some shillings per day. People come and go from our village from dusk till dawn. Some regulars believe I am a guru, preaching and meditating under this tamarind tree. When they ask, I do not lie. There is no point in lying. I clearly tell them I am a beggar. So, this tree is like a father that protects and a mother that nourishes. Who dares call me an orphan now? Come forward, come on, come forward," Thambi said with intense emotion, raising his fist. He then revealed the few remaining teeth in his wide smile.

"What brings you to the outskirts of the village this fine morning?"

"I am in search of a suitable job, one that promises respect and liberty, a job where I don't feel enslaved."

"Hmm...What is your heart searching for?" the beggar asked.

Shivaji immediately felt that Thambi knew the answer. "Honestly, I belong to the sea. Today, I explored the nearby village coastlines. Unfortunately, like other villages, the shallow waters have no small fish. During the cyclone, rising tides washed the small fish along the coastline. As I walked, I saw fish bones scattered on the sand."

"You must not follow the heart. The heart only follows the currents of the ocean."

Once again, Shivaji found the beggar's sayings incomprehensible.

"Don't become attached to the ocean. The ocean is not worth trusting. It will one day become your worst enemy."

"What are you saying? I am confused, baba."

Thambi closed his eyes, clenched his teeth, and tightened his face before exhaling in distress.

"Baba, are you okay?" asked Shivaji.

"Come here, son. Be seated."

Shivaji did not hesitate to sit next to a beggar who was considered untouchable by others.

"There is peace under this tree. My home is now your home. Make yourself comfortable, son."

Before sitting, Shivaji brushed aside pebbles and twigs.

"Now tell me, can you feel the soil?"

Shivaji nodded. "I sure do, Baba."

"What is on your mind?"

"Your riddles... I cannot understand their meaning. Is my life at risk? If it is, how do you know?"

"I am not God. I did not create your destiny. What is written, good or bad, will happen. No one can foresee their own or another person's future. I don't read hands or foreheads. I don't have knowledge of horoscopes or astronomy."

"Why do I feel your phrases are signs to warn me?" Shivaji asked.

"Vague images of betrayal, separation, transgression, and misfortune are what I see when I look into your eyes."

"I need more explanation. Can you elaborate?"

"No one can foresee the future, except God," Old Man Thambi replied.

"Then why do I feel you can see the future?"

"You, I, and others exist in this world for a reason. In our past lives, we have sinned. A sin so merciless that is unforgiven and unforgotten by God Himself is the kind of sin we committed. Rebirth is a chance to redeem ourselves."

"Wait! If we have sinned in our first birth, being reborn is certain. Isn't multiple lives better than one?" Shivaji asked.

The beggar laughed, rolling in the dirt.

"Being reborn repeatedly is not pleasant. People believe that when we expire, we enter either heaven or hell. Up there," he pointed to the clear skies, "is heaven."

"What about hell?"

"Son, are you serious?"

Ashamed of not knowing the answer, Shivaji dared not look at the beggar.

"You are in hell. Hell is below—the world we live in, the land we stand on. This is hell. The way out is if your good deeds outweigh your bad deeds. One bad deed can outweigh ten good deeds."

"How is that possible?"

"That depends on the severity of the bad deed. I have to tell you, God or a panel of Gods will decide if your soul is qualified to rest in peace after your death. So, it is His decision that sends you to heaven or hell. Heaven means the end of reincarnation, while hell means the beginning of a new life."

"Sorry to interfere, but what do you mean by a panel of Gods? God is one."

"Well, some individuals worship one God—for example, Jesus or Allah—while others, mostly Hindus, worship the many forms of one God, such as Brahma, Vishnu, and Mahesh."

"Are you sure you are not a guru or a saint? Because you certainly talk like one," said Shivaji, hoping for the old man to reveal his true identity if indeed he had one he chose to hide. The people who had encountered the beggar thought he was illiterate. But the manner in which he conversed suggested he was far more intelligent and wise than those who thought wrong of him. Shivaji, who was not as shrewd as the beggar, noticed that Thambi was quick when it came to changing subjects. The beggar's sayings sounded like poetry and riddles, but most of the time his explanations were partial. Shivaji felt he needed more from Thambi than what was given.

"The things you say, why are they left unfinished? It is like you give me a puzzle but supply only half of the pieces to solve it. I am not saying your talks are meaningless or impractical. Please don't misunderstand me. It's just that I..." Shivaji struggled to explain his point.

"Son, let life live. Surrender to the journey destiny has in store for you. And while on this journey, you must reconsider your actions and make sensible decisions. The people with whom you share a bond today are from your past. You and I, we met in our last life. That is why we have connected in this life. Remember, you have the choice to forget what I have said today. But please keep this in mind: you will be separated in this life, only to be reunited in the next."

"Separated...Reunited," said Shivaji, unable to understand.

Old Man Thambi arose. Swinging his half-full, half-empty jute bag over his shoulders, he started to proceed towards the outskirts of the village. "God be with you. The voyage awaits us. See you soon," he said, moving his hand side to side in a waving motion.

"Who is he? What does he mean? How does he know? Is there any truth behind his sayings? Should I be careful? How many questions can the brain store? How do I find the answers? Was he a messiah sent by the Lord above?" Shivaji asked himself as he watched the beggar vanish in the distance.

An Englishman dressed in a red and white uniform is understood without difficulty when he verbally abuses you. If an Englishman calls you an arsehole, bugger, dog, duffer, pig, scum, shite, or tyke, words of anger and hate are effortlessly understood by Indians. More than ninety percent of the villagers living in the Red Lilies District were unable to speak, read, or write English. Yet these uneducated people, from different castes and religions, with different personalities and upbringings, could still tell if an Englishman was insulting or abusing them. The detestation the British stored inside their hearts for the Indians was noticeable in their tone of voice, crude facial expressions, aggressive behavior, impulsive actions, and their fondness for the line bloody hell. At the start of a sentence there was bloody hell, at the end of a sentence there was bloody hell—bloody hell this, bloody hell that, bloody hell everywhere.

The very next day, at the break of dawn, the voices of the colonial rulers overpowered the throaty cock-a-doodle-doos that came from the roosters every morning. Several boisterous voices prowled into the creaks of the doors and windows of the village houses. To hear English words vocalized without revulsion came as a surprise to Shivaji.

A horn was blown, the wheels of the wagon came to a full stop, and several men dressed in British colors stepped down as an Indian servant opened the vehicle door. Shivaji and the others of the village rushed to the scene with their hearts beating fast. What were the British here for? What did they want from the villagers of the Red Lilies District? Families with their children formed a large gathering on the wayside, knowing not to get too close to the manipulating rulers. Shivaji and his family positioned themselves under the banyan trees that stretched across the roadside. The limbs of the banyan trees nearly touched the earth, which meant the children had the opportunity to entertain themselves by tugging, hanging, and climbing.

"Please don't worry. We are here as your friends. The British are aware of the cyclone which has brought ruin to the district. The lands have been destroyed. The houses damaged. Most of the men are now jobless," said the Indian servant.

"We know all of that. Get to the point. Tell them about your plans," a piercing voice intervened.

Shivaji scanned the assembly with his eyes. The voice seemed familiar to him. The servant exhaled noisily. It seemed as if he'd been forced to remember the speech word for word. "The British agents are here to assist the people of the Red Lilies District. The rulers of this land have a proposition."

"Mr. Traitor, are you sure it is a proposition? Or is it an evil scheme?" said the disruptive voice from the crowd.

One of the Englishmen leaned over the servant, overshadowing him with his broad shoulders and massive chest. He whispered into the servant's ear, "What is the foolish man saying?"

"Nothing important, please ignore him," replied the servant.

The British agent nodded, giving the servant a hint that it was time for his introduction.

"My fellow villagers, I introduce to you Agent Grahame. Agent Grahame will elaborate on the proposition. Pay careful attention; we have an offer that can change your lives. He will talk in English and I will translate into Hindi and Tamil. As for the opposing voice that keeps interfering, I ask you to be polite. I cannot stop you from talking, but if you can, please hold on till the end of the announcement," pleaded the servant with joined hands.

Silence filled the air; the children stopped climbing the branches of the banyan trees, the women lowered their eyes while veiling their faces with long scarves, and the men became excited about the proposal that could make a difference in their lives. The British agent stood upright with his enormous feet pressing into the soil beneath him.
"What a shame. Our motherland is being flattened by these colonial rulers," Shivaji said under his breath.

Agent Grahame talked in a genial manner. Not once did his tone seem brash. Whenever his eyes met a villager's, he quickly offered a wide grin. He even reached over to place his arm on the shoulder of a villager who stood in front of the crowd. The villagers were pleased to see such a fine gesture coming from a British official. Such a spectacle had never been witnessed before by the villagers of the red lilies district. As Agent Grahame finished a line, he patiently waited for the servant to translate his words into Hindi and Tamil.
"Ladies and gentlemen, the British Government will give you an offer you cannot refuse. The British know that villagers from the red lilies district are in trouble, and we are

here to relieve you from your troubles. We have a proposition that guarantees liberty; a proposition that promises wealth; a proposition that offers a bright future for your children. We ask you to become indentured laborers; we ask you to sign the agreement; we ask you to sail across the seas to paradise. Come aboard a two-month voyage to the Islands of Fiji, where you will be planting, harvesting, and milling sugarcane. This is the first time we need your help. No one is as hardworking and reliable as the villagers of this country. What you Indians can do in the farms, we Englishmen can never do. We don't have those skills and qualities that you villagers possess, and that is a fact. We promise a good home, good food, good clothes, and most importantly, a good life. Work in our sugarcane fields and get paid ten shillings a month. Believe me, I won't lie. Yes, this is the truth—ten shillings a month."

Chatter filled the area. The villagers were astonished. For them, ten shillings a month was more than reasonable. For others, they had never seen that kind of money all at once. "This proposal is most beneficial for the villagers who have lost their homes, crops, and jobs due to the horrible cyclone. Take advantage; don't let this opportunity pass you by. Men, women, children, and elders are welcome. Remember, this will bring to you what you all have been waiting for... liberty. You will be living on an island with no British rules or regulations. You work, we pay, and that is it. How you live your life and how you spend your money is your business. You will be treated as equals. In Fiji, the British will not suppress you. Within the next two weeks, please discuss this offer with your family members and come to a final decision. Every morning I, Agent Grahame, along with my commendable team, will visit the village to discuss the indentured laborer agreement. Any questions you have will be answered. Any suggestions you have will be considered. Now, I will take my leave. I hope to see you all tomorrow. Goodbye," the agent waved to the crowd, half of whom were enticed while the other half remained confused.

Like fire spreading in a forest, word spread in the village that there was a meeting for the Hindus, from all castes, at the Vishnu Temple. The villagers were aware of the motive behind the meeting. Together, they were to discuss the proposition set forth by the British. During the eight hours of job seeking, Shivaji bumped into many of his fellow villagers. Every villager had a question of his own.

"Do you think there is any truth behind this proposal? Or is it that we are being duped?" said an aging man, swatting the blood-thirsty mosquitos that buzzed around him.

"Can you believe it, ten shillings a month? That kind of money can fulfill all my needs. Soon, I will need to get my beautiful daughters married. The groom and his family will not dare to reject them once they see the amount of money I have to offer along with my daughters. You know what, young man, dowry is the nastiest invented ritual that a father has to submit to," said the elderly father as he continued to reveal his incessant hardships. "I am ready to stamp my print. Bring on the papers. There is no need to ask me twice. I have had enough of this country. It is time to move on with life. No more enduring—it is time for achieving. You are a wise man, Shivaji. I am sure you will embark on this sea voyage as well," said the teenager while herding the white bulls to the barn after an intense day of pulling, dragging, jerking, and heaving.

On his way home, Shivaji stopped in front of Venkatesh's door. After the first knock, Venkatesh answered. "Shivaji, it is nice to see you. Please come in."

"No Venkatesh, I need to be home soon. I wanted to ask if you are coming to the gathering at the Vishnu temple in the evening."

"Yes, I am."

"Is Anni coming?"

"Lachmaiya will be attending as well. What's the matter?"

"Nothing! I just wanted to know if everyone is attending. I am not sure if Vyjanti will be coming. She did not voice a single word about the proposal."

"Well, are you interested in the offer?" Venkatesh asked, hopeful that his friend would provide a clear answer.

"I don't know, Venkatesh. It is difficult to trust the colonial rulers. We are promised independence, but what happens if we get enslaved instead?"

"You do have a point. The whites are hard to trust. But I have to think about the future of my son. That kind of money can put him into school. I want the best for Karthik, for him to achieve what his father and forefathers did not."

"And what is that?"

"To be enrolled in a school, to get an education, to apply that education to further studies, to acquire a degree. With a degree in hand, apply for a government job. Once the government job is obtained, there is no looking back. From then on, it is all about rising to the top." Venkatesh was longing to experience the feelings of pride and honor from Karthik's miraculous future achievements.

"Venkatesh...Aye nanban," Shivaji snapped his fingers to pull him from his reverie.

"Sorry, yes I will be there."

"Be where?" Shivaji questioned his friend to see if he had returned to his senses.

"At the temple...This evening...Right?"

"Venkatesh, I will see you there," replied Shivaji while patting his friend's shoulder.

As soon as Shivaji entered the front door, Muthuraman examined him with a paternal stare. He bit his lips as if struggling to fight back his own words. "Son, you must attend the village meeting at the temple."

Shivaji did not appreciate the command. "Appa, is that an order?"

"Please, I want you to follow my instructions. Go to the temple; listen to what others have to say. This can be a precious opportunity for the villagers of this district to renew their lives after the cyclone. The British are not as bad as others perceive them to be. Today, we need help. Many of the villagers need help, including you. And the British are there to help."

"Nothing is free in this world, appa. If they are to help us, in return they ask for help as well. They need assistance with the planting, harvesting, and milling of sugarcane. They want to remove us from our motherland and export us to a tropical island that no one has ever heard of."

"They will not remove the villagers without their consent. The villagers have the opportunity to choose. Whether the villagers sign the agreement or not is a decision that will be made without pressure or force."

"At last, they are giving us a choice. Surprising, isn't it? This is the first time the British are asking for our consent. They did not ask for our consent when they conquered our motherland. Well, did they?" said Shivaji, his voice intensifying.

Placing his hand on his forehead, Muthuraman shook his head. "The hate that lives in your heart must depart. As long as we live in this country, we will never get to see independence. This is their land we live on. The island that the British want the villagers to labor on is free. It is free from their rule."

"How do you know that? What if the island is under British rule? What if they cheat us? What if they don't give us any money? What if they turn us into slaves? What if they don't let the villagers return?"

"Son, these are the type of questions that will be discussed at the meeting. The villagers must assist one another in answering such questions."

"Appa, are you attending?"

"No. There is no use for me to attend. I have no interest in agriculture. I have lived my life as a potter. I know nothing but pottery. What use will I be to the British in the sugarcane fields?"

"What if I say that I have no interest in this matter? I don't want to leave the village."

"Keep an open mind. I want the best for you. And I believe that this is it. This is your opportunity to prove yourself. If you were to earn ten shillings a month, we'd be able to marry off your sisters. In the future, you will have children—think about them. Don't you want to save money for them? Look at me! Just look at me! I am getting old. Soon these arms and legs will not work. I have provided for this family, now it is your turn to provide. Please discuss this proposal with your wife. All I ask is for you to give this a chance. Don't rule it out completely."

Double-minded about whether to be or not to be present at the meeting, Shivaji chose to leave the decision in his wife's hands. Breathing in with his sensitive nose, Shivaji inhaled a sweet fragrance. For him, the smell of jasmine meant that his wife was dressed for an occasion. Whenever Vyjanti was promised an outing arranged by her husband, she dressed her best with the symbolic jasmine flower placed in her hair. Then, with a loud bang, the door shut. Vyjanti, wrapped in an elegant red sari with pure white jasmine flowers inserted neatly into her hair, watched her husband move towards her. The image of thousands of scattered flower petals spread across the earth appeared in front of Shivaji's eyes.

"From where did you get the jasmine flowers?" he sternly asked his wife.

"How do I look?"

"You look fine. Can you please answer my question now?" Shivaji asked impatiently.

"Oh Deva, I was expecting compliments. Anyways, you have such considerate sisters. They both know how fond I am of jasmine flowers. Today, they went along with amma to the market where they bargained for a bundle of jasmine flowers. I tell you, these girls are so clever. With their sensible choice of words and competent speech, they managed to purchase the flowers for half the normal price."

"Impressive," said Shivaji. "After all, they are my sisters. I taught them well."

"Please don't flatter yourself! So, are you not going to ask me?"

"Ask you what?"

"Well, as you can see, I have jasmine flowers in my hair. You know what that means."

Before she could finish, Shivaji interrupted. "Yes, I do. It means that you are going somewhere."

"Both of us will be going."

"Of course, I am your slave. What you say, I will have to do. Right?" said the irritated Shivaji.

"Please, don't get upset. What is bothering you?"

Shivaji remained silent while he sat on the edge of his bed.

"If I sound officious and impolite, please forgive me. I believed that you'd be attending the meeting tonight. If you don't want to attend, please let me know."

"Do you think it is a good idea to attend? What benefit will we receive by going?"

"Well, I for one am keen to learn what our fellow villagers think of this proposal. I want to know how many are ready to take part in this sea voyage."

Shivaji fixed his eyes on hers. "So this proposal of becoming an indentured laborer—does it interest you?"

"Yes, it does. I think we should at least consider it. By the way, the meeting is taking place in an hour and fifteen minutes," Vyjanti informed her husband, purposely reminding him that the clock was ticking.

"Don't you think that the British will deceive us?"

"I believe that the offer they have put forth is not entirely false."

Dissatisfied with his wife's view, Shivaji exited the bedroom with his towel on his shoulder.

"Where are you going?" asked Vyjanti as her husband turned the corner.

Shivaji poked his face back into the room. "No more questions, Vyjanti. I don't have much time. I have to bathe, dress, and eat. Rush, rush, rush," said Shivaji.

As he left the scene, Vyjanti said to herself, "Oh Deva, I hope I am not forcing him into something we'll both regret later. Lord Shiva, please watch over us."

The vanishing of the sun left behind darkness on the route that led to the inner part of the village. Numerous bodies moved on foot, choosing the route past the British cigar factory. A shorter route was deliberately chosen by the villagers to avoid the fetid tanneries.

"Vyjanti..."

"What?"

"Please hold my hand. Don't worry about the others. I will not risk losing you in this darkness."

Vyjanti's heart palpitated. Never in the presence of others had she clasped Shivaji's hand. Fighting her nerves, her hand searched for contact. Her sweaty, cold palms revealed she was not comfortable with Shivaji's request.

"There is nothing to worry about. You are my wife, not my mistress. Imagine that no one is here, except you and me."

Vyjanti nodded in acceptance as she looked at her husband's calm face. A straight course, without bends or turns, led directly to the district center where the Vishnu Temple had been constructed decades before the birth of Muthuraman and his wife. A majestic line of gangly mango trees, their limp branches severely injured during the cyclone, hovered over the villagers. Stripped of leaves and fruit, the trees looked like eerie fingers waiting to pounce on the men, women, and children. Eyes did not blink as the villagers strolled past the frightening trees. Shivaji sniffed the air.

"What is it?" asked Vyjanti curiously.

"Can you smell the burning in the air? It's the cigar factory."

Vyjanti grew anxious. She knew how her husband felt about the cigar factory. She recognized the rage beginning to stir inside him, ready to erupt. Vyjanti predicted a rash move or sharp words from her husband. Something had to be said, something had to be done. She opened her mouth and stumbled upon her own words. "Umm...I did not...Well...It is that..."

"What did you just say?" asked her husband, his voice lacking delicacy.

"I am sorry. I forgot that the cigar factory was en route to Vishnu Temple. If I had remembered, I would not have pressured you to attend. I can be so unwise sometimes. I visit this temple with amma once a week. I should have known."

Shivaji's feet halted. He did not turn to face his wife. "When was the last time I visited a temple?"

"What?" Vyjanti asked in disbelief.

"When was the last time I visited a temple?"

Dumbfounded by her husband's question, Vyjanti let out a soft titter. "I honestly don't remember. In the past six months, have you ever taken me to the temple?"

A crackling sound came from beneath Shivaji's feet as he turned to face his wife. For a second, the dry mango leaves startled Vyjanti.

"Well, in the first week of our marriage, we spent a lot of time in the temple."

"Oh Deva, that does not count. Those were part of the marriage ceremonies and homecoming rituals. I meant, have we ever visited a temple together for a religious festival or casual prayer?"

"No," replied Shivaji. "For you, God resides in idols, pictures, and temples. You kneel in front of a statue and pray. You stand in front of a picture and pray. You step into a temple and pray. I don't need to do such things. Surely, I have told you this before."

Vyjanti rolled her eyes. "I know...God lives within your heart."

"Yes, that is true. I don't need to search for God in temples, statues, or pictures. Right here—this is where God exists," said Shivaji, pointing to the left portion of his chest. Vyjanti smiled at her husband. She felt pleased that after observing the cigar factory, her husband did not resort to indignant remarks or bitter expressions. Most of all, she was pleased he did not turn around and march back home after the sight of the factory. Shivaji and Vyjanti strolled past the ever-so-famous, ever-so-popular, ever-so-known British-owned cigar factory, ignoring both the smell and the view.

The concrete walls of the temple were decorated with an exotic carving of Lord Vishnu. In the midst of the sea, the Supreme God lay on the seven-headed Seshanaag with His wife, Goddess Laxmi, massaging the preserver's feet. On his visits before, Shivaji had never set his eyes upon the artistic creations on the temple walls. He was drawn to the antiquity of the hand-made temple. Vyjanti's eyes were fixated on her husband as he ran his hand across the carvings, ensuring his fingers touched every line and bend. Shivaji tilted his head at an angle to observe the eye-catching details the artist had put into the fine work. Challenged by the absence of light within the vicinity, he squatted to examine the carved waves on which the serpent floated. For a brief moment, Shivaji felt wetness in his eyes, which impaired his vision, until the fast reaction of his hand wiped away the tears before they fell.

The commotion of loud voices, the temple bells ringing unceasingly, the priest chanting divine mantras, the burning heat from the lit fire—nothing had the strength to distract Shivaji from the carved painting of the God, the Goddess, and the Serpent.

"It is unlike any other painting I have seen. It is exquisite. Is the painting fairly new?"

"No, this was carved before our time," replied Vyjanti with a gleeful smile. The feeling of satisfaction overwhelmed her as she realized her husband was showing keen interest in something other than fishing. "I have a feeling this is something you want to master. With time and practice, I am sure you will be able to carve a representation similar to this."

"Are you a mind reader?" Shivaji asked, bewildered.

"I have seen it in your luminous eyes. I have seen it in the smooth movements of your hand. I have seen it in the way your fingers caressed those lines on the wall. I have seen how you left the rest of the world behind while you studied the painting."

Shivaji's heart beat against his chest with adoration for Vyjanti's truthful words.

"You must study and learn this craft. I want you to give it a try."

Shivaji inhaled and then exhaled, releasing a loud sigh. "One day, someday, I definitely will."

"I hope that day is sooner rather than later," replied Vyjanti.

The fires lit by the village leaders in the surrounding area forcefully battled against the night's darkness. Nevertheless, the villagers came prepared with their kerosene lanterns. Close to an hour was spent seeking the blessings of Lord Vishnu through the idol inside the temple. With joint hands, eyelids shut tight, heads swaying side to side, the villagers formed a melodious choir of devotional songs. Once the harmonious voices ceased, the food first offered to Lord Vishnu was distributed to the villagers, who sat patiently on the floor with their hands extended. Soon after, the leaders directed the men, women, and children to form a grand circle. Every man who wished to speak was to proceed to the center, revealing his identity to the leaders. Women and children were not permitted to voice questions or opinions. Vyjanti knew that if she had something to say, she must whisper it into her husband's ear for him to share on her behalf.

Throughout the discussions, the villagers were drenched in perspiration. The mass of bodies and ignited lanterns combined to produce unbearable heat. Using the sleeves of their kurta, the men wiped the sweat from their faces. Even the lovely scarves the women carried were saturated from relentless dabbing. The fresh air was no longer fresh—it was contaminated by perspiration.

A blaring voice pierced the air when a villager burst out with questions about the proposal. "What is this Fiji? Where is this Fiji? How far is this Fiji? Can we adapt to the weather in this Fiji? What is there to eat in this Fiji?"

Villagers from all corners entered the circle with their own inquiries.

"Fiji is a dot on the map. I believe it is the size of our village," replied one.

"No, it is not a dot. It is an island not too far from India," said another.

"I don't know for sure. But I heard Fiji is an island in the middle of the ocean with no civilization whatsoever," said a leader.

Back and forth, the men rambled, unable to reach valid answers. The fact was no one in the village knew where Fiji was, what it was, how far it was from India, who resided there, what weather it had, or what it offered for food. The leaders and villagers raised pressing concerns: is there truth to the proposition? Do the British plan to enslave? Is the offer of ten shillings a month true or false? Have travel arrangements been made?

An hour of standing, deprived of rest, pressured many—especially families with children—to depart.

"My feet are aching," whispered Vyjanti, unable to stand still.

Shivaji could not bear to see his wife in pain. "I think we should leave. This is a waste of time. No one here knows the answers to these vital questions. The British said they will visit in the morning to discuss further. We have the questions, and they have the answers."

"Yes, that is true. Let's just hope they answer honestly," said Vyjanti.

As they proceeded to leave, they bumped into Venkatesh and his family.

"When did you arrive?" Venkatesh asked.

From the corner of his eye, Shivaji saw his wife head toward Karthik to embrace him. "We arrived on time. I did not see you inside during the prayer."

"We came just as the discussions started. Karthik lagged behind on the walk to the temple. He refused to use his feet. The only thing he used was his mouth. I had to carry him on my shoulders, tell him forest tales, and explain how cigars are made in the factory."

Shivaji burst into laughter.

"No, that is not the end of our miseries. Listen. As soon as we passed the cigar factory, he needed the loo. I told him there was no latrine in the middle of the village."

"Then what happened?" asked Shivaji.

"Well, he had to go, so he had to go. Before it was too late, I directed him behind the shrubs," said Venkatesh with humor.

Shivaji lifted his lantern toward Venkatesh's kurta to check for stains. "I can see you reached the shrubs on time," he said, patting his friend's shoulder. There was no need for Shivaji to persuade Venkatesh and his family to leave; they too felt the meeting was useless. The British held the real answers.

Positioning the lantern ahead, Shivaji guided his loved ones through the ghostly path. Vyjanti's eyes were captivated by the dangling lantern clutched in his hand. She smiled, reflecting on the natural swing of her husband's right arm whenever he walked. Often, from the bedroom window, Vyjanti had observed the same rhythm as he went to and from work. Though unaware of this habit, Shivaji always denied it when she teased him. Vyjanti would imitate the swing to annoy him, and Shivaji would brush it off, knowing she only wanted to pull his leg.

As he walked on, a disturbance stirred in Shivaji's mind. To free himself, he had to vent. "You know what bothers me the most?"

"What?" replied Venkatesh as he followed his friend.

"If this meeting was such an important event for the people of this village, then why was it held in a Hindu temple? Why was this meeting for the Hindus only?"

"I have known you for more than fifteen years, Shivaji. You have always considered Christians and Muslims equal to Hindus. You have always treated them with respect and dignity. You don't see a difference between the high and low class. You don't see a difference between a Brahmin Hindu and an untouchable. For you, all religions and castes are the same. You believe that everyone should be treated likewise. But nanban, that is not how others in this village think and feel. The Muslims did not attend this meeting because they do not wish to set foot in a Hindu temple. It is as simple as that," replied Venkatesh. "Well, then why not hold the meeting somewhere else? Who says that it must be held at a temple? Temples are for worshipping gods and goddesses. They were built for humans to offer prayers to the Lord. Temples are not for discussing and debating. It is disrespectful not to include our fellow villagers of the Islamic religion. They too are part of our village. Then why should we not include them? We should live united, not divided. Such decisions and actions like this will only separate us even more. It's a shame."

In order to stop this conversation from escalating further, Venkatesh decided to keep mum. Shivaji looked at his wife, who was paying full attention to the conversation. Her eyes glistened as Shivaji raised the torch to locate her face. "Another ten minutes until we reach home. Do you need to rest?" the considerate husband asked, knowing that her feet hurt from all that standing.

"I am fine, thank you. It is best if we carry on. If we stop, it will delay our progress."

The head of the pack then searched for the child. "Where is little Karthik hiding? Anni, are you and Karthik tired?"

"Not at all, we are both fine. Your delightful wife is keeping Karthik on his feet."

Karthik then raced to the front to meet his father. "Appa, did you know winged creatures are living in the mango trees?"

"Really?" replied Venkatesh as if he did not know.

"Yes appa, it is the truth. They are black in color. They have red eyes. They can fly in the sky. And they hang upside down from trees." Karthik took a deep breath only to unravel another set of questions. "Attai said they are awake during the night and sleep during the day. Why is that, appa? Why is it that we sleep during the night? Why can't we sleep during the day and stay awake during the night?" Karthik irritated his father with endless questions until they reached home. Venkatesh had no option but to answer in the most colorful way possible.

"One must have the patience to deal with a child's curiosity. Shivaji, I am looking forward to seeing you deal with fatherhood," Venkatesh whispered into his friend's ear.

"Goodnight, you rascal," Shivaji replied to his friend's playful comment.

"Where is Fiji?"

"Fiji is an island in the Pacific Ocean."

"Who resides in Fiji?"

"Fijians..."

"Who are these Fijians?"

"Fijians are the major indigenous people of the islands."

"Will they cause any harm to us?"

"Never...Uncivilized, uncultured persons, how can they be harmful?"

"How will we survive on this island?"

"The British will supply rations daily. A new home will be built for you on the land. Necessary materials will be provided for everyone to knit clothing. Every one of you will be taken care of in a suitable manner," said Agent Grahame.

Regardless of the draining sunshine, Agent Grahame managed to look fresh and alert for his audience. There was a constant beam on his face that vanished whenever he answered a question. For the British official, this morning allowed him to propel the villagers towards the intended direction. As for the Indian servant, who was not introduced and was not asked to introduce the British officials, he translated Agent Grahame's words accurately, ensuring that the villagers understood the Englishman who stood before them.

"How will we get to Fiji?"

"By ship...The passengers aboard will commence on a two-month voyage sailing across the oceans to reach the islands of Fiji."

"What ship? Will the ship be able to carry all of us? Won't it sink with too much weight?"

"No, the ship will not sink. It is a massive cargo ship that carries up to seven hundred passengers at a time."

"Who will sail this ship?"

"It is the captain of the ship who is in command. He is the one who will guide the ship to Fiji. We leave you in his hands."

"Can we trust the British?"

"We are here for you. We are in need of you. We come with promises. We come with peace. Please don't let our past identify our present."

"You promise us freedom. How so? Are we to be freed from the colonial system in Fiji?"

"Good question," said Agent Grahame while rubbing the side of his wet forehead. "There is no rule in Fiji. In Fiji, you are independent. With your hard work on the plantations, the country will prosper. Sugarcane will be planted, harvested, and milled. Once the sugar is prepared, it will be exported to other countries that need it. In the end, we will get paid, which means, you will get paid. For the first time in history, the British and Indians will work together to achieve success."

"Who are we working for?"

"You will be working for the Colonial Sugar Refining Company. This is the company that will pay you ten shillings per month. You will be spread to different areas on the island to fulfill your duties. We promise that families will not get separated. That is my word to you all. Keep this in mind, no families will be separated," repeated the agent in a high-pitched tone for every villager in the gathering to hear.

"Will we be paid ten shillings a month?"

"Yes, that is correct, ten shillings a month. It will be written in the official agreement. So, what can you do with that much money? Let me rephrase that — what can't you do with that much money? Earn, save, and spend. Renovate your home, purchase property, find your daughters suitable grooms, prepare a grand wedding, open up your own business, eat the rich man's food, wear the rich man's clothes, depart from the village, move into the city, send your kids to decent schools, and further educate them. Live the fulfilling, comfortable life you deserve."

The satisfied Agent Grahame peered at the village men and women. In these men and women, he perceived idleness. The villagers gathered in the assembly were enthralled by his speech. Their brains were engrossed with illusions of the most wishful accomplishments. But the agent was yet to meet his match. Amongst the still crowd, footsteps were heard. Appearing from the assemblage was a person who was not easily convinced, not lost in his thoughts, and not willing to comply with or trust the colonial rulers.

"How long are we to stay on this island of yours?" asked Shivaji with boldness in his voice.

"Well, first of all, it is not our island. As for your question, you will be given two choices in the official agreement form. Either you stay five or ten years — that is for you to decide."

"This form you talk about. Is it an agreement or a contract?"

"It is both — an agreement to set forth on this favorable expedition and a contract to work for the Colonial Sugar Refining Company. Both contract and agreement must be read and then signed. Like I said before, whether you choose five years or ten years, that is your decision to make," replied the agent as if he was defending himself from Shivaji's back-to-back questions.

"So, you want us to leave our beloved country? You are telling us that we must leave our family members behind. You expect us to live without seeing our fathers, mothers, brothers, sisters, husbands, wives, and children for so many years?"

"No, no...I am not saying that. Families are welcome. People of both sexes and all ages are welcome. As for the country you live in, let it be temporarily forgotten. Focus on the tropical island where you will be earning and saving more. We provide shelter, food, and clothing. You will have no expenses. This will allow you to save. And to save plenty of money, it will take years. Five years is perfect. By the end of five years, you will have plenty of money to take back to your motherland. Those who don't mind spending more than five years in Fiji are welcome to stay. Those who want to leave as soon as their five-year contract is over will not be held back. In fact, we will place you on a ship returning home."

"Do women and children have to work on plantations and in mills?" Shivaji asked the agent, looking directly into his stressed eyes.

"Women must work but will be assigned duties that are suitable for them. Children are not required to work on the plantations or in the mills. Do you have any more questions?"

"Yes sir, how can you prove that we will not be misled? How can you prove that we will not be lied to? How can you prove that we will not be cheated? How can you prove that we will not be oppressed? How can you prove that we will not be enslaved? You talk about togetherness. You talk about sharing. I ask you, why can't we share equality in this country? Why must we live apart? Why can't we live here together?"

Muddled by the array of questions put forth by the spirited villager, Agent Grahame was lost within his words. "I...Well...You see...You don't understand...One must not thi nk...Well..."

The up-front and hard-hitting collection of questions lifted the villagers out of their inactive state. Some were appalled by the questions delivered by Shivaji, while others were keenly waiting for the agent's reply.

"You will not be enslaved. Together we'll introduce Fiji to cultivation and civilization. History will be created. Think about your future, not about your past. We will be visiting this village each morning until the end of this week. Starting next week, I will bring in the paperwork. Remember, if you cannot provide a signature or print your name, a thumbprint will be required. The blissful journey awaits you, my friends. I hope to see you all tomorrow morning. Bring me a plate full of questions and I will dish you honest answers," said Agent Grahame as he waved farewell to the villagers.

"Agent Grahame, you are a sly devil. You have ignored my genuine questions on purpose. When you stumbled upon your own words, at that very moment, I knew that my questions would not be answered. My questions will never be answered by you or any Englishman who resides in this country. It is not that you don't know the answers to my questions. It is that you choose to purposely ignore them. For you, to answer correctly will lead to sabotage. And I understand that you cannot afford to sabotage what is in the works. You and your people have plans to become superior. To become superior you need our help. You need us and instead, you say that we need you. You may think of me as a blind man. But I am not blind. Nor am I deaf. Nor am I mute. If you think I am brainless, you are wrong. My brain belongs to me. It is not controlled by you or anyone else. And during this moment, my brain is telling me not to comply with, not to be lied to, and not to be misled," Shivaji said to himself.

As days passed, British officials, along with the temporarily hired translator, made regular visits to the village. All sorts of questions were asked, and all sorts of answers were given. Was there honesty behind the answers? Most villagers did not care, as long as there was an initial response. More than eighty percent attended the morning sessions, whether they had questions or not, their eyes wide, ears alert. They rose early, cleaned and washed, ate, and then attended the gathering. Shivaji was not among them.

For him, it was more important to continue the job hunt. He passed by family members, childhood friends, and familiar faces without yielding to friendly greetings or calls of his name. He pitied the vendors who closed shops to attend the sessions, the housewives who abandoned chores, the children dragged along, the working-class men who skipped work, and the unemployed who wasted their time in idle discussion. *"Were these sacrifices worth it?"* Shivaji asked himself.

Returning home from a day of "sorry, no vacancies" and "sorry, you are not qualified," his appa greeted him on the porch with a stern glare—a reminder that the month was ending. Finding a job seemed almost impossible, the district in ruins. Shivaji realized that shop owners, street vendors, rich farmers, and factory supervisors preferred hiring kin or acquaintances rather than outsiders. So why did he walk from village to village, seeking openings?

"I want to stay clear of the British proposition. That is why I try to inject hope into myself. But I fail. My system fights back. Instead of hope, I feel hopeless. Every day I leave to search for a job, yet I know I'll return empty-handed. I feel trapped—inside a black hole with nowhere

to go. How do I free myself? Is there a path out? A door? Is there anyone to drop a rope or ladder for me to climb?"

A rapid movement startled Vyjanti, causing her to lose balance. Seated back-to-back without facing each other, she was stunned as her husband moved from the floor near the bed to the window. Shivaji stared into the dim night. Fear—a feeling he hadn't known since childhood—gripped him.

"Vyjanti, do you think appa is serious? If I don't find a job before the end of this month, will he ask us to leave?"

"I cannot say," replied Vyjanti. "It is hard to understand appa. Sometimes anger speaks for him. Still, I hear him repeat that there are few days left in the month."

"If that is so, then we must leave now," Shivaji said, turning from the window.

"We shall not act irrationally. Where would we go? You and I are part of this family. Appa wants the best for you. I believe he wants you to sign the contract."

Vyjanti hid her eyes, unsure what to expect.

"Contract," Shivaji roared. "You know how I feel about the British. You know how I feel about this contract, or agreement, or whatever it is. I have no interest in this proposition."

Vyjanti held back her initial words but realized it was time to speak. *"My dear husband, you never asked how I feel. I want to express my thoughts and beliefs. If that is too much, tell me. If a wife should have no say, no voice, no role in key decisions, then I will shut my mouth."*

The fire within Shivaji softened as he recognized his mistake. "I apologize for not discussing this with you. If you don't mind, I want to know your feelings about the offer."

"Think about the happiness we can bring to our family by accepting this proposal. Appa can live in peace, knowing his son prospers. Amma can rest from stitching and knitting. Your sisters can marry men from respected families. You can pursue a new career. Remember the carvings? With money, you could learn and master that craft. Our children could have a secure future, attend valued schools, enjoy diverse classes, wear foreign clothes, and taste scrumptious foods."

Shivaji was dumbfounded by his wife's vision. *"If everyone wants me to...then I must,"* he murmured. "I want happiness for all. But this feeling kills me. If I step forward today, tomorrow my feet may be bound in chains. I dread slavery."

He drew in a deep breath and exhaled. *"Don't worry. I will take part in this sea voyage. I will learn to trust my enemies. I will conquer the fear within me. I will do all this and more, for a better future."*

"And I will be there with you from start to end. I will not let go of your hand. We are inseparable," replied Vyjanti with her affectionate smile.

"Only I will board that ship, not you, not amma, not appa, and not my sisters," said Shivaji firmly.

Vyjanti's circular eyes, filled with innocence, looked directly at her husband. The moisture in her eyes waited patiently to ambush him. For Shivaji, the slightest glance into her eyes debilitated his heart. Aware of this, Shivaji avoided eye-to-eye contact with his wife.

"I am your wife. It is my duty to be with you through thick and thin, through the highs and lows, through good and bad. You may forbid, but I will not listen. You may order, but I will not listen. You may request, but I will not listen. I will not be able to live a day without you. So let's just forget about five or ten years." Vyjanti rambled in a childlike, impassioned manner. "You cannot do this to me. If you leave me behind, I will...," she stalled, "I will stop breathing. I will find a way to stop my heart."

Shivaji listened carefully to his wife's melodramatic speech. He knew deep in his heart that nothing in this world could make her stay behind. As a husband, the most important rule in Shivaji's book was to protect his wife at all times. By departing to Fiji, he accepted the risk of endangering his own life. Yet he could not accept the same risk for his wife. He believed that for any husband to bring his wife and children on this journey would be dangerous.

"Why would it be dangerous? Dangerous for whom, you or me?" asked Vyjanti, teetering on the edge of agitation.

"I don't trust the Englishmen. I will not be able to endure it."

"Endure what?"

"If those white men inflict pain upon you in any way, I will not be able to endure it. I will lose my mind. Then, only God knows what I will do."

Fearing her husband's words, Vyjanti wisely shifted the conversation. "I will inform the family about our decision. I am sure appa will be delighted to hear that we have embraced this opportunity."

"He sure will," said Shivaji, biting his lip. Lines of tension formed across his forehead. Anxiety churned in his stomach. Not only did he have to watch his own back around the British, but he also had to remain vigilant for malicious eyes that might fall upon Vyjanti. "If those white men indecently look at you, I will pull their eyes out of their sockets," he said aloud, so his wife could hear.

"You will not do anything of that sort. My husband is no troublemaker. I expect submission and endurance from you. We both know there may be injustice on that ship—to what extent, we do not know. At any time, if you feel the British have overstepped, crossed limits, or broken promises, think of me before you act. We cannot lose one another on this journey. We must stay strong to create a better future for ourselves and our family members."

News traveled as fast as lightning in the small village in the Red Lilies district. Within a day, the entire village was aware of who decided to board the ship. Each passing hour, Muthuraman heard several names uttered. Whenever he heard the name of a person or family willing to place their thumbprint on the contract papers, he grumbled. He wished someone would come to his porch and inform him that his son had agreed to go to Fiji as well. A few days earlier, when he discovered that Venkatesh and his family had accepted the contract, he had fussed with his wife for hours.

"It seems everyone is going to the islands. Now I hear Venkatesh is going too. Venkatesh is going, then why not Shivaji? What is the matter with him? This is entirely your fault. You have spoiled him since he was a child. He does not think of anyone but himself. He must understand that there is no loss, only gain from this proposition!"

The wait ended for Muthuraman early one morning when his daughter-in-law announced that she and her husband were prepared to work for the Colonial Sugar Refining Company. As every morning, from his porch, he watched early risers pass by. Some people hustled to the village well to collect water, while others headed to the market to work or purchase groceries. Rocking back and forth in his chair, he greeted his friends with a companionable salute, inviting them to join him for tea. When he had no company, Muthuraman vigilantly watched the little children pass by, ensuring they were not involved in mischief.

Very fond of tea, he patiently waited for his daughter-in-law to place a cup of black tea with one spoon of sugar on the sturdy table on the porch. Vyjanti made it her daily routine to serve her father-in-law. Her mother-in-law had told her that Muthuraman preferred his tea to be made only by her.

"No one makes better tea than my daughter-in-law. Taste it once, and you will be asking for seconds," Shivaji's mother would overhear her husband tell visitors with pride.

While serving her father-in-law that morning, Vyjanti explained why she and her husband had decided to grasp this opportunity. Muthuraman jumped out of his chair, spilling hot tea on his dhoti. He released an ecstatic shriek. At first, Vyjanti thought it was the hot tea burning his skin. But it was not; the high-pitched scream was of excitement. He could not believe his ears.

"Is this true? Are you sure? What if," he swallowed hard, "please say it again?" he stammered.

Overhearing the excitement in Muthuraman's voice, the others inside the house rushed to the porch. As they set foot, Muthuraman's family watched him shouting in the yard to villagers passing by, "Come here, come now, everyone. My son is going to Fiji. Can you believe it? My son is going to the islands. All my concerns have washed away, all my tensions have vanished. My ideal daughter-in-law has revived this old man's faint heart with boundless contentment. I will distribute sweet treats all over the village this evening. Be alert! I will knock on your door with a handful of treats."

Annoyed by her husband's impulsive generosity, Shivaji's mother beckoned the remaining women into the kitchen to notify them that they would have to spend the entire day preparing sweets.

"What a foolish man! Without considering that we are still recovering from the cyclone and its aftermath, the old-timer decides to become extra munificent," Shivaji's mother whispered to her daughter-in-law.

Then unexpectedly, she changed the subject: "So, will you inform your parents?"

"Yes, amma, I will. I have decided to write them a letter."

"Please inform them to visit you before you leave the country."

"I surely will."

"By the way, where is Shivaji?"

"Amma, he has left."

"Where has he gone?"

"I am sure he went to meet Venkatesh anna."

"Did you know that Venkatesh and his family are going to Fiji?"

"Yes, mother, word spreads fast here in the village. I believe that my husband will try to convince anna not to participate in this journey. Amma, I feel that he is very troubled. I can see it in his eyes, and he is not content with the decision he made. I feel as if I have forced him to make this decision."

"You must not feel that way, Vyjanti. If I had a choice, I would not let you and Shivaji leave. The fact that you and Shivaji are leaving for so many years has torn my heart apart. But your father-in-law is a stern man. He believes that it is time for Shivaji to take charge. He wants Shivaji to be the sole caretaker of the family now. And with the undertaking of the indenture contract, the old-timer will finally see his dream of Shivaji advancing in life come true."

On his way to Venkatesh's residence, Shivaji came across disruptive claps and ear-popping whistles. "Who is making all that noise?" he thought. As Shivaji turned the corner, he spotted the young boy who used to sing catchy tunes on the roof of his house. The half-naked boy had grown since the last time Shivaji had seen him. He was without his famous instruments — pots, pans, and utensils. This time around, he was not seated on the roof. Instead, he was standing in front of his doorstep, clapping his hands and stomping his feet repeatedly. From time to time, his melodious voice ceased only to be replaced by a squealing whistle to grasp the attention of the villagers passing by. Shivaji stopped, looked, and listened.

"You can take away my pots; you can take away my spoons,
But you can't take away the sun; you can't take away the moon,
You can take away my clothes; you can take away my food,
But you can't take away my spirit; you can't take away my mood,
You see, man blames God, God blames nature,
I blame the devil masked as the destroyer."

After the sixth verse, the boy let out another wave of whistles, eager to lure more villagers passing by. "Uncle, aunty, father, mother, grandfather, grandmother, brother, sister, and children of all ages, I ask you to gather around. Please gather around, gather around to hear my voice," said the boy without tin utensils.

When Shivaji entered his friend's home, he was pleasantly greeted and fed. Karthik felt saddened that his lively companion Vyjanti was not present. Shivaji promised the child that when he visits next time he will not come without his wife. Karthik was gratified with his mama's uncle's promise. After entertaining Karthik with fairy-tale stories, Shivaji and his friend were left alone to converse. Shivaji did not know where to start. He did not know how to approach. His deadpan eyes were fixed on Venkatesh. His stare created an austere atmosphere within the room.

"What is on your mind? Come out with it, Shivaji?"
"Are you mad? What has gotten into you?" asked Shivaji bluntly. "You have a child. You have a wife. You have your own dwelling. You have your own property. You have everything you need here in this village. So, why do you want to leave?"
"Shivaji, you will not understand. You believe that the British are evil, blood-thirsty devils who will do anything and everything for their benefit. I don't believe that. I believe that

the British are offering the Indians a fair proposition. What they are proposing is far superior to the house and land I own in this village. I want a better future — a better future for Lachmaiya and Karthik. And Fiji promises a better future."

"Have you lost your mind? You have a small child. Can you prove to me that he will not be harmed? Can you prove to me that he will not get sick on the sea voyage? Can you prove to me that the British will not enslave him? Can you? No, you cannot, and that is a fact. How can you trust the Englishmen?"

"Shivaji, you must calm down. Nothing will happen to Karthik or Lachmaiya. I will never let anything bad happen to them. So, you came here to lecture me on why I must not go, right?"

"I don't want you to go. It is not safe for you, anni, and Karthik. Please listen to me."

"You are telling me not to go, but you are going yourself. From all the people, I did not expect you to accept this proposal. I was astonished when a fellow villager revealed that Shivaji and his wife have decided to travel to the islands of Fiji."

"You don't understand. I have not accepted the proposal for my benefit. I have accepted it for my family's sake. I live for them, not for myself. Not a single minute passes by without thinking about the decision I have made. Will the decision help us? Or will the decision obliterate us? Only God knows."

Feeling sympathetic for his friend, Venkatesh advised him to think positively. "Keep your mind on the future. Think of what we can do with the money earned in five years. I will be back in business. I will buy myself additional land. Then I will plant, grow, and harvest more crops. Wait and see, my friend — one day I will be the top produce distributor of this district. Forget district, I will be the top produce distributor for this state," said Venkatesh with a gleeful smile on his face.

"We are so different, Venkatesh. Here I am thinking negatively, and here you are distracted by this future of yours that is bursting with positivity. That is commendable, nanban. I wish I could think and behave like you."

"Don't say that. You are who you are. I know that you don't want history to repeat itself. You don't want to be enslaved. But, Shivaji, we are enslaved in our very own country today. The only chance to gain any kind of liberty is to leave this country. Who knows, perhaps Fiji will grant us liberty. No British rules and regulations to abide by — now imagine that. Think positive, Shivaji."

"You mindless fool, we are to comply. We are to labor for the British in Fiji. How can you forget that? It is their rules and regulations that we will be following. It is their company that we will be working for. And it is their money that we will be receiving," said Shivaji, unable to believe how naive his friend had become these days.

"Hmm, I see…" murmured Venkatesh. "Anyways, I have overheard that tomorrow is the first day of contract signing. The British officials will be coming by the village sometime in the morning with all the necessary paperwork. My signature is ready; it will be the first time in my life that I get the chance to sign an official document. You have no idea how excited I am. I am eager to seal the deal. You know what? I will be the first one in line tomorrow morning."

A guffaw came from Shivaji which rattled Lachmaiya. She entered the room filled with laughter. She asked Shivaji if everything was fine.
"Anni, your husband is mad," replied Shivaji.

"First, I deal with the roosters crowing. Then I have to deal with that nutty boy singing those ambiguous tunes. And now I have to deal with all the chitter-chatter ringing in my ears." Wishing to rest his eyes, Old Man Thambi lay on his stomach underneath the tamarind tree, which he called his dwelling. Not too far away, he spotted large crowds of people from neighboring villages pacing towards his location. The beggar moved his hand to the soil. He felt solid vibrations rising from the earth. In a matter of seconds, he assumed his begging-for-alms position. With his eyelids closed, he sat under the tamarind tree in a cross-legged position, reciting memorized verses from the sacred Bhagavad Gita. The people from the neighboring villages, who did not know him, were captivated by Thambi's enticing voice. They presumed the beggar to be some kind of saint. Thambi noticed that almost half of the crowd's attention was on him. He swiftly brushed his fingers through his hair, ensuring that it was combed neatly to the side. He then rose to his feet with the support of his loyal stick. Thambi paced back and forth in a slightly crouched form, endeavoring to make eye contact with the fortunate person he would bless today. "Biksham Dehi, give me alms. My fair sisters, my wise brothers, fulfill my wants with your generosity. Please son, please daughter, I am in need, give me alms," said the beggar as the flock of people entered the village.

Many of the villagers who knew that Thambi was an untouchable considered his presence to be an evil omen; therefore, they purposely avoided eye contact with him or hastily shooed him off before he was able to come near. Others who had never seen Thambi before reached into their shirt pockets or loosened the knots in their scarves in search of loose change. Some even went to the extent of peeping into their jute bags for bread or fruit to offer as alms to the beggar. After donating whatever they could get their hands on, the people waited to be blessed by the alleged saint. For many Indians, to receive an elder's blessings before proceeding to accomplish something is considered auspicious. Drifting from one person to another, Thambi did not realize that he too was forging ahead with the massive assemblage that kept increasing each minute. Venkatesh and his family believed that they had risen before the others in the village until they set foot outside their home. The pride Venkatesh felt believing that they would be the first ones in line to sign the contract had been crushed after witnessing the single-file line that practically had no end.

"Oh no, this will be a long day. Be prepared with more than a few stories to tell," Venkatesh said to his wife as they both took a glance at Karthik who was keen to step into the village path after witnessing the straight line of people.

For Karthik, the line was unusual. Usually, when he saw people on the village path, they were dispersed without any arrangement. It was his first time seeing a perfect line of people. "Let's go, appa. I want to stand in the line," he said as his eyes lit up with curiosity.

Identifiable faces of village men, women, and children were in search of the tail of the line. It seemed to them as if the line was never-ending. The families proceeded to the back of the line with the minors clinging onto their chests. Once the mobile villagers recognized the face of a close relative or friend who had a decent position in the lineup, they casually merged into the lineup, ensuring that nobody protested about the cheating act. Shivaji and his wife ambled past several familiar faces from the village. Both had no intention of cutting the line. At the same time, Venkatesh and his family were present in the middle of the line in search of their friends.

"Look appa, I see attai and mama," said Karthik, pointing in the direction of the married couple.

Venkatesh and Lachmaiya both waved their hands until Vyjanti noticed.

"Anna is waving at us. I have a feeling he wants to offer us a better position in the lineup."

"We shall not accept their offer. It is not fair to others who have been standing in line for hours," Shivaji replied to his wife.

"I knew you would not accept. And I will not be the one to reject the offer. I have never said no to anna," said Vyjanti with a giggle that managed to bring an upright formation on Shivaji's lips.

As Shivaji met Venkatesh, he drew near and whispered into his ear, "Sorry, I cannot...You know how I am."

Venkatesh turned around to see Shivaji and Vyjanti walk past him, towards the end of the line. He was not upset with Shivaji and his refusal. "I had a feeling he'd say no. In his view, to cut the line would be unjust," Venkatesh said to his wife.

Hindus, Muslims, Sikhs, and Christians from different villages were in a single filed line that extended one hundred and twenty yards. Bearing the explosive heatwave, the children wailing, the incessant yapping, and the slothful movement of the line, Shivaji regretted that he had decided to sign the contract on the first day. "I should have known better. This is a festival. And it is often that a high number of civilians attend the festival on an opening day. I need to slap myself across the face for this," Shivaji said to his wife who paid no attention to his words.

She was engaged in a conversation with an Indian woman who had arrived from a nearby village.

"The British agents informed us that we must come to this village to sign the indenture contract. They have visited all the villages in the red lilies district, but have chosen only a few areas to set up the contract signing," Shivaji overheard the woman say to his wife.

Shivaji scanned his eyes from side to side, attempting to see over the heads and shoulders of the villagers standing in front of him. What irritated him was that not a single person exhibited signs of annoyance despite the unbearable line. It seemed to him as if everyone was delighted to be there, overjoyed to meet the Englishmen, and motivated to sign the contract. Once in line, the villagers did not even think of retreating. Finally, after an hour and forty-five minutes, Shivaji and his wife made it to the front of the line. Four British agents, two British officers, and two Indian translators were present in the background. Seated in front of a wooden table that held bottles of ink, ink pads, ink pens, and stacks of paper was Agent Grahame. Wasting no time, he went over the rules, regulations, plans, and procedures that were to be followed in the contract while the Indian servant echoed Agent Grahame's words with his translations. He then introduced the registration form which required one's name, caste, age, occupation, district, body mass, height, and father's name.

"Let's make this simple. I will ask the questions and you will provide the answers. The answers that you provide, I'll write on the registration form. Is that understood?" asked Agent Grahame in a professional demeanor.

Shivaji waited for the translator to finish. A second after the Indian servant completed his last sentence, he faced the British agent and nodded his head to indicate that he understood.

"Name..."

"Shivaji..."

"Full name, please?"

"Shivaji Nair."

"Father's name..."

"Muthuraman Nair."

"Caste..."

"Hindu Brahmin..."

"Age..."

"Twenty..."

"District..."

"Red lilies district..."

"Body mass..."

"I don't know."

"Provide an estimate..."

"Around sixty kilograms..."

"Height..."

"I am sorry, I don't know."

"Hmm...I'd say five feet seven inches."

"Occupation..."

"Fisherman..."

"Thank you. Next!"

The question-and-answer process left Vyjanti aghast. When it was her turn to face the procedure, Vyjanti's nerves tightened around her throat. She knew the answers to the questions, but apprehension sealed her lips, not letting a single word escape. In the end, with the help of the translator and her husband, she managed to complete the process.

"What shall it be, five years or ten years?" asked Agent Grahame.

"Five years," replied Shivaji as his throat became dry.

Agent Grahame licked his fingertips to collect the first two papers from the top of the stack. He placed the two sheets of paper in the center of the table for Shivaji and his wife to observe.

"These will be the most important papers that you will sign in your lives," said Agent Grahame as he grabbed the ink pad. "Will you be signing with your signatures or will you be signing with your fingerprints?"

Shivaji swallowed hard. He felt the cold sweat on his back whenever his kurta grazed his skin. "This is it. There is no turning back now. I hope I am making the right choice. I don't know what to expect from this journey. God, I want my wife to be guarded against harm," he said under his breath. The uncertainty that Shivaji felt was exposed by the tremble in his right hand when he dipped his thumb into the ink pad. Agent Grahame tapped not once, not twice, but thrice on the particular area where the thumbprint was to be placed. When unable to distract Shivaji from his thoughts, Agent Grahame raised his voice.

"Sir, I need you to place your fingerprint on this paper now."

Shivaji inhaled to accept composure, submission, and optimism. He then exhaled to rid himself of resentment, trepidation, and pessimism. The upper part of the thumb was then placed on the paper, leaving behind an oval-shaped mark. By signing the contract, Shivaji felt that he had signed away his life.

The villagers of the red lilies district were no longer villagers but became indentured laborers under British rule. The contract signing continued for multiple days with a large number of villagers enduring the grueling lines. The only notable decrease in numbers occurred in the last five hours on the final day of signing. On that day, Agent Grahame announced that on the third day of the week, early in the morning, Englishmen would be coming to the villages to round up the indentured laborers and transport them to the vessel. Most of the villagers were disturbed by the announcement because it meant that they had only a single full day to spend time with their families who were to be left behind.

For Muthuraman and his wife, who were to bid farewell to their son and daughter-in-law, this was the opportunity to advise, encourage, inform, prepare, cherish, spoil, and bless them. On the second day of the week, Shivaji and Vyjanti were treated like the prince and princess of the district. Muthuraman gifted his son a hand-sewn, beige-colored kurta and doti which he asked Shivaji to wear for the departure. He also purchased a brand new sari for his daughter-in-law. Besides the gifts, Shivaji and his wife's favorite dishes were prepared by their mother. When Shivaji asked where the money came from to buy these expensive clothes and groceries, both Muthuraman and his wife purposely avoided the question.

"Small loans can be taken without hesitation because my son will be making plenty of money in Fiji," thought Muthuraman. Both of Shivaji's sisters spent the day in tears. Vyjanti was more than a sister-in-law to them. She treated them as if they were her children. The three ladies spent valuable time with each other. Vyjanti assisted her sister-in-laws with schoolwork and household chores. She was molding Shivaji's sisters into skilled housewives. Occupied with her in-laws, Vyjanti was unable to remove the thought of not having the opportunity to say goodbye to her blood mother and father. She cursed the British agents for deciding to leave so early. A letter written to her parents was sent. But Vyjanti knew that by the time her parents received the letter, she would be on the vessel. Her heart ached for her parents, and the ache was excruciating.

"Appa and amma, I wish that you were here, in front of my eyes, so I can tell you both how much I love you," she said under her breath.

What if all this was pre-planned? To avoid the villagers from changing their minds or turning their backs on the signed contracts, the British purposely chose to depart soon, thought Vyjanti. Her brain could not retain the distrustful thoughts for long since it kept wandering back to the faces she had to leave behind. During nightfall, the pillow of sorrow was drenched with her tears by the wife who concealed her face from her husband. Reluctant to disclose her current state, she remained speechless during that night. The husband knew of the situation but did not dare to confront it.

"Five years is equivalent to one thousand, eight hundred, and twenty-five days. How will I survive without a father, a mother, and siblings for the next five years? I will miss the admiration I received from my dear sisters, the compassion and affection that amma expressed, and the insensitive insults and lackluster lectures that appa uttered on a daily basis," Shivaji said under his breath. For him to rest, he waited for his untiring brain to intermit the endless thoughts of separation.

Finally, the day had arrived for the newly recruited indentured laborers to begin their excursion. After weeks of listening, considering, discussing, and approving, it was time for the villagers of the district to sail on the Ship Elbe. A countless number of men employed by the British government barged into the homes of the Indians. With no time to spare, the Englishmen ordered the villagers to march along the pathway that led to the outskirts of the village. Most of the villagers did not have the opportunity to properly bid farewell to their family members who were left behind. Some of them, who had been mistaken for recruits, were forcefully dragged out of their homes and ordered to join the leavers marching along the pathway. Those capable men and women pleaded, but the Englishmen saw and heard nothing. Loud cries swarmed the entire village. Women sobbed openly in public as their husbands waved farewell. Children tugged on their fathers' sleeves, begging them not to leave. Elderly men and women stood in front of clay idols and prayed to God for their children to have a safe journey. Desperate eyes of the remaining villagers peered far into the distance, ensuring they would not lose sight of their loved ones. Their eyes were exposed to the fading shadows that ultimately vanished in the distance. The first signs of loneliness were felt as soon as the remaining villagers entered their empty homes.

During that morning, the Nair family was in the middle of their breakfast when they received a loud banging on the front door.

"The time has come. Open the door. Let's go. Hurry, hurry, hurry," said an Englishman in a brusque manner.

The son and daughter-in-law of the house knelt to touch Muthuraman and his wife's feet. Shivaji and Vyjanti were blessed by their parents.

"Son, I wish you all the best. Make us proud. We will meet again. And the next time we meet, I hope to see a grandchild—or grandchildren," said Muthuraman as he reached over to embrace his son.

"Vyjanti, your husband is the only son I have. Protect him, be his savior. He must not lose his temper. You and I both know how easily he gets angered. He got that from his appa," said Shivaji's mother while holding back her tears.

Vyjanti held onto both of her sister-in-laws. "Don't cry. We will be back. These five years will pass by fast, I promise you. When your anna and I return, we are going to find you both the two most handsome groomsmen in all of India."

"Anna, please...please leave anni behind," said the younger sister, stammering because of her continuous weeping.

"Let's go, Vyjanti," said Shivaji. When leaving the compound, Shivaji did not look back at the saddened faces of his family members. As soon as Vyjanti turned around to wave, her husband pulled at her arm. Vyjanti was confused. It was not common for her husband to act in such an intimidating manner.

"Don't look back. The look on their faces will not let you sleep at night. It will disturb you," said Shivaji as he pulled his wife towards him.

Soon, the figures of both husband and wife were lost in the midst of the trail that was smothered with indentured laborers who were once known as villagers.

"Attention! If you want to be fed, sit on the floor. The chief officer wants to see you seated in straight lines. You will be provided with tin utensils. If you lose or misplace these utensils, then you will have nothing to eat with or from. So, if you don't have your plate and spoon in hand, your share of food will be dumped on the floor. Then, you will have to eat off the floor like a dog," said Brijnath.

"The only dog here is you. Dogs listen to their master. You listen to your master, Chief Officer Anderson. You traitor! You servant! Hell awaits you," said Old Man Thambi, waving his noble stick about like a madman.

"Old man, go wash your filthy mouth. Your words do not affect me," replied Brijnath.

"Baba...Baba," Shivaji called for the beggar.

Thambi turned at the sound of the voice echoing in his ears. His eyes met the presence of Shivaji. With his hands, Shivaji gestured to the elderly man to take a seat. Thambi suppressed his hatred and followed the direction.

"Well, coolies, begin forming rows and soon the crew members will distribute the food," said Brijnath.

This time, there was no confusion about how to form a straight line. The Indians had become familiar with the obsession the British had for straight lines. Straight, single-file lines were required for the contract signing, for entry to Ship Elbe, and now for the food handout. Families gathered their children, seated themselves on the floor, and waited patiently for the food.

"I hope they don't feed us white food," Venkatesh said to his friend.
"Let's just hope they don't feed us meat. We Brahmins are prohibited from consuming flesh," replied Shivaji.
"Well, do you think these Englishmen know the difference between a Hindu and Muslim? For them, we are all the same," said Venkatesh.

All heads turned when two members of the deck crew arrived with a large pot. The pot was seated on a wooden board with wheels. The children were energized by the sight of the deck crew rolling the pot towards them.

"Look amma, the pot is walking," said a small boy, his eyes filled with amazement.

Behind the Englishmen who rolled the pot were other members of the deck crew, carrying silver-colored plates and spoons. The plates and spoons were distributed to every adult passenger on board. The children were not given utensils of their own. Instead, they were to eat from the plates handed to their parents. Most of the villagers did not understand what the plate and spoon were used for. Others had never seen or heard of plates and spoons because they had been eating on banana leaves since birth.

"Why use such items when we have our hands?" asked Lachmaiya as she examined the tin spoons that were handed to her.

"What is that smell? I cannot recognize it," said Vyjanti. She was the first to be served. A portion, the size of a human fist, was tossed onto her tin plate. Vyjanti investigated the watery substance.

"What is this?"
"It is khichdi," shouted Karthik with enthusiasm.
"It does not seem as if they have prepared it with rice and lentils? There is more water than rice. Deva, how will I eat this?" said Vyjanti.

The displeasure she showed at the appearance of the food astonished Shivaji. "I have never seen her complain about the food," he whispered to Venkatesh.

The Indians were incapable of feeding themselves using the old-fashioned method of their bare hands. As they delved into the plate to scoop a small portion of the food, they felt only liquid between their fingers. This was unlike the khichdi they cooked at home; it was more of a lentil soup with tiny amounts of rice. Thus, the spoon became necessary to eat the food. Half of the passengers seated on the deck ejected the tasteless khichdi on their first try. Witnessing this, the British seafarers grew visibly upset.

"You coolies will need to clean the mess you have made. The next time I see you spitting food on the deck, you will be punished," said the deck crew leader.

Listening to the oversized intimidator, Old Man Thambi rose to his feet. "You listen now! We demand proper food. Even animals are not fed such poor food."

"Sit your old raggedy-ass down on the floor," barked the deck crew leader.

"This is unjust. We require better food!" The beggar released his fiery anger on the tin plate, sending it flying with a potent kick in the direction where no passengers were seated. The tin plate struck the wooden ladder with a crackling noise before plummeting to the floor, bent in all corners and angles—rendered useless.

The crew immediately responded. Several men forcefully grabbed hold of Thambi as he struggled, throwing punches in defiance. His inaccurately aimed blows did not strike any of the white faces surrounding him. Once seized, the crew dragged Thambi before the indentured laborers.

A handful of Indians rose to their feet.

"Eh, where are you taking him?" said one passenger.
"Leave him alone. He is too old to be punished," said another.

Shivaji moved forward, but his childhood friend blocked him.

"What is the matter with you? This has nothing to do with you. I don't want you to get involved," said Venkatesh, standing like a towering wall in front of his friend.

Thambi's body was handled as if it were a worthless mannequin. His arms strained against the persistent pulling, and his knees bruised as they rubbed against the dense floor. His blaring cries of insult pierced the ears of the men who manhandled him.

"Let go of me, you sinners! If you don't let go, I will put a curse on you. You Englishmen will pay for this. Hell awaits you," shouted Old Man Thambi, his voice fading into the distance.

The deck crew hauled the beggar down the steps to an unknown location. Chief Officer Anderson observed the incident from the deck above. Like an eagle, he scanned the Indians, noting every movement. His gaze fixed on the one who had budged when Thambi was mistreated. Slowly, Anderson descended the rusty steps to the lower deck. The disturbed Indians followed his movements with their eyes, only to be offended by his mocking belly laugh.

"You see what happens when you misbehave. If you defy us, we punish you. Now, I will tell you where the old man has been taken," said Anderson, as the indentured laborers whispered amongst themselves. He then met the eyes of his servant, Brijnath.

"Why are you not translating in Hindi or Tamil?"
"Sorry...very sorry, kulumber," replied Brijnath, hands folded.

"I want your attention, coolies. Keep your eyes on me. That foolish old man has been taken to 'the hole.' I am certain none of you have the slightest idea what 'the hole' is. If you challenge us, you will find out. Some who are sent to 'the hole' never come back. The severity of your crime determines how long you will stay there. As for the old man, he will spend the next five days in obscurity. Remember, coolies, do not misbehave."

Discussion after discussion, none of the Indians could tell if 'the hole' actually existed—or what it might entail.

The Englishmen began revealing their true colors. The first signs of cruelty formed distress in the minds of the Indians on the vessel.

"I don't want to be manhandled like some kind of animal," said one laborer.
"I feel as if I will vomit. The food the deck crew served was terrible. I hope we don't get the same khichdi this evening," said another.

Brijnath and the crew led the Indians to nearby barrels of water to wash their hands and utensils. "Use this water as if it were the last drops of your life. The water in these barrels has to last for at least forty-five days," said the servant.

Shivaji used a pail to retrieve water from the massive barrel. He assisted his friends and Vyjanti in cleansing the stains left from the khichdi. Once everyone was done, Vyjanti supported her husband in washing the utensils, making sure not to use too much water.

Across from him, a couple of Hindu Brahmins became embroiled in a feud.

"What do you think of yourself? Did you not hear the whites? We are to save water, not waste it," said the aggressor.

"What is it to you how I use the water? For God's sake, it is just water," replied the other.

"It is not just water; it is what will keep us alive. Imagine if we run out. What then?" said the aggressor, stepping between the barrel and the culprit.

"I need you to step aside. There is plenty of water for everyone."

"I am not moving until you realize that this water is essential for our future. I cannot let you splatter it here and there. Use it for washing your utensils, not for your arms and legs."

"Whatever you do with the water is your decision. But don't tell me what to do. If you don't move, I will take action," said the other.

As more Indians gathered, the deck crew noticed tension brewing. They quickly intervened, restoring order and ensuring that the lines for the barrels kept moving. Shivaji watched the minor war among his people and reflected:

Why do we fight amongst ourselves? Why quarrel with our own? Why cannot we direct our anger at the British for their wrongdoings? All we need is to channel the hatred we release on each other toward our true enemies.

Hours after consuming the rice and lentils, most of the passengers began to vomit. The Indians were not accustomed to keeping the watery khichdi down. Vomit, the same color as the soup, splattered across the deck. From elders to children, no one was spared. The deck crew was furious at the sight of their platform soiled. It was not expected for the English seamen to lower themselves to clean; instead, the crew leader fetched Chief Officer Anderson to manage the grotesque situation.

Anderson sniffed the foul air. He knew the bile on the floors had to be cleansed before the stench reached the Captain's sensitive nose.

"Bloody hell! What is the matter with you foolish people? Who will clean this mess? Well, I certainly won't. You make the mess, you clean it. The deck crew will provide you with the necessary materials: pails of water and rag cloths. Every day, before your evening meals, the deck must be washed and wiped. Refuse, and you will be punished. If the deck is not disinfected by evening, no coolie will be served dinner."

Brijnath did not translate Anderson's words this time. He was present, interpreting the harsh commands with an echoing voice for the indentured laborers. After each sentence, the chief officer's words carried the threat of punishment.

"If you don't do this, you will be punished. If you don't do that, you will be punished. Why is punishment attached to every instruction? Soon they'll say, 'If you breathe, you will be punished,'" Shivaji muttered under his breath.

"If you have questions, don't ask. If you have complaints, don't complain. It does not matter who vomited and who did not. Every adult with capable hands and legs must wash the deck. Fellow seamen, give the coolies pails of water and rag cloths," continued Anderson.

The indentured laborers froze. Who would step forward first? Who would be the first to obey such a humiliating command?

"Bloody hell! What is it now? You have your pails of water and rag cloths—what else do you need? Foolish coolies, do you want to be lashed?"

Shivaji heard the wooden floor screech beside him. Vyjanti had planted her knees firmly on the deck. She brushed aside strands of hair falling onto her face and dipped the rag cloth into the pail of water. With circular motions, she scrubbed the wooden deck. Other women quickly followed her lead.

Shivaji and the other men stood perplexed. Cultural norms frowned upon men cleaning floors—a woman's task—but on a British ship under British commanders, they had no choice. Within a minute, the men knelt alongside the women, assisting in the labor.

Soon, Lachmaiya felt sick. Her eyes dampened, her head spun, and her face turned pale.

"I think... I... help me... I need to..." she stammered as the khichdi surged from her stomach. Before she could cover her mouth, it spilled onto the deck. Venkatesh scrambled forward, scraping his knees on the hard surface.

"Lachmaiya, are you fine? Do you need water?"

"No, I'm fine. Forget the water," she replied.

"You must wash your mouth. I'll bring water," Venkatesh insisted.

"No, don't. We must conserve the water in the barrels. Remember what the Englishman said?"

Shivaji hurriedly cleaned up the mess, ignoring his own disgust. Around the deck, Indians continued to regurgitate, some unable to hold down the food, others overcome by the stench. The British seafarers watched with satisfaction, observing the indentured laborers struggle under their first assigned burden.

Hours of scrubbing left swollen knees and blistered hands, yet the laborers were ordered to form rows for the evening meal. Expecting a better meal after their toil, they were met with the same tasteless, watery khichdi, portioned the size of a human fist. Eating or refusing the dish brought the same torment: consuming it caused nausea and diarrhea, while skipping it resulted in hunger pains.

Vyjanti observed her husband. Shivaji, struggling to grasp the spoon, managed a single sip before nudging the bowl aside. The tasteless fluid slid down his throat, but he could not bring himself to eat more. Memories of family dinners in the village haunted him: the smell of spices, chutneys, and zestful food, the love of his mother and wife serving him with care. He had devoured his meals then, savoring every bite, licking the remaining grains off his fingers.

Now, the memory stabbed at his heart. Vyjanti, holding a tin spoonful of khichdi, hesitated. How could she eat while her husband could not? She placed the spoon back on the plate.

Shivaji's eyes followed her every movement. She forced a smile.

"Not today. Maybe tomorrow," she whispered.

"What about tomorrow?" Shivaji asked.

"Let's hope they serve better food tomorrow."

Before Shivaji could reply, Brijnath loomed over them, twisting the ends of his mustache, his devilish eyes inspecting their plates. He leaned close to Vyjanti.

"Let me answer that for you. Khichdi is what you had today, khichdi is what you will have tomorrow, and khichdi is what you will have every day on this voyage. Do you coolies think this ship is a fancy restaurant? What you crave will not be cooked in our kitchen."

The wrath that existed within Shivaji exploded like a volcano. Venkatesh, seated beside him, knew the extent of his friend's temper. Not allowing Shivaji to act physically or verbally, he intervened with a few words of his own.

"This food is not fit for humans. It should be fed to animals. You have poisoned our stomachs with this miserable dish. Because of the khichdi, we are suffering cramps. We refuse to eat this." The brave words of Venkatesh were heard by nearby indentured laborers, who realized it was their chance to voice complaints about the food. Voices erupted from all corners, leaving Brijnath staggered. Cold sweat formed at his temples. The escalation of complaints and demands ruled the lower deck until the sound of the vicious whip announced the true oppressor.

The initial screams of terror sent the Indians running for their lives. There was nowhere to hide. No direction offered refuge. The Indians were like caged beasts, straining to escape the menacing lashes. Chief Officer Anderson behaved like a ruthless animal trainer, striking his whip with immense force. Numerous indentured laborers, men and women, writhed on the floor in pain. Their clothes were stained with blood. Witnessing the horror, the children began to wail. Shivaji protected his wife, shielding every inch of her body with his own. Unsteady feet dashed past him, high-pitched cries echoed in his ears, and bodies plummeted onto the deck.

"Deva, what is happening?" Vyjanti cried, tears streaming down her face.
"Don't worry. You will not be harmed," Shivaji replied, pressing her face to his chest.

Along with others, Venkatesh and his family hid behind the water barrels. Brijnath oscillated his baton aimlessly in the air, hoping to strike a human face. He did not know if he was defending himself from the Indians who considered him a traitor or punishing them to stop objections. Whatever the reason, it did not take long for Brijnath to strike his first victim. The powerful swing cracked a man's jawbone. As the body hit the deck, a few teeth flew through the air. Soon, the man lay bleeding, mouth gushing like a river. Brijnath stood over him with a conniving sneer.

Shivaji dared to glance for Anderson. His eyes scanned the lower deck, meeting a horde of bodies closing in. "Vyjanti, we must rise to our feet. Do you hear me? We must rise. The crowd will trample us if we don't. Get up!"

Vyjanti was frozen in shock. The whip's lash against flesh, the baton crushing bones, and the agonized cries of mothers and children shattered her. Shivaji pulled her to her feet before it was too late, pressing her face to his chest again to shield her. Encircled by the crowd, he peered through scarves and turbans atop the Indian men's heads. Venkatesh and his family were nowhere to be seen.

"See what happens when you challenge the British," Anderson said boastfully. He swung his whip toward the cornered Indians. The eerie crack echoed across the deck, terrifying the indentured laborers. Bodies shifted, mothers hid children, husbands shielded wives, and elders huddled behind others, praying not to be struck.

"We are the British, not you. This ship belongs to us. You must follow our commands. Refuse, and expect severe punishment. Remember, you don't have the authority to rebel. You have no power. We do. Coolies, use your brains wisely."

Once translated, Brijnath moved next to Anderson. "How can they use their brains, kulumber?" he asked cheekily.

"Say what?"

"Kulumber, how can these coolies use their brains when they don't even have any?" Both the officer and servant roared with laughter.

Shivaji's eyes soared to the clouded skies. "What have we gotten ourselves into?" he muttered under his breath, clutching his wife.

Fear hovered in the minds of every Indian passenger. After the incident, there were no more arguments, disagreements, or protests. The bland rice and lentils were consumed the next morning without hesitation.

After the meal, the Indians washed their hands and faces, careful not to waste the precious water. Every rinse brought tension: How much water to use? Should feet be washed too? Should hair be washed before it became matted?

The deck crew leader monitored each person using the barrels. Excessive water use earned a swift whack from the baton. Then, the indentured laborers were assigned to cleanse the lower deck—a back-breaking duty to be completed within sixty minutes. Even when the deck was spotless, the British seafarers forced continued labor.

Shivaji splashed water on the deck while Vyjanti scrubbed in circular motions. The rigid floor cut and scratched her hands. Shivaji wrapped a loose cloth around her wounds, while spare pieces were used for others' bruises and lacerations. Men tore pieces from their turbans to nurse injuries.

As the laborers toiled, a predator watched from the upper deck, hands on the rails, completely still. A light breeze swept across the platform, lifting the scarf covering Vyjanti's face and chest nearly ten feet. Humiliated, she shielded herself with her arms. Shivaji raced, retrieved the scarf, and ensured she was properly covered.

"Deva, I am sorry. I...did not... I am so ashamed. Please...please, I beg of you to forgive me," pleaded Vyjanti, faltering in her speech as a result of distress.
"You are not at fault, Vyjanti. Let's forget that it ever happened."

Half of the Indians on board did not see the incident, while the other half respectfully turned their faces. Shivaji and his wife believed that no one on the vessel took pleasure in what had been shown. But that was not the case. The predator that stalked the inferior had his grisly eyes fixated on the sensuous exposure. Contradictory thoughts started to writhe inside Shivaji's brain. "I don't believe that anyone observed what happened minutes ago. But what if someone has taken pleasure in the exposure? What shall I do? Shall I let him be? Or shall I pull his eyes out of their sockets? My wife has put me in a complex situation, but I cannot blame her. This is not her fault," Shivaji said to himself.

He scanned the faces of the nearby Indian males, believing that eye contact might reveal who had watched. Since the indentured laborers were too involved with purifying the deck, Shivaji's experiment failed before it could begin. Many of the Indians feared that lagging in their duties would result in a serious penalty. So, they did not dare to raise their eyes from the platform.

For no reason, Shivaji scanned the upper deck. There he observed the predator resting his lecherous eyes on Vyjanti. The predator, Captain Sanders, had located his target. A bolt of lightning flashed within Shivaji's body. *If only that lightning could strike the captain,* thought Shivaji. His wife's words, "I expect submission and endurance from you," repeated in his mind. Shivaji was aware that sudden anger could result in extreme consequences for his wife. He felt as if a barrage of cannons and bullets had been unleashed on his chest. Shivaji believed the only way to survive the direct fire was to step back rather than forward. And that is what he did.

THE 5TH DAY

On the fifth day, the morning tides became lively, causing Ship Elbe to rise and fall persistently. The crash of the rapid waves startled the unprepared Indian passengers. As for the British seafarers, they were prepared for this encounter from the first day they set foot on Elbe. The Englishmen took their assigned positions to direct the vessel toward unmolested areas of the sea. Never having been placed in such an escapade, the Indians were a mess. Their belongings were tossed from one end to another due to the hyperactive movements of the vessel. The passengers situated close to the railings, including Shivaji and Vyjanti, scrambled to the center of the deck for safety. With the severe tilting of the vessel, any Indian standing by the railing was bound to get tossed overboard. Most of the indentured laborers felt nauseated. Whatever had been stored the day before was expelled onto the deck. Seasickness cleansed their stomachs of the distasteful khichdi that had been served.

The maniacal display of the Indians tripping and falling over each other, grabbing other people's arms and legs, chanting God's name repeatedly for protection, and vomiting so violently it seemed their intestines might emerge from their mouths, brought immense pleasure to the Englishmen. Soon, the British were able to relieve the Indians from the turbulent situation. Ship Elbe was efficiently operated toward calmer waters. The even sailing of the vessel allowed the Indians to recover their personal belongings. Extra pieces of clothing, turbans, scarves, jute bags, and sandals were strewn across the lower deck. The Indians scanned through others' belongings to locate theirs.

"Eh, are you trying to steal my sandals?" said the Hindu Brahmin.

"These sandals are mine. Why don't you have a look?" said the indentured laborer who was once a peasant from a low caste.

The Hindu Brahmin observed the sandals at close range. "Well, now that you have touched the sandals with your untouchable hands, you can keep them." Aware that the footwear was not his, the Hindu Brahmin still found it necessary to insult the peasant.

Shivaji was not far from the scene as he searched for his blood-red turban that had been placed on the deck before the abrupt rising and falling of the ship.

"I know these sandals belong to you. If I were you, I'd take these sandals and use them to smash his skull open," Shivaji said to the former peasant.

The vulnerable Indian shrugged his shoulders, not understanding what to say or do.

"When will our people start accepting each other as equals? We need to unite. We need brotherhood. I believe that unity can grant us liberty. On this ship, we should not differentiate between low caste and high caste. We should not differentiate between Hindu and Muslim," Shivaji said to the crowd of Indians that had gathered around him.

Vyjanti bumped and brushed against the indentured laborers to reach her husband. She feared that if the Englishmen were to see him in the center of the heated discourse, there would be severe consequences. Before she could speak or make a gesture to withdraw him from the crowd, Shivaji continued.

"For the British, we are not indentured laborers, we are slaves. That is why we must stand united. We need to stand together to make a change. We need to..."

The sound of a human body falling to the deck made several heads turn. Shivaji noticed a few members from the deck crew retreat into the dimness that led to the bottommost level of the vessel. The Indians clustered around the unknown body. Shivaji advised his wife not to move. If the body was lifeless, he did not want her to see it.

"Pardon me, please move aside." Shivaji pushed through the shoulders, arms, hips, and legs of the assembled Indians. His goal was to reach the compressed area where the body lay.

"Who is he?" said one of the Indians on board.

Shivaji heard that the unknown was a man.

"Look! He is moving," said an old-timer.

Shivaji was aware that the unknown was alive.

"Oh God, look at the black and blue marks on his body," said a woman from the crowd.

Shivaji now realized that the person was a living man with severe injuries.

As Shivaji reached the middle of the circle, his eyes fell upon the blood clots that had formed on the injured man's backside. First, the unknown twitched. Then he moaned. And then he mumbled a couple of words that were impossible to understand. He gently turned to his front side. The unknown was no longer unidentified.

"Baba, what have they done to you?" Shivaji stumbled to the deck. He instantly regained his mental strength, depleted by the sight of violence inflicted upon the beggar.

Shivaji tossed Thambi's left arm over his shoulder for leverage. Depending on his capable shoulders, Shivaji lifted the beggar to his feet. As soon as Thambi was lifted, the air was filled with the reek of human feces and urine. The indentured laborers who had gathered fled the scene, covering their noses with handkerchiefs and veils. The foul odor that came from Thambi's body and clothes did not disturb Shivaji. Noticing that the beggar's limbs were of no use, Shivaji called out for help.

"Please, someone, anybody...I need your assistance. I am losing my grip here. Please help me!"

To his surprise, from the collection of bodies emerged his reliable wife. She was the only female on board who did not let the odor and wounds of Thambi bother her. While the other Indian women onboard felt sickened by Thambi's condition, Vyjanti touched him. Shivaji's dauntless wife placed Thambi's right arm over her shoulders. She then followed Shivaji's lead to haul the beggar to the barrels of water.

"He needs water. He needs to feel refreshed," Shivaji said to his wife, breathing hard.

"Oh Deva, I hope he survives," said Vyjanti.

"I felt his pulse. He will survive."

"Look at his skin! It is abraded."

"Yes Vyjanti, I can see that. Don't worry; he does not have life-threatening injuries. He will survive."

The moment Shivaji and his wife arrived with Thambi at the water station, there was no sign of the deck crew leader.

"No Englishman is guarding the barrels at the moment, which means there is no restriction on the usage of water," Shivaji informed his wife.

The married couple placed Thambi on the deck with absolute care. Vyjanti fetched water using the buckets that were placed by the barrel. Once she placed the filled bucket beside her husband, Vyjanti left to retrieve more water. Shivaji first fed the beggar some water with his hands. He created a cupped shape with his hand, which looked like a nest, for the water to remain intact. Shivaji then bent his hands outward for the water to pour evenly into Thambi's dry mouth. The water served as both comfort and pain. Thambi drank, and he drank fast, relieving his dehydrated throat. But when the water graced his lips, it irritated the cracked skin. Vyjanti's tentative eyes searched for the men dressed in red. Shivaji clasped the bucket of water and sprinkled multiple drops on Thambi's pale body. Coming to his senses, Thambi repeatedly blessed Shivaji for his kindness.

"God bless you! May God bless you both," muttered Thambi as water rinsed his eyes.

"Vyjanti, I need your assistance. We need to lift Baba and move him to a safer area," said Shivaji.

With blurred vision, Thambi was still able to view the brisk movements of Vyjanti shifting the remaining pails of water back into the barrels. As soon as she finished the necessary task, Vyjanti supported her husband in moving the helpless beggar.

"Son, you and your wife are made for one another. I will pray for you both to come together in every birth, every life."

Old Man Thambi's words touched Vyjanti's heart. "I believed others. I judged without knowing. The people of my village said that he was troublesome. They claimed he did black magic. Some went so far as to call him a demon, while others said he was a madman. He does not seem to be anything like what others have said about him. He is not a man of evil curses and immoral wishes; he is a man of grateful blessings," Vyjanti said to herself.

Regaining strength, Thambi requested to be seated in the area provided to him when he first set foot on Elbe.

"My son, I thank you from the bottom of my heart. You have treated me like you would treat your own father. I am indebted to your humane services."

"No need to thank me, Baba. Now you must rest. Your wounds need to heal." Shivaji and his wife touched the beggar's feet before departing. Once more, Thambi blessed his saviors.

"Son, I have to talk to you. If possible, can you and your wife please stay for a while?"

"Talk to me...About what? Baba, are you feeling okay?"

"Yes son, I feel fine. These wounds must look severe to you, but for me, they are minor scratches. But let's forget about my injuries."

"Then, what is it that you want to talk about, Baba?"

"I have been in 'the hole' for the last five days. They had my grave prepared in the dungeon of hell. I was left in the darkness to starve. But what the Englishmen did not know was that I have lived my entire life battling starvation. I have lived seven days without eating and drinking, so five days was nothing."

Thambi's chronicle on 'the hole' had Shivaji and his wife enthralled. Both of them agreed to sit beside the old man when he gestured to do so.

"These Englishmen are clever. They had a back-up plan. If starvation did not lead to death, the British had another weapon: isolation. Son, I am a person who rambles on and on and on. I talk to you, I talk to him, I talk to her, I talk to God, I talk to myself—basically I talk to everyone. That is how I get my alms. So, at first, I waited. Then I waited some more, and then I waited some more. No one came to my rescue. No movement was seen. No voice was heard. Not a soul peeked into 'the hole' to see if Old Man Thambi was dead or alive. I felt as if the world and the people who lived in it had all forgotten the beggar of no real worth. For the first time in my life, I felt abandoned. The loneliness that resided in my heart led to insanity. I had no control over my senses. The insanity compelled me to end my life."

"Oh Deva," said Vyjanti as her hands rose to cover her opened mouth.

For a second, Shivaji imagined himself seated against the walls of the prison. It did not matter whether he kept his eyes open or closed. There was no trace of illumination. There was no trace of time. There was no trace of day or night.

The mental images which developed in Shivaji's brain suddenly vanished as Thambi resumed with his narrative.

"I believe it was the fourth day into my sentence when my trembling hands crept up to my neck. I sat in the darkness of solitude with both my hands prepared to mutilate the head from its body. I fought for life and I fought for death. Confusion had overpowered my brain. You would not be able to predict what happened next."

"What happened?" asked Shivaji, leaning forward with interest.

"A beam of light penetrated the darkness inside 'the hole' like a knife cutting easily through human flesh. Instantaneously, my eyes started to burn. I had not seen light for more than seventy-two hours. A voice distinctly bounced from the walls into my ear, 'Eh old man, you alive? Talk to me, coolie. Are you alive?'"

The words were in the Tamil language, and the voice sounded familiar.

'Yes, I am alive. Who is this? Is this the traitor talking?' I said, my throat dry and harsh.

I followed the beam of light from the walls to the floor. The light shone from a rectangular-shaped opening at the bottom of the door.

'So you're alive. You are one sturdy old man living with no food for four days. Well, old man, you are in here because you said that the food we serve is not for Indians but dogs. Now I present to you food that is really for dogs. Enjoy your supper,' said the arsehole.

You would not believe it—through the opening of the door, he slid a plate of biscuits."

"Biscuits?" asked Vyjanti, noticing the dark circles under the beggar's eyes, evidence of sleepless nights.

"Yes, my dear, biscuits—dog biscuits. I know how dog biscuits look. Back in the village, many people with black hearts tossed dog biscuits at me when I begged for alms. I am thankful to God. Never have I fallen to the state in which I had no choice but to devour food made for animals."

"So you did not eat the biscuits?" asked Shivaji hesitantly.

"No, son. This beggar may be old and fragile, but he has tremendous willpower."

"Baba, I hope you don't mind my saying this, but I have to disagree with you. You were on the verge of taking your own life. Why? How could you think of committing such an act?"

"The hole is like a prison cell. At times, it controls your mind. At times, it manipulates your instincts. At times, it torments your soul. Within that small compressed area, you battle against the eerie darkness, the dominant walls, the limited space, the harrowing voices, the deprived stomach, the craving throat, and much, much more. If you don't go to war with 'the hole,' it will gift you a slow, painful death. As you can see, I did go to war, I did battle. Somewhere in that battle, I lost my way. But God was there. God wants me to live; therefore, He kept me alive."

"Why, Baba? Why does God want us to live? Does God want us to live so He can see us suffer?" Shivaji asked the wise beggar.

"No, son. It is not God who is inflicting pain upon us. It is not the British who are inflicting pain upon us. It is our past sins that inflict pain upon us. We have placed ourselves in this position. We must pay the price for what we have done. Our past lives are connected to our present, and our present life will connect to our next. Son, what you lose today, you will gain tomorrow. Don't consider this your last life."

"Sorry, Baba, I don't understand."

"The cycle of life is hard to understand," said Old Man Thambi as he stretched his legs and arms. The beggar's eyes were heavy with sleep long denied. Thambi fondled his shabby white beard, released a loud yawn, and waved his hand in a back-and-forth motion. "Thank you for all the help. I am indebted to you both. But now you must excuse me. I need to rest my eyes," said Thambi as his voice started to fade and his lids began to close.

THE 9TH DAY

The British seafarers went beyond all limits, surpassed all boundaries, destroyed all barriers, and crossed all borders on the ninth day on Ship Elbe. Minutes before sunrise, a middle-aged Muslim embraced the beginning of his day with the formal Islamic prayer, Salah. With prescribed actions and words, the Muslim was fully absorbed in his prayers to Allah. The sound mind of the devotee made him entirely ignorant of his surroundings. He could not see, hear, feel, or sense anything but Allah.

Not far away, by the pool of water on the upper deck, stood Chief Officer Anderson. The chief was not an early riser, but on the ninth day of the voyage, destiny had him commit the most inhuman act of his life. With his stomach in need of food, Anderson stomped down the antique staircase from the upper deck to the lower deck. The kitchen was not far from the stairs. To satisfy his hunger, the chief proceeded to the northeast corner of the lower deck. Anderson did not care if he had to step over the motionless bodies to reach the indistinct pathway that led to the kitchen.

Just as he reached the bottom of the stairs, he was drawn to a whispering voice repeating *Allahu Akbar.* "There can be no other God than Jesus. Every passenger on this ship must worship Jesus. There is no Allah, there is no Ram; there is only Jesus. If one questions Jesus, if one addresses Jesus by a different name, if one does not believe in Jesus, that person will suffer," Anderson said to himself.

As he approached the Muslim, who was engrossed in his prayers, the sound of his leather boots crushing the wooden deck and his teeth grinding against each other were both audible. Even with the never-ending tension between the two major religions of India, Chief Officer Anderson, the overseer of the ship, did what no Hindu risked doing. The devotee remained kneeling with his hands extended and his forehead lowered, exhibiting complete surrender to his God.

As he turned his head to the right for the prayer to be completed, Anderson stood before him like the shadow of death. Before the Muslim opened his eyelids, he was introduced to genuine leather for the first time. He experienced the smell and taste of leather simultaneously when the chief officer booted him across the face. The lethal blow made the devotee yelp in pain. His body collapsed to the deck with one side of his temple scraping on the rigid wood. The Muslim was left with splinters on his face, which made his appearance grotesque.

"How dare you? Bloody hell, how many times have I told you coolies that there is one God? There is one God, and that is Jesus. I don't want to see you worshipping Allah or Ram," said the chief officer before striking the fallen devotee with another blow, this time to his ribs.

After the hit to the ribs, the devotee gasped for air. For a couple of seconds, he felt as if life was leaving his body. As soon as he felt air pump into his lungs again, the devotee struggled to escape Anderson's heinous acts. His fingers tried hard to dig into the floor, but the stubborn wood did not give in. There were no holes or cracks for his fingers to slide into and help propel his body out of harm's way.

The Muslim believed that with the support of his able hands, the opportunity was there for him to lift his body and escape the chief officer's remorseless actions. But once he discovered the lack of energy in his muscles and bones, the Muslim decided to shrivel up into a ball. The brutal kick to his face had temporarily paralyzed his brain. He could not figure out how to withdraw from the scene.

"Forget your God, believe in ours. Your God only brings you pain. You worship Allah, you get punished. You worship Jesus, there will be no punishment. Do you understand?" Anderson did not receive an answer to his question. The idle face of the Muslim evoked Anderson to begin a stomping spree. The incessant strikes to the devotee's ribs, stomach, and man-jewels led to high-pitched screams. A twisted grin formed on Anderson's face as the sufferer finally came to reveal his aliveness.

"I beg of you, please help me," cried the thrashed Muslim. His loud shouts had the indentured laborers tossing and turning. The Indians within the area, who had been fast asleep, were eventually rising to the villainous act.

"Eh, what is going on? Why are you beating our Muslim brother?" said one of the men from the numerous risen bodies scattered on the deck.

"What do you have against us Muslims? Why are we the ones that are continuously persecuted? Can you Englishmen for once torment the Hindus? Why must it always be us?" said a man from the Islamic religion.

The last set of questions resulted in commotion, with the Hindus denouncing the Muslims and the Muslims provoking the Hindus. Before the stimulated excitement led to shoving and pushing, then to slapping and punching, the chief officer seized the crowd's attention with his authoritative voice.

"Coolies, you are all the same for us Englishmen. Hindu, Muslim, and Sikh, you are all the bloody same. It is the color of your skin that defines you, not whether you believe in Allah or Ram. It is the country that you originate from that defines you, not the fact that one religion does not consume the flesh of an animal while the other does. Matter of fact, you are animals looking for the slightest opportunity to pounce on each other, as you did now. That is why the Englishmen are here to show you how to live. Jesus can be your savior; follow his path. If you choose to worship a God other than Jesus, then expect to be ill-treated."

The lectures on the religion of Christianity went in one ear and out the other. The Hindus, the Muslims, and the Sikhs belong to distinct religions. These religions encourage the faithful to perform good deeds.

"If the British say Allah gives pain, I say Allah also gives us the power to endure pain," said the Muslim devotee as he was helped onto his feet by other Indians.

THE 12TH DAY

The Muslims on the vessel did not know that their fellow brother's prayer had been disturbed by a kick to the face. Several questions were asked, but the victim did not reveal that he'd been abused while performing Salah. He believed that Allah would not want the savagery revealed. Allah knew how the Muslims on board would retaliate to such a heinous act. The unjust act, centered on religion, left the indentured laborers frustrated. They were not asked but ordered to surrender a religion they had inherited from their parents; a religion that their parents had inherited from theirs; a religion passed down by their ancestors; a religion that had existed for centuries. The demand was not to be challenged and was to be followed without question. Instead of joining their palms together, the Hindus would fold their hands to show the Englishman that the prayers were for Jesus and Jesus only. What the Englishman did not know was that the Hindus with folded hands were chanting the names of their Indian gods and goddesses under their breath. By the seventh day, the passengers on Ship Elbe were accepting the poorly made khichdi without complaint. The Indians did not even care to look at the yellowish, watery substance. The khichdi was first scooped into the spoon, then lodged into the mouth, then sent down the throat, then kept in the stomach temporarily, and then expelled from the mouth or rear. Too afraid to expel on the deck, the indentured laborers hurried to the railing to decorate the seas with vomit.

After his morning breakfast on the twelfth day, a middle-aged Brahmin father used his son as a mirror. He turned to his child for assistance with facial grooming. He asked his child where to snip and where to trim. Then he asked if it was even or uneven and whether it looked good or not. To answer, the child tilted his father's head from one side to the other. Before answering, he investigated with squinted eyes and pulled at the strands of facial hair with his tiny fingers.

"Ouch, not so hard, my whiskers will fall," said the father with a laugh.

Once the child was satisfied with his analysis, he provided a detailed response to his father.

"Appa, your mustache is not even. One side is longer than the other. You must snip more on the left side for both sides to match."

"What about the right side?"

"No appa, don't touch the right side. The right side is perfect. Work on the left side and then I will tell you how it turns out."

The father lifted his hand, which contained small scissors that had escaped detection during the body and baggage search when boarding the ship. With caution, he moved the scissors near his pointed chin. The metal blades clipped the mustache hair, which swirled in the air before it reached the deck. Hesitant to snip too much from the left side, the father paused. The unexpected stoppage excited the child. "Appa, what are you doing? I did not tell you to stop. A little bit more, snip a little bit more."

"Son, are you sure?"

"Yes Appa, I will tell you when to stop. Trust me!"

Some onlookers found the child endearing as he guided his father with confidence. The act made them reminisce about the sons, daughters, nieces, and nephews they had left behind in their villages. The Indian men hoped that the Brahmin father would share the undetected instrument. With the passing of a week, the men on board started to feel uncomfortable with the extravagant growth of their beards. Faces were scratched persistently. Most Hindus were not used to facial hair. Back in the village they often wore a clean-shaven look with the exception of a proud mustache. The men in need gaped at the scissors heading for the end of the mustache. The blades slid between the minuscule strands of hair. As the blades clamped, the flawed strands were removed.

"Perfect! That is it, Appa. No more, no more, that is it," said the child, his voice full of pleasure.

The father instantly lobbed his right hand into the air as his son dove into his chest with a mouthful of praise.

"Eh son, be careful. The scissors are sharp. You can easily get poked."

"Appa, you don't need the piece of glass that we have in our house. Your hands were steady. Not once did they tremble. You were outstanding."

"I could not have done it without you. Son, you are my mirror."

A rapid movement caused the father to wince. He felt skin on skin. The touch was rough. A tight squeeze on his wrist indicated he was overpowered. The tormentor's intruding fingers claimed the metal object by force. The father dared to glance upwards. In his sight was the face of a callous seafarer. Chief Officer Anderson stood before the unfortunate father and his son. With the claimed scissors in his possession, he released a derisive laugh. "Now I wonder? Yes, I really do. How in the hell did you manage to sneak this past us?" Anderson asked, without Brijnath's usual translations.

The father gestured for his son to look for his mother. In the back of his mind, he knew there were high chances of him being penalized for possession of a scissor. He did not want the vulnerable eyes of his son to witness cruelty. The child's feet dashed away in a hurry. His fast movements did not turn heads since all the focus was on the father and his nemesis.

"This teeny weeny metal object here is considered a weapon. You could have used this on a British seafarer. Do you want to see how much damage this weapon can do? Do you want to see how much pain this weapon can inflict? Do you want me to punish you?"

Silence bounced from one deathlike face to another. The Indians did not understand a word of English without Brijnath's precise translations. To them, the chief officer had a voice but no words. Anderson then drove the leather shaft of his boot into the victim's face. Blood oozed from the father's nose. He wiped the blood with his forearm, praying that his son did not witness the vicious scene.

"Talk to me. You bloody coolie! What is the matter with you? Why don't you answer my questions? Do you want me to cut off your tongue with the scissors? Or do you want me to cut off your ear with the scissors? Actually, I think I should cut off your shriveled-up balls."

The last statement filled the area with tumultuous cheers from the deck crew members who were eavesdropping from the upper deck. The upper deck was treated as the balcony seats of a theatrical show. From their prestigious seats, the deck crew members snickered and applauded Anderson's show of demeaning words and resentful acts.
"Eh fellas, why don't you come and join the show?" said Anderson as he summoned the Englishman to walk down the stairs.

The deck crew members came stampeding towards the Brahmin father like a pack of starved wolves eager to pounce on flesh. The father was now crowded by the Englishman, which caused him to perspire freely. His eyes searched for the presence of his son.
"Hmm, I think I may have a suitable penalty for this coolie. You," said Anderson as he pointed to the deck crew leader, "come here. Everyone, be quiet! There mustn't be any commotion. This shall be a lesson for all the coolies. If one breaks a rule set forth by a

superior, then he or she will pay the price." He then stared at the deck crew leader for more than a couple of seconds. "I need you to bring me a razor."

"What kind of razor, sir?"

"For God's sake, I need a bloody razor—the instrument we use to remove our facial hair."

"Sir, I need that to shave my beard in a few days."

"You imbecile, how dare you challenge me?"

"No, sir...I was not...I apologize...I did not mean to...I will get it right this instant," mumbled the deck crew leader. He dashed to the staircase, ascended the stairs, rushed through his cabin, grabbed the used razor, and delivered it into the hands of his superior.

Anderson caressed the sharp edges of the blade with the interior of his thumb. The blade was superlative. "As I predicted, the straight razor is sharp enough for the job," said Anderson. With the support of his right arm, Anderson revealed the instrument to the indentured laborers. A few had seen it used by others, a few had the privilege of using it on themselves, and the rest had never seen or heard of it before. The instrument was held in the air as if it were a crown waiting to be placed on a reputable king's head. The crowd of Indians on deck whispered to one another.

"He should have never used the tool in daylight hours?" said an Indian woman from the assemblage.

"Well, you cannot use a razor in the dark. What if the lack of light leads to a bloody mishap?" replied an Indian male, hoping others would participate in the conversation.

"Oh Lord, what will the British do now? I hope they don't cut the man's throat," a voice emerged from the crowd.

"Does an Englishman's life only revolve around delivering punishment?" asked an adolescent male.

"Where did his adorable son run to? I hope he is in the safe hands of his mother?" said another female with concern in her voice.

The chief officer beckoned the deck crew members to surround the Brahmin father. Words were exchanged between the chief and his comrades. These words were incomprehensible to the Indians. Then, as expected, the pack of wolves dispersed.

"Quick! Grab his arms, grab his legs and grab his head. You over there, I am talking to you. Hurry!" instructed Chief Officer Anderson.

The fast response from the deck crew members left no time for the Brahmin father to escape. But even if he did have the time, the real question was where to escape to. One did have the choice to plunge into the transcendent ocean. But the mystical ocean had prepared a deathbed for any living soul who planned to use it as an escape route. The father shrieked—shrieks of intense fear. Pressed against the wooden deck, his eyes searched for his family members. Unknown faces scooted across his pupils. "Is this the end? Will I be executed? I must see the faces of my dear wife and son before I am put to rest. Dear God, I beg of you, please reveal the faces I desire to see."

The desperate father repeated his prayers with urgency as he noticed the leather boots of the chief officer step towards him.

"Open your ears and open your eyes. May this be a lesson for all you bloody coolies," said Anderson as he displayed the straight razor under the flashing sun. For a second or two, the shine distracted the Indians on board from the shameful act that was about to happen.

Just as the cries of torment were unleashed, the focus of the bystanders deviated from the blade to the Brahmin father. A wave of panic stiffened the father's muscles when he felt Anderson's fingers on his cranium. With all his force, the father attempted to cut loose from the grasp on his arms and legs. His deep cries of help proved that he was unable to overpower the Englishmen with their massive hands and bulging arms. Anderson then grazed the skull with the blade initiating pandemonium.

The indentured laborers covered their mouths from the surprise, lowered their heads from the disgrace, turned their faces from the brutality, and dried their eyes from the sorrow, but refrained from walking forward and raising their voices against the malpractice. The sharpness of the blade made it easy for Anderson to remove the hair. The blade moved from the back of the head to the front.

The incessant outcry that emerged from the father's vocal cord stopped as he captured a glimpse of his son in the crowd. He felt his son's pain. The still child did not give his eyes rest. His lids did not flap. Realizing that such a fierce act could scar his son for the remainder of his life, the Brahmin father challenged himself not to make a sound. After some time, he decided not to face his inconsolable child. He unexpectedly turned his head from west to east, ignoring the razor and the probable outpour of blood.

"Eh worthless coolie, you need to be more careful. I nearly removed your bloody eyebrows," said Anderson with a cackle. "Now this is the perfect punishment for you. I know that you are fond of shaving and trimming. So, I thought I'd give you a hand with the cutting."

The Brahmin father set his vision on the encircling black strands of hair that were detached from his skull. Soon, he realized that there was no friction between skin and metal. At last, freedom was given to his limbs. The eyes that had witnessed the humiliation were no longer required to show pity upon the abused. The father ran his trembling hands across his bare pate.

"It is not that the British removed my hair that bothers me. It is that I was so useless in front of my child. The British have taken my pride, my honor, my dignity. The British have damaged my son. The British have induced fear into his heart. The British have done so much. And what have I done to stop them from building fear, inflicting pain, and eliminating free will? What have I done? Absolutely nothing," said the Brahmin father under his breath.

THE 15TH DAY

For what the Indians believed was the opportunity for life advancement was, in reality, turning into an excruciating journey to perdition. The once delicate skin now became pale, scaly, and stubborn. The once apt bodies had become dainty and gaunt. The lengthy strands of hair began to grossly intertwine due to the lack of washing and cleansing. All kinds of bacteria divulged their enormous appetites by picking at certain areas of the skin to nibble on. Men, women, and children were aware of their major weight loss but presumed that nothing would be done to improve the living and eating conditions. Most Indians lost their cheeks, which produced distinctly visible jawlines. The outline of an Indian's rib cage became perceptible as it grasped the outer layer of skin. When the Indians sluggishly paced back and forth, with nowhere to go and nowhere to hide, their movements seemed zombie-like. The servings of watered-down khichdi continued; therefore, the upset stomachs and vomiting continued. The cautious habit of minimal water usage persisted; therefore, the barrels contained enough water to last for months. The punitive attitudes and acts carried on; therefore, the usage of batons and whips persisted. Allah and Ram were covertly worshipped; therefore, Jesus remained immovable. By the fifteenth day, the indentured labourers had become familiar with the do's and don'ts on Ship Elbe. Every Indian found a vacant corner in their brain and utilized it to store the hatred felt towards the Englishmen. It was a given that they were required to endure the derogatory remarks, malicious demeanor, and inequitable penalties. There was no exit from the pilgrimage unless one had his or her life terminated. The indentured labourers believed that the most dreadful penalties had already been dispensed and tolerated. What could be worse than the different forms of punishment that occurred on the vessel, such as the brutal lashes to the human skin, the degrading insults, the strenuous chores, the growling stomachs, the disgusting rice and lentils, the intolerable vomiting, the excessive diarrhea, the dry coughs, the chest pains, the cuts and bruises, the itchy skin rashes, the limited use of water, and 'the hole' itself, thought the

Indians. After a merciless day consisting of adversities, during nightfall, the Indians were gifted lovely dreams of their respected villages. It was God's way of saying, "I apologize for the unbearable hardships destiny has placed upon you. I feel miserable when I see what the future has in store for you people; therefore, to redeem the faith you once had or somewhat have in Me, I decorate your brains with images of your beloved village, district, and motherland." These dreams were like soulful lullabies that placed one into a restful trance. Once the dreams commenced, there was no use for a person to rise until the first lights of the morning sun.

It was the beginning of the third week, during the night, that an explosive outcry shattered the barrier which divided illusion from realism. The loud cry from an Indian woman forced eyes to open, ears to ache, fingers to jerk, and bodies to leap. Shivaji behaved like a rodent poking its head out of the hole to investigate the sounds of distraction. As soon as the disturbed woman's voice entered his ears, Shivaji knew that evil was present in the darkness. The high-pitched screams made the hair on his arms rise. Finally, after several attempts, the feminine voice was properly concealed. Shivaji felt as if the partial cry was enclosed by a human hand. Then, amid the ongoing incident, he felt warmth. Human flesh rested upon his hand. Shivaji looked over his shoulder to see that his wife had risen because of the lingering cries. Venkatesh, Lachmaiya, and several other Indians near the area were too scared to rise to their feet. One had to rise. One had to lift their body to see the kind of situation the female was in. Shivaji used his forearms to crawl several feet ahead like a soldier in a battle. His body movements were detected by the other indentured labourers who lay flat on the deck with their heads lowered. All these men, women, and children were conscious only to remain ignorant of their surroundings. Two voices, one male and one female, simultaneously pleaded for assistance.

"Help please, I beg of you. Don't close your eyes and ears to this injustice. It's my wife. They are taking her away," said the desperate husband.

Shivaji dared to lift his eyes. He saw what the other Indians had seen, but like them, he did not act as if he was blind. In comparison to previous nights, this was the darkest night of them all. The Indian woman's utterances were incomprehensible as a result of the trouble she faced with the ruling hands that struggled to cover her mouth. The faces of the Englishmen, who had difficulty seizing the body of the Indian woman, were unrecognizable. However, it did not matter who was who. During that moment, all the British seafarers were the same. They were all evildoers.

"Those bastards, it's the members of the deck crew." Shivaji felt it boil, then sizzle, and lastly overflow. The bloodcurdling acts of the British were released as explosions inside his brain.

Three of the deck crew members pulverized the Indian husband by stomping his face with their boots and shattering his bones with their batons. Blood squirted like juice from the victim's body, but he still remained obstinate. "My wife, please help her. Please, she will be ruined. Don't let them embarrass her. My good people listen to her cries. I am begging you to rise, please rise. Teach the British a lesson; a lesson not to lay their fingers on a married woman," said the husband before he choked on his blood.

Shivaji could not bear to see more. Vyjanti realized that her husband was about to challenge the Englishmen. Her eyes met Shivaji's hands which had left the deck. She then witnessed the rising of his broad shoulders which revealed that her husband was prepared to stride towards the five deck crew members. Vyjanti's heart palpitated for her husband's safety. It was her duty to protect her husband, just as it was his duty to protect her. As her husband's knees unbent, Vyjanti dove to secure them. Shivaji felt the lockdown. His feet were tied with boundless love and utmost concern.

"Vyjanti," yelled Shivaji. "Let go!"

"No, I will not. You will go nowhere."

"Vyjanti, I demand that you let go of my feet. I am not blind like the rest. I will not let them take advantage of that defenseless woman."

Vyjanti noticed that Shivaji's eagerness to release himself upon the culprits made her loosen her grip. As Shivaji powered ahead, he managed to drag his wife along with him. "If you don't wish to stop, if you don't wish to retrieve, and if you do wish to get involved, then I will kill myself," said Vyjanti in the heat of the moment. She then covered her mouth, feeling regretful for uttering such drastic words. "Deva, I beg for your apology.

"Never before have I spoken to my husband in such a way. If only he could understand the fear I have within my heart," Vyjanti said to herself.

Shivaji looked down at his wife's traumatized face with remorseful eyes.

"Eh coolie, what do you want?" said one of the deck crew members as he noticed the lone Indian on his feet.

Listening to the Englishman's voice, Vyjanti felt petrified for her husband's life. She pulled on her husband's kurta, forcing him to descend. Soon, Shivaji was facing his teary-eyed wife.

"That is right! Sit your arse down. Anyone who rises will be beheaded. This is our matter, not yours. If any of you interfere in our matters, there will be consequences to pay," said the Englishman as he landed an echoing slap on the husband's bloodied face.

Ensuring he kept himself low-slung, Venkatesh capably maneuvered past several bodies to reach his temperamental friend. The sight of Shivaji's face revealed everything to Venkatesh.

"Get down! You will not associate yourself in this situation, Shivaji. Get down, right this instant!" said Venkatesh in an authoritative manner.

Shivaji accepted Venkatesh's words as advice from an elder brother. He united with the other Indians by flattening his body on the wooden surface. Shivaji submitted to his wife and friend's instructions, placing a heavy stone on his heart.

"Vyjanti, I will not forgive myself for this. To witness a sin is not a sin, but to neglect a sin is a sin."

Avoiding her husband's truthful eyes, Vyjanti lowered her head in shame. The sight of Shivaji's clenched fists made Venkatesh feel uneasy. He was certain that if Shivaji intervened, in all probability he would not live to see the next day. The British would have lashed him, hung him, or shot him to death in front of the indentured labourers on board. Picturing his friend brutalized to such an extreme forced a shiver down Venkatesh's backbone. He then turned to search for his wife. Once his eyes met hers, Venkatesh signaled with his hand that everything was fine. Lachmaiya acknowledged with a nod while holding Karthik close to her chest. Lachmaiya was aware of Venkatesh's situation and what might unfold if he made the wrong move. But she also knew that her husband was sensible and responsible. Venkatesh was first liable for his wife and son and then for the remaining passengers on Ship Elbe. If one reacted to the present situation, he or she would not only put their own life at risk but also the lives of their family members on board. Besides Shivaji, every other indentured labourer understood what defiance could produce, and that is the mere reason why the Indians chose to bear the sin of purposely not responding to the injustice.

Most women on the deck silently wept for the victims who were manhandled by the British seafarers. The struggle to remove the Indian woman from the scene continued. At times, she was pulled by her lengthy strands of hair. She was pulled and dragged away from her husband who was covered in red body fluid. Wanting to punish the culprits, her limbs thrashed desperately. One of the deck crew members covered the woman's mouth with his enormous hand. As soon as the Englishman felt the sharpness of the woman's

teeth dig into his unevenly textured skin, he released his hand from her mouth.
"Watch out! The tramp bites," said the Englishman, hastily shaking his bitten hand.

As soon as the Indian woman's mouth was liberated, she called for her husband. But her husband was not capable of responding. Although his heart was functional, he remained idle. The man could not hear because his ears were continuously ringing from the powerful blows he had received to his head from the baton. He could not see because his eyes were drenched with blood pouring from his forehead. He could not move because the British seafarers had crushed every bone in his body. In the back of her mind, the wife knew that her husband couldn't rescue her from the treacherous hands of the Englishmen, yet her unyielding cries for him persisted. The calls were of no use; what she needed was a miracle.

"Oh Deva, please assist her. Please don't let her fall into the hands of these wild beasts," Vyjanti prayed to the minuscule statue of Lord Shiva balanced on her palm.

"God will not come down to save her, Vyjanti. We need to save her. We need to rise. This is our moment to teach the British a lesson," said Shivaji.

Vyjanti closed her lids and clasped the idol firmly in her hand. This time, she prayed with more integrity. "I beg you Deva, show us a miracle. Strike with vengeance. Destroy these savages. Deva, you must save the woman from their lecherous desires," repeated Vyjanti in a soft voice.

Shivaji was not irritated by a person who believed in God—he believed in God himself—but it did irritate him when a person brought God into every conversation, situation, and happening. To link God with one's destiny was permissible, but to link Him to every move and every act was baseless. Shivaji believed that God had written our destiny before we came into this world, but He also gave us the power to believe in ourselves. And if we believe in ourselves, then nothing can stop us from altering and repairing our fate.

Shivaji kept mum. He felt like a prisoner whose hands and feet were tied with chain shackles. He waited for a rebellious voice to control the scene; a powerful voice full of confidence and determination, willing to overthrow the British seafarers. This brave Indian would first implant his thoughts and beliefs into the minds of the Indian passengers. Then, he would engrave the word 'hope' into the hearts of the indentured labourers. Ultimately, he would lead the Indians to revolt against the Englishmen. Shivaji viewed his body in the pupils of the female sufferer. He felt as if the moment had ceased. His surroundings did not matter. With time not moving, Shivaji had the opportunity to examine her face. A streak of blood poured from her nose to her discoloured lips. Her fair skin battled against the darkness of the night to remain vivid. There were no signs of tears or perspiration on her face. Shivaji felt as if the woman had accepted defeat. Her fragile limbs were tamed. Her hoarse voice had come to a halt. Her tussle was not evident. There was absolutely no fight left within her. The Indian woman's extended, lasting stare at Shivaji said everything.

"Why? Why did you not listen to yourself? Why did you listen to others? You could have saved my life, but you chose not to. Shivaji, you have sinned. This sin of yours will haunt you. You will pay for this, Shivaji. You will pay."

Shivaji felt numb. It was as if he had seen a ghost. He lost sight of the ghostlike face as the Indian woman was moved by the British seafarers to the upper deck. Her lively yellow sari revealed uncovered portions of her body due to the extensive tears. The lewd hands of the Englishmen did not resist clutching the delicate skin of the ruined woman. On the upper deck, lights were lit in the cabin where Captain Sanders slept. The five loyal seafarers dragged the poor woman by her hands. Once they reached the door to the cabin, her hands were freed. As she was let go, her body plummeted to the wooden floor. One of the deck crew members knocked on the front door. At the same moment, Shivaji's vision became blurred. He was not intimidated to see who answered the door. In a hurry, he swept his forearm across his eyes to dry the waterworks that impaired his vision. He gave his eyes another try while peering at the cabin filled with light. The door grated as it opened. The shadow of Captain Sanders was instantly recognized by Shivaji. No one was as gargantuan as the captain. The broad shoulders, bulging arms, massive legs, and humongous belly were plenty for Shivaji to confirm his decision on who the shadow belonged to.

"She is yours for the night," said the deck crew member who knocked at the door.
"I want her on her feet. I need to see her face," said Captain Sanders with a nasty smirk.

Even with support from the deck crew members, the overpowered woman stumbled on her feet. The captain lifted the loose strands of her torn sari to peek at the woman's sensitive legs. Those legs were now covered in scrapes from the nonstop dragging. Sanders' face turned sour. He felt disgusted. "Is that how you treat a woman? You imbeciles have scarred her beautiful legs." The captain placed his hand on top of the woman's chest. He felt what lay beyond the silk material with his hungry fingers. As the nasty smirk protracted from one ear to another, Sanders groped the victim's bosom. The surrendered woman did not react. Shivaji closed his eyes.

"I want to be disposed of from this ship, this life, this world," he said under his breath. At last, his clenched fists were allowed to breathe in air. His emotionless face touched the soiled deck. He felt blameworthy. Vyjanti's tears inclined near her temple as she lay on the deck with her head tilted to a side. She was able to notice the amount of pain Shivaji was in, even though his face was expressionless.

Captain Sanders plunged his hand into the maze of locks that covered the woman's face. With his index finger, he touched her soft cheeks. "There, there, no one will hurt you anymore. You are in good hands now, my love," he said. Sanders examined her face intently. He remained pleased with his choice until his eyes fell on the corner of her lips, which had turned purple. The captain shifted his focus onto the British seafarers.

"How did this happen?" he said, pointing to the woman's bruised lip. "I was very precise about how to handle her, wasn't I? I did not want her face to be damaged. Her beauty lies in her face. Can't you men see that?" He waited with very little patience for the scared deck crew members to respond to his question.

"Bloody hell, can someone answer me?"
"Captain, we are not sure how or when it happened. She was wildly swinging her fists at us. She screamed and screamed and screamed. I have to admit, she put up a good fight. The bitch even bit my hand. Look," said one of the seafarers who handled the woman, "this is what she has done to my hand."
"She's wild, she screams, she put up a good fight, and she bites. Hmm, that means she is the perfect woman to bed. As usual, I have chosen the best from the lot," said the impudent captain.

"What shall we do with her husband?" asked the talkative deck crew member.
Captain Sanders whispered into the British seafarer's ear. The message remained a secret from the Indian passengers on board, who desired to know.

"Now be gone!" ordered the captain, while he invited the doomed woman into his luxurious cabin. Shivaji listened to the sound of the closing door, the prominent footsteps of the Englishmen, the crude sniggering between the assailants, and the shameless muteness that hovered above the lower deck.

THE 16TH DAY

The ensuing morning led to wild guesses, backward theories, and opinionated statements regarding the Indian husband and wife, with the central question being whether they were dead or alive. If they were dead, where were their bodies disposed of? If they were alive, what kind of condition were they in? Discussions about the hapless couple materialized during the scrubbing of the lower deck, and then the active mouths were silenced because the Englishmen did not want a peep from the Indians during hard labour. Obsessed with preservation, Shivaji made sure to keep Vyjanti in front of his eyes as he cleansed the stringent deck.

After the incident of the previous night, Shivaji felt uneasy. Firstly, his soul was pestered by the fact that he had been unable to help the Indian woman from the heinous actions. If that was not enough, Shivaji's brain was implanted with involuntary images of dread. In his mind, the face of the exploited female was replaced by Vyjanti's. What if Vyjanti was Captain Sanders' choice? What if Vyjanti was the one abducted in the middle of the night? What if Vyjanti had sacrificed her body to satisfy the captain's sensual appetite? Shivaji remembered the time when Captain Sanders visually examined Vyjanti with his lustful eyes. He knew what he had to do: ensure that his spirited wife remained unseen by the Englishmen on board, especially the immoral Captain Sanders.

With that in mind, Shivaji paid close attention to his wife. Vyjanti did not lift her eyes while toiling. She was afraid to do so, since multiple seafarers were stationed at all four corners of the deck. Shivaji's hand movements ceased while he observed his wife lift her arm toward her face. While one arm was raised, the other did not retire from its assigned duty. With her fingers, she captured a loose strand of hair that fluttered in the light breeze. She flawlessly slid it behind her left ear, ensuring it was neatly tucked.

The brief scene, lasting less than two seconds, transported Shivaji back to his village days. He reminisced about the times he entered through the front doors of his house returning from the village market. Greeted first by his mother, Shivaji bent down to place his hand on her feet. Once blessed, he met his lovely sisters. After receiving cherished hugs, Shivaji continued to the porch. Standing there, he prepared himself for his appa's tedious lectures. At the first sight of his son, Muthuraman revealed the look of a disappointed father. To show respect, Shivaji endured five minutes of the lecture. Any longer, and it became suffocating. When he felt he would choke, he abandoned his father with a brand-new excuse.

"Useless! My son will remain a petty fisherman for the rest of his life. I ask you, God, what have I done to deserve a son like him?" Muthuraman said after Shivaji escaped the porch.

The newly married husband then entered the kitchen to interact with his precious wife. Shivaji found her engaged in preparing the evening feast. Before the sisters entered, he tried to make eye contact with her. With half of her face hidden by the traditional scarf, the task proved difficult. A bit shy and focused on her chore, Vyjanti avoided eye contact. Shivaji knew she was aware of his presence, but she still ignored him. He needed to make his presence felt, but how? Call it a miracle, or call it luck by chance.

As Vyjanti kneaded the flour, fine strands of hair fell out of place. Irritated by the loose strands waving before her eyes, she muttered, "Oh Deva, I must not have tied my hair properly," as she endeavored to maneuver it aside with her forearms. She glanced at her flour-covered hands, then fixed her eyes on her husband.

"I need your help. Please, can you move the disturbing hair to the side?"

"No," said Shivaji, displaying stubbornness.

"I ask you for a small favor, and you say no. Can't you see my hands are soiled with flour?" Vyjanti lifted both hands to show him, but Shivaji was not prepared to fulfill the request.

"When I needed my wife to look at me with her mesmerizing eyes, what did she do? She deliberately acted as if I did not exist. Now that Vyjanti needs Shivaji for a favor, all of a sudden, I exist."

With sadness in her voice, Vyjanti replied, "You don't need to do any favors for me. I will manage on my own."

Shivaji had a hard exterior, but his interior was delicate. Past his implacability lay empathy. He understood the heartache Vyjanti felt when he responded insensitively. As Vyjanti continued her battle with her hair, blowing air toward her forehead, she did not recognize the inseparable space between her and Shivaji. Using his index finger and thumb, Shivaji collected the strands drifting near her forehead. With care, careful not to pull too hard, he slid her unconstrained hair behind her ear. Vyjanti's face beamed with pleasure as she felt his fingers touch her sensitive ear.

"There you go. The disturbing hair will not bother you anymore."

Vyjanti's large, ball-shaped Tamilian eyes finally met Shivaji's gaze. Her inviting eyes sent a signal to him. He felt her warm breath on his face.

Shivaji then heard footsteps approaching the kitchen entry. The closeness and affection between the couple immediately receded as the two sisters barged in to assist their sister-in-law.

"My dear sisters...Perfect timing," said Shivaji, sarcastically.

"Imagination is oppressed by reality. Or is it that reality envies imagination? Whenever imagination unveils its enchantment, somewhere down the line reality intervenes as the nemesis. Reality is always prepared to devastate the satisfaction that imagination provides," Shivaji said to his wife.

Vyjanti did not wish to participate in the conversation. By not letting Shivaji act or react to the incident relating to the Indian woman, Vyjanti felt she had let her husband down. She also felt mortified by her uncaring attitude toward the violated woman during the occurrence. Before the sun disappeared into the midst of the ocean, Shivaji and his wife would regularly sit with their backs against each other. But that was not the case this evening. Shivaji noticed that his wife was reluctant to lift her eyes from the deck. Shivaji understood her feelings without her expressing a single word. The truth was that Shivaji had been restrained from involving himself in the incident. The bold threat that Vyjanti put forth had caged him. After that, he did not dare to test his wife. Her words were like a jagged dagger piercing his heart. At first, Shivaji chose to place the entire blame on Vyjanti, but then he realized how unfair that would be. "Only a coward hunts for someone to place the blame on," Shivaji said to himself.

Vyjanti did what any wife would have done for her husband in that situation. She was protecting him from death. If Shivaji had entered the scene as the rebellious Indian, the British seafarers would have gunned him down or beaten him to his last breath. And for a wife to see her husband executed would be unbearable.

"Why do you hide your eyes from me? Have you done something wrong? Or have I done something wrong to upset you?"

Vyjanti remained idle with a large portion of her face covered by a yellow scarf, a common color amongst South Indian women.

"Vyjanti, I am not upset with you. What you did last night—" Shivaji left his phrase incomplete.

"I don't know whether I did right or wrong as a wife. What I do know is that my husband would do everything and anything to protect me from danger. So why can't a wife protect her husband from danger? Yes, I do realize that I became selfish. Who knows—if I did not stop you from helping, she may have been saved. And if that is the case, then I blame myself. God will punish me," said Vyjanti, still unable to find the audacity to look at her husband.

Her sobbing became obvious even though her mouth was covered by the veil. Tears of remorse slid down her cheeks. It took a few steps, a warm embrace, a tender rub on the back, and the dabbing of tears to show that whatever the decision may be, good or bad, Shivaji would always stand by his wife.

"Vyjanti, I have said it once and I will say it again: never again do I want to hear you say that you will end your life."

"I promise, never again will those words be spoken," replied Vyjanti, who at last made eye contact with her husband.

Shivaji did not find it essential to notice the glistening stars of the night. The twinkle that existed in the stars above was visible in Vyjanti's eyes as well.

"God has given you the most beautiful set of eyes," said Shivaji.

"And with these eyes I only see you. I can see you when you are here, and I can see you when you are not here," replied Vyjanti.

"How is that possible?"

"Simple. When you are not present, my eyes automatically form and display an image of you."

"Vyjanti, trust me, I will never leave your side. I will always be present in your life."

THE 19TH DAY

For the last few days, all Shivaji could think about was the unforgettable face of the Indian woman. Those piercing eyes, which begged for liberty, were fixed on him. All she wanted was to be liberated from the oppressors who were mishandling her. Her expressionless face, indecipherable to others, was meant only for Shivaji to understand. Somehow, the woman knew that the one person who could save her from the defilement was Shivaji Nair himself. In fact, Shivaji even knew he had the power to free her from the hands of the untamed beasts.

"Why can I not forget her face?" Shivaji asked his friend.

"What happened was terrible, but it must be forgotten. You have to release it from your system," Venkatesh replied.

"Venkatesh, a woman was abducted in the middle of the night. She was taken to Captain Sanders' cabin. We Indians cannot be naive. We know what has happened and what is happening. I am certain that Indian woman is being sexually assaulted at this moment. How many days has it been since the incident?"

"Three nights ago," Venkatesh answered.

"For the past three nights, that woman has been trapped in a cabin—not with her husband, but with another man. Imagine her situation: her clothes shredded to tiny pieces, her face bruised, her body aching from brutal torture. That villain, the captain of this ship, must be constantly violating her without consent. She was once a loyal wife, and now she's a measly bedmate," Shivaji said, smashing his fist on the deck in frustration at his own inability to rescue her.

"What is the matter with you? Why punish yourself? Shivaji, why must you always be the savior? Do you want to be some kind of hero?"

"This has nothing to do with prestige. If I were to save her, it would not be for fame. A common man must help someone in distress. If not me, then someone else should have intervened. We should be ashamed—no one from hundreds confronted the British."

"So, who do you blame for this? Me? Or Vyjanti?"

"I blame no one but myself. Yes, my hands were tied in shackles, but who said shackles could not be broken?"

"If you had risen that night against the British, Vyjanti might have become a widow. She would have lost her husband, I would have lost my best friend. The Englishmen have crossed all boundaries with this incident. This voyage has become extremely dangerous. One wrong move or word can have grave consequences. We must control our emotions, be careful with our words, and vigilant about our surroundings. Disobedience is unnecessary," Venkatesh explained.

Shivaji could not discern right from wrong. If he had intervened to save the Indian woman, he would have risked his own life. His life, his existence, every breath he took was dedicated to Vyjanti. If he were gone, where would she go? What would she do? After all, Vyjanti was his main priority—not some woman he had never met, never interacted with, whose name he did not know. Yet it was a sin to ignore someone in need.

"If Vyjanti or Lachmaiya were placed in the same situation, would I not have intervened? How is Vyjanti any different from this unknown woman? They are all loyal, married women of the same descent and caste. Both are humans—then why differentiate between the known and unknown?" Shivaji asked himself.

The answer was clear: to save himself from near-certain death, for the sake of his beloved wife, Shivaji had sinned by not reacting to the indecent situation.

Meanwhile, the tale of the Indian husband who had been viciously beaten the night of his wife's abduction had finally dissolved. Rumors on Ship Elbe began to fade. No person, except one, knew what had happened to the missing passenger. Shivaji, consumed by guilt for not rescuing the woman, had turned blind to the fate of her husband.

After the common serving of rice and lentils and the purifying of the lower deck, the late afternoon brought the rare opportunity for the Indians to wash themselves. Nearly twenty days had passed since their last bath. The Englishmen allowed it for their own convenience—the stench of the Indians annoyed them. Supplying an extra three barrels of water cost the British nothing, yet hoarding it from the laborers had strategic importance: excessive bacteria, unwashed clothing, open wounds, rashes, and pus-filled bumps were all signs of disease. For the Englishmen, these signs could not be ignored.

The ship had a doctor, but he rarely appeared. He stayed in his cabin, fearing disease from the Indian passengers. Without introductions or presence, the doctor was effectively nonexistent for the laborers. Captain Sanders knew the doctor was necessary for the ship's operation. Useless to the Indians, the doctor's services were reserved for the British crew.

The announcement of unrestricted water usage sent the Indians rushing to the barrels. A single laborer had two minutes, a family of two three minutes, and a family of three or more five minutes. Standing in line, clutching filthy clothing—saris, kurtas, dhotis, and pajamas, often riddled with holes—these rural Indians, living in poverty, waited eagerly. Less clothing to wash meant more time to bathe, and for once, their bodies could feel the cleansing touch of water.

For once most of the lower deck on Ship Elbe was nearly deserted. As Shivaji waited in line, he visually examined the bareness. His eyes roamed from the corner where he and his wife were to the cabin above where Captain Sanders slept. *At this moment, he is probably undressing the ill-fated woman to fulfill his sexual craving,* thought Shivaji. The image of the captain sliding his desiring fingers beneath the Indian woman's blouse disturbed him. Shivaji cursed himself for such lewd, imaginative thoughts. He returned his focus to the lower deck. His eyes moved from the cabin to the dim passage that led to 'the hole'. As soon as he remembered 'the hole', Shivaji scanned the line in search of Old Man Thambi. "Is Baba in line?" he asked his wife, curiously turning to examine the faces behind him.

"Is that him?" Vyjanti asked, panic in her voice. She pointed toward the south-east corner of the vessel. Shivaji responded quickly, "Vyjanti, stay with Venkatesh and his family; I will attend to Baba."

Before Vyjanti could protest the impulsive decision, Shivaji was en route to the aged body that lay still on the deck. His heartbeat soared. The pulse of his heart throbbed against his ribcage. He did not know whether Old Man Thambi was breathing. Closing in, he noticed that Thambi's back was turned in his direction. There was no sign of movement. Shivaji could not see the color of Thambi's skin. He needed to know if the beggar was pale. "Please be alive, please be alive," Shivaji kept repeating as he gasped for air. Shivaji's movements were observed by several members of the deck crew but went unnoticed. The Englishmen knew of the stationary beggar who remained idle while the mobile Indians proceeded to the barrels of water. They did not care if he was alive or dead. Shivaji slid beside Thambi's body. With force, he nudged the beggar's shoulder. Thambi reacted as if woken from a bad dream. The old man tossed his arms in the air wildly as if defending himself from evil.

"Baba, it's me. Thank God, you are alive," said Shivaji, attempting to soothe the rattled beggar.

Thambi's initial response quickly tired him. The old man let out close to a dozen coughs in a row. Agony was printed on his face whenever he released one of those heavy barks. Shivaji had never seen the beggar in such a devastating condition before. His limbs seemed as if they would fall off. His bones seemed as if they would shatter with the least movement. His throat seemed as if it had not received water for days. Thambi fought to open his lids, which were like dependable curtains that protected his eyes from the golden sun. With his fingers, Thambi rubbed the darkness from within his eyes. He examined Shivaji from top to bottom, then bottom to top, as if he were a stranger.

"Baba, are you okay? It seems as if you have seen a ghost. Do you recognize who I am? It's me, Shivaji."

"Son, those days in 'the hole' have affected me. They may have crippled every inch of my body, but they have not crippled my spirit. My spirit is still alive. It was alive when that unfortunate woman fell victim to the captain's sexual desire. It was alive when the husband suffered the misery of witnessing his wife being forcefully violated. Imagine what he felt in that moment—the feeling of not having the power to free your wife from the hands of wrongdoers. If it was not for the lack of power, if it was not for the loss of movement, I would have interfered. Damn these arms and legs; at the time they were most needed, they were of no use," said the beggar as he looked helplessly at his quivering hands.

"One person needed to rise to his feet, just one person. That one person may have introduced a new revolution. With his actions, he may have created a wave of uprising in others. The confrontation may have ignited defiance in the hearts of the other Indians on board. Such a deed may have saved the Indian husband and wife," Thambi added.

"Baba, we have closed our eyes, turned away our faces, lowered our heads and imprisoned our brains," said Shivaji, feeling repentant.

"I understand that you are restrained by the love of your wife. But what if that husband was you? What if that woman was your wife?" Thambi's questions made it difficult for Shivaji to breathe. "You, I, and every other Indian on board have all committed a dreadful sin. And for this sin, we will pay. Why? If you ask God, He will tell you to look deep within yourself. He will tell you to ask yourself that question...Why?"

The man that Indians in the village called senseless made complete sense as the guru relayed his words of wisdom to his disciple.

With his hand, Shivaji signalled Vyjanti and the others that Thambi, who seemed as if he was not breathing, was indeed breathing. As soon as Venkatesh received the signal, he left the queue to assist Shivaji in maneuvering the powerless beggar. Shivaji believed that a wash might perhaps cleanse the rust. Once cleansed, Thambi may return to his witty self again. But the same could not be said about how he had been since boarding Ship Elbe. The dungeon of doom, 'the hole,' had gnawed at his bones and sucked his blood during those five days. When Thambi was released from 'the hole' it seemed as if he went to hell and came back. Since the day of his release, the beggar had been in a resting position. First, he tucked his knees inwards, near his chest. Then he tried to cover his upper body with skeletal arms used like a blanket. Most of the day and night, the beggar remained in this specific position without food and water. Any other human in his position would have died. But Thambi was no ordinary human. He was a mendicant, a man who begged for alms for hours to feed his stomach. For him to live without food and water for days was not hard. To adapt to the hot summer day and cold winter night was not hard. To endure sticks and stones was not hard.

"It will take some time, Baba. You will regain your energy. Your sluggishness will disappear," Venkatesh offered words of comfort to the beggar. The line of indentured labourers eyed Shivaji and Venkatesh as they carried Thambi by placing his arms over their shoulders for support. At times, Shivaji noticed that there was no life in the beggar's feet. During the transfer, the sound of Thambi's feet dragging on the timber was heard. When in line, Thambi was unable to stand for long periods. After a few minutes, he collapsed. Luckily for the old man, Shivaji and Venkatesh were prepared to catch his fall. Both childhood friends managed to steady Thambi's body whenever he slouched. The three additional barrels of water, along with the initial two, were utilized simultaneously. The Englishmen ordered the indentured labourers to form five different single-file lines. The lines proceeded toward the water barrels in an efficient manner. The waiting period for the Indians was not as harsh this time. Some exceeded their five-minute limit, which was ignored by the other Indians and oddly missed by the British seafarers. It may have been the importance of purifying the Indians to avoid health-related issues that led to the leniency. If the situation had been different, the whip and baton would have been used on the perpetrator by now.

Old Man Thambi patted the heads of Shivaji and Venkatesh with his unsteady hands, blessing them for their assistance. "God bless you and your family with happiness." His eyelids fought against the irritant sun as he attempted to make eye contact with Shivaji. Shivaji used his forearm to shield the beggar's weary eyes.

"Son, I pray to God for you. I ask God for a change to be made. But how can one change what is destined to be? Your past is accountable for your present. Your past sins are so severe that..."

Thambi left the sentence incomplete, as if beckoned to say no more. He wished that Shivaji would not interrogate him further.

"Please continue, Baba," said Vyjanti, distress in her voice. "Is my husband in danger? Baba, are you hiding something from us? Is there something you know that we don't? Please, tell us everything you know."

Thambi remained idle, his face devoid of emotion. He felt he was in no position to express what he knew. The beggar was no God. He was no fortune teller, no magician, no saint.

"Sometimes, I wonder! Are you a messenger?" asked Shivaji, observing how close they were to the barrels of water, meaning the line was moving at a respectable pace. "Baba, if you know everything about my past, present, and future, what does that make you?"

The beggar remained silent, concealing his eyes from those nearby.

"Remember," Shivaji continued, "there was a time when you said no person in this world could tell you about your past, present, or future except for God. Do you remember?"

Finally, Thambi's lips parted. "Yes, that is true. No one can, except for God. And I am not God. What I say, I say. Consider my presence a sign, or a signal, in the lives of others. I try, but I fail."

Venkatesh, initially reluctant to intervene, could hold back no longer. "What do you try?"

"I try to help others understand that their past lives are connected to their present life. I try to inform, I try to advise, I try to educate, I try to warn, I try to indicate—but I fail." The beggar released a frustrated sigh. For once, his own words seemed tangled. It was as if he spoke with his teeth bound together by steel wires. His speech had restrictions—but who set these restrictions? Only Thambi knew. "I fail. I fail because no signal or warning can prevent what is engraved by God. I pray—oh Lord, I pray. I pray for the ones who don't deserve the punishment. I fight. I fight for those whose current lives revolve around good deeds. But I am unsuccessful. The sins of one's past life play an overruling role in their present life."

Venkatesh believed in rebirth, but found it difficult to accept that a beggar might exist in this world to partly inform and warn people about what may or may not happen. In other words, Venkatesh considered Thambi a deranged vagrant. "Baba, please forgive me if I am disrespectful, but do you believe you have come into this world for a special reason?"

"Isn't every human brought into this world for a special reason?" Thambi countered.

Venkatesh turned his unfeeling face toward his friend. Shivaji knew how Venkatesh felt about the beggar when he saw him rolling his eyes.

"Baba, you are the wisest of them all. You are a saint. Please forgive me if I was disrespectful," said Venkatesh half-heartedly.

"I am not a saint," Thambi replied.

"Yes, Baba, I understand. Can you please tell us about the husband who was severely beaten the other night? Where is he? Is he still alive?"

Thambi chuckled. He knew what Venkatesh thought of him. It did not bother him; he was used to people calling him a nutcase.

"Son, I may seem mentally bizarre to you, but at least I don't unhook myself from reality when others are suffering." Thambi's words cut like a blade, piercing the hearts of those listening. While Venkatesh remained silent, unable to respond, Vyjanti sought forgiveness from the heavens, where she believed her Lord Shiva resided. Since the incident, Shivaji had been tortured with remorse. He waited patiently for Thambi to answer Venkatesh's question about the unfortunate Indian husband. Shivaji believed Thambi—but only what he could understand. Whatever he managed to dissect, interpret, and comprehend, he trusted completely.

"Before the sun appeared over the horizon, before the gulls started to chirp, before the human eyes first opened, before the bloodstains left on the deck were washed, I heard…" Thambi paused, building suspense. A forceful attack of dry coughs interrupted him, one after another.

Once the coughing ceased, Shivaji suggested, "Baba, I think you should not talk so much. The answer can wait."

"No, it cannot. I am sure Baba is fine," said Venkatesh.

"Don't be inconsiderate. His throat is drier than a desert. Let him relieve his dryness with water. We are close to the barrels. Soon our turn will come."

The beggar felt touched by Shivaji's concern. No one in his life had been more benevolent or courteous than Shivaji. Thambi considered Shivaji a son, but in this moment, he felt as if Shivaji were more like a father.

The shoulders of both Shivaji and Venkatesh began to ache from carrying the helpless beggar. Fortunately, they were soon to reach the barrels of water. Waiting in line did not trouble Shivaji, Venkatesh, or the wives, but Karthik grew impatient, tugging at Vyjanti's sari to grab her attention. For once, Vyjanti did not respond with a playful expression, riddle, or folktale. She was lost in the ongoing conversation between the men. Like the others, she waited eagerly for Thambi's delayed response.

"I am fine. These coughs happen regularly. So, where was I?" Thambi asked himself. "Yes, what did I hear? I heard discreet messages passed in some obscure language. I can beg for alms in Hindi, Tamil, and Telugu; therefore, I understood it was neither of them. It was not Angrezi, English. I know a bit of that too: 'How you do, I do good, what name you, name my Thambi, give me shilling, and bloody hell.'"

"If not English, then what language?" asked Venkatesh, incredulous.

"It was the language of deviousness. Spoken by members of the deck crew. A few hours before sunrise, while the Indians had their faces covered, backs turned, ears closed, and lids shut—some from unconsciousness, others from consternation—the British seafarers prowled into the darkness. They collected the lifeless body of the husband, who had lain in a pool of blood for hours. His face, from which blood poured, had been severely damaged by the batons. Covered in gore, fine lines ran downward from his eyes to his cheeks. These lines revealed the initial color of the man's skin. On his face were the tears of a husband who could not save his wife. These tears carved paths separate from the ocean of blood."

Old Man Thambi recounted the pitiless night as if he were an experienced storyteller, narrating this regularly. Vyjanti and Lachmaiya listened with eyes wide and lips parted, absorbed as if in a spellbinding tale.

Venkatesh interrupted, "How do you know this? Where were you when this was happening?"

Thambi did not seem pleased. "I witnessed everything with my own eyes. I was not like the others. I was not like you. I had my eyes open. I did not have my face covered. Only if my limbs had remained faithful, I would not have let the bastards commit such a monstrous crime. I curse myself, I curse my worthless legs, my useless arms, my helpless body. If it were not for 'the hole', I would have saved his life. But I did not. I lay there like a cripple, with no working bones or joints."

"You mean to say..." Shivaji was unable to finish his sentence.

"Son, he is no more," the beggar replied to Shivaji. "Those devils—who will be reborn as stray dogs and despicable flies—tossed a living human over the barriers and into the vast ocean."

Shivaji caught his wife's startled eyes. He gently touched Vyjanti's graceful hand, letting her know he was there. The touch brought comfort, a quiet reassurance that her husband was at her side, protecting her from misfortune.

"Deva, why is there so much evil in this world? Are these people not scared of God?" Vyjanti asked, her voice trembling with a mix of grief and indignation.

"The ones who are not scared of God," Thambi replied, "are the ones who have no heart."

Shivaji closed his eyes for a few seconds, wishing he had never boarded the vessel. Within that fleeting moment, the image of the deprived woman's haunted face flashed vividly before him.

"Baba, whatever happened to the Indian woman who was abducted? Where is she? Is she alive?" Shivaji asked urgently.

Before Thambi could answer, the deck crew leader called the next person in line forward. It was time for Shivaji and his wife to purify their bodies.

THE 22ND DAY

as it the water they had splashed over their bodies a couple of days ago? Or was it the chilly breeze that rammed into the outer layer of their skin? Or was it simply pneumonia? The Indians did not know the exact reason their bodies shivered. The flawless blue skies were invaded by sinister clouds, which seemed prepared to rule and conquer. The clouds gathered to form a massive battalion. Even the ocean waves began to rebel, prompting the vessel to sway in a seesaw motion. By evening, Ship Elbe and its passengers were engulfed in what felt like high-explosive artillery fire. Above, the skies were charcoal with shades of fire-power; below, the sea surged with violent waves. Torrents of rain fell like missiles. The barrage of precipitation was so extreme that if one were to hold a tin cup, it would overflow in ten seconds.

Chief Officer Anderson ordered the deck crew to take position. The British seafarers raced frenziedly to the sails. Each crew member, for the first time since Ship Elbe departed India, displayed panic on their faces. The Indian passengers felt these events were the final moments of their lives. The rapid currents of air and constant tilting of the vessel made the Indians appear like rag dolls, tossed from one end to another. Their bodies seemed weightless as they rolled across the deck, unable to cling to anything sturdy. The cries of children, the yelps of mothers, and the advice of fathers were all drowned by the roaring ocean waves slamming against the belly of Ship Elbe.

Positioned by the railing, Shivaji and his wife had an advantage, unlike the other passengers. "Grab on! Don't look beyond the railing," Shivaji shouted to his wife and friends.

Venkatesh and his family obeyed Shivaji's instructions. Lachmaiya followed her husband's lead as he firmly clasped the barrier to prevent being tossed overboard. Like a bird shielding its eggs, Venkatesh and his wife kept their son protected. The child was so well hidden that Vyjanti had to ask Lachmaiya where he was. Nestled between his parents' heated chests and arms, Karthik whimpered softly.

Other passengers nearby, struggling to maintain balance, watched the actions of the wiser Indians. Unable to stand upright due to the ship's constant shifting, the stranded passengers crawled on their knees toward the barriers. Each thud of a wave against the vessel sent large amounts of water splattering onto the deck, like a volcano erupting, spewing magma and ash. The ejection of seawater sent bodies tumbling in every direction. The helpless Indians collided with one another, brushed against sharp edges, and banged into solid objects. Skulls were damaged, limbs injured, and bones fractured amidst cries of pain.

Then a sudden, dominant heave of the vessel sent bodies sliding toward Shivaji and the others. So many bodies came hurtling into the railing that Shivaji cringed at the sound of cracking bones, mingled with the ear-popping drip of water.

"Vyjanti, listen to me," Shivaji blurted, trying to overpower the chaos. When she did not respond, he tried again. "Vyjanti, look this way. Listen to me, Vyjanti."

Vyjanti, inhaling and exhaling fear, finally turned to face her husband.

"Stay put, Vyjanti. You will not move from here. The others need help. I am sure some are injured."

Without waiting for a response, Shivaji used the railing to reach the wounded passengers who had collided with the barriers. Vyjanti wanted to help but could not stop her husband. She did not know whether to close her eyes and pray or assist him in aiding the others. Shivaji waited for the vessel to stabilize, but the ferocious waves persisted. He needed a brief lull to release the railing safely. He heard his wife's voice in the background, calling him back, but he did not allow it to sway him. Counting to three, he freed his hands and fell onto his knees as the platform below shifted violently.

With raindrops pelting his face, Shivaji crawled forward to reach the nearest passenger. He gripped a female hand; in this life-or-death moment, it did not matter if she belonged to another man. Ensuring her hand was safely placed on the railing, Shivaji moved to another passenger—a woman in her sixties. Her fragile physique did not exhaust him.

When rescuing a male passenger twice his size, Shivaji had to pause several times. Numbness in his arms slowed him, but once sensation returned, he continued dragging the heavier body toward the railing. His last passenger was a young man roughly Shivaji's size. Hauling him was like dragging his own body. Shivaji carefully held his arms, noting a dislocated elbow.

"Nanban, can you hear me?" Shivaji called in a high-pitched voice.

"Yes," replied the young man.

"I am here to assist you. You need to be moved to a safer area."

"No, please. I cannot feel my right arm. The slightest movement causes unbearable pain."

"If I don't move you near the railings..."

"You don't understand. You cannot imagine the pain I am in. Leave me alone," said the young man, not letting Shivaji finish.

Shivaji ignored the protests. "Sorry, nanban, but you are coming with me," he said, dragging the passenger by his feet. The young man whined, pleading as the initial movement had aggravated his elbow. His cries rang sharply in Shivaji's ears.

"You will thank me later," said Shivaji as he slid the body close to the group of saved passengers near the railing. He advised the other Indian passengers to support the young man with the dislocated elbow. The exhausted Shivaji lifted himself off his knees onto his feet, using the dependable barrier for support. He knew he needed more energy to protect his wife from the descending raindrops, the insistent splashes of seawater, the unpredictable movements of the vessel, and the calamitous scenario on deck, where bodies dropped, rolled, and crashed. The deck resembled an untamed circus, tents set ablaze, leaving performers scrambling for their lives. Everyone ran, but no one knew where the exit was.

"You left! How could you? Did you not think of me before saving others? Deva, why does my husband always have to play the role of the saviour?" Vyjanti exclaimed, looking toward the heavens in search of God.

"Vyjanti, why are you looking at the sky? I realize you have a lovely face, but do you believe the God of Rain will be swayed by your elegance and end this relentless storm?"

"Stop it," Vyjanti said, her face flushing. "This is not the time for humor."

Browsing the interior of the vessel for the beggar, Shivaji noticed the door to Captain Sanders' cabin was left open. "When did he leave his shack? And where was his prized bedmate?" Shivaji wondered. He sheltered Vyjanti with his left arm, his other arm intertwined with the railing bars for a secure hold. Vyjanti buried her face into her husband's chest. One side of her face rose and fell with each of Shivaji's breaths. She remained silent, focusing entirely on his heartbeat, placing her ear over the left side of his chest and feeling it palpitate rapidly. She stole a glance at him, noticing his eyes fixed on the unlatched cabin door. He waited for the Indian woman to free herself from unending misery. It had been exactly seven nights since she was first abducted by the Englishmen.

"Why is she not moving? This is the perfect chance for her to escape," Shivaji whispered to his wife.

Vyjanti did not hesitate to understand whom he meant. "Escape? Where would she go? Where could she hide? And if she did find a place, would the captain not discover it?"

Shivaji knew her words were true. The Indians on board were helpless. To be placed on Ship Elbe was like being sent to hell. He began to believe that every person—Brahmin, untouchable, farmer, villager, or beggar—was on the vessel for one reason: the sins of their past and present lives. "A short while ago, I helped four Indian passengers; why did I not save the Indian woman?" he asked himself. Deserting this thought, he turned to his wife. "Vyjanti, are you fine?"

Before she could respond, powerful currents lifted the 1,693-ton vessel. Those near the railing held on for their lives, while those farther away were thrown across the deck, some crashing into barrels, others overboard. Vyjanti held firmly to Shivaji's forearm. He looked into her eyes. "No matter what happens, don't let go, Vyjanti."

As the vessel surged, passengers felt giddiness in their stomachs. Many vomited from the unstable motion. Ship Elbe then fell hard, the violent currents hammering its belly and spreading water across the lower deck. Passengers from the Red Lilies district were reminded of the devastating floods in their villages. The water on deck petrified the indentured labourers; many feared it would sink the ship. Death seemed eager to claim them.

"Oh Deva, please take me, but let my husband live," Vyjanti prayed, dissolving into tears.

"Vyjanti, we will be fine. Nothing will happen to you, I promise. Now keep your eyes on me." Immersed in the chaos, Vyjanti did not listen.

"Vyjanti, I need you to look at me," Shivaji commanded.

Her eyes scanned the deck filled with hysterical passengers. First, she saw her brother and his family: Venkatesh, Lachmaiya, and Karthik remained in the same positions. To her, Venkatesh seemed like a protective umbrella shielding his wife and son from the rain and wind. Then she saw an Indian mother dragging her child, no more than seven, by the arm to the edge of the railing. The boy resisted, sobbing and stomping, but the mother was firm. Reaching the barrier, she instructed her son with abstruse hand gestures. Vyjanti strained to interpret them, but it was too late. In a flash, the child climbed onto the railing separating the vessel from the ocean. Resting his innocent eyes on his mother, it seemed as if he said, "Amma, I am ready." The mother closed her eyes and pushed. With little force, the child fell. Before opening her eyes, the mother followed the same action. She did not look back. One blink from Vyjanti, and both were gone.

Shivaji wished he had not witnessed the act. He noticed his wife had become unresponsive. "Vyjanti, I hope you did not see that."

She remained silent, gripping his forearm. The vessel's trembling subsided; the hard rain became light, the powerful winds shifted course, and the deck's motion lessened. Gradually, the crew steered Ship Elbe away from the storm. Shivaji could not tell whether his kurta was damp from raindrops or Vyjanti's tears. She pulled her face from his chest and realized no Indian had moved from their spots; it seemed everyone awaited confirmation that the vessel was safe.

"Look, it's Baba," Vyjanti said, wiping her remaining tears.

Old Man Thambi was huddled with several Indians under the staircase to the upper deck. For once, dismissing caste and religion, the small group clung together, watching the clouded skies.

"If something like this happens, it does not matter who is who," Shivaji said, shaking his head.

"What do you mean?" asked Vyjanti.

"Look for yourself."

"I see Baba. He is safe."

"Yes, thank God he is fine. But you missed the point, Vyjanti. An hour ago, before the storm, Muslims avoided a beggar, Hindus avoided touching one. Look at them now; they huddle under the staircase with a beggar in the middle."

"We all fear for our lives and those of our loved ones. In such incidents, we must unite to survive. That is what the Hindus, Muslims, and the beggar are doing—they are keeping each other warm, keeping their blood circulating," Vyjanti explained, trying to be practical.

"So what it took was fear of death for a Brahmin to touch an untouchable? Now, isn't that remarkable."

For the remainder of the day, there were no commands given, no orders followed, no food cooked, and no food served. Both the Indians and the Englishmen on board kept unnaturally still. They felt it unwise to move about on the deck. No one knew if the black curtains of night would lift in the morning to reveal the sun. The chill in the air made bodies shiver, and the damp clothes worn by the passengers only worsened it. Shivaji and his wife listened as Lachmaiya sang Karthik a soothing lullaby. The sound of her voice was ethereal—so pleasant that Karthik and many nearby Indians fell asleep almost instantly. But for Vyjanti, even a heavenly voice could not quiet her thoughts.

Shivaji advised his wife to rest her eyes. He told her that while she slept, he would remain awake. After all, there was no promise the storm would not return—and if it did, Shivaji would be the first to know.

"No, that is not fair. You need rest as well. We shall both rest our eyes," she replied.

"Vyjanti, do you ever agree with anything I say or do?" Shivaji asked with a trace of wit.

"Deva, that is so untrue. It is my duty to abide by and agree with everything you say."

"Which means you will now shut your eyes."

"Very clever," Vyjanti said with a small sniffle.

But as soon as she closed her lids, images of the mother and her child forced her eyes open again. Startled by the relentless visions, she sobbed into her husband's comforting arms.

"Whenever I shut my eyes, I see them," she whispered. "The child stands on the edge of the barrier with no other choice but to end his life. Can you imagine what the poor boy was feeling at that moment? What kind of mother guides her child to death?"

"Vyjanti, in drastic situations the brain does not function properly. We act on impulses, and those impulses lead to reckless decisions," Shivaji said softly.

"If that is the case then why doesn't everyone on board jump into the ocean to end their lives?"

"I think we should not talk about this matter," Shivaji said, a hint of irritation creeping into his tone.

"As you say, I will not talk about it," replied Vyjanti, clearly confounded.

She could not understand how a mother had compelled her own son—her flesh and blood—to end his life in that manner. After several minutes, she murmured under her breath, "I probably don't understand because I am not a mother."

"What?" asked Shivaji, unable to catch what she mumbled.

"I am sorry. My mind keeps drifting to the real-life incident. I need to know why she killed her son and then herself."

Shivaji did not want his wife thinking or speaking about the tragedy. He knew Vyjanti would torment herself over it. He felt the urge to scold her but reminded himself of her vulnerable state. What she had seen—what they had all seen—was hard to digest.

"You know, she probably did it to free her son and herself from misery," Shivaji said quietly. "She could not bear the oppression any longer. She chose suicide over both defiance and compliance."

"It may have been the storm," Vyjanti said as the tears on her face began to dry. "Perhaps she assumed the storm would destroy the ship. If it went under, no one would have survived anyway. So why let a child endure such horror? Jumping over the barrier may have seemed the only escape from this hell."

"Hell," uttered Shivaji. "Yes, this is hell. But suicide is a sin. I honestly believe God exists—and He is opposed to suicide. When a person takes his or her own life, it ruins God's plans. God has plans for every person in this world. Everything is written beforehand; our fates are sealed before we are born. Suicide denies us the fate chosen for us. We should not leave this world until it is our time."

"I never knew you could talk like..." Vyjanti began.

"Talk like what?"

"Like a saint."

"The only saint here is Baba."

"Then I am sure he knows why the mother forced suicide upon her son and then herself," Vyjanti murmured.

THE 23RD DAY

The Indians and Englishmen were blessed with the arrival of sunshine, which meant the heavy storm clouds had finally cleared. The early morning brought skies as clear as the pale skin on an Englishman's face. Puddles of water still pooled across the deck floor. Personal belongings—saris, kurtas, pajamas, shawls, sandals, and tin utensils—lay scattered everywhere on the ship. Dried blood stains were visible on the brows, hands, elbows, and shins of many injured passengers. A number of Indian families sat on the deck with both hands placed on their heads, exemplifying the depth of their distress. Some pounded on their chests as they bawled over the loss of a husband, wife, or child who had fallen victim to the storm. Ship *Elbe*—a vessel once maintained by the indentured labourers for its cleanliness and order—was now a total mess. The chief officer ordered the Indians to immediately collect their personal belongings before he dispatched the deck crew members to hurl them overboard. There was no sympathy in his voice, no mercy for the Indians. Everyone on board knew that the ruinous storm had captured many lives—some taken by choice, others against their will.

"Everyone present is fortunate to be alive. Don't thank your Gods. Thank Captain Sanders. He steered this ship to safety. If it was not for our superior master, you coolies and the ship would have drowned," said the traitor, Brijnath, as he strolled past the Indians scrambling to gather their belongings.

The Indians felt nervous that if their possessions were not recovered in time, the British seafarers would dispose of them. With that in mind, they moved about in a frantic, chaotic rush. Old Man Thambi, the only person who did not find it necessary to participate in the search, suddenly leapt to his feet. It seemed as if he had beheld a ghost. The petrified expression on his face indicated trouble. "Hurry... Quickly, find your possessions. The dogs are prepared to bite."

Nobody understood what the beggar meant until the Indians noticed the deck crew members standing with batons clutched in their fists. Their hands were prepared to strike, their feet ready to unfetter, and their ears keenly waiting for Anderson's command to unleash violence upon the suppressed Indians. Panic spread among the indentured labourers. Some hid near staircases, railings, and barrels, hoping to escape the looming brutality. Shivaji advised Vyjanti, Venkatesh, and Lachmaiya to collect as many items as they could. "Don't worry if the item is yours or not. Collect whatever you see. We can return them to their rightful owners later," shouted Shivaji, loud enough for others to hear as well.

The practical words spread quickly. The nearby Indians followed Shivaji's lead, and they, in turn, passed the message along. At last, the indentured labourers were working as a team. Shivaji's quick thinking inspired the Indians on board as they rushed about, leaning forward and bending down to gather the scattered belongings. Soon their arms were so full they could carry no more. Fortunately, Shivaji was one step ahead—he began forming a large pile in the center of the deck. It did not take long for the others to contribute. Soon, many areas of the lower deck were left spotless, and the pile of possessions in the middle of the deck had grown nearly seven feet tall.

The ominous slaps of batons against palms ceased. The deck crew expected their leader to permit a thrashing, but Anderson remained silent. Brijnath inched toward the chief officer to exchange words, but was signalled to hold back. With a curt wave of his index finger, Anderson dismissed the all-in-one servant, translator, and traitor. He had no desire to hear a word from him.

"The insurgent... he is the one. Yes, he is the one with the brains. A coolie with a functioning brain is a dangerous threat. Something must be done," muttered the chief officer under his breath.

Shivaji did not partake in the frantic collection. Instead, he asked Vyjanti to gather their belongings from the pile while he stood back and observed. Watching his wife, friends, and fellow passengers search through the hundreds of items, he felt his spirit stir with pride. The Indians were assembled without bickering, barking, or biting. For once, they acted as one. Men and women from different castes and religions worked side by side. Hands brushed as they passed items to their rightful owners. Shoulders bumped as they picked up or set down belongings. Questions were answered and suggestions acknowledged—not with hate but with respect. For the first time aboard *Elbe*, the Indians trusted one another. No one seized what was not theirs. Instead, items were returned or left behind for their owners to claim.

Shivaji watched Vyjanti wave her arms in joy. She was all smiles when she found her jute bag, still holding her spare clothes and small idol of Lord Shiva. She hurried to Shivaji with the bag slung over her shoulder. "You keep this. I'll search for your belongings now," she said, leaving her sack with him.

Before Shivaji could reply, Vyjanti was back among the women, searching the pile, which looked smaller than before. Meanwhile, the men clustered near the tin utensils, sorting plates and spoons so that families could claim at least one of each. Not everyone received their own plate or spoon—the storm had swallowed many along with lives—but the helpful men ensured that every family had something to eat with. There was no possible way to tell which utensil belonged to whom, but no one complained. For the first time, a Brahmin ate from a plate once used by an untouchable, and a Muslim did not mind using a spoon that a Hindu had touched. Change was taking root, and that made Shivaji hopeful.

"Let us stand as one, let us stand united.

Let us not separate, let us merge together.

Let us eliminate the hate we carry in our hearts.

Let us erase status, caste, and religion.

Let us not be suppressed, let us not be oppressors.

Let us be free, let us become liberated."

The enchanting voice of the beggar left the Indian passengers moist-eyed. Shivaji had not realized that Old Man Thambi stood behind him until the inspiring poem was spoken. Respectful of his elders, Shivaji touched the beggar's feet.

"God bless you, in this life and the next," said Thambi.

"I am happy to see you safe and sound after the storm, Baba."

"Yes, it seems God does not yet want me by His side. Whenever I feel my time has come, I live to see another day."

"Baba, those words you recited—it was as if you pulled them straight from my own thoughts and shaped them into poetry."

Thambi laughed hysterically. "I did."

"You did what?"

"Let's just say I borrowed them from you."

Once again, Shivaji was left puzzled by Baba's twists and turns. Instead of explaining, Thambi, as always, shifted the subject. "The Englishmen—they fear you. To them, you are a threat."

"Why?"

"You are not like the others. You have a voice. And with a voice comes a mind. That is dangerous to them. Be careful. Watch every step, every move. Protect your loved ones. These arseholes have no heart."

"Baba, I will do as you say. But I am not worried for myself. I am only worried for Vyjanti."

"Don't be foolish. Your life matters. If there is no Shivaji, how will Vyjanti survive? I tried to find a way to keep you distant from harm. I tried—I really tried—but God is stubborn."

Before Shivaji could interpret the cryptic words, Vyjanti returned, holding his bag. With her right hand she touched the elderly man's feet, and Thambi blessed her, tears dripping from his eyes.

"Baba, why are you crying?" Vyjanti asked, concern etched on her face. "Please forgive me if I have done something wrong."

"No, no, no... You have done nothing wrong. I wish..." Thambi trailed off and walked to his resting place, leaving Shivaji and his wife to wonder what he had left unsaid.

With restless eyes, throbbing heads, aching limbs, and empty stomachs, the Indians on board were, for once, looking forward to the unsavory mixture of water, rice, and lentils. Food in the stomach not only satisfied hunger but eased headaches and lifted spirits. But to receive food, the indentured labourers first had to earn it. The deck crew leader ordered them to cleanse the lower deck. Only when the puddles were dried and the debris cleared would they be allowed to eat.

The Indians were exhausted, yet still they were shown no mercy. Their sluggish movements irritated the deck crew. Brijnath came stomping down the staircase with a lethal whip in hand. The traitor gleefully passed it to the deck leader, eager for him to release it on the backs of the Indians. The crack of the whip was a sound the indentured labourers knew too well. Instantly, they forced their weary bodies to push harder. Those who failed to increase their pace felt the lash tear into their backs. Their yelps of pain filled the deck. The lashes drove their hands to move faster and their knees to hold stronger. Only when the cleansing ended did the labourers finally pause—waiting, desperate and trembling, for the arrival of food.

"Appa, I can hear my stomach growling. It sounds like a tiger," Karthik said to his father.

"Not to worry. Soon we will be offered the most tasty, flavorful, and zestful khichdi ever," Venkatesh replied sarcastically.

The indentured labourers were relieved to see the faces of the regular Englishmen who distributed food each day. But the seafarers were not rolling the large pots of khichdi. Instead, their hands held steel pails.

"What is this?" Lachmaiya asked her husband.

Venkatesh remained silent. He picked at the food with his fingers. Then, he clutched it in his hands and brought it close to his nose. From the corner of his eyes, Venkatesh noticed Karthik moving the food towards his mouth. "Stop, Karthik! Not now. Let me taste it first. I want to know if it is safe to consume."

Karthik stopped immediately. He placed the hard, brownish-colored, rectangular-shaped bread onto the plate. Venkatesh took a sniff. The bread had no scent. "I will taste it first," said Venkatesh.

"Hold on, Venkatesh!" said Shivaji as he grabbed his friend's arm.

Shivaji examined the line of Indians; most of them were displaying repulsive facial expressions, while some of them were vomiting. The Indians were rising in protest, an act that staggered the Englishmen. The Indians demanded answers: "What are you feeding us?"

In the middle of the outcry, Brijnath burst out in laughter. "Invented by the English and fed by the English. Coolies, I present to you, dog biscuits," said Brijnath with a smile from ear to ear. "Since the cook was not able to prepare khichdi because of the devastating storm, for the meantime, you are to feed on these appetizing biscuits."

Enraged voices persisted despite the whip being unleashed to instill fear. Shivaji understood that the hostile situation could become disastrous.

"Nillu, nillu—stop, stop!" Shivaji raised his voice to the group of disturbed Indians.

Gradually, the Indians began to settle down. The pumping fists, the constant jaw movements, the daunting stares, and the biscuit tossing ceased. At that moment, the British seafarers were convinced that Shivaji Nair had power over his people and might lead a revolt. The Englishmen became concerned that the Indians would soon only listen to Shivaji.

"I must talk to Commander Anderson. This Shivaji, he is a disease. And before this disease spreads and infects others, it has to be eliminated," Brijnath said under his breath.

The Indians felt that by being fed dog biscuits, the English seamen had injured their self-respect and dignity. Trapped between the decision to consume or reject the dog biscuits, the Indians turned to their family members for instruction and advice.

"We are not animals. This is not the food we eat," said a helpless father to his weepy-eyed daughter.

"I cannot bear the hunger. We must eat. I don't care what others say or think. If we don't eat, it will be hard to carry on," said a wife to her husband as she moved the biscuit closer to her mouth.

"Are you an animal? Why are you chewing on that biscuit? Spit it out. If we eat this now, the Englishmen will have a reason to serve dog biscuits every day. Stop, right this instant!" said an infuriated husband to his starving wife.

From the three hundred Indians assigned to Section A of the ship, half consumed the dog biscuits while the other half allowed starvation to persist. Venkatesh and Lachmaiya could not bear to see Karthik suffer. Lachmaiya smashed the biscuits into crumbs for her child to easily swallow. When Lachmaiya fed her son with her hands, she felt as if she were feeding him poison. "I am feeding my child food that is eaten by dogs. May the hand with which I serve him fall off," Lachmaiya said out loud, nearly in tears.

Karthik made repulsive facial expressions while chewing on the biscuits. "It tastes like... I don't know what it tastes like." He started expelling the crumbs from his mouth directly onto the plate. "It is gross, amma."

Shivaji and his wife both decided to shove their plates aside. Be it pride, ego, or stubbornness, they were determined to starve until the Englishmen offered a plate full of diluted khichdi.

As the Indians lined up to wash their hands and utensils, the door to the secretive cabin located on the upper deck flung open. The opened door revealed absolute darkness. No one was able to see Captain Sanders, his table, his chair, his bed, his uniform, his boots, or his bottles of rum.

From the off-limits bedroom came the demoralized Indian woman who had been stripped to her bare skin and repeatedly raped for the last eight nights. Her sari was torn in many places, exposing parts of her thighs. Her hair was a tangled mess, her eyes blood-red, and her lips severely damaged. The woman's arms revealed numerous scrapes and bruises.

Her fatigued body was inflexible. It seemed as if she was not using her feet as she slowly descended the staircase. She had a blank expression on her face as she moved closer to the area where she and her husband were first assigned to reside. The indentured labourers stared as if they had encountered a ghostly spirit. To them, she behaved like a woman who had lost her mind. It seemed as if her body was there, but her soul elsewhere.

There was finger-pointing and chitter-chatter amongst the mob of Indians near the water barrels. She had not been seen or heard of for the past week, compelling the Indians to believe that she had been executed.

When she reached her designated area, the woman had difficulty seating herself on the deck. Unable to balance, she fell sideways. At that moment, many Indian females surrendered their place in line to help the disturbed woman. Vyjanti and Lachmaiya both ran across the deck.

As the Indian women approached her, she let out a paralyzing cry for her husband. Vyjanti noticed that her body started to tremble. Knowing that the victim might act recklessly, Vyjanti extended her arms. At that moment, Vyjanti believed that her touch, her warmth, and her closeness were needed. She reached over to console the battered woman.

THE 25TH DAY

After sustaining three consecutive days of life-threatening hunger, Shivaji, his wife, and other unwavering Indians eventually received edible food. On the morning of the twenty-fifth day, the cook on board had prepared watered-down khichdi that most indentured labourers had become used to despite its flavourlessness. But compared to dog biscuits, the khichdi was like delicious idli or dosa to the Indians. In reality, the khichdi served that morning was probably the worst since the vessel set sail.

The Indians, who had objected to the dog biscuits—which had resulted in stomach cramps, headaches, fainting, and vomiting—did not care how stale the rice and lentils were. Taste was no match for their desperate craving for nourishment. It was afterward that the Indians predicted that both rice and lentils were flooded in seawater because of the recent storm. Their stomachs developed acute pain. Most of the day, the indentured labourers struggled to endure the discomfort. Many of them felt as if poison was swarming inside their organs. For the unfortunate ones, the pains lasted for hours. For the fortunate ones, it did not last too long, since whatever went in soon found its way out.

The Indians who refused to eat dog biscuits changed in appearance. After consuming water only twice a day, these Indians shed many pounds. While no difference in Vyjanti was seen, it was not the same case for Shivaji. He had lost the oval form of his face. The bones of his jawline firmly embraced the outer layer of his skin. Vyjanti noted how the past three days worked their magic on her husband. Unfortunately, it was not good, but bad magic.

"I will be fine. Don't worry about me. It seems like we will be fed khichdi regularly now. I will recover in no time," Shivaji tried to convince his wife.

Vyjanti did not feel convinced. She was still concerned for her husband. "Hmm... I have an idea. From now on, you will eat my share."

"Sorry Vyjanti, but I will not do that."

"Why?"

"If you think the amount of rice and lentils we receive is plenty, then I must say you are being impractical. I will not take your half and watch you starve for the remainder of the day."

"You look unwell. Had my appearance changed, would you not do the same for me?"

"I may look unwell, but I will survive," Shivaji replied defensively.

Compassion worships one religion, and that is humanity. Humanity does not belong to a single caste, nor does it uphold a certain status. In the past few days, Indian women from all castes and religions showed compassion to the victim who had been detained for eight consecutive nights to fulfill the needs of a sexual predator. The Indian women helped the sufferer by cleaning her with water from the barrels, feeding her khichdi from their plates, involving her in daily conversations, and lending a shoulder for her to release pent-up emotions.

Shivaji did not permit Vyjanti to help the woman who had been the recent center of attention. After the conversation with Old Man Thambi, he kept a close eye on his wife. Vyjanti was kept in front of his eyes continuously. Shivaji was also extra vigilant when it came to Venkatesh and his family members. When fulfilling the daily chores assigned to them, Shivaji kept his eyes moving, ensuring that he knew his loved ones' whereabouts. While seated to eat breakfast and dinner, he shot rapid glances towards the members of the deck crew, looking for any sudden movements. Shivaji anticipated evil from the British seafarers. After furtively observing the Englishmen, he sensed that their eyes were not on his loved ones but on him. Despite Shivaji fixing his eyes elsewhere, he still felt their eyes on him. "Baba was right. I have become their main enemy," Shivaji said to himself.

Like most days, after the evening dinner, the Indians proceeded to the water barrels to rinse their hands and feet. While standing in line, Shivaji repeatedly looked over both his shoulders. He was sure that the Englishmen had plans for him. "Come on, this is your chance, come get me. Come from the left, come from the right and come from the back. And if you have the nerve, come from the front. I am ready. Come on, I want to get this done and over with," Shivaji said under his breath. Shivaji did not want to continue waiting extra minutes, hours, or days speculating whether he'd be ambushed by the British seafarers or not. He wanted it to happen then and there as he stood in line.

"Oh Deva, what is the matter with you? Why are you moving about so much? Is there something you are not telling me?" Vyjanti asked her husband.

"No, not at all, I am just..." Shivaji hesitated. He needed an answer to his wife's question and he needed it fast. Any answer would do. And it did not matter if it was a lie.

"I was in search of Baba. I have not seen him today. What about you, have you seen him?"

"No sorry, I have not. But I am sure he must be fine."

Conversing with Vyjanti, Shivaji forgot about the British seafarers who were on his tail. To escape from Vyjanti's chatter was close to impossible. Yet, Shivaji did not find it bothersome. His brain, which had been dominated by vexation, was now at peace, thanks to his wife.

Shivaji and his wife viewed the faraway sun dive into the ocean. The apparent layers of red, orange, and yellow lines progressively descended in the company of the sun. It took some time for the enormous body of the sun to perish into the waters. Every passing minute of the breathtaking scenery left the husband and wife in awe of God and His masterful creations.

Shivaji placed his hand on his wife's hand. He experienced the same feeling now as he did when he first reached for his wife's hand during their wedding ceremony. Hand in hand, the bride and groom walked around the pious fire. The first touch of Vyjanti's hand during the saat phere, seven rounds, was all it took for Shivaji to feel endless contentment.

After a stressful day of keeping a careful eye on Vyjanti and the others, Shivaji needed his wife's hand. Her touch relaxed his nerves, calmed his mind. He noticed the delicate wind playing with her long tresses. The feeling of jealousy intervened. "No person or thing can touch my wife other than me," said Shivaji under his breath. He challenged the light breeze by running his fingers through Vyjanti's hair.

"There are people around us. What will they think about your obscene actions? First you hold my hand, then you slide your fingers through my hair and now," Vyjanti paused for a moment, "What's next?"

"Others should not have a problem with a husband expressing love to his wife."

"Oh Deva!" said Vyjanti, discharging a rush of air from her mouth. "I predicted your answer before you even said it. You see how well I know my husband."

"Yes, no one understands me better than my wife," replied Shivaji.

Vyjanti felt hesitant to ask Shivaji why he did not permit her to visit the traumatized woman who, from all the Indians on board, required the most attention. Thus, she used a different tactic. "I have noticed that you have been restless for the past couple of days. I know that something is bothering you."

"Vyjanti, we need to be alert. We need to be careful. Baba feels that the Englishmen are keeping a close eye on me. They believe I am a threat, a person who can harm their unethical system."

A sudden emotion of anxiety dispersed within Vyjanti's blood circulation. Her heart pounded on the walls of her chest. Her eyes became teary. Her lips started to quiver. She did not know what to say.

"I need to protect. I am watching over you, over Venkatesh, over Lachmaiya, and over Karthik. I don't want you to leave my side. I want you to always remain close to me. From today onwards, I will not sleep during the nights. I will be on guard every minute of the day."

Vyjanti could not bear to hear more. "That is impossible. You need to sleep. How will your body function without rest?"

"You don't understand. These Englishmen have no limitations. These people are capable of doing anything and everything."

Vyjanti's dampened eyes were now profusely leaking. Deep within, she felt that all this was her fault. "If it was not for my decision, he and I would have never boarded this ship. Now because of me, his life is in danger," Vyjanti said to herself.

"Why are you crying? Nothing will happen to me or you, I promise. This is entirely my fault. I am no saviour. I am not God. Then why do I reach out to others? I don't know why I have this habit of confronting injustice. It is my untamed mouth, erratic means, and radical behaviour that have put our lives at risk. I apologize, Vyjanti."

Vyjanti covered his mouth with her gentle hand. She closed her eyes to prevent tears from becoming visible. "Please, this is not your fault. I have forced you to take part in this journey."

Shivaji instantly took hold of the hand which covered his mouth. He realized that Vyjanti had more words to say, but he did not let her proceed.

"Listen, this is not your fault. The decision to sign the contract was not yours alone. We both chose to be part of this expedition. So, here we are. Why cry about it? Let us make the best of it."

With the back of her hand, Vyjanti attempted to dry her dampened cheeks.

"Now my focus will be on protecting you. You are my priority. As a husband, I must protect you. I must not get involved in other people's matters. I will not help, direct, advise, or persuade the other Indian passengers on board. From now on, I will keep my conversation with others on board minimal. I must be invincible to these Englishmen.

All the eyes that search for my whereabouts and examine my movements will soon need to search for a different rebel. You know why? Because I am no rebel. I will be like other Indians on this ship who have no problem submitting and enduring."

"You have to promise me that you will not be harmed."

"Vyjanti, nothing will happen to you..."

"I am not talking about myself; I am talking about you. If something happens to you, I will not be able to live."

"I promise that nothing will happen to me or you."

Shivaji tried convincing his wife that she must rest her eyes, while Vyjanti tried convincing her husband that he must not stay up all night. Since both were too concerned for one another, it took nearly three hours for one of them to eventually fall asleep. Vyjanti had fallen victim to Shivaji's clever bluff. After many arguments and disagreements, Shivaji thought of an idea.

"Fine, Vyjanti. You win. We will both close our eyes and take rest."

Vyjanti happily agreed to Shivaji's final decision. For at least an hour, both Shivaji and his wife lay on the rock-hard floor. Eyes closed yet wide awake, both waited for the other to fall asleep. Vyjanti finally opened her eyes to see if her husband was unconscious. What she beheld was Shivaji lying on his back with his face pointed to the moon and the stars. Not once did his eyes flicker. His chest rose with every inhale. After every exhale, his nose made an unusual sound. At first, Vyjanti felt skeptical about the noise deriving from his nostrils. She had never heard Shivaji make such abnormal noises before. Should I shake him to see if he is sleeping? thought Vyjanti. Instead of deciding to jerk his kurta, she placed herself beside Shivaji and closed her eyes. Within minutes, Vyjanti was unconscious. The sight of her husband asleep gave her the chance to rest her overloaded mind, burdened with doubts and tension. What she did not know was that Shivaji had deceived her with his unselfish act.

"I am sorry, but it is for you. I will not let them get to you or me. I will fulfill my promise to you," Shivaji whispered in a lowered voice, with his eyes open and ears alert. As the night persisted, Shivaji noticed what he had never noticed before: Ship Elbe was flooded with eerie silence. There were no sounds of whips and batons lashing against human flesh, no sounds of filthy rags pressing against the wooden deck, no sounds of complaints and concerns during the food sessions, and no barking or howling from the Englishmen. A match between consciousness and unconsciousness took a toll on Shivaji. Sessions of unconsciousness prevailed, but most of the time, within a few seconds or minutes, Shivaji received a signal from his brain to open his eyes. To protect his wife and himself from any sabotage, Shivaji had to find ways to stay alert. To keep his lids from closing, Shivaji pinched his arms, slapped his face, and shook his head. Then, his attention was pulled to his wife's loud moaning. Her moaning turned into words. "No, no, please don't," Vyjanti mumbled in her sleep. As far as Shivaji knew, this was irregular. This was the first time he had heard Vyjanti talk in her sleep. He surmised that his wife was in the middle of a miserable dream. To help her out of this nightmare, Shivaji needed to bring her to a conscious state. But he felt reluctant to do so. He knew that if she rose, she would question him. Before agreeing to close her eyes, Vyjanti expected her husband to be fast asleep. Now, if she saw Shivaji with his eyes wide open, Vyjanti would immediately sense deception. Shivaji felt that the hurt his wife suffered from the dream would be less severe than the hurt she would feel if she awakened to his dishonesty. Keeping that in mind, with discomfort, Shivaji observed his wife as his vision became hazy. Eventually, Vyjanti's dream ended. The words she voiced in her sleep stopped. She returned to her normal position, sleeping tranquilly, with her left arm extended to comfort her neck. Shivaji unrolled his extra kurta over her sari-clad body. This act was done on nights with cold winds. He gazed at her serene face.

"Her beauty is something that I have always overlooked," Shivaji said under his breath. "The extra-curvaceous figure, the pink, luscious lips, the big, rounded eyes, the long, lusty lashes, the sharp, feminine jawline, the perfectly-shaped nose, and the not-too-pointy chin—how could I fail to notice these admirable features that my wife possesses?" What he always noticed was the tiny mole located right above her lip on the left side of her face. The small, dark blemish contributed to her attractiveness. Shivaji noticed it the first time he had set eyes on her. Reflections of the past captivated him, emancipating his brain from the overlong and lifeless night.

In the villages of the Red Lilies district, almost every man, woman, and child was of dark complexion. The dark appearance which the Indians carried was nothing to be ashamed of. Most of the Tamilians believed that most civilians of India were of that color. The only people with fair complexions within the district were the Englishmen and a small number of Muslims. What the villagers did not know was that Indians from other districts and states had a slightly lighter complexion. Most villagers did not travel outside the district to witness an appearance different from theirs. But when these villagers looked at Shivaji, they did not see a reflection of themselves. Shivaji was not milky white, but he certainly was different from others. The buttery color of his skin did make heads turn.

Unfortunately, his complexion made him an outsider during childhood. He was picked on and bullied by his peers in school. He was not acknowledged by his teachers for his superb grades. Even the village headman frowned upon seeing his appearance. Shivaji used to ask his mother why others mistreated him. His mother constantly replied, "They envy you, my son." Shivaji's mother felt that since no one in the village was fairer than her son, everyone was jealous of him. "Everyone wishes they could be as light as you," she told him.

During adulthood, people and their views changed. Shivaji profited from his skin color. He noticed that he received more attention from the ladies in the village. Younger women waited for a chance to talk to him, while elder women dreamt of him in their arms. Shivaji never expected the opposite sex to give him such attention. Though he did not mind, he also did not show interest. While strolling down the village road, women gave him lewd stares. At the village market, he felt a woman's hand or feet purposely brush against his skin. And while escorting his father to another villager's home, the women in the family stole glances at him from open doors and windows. Shivaji found nothing wrong with casual talks, but if a woman expected more, he did not hesitate to withdraw. If a woman requested to meet in private, Shivaji refused, no matter how seductive, flirtatious, or inviting she was. When Venkatesh first asked Shivaji about his pigmentation, he replied with the help of his father's explanation. "Appa used to say that I got it from his father."

"How does that make sense? You are saying that you got it from your grandfather. If that is so, don't you think your appa should be fair in complexion?" Venkatesh asked his friend.

"I try not to think about it. I am not saying that I never did. I did. But it's pointless. Honestly, I don't know what the big deal is."

"Nanaban, it is a big deal. You make us dark-skinned men look bad."

Shivaji shook his head in disgust. "Venkatesh, the color of my skin does not proclaim that I am handsome. Trust me, you are more handsome."

"I know that," replied Venkatesh, with no humor in his voice or on his face. "But you are the one who will end up with the most beautiful spouse. In the marriage bazaar, you are in demand. Fathers with unmarried daughters will bid a high price for you."

"Are you saying that I am some kind of popular item?"

"Yes, that is exactly what I am saying."

When searching for a bride, Muthuraman desired a family that could bid the highest price for his one and only son. As for Shivaji's mother, she was on the lookout for the most attractive of them all. Keeping in mind that a female did not have to be fair-skinned to be considered beautiful, Shivaji's mother wanted a daughter-in-law who surpassed her son in terms of appearance. Basically, she hoped for a 'Ram & Sita' kind of pair. Thus, when Shivaji was brought to the fair, numerous fathers approached Muthuraman, offering all sorts of valuables in exchange for their marriageable daughter. While Shivaji opposed dowry, Muthuraman considered it a tradition.

In a span of fifteen days, Shivaji was forced to visit three different households, whose families were prepared to offer loads of gold, a decent sum of money, well-knit clothing, tin pots and pans, and cattle to help with labor in the sugarcane fields. Muthuraman did not care much for the clothing, the cookery, and the livestock, but his eyes lit up greedily when the father of the daughter announced gold and money. Since Shivaji had no interest in choosing his future wife, he left it to his mother to make the proper decision. Actually, it was Shivaji's mother who rejected the daughters that were presented.

"But that was the best offer; a large amount of shillings, a handful of gold, and on top of that Shivaji would receive half of their land. How can you say no to that?" Muthuraman questioned his wife.

"My son does not need money, gold, or land. He needs a beautiful wife who shall take good care of him."

"What about us?"

"All we need is a daughter-in-law who will give us love and respect," answered Shivaji's mother, hoping Muthuraman would stop pestering her.

The Nair family was informed of a Tamil Brahmin family living within the district but far from their village. The family was not offering land or cattle but a sufficient amount of money, gold, clothing, cookery, and unlimited ration every week until the marriage date. Muthuraman argued that other families were offering more, but Shivaji's mother ignored her husband's nonsensical remarks. The next day, Shivaji and his family traveled on a bullock cart to this unknown village, which en route contained lots of twists and turns, ups and downs. Seated in the bullock cart, with the sunlight bothering their eyes, Muthuraman and his wife complained about the unbearable heat. Shivaji paid no attention to his parents' constant grumbling. Instead, he was absorbed by the intriguing scenery.

The enchanting village was full of greenery. It was unlike his village. It seemed like a place from one of the storybooks Shivaji had read in grade school. All kinds of trees—mango, tamarind, coconut, and jasmine—were scattered across the landscape. The houses in the village were surrounded by colossal hills. These nurturing hills served as protectors on guard. Standing tall and wide, the hills protected the villagers and their homes from heavy winds and major floods.

While traveling, Shivaji noticed the pathway. Oncoming traffic would be problematic. Due to the narrow route, the driver had to be a perfectionist to direct his cart to the side for oncoming traffic to pass by, thought Shivaji. The bullock cart driver finally made a sound with his tongue to stop the bulls from advancing. "This is Ramesh Krishnan Iyer's residence," said the driver, pointing at the house made of wood, leaves, and straw. Shivaji did not feel nervous when he reached the residence of his possible bride-to-be. He did not have butterflies crisscrossing in his stomach like the other times he had been greeted by the father and mother of a daughter.

As he walked on the compound, he noticed that most of the village men, women, and children had surrounded the house with smiles that extended from one ear to the other. Even with all the eyes staring at him as if a noble prince had set forth onto their land, he did not turn bashful. Shivaji felt relaxed. He knew that it was not required for him to fall for or accept Miss Iyer. In fact, it was not his decision. "I have already fallen for the beauty of this wonderful village; therefore, I have nothing else to look forward to except the ride back home," Shivaji said under his breath.

In the sitting area, murukku (circular-shaped snack) was served along with payasam (a drink made with milk and sugar). As usual, Muthuraman praised his son, eager for a high offer, while Shivaji's mother kept quiet, hoping that whoever she was, she was the one.

"What is her name?" she asked the mother.

"Vyjanti," replied the mother.

Shivaji's mother examined Vyjanti's parents carefully. She noticed that both were not as dark as other Tamilians in this district. Both mother and father had preserved themselves well. The mother was not too tall, and the father was not too short. Both were in their early forties, without a wrinkle on their face or a grey hair on their head. Shivaji's mother felt ecstatic when she discovered that Vyjanti worships Lord Shiva, cooks all South Indian dishes to perfection, and ensures that both house and compound are spotless.

"I would like to add that Vyjanti is not able to sing gracefully, but she will try," said the father, looking a bit ashamed.

Shivaji had heard other marriageable women sing. One had the voice of a chirping bird; another had the voice of a shrieking monkey, and another cried even before she was asked to sing. "Who invented this custom where a female has to sing to impress a male and his family?" Shivaji said under his breath.

"You are the first to come see Vyjanti. Shivaji, my son, I really hope my daughter impresses you," said Ramesh Krishnan Iyer, a man who did not lie, not even for the sake of his daughter.

"Impress? Why does she need to impress? This is no competition," Shivaji said to himself.

The head of the Iyer family signaled for his wife to fetch Vyjanti. Seated beside his father, Shivaji glanced at him. Muthuraman seemed deep in thought. He is probably regretting the fact that other families were rejected despite offering more than Mr. Iyer, thought Shivaji.

Moving his eyes across the room, Shivaji glanced at his mother, who was involved in a conversation with Vyjanti's eldest aunt. He then heard a jingling sound—a sound he often heard when his sisters danced and pranced around the house. "She is wearing anklets," Shivaji said under his breath. He knew it before he consciously perceived it.

A heavenly fragrance wafted to his nose. Shivaji inhaled the tempting aroma, not wishing to release it with an exhale. The sweet-smelling perfume and the clinking of metal became more evident. She then appeared in a yellow sari, not as bright as the sun, but bright enough to complement her olive-colored skin tone. The silk sari could not be considered a South Indian garment unless it had heavy borders. Vyjanti's sari consisted of heavy borders in a darker shade of brown, which blended perfectly with the yellow. The sari was beautiful, but not as beautiful as her.

"It is not the sari that makes her stand out; it is she who makes the sari stand out," Shivaji whispered to himself. He noticed her strapped anklets, her nose ring, and her gold bangles, but for him, these were just unnecessary accessories that did not enhance her overall appearance. Shivaji tried his best to prevent his mouth from hanging open. He made sure that his eyes did not pop out of their sockets and restrained himself from blurting out something that would embarrass him.

Vyjanti was seated next to Shivaji's mother under the guidance of her aunt. Her forehead was lowered, her eyes fixated on the ground, and her hands trembled from nervousness. Shivaji's mother asked several general questions, to which Vyjanti replied softly.

Shivaji did not realize what he was doing. He bent his neck to introduce his eyes. Once he presented his gaze to her, he expected her eyes to respond in return. As Shivaji bent low to catch a glimpse of the exquisite face under the scarf—which covered not only Vyjanti's head but also most of her face—he forgot that his father was seated next to him. Muthuraman purposely cleared his throat, making Shivaji aware of his actions.

Positioning himself back in his seat appropriately, Shivaji witnessed the joy on Vyjanti's mother's face. At that instant, he knew that his mother would accept Vyjanti.

"Vyjanti, please stand," said Mr. Iyer, not able to look his daughter in the eyes. "You must walk."

To walk for the probable groom and his family was a regular custom, in which the daughter to be wedded had to prove that she was not blind or disabled. Shivaji felt ashamed each time a daughter of a household had to fulfill this custom. He believed it was degrading to women. In the past weeks, whenever a female had to comply with this act, Shivaji kept his head lowered. But today was different; he did not repeat this habitual act. This was his chance to steal a better look at her beauty.

As Vyjanti rose from her seat, one could tell how hesitant she was. Shivaji sensed that she did not want to proceed. She did not know when to start or when to stop. Eventually, Vyjanti walked slowly towards the door she had entered from. She may not have realized that while walking, her scarf had slipped from her head.

"So it's jasmine," Shivaji said to himself. A white jasmine flower was tucked in between the strands of Vyjanti's hair. As Shivaji observed her, he noticed that Vyjanti was also the perfect height—not too tall, nor too short. Besides the noise made by the anklets, her movement was soundless. Vyjanti moved like a peacock, with grace and finesse.

As she neared the entrance, Shivaji waited for her to turn so he could finally make eye contact with her. She turned. Her fingers kept fidgeting while she dared not set eyes on her possible husband. She was battling with herself. This was also her chance to observe the gentleman prepared to marry her. But her nervous behavior kept puncturing her confidence. Vyjanti feared for herself and her family. If she were to be rejected, her family members would be disheartened. A rejection, no matter how long it is kept hidden, eventually spreads like fire within the village. Once spread, villagers talk nonsense about the rejected daughter and her parents.

"I should place my eyes on him," Vyjanti said to herself while nearing her seat.

Shivaji finally stored an image of Vyjanti in his brain. It was as if he had taken a photo. As soon as Vyjanti rested her eyes upon his face, Shivaji mentally clicked the photo—capturing her hazel-colored eyes, tight-lipped smile, and the tiny black dot above her lip. He was assured that this image would replay in his mind regularly.

"He is fair, which is very peculiar. I did not expect that," Vyjanti said to herself. "It is not his complexion that defines his handsomeness. It is not his spellbinding eyes, nor his evenly shaped thin mustache above his lip. Then, what is it?" she asked herself.

Shivaji felt something he had never felt before. Never had his heart beat so passionately for a woman. One glance from Vyjanti was enough for him to decide that she was the one. Now he had to see whether his father and mother had any issues. Shivaji understood that his mother's decision mattered most. After all, she knew what was best for her son.

"Who'd be better than a mother to choose the perfect bride for her son?" Shivaji said under his breath.

Both Shivaji and Vyjanti, strangers to one another, felt uncomfortable. For a few seconds, their eyes met and then diverted. The young man and woman were both prepared to leave their future in God's hands. Thus, a couple of stolen glances at one another did not hurt.

The moment Vyjanti seated herself, she was ordered to put her vocal skills to use.

"Vyjanti, you have to sing," said Mr. Iyer, after clearing his throat. Vyjanti's father felt awful ordering his daughter to sing. He knew Vyjanti did not want to sing but had no other choice. There was no escape from this ritual. It had to be fulfilled to satisfy the potential groom and his family members. By singing the chorus of a folk or religious song, the daughter of the house proved to her possible husband and in-laws that she was not mute.

Vyjanti was aware of how she sounded when she crooned. She did not feel comfortable singing in front of her family members, and here she was expected to sing in front of absolute strangers. She searched for her inner voice. Her vocal cords were tied in a knot. Coyness had sealed her lips; for that reason, no sound was produced.

"Vyjanti, please sing a few lines for our visitors," said Mrs. Iyer, hoping to encourage her daughter. "Please, Vyjanti, this family has traveled miles to come see you. Your voice must be revealed," added Mr. Iyer.

Vyjanti swallowed so hard that Shivaji saw her Adam's apple move. Her eyes were glued to the floor, her body remained frozen in the seat, her temple was lowered to conceal her face, and her heart banged against the walls of her chest.

"Vyjanti!" shouted her demanding father.

Vyjanti shuddered at her father's loud voice. Shivaji felt sorry for her. The position she was in was preposterous. He imagined himself in the same situation, where nervousness resulted in stomach cramps, cold sweat, and slurred speech. Why must a woman walk when told to walk, talk when told to talk, smile when told to smile, and sing when told to sing? thought Shivaji.

Vyjanti bit her lips. Then, her lips parted. Just when everyone thought Vyjanti was about to sing, Shivaji interrupted.

"Vyjanti does not have to sing."

The elders in the room looked at one another in shock. Muthuraman ogled his son with a menacing facial expression, literally saying he wanted to choke him.

"Son, please don't interfere. It is disrespectful to the elders. This is a custom that must be fulfilled."

"Sorry, but I don't think it is necessary. We all know that she is not mute. She has responded to Amma's questions," Shivaji said, wishing that his mother would intervene to assist him.

It was the first time, without hesitation, that Vyjanti moved her eyes from the floor directly onto the brave and bold man seated across from her. She was impressed by his comments.

"I apologize on behalf of my son, Mr. Iyer. He does not seem to realize how important these customs and traditions are," said Muthuraman with his hands folded together.

"No need to apologize, Mr. Nair. We don't mind. If your son does not want Vyjanti to sing, then that is fine with us," replied Mr. Iyer, pleased that his daughter was saved from humiliation. Mr. Iyer believed that if his daughter were to sing for everyone, the final result would be a definite rejection.

Muthuraman was not thrilled with Shivaji or Vyjanti's family members for disregarding the regular custom. As for Shivaji, he did not understand the reason behind the ritual.

"How can someone judge a person's humaneness or courteousness through his or her voice?" asked Shivaji, delivering his final blow. Shivaji didn't need to add the last phrase, though he did. He wanted his father to understand how senseless these rituals were.

Vyjanti felt like giggling at Shivaji's comment, but she knew it was not appropriate. Like a dummy, she remained without motion or sound, praying that no one would change their mind and order her to sing again. The chewing of the murukku seemed loud since no one dared to speak after the uprising of the adolescent male.

"The murukku is very tasty," said Shivaji as he handed the plate of snacks over to his father.

Since he was still upset with his son's rash actions, Muthuraman rejected the offering immediately.

"Vyjanti made it. She prepared it this morning. Her murukku is a favorite among the villagers nearby. Many villagers come by asking her if she can prepare it for them. Some even pay for the murukku," said Mrs. Iyer, hoping that this topic could help restore the smooth back-and-forth conversations that occurred at the beginning of the visit.

Some other topics were introduced and discussed. More questions were asked, and more answers were given. Then, the Iyer family desired an answer: Would the first family who had come to see Vyjanti accept or reject? The answer to this question harassed Vyjanti's mother and father as they waited. There were no signs of a yes or no from either of Shivaji's parents.

"You can discuss this matter in private, Mr. Nair. My family and I will step out of this room for a couple of minutes. When we return, you can provide us with the answer. Is that alright with you?" Mr. Iyer asked Muthuraman.

Muthuraman nodded with a straight face. He already had the answer but agreed to Mr. Iyer's request out of courtesy. Shivaji could not tear his eyes away from Vyjanti's movements. He saw Vyjanti wait until her mother signaled her to leave the chair. This meant that she obeyed her parents. So whoever her parents asked her to marry, she would marry without hesitation, thought Shivaji.

As Vyjanti rose from her seat, she ensured that her sari was in place. She also found it necessary to adjust her long scarf, which tilted slightly to the left. This proved to Shivaji that she was neat and tidy. She then followed her parents out of the room, never once looking back. This showed Shivaji that she was a follower who supports a leader and, once committed, would never break that commitment. These judgments based on Vyjanti's movement from one part of the house to another helped Shivaji better understand the kind of person she was.

With the Iyer family not present in the room, he waited for one of his parents to start conversing. Muthuraman was in no mood to talk, while Shivaji's mother knew that if she spoke first, it would be considered an insult to her husband. She felt that her son had created a major dilemma. If Shivaji chose not to voice his opinion, there'd be no offended Muthuraman. Only then could Shivaji's mother effortlessly say, "Yes, she is the one. I want Vyjanti and no one else."

"Why did you have to insult me in front of the Iyer family?" Muthuraman asked his son.

"I am very sorry that you feel that way, appa. In all honesty, I was sharing my view. You and Amma are not the only people here to see Vyjanti; I am too. So if I did not want her to sing, why is that a problem?"

"You see, Shivaji's mother, this is how your son talks to me. Shivaji, you have no sense of decency."

With her hands, Shivaji's mother gestured to her son not to escalate the situation with his legitimate reasoning. She feared that her husband might misinterpret Shivaji's explanations. In fact, it was a given that Muthuraman would devour the explanations as insults.

"Son, all I want to know is why you intervened. Why did you not let that girl sing?" asked Muthuraman brusquely.

"I have a few reasons. Firstly, her appa had mentioned that she did not sing well. Then why let her embarrass herself in front of guests? Secondly, if she did sing, you both would have judged Vyjanti on the quality of her voice. Is that not unfair?"

Before Muthuraman could counter, Shivaji's mother raised a significant question: "Why is it important to you on what basis we judge her?" She intentionally asked, feeling that her son was hiding something from her.

"Amma, if she sang poorly, my odds of marrying Vyjanti would have been close to nothing," replied Shivaji, realizing afterward that he had exposed his true feelings for the Tamilian beauty.

"Hmm, did you hear that, Shivaji's father?"

"Yes, I did. I am not deaf," Muthuraman replied with a grunt.

Shivaji moved his eyes from side to side, hoping that one of his parents would reveal the final decision. He felt his heart beating twice as fast as usual. Perspiration formed on his brow, his legs kept shaking, and his throat began to parch. He did not know whether his mother would approve or disapprove.

With every marriage arrived dowry, which the groom's side of the family collected. If Muthuraman were in full control, he would have preferred Shivaji to wed all the ladies shown to him. With his son marrying various women, Muthuraman would have easily collected dowry from all families. Shivaji understood his appa's lack of interest in choosing the proper bride, which is why he permanently fixed his gaze on his amma, confident that she understood his inner feelings.

"So... do you like her?" Shivaji asked his mother.

"Do you?" replied Shivaji's mother with an impish smile. What the luminous sun could not do, a mother could. Her smile ignited the room, gifting it a diverse form of brightness.

"Yes, I do. She is beautiful. She entices like no other. She mesmerizes like no other. She touches the heart like no other," replied Shivaji before sealing his lips. He felt ashamed revealing too much to his mother.

"Amma, it is in your hands to accept or reject. Whatever decision you make, I will accept. You have given me life, so therefore God has given you the right to choose my life partner. I trust in you."

Shivaji's emotional words left his mother speechless. She remembered her son as a child, regularly coming to her to share his feelings, ideas, complaints, concerns, successes, and failures. But as he grew older, Shivaji did not find it necessary to share what floated in his mind with both parents.

"It has been a while since you shared your feelings with me. Thank you," said Shivaji's mother, restoring faith in her son's heart.

Soon after, the Iyer family entered the room with Vyjanti. Everyone looked at each other's faces for an answer. Mr. Iyer stared at Muthuraman. Muthuraman stared at his wife. Shivaji's mother stared at her son. Her son stared at Vyjanti. Vyjanti stared at the floor.

"It will be an honor for our family to accept the respectful and beautiful Vyjanti as our daughter-in-law," Shivaji's mother announced to everyone in the room.

The Iyer family transformed the expressions on their faces from uneasiness to cheerfulness. Then Shivaji's mother added, "The best part is that my son has a strong liking for Vyjanti."

The last comment persuaded Shivaji to hide his face from everyone. For a moment, he could not believe that his mother had actually said that. He casually rubbed his forehead with his fingers in a manner that covered most of his face. Shivaji hoped that no one was looking at him. Nobody was looking at him—except for his soon-to-be wife.

After setting the date for both families to converge for the matching of horoscopes, it was time for Shivaji and his parents to return home. Shivaji did not want to move. He wished to spend more time with his future wife. He felt the urge to ask Mr. Iyer to sanction a private meeting between Vyjanti and him somewhere within the household. But the urge was no match for his timidity. He knew that his request would never be approved. No father would allow his daughter to mingle with a man before marriage, even if that man was her soon-to-be son-in-law.

Shivaji wished to tell Vyjanti how attractive she was, how fortunate he felt to have met her, and how excited he was to share his life with her. Mr. Iyer politely walked Shivaji and his family to the front of the house. Muthuraman summoned the bullock cart driver. The driver and his massive, white-colored bulls came storming down the trail that led to the house.

Shivaji collected whatever courage remained in him and looked over his shoulder. There was no sign of Vyjanti near the door. Shivaji felt disheartened. He had expected Vyjanti to be there, seeing him off.

"She may not feel what I feel for her. I hope she is not being forced to marry," Shivaji said to himself.

After Shivaji and his family members seated themselves in the cart, the driver once again communicated with his bulls in an unfamiliar language produced with his tongue. Once the beasts received the peculiar sound, they began to move their powerful legs.

As the cart pulled away, Shivaji turned around for the last time. He saw the respectable Mr. Iyer waving his hand rapidly to bid farewell. Standing by the front door was Mrs. Iyer, most of her face covered by her long scarf. As the driver warned his animals that the cart would soon be moving downhill, Shivaji noticed a spot of yellow in the midst of boundless greenery. In the backyard, positioned next to a jasmine tree that bore an army of snow-white flowers, was Vyjanti. Though she was far away, Shivaji felt her eyes on him. A wave of relief calmed his restless mind. He started to believe that she might like him after all.

"Why else would she be there to see her future husband depart?" thought Shivaji.

During the ride back home, Shivaji kept thinking of Vyjanti. What she might want, what she might need, what she might like, what she might dislike, what she might think of him, what she might think of his parents—Shivaji's brain was crowded with all kinds of thoughts.

"She seems to be fond of flowers, especially jasmine," Shivaji said under his breath. "I have seen lines of jasmine trees planted in the fields of the village. I breathed in the sweet fragrance of jasmine within the household. I noticed a bundle of jasmine flowers placed in Vyjanti's hair. And I have seen a blossoming jasmine tree in the backyard where Vyjanti stood. Jasmine, jasmine, jasmine... is there some kind of meaning behind this plant?" Shivaji asked himself.

Shivaji's mother noticed that her son was deep in thought. "What are you thinking about? Or should I ask, who are you thinking about?"

"I will plant a jasmine tree in our compound."

"Why?"

"I must gift it to Vyjanti as a welcoming present."

Shivaji's mother could not resist laughing. "To nurture a tree requires a lot of time and effort."

"Not to worry, Amma. I will put in the time and effort. I'll wait for the day she arrives as my newly wedded wife to first see and then understand how much her husband..." Shivaji almost forgot that he was talking to his mother.

THE 26TH DAY

The prolonged night made Shivaji impatient. His eyes were fixated on the skies, waiting for the first rays of the sun. He then released a loud sigh, heavy with exhaustion. He was aware that soon the deck crew leader would command the indentured labourers to rise.

"Why are you up so early?" asked Vyjanti.

Shivaji was startled by Vyjanti's suddenly sharp voice.

"And why do you look so tired?"

Shivaji turned to face his wife.

"Oh Deva, look at your eyes. They are so red."

Shivaji gulped. His brain needed to process something—anything—suitable to reply.

Vyjanti brushed aside the kurta, which she had used as a blanket, to lift her torso. She remained seated on the deck as she gathered her loose strands of hair. Shivaji's attention moved to Vyjanti's delicate hands, which effortlessly twisted her hair into a neat bun. Vyjanti examined her husband's drained eyes.

"Did you sleep last night?"

"Yes, I did. But why do you ask?"

"It's your eyes. They look like they are fighting to stay awake."

"I did sleep. I have risen early to watch over you. From now on, every day I will rise before you."

"That is unnecessary. Trust me, I will be fine."

Shivaji wanted to respond but held himself back.

"If you have no fears, if you are not distressed, then why did you suffer in your dream last night?" Shivaji wished to ask his wife, but hesitated. If he probed, Vyjanti's doubt about him staying awake all night would unravel. Shivaji knew that Vyjanti's dream was troubling, but he did not know its cause. It bothered him not knowing what was troubling her.

Soon, Karthik came running into Vyjanti's arms for his regular morning visit. Since the child had boarded the vessel, he made it his duty to reveal his bright, cheerful face to Vyjanti every day. Vyjanti always had new stories to tell, new games to play, and new questions to answer. With Karthik, she also became playful and carefree. Shivaji often watched the child and his wife share a delightful chemistry. The image of them bonding calmed his senses.

As Vyjanti and Karthik interacted, Shivaji drifted into a world of imagination. In this fantasy, he observed his wife rocking an infant in her arms. In the bedroom of the Nair household, Vyjanti sings a lullaby to their newborn daughter. Hoping the child would soon fall asleep, Vyjanti's eyes briefly met Shivaji's, beckoning him to come closer. The newborn, sensing that her mother had ignored her, protested with an emotional cry for attention. Surprised by the child's outburst, Vyjanti asked her husband to sing along with her. Unable to remember the lullaby's words, Shivaji hesitated.

"Just follow my lead," Vyjanti said to her husband.

And then, the fantasy was interrupted by Karthik. After chatting with his athai, the child leapt onto Shivaji's lap. But this time, Karthik was serious; he meant business.

"Mama, you know what happened?"

"What happened?" Shivaji asked the minor, who pouted in dismay.

"Appa scolded me. Since you are his childhood friend, it is best if you talk to him."

"Talk to him about..."

"Well, you must tell him not to scold me, especially not in front of other children. It is really embarrassing," said Karthik, with a few tears brimming in his eyes, showing that Venkatesh had done wrong.

"Karthik, can I ask why you got scolded?"

"It was not my fault. Yesterday, the other kids and I were bored. So we decided to have some fun. My friends Anna, Raju, Gulu, Feroz, and I were kicking tin plates from here to there, as if they were balls. But Appa did not like the idea of using the plates this way. So he gave me a stern lecture in front of all my friends. Appa was upset with me for treating our utensils as toys. He took away our ball—I mean, our tin plate," said Karthik, his voice trailing in a soft whimper.

Shivaji fought to suppress a smile. Before the failure to conceal it was apparent, Shivaji consoled the child: "Don't worry, Karthik. I will talk to your father about this matter."

"Will you scold him for me?"

"Yes, I will. He will receive an earful."

The pleased child rose from Shivaji's lap and returned to his attai. Then unexpectedly, Shivaji heard a splash. He felt a sudden jolt of panic, imagining someone had fallen into the endless ocean, never to be seen again. He turned around to see Vyjanti—there she was, standing on the edge of the deck, perilously close to the water. The lone barrier separating her from the waves was the timber railing.

"Vyjanti, come back!" shouted Shivaji.

"Oh Deva, you will never believe what I saw," replied Vyjanti, rushing toward her husband, brimming with excitement. Shivaji rose to his feet, hoping she had seen the first glimpse of the islands.

"I saw a giant fish," said Vyjanti, gasping for breath.

Shivaji was left speechless. He began to think his wife might have lost her mind.

"What did you see?" Shivaji asked, as if he hadn't heard her properly the first time.

"A giant fish! I saw a giant fish. It erupted from the ocean, leaping high into the air."

"Then what happened?"

"Just as it came up, it went down. It plunged back into the ocean."

"Vyjanti, are you sure?" Shivaji paused. "Are you sure you are not imagining things?"

"Yes, I am sure. Please, believe me. Did you not hear a splash in the water?"

"Yes, I did."

"Well, that was the fish. I have never seen anything like it before. It was a sea creature with dusky grey on its back and pure white on its belly. Its nose was shaped like a bottle—can you believe that? It had tiny, almost unnoticeable eyes. Its skin shimmered under the sun. What a beautiful animal."

"Attai, did it have a tail?" asked Karthik, completely engrossed by Vyjanti's vivid description of the creature.

For a moment, Shivaji had forgotten that the child was still present. He knew that this conversation would stretch on for hours due to Karthik's fascination with animals.

"Yes, it had a tail. Umm, or was it its legs?" replied Vyjanti, placing her index finger to her lips. "Actually, now that I think of it, it had small feet. You know what? On its back, it had arms. No, no, no, it had two small hands under its belly. Wait, that can't be," Vyjanti continued, trying to make sense of the animal's extraordinary form.

A small crowd, including Venkatesh and Lachmiaya, gathered around Vyjanti to hear about the mysterious creature in the ocean. The indentured labourers were so absorbed in her story that they skipped their regular morning visit to the head. Each person in the group had at least one question about the enigmatic mammal.

As for Shivaji, he had no interest in the fish at all. He did not care whether it was big or small, short or tall, white or black, grey or blue, smart or stupid, or known or unknown. He decided to distance himself from the conversation by closing his eyes for a short while. Not more than fifteen minutes later, Shivaji was awakened by screams, signaling it was time to form lines for the morning breakfast handout.

As usual, the servings of lentil and rice covered the tin plates. Facial expressions of disgust were evident, but it was of no use. The British seafarers offered nothing other than khichdi and dog biscuits. Some Indian passengers had become accustomed to the common dish. For them, anything was better than the repulsive dog biscuits.

Shivaji reminded himself to be vigilant while consuming the food, standing in line to wash utensils, scrubbing the wooden floors, and visiting the head. He was prepared for an Englishman to attack from behind or interrupt him mid-task. He even tasted the khichdi from Vyjanti's plate before she could, suspecting the British might poison it.

Later that night, for the first time since boarding Ship Elbe, Vyjanti spoke of her in-laws.

"I miss amma, appa, and my sisters-in-law. I hope they are well."

"I am sure they are fine, Vyjanti. Appa is most likely busy with his pottery. He is probably the same with or without us. The only difference is that now he doesn't get to scold or lecture me anymore. He must surely miss that," said Shivaji, hoping his words would soothe her.

"What about amma?"

"Amma is probably busy with cooking and cleaning. I am certain she has no time for knitting because now she has to do your share of the work too."

Vyjanti pouted. "You are making me feel bad."

"Sorry, Vyjanti. I did not mean that. I am sure amma is fine. She has capable daughters to assist with daily chores. Don't worry about her."

"Yes, that is true. Amma has capable daughters. I miss them dearly. Five years from today, they will have grown up. I cannot wait to see them."

Shivaji burst out laughing. "We haven't even arrived in Fiji, and you're talking about five years from now?"

"Yes, I am. Is that a problem?" replied Vyjanti, slightly offended by Shivaji's laughter. "Oh Deva, how will these five years pass? Time is moving at a snail's pace. When will we set foot on the islands?"

"Stay calm. Have patience. We'll be there soon. I have been trying to count the days since Elbe set sail. I believe we have another seventeen or eighteen days to travel."

"Oh Deva, that is so much to bear," said Vyjanti, not realizing that her tone had escalated.

Shivaji rested his index finger on his lips, signaling Vyjanti to keep quiet. "You have to speak softly. We don't want to awaken the sleepers."

To show she understood, Vyjanti nodded as she lay beside Shivaji on the deck.

"Vyjanti, do you not think of your parents?"

"What kind of question is that? Of course, I do," she replied loudly.

"Ssshhhhh... Please, Vyjanti!"

"Sorry, I forgot. Yes, I do think about them every day. I still regret not being able to see them before leaving," Vyjanti softly admitted.

"Why do you say that? It is not like you will never see them again. These next five years will pass quickly. Now, erase all those thoughts from your mind and rest your eyes," Shivaji advised gently.

Vyjanti yawned. "Yes, I think you are right. Though I must say, your eyes reveal that you have not slept for days."

Shivaji responded hastily, "I have slept. And I will sleep tonight as well."

Vyjanti looked deep into her husband's eyes. Apart from the tiredness, she saw his past, present, and future.

"If it were not for you, Deva, my life would have been irrelevant," she whispered. With those words, Vyjanti closed her eyes, slipping into a peaceful slumber. Her face was a serene portrait, reassuring Shivaji that there were no troubles in her mind.

Staring at his wife's lovely features, Shivaji felt a deep sense of ease. For a second, he realized there was no need to protect her. In that same moment, he decided to abandon his protective vigilance. And then, a second later, he surrendered to sleep himself.

A wave of loud sounds assaulted Shivaji's ears. The piercing cries were so intense that they forced him to emerge from his deep sleep. He rubbed the slack and fatigue from his eyes. Shivaji heard bodies shift and then footsteps crunching against the wooden floor. Another cry erupted, only to be silenced seconds later. Shivaji scanned the darkness for the source of the commotion. By now, Vyjanti should have reacted to the situation, he thought. He looked down beside him. There was no sign of her. Anxiety rooted itself deep in the pit of his stomach. He began to panic.

"Where is she? Where is my wife?" Shivaji muttered to himself.

Quickly, he rose to his feet and called for her, unaware that his shouts would awaken both the Indian passengers and British seafarers.

"Vyjanti!" he yelled, desperation shaking his voice.

Finally, a response came.

"Deva! Help! Please, help me!"

Shivaji followed the cries with eyes sharpened by dread. His heart nearly stopped when he witnessed five members of the deck crew manhandling Vyjanti. He did not know why, nor for how long, but he knew he had to stop them. Shivaji ran as fast as he could, leaping over the motionless bodies that littered the deck. For the first time in his life, he believed that his fellow Indians were powerless. Yet, with respect, he avoided stepping on any of the fallen.

His mind raced. There was no time to understand why this was happening, nor to plan his next move. As he sped across the deck, the old timber beneath him creaked ominously. He caught a glimpse of Vyjanti, dragged toward the staircase leading to the upper deck. Her feet scraped the floor helplessly, and her sari was disheveled. Her crucial scarf, which concealed her chest, had been ripped away, leaving her in only a short blouse. The partial exposure forced her to feel ashamed and vulnerable. She could not decide whether to cover herself or fight for escape.

Witnessing the atrocity, Shivaji pushed his body harder. Then, in a flash, he felt a violent impact. His body collapsed, sliding eight feet across the deck as his face kissed the jagged timber. Blood streamed down the right side of his face. Vyjanti's shrieks became more excruciating, her terror palpable.

She bit, scratched, kicked, and spat, but her efforts were futile. The deck crew were relentless, ordered to complete their task without mercy, and anyone who intervened would be eliminated.

Shivaji tasted blood for the first time. The fall had knocked the wind from him. For a few seconds, he forgot where he was, what he was doing. His mind began to play cruel tricks.

"Deva... I ask for your help. Get up, please get up," Vyjanti pleaded, tears streaming.

Shivaji regained his senses and forced himself upright. Pain radiated from his left leg, but there was no time to assess it. Hideously, he limped toward Vyjanti.

From behind, Chief Officer Anderson appeared, baton in hand. Without mercy, he struck Shivaji on the back of his head. Once again, Shivaji fell to the deck. Anderson targeted his knee first, then his skull, deriving cruel pleasure from assaulting the one man among four hundred passengers who might one day resist British rule.

Vyjanti witnessed the blow to her husband and twisted frantically, struggling against the tight grips that limited her movement. She could do nothing but call out for Shivaji, for her brother, for help. Her desperate cries went unheard.

Shivaji's vision wavered, flickering between darkness and blurred figures. An agonizing monotone reverberated in his head. It was Vyjanti's voice that stirred his spirit. With the remaining strength in his arms, he crawled toward her.

Anderson taunted him mercilessly. "You want to save your wife? Then move, you arsehole. Come on, move!"

The baton fell repeatedly on Shivaji, the sound of wood against flesh echoing across the deck. The indentured labourers remained motionless, paralyzed with fear. Venkatesh watched helplessly, torn between protecting his friends and saving his wife and child.

"You will not leave Karthik and me. If something happens to you, how will we survive?" Lachmaiya whispered to her husband, placing a stone against her chest. She knew if Venkatesh left to rescue Shivaji and Vyjanti, he might never return. Karthik held his father's hand expressionless, and Venkatesh stared into the boy's eyes, realizing the danger his friends faced.

Shivaji endured blow after blow. Anderson roared with each strike, ensuring every Indian on board knew who was in control. Bruises swelled, blood streamed from his forehead to his chin, and his upper body turned an angry red. Finally, Anderson, exhausted, huffed and released the baton, kicking Shivaji's battered body.

"This is what happens to a person who revolts," Anderson sneered, chuckling. "I will not kill you, but I will let you suffer. Watch how the British, whom you despise, violate your wife." He spat on Shivaji's bloodied face before vanishing into the shadows.

Vyjanti's eyes were covered by the enormous hands of an Englishman, leaving her unable to see the aftermath. Shivaji did not cry out, knowing that any sound would torment her further. Lying on the deck, only his fingers functional, he watched helplessly as five merciless seafarers dragged Vyjanti toward the halfway point of the staircase, still under their control.

Vyjanti did not give up, would never give up. There was no way she would fall victim to an Englishman's lustful intentions. She had a fierce determination that gave the British seafarers much trouble. Vyjanti clamped her teeth down hard on the palm of one of the men. Releasing a loud shriek, the Englishman staggered back, freeing her face. At last, Vyjanti could clearly see her husband's battered form. Observing Shivaji's severe condition, her heart settled slightly, though worry still gnawed at her.

In pain and shock, the Englishman nursed his hand while sitting on the steps of the staircase. Seeing that Vyjanti had escaped his mighty grasp, the remaining English seamen lunged toward her. The men moved like a pack of hyenas, snarling and closing in on their prey.

Vyjanti called for her brother. "Anna, please help us!" Her voice grew hoarse from screaming repeatedly, but she did not stop. Her cries intensified as the culprits closed in. Shivaji recognized his wife's voice, but he lacked the strength to respond. Blood gushed from his mouth whenever he tried to speak. Shivaji had no idea which bones were broken or which muscles torn. He felt as if his entire body were paralyzed.

Venkatesh consoled his wife and child. He and his family heard Vyjanti begging him to rescue her from this peril.

"I must go. I am sorry, Lachmaiya. I can no longer ignore Vyjanti. I would be committing a sin by standing idle."

Lachmaiya whimpered. She understood he was right, but a wife did not want to let her husband face such danger. "Please don't leave us. Karthik needs a father."

"No one is rising. Shivaji and his wife need my help. If something happens to me, please take care of Karthik."

Before Lachmaiya could respond, Venkatesh broke free from the prison of hesitation. His thin legs propelled him forward toward the standing crew members. Vyjanti's eyes locked onto the four men who were about to seize her.

"Come on, don't be afraid. Our master expects your arrival," one of the deck crew members sneered.

"Why are you downstairs? Let's go upstairs. Trust me, you'll be satisfied," said another, leering at Vyjanti's cleavage.

The culprits reached out to grab and grope her. After descending the staircase, Vyjanti could not evade them completely. The Englishman whose palm had been bitten was now on his feet, ready to seek revenge.

In the nick of time, Venkatesh arrived waving his fists defiantly. He expected the deck crew members to step back, but they did not. Instead, their hands reached for their waists, pulling out fourteen-inch wooden batons. The Englishmen were startled by the audacity of an Indian daring to intervene.

"Run, Vyjanti!" Venkatesh shouted, his voice cracking with urgency.

The Englishmen turned their focus to Venkatesh, cornering him with no possible escape. From the corner of his eyes, he saw Vyjanti pacing toward him.

"Don't worry about me. Save yourself, Vyjanti," he called out.

The British seafarers did not hesitate to mercilessly beat the victim down. Their hand motions were faster than the speed of lightning. Venkatesh faced one blow after another. However, it was the blow to his stomach that made him fall to his knees. Wisely, he protected his head with his hands as the Englishmen continued with the unending punishment. Venkatesh tightened his lips, ensuring he did not cry out in pain. He did not want his son to know that his father was suffering. Lachmaiya kept her eyes shut with Karthik held firmly against her chest. She did not dare to peer at the darkness of their cruelty. She was in a trance in which she recited the name of Lord Vishnu continuously. Lachmaiya asked the God of protection to salvage her husband from the hands of the British seafarers.

"Oh Deva, what have they done to you? Talk to me, Deva. Please talk to me." Vyjanti desperately waited for her husband to respond. Shivaji opened his eyes. Vyjanti noticed water emerge from Shivaji's eyes and sail towards his temple. "Don't worry, nothing will happen to you. You will be fine. Anna has ascended. He will help us," said Vyjanti, trying to lift her husband's shattered spirit.

Shivaji tried to utter something, but instead of words blood spilled from his mouth. Vyjanti became hysterical. She never imagined seeing her husband in such a dreadful state. Vyjanti sobbed as her husband coughed up blood. With immense care, she moved Shivaji's body to the side, ensuring he did not choke on the blood. "Deva, take me, not him," said Vyjanti while she closed her lids to offer her prayers to Lord Shiva. As she folded her hands to the one above, the devils below moved towards her. The deck crew members were finished with Venkatesh, leaving him unconscious on the floor. Venkatesh was still alive because the Englishmen knew that it was more important to divert their attention back onto Vyjanti.

She was the one that the master had chosen. She was the one that the master had his eyes on for days. She was the one that the master wanted in his bed. Vyjanti felt as though she had eyes on the back of her head. She heard the footsteps get closer and closer. Vyjanti wished that she had a weapon of some kind in her hands at the moment. With nowhere to run or hide, she took a glance at her last hope. She looked at her motionless brother who lay on the deck. Tears rolled down her face. By now she did not know how many of her teardrops had hit the floor. For a moment, she pictured the Indian wife who had surrendered to the white men and their evil acts. She pictured the woman not fighting to protect her body from the forced sexual assault. The frightful image sent chills up her spine.

The British seafarers whispered amongst one another. Vyjanti listened to the words that no one believed she could interpret. But she knew that the five deck crew members were discussing a plan to surround her from all corners. Shivaji's vision was blurred, but he was capable of sighting the leather boots of the Englishmen who were inches apart from his wife. With his hands shivering uncontrollably, Shivaji managed to use his index finger to point at the sinners on the move.

And then, Vyjanti released a loud shriek. The deck crew member, who Vyjanti bit, attained his revenge by yanking the defenceless woman by her long tresses. The other deck crew members whistled and cheered as they viewed one of their men act barbarically. Shivaji felt useless. In front of his eyes, the Englishmen were putting their hands on his wife and he could not stop them.

Vyjanti knew that she could not let this happen. "This must be reversed. There must be a way out of this," she kept telling herself. Her desperate calls for help seemed pointless; therefore she put her mouth to rest. Even when the British seafarer was dragging her by the hair, Vyjanti did not feel any pain. It was as if God had descended on earth to grant her supreme powers to tolerate the suffering.

As the Englishman released the hair to control the upper portion of Vyjanti's body, she briskly rose to her feet. Astonished by her sudden movements, the deck crew member took a few steps back. Vyjanti extended her fragile arms towards her attacker. Her palms connected with his abdomen, knocking him down onto the staircase. The Englishman landed on the staircase with his back colliding against the edge of the steps. Vyjanti felt the hands of the Englishmen graze her uncovered waist. She hurried towards the railing without looking back to see how far or how close behind the British seafarers were.

Moving as fast as her feet could, Vyjanti's brain repeated images of the mother and son who committed suicide. Vyjanti knew that if she was captured by the English seamen her life would be ruined. She would not be able to show her face to Shivaji and others from her village again.

"I'd rather kill myself than let Captain Sanders tarnish my image, extinguish my dignity and obliterate my soul. He will not be able to seize my body which is for my husband and my husband only. Never will I let this happen," Vyjanti said under her breath as she placed her hands on the wooden railing.

Although Shivaji did have the ability to look and listen, he did not have the ability to properly move. So when he perceived his wife rushing from the staircase to the barriers, he struggled to use every bone and muscle in his body to move forward. An unbroken Shivaji would have outraced the Englishmen who started to inch closer towards his wife. While the broken Shivaji crawled forward, using his bloodied limbs. He knew exactly what his wife was thinking. Vyjanti was to end her life; a decision she made without consulting her husband.

For Shivaji, it was a must for him to catch her attention. He managed to unleash a raucous call for his wife through the boundless amount of gore that covered his mouth. "Vyjanti," yelled Shivaji again. His voice did not have the robust essence it used to have. Vyjanti finally looked over her shoulder, not because she heard Shivaji's voice, but to observe how far or close the deck crew members were from her.

She beheld the animals nearing with their claws ready to dig into her flesh. She then placed her eyes on Shivaji who proceeded towards her at a slow pace. Forcing his arms and legs not to submit, Shivaji moved forward.

"Oh Deva, please forgive me," Vyjanti said under her breath.

Shivaji helplessly watched his wife lift her body over the railing. For a second, she balanced herself on the edge of the barrier. She then launched herself backwards into the void. Within a flash of a second, she was gone. Shivaji released a heart-wrenching outcry, loud enough to resonate in the ears of every passenger on board. He uttered his wife's name from his mouth. The husband cried for the person he loved the most. He shed tears of blood. He felt as if his heart shattered into a million pieces, never to be mended again.

Shivaji did not know which emotion to grasp to express. Did he feel enmity, or did he feel misery? He did not know. Shivaji stretched out his right arm, wishing to prevent Vyjanti from falling into the devouring waters of the Pacific.

"Hold on, Vyjanti. Please take my hand. I will not lose you. Never will I let you go," said Shivaji, his mind frenzied and incoherent. Shivaji acted as if he were mad. For the first time in his life, Shivaji did not have control over his mind. Over and over again, he called for his wife. He believed that she would respond, but the only sounds to be heard were the murmurs and commands of the British seafarers.

The Englishmen communicated amongst themselves. Their prey had escaped, which meant there was much explaining to do. The Englishmen reluctantly proceeded to the upper level to inform their master that he would have to wait for another night to fulfill his sexual needs. The indentured labourers, who lay flat on their stomachs with their faces buried in the deck, heard the commotion but could not see the tragic incident unfold. Shivaji wailed on the top of his lungs for every Indian passenger to hear the upsetting sounds of mourning. What he felt, if not already, would be felt by every Indian who had accepted the role of an indentured labourer, thought Shivaji.

"You will all pay for this," roared Shivaji. Whether his message was for the people of his kind or the people who despised his kind, Captain Sanders did not like it. All the high-pitched shouting and wailing kept him from resting. He left his cabin to maintain order. On his way, he crossed paths with the five deck crew members who hung their heads low in shame.

"Why is there so much commotion?" Captain Sanders asked his men.

The English seamen did not dare look into the commander's eyes.

"What is the matter? Are you all deaf? Can't you hear the words coming from my mouth?"

One of the deck crew members then described how the Indian woman had escaped from them, only to fall to her supposed death. The Englishman was in the middle of explaining in detail how Vyjanti climbed over the barrier when unexpectedly Captain Sanders lifted his hand and slapped the subordinate across the face.

"You men are a disgrace to the colonial system, power, and rule." Before he could release more anger on the deck crew members, his attention was drawn to the consistent threats made by Shivaji. After seeing his wife plunge to her tragic death, he still did not believe she was gone. For him, the fact that Vyjanti took her own life did not register.

Deep within him, Shivaji felt as if she was somewhere on the deck, waiting for him to recover from his injuries. He was on the verge of erasing the past and imagining a new scenario in which Vyjanti existed.

"Where is she? Where is my wife? If you don't unveil where she is, you will regret it. You talk about sins, wrongdoings, bad deeds—what is the use of that? I say that you have sinned. You must, I say you must, return her to me. If you cannot do that, there is no use for me to believe in you."

Shivaji's incomprehensible words and frantic behaviour were heard by everyone on board, but no one understood who it was intended for. The chief officer did not have any sympathy for Shivaji. He stepped on the hand of the delirious husband, now a widower. Shivaji battled the torture by not releasing an outcry. His bold defiance disturbed Anderson, who pushed down on the hand with even more force using his boots. The chief officer hungered to hear the victim scream in pain.

But Shivaji did not give in. Anderson felt as if the measly Indian was outlasting him in the present battle. With that in mind, he clasped the baton immediately. With much force, the lethal weapon struck Shivaji's head. Numbness invaded his brain. This time, Anderson's blow resulted in complete loss of consciousness. Unluckily for Shivaji, the blackout persisted. He would not rise as a protective husband or resolute insurgent for a while.

THE 30TH DAY

At the speed of light, diving headfirst towards the still currents of the miserable ocean was a living human being. The wind crashed against her pale face. Her draped sari began to unravel. Every strand of hair on her scalp loosened under the effects of the uncontrollable motion. Her arms and legs became lifeless, bidding farewell to gravity. The pressure of the air did not let her inhale or exhale. As she traveled from warm to cold, dry to wet and life to death, Vyjanti beheld the covering of the ocean. Her heart pulsated, her ears ached and her nostrils were blocked. At last, Vyjanti pierced the walls of the ocean. The powerful impact of the black waters versus the defenceless head left Vyjanti senseless. Her flesh ripped, limbs shattered, lungs flooded and heart ceased. Vyjanti had emancipated herself from defilement and servitude.

"Vyjanti!" cried Shivaji as he left the darkness of ignorance to enter into the darkness of actuality. He listened to his voice echo against the walls. The walls surrounding the limited area refused to let light enter. Shivaji sat with his back leaning on the solid blockade that had him caged like an animal. He shifted his eyes from one side to another, wanting to perceive an image of something, anything. Unable to see his own hands, he felt the mixture of anger and frustration inside him. Thus, he incessantly released ear-splitting cries. The abrasive uproar did not help. The high-pitched sounds bounced off the walls and landed directly in his ears, causing the drums to vibrate with force. Shivaji was not able to move his legs due to the limited space provided to him. His limbs ached because he had not moved a muscle for over three days. Shivaji tried to lift himself, but there was no strength in his arms and feet. He then felt his stomach grumble. The soreness that was gathered in the pit of his stomach meant that he had not eaten for days. From time to time, Shivaji raised the torn sleeves of his kurta to cover his nose. An offensive stench dominated the miniature area. Following his senses, Shivaji sniffed his dhoti. When he learned that he had urinated on his clothes, Shivaji did not feel embarrassed. He did not know when he did it, but if he had to do it again, he would do the same as before. There was practically no space to move in the enclosure; therefore, he had no other choice but to urinate on his attire. Perplexed by the situation he was in, Shivaji tried hard to bring the pieces together. Where was he? Why was he there? Was it all a dream? As soon as he endeavoured to assimilate the situation he was in, his brain started throbbing excessively. Within seconds, he had no choice but to release the train of thought that may have led to an understanding of his position. He swallowed hard, wanting to moisten his dry throat with as much saliva as possible. Trying to provide some comfort to his throat, Shivaji came up with an idea. To assure himself that he was not in the middle of a dream, Shivaji smacked himself across the face many times. As he did that, he felt the lengthy growth of his beard. He then felt both of his hands, ensuring all his fingers were intact. One hand at a time, he felt his arms in search of cuts and tears. There were no cuts or tears but many sensitive bumps along the way. His hands moved down to his knees and shins. Shivaji regretted placing his fingers on his shin. The gentle touch led to intolerable pain. He finally understood the reason why he struggled to maneuver his right leg. Shivaji remembered that Chief Officer Anderson had severely damaged it with his baton. While his fingers searched for more injuries, he felt dried stains of blood on most parts of his body. Eventually, he came across his ribs which seemed to be more noticeable than before. The bones of the rib cage were easily felt by his fingers despite the top layer of skin. With that in mind, Shivaji realized that he had been kept in this location for more than a few days. The empty stomach, visible ribs, numb limbs, cracked lips, thirsty throat, irritant eyes, pounding head and aching heart compelled Shivaji to believe in past lives. "Somewhere before this life there was another life in which I must have made others fret, weep, endure and suffer. I must have taken a life; that is why God has taken mine. He has taken Vyjanti from me. Vyjanti, my beloved wife, I don't exist without you," Shivaji said to himself while tilting his head back and resting his eyes on the ceiling of the prison.

Shivaji passed the day with involuntary sessions of unconsciousness. The darkness, in which he spent hours, minutes and seconds, did not segregate night and day. In 'the hole' a person remained in complete solitude, oblivious to his or her surroundings. Shivaji was not aware of where he was other than the fact that he was still on Ship Elbe. Placing his ears against the wooden floor, he was able to hear the tides of the diabolical ocean that consumed his wife. He then embraced the walls that held him captive. He listened for a sound or a voice. In return, he attained nothing but silence. Whenever Shivaji remained conscious, he thought about Vyjanti. And whenever he thought about Vyjanti, he blamed himself for her death. The thought of her running to the barrier, uplifting herself onto the ledge of the barrier, balancing herself until the body was steady, looking at him for the last time and then letting go of the railing haunted Shivaji. There were moments when he wailed loud, but the dense walls of 'the hole' forbade his voice from traveling into the ears of the passengers on board. Sometimes, he curled up into a ball, letting his tears descend onto his face as he pictured his wife. Then, at times, he searched the blackness, desperate to catch a glimpse or a reflection of Vyjanti. Deep within, he did not want to accept reality. He kept telling himself that sooner or later she would whisper a few lines of encouragement in his ear. He patiently waited for Vyjanti to tenderly brush her fingers against his hand. Shivaji kept his eyes wet, hoping that soon his wife would come to dry them with the corners of her scarf. With no results to his searching and waiting, Shivaji became maniacal. Throughout the night, Shivaji furiously pounded the walls until his fists became unresponsive. With the absurd stint of self-inflicting pain, he unleashed blatant cries wishing that someone could understand his misery. Shivaji wanted someone, anyone, to notice that he had finally submitted to reality, that he had finally accepted the truth.

THE 31ST DAY

There was no trace of time. Shivaji was unable to keep track of the hours and minutes spent in the cubicle. The eerie silence made him feel as if he had been in 'the hole' for a lifetime. Listening to the cries of his aching stomach, Shivaji knew that if he did not receive food, he would soon die of hunger. Unexpectedly, he burst into laughter. With the thought of death revolving in his mind, he felt relieved. The truth was that he did not want to live anymore. His life meant nothing to him after the death of his wife. He did not care if he lost his life due to starvation. He would not retaliate if the British seafarers entered 'the hole' and beat him until the last breath left his body. He would not complain if the Englishmen were to hang him to death, feed him poison or toss him over the barriers.

"I ask them to eliminate my presence from this world. If they want to kill me, then kill me. Puncture my heart, slice my throat, cease my breathing, smash my brains in—they can do as they please. But if they ask me to kill myself, that I will not do. I will not take my own life. Vyjanti, my dear wife, what you did is sinful. To commit suicide is immoral. You believed in God, then why? Why did you alter the destiny God had set for you? He created a path for you to travel on, but instead you chose to proceed on a different route. Why did you leave? Did you not think of me, your husband? Answer me, Vyjanti?" Shivaji vented to the unresponsive walls.

The walls of the prison did not have answers or explanations to his questions. When Shivaji realized that he was talking to an obstruction and not a human, he felt ashamed of himself for the strange behaviour he had displayed. What was happening was not supposed to happen. Unexpected mood swings, not being able to remember, the confusion between fantasy and reality, the inability to suspend imagination, and talking to oneself were the major side effects Shivaji had inherited from 'the hole'. It was as if 'the hole' was taking over his brain. Once he regained his normal self, Shivaji punished himself for letting the dungeon control his soul. Sometimes he bruised his knuckles, and other times he tore his forehead by constantly hitting the rock-hard walls. Shivaji was in an ongoing battle with the combative prison in which he resided.

Someone was nearby. The footsteps became apparent. Shivaji launched himself against the walls in front of him. He placed his ears firmly against the walls, only to confirm that the sounds of the footsteps he heard were indeed real. Having heard no sounds of movement for days, except for his own, made him uneasy. He feared being released. He did not want the Englishmen to enter 'the hole' only to exit with him in their hands. Instead of being set free, he preferred to rot to death in the lifeless prison. As the footsteps became louder, Shivaji hurried to his normal position with his back leaning against the wall. Since he was unable to release his bruised knuckles on the prison door, Shivaji thought of a different idea. To force the unidentified person to retreat, with his usable left leg, Shivaji kicked the walls from which loud sounds erupted. Hopeful that the sounds would scare the person off, he began to kick with more force.

"Go away! Don't come near me. I am not going anywhere. You cannot take me alive. Only return when there is no life in this body."

"Stop this nonsense, I am here to see if you are still breathing," emerged a manly voice from beyond the walls. The words were in Hindi, thick with a deep British accent, which left Shivaji puzzled. The voice was never heard on Ship Elbe before. It did not belong to any of the British seafarers that Shivaji had encountered since he came aboard. The unfamiliar voice managed to stop his leg and foot.

"Leave me alone. Come back when I die," replied Shivaji in Hindi. Shivaji noticed that when he spoke in Hindi, it was not as coherent as his Tamil. Most of the South Indians on board were able to understand Hindi but not able to speak it proficiently. Shivaji and Venkatesh were the few Tamilians on board who had attended school, and for that reason, both had the ability to communicate in various languages to an acceptable degree.

"Sorry, but my profession is against death. I don't promote death; I steer people away from it. I don't benefit from lifeless coolies; I benefit from healthy coolies, which is the main reason why I am here with a plate of nourishment for you to consume. I know you must be very hungry. You have probably not eaten for several days."

"Yes, I have not eaten for days. But I wish not to gratify my stomach. The expedition, the ship, the British seafarers, the Indians on board, the mighty God above—every-one—you all have taken Vyjanti away. You're against death? Is that so? Then where were you when my wife was abducted? Where were you when she was manhandled by the deck crew members? Where were you when she was compelled to leap over the railings? You were not there."

"Coolie, I am sorry for your loss. There was not much I could do. I'm practically anonymous to the commanders on this ship. I don't take part in the things they do. Simply, the lives of the coolies on board play a significant role in my life. You staying alive benefits me. My pay is based on the number of healthy bodies on Ship Elbe. Hale and hearty coolies mean pockets full of shilling," replied the faceless person in his raucous voice.

"I don't even have to look at you with my eyes to see what color your skin is. You whites are greedy. You have greed for power, status, fortune, and fame. The British want it all, and they are willing to go to any extent, not to achieve it, but to steal it." Shivaji began to pick up from where he had left off. Gradually, he started to reform. The unstable state he was in eased. Once again, Shivaji was talking like a revolutionary.

"A few of the deck crew members have told me about your wife. I know how you feel; I understand your pain. I once had a wife, just like you did. Now that she is gone, I have four children at home that I must feed. The children rely on me, and it is my responsibility to look after them—just like it is my duty to cure the Indians on deck from all kinds of maladies. Call me greedy, call me selfish, call me whatever name you want."

The voice of this unknown person started to develop emotion. Shivaji knew that the person behind the obstruction was an Englishman. What surprised him was that he was an Englishman who had feelings. He was the first Englishman to share his own story with him. For once, Shivaji realized that not all white men were oppressors.

As the conversation came to a halt, the British male slid open the rectangular opening at the bottom of the invisible door. He then carefully moved a tin plate full of khichdi and a tin cup full of water into 'the hole'. At first, Shivaji was blinded by the harsh light of the evening. He felt as if someone had smeared his eyes with red chillies. Shivaji screamed at the unknown person to close the opening immediately. The Englishman obeyed. The quick response from him left Shivaji appeased. Never before had a white man listened to his command, he thought.

"Eat up, coolie! Your stomach will be thankful after you devour the food."

"I am not going to eat anything," replied the stubborn Shivaji.

"Well then, I have completed my duty. It is your choice if you want to live or die. Before parting, I must say that in the last several days I have witnessed children suffering from malnutrition. These children are brought to my private cabin only when things get severe.

When a child vomits after eating or drinking, that is when I consider it to be disastrous. Vomiting and diarrhea are lethal punishers that have combined to destroy the lives of these children."

Shivaji kept his eyes closed as he imagined innocent children attempting to endure the torture that had descended upon them.

"Look at them and then look at yourself. Place yourself in their shoes. Can you? These children are not well, yet they still want to see tomorrow. You are well, but you don't want to see tomorrow. These children want to live despite suffering from the harmful effects of malnutrition. You don't suffer from a disease, but you still want to end your life."

Shivaji intervened, "I am not ending my life. I will not commit suicide. The cause of my death will be involuntary."

"Choosing not to eat and drink is equivalent to suicide."

Shivaji kept silent for a while. What the Englishman voiced did have some truth behind it. However, Shivaji did not consider the Englishman's words valuable. Instead of telling the Englishman if he would consume the food or not, Shivaji asked, "How long have I been in 'the hole'?"

"Five days," replied the Englishman. "Several more days without food and water and your moment to bid farewell to life will arrive."

THE 32ND DAY

In disguise, layered in the shades of blackness, arose the first signs of light to present the newborn day. Once again, Shivaji had risen from the insistent dream in which he had seen his wife falling into the waters of death. Breathing heavily, he noticed that his entire body was covered in perspiration. He managed to remove his soaked, long-sleeve kurta. Shivaji then used his kurta as a cushion which he placed beneath him. After the visit from the ship doctor, there was no one else who passed by for Shivaji to converse with. Shivaji began to doubt if he would ever get the chance to talk to the inscrutable Englishman again. Although the discussion between the two men lasted no more than a couple of minutes, Shivaji felt as if he had connected with him. He wanted to hear about his views on the colonial rule and regime. He questioned why the sensible man chose to assist and treat the Indians on the vessel. Shivaji also felt that the Englishman wanted to say more, but his rude behaviour and impulsive answers would not permit the ship doctor to do so.

Who is he? Why is he on Ship Elbe? Why is he not an oppressor like the rest of them? Why does he care if I live or die? A variety of questions ran through Shivaji's mind until his stomach began to howl. The devastating hunger was now affecting his senses. Shivaji experienced shooting pains in his head. He felt extreme coldness in his hands and feet. Utmost exhaustion was visible in his eyes. Whenever his eyes were set to rest, a sharp pain would enter his skull or the chill in his hands and feet would battle to keep him alert. Shivaji understood that the only remedy for this was to eat the stale food left behind from the previous day.

His eyes wandered the limited space around him. The darkness concealed the tin plate and cup. The double-minded Indian did not know what to do. He could either sensibly move his hands to grab hold of the edible material or wildly sway his hands to knock it down. The decision was his to make; a decision that would determine whether he wanted to live or die.

"On one end there is the pride of being an Indian. If I eat the food, I would not be loyal to my land and its citizens. A rebel should never comply. Why should I take advice from an Englishman? I must not believe that he is different than the others. After what they have done and will do, there is no way I can trust them. This food is given by a man whose skin may be pale white, eyes blue or green and hair any other color except for black. Who knows, the food may as well be poisoned," Shivaji said to himself, not realizing that once again he was talking to the walls of 'the hole'.

"Wait a minute, poison in the food. If that is so, then why must I not eat it? Yes, I should eat it. After all, I do want to die. But if I do eat it, that will be considered as ending my own life. I know that the food is poisoned. Well, do I? I am not sure." Shivaji kept going on and on, back and forth, attempting to make sense of what was true and what was false.

"On the other hand, what does Vyjanti want? Who cares what she wants. Vyjanti left you, you imbecile. You sit here musing about what Vyjanti wants you to do despite knowing the fact that she has abandoned you. She was traitorous, unfaithful, disloyal...Shut up! She is my wife. No, no, no she is not my wife. She still lives in my heart. If Vyjanti was here she would not let me starve, she would feed me the khichdi with her own hands. So you are saying Vyjanti would feed you poison. Stop talking! No, you stop! I've had enough of this nonsense. Don't ever talk ill of my wife again. She left this world only to enter a far better place. Vyjanti, at first, I asked you to return. But now I say that we'll both meet again in a different time, different place and in different bodies."

To live his life without Vyjanti meant to live without a purpose. Since the loss of his wife, Shivaji searched for a path that would lead him to the end of life. But natural death did not come easily. He felt that the sooner he left this life, the sooner he would be reunited with Vyjanti. Shivaji did not see a future, because the future he strived to build was mainly for the woman he truly loved. There was no need for him to work and save money because he did not see himself returning to the village to inform his family members that Vyjanti was no more. It was pointless for Shivaji to liberate himself from the oppressors because he believed that he was no longer worthy of happiness.

The hours of the day progressed, yet there were no signs of movement towards the plate of food or cup of water. Shivaji was fighting with his stomach. He pulled the kurta from underneath him and strongly tied it around his waist, expecting the technique to suppress the hunger which tortured his abdomen. On the soiled floor, Shivaji withered in pain to the extent where it became unbearable for him to continue. At times, he felt as if his digestive organ would burst. His fatigued physique begged for rest, but the loud cries of the stomach would not permit sleep.

As the night began to prepare for its shift, Shivaji started to lose his mind again. With his knees held close to his abdomen, the helpless Shivaji lay on the floor, unable to control the tiny voice within his brain.

"Shall I eat or shall I starve? If I eat I will live, if I choose not to I will die. Why is it my choice? Was it Vyjanti's choice? Yes, it was Vyjanti's choice to end her life. Is God avaricious? He writes our destiny and then presents us with life. Why can't he let us determine our fate? Are we not capable of doing so as human beings? Now at the end of the road, God has allowed me to decide between life and death. Vyjanti was probably given the same opportunity before she decided to kill herself."

At times, Shivaji talked to himself in a calm manner, and then sometimes he turned to the walls to vent with passion. He had no balance whatsoever. His thoughts bounced from one subject to another.

"God is responsible for the death of my wife. Why? Because..." Shivaji pondered, "Why am I blaming The Lord, when I should be the one to blame? I was not able to protect her. I am the one who let my eyes close. If it was not for the blunders I made, Vyjanti would still be alive. I should have put my foot down when I needed to. Yes, I should have stopped her from boarding the ship. I should have never agreed to take part in this expedition. It is not God's fault, nor is it Vyjanti's fault, this is entirely my fault."

With force Shivaji pounded his fist on the floor, unleashing his aggression by inflicting damage to his hand. His loud wails stabbed through the caged walls of 'the hole'.

"Please, someone, something, anyone, anything, give me a sign. How do I escape the mind and its released demons? Am I going insane? No, I am insane. I know I am talking to myself. I sometimes even talk to the walls. Can you believe that? Wait, who can believe that? Wait a minute! Who am I talking to? Is anyone there? If someone or something is listening, please appear. I ask you to show me your face. Vyjanti! Vyjanti, are you there?"

Shivaji wanted to hear a voice. He crawled next to the impassive walls. He placed his right ear close to the firm obstruction, waiting for a response.

"Vyjanti, are you there? Hello, is anyone there?"

Shivaji knew that the chances of his wife being situated behind the inescapable walls were close to zilch, yet he still hoped for a miracle. He then used his smallest finger to clean his ear. "Perhaps my ear is covered with too much filth and because of the filth I am unable to listen properly," he said to himself.

Once more, Shivaji leaned against the walls to hear a response that could provide him the answers to his questions. When unable to catch a voice, he switched to his other ear. Now with his left ear, which he treated as a new hope, Shivaji listened carefully but still there was no responsive voice discovered.

For the first time in his life, he felt the need for assistance.

"So, this is how it is. If I don't eat, that will end my life. But to end my life in that manner would be considered self-murder. If I do eat, I may live to see another day. God wants me to devour. Vyjanti wants me to devour. Then, why am I holding back? I know that I don't want to live, but I have to live. Why must I continue with life? What do I have that is worth living for? Vyjanti is dead. She is no more. She waits for me in another life. If that is so, then I must end this life to enter another. But is that definite? Is it certain that Vyjanti and I will meet again? Dear Lord, if you do exist, I beg for you to help me. I need a sign. My body needs food, but my brain rejects it. What should I do? Should I resist or submit?"

These questions were asked recurrently to the walls until Shivaji's lids covered his eyes, relieving him from his erratic views and behavior.

THE 33RD DAY

"Please forgive me for I have sinned," Shivaji heard the familiar voice repeat. The significant words played like a tape recorder in his mind as he rose from his sleep. Grasping his senses to become attentive, Shivaji gently lifted his torso. Sitting on his buttocks with his legs crossed, Shivaji collected all the images and sayings that flowed in his brain while he was unconscious. If he did not hurry, the dream would fade, resulting in the loss of the succession of imageries. He knew that the slightest neglect towards a dream would backfire. Several times before, when Shivaji had a dream—either good or bad—it would evaporate immediately if not provided full concentration. Shivaji, on the morning of the thirty-third day on the vessel, knew that there was no way he should lose focus. By interpreting his dream he would probably find the answers to his questions. Perhaps this illusion, once figured out, would provide a sign that would allow him to determine his fate.

The collection of images returned Shivaji to India, to Red Lilies District, in his respective village, inside his family home. He discovered Vyjanti seated across from him on the kitchen floor. In between them was a single tin plate with all the tasteful dishes that forced his mouth to water. Vyjanti sat with her chin rested on her knee, glaring at her husband as if she were ready to throw a fit. Shivaji noticed that his wife was upset with him. So he did not meet eyes with her. He fixed his gaze elsewhere, hoping that Vyjanti would not bombard him with questions.

"Why are you not eating food? Are you on a hunger strike?" she asked in a witty manner.

Shivaji stared at the plate of food, unable to release a word from his mouth. Vyjanti became conscious that her whimsical question did not appeal to her husband. Thus, she decided to give it a rest. In a serious tone, Vyjanti asked, "Are you in search of death? You and I both know that if you continue like this soon you will be no more. I don't want that to happen. You have lived life with me, now it is time to live life without me. Our journey is unfinished. You and I will reunite to fulfill our life together. This is not the end and this is not our end. It is a grievous sin to not live the life that God has etched for you. Don't make the mistake I have. Yes, I have sinned. Will I be punished for my sin? Only God knows. I believe that He will understand why I have taken my life. I hope you understand as well."

Shivaji remained placid as his wife talked, wishing that she would not notice his tearful eyes. Vyjanti placed her hand into the tin plate to gather a small portion of dosa covered in chutney. She brought the small portion of food to her husband's mouth. Shivaji did not propel backwards; however, he kept his lips sealed together.

"You must eat. If you eat, then I will know that you have forgiven me. My soul will be at peace if I am exonerated. Please forgive me for I have sinned, please forgive me for I have sinned, please forgive me for I have sinned," continued Vyjanti as her voice reverberated in the affected prisoner's ears.

Sobbing uncontrollably, the widower voyaged from an involuntary trance back to the reality of existence. Shivaji desperately moved his arms in the lonesome darkness, searching to make contact with his wife. The state of illusion, which not too long ago had full control over his mind, felt real. It seemed as if Vyjanti was there, right in front of his eyes, seated across from him. Shivaji called for his wife over and over again. But the walls only produced an echo of his voice, which began to frustrate Shivaji.

"I don't want to hear myself, I want to hear you. Where are you Vyjanti? Don't leave me again. Please respond."

As he moved about with both his arms and legs in motion, Shivaji heard a clatter. He felt his knee softly touch the tin plate. Was this a sign? Other than his voice, this was the first actual sound that entered his deserted ears after quite some time.

"Probably, she wants me to consume the food. In the dream, she did voice that to avoid death I must eat and only then will her soul rest in peace," Shivaji said to himself.

He remained silent as his brain entered a war zone. His brain, divided in half, was once again in a battle.

"What am I waiting for? The dream is a sign. I must listen to what Vyjanti wants me to do. You don't need to listen to anyone. Dreams are illusions which are not meant to be taken seriously. That was not Vyjanti. That was just your mind playing tricks with you. It was Vyjanti and she needs me. Her sin is the reason why her soul is not at peace. If she sees that I have not taken my own life, like she had taken hers, perhaps then Vyjanti will be released from misery. I will go to any extent to lead Vyjanti into the path of eternal bliss even if she is not existent in this world. Well, she is not existent. She has betrayed you. Vyjanti has left you to suffer alone. Shut up! Vyjanti exists in my heart. I know she would not want me to do what she had done. She wants me to be free of transgression. I must survive to see what lies ahead for me. What is the reason behind living a life which is controlled by the British? They are the strings, while you are the puppet. And as you know the strings operate the puppet. You should not intake the food that has been given to you. Believe me; death will lead you to heaven. It is time for you to think about yourself, Shivaji. I have always cared for my loved ones. I have always put them over myself. I have not changed then and I will not change now. Call me whatever you want, mindless or foolish, I don't care. I will do what my wife prefers me to do. I will live till God wants me to live. I will make sure that your soul rests in peace, Vyjanti," Shivaji told himself as he grasped the tin plate and moved it close to his body.

He devoured the food as if he was some kind of untamed animal who had not eaten for months. The stale food, which reeked of foul odor, became hard to swallow. The rice and lentils were not watery like they were on other days on the vessel. Shivaji felt the morsel power its way down his throat. Even the water provided to him with the food did not help with the consumption. As he chewed, Shivaji was able to hear how solid the rice had become over the past few days. He knew that the decayed food, which had been entirely covered in bacteria, would be injurious to his health. Yet the fact did not seem to bother him. He did not leave a single, measly piece of rice behind. Shivaji had never eaten stale food before. He was unaware of the aftermath.

A couple of hours later, the stale food **finally** revealed its true colors. Shivaji felt as if **poison were** circling inside his intestines. His stomach pleaded for mercy. Shivaji **writhed** in pain. He begged for someone or something to put him out of his misery. The unbearable stomach pain was not the only factor that made him suffer—he also felt as if his chest were about to explode. A burning sensation moved **upward** from his intestines and directly into his chest.

Without warning, the food he had consumed found the urge to free itself. For minutes, Shivaji vomited profusely, removing every bit and piece of the decayed food. The dry **expulsion** of rice, lentils, and water **burned** his throat. With most of the undigested food no longer in his system, Shivaji managed to position himself up against the walls. He did not want his sensitive nose to encounter the smell of vomit. **However**, when concealed in **a** limited space with practically no ventilation, Shivaji couldn't escape the stench.

He did not know whether to use his hands to cover his nose or rub his stomach to relieve the persisting discomfort. Fortunately, the chest pain started to recede as he breathed heavily through his mouth. Shivaji decided to block his nose from letting air enter through the passage. Now he was to inhale and exhale only through his mouth, which he did until **his lungs began to tire** from the overload.

Later in the day, he accepted defeat. Shivaji adapted to the foul odor that remained within **'the hole'.** But when he was forced to hold on for a long time, Shivaji cursed his fate. He believed that if he had held on **a bit longer,** his stomach might not have required the expulsion of feces. Shivaji could not recall the last time he had visited the loo. Whatever day that was, he did not care. He did not want to share his residence with the smell of his vomit and feces.

Despite his efforts to bear it, once again, Shivaji had to submit. The stomach cramps were too much for him to handle. He had no other choice but to pull down his dhoti. "I can't believe this. I can't believe that I am living in a cage, sleeping in a cage, eating in a cage, vomiting in a cage, and **defecating** in a cage," Shivaji said to himself. He felt ashamed that he was nothing more than a useless caged animal.

"This is what you desired to see? Do you want me to live like this?" said Shivaji as he pointed to the ceiling of the dungeon. "What have I done to deserve this? All I wanted was a better future for my wife and family. Was that too much to ask for? Look at what I have become. Look at where I am now. Do you have the answers? Can you give me an explanation?" roared Shivaji as he violently banged his fists against the walls.

It seemed as if the wick to an explosive bomb had been lit. Shivaji was on fire. He made sure to create dents on the walls that held him captive. "You bastard, you think that you are the ruler of this world? Come on, you arsehole, you think that you are the ruler of this body? Do you think that you are the ruler of my soul? I will punish; I will retaliate. You take away my liberty. You take away my dignity. You take away my wife. I will cut off your member and take away your manhood. I will slap your face and take away your pride. I will strangle your neck and take away your life. And I will piss on your flag and take away your dominance."

For a short period, it did not seem as if Shivaji was there. Someone else—something extreme—had conquered his soul. After every line, the deranged prisoner stained the walls with his bloody knuckles. Curse words were released from his mouth like never before. Not once did his eyes blink. Not once did his fists **flinch.** Not once did the level of his voice **falter.** The severe mental distress **that** 'the hole' created made Shivaji go ballistic, and there was no one there to stop him.

THE 34TH DAY

With a throbbing sensation in his brain, minor cramps in his stomach, and sharp pains in his chest, Shivaji rose to the sight of a familiar face that had been haunting him for days. As he opened his eyes, an image of the Indian woman who had been stolen from her husband and presented to Captain Sanders hovered above his face. The impassive face petrified Shivaji. The face of the despoiled female was swollen and bloodied. Her nose was severely damaged, and her lips were badly bruised. The dark circles around her eyes made her appearance almost witchlike, while the blackness in the cell added to the eerie atmosphere.

Shivaji wanted to flee, but there was nowhere to go. Surrounded by concrete walls, he had no choice but to close his eyes. As he shut his lids, Shivaji remembered his wife and started chanting the name of Lord Shiva. For him to chant the name of a Hindu God—or any God, for that matter—was unusual. Though Shivaji was a believer in the Lord, he was not the kind to seek help from Him. He was not like his wife, who turned to God after every problematic situation.

Shivaji reminisced about the times when he used to peek into the prayer room to watch his wife sit before the various brass and clay idols. Since her mouth was occupied with spiritual words, Vyjanti inhaled and exhaled through her nose. Her hands were folded together in respect to the one above. With her eyes closed, Vyjanti swayed her head from side to side as she chanted the three divine words that informed the members of the household to participate in the daily prayer. Muthuraman, his wife, and daughters all moved toward the uplifting voice as Shivaji stood beside the door, unable to remove his eyes from Vyjanti. He carefully listened to her as she repeated, "Om Namah Shivay, Om Namah Shivay, Om Namah Shivay."

Shivaji did not want to, but he had to, store his memories aside to return to the world of isolation. As he dared to separate his closed lids, Shivaji wished not to see the dreadful face again. Fortunately, there was no sign of the tormented female. As the day progressed, he examined the connection between Vyjanti, who was no longer living, and the ruined widow who still was. Like every other person, Shivaji decided to ask God for answers.

"Every person has the right to ask God why and how. Well, today is my day to do so," Shivaji said under his breath. "Why does her face keep reappearing? Does she blame me for the misfortune? Was I the only Indian on the deck that night? Why must I be accused?" Shivaji vented as he stared at the left portion of his chest in which his God resided. "You live in here," he said, beating his chest fiercely, "not above in the skies."

He did not realize that his knuckles on both hands were swollen and discolored—red, black, blue, and purple—causing searing pain each time they struck his chest. Shivaji cried in pain, but still he did not relinquish.

The interrogation continued. He did not expect God to respond to his questions. Shivaji used Him as an excuse. Deep within, he knew that the answers were buried somewhere in his mind. Shivaji needed to overcome the mental blockage that restrained him from bringing those answers to the forefront. Hours passed, yet Shivaji still worked on connecting the pieces of the puzzle. He did not let the pain he was suffering become an obstacle in his conversation with God.

"I did not save the unknown Indian female, so therefore no one was there to save my wife. Or was it the fact that my wife did not let me save the Indian female—that is why God punished her? Hmm, instant karma! At a time like this, the only face I need to be seeing is my wife's. Then, Lord, why am I seeing the face of a stranger? What significance does she have in my life? How does she relate to Vyjanti's death? I wonder if she is alive. Had she appeared in front of my face to let me know that her life has ended? She may have been killed or committed suicide. If that is true, then obviously I am to blame. Is that not true? Yes, I am talking to you. Aren't you within me, living inside my heart? Or are you my voice—the same voice that is in use at the moment—my conscience? Answer me!"

Shivaji pounded his battered fist in the air, demanding immediate attention from his Lord. After a session of deep breaths, Shivaji pondered once more. This time he did not consult God. Why blame others, he thought.

"I am the one who should be held responsible for everything. Vyjanti is not in this world today because of my decisions," Shivaji said to himself. He started to believe that his wife leaving this world was a sensible decision on her part. "In a way, Vyjanti is now at peace. Wherever she is now is far better than living in the midst of the Pacific Ocean, residing on the deck of a cargo ship, fighting to survive the hate and violence displayed by the British seafarers on a day-to-day basis. Vyjanti, you would have never found bliss with a disgraceful husband. You see, even God knew that you deserved a better life than what I had provided you. That is why He accepted you into His world. If you can, please forgive me," Shivaji pleaded, tears raining from his eyes. "If we meet again, I promise you that your life will be my canvas. And I will decorate your life with appealing lines, forms, and colors."

THE 35TH DAY

The brain of a person residing inside "the hole" was similar to a balance scale. One side of the scale measured sanity, while the other side measured insanity. Within the prison, most of the time, the scale tilted on the side of insanity. Any captive, bright or dull, was no match for the lethal prison. The prison made the wisest of the wise lose their minds. Everyone had a different reason for their breakdown. Some became maniacal due to complete isolation, while others went mad after accepting their miserable fates. Some even became unhinged due to starvation and dehydration. The aching stomachs did not receive a single morsel of food, and the parched throats did not receive a single drop of water.

For Shivaji, the walls of the prison were his enemy. On the walls of seclusion, he foresaw his future without Vyjanti. Using the walls as a canvas, Shivaji painted his imaginative destiny. But his tints, hues, and shades created a dismal picture since the person who brought color to his life was no longer alive. Many times a day, Shivaji had lengthy conversations with the walls. Sometimes, he treated the walls as his own conscience. It was as if the walls presented a mirror image of him. He talked to himself, voicing all sorts of questions involving God, his wife, incidents of the past, and the unpredictable future.

After nine long nights in "the hole," the captive was eventually liberated from the tormenting walls of confinement. With his brain half asleep, eyelids partially open, and limbs somewhat active, Shivaji was pulled out of the cage by the deck crew members. The sounds of chatter resonated within his ears as he tried to discern the words spoken. Shivaji heard the Englishmen uttering something about the islands of Fiji. What exactly was said about Fiji, he did not know. Somewhere within his mind, Shivaji understood that he was being dragged. He was aware of the fact that his arms and legs had no life. This particular truth disturbed him. Not having control over his own body meant he was unable to walk on his own. He felt as if the Englishmen were helping him. Shivaji did not want or need help from the British. If it were not for his powerless limbs, Shivaji would have battled the three Englishmen till his last breath. He preferred to die rather than accept assistance from his enemies.

The British seafarers continued through the tenebrous passage. It was certain that these Englishmen were well familiar with this area of the vessel. The absence of light in the passage did not seem to bother them. Not once did they trip or fall. The area was located within the belly of Ship *Elbe*. The passage ran to an opening which presented a staircase. The staircase, made of timber, led to the lower deck, which was divided into three different sections. Situated before the opening were a couple of doors. One of the doors led to the kitchen, where the morning and evening meals were prepared by the chief cook. The other room was a storage area that was not often used by the British seafarers.

The two members of the deck crew, along with the third who was there for security reasons, had been instructed by Chief Officer Anderson to transport Shivaji to Section A of the lower deck, where he was first assigned to reside. As Shivaji was dragged, he felt his feet colliding against the empty bottles left behind in the dark passage. These bottles, once filled with intoxicating beverages, had been gifted by the captain or chief as a reward to the British seafarers for a job well done. Not willing to share the precious reward with the other seamen on board, the selfish Englishman would hide in the dingy passage to consume the forbidden drink.

As Shivaji got closer to the opening, his eyelids began to flutter. The intense light from the sun was expanding into the secretive areas of Ship *Elbe*. The last time Shivaji had seen light was more than a week ago. At that moment, he was only familiar with dimness. For Shivaji, illumination had betrayed him. Though he needed more time to trust and adjust to the rays of light infiltrating his eyes, Shivaji's uncontainable obstinacy would not let him surrender easily. He fought his battles with intensity. With the burning sensation irritating his eyes, he still managed to see what had been stored in the room close to the kitchen. The door to the storage room was left wide open for him to perceive the numerous bundles of sugarcane firmly knotted together. Covering the entire room, the bundles stood six feet tall. Shivaji closed his eyes for a second and asked himself whether what he had seen was truly real or imagined. As he reopened his eyelids, Shivaji confirmed that the bundles of sugarcane were real.

Before he could process questions such as why the stalks of grass were being delivered to Fiji, Shivaji felt his front crashing onto the solid floor. Immediately, pain rushed to his face. Falling face first onto timber resulted in massive soreness. Struggling to turn his body to the side, Shivaji noticed blood dripping from his nose. Soon his lips were covered in red. He attempted to raise his hands to wipe the mess but was defeated by his lack of power.

"Hey coolie, start using your feet!" bellowed one of the deck crew members who had transported Shivaji.
The Englishman, who behaved as if he was the captain of the vessel, also had some words for the enslaved. "What are you waiting for? Do you think we are your servants? Crawl, you useless Indian, crawl. Start moving because we are not going to lift your arse up these stairs."

The British seafarers felt no shame expecting a captive to rise to his feet after living eight days and nine nights in a prison with barely any food, water, space, or company.

The British seafarers provoked the enslaved insurgent. The taunting and teasing rekindled life within Shivaji. He believed the deck crew members were testing his will. Shivaji had to muster immense strength and determination to climb the staircase. With minimal power left in his body, the task seemed close to impossible. The English seamen continued their disrespectful behavior, using foul language relating to Shivaji, his family, his religion, and his fellow Indians on board. How Shivaji wished that he was in better condition—if that were so, the situation would have been entirely different. He pictured his fist connecting with the faces of the deck crew members—blood pouring from their mouths and noses, teeth flying all over the place, bodies crashing onto the floor, faces black and bruised, and voices crying for help—these were the many images that formed in Shivaji's brain.

The Englishmen kicked Shivaji in his torso, demanding he rise to his feet. Shivaji felt the imminent spirit within him longing to discharge. In his view, the taunts were not directed only at him. "These bastards are challenging me, my people, and my nation. We must rise. Lord, I ask you to give me the power of all the Indians on board, so I can demonstrate our perseverance by reaching the top of the staircase without assistance," said Shivaji under his breath.

He used the insults as fuel to prove to the British that Indians still had fight left within them. He wanted to let them know that the Indians were still powerful and dangerous. Despite the harsh punishments, tasteless food, extensive chores, shameless obsessions, and unreasonable rules and regulations, the indentured labourers still fought to see the next day. Then and there, Shivaji understood that the name-calling, degrading insults, and biased remarks were all signs for him. It was a message sent by God to the prisoner who had temporarily lost his path when imprisoned in "the hole."

This was his chance to decide whether he wanted to depart from or continue with the life God had chosen for him. There was no moving backwards. The choices were either to move forward or remain still.

Shivaji felt life in his fingers. The lurching movement of his fingers signalled his hand to operate. While resting his palm on the first step of the staircase, Shivaji felt strength in his arms. The nerves, tendons, muscles, and bones were now operational. By forcefully using his struggling arms, Shivaji elevated his torso to the next step. He then started to receive assistance from his legs, which began to move in tandem with his arms. Shivaji believed he had no control over the movement of his limbs. It was as if his limbs had a mind of their own.

"Where did this burst of energy come from? How in the world do these limbs function so well after the excruciating days in captivity? Is it I, or is it someone else? Is it God controlling both my arms and legs at this moment?" Shivaji asked himself.

As he writhed like a snake upward, the British seafarers eyed the indentured labourer who had the heart of a lion. In their eyes, Shivaji had all the characteristics of a true leader—an Indian who was a threat to colonial rule.

"This is impossible. How...How...How does he..." uttered the stammering deck crew member.
"Quick, grab hold of his legs. We must not let him defeat us," said the Englishman who staggered behind during the transfer.

If Shivaji were to reach the top of the staircase in his condition, it would be a slap in the faces of the British seafarers. These Englishmen did not want to be placed in a situation where they would be forced to swallow their pride.

"Stop, coolie!" barked the Englishman, confident that his loud voice would slow Shivaji down. He carefully observed Shivaji's movements. "Hmm, this coolie has heart. After all that he's been through, he still has the nerve to resist dominance. Too bad he is not British. We need more people like him in our line of work, especially a man who never lets go of who he is and what he stands for."

"Shut up! You are not here to compliment a measly Indian. Bring his arse down," ordered the Englishman acting as the leader of the group.

As the two deck crew members hurried onto the staircase, Shivaji had progressed halfway to the top. The barrage of footsteps started closing in on him. He knew he was not too far from the endpoint. With that in mind, Shivaji scurried higher, his knees crashing into each step. The contact between his knees and the steps was painful but did not stop him from ascending.

The British seafarers witnessed the man transform from powerless to powerhouse. They viewed Shivaji as a four-legged beast with more agility and endurance than them. Five steps from victory, Shivaji realized that his legs were no longer operational. He glanced over his left shoulder to see two deck crew members holding his legs. Both seafarers had one leg each to control. The strength of the Englishmen was too much for Shivaji to handle. Gradually, the seamen hauled Shivaji down to the bottom of the staircase. Shivaji did not holler nor howl. He remained silent. Every part of his body became dysfunctional except for his arms, which struggled to hold onto a tread. His efforts failed because his hands could not grasp the step. Shivaji was prepared for the short-lived moments of independence to be replaced by unethical confinement.

No other indentured labourer on Ship *Elbe* had experienced what Shivaji felt in those minutes of absolute independence. He was so close to proving to the supporters of colonial rule that there would come a day when Indians would step forward, raise their voices, take action, and retaliate if necessary. A day would come when Indians would be considered equals. The fear of this possibility was what Shivaji sought to instill in the minds of the Englishmen present at the scene through his vital actions.

"You men have challenged the Indian. Well, the Indian did accept. But you people and your system could not see the Indian achieve freedom; therefore, there had to be interference. Why did you interfere? Was it because of fear?" Shivaji rambled under his breath. His loss of not being able to climb to the top of the staircase in reality was not total. Shivaji knew that if he had succeeded, the British would have tossed him back into 'the hole.' If that were the case, Shivaji would not have survived another stint in the mortal cell.

What Shivaji did know was that even climbing a few steps would be enough to inject threat and alarm into the minds of the Englishmen. These British seafarers were incapable of digesting a single ounce of insurgence, which made it easy for Shivaji to teach them a lesson. From this occurrence, Shivaji understood that God had provided him with a sign. He always believed that God often showered His children with indications—but not all of His children were capable of noticing them. Certain factors, aspects, situations, and occurrences prevented a person from recognizing these signs. God writes everyone's destiny but also provides opportunities to alter what has been composed. Some people are fortunate enough to notice these signals, which have the power to change lives. On the thirty-fifth day of the sea voyage, Shivaji was the fortunate soul to understand what The Almighty had signalled. While clashing between the decision to live or die after his wife's passing, Shivaji reached to God for assistance. God prompted him to accept life over death by implanting the heart of a soldier into the body of a ravaged Indian.

The deck crew members placed Shivaji at the bottom of the staircase. Both men held him down by placing their knees on his lower back. The widower did not shift. He knew what awaited him. The Englishman, who acted as if he were in charge of the operation, marched toward the unmoving captive.

"I may be inactive now, but that does not mean I will remain inactive forever. In the past, I was considered a threat when in reality I was not. Because of this confusion, my wife was taken from me. Now I am telling you to consider me a threat. I am not an obedient slave. How, when, and where I will retaliate, I do not know. Expect control to be challenged, expect rule to be rattled, expect transgression to be trampled," said Shivaji with pride in his voice.

The deck crew member holding Shivaji to the floor retaliated with violence. He managed to hold Shivaji in a headlock while the other crew member, secretly in awe of the captive's fortitude, remained idle. The Englishman tightened his grip around Shivaji's neck, ensuring that no further incomprehensible threat was released. Shivaji gasped for air as he writhed to break free.

"Don't apply too much pressure. We don't want the rebel to choke to death. He needs to suffer more in his life," said the British seafarer in charge. He knelt beside the captive, whose face showed no panic. The tall Englishman covered Shivaji's body with his shadow. He then removed the turban wrapped around Shivaji's head. Once unravelled, the headwear was disregarded and tossed into a corner. He then patted Shivaji on the head as if he were a pet animal.

"Believe me when I say this: you and the other coolies will suffer more on the islands of Fiji. Hell awaits you, my unruly friend."

The deck crew members did not let Shivaji respond. Whenever he felt the urge to speak, the British seafarer administering the headlock used his spare hand to block his mouth. Then, the Englishman in charge revealed what he had buried in his trousers. The lethal baton entered the scene. It was positioned above the ineffective Shivaji's head. He viewed the movement of the weapon from the corner of his eyes as the British seafarer extended his arm toward the ceiling. The baton was then lifted into the air. Before the pulverizing torment lanced past his skull and into his brain, Shivaji closed his eyes. He welcomed the violence only because he knew this was not the end of his journey.

THE 36TH DAY

Revived by unfamiliar sounds in the ocean, Shivaji attempted to lift his eyelids. He was unprepared for the sunlight invading his eyes. Since his wife's death, he had seen only darkness. Now that daylight was creeping back into his life, Shivaji felt the need to acclimate.

Curious, he listened to the sounds emanating from the waters below. It seemed to him as if someone were flapping their hands against the water. Shivaji wanted to know the source of the sounds—who or what was making them. But the pain from the previous day lingered. The best he could do was turn to his side. While shifting, he felt tightness in his muscles, soreness in his bones, and a vibration in his head. Soon, he was facing the barriers that separated man from the sea.

He could hardly believe his eyes. He was back where it had all begun. Dumbfounded by his surroundings, Shivaji began to believe that most of the past events—the demise of his wife and the days of confinement—had been some kind of dream. The feeling of hope lifted his spirit. Ignoring the fact that even the slightest movement caused pain, Shivaji turned around, wishing to see Vyjanti. Since boarding the vessel, every morning Vyjanti had been conscious, waiting for her husband to rise. With that in mind, Shivaji expected to find his wife resting beside him.

"I need to see her comforting eyes," he whispered.

But the space beside him was empty. He listened to the chatter of the indentured labourers. Amid the many voices, perhaps one belonged to Vyjanti, he thought. Shivaji scanned the crowd, bouncing from one face to another, but he could not locate her. He rolled onto his back, positioned his neck comfortably, and closed his eyes.

"It is something I had to accept, and I have. Vyjanti is no more, and she will not return in this life," he said to himself.

Although his ears were occupied by chatter, he did not ignore the strange splashing sounds. Minutes later, they became louder and more frantic. Shivaji pictured the children from his village by the nearby lake. Children of all ages, castes, and religions kicked and slapped the water joyfully. No one could determine which was louder: their laughing and shouting, or the powerful sounds of their flesh hitting the water.

Abruptly, Shivaji moved to the barrier. He rested his eyes on the exposed space between the rails. Whistles, trills, squeaks, and grunts formed a communicative harmony. Shivaji felt as if the new sounds were trying to convey something. Perspiration ran directly into his right eye, forcing him to rub it. Just as the irritation subsided, a sea creature rocketed from the water. Like a shooting star, it vanished quickly. As it plunged headfirst into the ocean, water splashed onto Shivaji's face.

Though startled, he managed to glimpse the animal and wanted to see more. Using his forearms, he lifted himself onto the railing. Through the space between the rails, Shivaji observed the vessel steering the ocean waves aside. The water's color had changed since *Ship Elbe* left India—shades of blue and green had intermingled to form a picturesque view. While admiring God's majestic creation, Shivaji reflected on how pleased Vyjanti would have been to see the waters look clean for once.

"We must be near the islands," he said, scanning the waters for more activity.

Loud splashes signaled bodies hitting the water. At first, Shivaji feared someone had leapt from the deck. Images of human bodies flying from the vessel flashed before his eyes. He closed his eyes firmly until the visions disappeared. Slowly, he reopened them, squinting to observe the vast ocean. Not far from the vessel was a herd of twelve bottlenose dolphins. The waves invited the creatures to explore the surface.

In his lifetime, Shivaji had never seen anything like this. The dolphins, to him, were oversized fish. He did not blink as he watched the grey mammals travel elegantly alongside *Ship Elbe*. Some soared into the air before plunging into the water; others vanished into the depths, only to resurface again. Occasionally, they swerved to avoid major waves. It seemed the dolphins anticipated the waves before they formed. Their speed made Shivaji wonder if humans could ever trap them—a thought that sent chills down his spine.

Shivaji noticed how the dolphins behaved like small children racing each other, taunting and playing, whistling and grunting without colliding. Even when diving beneath the surface, their shadows remained visible on the rippling water. From time to time, they raised their heads above the surface, like a baby first leaving its mother's womb. Shivaji was struck by the lighter grey of their undersides, which sparkled under the sunlight. Among the twelve dolphins was a calf, closely following its mother. The infant's dark eyes seemed to look directly at him.

The calf swam closer to the vessel, ignoring its mother's calls. The mother followed, leaving the rest of the herd behind. Shivaji, using the little strength left in his hands, urged them to return to the water.

"Shoo, shoo, shoo, go away. I don't want you separated from your family. Please leave," he whispered hoarsely.

But the calf floated on the surface, snapping its jaws repeatedly as if trying to warn him. The mother appeared beside the calf, issuing grunts and nudges. When the infant still refused to move, the mother asserted her authority by gently butting its head. The calf, annoyed, sprayed water back at the mother.

Astounded, Shivaji finally used his exhausted voice:

"Please listen. I beg you to leave. Stay away from this prison. If you come near, you will be enslaved. You are free animals; we are imprisoned. That is why you must return to your herd."

After hollering, Shivaji gasped for air, feeling faint. He had to ensure the mother and calf safely departed. The view blurred as he teetered on the edge of unconsciousness. Still, he watched the pair reunite with their family in the Pacific waters.

Senseless for hours, Shivaji finally awoke when Karthik displayed a childish antic. With a tin cup full of water, the child tiptoed to his unconscious mama and tilted the cup so water fell directly onto Shivaji's face. The posture resembled a gardener watering a treasured garden. Startled, Shivaji rose to his feet. Once he recollected where he was, he noticed the minor beside him.

"Karthik, is that you?" Shivaji asked, still feeling as if trapped in a dream.

"Yes, mama, it's me, Karthik. Appa and Amma told me not to bother you. I don't know why."

"Where are your appa and amma?"

"Shush, not so loud! They are sleeping next to us," whispered the child.

Shivaji surveyed the scene, surprised to be talking to a child in the middle of the night. Used to his caged life in darkness, he no longer acknowledged daylight.

"Where were you? Appa was very worried. I missed you. I even used my drinking water to help you rise, mama," said Karthik in his adorable voice.

Shivaji could no longer resist. He dried his eyes with his sleeves and extended his arms, expecting Karthik to run to him. But the child stood still, eyes glued to the floor.

"Why are you hiding your eyes?" Shivaji asked.

"I'm sorry. Appa and Ammi told me not to come near you," Karthik replied.

"Why?"

"I promised them," said Karthik. "They said not to bother you or ask many questions. Appa said you need time to recover."

Shivaji expected this from his friend Venkatesh. If it were someone else, they would have assumed Shivaji dead. Most indentured labourers who witnessed the sins inflicted on Shivaji and Vyjanti believed both were destroyed by the British. Venkatesh, however, had faith in his friend's survival and prayed for his liberation from 'the hole.'

"It is fine, Karthik. You may come near me. I don't need time to recover. All I need is for you to embrace me," Shivaji gestured.

The hesitant child worried: "What if father punishes me?"

"He will not find out. Listen to the obnoxious sound your appa is making."

Karthik chuckled. "It comes from his nose," he said.

Shivaji smiled, confident the child would move toward him, and widened his arms. "Your father won't know, I promise."

"Are you sure?"

"Yes. No one will know. It will be our secret."

Karthik smiled and moved closer, ignoring the stench of Shivaji's clothes, the prickly beard, and the rashes covering his face and hands. The warm embrace reminded Shivaji he was still loved. He mattered. Others wanted him to live. Karthik's touch made him feel human again.

"Mama, where is Attai?" asked the child, resting his face upon the chest of an Indian whose heart had battled and survived countless trials. Yet Shivaji knew the weight of the question and braced himself to answer.

THE 37TH DAY

While most Indians on *Ship Elbe* were immersed in various dreams, Shivaji had risen before dawn. Awakening to the sounds of bodies tossing and turning, husbands snoring uncontrollably, wives whimpering softly, and elders breathing heavily, Shivaji understood how different it was from rising in a place enclosed in silence and darkness. The more he tried to dismiss 'the hole' from his mind, the more it crept back in.

He looked over to see Karthik nestled between his parents. Shivaji recalled the question the child had asked.

"From where do I get the courage to tell Karthik that his attai is no more?" he asked himself. Not long ago, Shivaji had been as frank as possible. He looked the child in the eyes and said,

"Karthik, I don't know where she is. But what I do know is that we will never see her in this life again."

With a blank face, Karthik asked, "Why? Is Attai far away?"

"Yes, my child. She is unreachable. But that does not mean we can't find her. For those who truly love her, like you and I, all we have to do is look within our hearts."

"I don't have eyes in my heart, so that means I will not see her."

Shivaji noticed his mouth curl upwards. "Wherever she may be, let us pray she remains happy." As the conversation progressed, Shivaji touched his lips with his tongue to moisten the painful cracks caused by dryness. To his surprise, he tasted salt on his lips and in his mouth. Tears started to gush from his eyes. These were not tears of hurt; rather, they arrived as a form of remedy. Shivaji believed that wherever Vyjanti may be, it was a better place than where he was.

"Mama, I really miss her," said Karthik.
"I do too," replied Shivaji.

His thoughts were interrupted when he was startled by movement next to him. Before he could move his neck, Venkatesh had already embraced him.

"I knew you were alive. Thank God, you are here. What happened? Are you in good health? Have you eaten? You look very weak. Do you need water? I think we must get you some to drink. Why are you not saying anything? Do you need to rest? Are you wounded? Did the British hurt you? Shivaji... talk to me."

Venkatesh examined his friend from head to toe, fearing the Englishmen had shattered his bones. He checked Shivaji's visible ribs, uncovered due to tears in the kurta. Irritated, Shivaji rejected his friend's supportive hands.

"I am fine. There is no need for that. I don't need help," Shivaji replied pompously.

Venkatesh did not quarrel. He knew Shivaji better than anyone. Whispering, he said, "Now that's my good, old friend Shivaji! He will never change." He knew Shivaji would assist others without hesitation, but refuse help for himself. Shivaji's motto, *"I can take care of myself,"* made others think twice before offering advice or orders. Even from family, Shivaji rarely accepted help. Venkatesh, as an elder brother, often reminded him that it was okay to seek support from trusted friends and family, but Shivaji habitually disregarded it. So when Shivaji behaved impolitely, Venkatesh held no grudge. In fact, he was slightly pleased to see his friend remain the same to some extent.

Venkatesh and his wife were uncomfortable discussing Shivaji's loss. Lachmaiya struggled to carry on a conversation with him. Whatever she asked, Shivaji seemed disinterested, and when he did reply, it was only one or two words. Sometimes, Venkatesh tried to capture his friend's attention, but Shivaji seemed lost in his own world.

The couple understood the grief of losing his wife, but not the remorse Shivaji had internalized. Not asked to perform general duties such as cleaning the deck or purifying his body due to raw wounds and low energy, Shivaji felt useless. Seated against the railing with a damaged knee, he watched his friends obey every command: listen, speak, stand, sit, work, and eat when asked.

"Soon, we will shit and pee only when told," Shivaji muttered under his breath. He still had a fire of radical determination burning within. To bring change, he needed the support of every Indian on *Ship Elbe*. Though the task seemed impossible, it was not beyond reach. Whenever the flames within his soul surged, Shivaji suppressed them himself. He wished to change the unethical system, but without endangering others. He could not bear seeing another human lose their life because of his actions.

Unable to take part in the morning handout, Shivaji waited for the Englishmen to place his share of food. But Lachmaiya carried it to him near the barrier. Venkatesh knew if he delivered it himself, Shivaji would reject it. Instead, he asked his wife to do it, reducing the likelihood of refusal.

When the deck crew served food, Venkatesh requested another plate of khichdi for Shivaji. The interrogation was simple. When asked who needed the food, Venkatesh replied,

"It is for the man who has lost his wife. He has not eaten for days. Please be kind and fill this plate as well."

The British seafarers understood Shivaji's condition. He was no longer a rebel, but a helpless slave, so feeding him was harmless. Without further discussion, the plate was filled. Venkatesh did not ask for a larger portion openly; instead, he secretly added extra khichdi to Shivaji's plate. Lachmaiya noticed and understood her husband's sacrifice. Though initially frustrated by his choice to wait until the next handout, she knew Shivaji needed the food more.

"Shivaji is fortunate to have such an unselfish friend," she said, placing the tin plate next to the widower, who once again seemed lost in thought.

"Shivaji!" Venkatesh called twice, expecting a reaction. Lost in thought, Shivaji did not hear him. Venkatesh snapped his fingers to catch his attention.

"What happened?" Shivaji asked, moving his eyes agitatedly for signs of danger.

"Did you not hear me calling?" asked Venkatesh, exasperated.

"No, what is it?"

"Lachmaiya has brought you some food."

"That was unnecessary. You must have faced trouble. Didn't the British bother you?"

"No, we asked politely, and the deck crew filled the plate."

Shivaji studied Venkatesh, asking, "Have you all eaten?"

"Yes, we are full. This is your share," Venkatesh said, moving the plate closer.

"The portion of khichdi—"

"Why so many questions? This feels like an interrogation. Do you not trust me?" Venkatesh said passionately. "You want to know why your serving is larger? Because I told them you haven't eaten properly for days. Now stop this nonsense and eat."

Venkatesh knew deception wasn't ideal, but it ensured Shivaji actually ate. His friend's appearance had deteriorated, and Venkatesh wanted him to regain strength.

"Go ahead, Shivaji. Don't waste time," he urged.

Finally, Lachmaiya said, "Yes, Shivaji, you can't refuse khichdi. Don't punish your stomach."

Shivaji realized Venkatesh had sacrificed his portion. Instead of questioning, he bargained:

"I will eat only if you eat with me."

The clever Venkatesh replied,

"Nanban, I told you my stomach is full. This is yours. Please eat."

"So you won't eat?"

"Yes, I will not."

Shivaji grinned. "The deal is: if you eat, I eat. If not, I don't. Since you won't, I won't either."

Venkatesh, no match for Shivaji's stubbornness, complied, which ultimately benefited both friends.

Karthik watched his appa and mama share a plate of food. He had never seen two grown men eat from one plate. Village children often fought over shared food, but Shivaji and Venkatesh's battle was unselfish.

"Venkatesh, take the last piece!" yelled Shivaji, almost exploding.

"Calm down! I am older; you should listen. Eat the remaining khichdi," replied Venkatesh.

"Are you asking or ordering?"

"Asking. Please eat."

"No, I will not."

"Shivaji, you look like a skeleton. You need it more than I do."

Meanwhile, Karthik, quick-witted, quietly crawled to the pair and finished the leftover khichdi. Lachmaiya hid a smile behind her scarf.

"Appa, I solved the problem," said Karthik.

Venkatesh was astonished. He looked at his wife, who had turned away.

"How did you get here?"

"Simple, walking and crawling."

"What problem did you solve?"

Shivaji intervened: "What problem? There is none. Did you think we were fighting?"

"Yes, I thought you and Appa were fighting over the last khichdi," replied Karthik.

"No son, I mean yes son," Venkatesh stammered, "Mama and I were arguing. But the argument was not out of hate, but out of love."

Karthik struggled to understand his father's explanation. As Venkatesh continued, his son felt the urge to intervene, but knew it would be disrespectful to do so mid-conversation. So he shifted his eyes from his father to the empty tin plate on the floor. While Venkatesh preached about friends and enemies, love and hate, selfishness and unselfishness, Shivaji followed Karthik's button-shaped eyes.

As soon as Shivaji noticed the empty tin plate, he erupted with rejuvenating laughter. His laughter startled Venkatesh. Words that had been trapped in Shivaji's mouth spilled out uncontrollably. Unable to stop the laughter rising from the pit of his stomach, Shivaji pointed at the plate to show his friend what the playful child had done.

Venkatesh could not believe his eyes. "Karthik, what have you done?"
"I solved the problem, Appa. I finished the khichdi so that you and Mama would stop fighting," said the child, teasingly.

Upon hearing the answer, Venkatesh succumbed to laughter himself. Somewhere amid the joy, Shivaji momentarily forgot the death of his wife. Though brief, once he realized the lapse, he did not forgive himself. His emotions and expressions shifted intensely, becoming difficult for Venkatesh to handle. Unsure whether it was safe to speak, Venkatesh stood silently as Shivaji covered his face with his bare hands.

Shivaji believed he did not deserve to smile, laugh, or have fun.

"It has not been more than two weeks since my wife's passing, and here I am laughing. If I am to laugh again, then I plead to the God of Destruction that I shall die laughing," he said aloud.

With Venkatesh's help, Shivaji relieved his parched throat and cleansed his grimy body using barrels of water. He was fortunate that no Indian or Englishman objected to the excess use of water. As Shivaji washed his face, the Indian bystanders whispered behind his back. They expressed pity for him and discussed Vyjanti's death.

To assist in washing himself, Shivaji lifted his kurta, revealing the severe wounds inflicted by the British. Venkatesh, bearing many cuts and bruises himself, had tears in his eyes at the hideous sight. The Indians in line were stunned; many women, unable to handle the sight, covered their eyes with scarfs, veils, or hands. Every splash of water against Shivaji's torn skin caused unbearable pain. Fighting to suppress loud cries, Shivaji closed his eyes, gritted his teeth, and clenched his fists.

Venkatesh closely observed the agony. At times, his hands froze, unable to bear witnessing Shivaji's misery. Yet Shivaji insisted on continuing, ordering his friend despite the burning sensation:

"Don't stop, Venkatesh. Perhaps I deserve this pain."

Venkatesh tamed his shuddering hands, then resumed his task, unsure how emotionally draining it would be. Though the water caused pain, it also brought renewal. Shivaji felt reborn. His senses sharpened, his muscles and joints moved more freely, and his mind cleared. He used the blistering sun to dry his wet hair and body. Seated next to Venkatesh in silence, he absorbed the world anew.

Venkatesh remembered the last time he had seen Vyjanti. Images of a sister running to her brother, surrounded by culprits, tormented him.

"I feel so ashamed. I should have saved her. Will Shivaji ever forgive me for this?" Venkatesh asked himself.

What he did not know was that Shivaji blamed only himself for his wife's death.

"She trusted me, and I broke that trust. She believed in me, and I destroyed that belief. She wanted me to protect her, and I failed. She asked me to comply, and I did not. She asked me to restrain myself, and I could not. It was I who killed my wife. I am the reason she is no more," Shivaji said, weeping openly.

Venkatesh was left numb. He had not expected his friend to break down. He had seen Shivaji cry only a few times during early school years. Seeing him weep among seafarers and laborers left Venkatesh petrified. He remained silent, waiting for the widower to speak from his bleeding heart.

"At first, I searched for others to blame. I think it is common in people to blame God when tragedy strikes. I, Shivaji Nair, blamed God. Then I blamed the colonial system and its followers, who caused my wife's death. My mind then pointed to the Indians on board for not helping in the urgent situation. I remembered the village and my family, and held Appa responsible for pressuring us to board the vessel. Many people could be blamed, but in the end, I realized the true cause. Nanban, in the eyes of the Englishmen, I was a menace. And to destroy this menace, the British wanted to sabotage the purity of my wife."

"Which the British could not," said Venkatesh, cautiously. He understood the seriousness of the conversation.

"What do you mean?" asked Shivaji.

"Those devils could not capture Vyjanti. Their salacious plans failed. Vyjanti was humiliated, but not despoiled," Venkatesh replied confidently.

"Honestly, I don't know what was going through her mind that night. All I know is that whatever occurred in the cabin doesn't matter. In my eyes, my wife remained pure. I wish she were listening. Well, she is—she resides in my heart."

"Shivaji, I don't think Vyjanti could have lived with that stigma attached to her soul. My sister—"

Before Venkatesh could finish, Shivaji interrupted:

"So you are saying Vyjanti's suicide was reasonable?"

"No, Nanban, don't misunderstand me. Suicide is a sin. She made a hasty decision. Then again, what choice did she have? Either the British would end her life, or she took it herself."

"You don't understand, Venkatesh. I need to..." Shivaji could not finish. Tears choked his words.

Venkatesh, seeing the depth of emotion, intervened:

"Let's not talk about this anymore. Vyjanti wants you to live. She is watching over you. I don't know your plans, but remember: I am here for you. From now on, Lachmaiya and I will take care of you. You are not alone. You have us, Shivaji."

THE 40TH DAY

Shivaji physically improved with each passing day; the aches in his muscles, joints, and bones gradually subsided. The frequent headaches diminished, and the limp in his walk vanished. But this return to good health was not without consequence. As soon as the oppressors noticed him walking without Venkatesh's support, they ordered him to resume normal duties. Shivaji, lacking the will or power to revolt, obeyed without regret.

The feeling of being useful, of being needed, of being recognized, brought a flicker of life back into Shivaji. For the first time, he fulfilled his duties without his conscience tormenting him for being downtrodden by the British seafarers. He cleansed the lower deck floor, washed his hands and feet, and ate the rice and lentils without assistance.

Venkatesh always feared that his friend might neglect an order, disobey a command, or retaliate, for he did not want to see Shivaji sent back to 'the hole'. In fact, he believed that if Shivaji was once again seen as a threat by the British, the punishment would likely be death. With that thought in mind, Venkatesh kept a vigilant watch over his friend.

"Have you seen the ocean?" Venkatesh asked.

"Yes, I have. Is there something wrong with it?" replied Shivaji.

"No, Nanban. Nothing is wrong. It's just the color."

"What about the color?"

"Well, it's changing. The ocean no longer has waves of grey. When I look over the barrier, I see fluorescent blues and greens."

Suddenly, Shivaji fumed. "Why did you look over the barrier? Don't you know it only separates you from the ocean? Don't trust the railing. I once did. They are not there to save lives; they are there to end them," he said, his voice tinged with pain.

Venkatesh chose not to challenge him, keeping silent, hoping he did not disturb Shivaji by referencing the barrier Vyjanti used to end her life. Venkatesh and his family kept Shivaji occupied with conversations throughout the day, prioritizing distraction over reflection. But for Shivaji, ignoring Vyjanti entirely for even a single day was impossible. Sooner or later, amid discussions and tasks, her memory surged back.

Sometimes, Shivaji made eye contact with his conversation partner, yet his mind wandered in the past. As for the other Indians on board, they avoided him entirely. They did not look up, extend a hand, or greet him. No one stood face-to-face or shoulder-to-shoulder; no hellos, no polite inquiries. The Indians were ashamed for not helping Shivaji when he most needed it. Part of Shivaji felt that his fellow Indians had disowned one of their own that unforgettable night. With that feeling, he interacted only with Venkatesh, Lachmaiya, and Karthik. Yet he had forgotten one person who had wanted to help that night, but was denied by fate.

After the evening meal and the washing of hands, feet, and utensils, Shivaji encountered his old friend, the beggar, Thambi. Instead of greeting him verbally, Thambi immediately embraced him.

"I am so sorry. Please forgive me. You have done so much for this beggar. What have I done for you? Nothing. I have done nothing," Thambi said, chastising himself.

He beckoned Shivaji to sit down, and the widower obeyed. Shivaji noticed Thambi was more active than before: he had regained weight, movement in his limbs, and no longer suffered from his persistent hacking cough. Though pleased by Thambi's improvement, Shivaji pondered his whereabouts during the calamity.

Thambi preempted the question. "I had been tied down, nailed to the floor, trapped in a cage, whatever you may call it."

Shivaji was momentarily speechless. "Sorry, baba, I don't understand."

"I wanted to help that night, but I was forbidden. I asked for change. I battled the Almighty. It's no easy task to clash with Him. For you, I first confronted, then objected, then tussled, and finally begged. I was the lawyer, He the judge. I presented my case, but He did not listen. As I always say, what is written in destiny cannot be changed. Our past-life sins cannot be erased."

Shivaji grew irritated with the repeated phrases. "This system God created is pathetic. Why are sins carried from life to life? If Vyjanti sinned in this life, punishment would be fair. But in this life, my wife committed no sins, yet God destined her for such a short life."

"Short life, you say? She did not have a short life. Her life was great in every way, my son. She lived well. Her parents, siblings, in-laws, and husband provided eternal bliss. When she left, she left with dignity. She was a fearless warrior, loyal to her husband till her last breath. She acted to prevent those devils from taking advantage of her."

Hearing this, Shivaji's eyes moistened. He wanted to unleash his stored rage, but lacked a target. "Who deserves to feel my wrath?" he asked himself.

"What you harbor can only destroy you. Release the hatred, the poison, the anger, the burdens. Let go of the buts and ifs," said Thambi, as if he held a magnifying glass to Shivaji's mind. "You must accept that God is in charge."

"Baba, at the moment, we both know who is in charge. The British rule. It was because of their rule, their orders, their wants, and their needs that I have lost my wife. So tell me, should we view them as our God?" Shivaji asked disrespectfully.

"Son, it is not you speaking to me, it is your anger. At the moment, your God has strayed from His destination. Find Him, then return Him to His rightful place. You know where your God resides. But remember, as you search, you must destroy the rage that blinds you."

The discourses between mentor and disciple continued as nightfall crept stealthily across the congested deck. Shivaji knew it was time to rest, but many questions still churned in his mind.

"Why are we here? Why did we sign those indenture contracts? Were we destined for this ship? Why did God not prevent us from boarding?" Shivaji asked, unaware that his questions sounded almost like an interrogation.

Despite the somber tone, Thambi suddenly burst into laughter, leaving Shivaji aghast. He did not consider the laughter insensitive, for he knew the last thing Thambi would do was insult him.

"Let me tell you a story," said Thambi, his face serious, humorless. "It is about a monkey and a crocodile."

By now, Shivaji had grown accustomed to Thambi's sudden shifts in mood—from happy to sad, funny to serious, energetic to lethargic. These shifts no longer surprised the widower. Though unused to storytelling, Shivaji listened with open ears, treating the tale like a fairy tale.

"A long time ago, on the banks of Kolavai Lake, stood a lone jambul tree, home to a monkey. The monkey protected the tree and its fruit. The tree had a muscular trunk as a base, splitting into limbs that reached skyward, bearing lush green leaves. The thousands of leaves covered the upper canopy, leaving the bottom exposed.

"On the branches hung ripe, round, plum-colored fruits that delighted the tongue. The monkey used the tree as shelter from rain and wind, as a bed to sleep on, and leaves as blankets during cold nights. The tree also provided daily nourishment, so the monkey never had to search elsewhere for food. By all accounts, the primate's life was comfortable and sufficient.

"But the monkey was friendless. It felt distant from the world, spending its days swinging from branch to branch, warding off intruders. It dreamed of an adventure beyond its isolated existence. Many wild animals visited, seeking friendship in exchange for fruit. But the monkey was cautious, knowing they would leave once their hunger was satisfied.

"One day, a crocodile emerged from Kolavai Lake. Its vertical-slit pupils scanned the water and sky for predators. As it floated by the jambul tree, it heard the monkey's playful sounds. The crocodile searched the branches until a round fruit struck its head. Undeterred, it watched the jamun floating on the water, but, being carnivorous, ignored the fruit, focusing instead on the elusive primate, which howled at the approaching reptile.

'How are you?' asked the crocodile.

'Shoo! Go away! I don't want you near my home,' replied the monkey, alarmed.

'I will not hurt you, my dear friend.'

'How dare you call me your friend? I am not your friend!'

'Sorry, if I have upset you. I could not resist exploring this magnificent lake. I am new here, an adventurer, and I seek only exploration. If I have intruded, I ask your forgiveness,' said the polite reptile.

'So you are an adventurer?' asked the monkey, curiosity piqued.

'Yes. I have traveled far and wide, seen many wonders, walked the highest lands, swum in the deepest seas. But this place is new. Does it belong to you, sir?'

Feeling his pulse quickening, the monkey moved to lower branches. 'First, this is Kolavai Lake. Second, it belongs to no single being. God created it for all creatures. Many drink, bathe, swim, and live here freely.'

'And you? What brings you to this lake?' asked the crocodile.

'Once in a while, I come to the lake to relieve my dry throat. Other than that, you will never see me place my hands or feet in the water. I don't leave my jambul tree for more than a minute. This place here,' said the monkey, pointing to the evergreen plant, 'this is my home.'

The crocodile kept its webbed feet still as it propelled closer to the jambul tree. Noticing the movement, the monkey climbed higher into the branches, slanted in various positions for safety.

'Don't be afraid. I am not here to harm you, nor to seize your home. I am here to ask for a favor.'

The cautious primate replied, 'What favor do you seek?'

'I ask you to share the jamun that grows on your tree.'

'Why should I share with you?'

'Please, I have not eaten for days. I am very hungry.'

'Wait a minute! Your kind does not eat fruits. Your kind eats other animals.'

'That is not true. Who told you this fib? Our kind eats only fruits and vegetables.'

'Hmm, is that so?' The monkey tried to recall if it had ever seen a reptile consume flesh.

'Yes, it is the truth. For many days, I have traveled with an empty stomach, unable to find nourishment. Finally, my eyes fell upon the jamun hanging from your branches.'

The monkey's innate kindness would not allow a refusal, though it remained cautious. 'Well, if that is true, why did you not devour the jamun I launched at your head a few minutes ago?'

For a moment, the crocodile was tongue-tied. 'Oh my goodness, I did not even notice the object that struck my head. Where is the jamun now?' It created ripples in the lake as it turned to check. Luckily, the deformed fruit floated nearby. The crocodile nudged it with its snout.

'Friend, I sense you doubt me. To prove I eat only fruits and vegetables, I will eat this jamun right here, right now, in front of you.'

In less than a second, the fruit was gone. The crocodile bit into it with razor-sharp teeth, while the monkey covered its eyes, intimidated by the reptile's formidable features.

'Delicious,' said the crocodile, licking its teeth. 'But one will not suffice. I need at least a dozen to fill my stomach.'

The monkey, a hoarder by nature, wanted the crocodile gone. 'I will not give you my jamun. There is no point in lingering near my home.'

The crocodile, not easily defeated, persisted. 'Please, don't turn me away. Let us make a deal. For a dozen jamun, you may ask for anything you want. I promise to grant it.'

The monkey remembered the reptile was an adventurer. Born and raised in the jambul tree, it had named the tree its legal guardian after being abandoned by its parents. Now, as the tree aged, the monkey served as a dedicated caretaker, which ensured a solitary life. It spent days swinging between branches, chased away other animals, and ate only the same fruit repeatedly.

The crocodile's promise sparked a rare opportunity, and the monkey did not dismiss it.

'So, whatever I wish, you will fulfill?' asked the monkey, seeking complete assurance.

'Trust me! I am loyal. Whatever your wish, I will grant it,' replied the crocodile convincingly. 'But first, tell me what it is.'

'Well,' the monkey hesitated, 'since you are an adventurer…'

'Yes, yes, please go on, I am listening,' said the impatient crocodile, cutting no corners.

'Let me try again. I know you are an adventurer. Will you show me around? Though I have lived by Kolavai Lake all my life, I have never seen its real beauty or felt its essence. I want to explore the waters, witness what lies above and below, meet new creatures, hear new sounds, smell new scents, taste new foods. The thought excites me so!' The monkey leaped to another sturdy limb in excitement.

'My friend, it will be my pleasure. I promise this will be your most unforgettable adventure.'

'Thank you,' said the monkey, pleased and relieved.

'Adventure is greatest when the adventurer knows not what to expect. We both venture into the unknown, which makes our expedition incredible,' said the crocodile, like a merchant enticing a buyer.

Amidst the excitement, the monkey remembered its home. If it left, who would protect the tree from intruders?

'If the jambul tree is left unattended, who knows what might happen? What if all the jamun are gone by the time I return? I can't risk losing my only food source,' said the monkey, regretting not thinking of this sooner.

'Don't worry about food. Along the journey, we will find plenty. I will help you return with enough to last an entire year. Even if your tree is stripped bare, there will be no need to grieve,' said the crocodile, reassuringly.

Any doubts or concerns the monkey had were formed into questions, directed at the crocodile. With immense patience, the reptile answered them exhaustively, hopeful that the primate would not change its mind about embarking on the journey.

'To fulfill a wish or make a dream come true, one must be willing to sacrifice. In your case, to experience this desire, you must risk the security of your home. Life is about give and take, take and give. We can't have everything we want, my friend. It does not work that way.'

The crocodile's words made sense to the monkey. This was its chance—the first opportunity since childhood to venture beyond the confines of its jambul tree. Whether sent by God or fate, the reptile appeared as a savior, guiding the primate toward independence.

Bidding farewell to the jambul tree was no easy task. The monkey was confident it would return, yet it would deeply miss the motherly support and fatherly protection the tree had provided since its early days. Carefully selecting the plumpest jamun, the monkey let them sail into the lake for the crocodile to gather. Instead of the twelve requested, it sent eighteen—just in case the journey offered no other food.

Once the crocodile had collected the floating fruit, it beckoned the monkey. 'My friend, you will need to climb onto my back,' said the reptile, approaching the shore. 'From now on, I am your boat and you are my passenger. Stay on my back at all times.'

The monkey hesitated. Being so close to the crocodile was intimidating. Its webbed feet, leathery skin, armored scales, powerful muscles, enormous jaw, and knife-like teeth made the primate shudder.

Noticing the monkey's hesitation, the crocodile asked, 'Let me guess—it's my appearance?'

'It's because of your appearance that no one comes near you. Others judge me before they know me. Why look at my face and body, but not my heart? God gave my kind this form. I've accepted it. If you cannot see past my appearance, our journey together is pointless.'

Feeling sympathy, the monkey replied, 'I'll be honest—I was nervous when I first saw you enter my home. But as we spoke, I began to trust your words. Some may say you have sharp teeth, others venomous eyes, or grimy skin—but none of that matters. I know you will not deceive me.'

'This appearance has never allowed me friendship, until now,' said the crocodile as the monkey leapt onto its back. Startled by the primate's weight, the crocodile asked, 'I never knew your kind was so delicate. Do you eat anything besides jamun?'

'I've lived my life eating the same fruit day after day. But that will change on this journey. I'm desperate to experience new foods. What do you recommend?'

'Friend, I have all kinds of fruits and vegetables at my habitat. Everything there is delicious.'

The monkey could not contain its excitement, using the crocodile's durable back like a trampoline, bouncing up and down.

'So, will you travel to my habitat?' the crocodile asked.

'Sure, but how far is it?'

'Not too far from this lake. If we leave now, we'll reach the swamp by evening.'

The monkey hesitated. 'Hmm, that seems like a long journey. Maybe we should stick to exploring Kolavai Lake today.'

'Why not fill our stomachs first? This lake doesn't have the variety of foods the swamp does. To taste new fruits and vegetables, we must go to the swamp. We'll enjoy the food and return to Kolavai Lake tomorrow morning.'

'I'm not comfortable traveling to a place I don't know.'

'You are in safe hands. I will be with you—by you, for you. After all, it is my habitat. Trust me, there is nothing to worry about.'

'But what about Kolavai Lake? Weren't we supposed to explore it today?'

'The lake is here today and will be here tomorrow. Trust me, it will not disappear,' said the crocodile, snickering.

Craving any food other than jamun, the monkey agreed. Delaying the exploration of Kolavai Lake for the promise of new flavors seemed reasonable. The plan set by the crocodile was accepted.

As friends who trusted each other, the monkey and crocodile happily proceeded to the swamp. Along the way, they were so engrossed in conversation that neither noticed the marvelous sunset painting the sky in vibrant hues. The primate, who had lived in isolation, longed for company, and never explored its surroundings, felt as if it had finally emerged from its mother's womb. This journey felt like a new birth.

'You know, if it weren't for you, I don't think I'd ever leave my tree. I know, for sure, that all my dreams will come true on this expedition. I can't thank you enough for what you've done for me,' said the monkey.

For the first time since their journey began, the crocodile turned its head to face the monkey. The primate shivered at the sight of the reptile's vicious teeth, unsure why they remained visible even when the mouth was closed. The urge to ask lingered, but the monkey remained silent.

'There is no need to thank me,' replied the crocodile. 'You have given me food when I needed it most. I must repay you by letting you into my home to enjoy the scrumptious foods I have gathered.'

'All this talk about food is making me hungry. How far is your home?' the monkey asked, growing impatient.

'Not far. Let us not worry about time and distance.' The crocodile assumed the role of guide, pointing out various plants and animals, mountains and waterfalls, rivers and streams. It was as if they were etched into a living portrait of God's flawless creations.

As the sun began to hide its face, the monkey heard sounds it had never encountered. 'What is that?'

'Owls,' whispered the crocodile.

'What are they doing?'

'Hooting. They are nocturnal animals.'

'Nocturnal?'

'It means they sleep during the day and wake at night.'

The monkey giggled. It had never seen or heard of such a creature. 'Strange. What business does it have at night?'

'Hunting,' the crocodile replied, accelerating its stubby feet. 'Friend, make yourself invisible. Lower your head—I don't want the owl to swoop down and snatch you.' Without wasting a second, the crocodile surged forward at top speed. Hesitant but trusting, the monkey gripped the crocodile's head, narrowly avoiding owl's talons.

After the escape, the monkey, drenched from the splashing water, shook itself vigorously to dry its fur, sending droplets onto the crocodile's face.

'I am sorry,' said the monkey. 'Swimming at high speed makes water fly everywhere. I should have remembered that unlike me, you are used to water.'

'True,' replied the monkey. 'Back at Kolavai Lake, I rarely went near the shore. Occasionally, I drink or collect fallen jamun. Honestly, I can't even remember the last time I bathed. No wonder I have so many lice. How do you endure being wet all the time? Don't you feel cold?'

'I never feel cold,' said the crocodile proudly. 'I am not warm-blooded like you.'

'Huh?' the monkey asked, confused.

'I am cold-blooded.'

The monkey was stunned. 'And here I thought every creature was warm-blooded. There is so much I have to learn about this world and its inhabitants.'

Befriending the reptile had not been a bad idea. As time passed, the monkey felt increasingly attached to the crocodile. It relied on the reptile for lessons and guidance, but also felt comfortable sharing personal stories and feelings. A connection had formed, as if they had known each other in a previous life—or perhaps the monkey had simply never given itself the chance to bond with another creature. Now, free from habitual isolation, it addressed the crocodile as a true friend.

'So, friend, how much longer until we reach the swamp?' the monkey asked, smiling broadly. The grin revealed a set of rotten teeth that had never been properly cleaned.

'Almost there,' replied the crocodile. It paused, considering whether to speak, before asking, 'Forgive me if I sound rude, but why don't you take care of your teeth?'

'I don't know. Does it matter?'

'Well, if you clean them, they will remain strong, sharp, and durable—just like mine,' said the crocodile, opening its mouth to reveal perfect teeth. 'With my teeth, I can break, cut, rip, rupture, snatch, shred, split, and separate.'

'Why is that necessary?' asked the monkey, frowning. 'I don't have strong teeth like yours, yet I can still bite into my food. Dirty, decayed teeth work fine for fruits and vegetables. If I were eating flesh, then perhaps teeth like yours would matter.'

After hearing the last comment, the reptile felt as if its tongue had tied itself into multiple knots. The crocodile did not know whether to add a witty remark or change the topic, so it remained silent.

Before the creatures reached the swamp, darkness had cast overbearing shadows across the entire area. The monkey did not possess the same vision as the crocodile, who could see everything above and beneath the waters. Surrounded by dimness, the monkey felt nervous. Back in its habitat, when the sun slipped behind the mountains, creatures hid in caves, burrows, holes, and trees. In Kolavai Lake, the monkey never left the jambal tree at night, aware that predators lurked nearby. And now, it was passing through a swamp filled with complete darkness and eerie silence.

'Why am I fretting? I have my new friend by my side. I must rely on the crocodile to protect me,' the monkey said to itself.

The crocodile, which had been silent since entering the swamp, finally put its feet to rest. The monkey noticed the raft decelerating.

'Are we planning to rest before continuing?' asked the primate.

'Continue where? My friend, this is the swamp. This is where I was born and raised.'

'It is a shame that I cannot see how beautiful your habitat is.'

'Beautiful—that's a first,' countered the reptile.

'Why do you say that?'

'Let's not talk about that,' replied the crocodile, ignoring the simple question. 'First, I must ask: are you scared of water?'

'I am not scared of water,' answered the monkey honestly.

'Well, then I am sure that you won't mind getting wet from head to toe.'

'I sure would,' replied the monkey bluntly. 'I hate getting wet. It takes forever to dry my body. I am not hairless like you, nor do I have skin like yours.'

'My friend, you must understand. My home is not above the waters—it is below them. To taste all the different kinds of fruits and vegetables, you must dive into the waters.'

'How will I do that? I don't know how to swim,' said the monkey, flinging its dangly arms in frustration. The primate was annoyed at the lack of prior warning that the reptile's home was beneath the waters. It had assumed the food was stored in caves, burrows, or shrubs, like most land animals.

'Don't worry, I am with you. We'll dive together. All you have to do is hold firmly onto my neck.'

'But what if—' the monkey stalled, uneasy about diving. 'What if I cannot hold my breath long enough?'

'You will not need to hold it for long. I will bring you above the surface every minute for a breather.' The crocodile knew exactly how the monkey felt. Instead of halting its persuasion, the crocodile lured its friend with a meticulous description of the exquisite foods beneath the waters, over and over again.

'Is it necessary for me to come with you?' asked the monkey.

'It sure is, my friend. I want you to visit my home, but most importantly, I want you to explore. I want you to see, taste, touch, and hear things you have never encountered before. Beneath the waters exists a different world—completely diverse from the one you know. Trust me; this will be a memorable experience.'

The hesitant primate knew it should not let this opportunity slip, though an unfamiliar feeling signaled caution in its heart.

'To achieve and evolve in life, one must take chances. Now is your time to explore. Don't let this opportunity pass by,' said the reptile, spellbindingly.

Even though the monkey did not know what to expect from the swamp, it chose to enter unfamiliar territory. Knowing it could not hold its breath for long, it still clung to the crocodile's neck, determined to experience something new. The primate's fears were overpowered by its desire to explore.

Once the swamp water touched its fur, the monkey took a deep inhale, closed its eyes, and pinched its nose to prevent water from entering its lungs. The waters of Kolavai Lake were not much different from the inscrutable swamp—cold and foreboding.

'Open your eyes,' the crocodile instructed.

After hearing this twice, the monkey freed its eyelids and beheld wonder. 'This is an entirely different world from where I come from,' it whispered to itself. Astonished, the monkey forgot to release its nose, holding tightly onto the crocodile's neck, and wrapped its tail around the reptile's upper chest for extra security.

The monkey marveled at how fast the crocodile swam underwater compared to above. It had so many questions, but opening its mouth risked inhaling water, so it kept silent, focusing on the underwater sights.

It discovered intertwining roots of trees it had never seen, looming monstrous trees far larger than the jambal tree. Their shadows hovered over the water, dominating the submerged world. Despite the dim light, the monkey observed creatures and plants in abundance.

Numerous schools of fish swam in tight circles, scattering in all directions as the crocodile and monkey passed. The primate was baffled by their fear. 'Why are they afraid of the crocodile?' it asked itself.

While moving towards the area where the crocodile stored the goodies, the tourist and guide came across small, black-colored dots. In groups of hundreds or more, these teeny-weeny creatures swam in circles near the bottom of the swamp. Were they insects, fish, or some kind of amphibian? The monkey did not know. It examined the pesky little creatures and discovered that they did not have hands or feet, but they did have a tail shaped like a sword. Of course, the primate was fascinated, but when a creature with a shell on its back glided through the waters, the monkey was impressed. To its surprise, the exotic creature was in no hurry to flee, giving the monkey a chance to observe it closely.

'Hmm, so the shell is for protection. With the shell on its back, no predator will be able to bite its flesh,' said the monkey to itself, wishing that its own body were similarly protected.

Being the perfect guide, the crocodile swerved near the mysterious creature so the monkey could get a better look. Up close, the primate noticed how ancient the creature appeared, with wrinkles across its hairless face, stubby feet, and tiny tail. Once it sensed that the guide and tourist were intruding, the creature disappeared. No face, no feet, no tail—only the shell remained. The monkey almost fell off its seat.

'Where did it go? Oh my, that was like magic. One second it was there, the next it was gone. It is probably hiding in its shell... no, it can't be hiding... actually, I think it is hiding,' the monkey muttered to itself, unsure what to believe.

With so much to take in, the monkey had not realized how long it had held its breath underwater. At the moment, air was not essential, but it felt no harm in surfacing. So the monkey tapped on the crocodile's noggin. The reptile understood and swam to the surface. Able to communicate both underwater and above, the crocodile informed the monkey they were less than a minute away from the stored fruits and vegetables.

'I am very impressed with your endurance. It is hard to believe that your kind can hold its breath underwater for so long,' said the crocodile pleasantly. 'I am sure you can manage a few more minutes. Let's first collect as much food as possible, then surface to enjoy our meal.'

The monkey trusted its friend completely and nodded, signaling that it was unnecessary to surface yet. It did not take long for them to reach the designated area. As soon as the crocodile declared the empty area its home, the monkey urgently searched for the fruits and vegetables—but there were no signs of food.

All sorts of thoughts swirled in the primate's brain, most negative: was this some kind of prank? No matter how pessimistic, it did not let its trust in the crocodile falter. Relief came when it spotted shrubs not too far away. The monkey pointed excitedly.

'Friend, I must say, you are clever. How did you know the food was hidden behind those shrubs?' asked the reptile.

The monkey, able to hear but not speak, felt its stomach grumble. Its enthusiasm was boundless. Finally, it felt like a true explorer, someone it had longed to become since childhood.

'The food is behind the shrubs,' said the crocodile, signaling the monkey to step down. Letting go of the crocodile's neck, the monkey flapped its arms like a bird and kicked its legs like a horse to reach the shrubs. Not born to swim, it struggled through the swamp waters. The reptile guided the primate with its tail, directing it toward the shrubs.

Now before the monkey, the shrubs concealed the long-promised fruits and vegetables. It began to clear the path with its hands, ignoring thorns or branches. Until its hands met a solid object. Its face pressed into the bushes, the monkey could not see what it had grabbed.

Finally, it freed its hands and eyes to inspect the object. One look and the primate accepted its fate. Standing between the shrubs, it peered through a small opening—and the sudden blow forced it to gasp. Instead of air, a large amount of water entered its lungs. The monkey dropped the object—a bone—and saw the scene before it.

A cemetery. Bones from all kinds of animals littered the sandy ground. Some were fresh; others decaying. Skulls, ribs, hands, and feet were detached from bodies. Most terrifying of all, the monkey saw a skeleton of its own kind.

'So this is it. I never imagined that aiding, befriending, and trusting someone would lead me here,' the monkey whispered, struggling to breathe.

It was time to surface, but the imposter would not allow it. The crocodile's scheme was to be fulfilled at any cost.

'There is no place to run; there is no place to hide. This is the end of your journey,' said the reptile in a newly hostile tone.

The voice, once polite, became menacing. As the primate exited the bush, it faced the traitor.

'You used my hopes and desires against me. You forced me to abandon my home. You pressured me into exploring the swamp. You misled me into believing there was food behind the shrubs. I have fallen to the lies of a con artist,' the monkey muttered under its breath.

'At first, I thought you'd never give in. It is never easy to lure a creature of your kind into my trap. But I usually succeed due to my consistency. The collection of bones is the proof of my success,' said the crocodile, its tongue brushing the monkey's face. 'Let's not make this complicated. Close your eyes and acknowledge defeat. Soon your remains will be added to my cemetery.'

The monkey obeyed, convinced that there was no use living another second, minute, hour, or day. If it were to survive, the primate would return to its solitary life once again. There was no purpose in going back to its old life, nor in attempting a sociable life where trust had to be earned before it could rely on another. Betrayal, it knew, was inevitable. The closing of its eyes signified capitulation.

Finally, the rapturous crocodile added, 'Don't worry! It will not hurt as much as you think it will.'

After hearing the tale, Shivaji was left flabbergasted. Throughout the narration, he had not uttered a single word, yet his brain worked overtime. While the guru returned to his assigned position, the disciple ruminated over the monkey and the crocodile. Understanding Old Man Thambi was sometimes possible, but more often, near impossible. Shivaji sensed a hidden meaning in the beggar's tale. Thambi was known to weave riveting stories of the past, present, or future, but deciphering their essence had always challenged the widower.

'Probably, the crocodile symbolizes the British, and the monkey symbolizes the Indians,' Shivaji whispered to himself.

Standing motionless on the deck, oblivious to the unlit heavens, the silence around him, the weakening strength of his legs, and the dampness of his clothes, he was absorbed in thought. It was as if the world had ceased to exist.

'I think I finally understand the story. Baba has the crocodile as the British and the monkey as the Indians. The crocodile lures and deceives, just like the Englishmen have done to the Indians. The monkey trusts and accepts, just like the Indians boarded Ship Elbe. Now, if I am correct, the Indians will be devoured by the British. When? How? And where?'

Shivaji asked himself, angry yet helpless.

'Are we Indians fools, ready to be fooled? We have fallen into their trap. Deep down, I always knew not to believe, trust, or rely on the British. This is a trap planned and practiced for days, months, and years. Indians have been falling into this pit for ages, and will continue to entangle themselves in this web of their own idiocy,' Shivaji cried to the passive waves.

He cursed himself and the other Indians on board for agreeing to become laborers. 'How on earth did we sign the indenture contract, knowing these were the same people who had detained and conquered our land?'

Thambi's narrative had supressed whatever remaining faith and hope Shivaji had. Unlike his friend Venkatesh, he did not underestimate the beggar's words. Shivaji knew that everything Thambi said carried meaning. His words flowed like poetry, his riddles revealed hints, his outbursts signaled danger, and his teachings served as cautions and cues. Shivaji was convinced that Thambi had revealed the unalterable path the indentured laborer would tread, a road from which deviation was impossible.

THE 43RD DAY

The seafarers on board noticed various alterations. The most drastic change was in the weather. Previously, the heat had been endurable, but in the past several days the rising temperature led to heat strokes, blackouts, rashes, and swellings. The dehydrated indentured labourers had no choice but to overuse the water in the barrels. The British seafarers literally pushed or pulled the Indians away from the barrels whenever they exceeded the time limit, sometimes striking them with batons for cleansing their mouths, hands, and feet for too long.

"There is no future. Certainly, there is no future for a labourer," Shivaji whispered to himself. At times, he felt as if he did not want to live. Several times, he refused to join the line leading to the water barrels, remaining seated next to the railing while the others quenched their thirst. On the few occasions he did accompany Venkatesh, Lachmiaya, and Karthik, he was practically forced by his friends to sip water. Shivaji felt there was no purpose in his life anymore. He did not wish to take his own life, nor to have it taken.

Shivaji longed for freedom, but first, he needed to free his mind from unwanted blame. The remorse he felt after his wife's death still tormented him. Thoughts of vengeance surfaced constantly, but he knew Vyjanti would never consent to such destruction. During the night, like a nocturnal owl planning a scheme to trap and kill its prey, Shivaji remained awake for hours, strategizing how to annihilate the British seafarers. Yet, when the sun rose, his malicious ideas evaporated.

On the morning of the forty-third day, Shivaji's criminal thoughts remained intact. He stepped forward, ready to respond to his wife's death, but his feet and hands felt locked. He felt like a prisoner chained to an invisible obstruction. The entire scenario seemed paranormal. Then, in front of his eyes, Vyjanti appeared. She lingered for no more than a second before disappearing in the blink of an eye. Shivaji could not discern whether her face bore a smile or a frown. What he did notice was her attire—dressed from head to toe in black.

"As far as I know, Vyjanti never wore black. She despised it. She did not permit that color in her life, which was always vibrant—red, orange, blue, green, yellow," Shivaji murmured. He waited, hoping to catch another glimpse, but none came. He instantly understood her message. Entirely clad in a color representing evil, hostility, and melancholy, Vyjanti was warning him not to proceed with violence.

"I know that if I take the life of an Englishman, my life will not be spared. Even so, why do I feel a strong urge to move forward? Why do I want them to kill me?" Shivaji asked himself. "She became visible only to protect me. Vyjanti does not want me to succumb to violence. My limbs are chained because she wants me to live. Perhaps, I am destined to achieve something worthy in this fight against injustice and in the battle for liberty."

Once the harmful thoughts of retribution dissolved, Shivaji seated himself against the railing to welcome the active sunrise. He did not notice how or when he regained movement in his limbs. Instead, he focused on the moderate pace of the vessel. The lights on the upper deck were lit, and he heard voices issuing orders. He looked to the waters below, wary of Mother Nature's possible fury, but the ocean remained calm. Turning his gaze to the heavens, he saw no clouds gathering into a fatal battalion.

Shivaji noticed that the continuous vibration of the floor beneath him was no longer lively. The relaxed movement of the vessel hinted that something disastrous was imminent. His mind teemed with fatalistic thoughts, never considering that the ship's leisurely pace might lead to something propitious. Shielding his eyes from the sun with his left arm, he sniffed an unfamiliar freshness in the air. Neither in India's villages nor the Pacific waters had he encountered such a scent. Perspiration streamed from his forehead, the heat and sweat burning his skin.

"It seems the sun has been angered. Never before have I felt such extreme heat," he whispered. He rubbed his face against his collarbone to let his tattered kurta absorb the sweat, but no matter how much he tried, the flow did not stop. "The sun can dry crops, plants, rivers, and streams, so why not the human body? Why can't it dry the sweat pouring from my forehead, armpits, and shins?"

As he pondered, his eyes met a massive landmass surrounding the vessel. Compared to the cargo ship, the island was monstrous. The closer the vessel came, the more it seemed as if the island would swallow the ship whole. Silent and empty, it appeared unused and rejected.

Celebration erupted on the upper deck as the Englishmen eagerly prepared to set foot on the island. The noise awoke the Indians below. After struggling to comprehend the commotion, the indentured labourers caught sight of the angelic sands, colorful trees, and grassy hills. Not a single Indian raised a hand to clap, cheered, or smiled. The foreign land left them mystified, torn between excitement and terror. Some felt relief that their voyage on Ship Elbe was nearing its end, while others were anxious, convinced the worst was yet to come. Though all manners of emotion coursed through them, none were verbally expressed.

From the hundreds of islands that form Fiji, the largest island welcomed the first shipment of indentured labourers from South India. Exiting Ship Elbe was inefficient, due to the lack of communication and understanding between the Indians and the Englishmen. Luckily for the British, as soon as the indentured labourers set foot on the beach, close to a dozen white officers were already on scene. The officers began to gather and divide the Indians into several groups, assisted by trained canines.

As Shivaji placed his feet on the shoreline, he felt the burning sand cuddle his toes. Before taking a step forward, he felt a wet nose rub against his leg. Instantly, he turned around to see a furry animal covered in a beige coat, growling furiously. Shivaji's heart bounced in panic. In his village, whenever he crossed paths with a dog, he trembled in fear. He remembered his appa telling him there were two ways to handle a dog:

"If you are daring, stand your ground and lower your arm to the ground to find a stone. Even if there are no stones, the dog will believe you have something to throw and will flee. If you are not daring, run as fast as you can. And if there is a tree nearby, climb to its branches."

Unfortunately, there was no time for Shivaji to lower his arms, nor any tree nearby. He inhaled loudly, attempting to conceal his uneasiness. Just as the canine revealed its full-mouthed bark, the owner yanked the leash vigorously, causing it to howl in pain. Astonished, Shivaji watched as the dog quickly disregarded the pain and obeyed another command. For a moment, he thought how similar he and the other indentured labourers were to this animal. Both were ordered here and there, to do this and that. The only difference was that the canine had a leash.

"Soon the British will place a rope around our necks, ordering us to go, stop, sit, and bite," Shivaji murmured. He waited to locate Venkatesh and his family, scanning the enormous crowd of bewildered people. Some Indians were being tossed and shoved, while others were dragged by British guards into assigned areas. When chaos escalated, the guards resorted to their last option—the faithful baton.

The twenty-five minute sequence of havoc eventually began to settle. The Indians were initially frightened by the canines howling and growling between their legs, believing the dogs would be set loose on them. In reality, the British were simply organizing the labourers into smaller groups without dividing families.

Shivaji huddled among the indentured labourers—male and female, Hindu and Muslim, covered and uncovered—eager to rest his eyes on Venkatesh. His concentration shattered when a shot fired into the air pierced the chaos. Many women and children screamed, while the men instinctively covered their ears. Shivaji, however, did not flinch. The sound was familiar to him; no rifle or bullet could evoke fear.

The shot came from a Lee-Metford rifle, held by the British commander. Automatically, all eyes turned to him. Standing close to six feet tall, weighing nearly two hundred pounds, his head high, shoulders lifted, chest expanded, and face devoid of emotion, he radiated authority.

"The total count of indentured labourers from Ship Elbe is three hundred sixty-seven. The total number of British guards on site is twelve. Since we are outnumbered, the task will be difficult. Men, we are to escort these coolies to the depot on foot. Each guard will have close to thirty coolies in their group.

If these Indians cause any problem whatsoever, do not hesitate to use your baton. If one of them dares to ignore or defy your command, make sure to respond with extreme violence. God forbid, if one of the coolies raises his hand or foot towards you, please let me know. I do not tolerate physical or verbal retaliation, especially from these no-class, low-grade peasants. Understood?" the armed British commander asked his team members.

His men, dressed in red and white, all replied in sync, "Yes, sir!"

"Don't forget that once we deliver the coolies to the depot you must return to the shore again. By then, the British seafarers of Ship Elbe will be done unloading the bags of sugarcane ordered by the Colonial Sugar Refining Company from India. With their assistance, you are to carry these heavy bags to the depot for safekeeping," said the man in charge.

There was no interpreter to translate what the British commander had said, yet the indentured labourers understood that they were required to follow the leader with their mouths shut. They knew this was not the time or place to ask questions, raise complaints, or make demands. Still unable to locate Venkatesh and his family, Shivaji felt tense. "What if something happened? What if they did not leave the vessel? What if they were separated into different groups? What if Karthik was not by his parents' side?" Shivaji asked himself. After the loss of his wife, his every question turned pessimistic.

Shivaji was so involved in locating his friends that he had forgotten about his other companion, Old Man Thambi. With no food in their stomachs for over fifteen hours, the indentured labourers were ordered to march ahead. Many glanced back to catch a final glimpse of the vessel that had been their lamentable home for the past forty-three days. For the Indians, Ship Elbe brought memories of hardship; whenever they recalled the voyage, thoughts of blood, sweat, and tears emerged. For Shivaji it was too hard to look back—the vessel had taken what he had lived for. To him, Ship Elbe represented death. In his view, the vessel and its seafarers were partly to blame for the deplorable life he now led.

Fifteen minutes of steady walking resulted in exhaustion. With aching muscles and growling stomachs, most Indians felt as if they might faint. Some needed food, some needed water, some needed rest, some needed to relieve themselves. No food, water, or breaks were given.

"So these Indians are supposed to be diligent farm workers? How is that possible? Look at these measly labourers! They are huffing and puffing after fifteen minutes of walking," the officer in command sneered with pride in his voice.

What the British commander did not know was that these Indians were moving forward on empty stomachs and with severe dehydration. If these indentured labourers were given a proper meal—or even one meal per day, as they had back home—they could outperform every British guard on scene.

Before the short hand of the clock reached nine, the indentured labourers arrived at the depot. The area around the depot seemed deserted. There were no signs of Indians inside or outside the depot. Nonetheless, officers of the colonial system were present, dressed in their usual red and white uniforms. For the indentured labourers, all the Englishmen began to look the same. It was as if they were all close to six feet tall and weighed at least two hundred pounds. All of the men had similar, dense, and unkempt beards. These beards were not entirely black but contained lighter shades of red and brown. Their eyes were not always black or brown; some were blue or green. These domineering men walked with grandeur and spoke with absolute confidence. Even when the British remained still, their posture exuded authority. Their shoulders were even, backs straight, chests overextended, and feet close together.

The British commander who had led the Indians to the depot ordered his team to usher the labourers to the washing area. Not far from the depot were barrels filled with water. These wooden containers were three times the size of the barrels on Ship Elbe.

Immediately, the Indians began drenching themselves in lukewarm water. In the last few days on Ship Elbe, the indentured labourers had not been permitted to bathe. For that reason, they cherished the opportunity to cleanse their sweat- and dirt-covered bodies. However, this time, the Indians felt their skin burning. Was the boiling sun in combat with the salt water? Perhaps the water in the barrels had been tampered with by the British, thought Shivaji. Whatever the cause, the burning sensation troubled the Indians even after washing. With limitless drops of water pouring from their bodies onto the earth, the Indians were sent to open areas to dry themselves in the sun. With no hint of air brushing his face, Shivaji understood that the task of drying his body and clothes would be brief.

Realizing there were no British guards close by, Shivaji began to observe the island. He scanned the area to see grass in shades of yellow and brown, trees with no branches, trails with no clear start or end, and hills devoid of cows and goats. The island of Fiji was vastly different from his village, district, and country. Whatever he had seen, he did not like. But Shivaji knew this was just the beginning. "I should not compare or judge at this moment. There is more to witness and experience on this island," Shivaji told himself.

As soon as the British commander felt that the Indians were dry, he marched back to the depot with his team, groups of labourers following behind. Armed guards were positioned at the depot entrance. The hatred etched on their faces made the Indians uneasy. Their hearts raced, stomachs trembled, and eyes filled with tears. The indentured labourers hesitated to enter the unwelcoming storage area. Fear gripped their throats. As they were led inside, the wives stayed close to their husbands, and children clutched their fathers' hands and held onto their mothers' waists. No one knew what to expect.

Inside the dull depot were more British officers of the colonial system. The difference among the officers was that their uniforms displayed numerous badges, which made no sense to the Indians. To the indentured labourers, all the Englishmen were the same. These Indians did not know—and did not need to know—that the officers serving as barriers were Immigrant Inspection Officers. These officers decided whether a coolie was in good health after the gruelling voyage on Ship Elbe. If the labourer was fit, he or she would receive a certificate of fitness and proceed to the next step. If the labourer was ill, he or she would be sent to the civil hospital, which was not far from the depot.

There were ten lines, each with an Immigrant Inspection Officer. These officers called labourers one at a time, except for families with small children, who were allowed to present themselves together. As the officers examined the Indians from head to toe, Shivaji kept his own observation team at work. The team of two—his eyes—carefully watched the Englishmen sign a basic, letter-sized form, which was then given to the labourer to hand over to the British guard standing nearly twenty feet behind the officer. Many Indians were inspected visually, while some were examined diligently.

"So how does this work? Does an Indian need both arms and legs in working condition to be sent to the British guards?" Shivaji asked himself, impatiently waiting his turn. Like a child searching for loved ones, he turned from side to side, hoping to spot Venkatesh, Lachmaiya, or Karthik. Instead, he caught a glimpse of his dear friend, Old Man Thambi. Shivaji wanted his eyes fixed on Thambi, but with so many shifting bodies impeding his view, the task became challenging. To regain sight of the old man, Shivaji began pushing and shoving the other Indians in line. All he knew was that Thambi was not in the same queue as him, so Shivaji cut into different lines, desperate to come face to face with his friend. The budging did not sit well with the indentured labourers, who felt elbows thrust into their ribs, beards brushing their faces, and feet crushing their toes. Some of the Indians did not repress their protests.

"Oye, watch your step," said an elderly man who looked about the same age as Shivaji's father.

"You have no decency. Didn't your parents teach you manners? How can you shove a female?" asked a Muslim woman whose face was partially covered by a veil.

"Is he trying to cut the line to be examined first? If that is the case, then he needs to be detained by the British officers," said an Indian husband standing close to his wife and daughters.

"Maybe he is in search of his deceased wife," said an Indian who recognized the widower.

Shivaji paid no attention to the calls pitched in his direction. These bitter sayings had the power to pierce the heart, but Shivaji did not let that happen. He avoided the taunts and barged through the crowds. Not once did he think about the British and their lethal weapons, nor about the grievous punishment that might follow his bold act. Once again, the rebel within him began to surface. And this time, there was no Venkatesh or Vyjanti to tame him. Shivaji wanted to reunite with his mentor. He needed someone he knew to be with him on this far-off island.

The area where Shivaji had caused the disturbance was filled with many British guards. Though, before an Englishman could lay a hand on Shivaji, Thambi appeared.

"Baba!" yelled Shivaji, ignoring the fact that his voice could easily be detected by the Englishmen. "Look, Baba, it's me, your friend, Shivaji."

The beggar, standing near the front of the line, listened to the familiar voice echo in his limited hearing. He then took a full three-sixty turn to see the widower standing close to him. His facial expression stunned Shivaji. Never had the widower seen the beggar oppressed by concern.

"What is the matter, Baba?"

There was no response.

"Baba, can you hear me?" asked Shivaji, unaware that his loud voice was indeed audible, despite the cacophony of the depot.

With a shiver in his voice, Old Man Thambi replied, "You must leave! For so long you and I were travelling the same road. But now our roads are different. It is time for us to part."

"What is that supposed to mean? Don't say that. We will not be separated," replied Shivaji, desperate to instill confidence in the beggar.

"This is not my decision. It is His decision," said Thambi, pointing his finger toward the ceiling.

As the beggar leaned forward to console Shivaji, his wooden stick fell from his hands. Once the stick hit the floor, it was gone. Instantly, Shivaji knelt to find it. "Someone must have accidentally kicked it," he said under his breath. Amid a countless number of legs and feet, the stick had disappeared.

The old man pulled Shivaji to his feet. "Forget it. It is of no use anymore. Someone must have walked over it. I have a feeling it's in multiple pieces."

"How can you be so sure? You need that wooden stick. Baba, you rely on it to walk around."

"Son, let it go. It was meant to be my relief and support for a certain time only. When the time came for it to leave, it did. Bonds, ties, connections, relationships don't last forever. But if it is meant to be, they transfer from one life to another."

Deep in his heart, Shivaji felt that this conversation might be his last with Old Man Thambi. His eyes burned. His lips were dry. The widower consoled the beggar silently.

"I will be there in the next life, in a different form, with a different face. Once again, we will meet. But we will not meet as widower and beggar," said Thambi, confident that Shivaji was following his meaning.

"How will I know that it is you?" asked Shivaji.

"You will not know. No one knows. But do expect a heartfelt connection."

Shivaji let go of the beggar. Like a worshipful son respecting his father, he bent down and touched his guru's feet for a blessing. Thambi placed his trembling hands on Shivaji's head. The follower did not meet his guide's eyes. Shivaji was so dispirited that he retreated to his line without bidding farewell. By letting go of Thambi, he accepted the notion that his sins had caused the people he loved to disappear from his life.

As he walked back to his initial line, Shivaji felt the presence of his enemies closing in. From the corner of his eye, he observed red and white uniforms. His ears caught the sound of batons repeatedly striking against the palms of Englishmen. Shivaji pushed and pulled harder through the crowd to retain his position in line. Indians shouted insults at him, but the words did not bother the widower. By tugging on sleeves, stepping on toes, and writhing past bodies, Shivaji reached his original spot.

He looked back to see if the British guards were behind him. Instead of following, the guards rushed toward a commotion in a different area. Shivaji did not know the reason, but the men with batons headed toward the uproar. The chaos erupted from the same area Shivaji had left moments ago. Many Indians had left their spots in line to witness the dramatic scene. Shivaji felt a sharp pang in his abdomen. The fear of losing Thambi gripped his mind. From a distance, he could see four armed guards, one disarmed beggar, and numerous bystanders. The British guards, powerful in every aspect, were struggling to detain Thambi.

The beggar did not restrain himself from unleashing verbal bombs.

"At first, we were enticed, and now we are being deceived. The British say that I am of no use to them, that I am not capable of performing duties in the sugarcane fields. These whites have a problem with my appearance. I am too old, and I am too small—that is what the Englishmen say. These whites cannot judge me; only God can. I want everyone to understand that the Englishmen know we are more capable than them. If we were not capable, we would not have been selected to work on this tropical island," shouted Thambi as he struggled against the British guards, who were unable to get a firm hold of him.

The beggar was indeed performing a comical yet defiant act for the indentured labourers, playing a cat-and-mouse game with the British guards. He knew all eyes were on him. In the spotlight, this was his opportunity to shine. The unfolding scene made it impossible for Shivaji to watch Thambi continuously, but he could still hear the beggar's words.

"Why can't these guards stop me from moving my feet? Why can't they stop me from moving my hands? Why can't they stop me from moving my mouth? Dear God, these white folks are having so much trouble detaining me, yet they still insist that I have a disease, that I am suffering from malnutrition. Most of you probably believe the Englishmen, but I know for sure that my son does not believe these lies," Thambi shouted, before his next words were obstructed by a human hand.

Instead of grasping his arms or legs, one of the British guards covered the beggar's mouth. As soon as he felt the hand over his mouth, Thambi bit down on the guard's fingers. The screams were so loud that they echoed across the depot. The remaining British guards rushed to their colleague's aid, yanking on the old man's hair, which luckily released the guard's fingers. Wailing in pain, the guard examined his numb hand.

Thambi, who seemed to have lost his mind, laughed hysterically. "I was told by the Immigrant Inspection Officer that I will be sent to the civil hospital. Why must I go to a hospital? Do I look ill?" he asked the Indian bystanders.

As he voiced his protests, Thambi felt a baton strike the upper portion of his right shoulder. Immediately, the old man plummeted to his knees. At that moment, he knew that his last brouhaha was over. He no longer dared resist the British. His sayings, which had begun and ended with insults, were silenced. The spirited limbs that had helped him escape the oppressors were now lifeless. One might expect the beggar to flinch in pain after the blow, but he did not. Instead, Thambi mumbled a few words to himself.

He was escorted out of the depot by multiple British guards, offering no resistance. As he reached the exit, his last words drifted into Shivaji's ears: "Be the first within our community to disturb the unethical system."

Where the beggar was led, no one knew. During the voyage on Ship Elbe, he had once been removed from the lower deck, only to return later in full strength. With that in mind, the Indians anticipated Thambi's return—sooner or later. Shivaji, however, did not. He accepted that his mentor would not reappear in his life. For others, losing Thambi did not matter. But for Shivaji, it was like losing a father. The widower had no tears to show, but he mourned his guru silently.

With the beggar's departure came an eerie silence in the depot. The elders began to question themselves after witnessing what had transpired with Thambi. The old folks had developed the jitters, wishing that the Immigrant Inspection Officer would overlook their bran-like skin and frail bones. To journey to the islands in such a hostile state, leaving behind village, family, and friends only to be rejected for work due to infirmity would break any elderly man or woman.

For Shivaji, it did not matter whether he would be sent to the fields or the civil hospital. He knew his chances of being sent to work were higher, as he was at the prime age to fulfill any duty. Ship Elbe had shown him that the indentured labourers would be maltreated in the fields just as they were on the vessel. In Shivaji's view, all British were the same. Ships, hospitals, or fields—the system of slavery persisted. The immoral system would not change in Fiji, he thought.

Waiting in line to be examined by the Immigrant Inspection Officer, the Indians had stood on their feet for hours. Shivaji did not track the seconds, minutes, or hours. His mind was fixed on Thambi's last words. What surprised him most was that he did not act when Thambi was manhandled. Normally, he would have lost control—especially in situations where a close friend needed help. Usually, others intervened to protect him, like his deceased wife Vyjanti and childhood friend Venkatesh. But in this last incident, there was no one. One would expect him to fly into a rage, but he did not. Shivaji developed self-control. He restrained the anger boiling inside him and tamed the creeping remorse as the situation unfolded. Perhaps, there was a divine purpose for him to understand. Old Man Thambi had been destined to exit the picture. With his departure, Shivaji lost a true friend but gained the power to govern his actions and emotions.

"Next..."

Shivaji was lost in thoughts of the individuals who had left his side in the past few months. Images of familiar faces flickered through his mind, appearing and disappearing in rapid succession.

"I repeat, next in line, please," said the Immigrant Inspection Officer, raising his eyes from the papers lying before him. The officer resembled most of the other Englishmen working for the colonial system—big, strong, and heavily whiskered. He dressed according to the standards of an officer, with hair groomed, shirt tucked, belt fastened, and laces tied. His medals and badges gleamed, despite the dim lighting in the depot. Everything about him radiated authority and importance.

"Listen, coolie, you better come over here before I leave my post. And if I leave my post, then your arse is mine. Don't force me to shove my baton so far up your arse—" Before the officer could finish, Shivaji returned to the present. Fortunately, the indentured labourer behind him tapped his shoulder, snapping him back to attention.

Shivaji was examined from head to toe with deliberate malice. He was ordered to turn around, lift his arms, show his feet, and open his mouth. Shivaji complied without hesitation or resistance. Though he did not understand how the procedure determined the result, he was confident that he would be sent to the fields—and he was right. It took the officer two minutes and thirty-five seconds to declare Shivaji a fit labourer permitted to work in the sugarcane fields. Shivaji was also assigned a five-digit immigrant number: 198423. Once his papers were stamped, he was directed toward a group of Indians assembled and supervised by a responsible British guard.

After the examinations, the indentured labourers were organized into bands of thirty to forty people. Each band was supervised by three guards, who worked as a team to control, manage, and guide the Indians. Bands with more children and elders were allowed to spend the night inside the depot, while those with fitter, younger labourers were instructed to sleep outside. At first, Shivaji felt fortunate that his band was allowed inside, while others were hurriedly ushered out.

As the depot doors closed, Shivaji felt a wave of stifling heat against his skin. The smell of hundreds of bodies packed together polluted the air, making it difficult to breathe. The crowded Indians were expected to eat and sleep in the depot without space to move comfortably.

When seated to consume the regular khichdi distributed among them, Shivaji felt utterly uncomfortable. There was insufficient space to fold his legs, making it hard to sit properly. Half the time, food that should have reached his stomach fell to the floor, as neighbours accidentally bumped him. While other Indians conversed with friends and family, Shivaji remained quiet, unwilling to introduce himself to strangers or engage in idle chatter.

"It seems my brothers and sisters have nothing to worry about. Do they not consider tomorrow? What if today is their last day and tomorrow is the end?" Shivaji asked himself. "Do they not realize the British have not employed them as field workers, but as slaves? Shillings, shillings, shillings... Is that all an indentured labourer cares for? Is this our future, to be dehumanized as mere servants?"

As his thoughts multiplied, Shivaji began to feel mentally drained. What troubled him most was that he no longer fully understood his own feelings. After the death of his wife, Shivaji had repressed his desire to fight for independence and resist enslavement. Yet, at times, circumstances and the acts of others caused those feelings to resurface. Alone, no one could detect the restless fighter dwelling within him. His face bore innocence, yet the wounds in his heart pushed him toward defiance and resistance.

Amid the hundreds of Indians gathered inside the depot, Shivaji repeatedly raised his head and strained his neck, scanning the crowd for Venkatesh, Lachmaiya, and Karthik. "God, please watch over my friend and his family," he silently prayed. "If not here, then where? Perhaps Venkatesh has been placed outside the depot. It is a shame I could not stay by his side during the evacuation on Ship Elbe," Shivaji said to himself, filled with regret.

The sunlight filtering through the window rails began to fade. Shivaji predicted the depot would be shrouded in darkness by nightfall. He fantasized about lying outside under the stars, breathing in the fresh air, with his wife close by his side. Unfortunately, these fantasies remained just that—fantasies, never to exist in reality.

The depot resembled more a prison than a shelter, with walls and floors made of cold, unyielding concrete. Once enclosed in the suffocating space, a person could easily feel trapped forever. The only concession was that if one needed to relieve oneself, he or she had to exit the depot. There was no loo inside, leaving labourers struggling to control their bladders. Asking the British guards for guidance or requesting directions seemed impossible. As a result, the congestion worsened, and the air was tainted with the pungent smell of urine.

When it was time for the indentured labourers to rest, sudden brightness lit the area, startling women and children. The British guards entered the depot, carrying small lanterns that could blind the eyes. They distributed blankets and a set of new clothes to each labourer—but not with care. Instead, the items were hurled at their faces with force. When a blanket struck the side of his face, Shivaji felt the full weight of humiliation. *"I am sure the Englishmen don't treat dogs this way. So what are we now, lower than dogs?"* he asked himself. He bit his tongue, unwilling to let his fierce emotions escape as harsh words.

Once the British guards left, most of the Indians clutched their blankets. Strangely, the night contrasted sharply with the day. Where the sun had brought waves of stifling heat, the pale moonlight and glistening stars carried chilling winds. As the cold embraced his body, Shivaji admitted that sleeping inside the depot was far preferable to being outside. Yet he did not forget the hundreds of indentured labourers—some minors, some elders—enduring the raw temperature outside.

As the night deepened, most of the Indians fell into sleep. Shivaji remained awake. Thoughts of his wife, Vyjanti, kept his eyes open. He felt her presence, intangible yet persistent, nearby. A sudden, uncontrollable urge made him reach into his jute bag. His hand moved as if detached from his body. Fingers brushed past clothing until they met the steel idol at the bottom of the bag. Shivaji clenched it tightly, gazing at the statue as memories of Vyjanti flooded his mind.

Vyjanti had always sought Lord Shiva in moments of distress. Whenever she needed guidance, solace, or to share her deepest thoughts, she knelt before her Lord. Shivaji sometimes felt he had to compete with God to ease her distress, which he knew was impossible. Tears streamed down his face as visions of Vyjanti formed in his mind: her hands folded, eyelids closed, lips moving in silent prayer beside the statue of Lord Shiva.

In that moment, Shivaji forgot the overcrowding, the cold, the discomfort, and the lateness of the hour. Only Vyjanti's presence—real or imagined—held sway over his heart and mind.

THE 44TH DAY

A horn was blown. At first, the indentured labourers presumed it to be the crow of a cock. Yet this was not their village—it was the depot where they were temporarily confined. The frigid night had brought with it dry coughs, sore throats, and runny noses, particularly among those who had slept outside. The blankets provided were insufficient, offering little warmth.

When Shivaji awoke, he instantly felt the idol clutched in his hand. He did not know when he had fallen asleep. It felt as if Vyjanti herself had laid him down, tending to his need for rest. *"She knew how necessary it was for me to sleep. Without rest, I would not have been able to lift my hands and feet. My love, you are still here to serve and protect. I thank you from the bottom of my heart."*

In walked the British guards, suited and booted, muttering among themselves. Their appearances had not changed since the previous day—shirts perfectly pressed, trousers spotless, buttons fastened, boots gleaming. Stepping ahead was an Indian translator: middle-aged, beardless, spectacles perched on his nose, hair slicked with oil, dressed in beige—oversized trousers and long-sleeved shirt. Short, slim, and entirely obedient to the colonial system, he was a traitor to his own people, showing no respect for those who shared his language, skin color, birthplace, or faith.

"Now listen, coolies. Today is a very special day. You are required to wear the clothing provided by the British. Plantation owners from all over Fiji are visiting. We must prove that you, the indentured labourers, are in good health and capable of working in the fields," the translator declared.

The Indians exchanged confused glances, unsure whether to protest or comply. Many feared separation from friends and family. The indenture contract had promised that families would never be separated. But these were the British—a people who had broken every rule and principle of humanity during the voyage.

"The women will receive new pieces of clothing to hide the tears and holes in their sarees, while the men will be provided beige and white kurta and pajama. After the morning nourishment, each of you will change into these fresh garments. Then, the guards will escort you to the back end of the depot, where the British commander will assign you to an owner."

Owner... How can one man, who is not God Almighty, own another? Shivaji whispered to himself. *"Overseer, manager, supervisor, guide, mentor—yes. But owner? No. God does not own us; He runs the universe. With God, we are loved, not hated. Free, not imprisoned. Human, not inhuman. Selected, not forced. The British and God—both punish, but only God punishes with reason. The British punish without reason."*

Shivaji's discomfort was not just with the oversized kurta that swallowed his hands, but with the pajama, which he had never worn, having worn only a doti since adolescence. Yet the clothing was the least of his worries. His eyes scanned the herds of labourers, desperately searching for Venkatesh, Lachmaiya, and Karthik. Occasionally, his gaze met that of the British guards, and he immediately turned away, pretending nothing had happened. Humiliation in front of hundreds of people was to be avoided at all costs.

The British commander, positioned on a raised platform with the Indian translator, radiated authority. He had meticulously planned every detail: assigning guards to each band, arranging the labourers, distributing clothing, and orchestrating the sale and assignment of workers. His confidence was absolute. Around the platform, wealthy white men in long coats and oversized hats surveyed the scene. Some were old, nearing retirement; others were of similar age to Shivaji and Venkatesh. Plantation owners, many supplying sugar to the Colonial Sugar Refining Company, feasted their eyes on the labourers, selecting their favorites before the event even began.

Shivaji's stomach churned. He had never witnessed so many Englishmen gathered in one place. Unease twisted within him, and he realized he was about to face something entirely new, a spectacle of power, control, and the dehumanizing weight of colonial ownership.

"Welcome to this propitious occasion. Soon, we will start the auction. But before that happens, I must add that this lot of coolies arrived from southern India. In this part of India, crops such as rice, cotton, chilli, pepper, tea, coffee, and coconut are cultivated. So imagine what these Indians can produce on this island with their miraculous hands. These coolies are far more accomplished than labourers from other parts of India. That is why the bidding will start at a higher price," announced the British commander.

The buyers expressed their feelings with vociferous objections, but that was of no concern to the commander or the colonial system he served. "Well, I always say, you get what you pay for. To receive good quality, one must pay a good amount," continued the man in charge of the event.

Meanwhile, the Indian translator stood patiently behind him. There wasn't any need for him to utter a word. The British commander did not find it necessary to let the indentured labourers know of the occasion that was to commence. In due course, the commander ordered the translator to inform the families to stay together. To simplify his task, the traitor shouted at the top of his lungs advising families to stay together; otherwise there was the possibility of separation. The message was repeated continually until the man's voice became hoarse. Then the translator began communicating with gestures, instructing a band of ten coolies to walk the platform of degradation. In these groups of ten, at least three to five were members of one family.

As the coolies walked the platform, displaying their physical structure, purchasers either whistled or hooted. If the plantation owners applauded, that meant a coolie of decent age and robust body was on display. Higher bids were presented for the tallest, fittest, and healthiest. On the other hand, lower bids were placed on coolies who had disabilities. If an Indian was missing an arm or leg, a single bid often would not be registered. To get rid of these unfortunate labourers, the British bundled them into package deals. Basically, these incompetent coolies were handed over without extra charge to the plantation owners who purchased the most labourers. Thus, by purchasing fifteen coolies, several more coolies who were disabled came free.

"So what if he does not have an arm or leg? So what if he will not be able to labour in the farms? Not all coolies are made for the fields. These coolies can be put to use in other positions and locations," the British commander explained to plantation owners, who did not object—knowing there was nothing wrong with obtaining extra help around their estates.

Bids for elders and children were fairly low. There was little demand for coolies who were too young or too old to labour in the fields. To avoid an emotional catastrophe, the British enforcement kept their promise not to separate family members. In that case, plantation owners had no choice but to take the children and elders who belonged to a family. These wealthy estate owners sought Indians aged twenty to forty. Men and women in their prime were best suited to endure an excruciating day of work in the sugarcane fields. While the fair-skinned hustlers decided each labourer's worth, the indentured labourers did not understand what was happening or what would come next.

Hundreds of indentured labourers clustered at the side of the platform. The vociferous shouts, rambunctious laughter, lecherous stares, and discourteous finger-pointing created a chaotic atmosphere that made the Indians nervous. Even Shivaji, who feared mostly for the safety of others, felt anxious because he found it difficult to interpret his surroundings. Words such as "shilling" and "sold" rang out repeatedly. Fortunately, the widower was familiar with both words; he could pronounce them and knew what they meant. It was not hard for him to pair the words and conclude what the event signified. Still, his brain was overly active—searching for his loved ones, focusing on the British's actions and words, and predicting what might be done to him in the future.

The commotion escalated when a new group of labourers walked the stage. The Englishmen pitched bids one after another. So many voices and so many numbers were thrown at the British commander, who paced the stage and did not miss the purchaser with the highest bid. There were occasions when more than one buyer sought the same labourer. Bids for healthy, well-built Indians soared to extraordinary heights. At times, verbal arguments and physical confrontations erupted between Englishmen bidding for the same person. British guards were then assigned to settle the disputes. In the end, the buyer with the highest bid—conflict or no conflict—escorted the purchased coolie into a new world of disaster. The Indians did not know that misfortune awaited them; it was as if they were being thrown into a bottomless pit.

Group after group, the coolies were ordered to march the stage. Sometimes an interested planter requested to examine a labourer or group more closely. When permitted, the Englishman would circle the Indian, looking for signs of infirmity. At times the coolie was asked to lift his arms and feet, bend his knees, and open his mouth—inspections carried out in the middle of the bidding session. Often a buyer would be on the platform inspecting a group so intently that he forgot the other buyers; this frequently resulted in another buyer claiming the labourer. It was rare for a plantation owner to purchase a full group of ten; if it happened, the purchaser likely did not want to be drawn into a bidding war. Some bidders searched tirelessly for the best suited; others sought to buy as many coolies as possible without focusing on appearance. Some felt that being too particular might result in no purchases at all, so they bought in groups of ten.

Due to the heat and crowded bodies, the Indians were drenched in perspiration. Not as tall as many around him, Shivaji had difficulty getting a clear view of the prestigious stage. When he did glimpse it, a rush of hope flowed into his heart. Unable to control his emotions, he began to push and shove—prepared to do whatever was needed to reach the stage. It helped that the British guards were focused on bidders and the bidding rather than on the crowd. Shivaji flashed past numerous bodies without colliding or falling. In that moment, he felt like a soldier avoiding land mines to reach safety.

Only when Shivaji had reached the stage did the Englishmen react. As he stepped onto the platform, he noticed how similar it was to the deck on which he had scrubbed for hours during the voyage. An immediate reflex urged him to retrieve something, but he knew that was no longer possible. The widower ran across the stage. The crowd's attention snapped away from the auction when they saw his impulsive act. At the end of the line, Venkatesh, Lachmaiya, and Karthik stood with tears of relief rolling down their faces. Finally, the childhood friends were reunited. Not able to stop in time, Shivaji crashed into Venkatesh's chest. The friends embraced as if meeting after decades. Karthik watched with a glint in his eye, moved by the intense emotion on his parents' faces. Lachmaiya concealed her face behind the new scarf provided by the British, hiding the stream of tears.

The plantation owners did not welcome Shivaji's interruption; they halted the bidding after seeing him attend to his loved ones. Shivaji faced the crowd of riled Englishmen with no fear. He was mentally and physically prepared for a beating. "Be it batons or whips, daggers or pistols—bring whatever you have," he told the British guards charging toward him.

"Look at this disgraceful beast. He thinks he stands a chance against our team of British enforcers," one plantation owner sneered, throwing up his fists.

"Kill the Indian. Hang him. Slice his body into pieces. Who is he to interfere?" another planter roared, veins bulging with aggression.

"Were the entire team of guards sleeping? How did a dimwitted coolie run past our guards? I will not stay here another minute. I will not participate in an auction where a measly peasant can cause such disturbance. I have no respect for a leader who has no control over his coolies," said one buyer, pointing at the commander.

All the finger-pointing, uttered threats, and hurtful sayings made the British commander furious. "I feel like strangling this disobedient Indian. Perhaps a hundred lashes would do the trick. Actually, smashing his bones with a baton would compensate for this unnecessary disorder. Well, it does not matter what the punishment is, as long as it is severe enough to stop his defiant acts," the commander debated while nearing the rebel.

Immediately, Shivaji was surrounded by uniformed Englishmen. He struggled to repel the many arms and legs flung at him. Venkatesh tried to hold onto his friend's left arm but lost his grip as the British guards forcefully dragged Shivaji across the platform. Meanwhile, Karthik, numb with fear, stood behind his outraged mother, who cried for her husband to retreat. Fleeing past the British enforcers was indeed forbidden, while defending oneself against them was far more dangerous. Shivaji knew in the back of his mind that he was going to receive a beating that would pain him for weeks. What stunned the indentured labourers, estate owners, and British enforcers was that his actions revealed he was prepared to endure the suffering.

During the unrest, an Englishman stepped forward, clad in a double-breasted suit and a high-top hat. The gentleman had a slender face adorned with mutton-chop sideburns. Unlike the other Englishmen the indentured labourers had encountered, he was average in height and weighed no more than a hundred and fifty pounds. From his hand motions and body language, one could presume he belonged to the upper class. He ordered the British guards to release Shivaji.

The guards ignored his command—they did not recognize the man as an enforcer. He was not dressed in red or white, nor armed with a rifle or baton. Instantly, the guards knew he was not part of the British enforcement. *Who was he to give orders, and why should we listen?* crossed their minds.

"You must obey. I said let go of him. This coolie belongs to me. I, Ernest Stanfield, will make an offer that no one will dare challenge," said the plantation owner.

The British commander gestured for his team members to stop. Shivaji noticed that his knees were no longer scraping the platform. The British guards halted but still held onto the rebel's arms.

"This man has me interested. Let's hear what he has to say. Continue, Ernest," said the British commander with a smirk.

"I am willing to purchase every coolie who stands on that platform at this very moment. Yes, I want them all, especially the one whose soul is on fire. I have never seen a coolie with such audacity."

"Are you sure? The cost will be fairly high."

"Don't underestimate my financial power. I will pay a huge amount for every single one of them, including the child," said Ernest as he removed his hat and bowed before Karthik.

The child did not know what to say or how to react to a gesture so foreign to his culture.

"Why must you buy them all at once? Don't you think it is necessary to choose and pick?" the commander asked, wanting to know the planter's true intentions.

"Why does that matter to you? I am not here to waste my precious time. In my view, all Indians are the same. I expect them all to be skilled labourers in cultivating and harvesting. And if they are not skilled, I will train them to be expert farmers."

"Sir, the manner in which you converse is highly inappropriate," said the British commander, offended by the rudeness in the plantation owner's voice.

"I am not here to talk about respect or disrespect. I am not here to talk about who has manners and who does not. Let's strike a deal, and I will be on my way. As I said, I want to purchase these eleven labourers," said Ernest, pointing to the coolies on stage.

"There are ten coolies on stage for sale. The Indian who disrupted the bidding session is not for sale at the moment."

"Well, if he does not come with this batch, then I must forfeit the deal."

The bystanders witnessing the back-and-forth between the commander and plantation owner began losing patience. Outcries to resume the bidding pressed the man in charge to advance. The British commander did not understand why Ernest Stanfield was so desperate to attain the short, thin, pesky Indian. What did he see in Shivaji that others did not?

The commander then walked directly toward the plantation owner. "So, what is the offer that you are willing to make for these coolies?"

Amid the commotion, Ernest leaned toward the commander and whispered in his ear. The amount offered was known only to the ruler of the premises. As the British commander revisited the stage, the bystanders immediately started proposing high amounts for the current labourers.

"Sold... Gentlemen, please stop the bidding. This batch is sold to Ernest Stanfield."

At first, the other planters felt cheated, but when a different batch of ten coolies arrived on the platform, they began whistling and hooting again. Shivaji and the others of his batch were then escorted off the premises. Once removed, the indentured labourers were no longer associated with the British enforcers who governed the depot. Instead, the coolies now belonged to the richest sugar plantation owner in the district, Ernest Stanfield.

Again, Shivaji was on the move. He was very careful not to lose sight of Venkatesh and his family members. Marching over the hills, along the pine trees, around the thorny bushes and across the flowing streams, Shivaji and the others hoped that the distance to their placement was not too far. The batch of eleven indentured labourers was ushered by Ernest and his brothers, Edward and Edwin, both younger than the plantation owner. With their lips sealed and brains overworking, the Indians were en route to the plantation that was once controlled and operated by a reputable Englishman named Hugh Stanfield. It was he who entrusted the responsibility of leadership to his eldest son before dying. Hugh felt that his eldest son was the best candidate to handle the plantation. The father did not choose Ernest over Edward and Edwin because he was older. It was because Ernest did not make impulsive decisions. He was a level-headed individual. Very rarely did he lose his temper. He had shown more interest in production rather than punishment. Unlike other planters and overseers in his district, who did not hesitate in flogging a peasant, Ernest had to rethink the problematic situation to decide whether punishment was necessary. Although he was a no-nonsense and straight-laced gentleman, Ernest would not discipline to the point where a labourer was unable to perform his or her regular duties accordingly. He believed that all coolies were needed in the sugarcane fields each work day, able-bodied and in tune with the schedule. If one was not able to perform due to open wounds, shattered bones or extreme illness, that would disturb regular production. Ernest demanded the same results from his coolies day to day. He aimed to not let anyone or anything hinder work in the sugarcane fields. Hugh found his son reasonable when it came to handling the Indians. But the one thing Hugh disliked about his eldest son was that Ernest had a strong craving for wealth. Due to his fixation on wealth, Ernest did not find it necessary to marry or make friends. The planter was so occupied with the management of coolies and the production of sugar that he did not have time to form new relationships. Hugh always told his son that wealth can buy you power and fame, but it will not buy you a wife and children. The father was concerned that his son would end his life in forlornness. There were times when Ernest left his estate for days to negotiate deals with companies that demanded quality sugar. Sometimes he left the farm to attend the latest auction organized by the British enforcement. Loaded with fortune, Ernest still hungered for more. To further advance in the sugar plantation business, he left the estate in the hands of his brothers; without his presence, Edward and Edwin took on the obligation to supervise the estate. The days Ernest was absent were days of savagery. Edward reformed the farm into a place that was hell on earth for the indentured labourers. Whenever Ernest returned to his land, he ensured that the pockets of his trousers were dangling with riches. It was his obsession that made him the wealthiest plantation owner in the district. Ernest, with the help of his adolescent brothers, had been running the sugarcane farm for the past seven years. With each passing year, the planter produced more profit. Ernest knew he was a commendable businessman. On top of that, he recognized the importance of the indentured labourers on his estate. These Indians were the backbone of his plantation.

"Keep a close eye on the firebrand," Ernest said to his brothers. "Don't let his innocent appearance create misconceptions. He is what our estate needs to maintain the best performance from our coolies. The more the coolies produce, the more profit we gain."

"Brother, I don't understand why you selected him. This Indian is not fitted for our plantation. He will only bring trouble to us," Edwin voiced.

As soon as the youngest finished his sentence, Edward dove in, "What if he encourages our coolies to protest or revolt? He sure has that kind of personality. Did you not see him at the auction? He had the nerve to interrupt the bidding process."

"Yes, I saw the occurrence. Though I must say I am not blind like you, Edward. A man with such fortitude is needed on our property. I have plans to use him as a slave-driver."

"Slave-driver... Don't we have Gurdayal Singh in that position?" asked Edward as he probed Shivaji from top to bottom.

"Gurdayal is a faithful peasant, but he is ageing. His arms and legs don't have the strength they once had when I first purchased him. He is no longer able to wield the whip with authority. Before, the coolies on our estate were intimidated by him. Now that fear has disappeared. Once again, we need to implant terror in our indentured labourers."

"So you believe this firebrand of yours will be able to do that?" Edward asked.

"Yes, absolutely," Ernest replied with confidence. "Hmm, 'firebrand' — now that is the perfect name to call this Indian."

After trekking for nearly an hour, the indentured labourers felt short of breath and discomfort in their limbs. It was fair to say that their past few days had been strenuous. But that could also be said of every other day since the Indians boarded Ship Elbe. In the past six weeks, Shivaji had endured all kinds of pain, mentally and physically. He did not know if he had the strength to handle more. The widower had his share of mental breakdowns. Yet his hands had still not had the chance to suffocate an oppressor.

As soon as the escorted labourers reached the sugar plantation on which Ernest and his brothers thrived, they were assembled in front of the coolie line. The coolie line was a single row of despicable hovels in which the indentured labourers were to reside. The roofs of the huts were made of grass, twigs, banana, and coconut leaves. Twigs and dirt were used to create the walls of the huts. These eight-by-eight-foot huts did not have beds, which meant that the indentured labourers were to sleep on the earth. Also, if a natural disaster, such as an earthquake or tropical storm, were to occur, the huts were bound to collapse. Deprived of a window, toilet, and pipeline, it was clear that the Indians would have trouble adjusting to their new home. The appalling view of the single row of huts indicated to the Indians that their lives were only about to get worse.

Shivaji and the others explored the premises with their roaming eyes. Venkatesh was in search of others of his kind, the exploited and oppressed. "Perhaps the Indians are busy in the farm," he said under his breath.

At this point, the indentured labourers had clearly understood their purpose on the farm owned by Ernest Stanfield. These men and women were now to be considered merely help for the plantation owner. It was his orders that were to be followed. It was his demands that were to be met. He was the landlord, overseer, sirdar, and kulumber. His decisions mattered, his alterations were to be considered, and his various forms of punishment were to be inflicted. Ernest had his own set of rules and regulations, which set him apart from other planters. He instructed his youngest brother, Edwin, to fetch Gurdayal Singh from the fields.

"Fetch the peasant. I need his assistance. He must translate my words into Hindi for these coolies to understand," said the planter, grinning at Karthik, who in return stuck out his tongue.

The overprotective mother concealed her son's face behind her scarf. Lachmaiya did not want the malicious eyes of an Englishman to fall upon her son. Her heart sank as she prayed that the planter would not step forward. Venkatesh and his friend planted their feet firmly on the ground. Only if the father and mother of the child felt that the planter had crossed the line were they to respond with violence. The safety of the child was far more important than their lives. But what Shivaji and Venkatesh did not understand was that if they were not alive, then there would be no one to protect Karthik.

Instead of becoming furious, Ernest responded with a chuckle. He found the child amusing. Soon after, Edwin came pacing towards the coolie line where the newly recruited labourers stood. Following him was an Indian male who appeared to be in his mid-fifties. The man had a poignant face, once seen, never forgotten. With an oval-shaped face, deep-set eyes, hair covering only the sides of his pate, and a clear-cut mustache above his upper lip, Gurdayal Singh was the only Sikh in the entire district.

With his arrival, Ernest began his lecture. Gurdayal, the Indian overseer on the plantation, was not ordered to translate. Ernest did not find it necessary to tell Gurdayal why he was summoned because the planter knew his coolie was aware of his duties. Gurdayal had translated for new recruits before. As a matter of fact, Gurdayal was asked to translate in Hindi because he was the only Indian who completely understood English on the plantation.

"Coolies... Coolies... Coolies! You are my precious coolies. I am pleased to say that you belong to me. As of now, you are to work for me and me only. Now let me introduce you to my very own Gurdayal Singh," announced Ernest, while the peasant translated in Hindi.

Shivaji was confused because the Sikh was not wearing a turban. The few Sikhs he knew and had encountered in his district wore a piece of cloth on their heads.

Ernest continued, "He is one of the most faithful coolies working on the plantation. This man is to be worshipped. He is the only coolie on this estate who has never defied my first and foremost rule: never say no."

Shivaji and the others found it unusual that the infamous labourer was praising himself. Nevertheless, they understood that he was only fulfilling his duty by translating the words of the plantation owner.

"You need to obey my every command. If I say do this, you must do this. If I say do that, you must do that. I will control your every move. When I say run, you run. When I say stop, you stop. When I say stand, you stand. When I say sit, you sit. What I despise most is a coolie who has the urge to revolt. Don't you dare talk back to me, don't you dare ask a question, and don't you dare touch me. Retaliation is the worst sin on this plantation. The sinner who retaliates with violence will be flogged until his last breath," said Ernest, madness in his voice.

Shivaji, who seemed uninvolved in the planter's discourse, was keen to make eye contact with the translator. But that seemed impossible because the peasant spoke with his forehead lowered and eyes facing the ground. His body language communicated that he did not want to be there. There were no signs of egotism in his voice. At times, his voice became faint, making it difficult for the indentured labourers to hear the words.

"Gurdayal, you must talk louder. What are you, a pantywaist?" Ernest asked his labourer.

Humiliated by the boorish remark, Gurdayal replied, "Yes, sirdar."

"My second rule is that you must refer to me as sirdar. I don't need to define the word for you, since it originates from India and by Indians. I am the head of authority, which is why it is required for indentured labourers to address me by that name."

As the owner of the estate continued to address his staff, Shivaji examined the translator. Gurdayal did not seem like a man who was easy to approach. He had fiery eyes, broad shoulders, and stubby legs. He was dressed in raggedy clothes with multiple tears. What made the labourer prominent was the grisly scar etched on his face. The scar was only visible from close distance and in sunlight. But once noticed, it remained a topic often talked about. Shivaji wondered how the Sikh received the scar, which extended from the side of his left temple to the bottom of his jawline.

"My third rule is that everything will be done according to my time. You must rise at the break of dawn. Before the sun restfully positions itself in the sky, the coolies are to report to the farm. By noon, the indentured labourers will be provided with a fifteen-minute break. Then, later in the afternoon, the labourers will be awarded another fifteen-minute break. After that, there will be no more breaks. Finally, as the sun diminishes, the indentured labourers are to retire. Let me add that the coolies on this plantation are required to work six days a week and fifteen hours a day. Rain or shine, you must work. Intense headaches, severe blisters, upset stomachs, damaged bones—I don't care. All the Indians on this estate must labour, and they must labour hard. If you fail to arrive at the sugarcane fields on time, there will be a deduction in your payment. Lateness can also result in punishment."

As the indentured labourers heard the set rules and principles, Lachmaiya whimpered. She wanted to raise her hand and voice her concern. She needed to know if children were required to labour in the sugarcane fields. As a mother, she would not be able to see her child aching from the burdensome duties of the sugarcane fields. Before Lachmaiya raised her arm, she remembered what the planter had said earlier about not daring to ask him a question. Immediately, she repressed her concern. The sensible mother of Karthik foresaw that her question would lead directly to verbal or even physical abuse. So Lachmaiya did what every mother would have done: inaudibly prayed to God.

"My fourth rule is that you are never to leave this property unless instructed to do so. Also, you are not permitted to work for a different planter or plantation as long as you are under my control. If you are seen off the premises, you will be lashed. If you are seen escaping from the premises, you will be lashed to death. No coolie has ever escaped from this plantation. And no coolie will ever escape from this plantation. That is a promise not to be forgotten. I must admit that several Indians have tried—and they have failed miserably. For that reason, I strongly advise every single one of you to eliminate your desires for absolute liberation. Don't misinterpret my suggestion. Your freedom will not entirely be taken from you, but it will definitely be restricted. You can live freely in your hut, you can explore the coolie line, you can cook and eat whatever you have, you can follow your religious beliefs, and you can worship your own God. Your soul belongs to you, your body belongs to me," said Ernest.

The more Shivaji thought about it, the more he despised the truth. What frustrated him was that he, like many other Indians, had formed an unfavorable conception of Englishmen in general, and now the small doses of fairness shown by the plantation owner were slowly altering that conception into a misconception. Ernest did talk about beatings and whippings, rules and restrictions, but he was also the first to present the concept of limited emancipation in the lives of the indentured labourers.

"Now let us proceed to the final rule, which is that you are not permitted to inquire about your salary. I don't answer questions related to financial concerns. Listen carefully: I don't pay at the start of the month; I pay at the end of the month. Coolies will be paid in full, ten shillings, on the last day of the month. A labourer must work at least twenty-six days per month to receive the full amount of ten shillings. If you miss a full day of work, expect your pay to be cut. If a labourer performs his or her duties far beyond my expectations, that individual will be rewarded with an extra shilling. And if a labourer performs incompetently, that individual will receive a cutback. The duties on the plantation are incredibly laborious. However, that does not matter. What matters is that the work must be done. I will not tolerate a peasant who lags. I will not tolerate a peasant who underperforms. And, under no circumstances, will I tolerate a peasant who initiates trouble."

It was the ten shillings a month that lured Indians to grind for the Englishman, and that is why the coolies needed Gurdayal to translate in order to fully understand the concept of how a labourer is paid. For some Indians, it was a matter of reassurance. As for Shivaji, the collection of shillings was unnecessary. "Why must I earn, if I have no future?" he asked himself.

There was a moment of absolute silence when Ernest finished explaining his five rules. The band of labourers had mixed feelings about the orders voiced by the planter. Anxiety had crept inside some of their souls upon hearing about the violent punishment they were to sustain if a command were disobeyed. Others felt excited after listening to the dialogue regarding the shillings that were to be handed to them at the end of each month.

With half of the day finished, Ernest felt that the indentured labourers should rest instead of beginning work in the sugarcane fields. "Edward, please take the coolies to their huts. I want you to assign the families to separate huts of their own. As for the lone birds, they can share one hut. Now that leaves us with the firebrand. He is to reside with the most loyal peasant on this estate," Ernest said to his brother.

"Edwin, I need you to gather rations from the cottage and distribute the goods evenly among the coolies. Also, don't forget the blankets. We do not want our recruits to suffer during the frigid nights. These Indians must be fed and clothed appropriately for them to perform their duties faultlessly. Don't hesitate to ask Gurdayal for help. He will be more than pleased to assist you."

Edward, unlike his elder brother, did not have a tender spot in his heart. There was not a single drop of empathy or repentance within him. The Englishman was obsessed with dominance. He expressed it through his flagrant behaviour, lecherous acts, ridiculous instructions, and immoral forms of punishment. As he led the coolies to the line of huts, Edward acted abominably. He did not feel the least reluctant when he shoved an Indian and spat on his shin. "Move aside, you swine," he said to one of the male coolies in line. The peasant did not respond to the humiliating act physically or verbally. He behaved as if nothing had happened.

Shivaji eyed the Englishman like a poisonous cobra, following the movements of its enemy. The widower knew that in the future he must not embark on the path Edward had taken. If, by chance, they were to cross paths, the outcome would be unpleasant.

There were a total of sixteen huts, twelve of which were already occupied by coolies on the plantation. These huts were all the same size: eight feet by eight feet, with five feet separating each one. The coolies felt congested. There was no room to move and no fresh air to breathe inside the huts. Each hut contained three or more coolies. Due to the lack of space, men usually spent their nights outside in the cold. There was no latrine inside the hut. If one needed to relieve oneself, they were to stand or sit among the trees and shrubs behind their hut. During the nights, if a child or wife needed to relieve themselves, they were escorted by the husband into the sugarcane fields.

Another problem the coolies faced was the lack of firewood in or around their huts for preparing meals. To collect the necessary material, the labourers had to visit the southern section of the estate, which was very much like a desolate forest containing pine trees and streams. The northern section, which occupied forty percent of the estate, was dedicated to planting, nurturing, and harvesting sugarcane. There were three cottages—one for each Stanfield—located in the western section of the estate. Next to the cottages was the animal shelter, in which horses, pigs, roosters, and hens were kept. The western section was a forbidden zone for the indentured labourers; they were not to be seen in or around the premises unless instructed by one of the Stanfield brothers.

Lastly, in the eastern section of the estate resided the coolies in their huts, without the basic necessities required for comfortable living. The Stanfield brothers had the freedom to step onto the eastern section whenever they pleased. Since it was their land, it was considered civil for them to barge into the huts without advance notice. Rules only applied to indentured labourers, not to the Stanfield brothers.

From the group of eleven coolies, ten were designated to specific huts, leaving Shivaji temporarily homeless. The widower was upset that he was not assigned to live with Venkatesh and his family. Nevertheless, he felt relieved to see that the family had not been separated and were assigned to a hut with no one else besides themselves. Shivaji asked himself, "If all the huts are occupied, then where do I live?" What he did not know was that Ernest and his brothers had different plans for him.

With help from other labourers, Edwin and Gurdayal moved bags and containers of rice, lentils, salt, and oil to the coolie line. Once the bags and containers were transported, Gurdayal and the other labourers were sent back to fetch the blankets and utensils that were also provided to the recruits. Meanwhile, the Stanfield brothers oversaw the distribution of goods. One labourer per hut was instructed to step forward to collect the monthly ration, which Edward and Edwin distributed evenly.

As Shivaji watched Venkatesh happily collect his share, he ruminated on why he was neglected. "No hut, no food... what is going on?" he asked himself. The widower stood aside as the indentured labourers moved their rations to their huts. Soon, Gurdayal and his team returned with the essential materials. The coolies, who looked no different from the latest recruits, carefully handed over utensils and blankets to the newcomers. They knew that accidentally dropping any of the materials would lead to punishment. No mistakes—minor or major—were tolerated, especially with Edward on scene.

At last, Shivaji felt a small sense of importance after receiving a blanket, a tin plate, and a tin cup. The blanket, made of wool, was infested with vermin. Cockroaches, the size of a human thumb, slithered from the ends of the blanket onto the ground. These pests terrified the women and children. Karthik released a high-pitched scream the first time he saw one drop near his feet. Additionally, the blanket reeked of urine and vomit—a combination that released an intolerable odour. No matter how repulsive, the indentured labourers had to use the blankets to endure the cold nights.

After the materials were divided and distributed, Ernest stepped onto the eastern section of the estate. First, he signalled for Gurdayal to translate his words. He then instructed the helpful labourers to resume their duties in the sugarcane fields. The plantation owner revealed a wide smile, indicating to his brothers that he was pleased with how quickly his orders were executed.

"So, here I am, on the eastern section of the property. These will be the homes you will reside in for the next five to ten years," said the owner of the estate, pointing to the wretched shacks. "Every month, you will be provided with rations. The portions you have received will last for an entire month. If you believe the portions are small, then you must adjust. It's simple: eat less. Remember, you will not be given extra handouts."

The new recruits stared at the bags and containers, unsure whether the amount of ration supplied was sufficient. In his mind, Venkatesh immediately decided to ration food, probably eating only once a day, so that his wife and child could rest with full stomachs. He believed that this decision, made without consulting Lachmaiya, was obligatory.

Ernest continued, "Whether you prepare meals inside or outside your hut is for you to decide. Once a week, you will have the opportunity to gather wood from the forest. Remember, if you don't collect the wood, you will not be able to start a fire. There are no restrictions on water—you have a well in your area. You may fetch water during the morning and night. Basically, on your off days and hours, you can dance, sing, cook, clean, eat, shit, piss—whatever you like. But when you are in the fields labouring, you will not be permitted to relieve yourself. That means you are not allowed to shit or piss on my time. That must be done on your own time. Don't forget, your bodies belong to me. They react to my command; they respond to my orders."

The indentured labourers struggled to adapt to the unstable flow of positives and negatives demonstrated by Ernest Stanfield. At times, he portrayed himself as a man with a soft corner for the unfortunate Indians. At other times, he was the dictator who had no room in his heart for them. For most of the coolies who had lived on the estate for years, the planter was just another oppressive Englishman who turned indentured labourers into slaves.

"We were captives on Ship Elbe; now we are captives on this plantation. We were owned by Captain Sanders on the vessel; now we are owned by Ernest Stanfield on the sugarcane estate. It seems as if our destinies are not in the hands of God, but in the hands of these oppressors," Shivaji murmured under his breath.

"Since it is winter in the tropics, we will begin cultivation. If you are untrained, you will be trained. If you have no experience in the fields, you will gain it. I have the finest peasants in the district to show you how things are done. Soon, you will all be experts in farming," said Ernest, attempting to instill confidence in the group of coolies.

"We now have fifty-three indentured labourers on this plantation. Every one of you must complete your assigned duties, regardless of setbacks—whether intense weather, serious injuries, or lack of nutrition. I will do whatever I can to keep my labourers healthy and strong. Every hand, every foot is needed to run a successful plantation, and I will not allow them to weaken or waste away. Others may have hundreds of coolies, but I will still have the finest plantation in the district. That is because I turn my coolies into the best workers. One of my coolies here is equal to two of theirs," Ernest added, arrogance audible in his voice.

Indians on plantations with over a hundred labourers laboured less than those on smaller estates. More workers meant the workload was shared—but more overseers and drivers often meant more punishment.

"A medic comes to the plantation once every three months to examine and treat coolies. He will treat physical ailments, not mental suffering," Ernest added, his tone void of humour.

As Ernest continued outlining the estate policies, Shivaji scanned the eleven coolies at his side. More than half were men, ranging from adolescents to middle-aged. Shivaji wondered who they were, where they had come from, and whether fire burned in their hearts. Could they refuse, protest, or endure? He did not want to be the only insurgent among the fifty-three indentured labourers.

Much to his relief, he saw Venkatesh looking his way. Shivaji offered a tight-lipped smile, signaling to his childhood friend that he was fine, even though he was not. For a moment, a strange, invisible force seemed to separate him from Venkatesh, Lachmiaya, and Karthik—but in reality, they were not distant at all.

"I am fortunate to be on the same estate as Venkatesh," Shivaji thought, forcing his mind toward optimism.

His focus was suddenly shattered by a loud voice. Edward had noticed the firebrand not looking at him and took it as disrespect. "Coolie," he shouted, waiting for Shivaji to respond. "Look over here, you deaf arsehole!"

Shivaji calmly met Edward's eyes, showing that not an inch of his body wavered.

Edward's anger boiled over. "Lower your eyes before I pull them out of their sockets!"

Shivaji only understood the word *eyes*. Recognizing the threat, he remained unde-terred. He was there to disobey, not obey. Calmly, he observed Edward approaching with fists clenched.

Venkatesh felt the urge to intervene but planted his feet firmly. *Why is this necessary? Shivaji, why must you do this? What is achieved by defiance? Look down... please, look down,* he thought, holding back the words for the sake of the child who needed his father alive.

"Stop, right this instant!" Ernest commanded.

With Shivaji only four steps away, Edward hesitated but refused to obey at first.

"Listen, Edward. You will not lay a finger on the firebrand."

The younger brother had no choice but to stop.

"Brother, this coolie has no decency," Edward muttered.

"Before you elaborate on decency, I have a question," Ernest said firmly.

"Yes, brother," Edward responded.

"Do you think it was appropriate for you to interfere while I was talking to the coolies? Where has your decency gone? This coolie has disrespected his owner, but you have disrespected your brother."

"Brother, you don't understand. This firebrand of yours will turn on us. He is a threat to our system. Today he displayed insolence; tomorrow he will display violence. Please give me the order to hang this peasant," insisted Edward.

Ignoring his brother's request, Ernest continued from where he had left off in his speech. Edward felt unnecessary to remain on scene after being rebuked and ignored. As he departed, Edward glared at Shivaji with cold eyes, promising retaliation in some hurtful form. Even then, Shivaji did not remove his eyes from where they stubbornly rested. *A dirty look earns a dirty look in return,* believed the widower.

"You will need to rise early in the morning. Get as much sleep as possible. I don't want fatigued labourers; I want active and effective ones. Nobody from this batch knows how to reach the sugarcane farm. That is why you must rise on time and follow the adept coolies of this estate. They will lead you to the sugarcane fields. If you don't rise on time, I will dispatch my brothers to fetch you. How they handle you, in whatever manner, is not my concern. I must say that I very rarely punish. However, remember that what I do not often do, my brothers are there to do on my behalf," said the planter, standing face to face with Shivaji.

The widower felt Ernest's words were intentionally directed at him.

"Coolies, now you must rest. I will take my leave. We will soon meet again," concluded Ernest. Before leaving, he ordered Gurdayal to return to the sugarcane farm. Instead of being rewarded for his service, Gurdayal was ordered to continue labouring for the remainder of the day.

Shivaji was instructed to gather his jute bag, containing his personal belongings. He also clutched the ragged blanket and second-hand utensils provided by the estate owner. Edwin escorted the firebrand to the hut where he was to reside. During the brief walk, Edwin did not once raise his hand to hit, extend his leg to kick, or shove the widower. Shivaji did not understand the lad. "If it were any other Englishman, he would have physically or verbally assaulted me by now," he thought. The widower looked behind him and saw that the other indentured labourers had already concealed themselves inside their huts.

"What is your name?" Edwin asked the widower.

Shivaji did not believe it at first, but when Edwin repeated the question, he felt the need to clean his ears.

"Your name. Do you understand what I am saying? N A M E..."

Shivaji understood what Edwin was asking. It had been a long time since an Englishman asked for his name. The question stunned him, as he was accustomed to being called names like coolie, peasant, asshole, arse, swine, and bastard.

"Do you know any English? Naaaaammme..." Edwin asked for the last time.

Finally, Shivaji retorted, "My name is Shivaji."

"How in the world do you know English? Where did you receive your education? Aren't you a measly peasant from a village?" Edwin asked, preparing to investigate further.

Shivaji did not respond. He felt the questions, which he partially understood, were useless. There was no way he would reveal his personal life to an Englishman. The widower remained extremely cautious. "The less I say, the better. These people can use my words against me," he thought.

After a few attempts, Edwin gave up his inquiries. He presumed the questions were too diverse for Shivaji to answer. As both lead and led tried to unravel each other, neither realized they had reached the end of the line. Edwin opened the door to the last hut in the line of sixteen.

"This is it. From now on, this hut is your home." With those words, Edwin departed the Eastern section, leaving the widower alone.

As Shivaji entered the hut, he felt the need for air. It seemed the confined space had inhaled the air and forgot to exhale. With no windows, Shivaji knew he would constantly battle the interior of the hut. The widower's eyes fell on the steel pots and pans, tin utensils, ragged clothing, infested blankets, and ration supplies. He felt relieved to share residency with another labourer. No more isolation. His past experience of spending countless hours in "the hole" was a painful memory. It was only then he understood how crucial it was to see a face, hear a voice, or feel a touch.

The hut seemed fit for only one person. Shivaji felt crammed after placing his belongings in the corner. But insufficient space was the least of his worries. The worst was yet to come. "Will there be an end to this journey?" he asked himself, sitting on the dingy floor.

As the sun began to descend, he felt the need to close his eyes. It was necessary, but excruciating. Whenever he tried, images of his wife covered in blood appeared. He could no longer shut his eyes. His heart ached to see Vyjanti in such a state. Shivaji wished she would appear as a newlywed bride, not a bloodied corpse.

Such disturbing thoughts could have led to dangerous outcomes, but this time, Shivaji was prepared mentally and physically. Hours passed, yet he remained vigilant. He focused on the spiders who had built their webs near the ceiling. Their masterful designs fascinated him.

He then shifted focus to the uncleanliness of the hut—pots and pans unwashed, clothes scattered, walls covered in dust, and ceilings adorned with webs. This distasteful sight could not be ignored. Shivaji rose and began gathering the scattered clothing. Once folded, he grabbed a rag as hard as concrete. It seemed unused for decades. There was nothing else to clean the walls. Shivaji refused to use his kurta or pajama, or his roommate's torn clothing.

Before using the rag, Shivaji ran his index finger along the wall, producing a line of filth. He observed the finger: so much grime that it concealed the upper portion entirely. Shivaji cleaned the walls with both hands, taking care near the spider webs, fearing he might destroy them.

Once the walls were spotless, his muscles and bones begged for rest. But he was not done; the pots and pans needed washing. He remembered the plantation owner's mention of a well. "What can I use to fetch water?" he wondered, scanning for a bucket or pail. Unable to find any, he decided to carry the water manually with the pots and pans.

As he approached the door, he met Gurdayal Singh, drenched in sweat from the sugarcane fields. Gurdayal eyed the pots and pans. Shivaji gradually lowered them to the floor.

"I was going to wash these for you," said the widower.

Without responding, Gurdayal walked past his roommate. Shivaji did not know if the haggard man had even noticed that the hut was now somewhat purified. "I am sorry, but I found it necessary to clean the hut."

Once again, there was no reply. Gurdayal removed his shirt and sandals, spread his body on the rocklike floor, and pulled his blanket over his face. The non-social peasant did not want to speak or hear anything. Shivaji believed that a person who does not want to respond or react should be left alone. After all, some people in the world preferred detachment over fellowship. Nonetheless, the peasant's behavior irritated Shivaji.

"What is the matter with the old man? Did he not want a roommate? Was it because I touched his belongings? Or was it because I was not submissive towards his masters? Whatever it may be, he will have to deal with it, because this hut does not belong to him alone; it now belongs to me as well," Shivaji said to himself.

With nothing in their stomachs and dirty clothing on their backs, both indentured labourers separated themselves as far as possible in order to shut their eyes and welcome a new day. For Shivaji, resting on soil was not problematic. During the voyage, he had slept on wood for forty-two nights. Therefore, compared to wood, soil felt like a cushion. Shivaji did not feel the need to use the blanket. He did not understand why others would. The foul odour emanating from the blanket could induce regurgitation, so he set it aside.

Just as his eyes were about to discard the key of consciousness, a peeved voice arose from within the hut.

"You have left the door open," said Gurdayal.

Shivaji wanted to respond impolitely, but his religion and culture, which shaped his upbringing, did not permit him to misbehave with an elder. So he rose to his feet, walked a few steps, and gently closed the door.

On a nightly basis, the indentured labourers were to endure noise. Unharmonious sounds of crickets chirping, toads croaking, bats screeching, and dogs barking resulted in sleepless nights. On Shivaji's first night in the hut, the dogs kept him awake. At times, he felt as if the canines had surrounded the hut. The constant barks and growls pained his ear.

These dogs were nothing like the ones in India. Dogs in India were beaten with sticks or shooed away. If Shivaji had opened the door and stepped outside, he risked being attacked.

"How can one attend the loo in the middle of the night with bloodthirsty hounds roaming the premises?" Shivaji questioned himself. During the day, Indians were enslaved by the British; at night, they were enslaved by the canines. The widower felt as if there was no means of freedom on the Stanfield brothers' plantation. At night, minutes seemed like hours, and hours seemed like decades. Shivaji tossed and turned, changed positions, and stared at the wall, yet nothing helped him fall asleep.

Outdoors, the enemy was the hounds; indoors, the enemy was the mosquitoes. One after another, Shivaji felt something land on his skin—face, arms, legs, or back. Then he felt his blood being sucked out, as if pricked by a needle. Once their bellies were full, the mosquitoes departed only to land on another body.

It was challenging for any individual to fight these pests because they were so minuscule. Shivaji began to whack the mosquitoes. It did not take much impact to kill them. After a while, he realized it was dangerous to continue. He became conscious that the mosquitoes drank the blood of not one but many people. So when his hand struck a mosquito, it was not always his blood that splattered, but the blood of others as well.

The bites usually led to irritation and swelling. Shivaji could not resist scratching the itch, unaware that such actions only worsened the bites. As the night advanced, the widower felt the temperature drop. "How can a tropical island that produces sweltering heat by day generate such cold winds at night?" he pondered.

With so much to bear, he felt as if everyone and everything had turned against him. "The Stanfield brothers, the farm, the hut, the blanket, the dogs, the toads, the crickets, the bats, the mosquitoes, and Gurdayal Singh are all on a mission to destroy my soul. And up till now, their mission has been successful," Shivaji said under his breath.

To consider everyone as the opposition did not promise bliss. Shivaji knew this but still preferred to begin a war against his enemies. Since he established a new battle, the constant struggles with his demons were temporarily shelved. A determined soul and fearless body were required to challenge his enemies. Determination was needed to annihilate thoughts of past sins and errors. Fearlessness was required to endure the definite punishment that would be inflicted upon his body.

Revolting against the British and its colonial system normally led to some form of penalty, and Shivaji had accepted this. His mantra was insurgence, and he knew there was no retreat from his chosen path. Presently, there was no optimism in his life, and dwelling on past pessimisms was futile. He was to forgive, forget, and focus. Though he never considered dismissing Vyjanti from his life, she was there to be, forever.

THE 45TH DAY

Cock-a-doodle-doo! The rooster crows, the proper outfit is worn, the water is gathered from the well, the collected wood is ignited, the pots and pans clatter, the rice and lentils are cooked, the indentured labourers feed themselves and then proceed to the sugarcane fields where their overseers expect their arrival. Shivaji was not able to rise from the calls of the wild roosters that meandered on the estate. Nor was he able to rise from the clatter of the pots and pans. Nor was he able to rise from the sounds of the brimming khichdi cooked. Nor was he able to rise from the steady movement of Gurdayal's feet within the hut. But Shivaji did rise once he heard the door to his hut close with a thud. He searched the area with his eyes, which were heavy with sleep. There was no sign of his roommate. At that moment, he realized that Gurdayal and the other labourers were en route to the sugarcane fields. Instantly, he rose to his feet. Shivaji panicked. His heart began to race. He knew he was late, but he did not know why he was overreacting to the situation. "Why should I fear these Englishmen? I am not to abide by their instructions. Shivaji Nair will not report to the fields on time," the widower said aloud. This was his first step in his revolution against the Stanfield brothers and their erroneous system. Casually, the widower dressed himself in the soiled kurta and pyjama. He then ate the remaining khichdi left behind. "Hmm, the crabby man is not heartless after all," said Shivaji, believing that the food had been set aside for him by his roommate. After devouring the rice and lentils, Shivaji closed the door behind him and set off leisurely to the sugarcane fields. The only problem was that he did not know in which direction he was to go. He scanned the line of huts for any Indian; none was to be seen. He remembered Ernest saying that the sugarcane fields were located towards the north. So the firebrand began walking towards the north at a comfortable pace. Before reaching his tenth step, Shivaji's eyes met the ground which was covered in footprints. The soil, which was practically the colour of blood, seemed to burn under the blistering sun. "This soil is probably covered with the blood of our Indian brothers and sisters who must have been tortured and tormented by the Stanfield brothers," Shivaji said under his breath, not able to control his resentment. He followed the path of crucifixion, walking for about fifteen minutes on a desolate course, until he heard voices.

"Brother, your firebrand is here, on site, on time, in uniform and at your service," said Edward with sarcasm in his voice.

As Edward and Edwin moved forward to seize the widower, Shivaji glanced at the fifty-two indentured labourers engaged in the planting of sugarcane. The labourers were gathered into bands of five and designated to various sections in the field. Indian adults and children, able and limp, were dispersed in the fields with their hands and feet moving incessantly. The Indian men had cane knives and hoes in their hands, while the Indian women had pails of water and sugarcane stems in their hands. The children, seven of the fifty-two coolies purchased by the owner of the estate, were collecting and stashing the debris on the ground. Although the duties of these kids were simple, the promise made by the British that children were not to labour in the fields had not been kept. Abruptly, Shivaji felt his arms lose their power as he was detained by Edward and Edwin. While being dragged by the Englishmen, who were at least four inches taller than him, Shivaji tried to plant his feet on the earth. As he struggled to do this, both sandals betrayed him, exposing his flesh. Shivaji screamed in pain when his feet kissed the flaming ground. No labourer could work in the fields barefoot. No one's flesh was indestructible. The younger brothers placed the widower in front of their elder brother's feet. Shivaji, whose face was now covered in dirt, could not believe how effortlessly he had been manhandled by Edward and Edwin. His struggle to resist did not match the vigor of the Stanfield brothers.

"Tsk, tsk, tsk... You have let me down. I was not expecting this from you. On your first day, you have arrived late to the fields. On top of that, you are not even in proper uniform. That is not acceptable. Not acceptable at all. Though since it is your first day, you will be spared," said Ernest with no sign of displeasure in his voice.

"Brother, what are you saying? This coolie will not receive punishment? Why must you be so soft-hearted?"

"Be careful how you talk to your elder brother," replied Ernest, feeling challenged by Edward's insult. "Who are you to call me soft? One man down means two hands not at work. It will hinder our total production for the day or several days depending on how serious his injuries may be after the lashes."

"Brother, you have shillings circling your brain constantly. What about teaching this Indian a lesson? What about providing a message to other indentured labourers on site? If this coolie is flogged, he and the others will learn a valuable lesson, which is to always be on time. These coolies should not feel that we are lenient when it comes to discipline," said Edward, hoping that his elder brother would alter his initial decision. "Only ten lashes. No more than that, I promise."

Ernest was left dismayed by his brother's argument. The owner of the estate started to tap his parched lips with his index finger as he contemplated. "Do as you please. I will not be here to witness this."

"You have made the proper decision," replied Edward with a thrill in his voice.

"Yes, but no more than ten lashes. Edwin is to overlook your actions. If you defy my order, I will have you removed from the sugarcane fields permanently. At noon, I will return to inspect the work that has been completed by the peasants."

Edward, who received immense pleasure when flogging the labourers, could not afford to lose the privilege of overseeing the fields. He was an overseer who thrived on the suffering of his coolies. "Edwin, hand over the whip!" demanded the savage beast.

Shivaji was unfamiliar with English words such as 'whip' and 'lashes.' He was unable to comprehend what the Stanfield brothers had decided. But once his ears recognized the sounds of the whip penetrating the air, Shivaji knew that he was to prepare his body for unimaginable pain. For the punished, nothing is worse than the delay of the pounding. It tends to toy with the mind. At that moment, a sufferer tends to feel sorry for him or herself. One asks oneself, "What have I done? What have I done to deserve this excruciating punishment?" Feelings and thoughts of that nature are prohibited for an insurgent. Shivaji had foreseen this. He had accepted this. Thus, Shivaji committed himself to withstand every kind of abuse. Edward believed that by flogging Shivaji, he was sending a message to the other indentured labourers on the plantation. That message was not to violate any of the five rules appointed by the owner of the estate. What Edward did not know was that Shivaji was sending a message to his fellow labourers as well. Shivaji wanted to show that it is moral to fight for freedom and justice no matter how violent the result may be. He wanted others to begin work at a time that was reasonable for everyone. And by everyone, he meant owner and peasant. Shivaji wanted labourers to be dressed in whatever they felt comfortable in. "Why must the Indians dress in clothing handed to them by Englishmen at the depot?" he asked himself. He wanted both dhoti and pyjama to be permissible on the sugarcane fields. To attain freedom and justice based on time and clothing, Shivaji had to endure and express. While proceeding to the sugarcane fields, he pledged to sustain his acts of defiance until he saw a change in the rules set forth.

May it be ten lashes, may it be a hundred, Shivaji was to accept the unbearable suffering without resistance. Edward commanded his brother and the loyal peasant to pin Shivaji to the earth. The unsteady Edwin detained the legs, while Gurdayal clasped Shivaji's hands, displaying literally no emotion on his face.

"Gurdayal, is this your first time punishing a labourer?" Ernest crudely asked the peasant.

"No, sirdar."

"Then I should not be instructing you on what to do and how to do it."

"Yes, sirdar," replied Gurdayal as if he was a trained animal who only knew the difference between and meaning of yes and no. Instantly, Gurdayal started undressing the widower. Even then, Shivaji did not move an inch of his body. He remained idle, feeling no need to resist or retaliate. For a second, he imagined his wife on the scene. "Vyjanti would not have been able to see me in this state. She probably would have intervened or fainted after the first lash," said Shivaji under his breath. The flexible whip was then swung effortlessly before it landed upon the firebrand's uncovered back. The connection of leather against skin made him jolt. He held back the cry that was about to escape from his mouth. Just as the widower heard the sounds of thunder, the lightning struck his back again. To somewhat reduce the pain, Shivaji clenched his fists, curled his toes and gritted his teeth. With immense force, Edward delivered another lash. It was not often that lacerations were shown on the third blow; however, Shivaji was unfortunate. He felt the urge to rise to his feet to prevent further discipline. The soreness insisted he grasp the untamed tool. But Shivaji had to resist these urges. As he opened his eyes to the cruelty, another blow was inflicted upon his back. This time, Shivaji was able to feel the streams of blood trickle down to his lower back. After the fifth lash, when Edward drew the whip back, blood splashed into the firebrand's eyes. There was no water to flush his eyes. Shivaji was tempted to release his hands from Gurdayal's firm hold. Witnessing such an act was unbearable for the loyal peasant. But whatever the sirdar ordered, he was to do. There were no ifs or buts about it. When Gurdayal noticed the widower using his strength to free his hands, he immediately tightened his grasp. During that moment, what he had seen in the firebrand reminded Gurdayal of himself. The loyal peasant also could bear hardship. Reminded of his troubled past, Gurdayal became sympathetic. He let go of Shivaji's hands, not thinking about the consequences. The loyal peasant was fortunate that Edward did not see the compassionate act because he was too involved with beating the firebrand. One more devastating blow was administered, this time flaying the left side of the victim's temple. The whip did not have a single destination on which it landed. It was unpredictable, unable to decide its whereabouts. The tool was not to be tamed. On the other hand, the sufferer who received lashes from the whip was to be tamed. Shivaji wiped the blood from his eyes with the back of his hand. A few seconds later, he sensed additional blood descending from his temple onto his face.

There was no twinge associated with the seventh lash. For the meantime, the numbness of his body had rescued Shivaji from the torture. Shivaji had experienced the pain of a baton thrashing against his skull. He also experienced the pain of bones crushing and ligaments tearing. Then, there were those painful days spent in "the hole". Shivaji had experienced much agony, but nothing was more agonizing than the six hurtful lashes. As Edward persisted with the flogging, Shivaji had descended into a reverie. For the widower, this was his moment to reflect upon his deceased wife. He reminisced about the times when Vyjanti used to guide him onto the righteous path. Shivaji went back to the night when his wife told him that she expected submission and endurance from him in regards to the journey from India to Fiji. "I still follow your guidance, Vyjanti. I have submitted to my inner beliefs. I believe I have what it takes to fight the British system. That is the freedom to speak when we want to speak, act the way we want to act, eat when we want to eat, rise when we want to rise, sleep when we want to sleep, dress the way we want to dress, reside where we want to reside and work where we want to work. I have also endured and will endure until my last breath. For one to achieve, one must endure. To attain liberation, I will have to endure the intense beatings, crass insults, startling deceits, backbreaking labour and repulsive living conditions," Shivaji mumbled to himself. Gurdayal snapped his fingers for the widower to regain alertness. Coming back to the situation he was part of, Shivaji felt the last hit which did not have the same impact as the others. When and how the last few blows were administered he had no idea whatsoever. Edward was not pleased. He wanted Shivaji to moan in pain, resist his detainment, attempt to escape or beg for forgiveness. But that was not the case. Edward felt as if Shivaji was about to win this battle. He did not want that to happen. In his view, to lose a fight to an Indian was disgraceful. Unable to accept defeat, Edward readied his lethal whip for another lash.

The firebrand desired to say, "You show no mercy; I feel no pain. You have no courage; I have no fear. One, ten, or a hundred lashes — it does not matter. Keep them coming; I will endure," but he knew that his roommate would not translate his words in English for the culprit to hear.

Before Edward flung the whip above his head, Edwin intervened. He had released Shivaji's motionless legs and walked directly to his elder brother. "That is enough. No more lashes."

"Move aside," said Edward, acting as if his brother did not exist.

"Brother Ernest said ten lashes only. I will not allow more than that," replied Edwin in a strict manner.

"And what if I do?"

"I will report you to brother. One more lash inflicted upon this Indian's flesh will lead to dismissal from the sugarcane fields," Edwin threatened his elder brother.

Edward had an evil grin on his face. He ogled at his brother, frightening him with his piercing eyes. The elder brother was not disturbed by Edwin's warning. Instead, he felt proud that his younger brother was learning to become an authoritarian. "As you say, Edwin," he said calmly. The savage beast then ordered Gurdayal to lift the wounded Indian to his feet and assist him back to the coolie line.

En route to the hut, Shivaji walked faltering due to the blisters under his feet caused by the searing earth. Every step resulted in discomfort. At times, he had to stop to let the ache lessen. He secretly wished that Gurdayal had the appropriate tool to chop his feet off. Perhaps no feet were better than feet with swellings, thought Shivaji. As for his back, the lesions began to tear wider and longer with every movement. When Shivaji felt the tear widen, he bit his tongue to stifle a shriek. The pain was unbearable, but had to be endured. The widower had never been abused in such a drastic manner. But he knew that to further his stance against the Stanfield brothers, he had to become familiar with such maltreatment. Punished by his spiteful enemies and the fiery soil beneath his feet, Shivaji headed towards the coolie line without the help of his roommate. Gurdayal kept his distance because of the widower's stubbornness; he did not want to intervene. Shivaji was not the person to seek help from a traitor. After he saw the loyal peasant assist Edward during the beating, Shivaji had lost all respect for him. He knew that Gurdayal was a translator for the Stanfield brothers, but he did not know that he had taken part in the callous punishments administered upon the indentured labourers of the plantation.

"Let me help you," said Gurdayal as he saw Shivaji fall to his knees.

Unexpectedly, Shivaji felt his legs give way. He reached behind to touch his feet. Even the slightest touch led to a searing pain. He then brought his hands forward. To his surprise, both hands were smeared with blood. Shivaji did not have to think about what had happened or how it had happened. He knew that the blisters had burst.

"You must let me assist you," pleaded Gurdayal.

"I don't require assistance from someone who assists the oppressors," replied Shivaji bluntly.

Gurdayal chortled. "I have walked the line of fire. The same fire that burns inside of you once burned inside of me. What you have endured is no comparison to what I have endured."

"How can you say that? You don't know who I am or what I have been through?" cried Shivaji.

"Well, if that is so, then we shall talk about our pasts and ease the ache that shelters within our hearts. Let me help you," said Gurdayal as he lifted Shivaji to his feet. "You have a story to tell and so do I. Let's share."

Shivaji assumed the loyal peasant to be only loyal to his owners. "I will not share my personal life with you. Yesterday, you were not interested in talking. Today, you want to reveal your personal life. That does not add up. You must be an informer. There is no doubt that what I will say to you will get passed on to the Stanfield brothers."

"That is not so," said Gurdayal while positioning Shivaji's arm over his shoulder for support. "I am no informer. I am no deserter. I am no traitor. I am a slave driver on this estate; a slave driver who is forced to hold the whip and forced to engage in repression. What I do for the sirdars on this estate is disgraceful. These Englishmen order me to sin and I commit sin after sin after sin."

Shivaji kept mum. He was actually interested in what the loyal peasant had to say.

"I am sorry that I did not talk to you last night. I was in no mood to do so. I did not want to tell you that I had inflicted fifteen lashes upon a labourer who was under my supervision," said Gurdayal as both men began to step forward.

"I believe that you still have the power to choose whether to beat the labourers or not. These are our people. These are people who come from our land, people who have the same responsibilities, concerns and values as we do. These are the same people who have been misled, oppressed, assaulted and discriminated against like we have. Then how—how do you let your hand raise the whip upon these ill-fated men and women?" Shivaji asked as his voice became emotional.

"That is because if I don't raise my hand, they will raise theirs."

"Who are they?"

"Well, the Stanfield brothers, particularly Edward. As an overseer for a group of sixteen indentured labourers, I am required to inflict pain upon them for their wrongdoings."

"What might these wrongdoings be?" asked Shivaji as if he was an investigator.

"Let's say: if a labourer is not keeping up with the pace, spreads the cane on the earth incorrectly, is seen talking to another labourer during working hours, shirks an appointed duty, fails to fulfill duties by a set time, requests to use the loo during working hours, inquires about pay during working hours, speaks to a sirdar coarsely, does not wear proper clothes in the sugarcane fields, or does not arrive on time — he or she is to be lashed."

"I am familiar with the last few examples you have mentioned," said Shivaji.

Gurdayal did not smile at the comment. His facial expression displayed remorse. "I am to hit these peasants whenever one of the rules the Stanfield brothers created is violated. So imagine—just imagine—how many times I have to use that lethal weapon. When I first came to the plantation, I did not use the whip on a labourer when I needed to do so. Even when I observed a labourer not doing what was asked of him or her, I did not use the whip. But the result was devastating. I, who did not obey my duty, was flogged. The labourer who should have been flogged was flogged. And the remaining labourers in the group of sixteen were flogged as well."

The fuming Shivaji responded, "That is unjust. These rules are more like restrictions."

"Now do you understand the position I am in? I would rather inflict pain upon one labourer instead of the entire band that I oversee. If it was possible, I'd prefer the sirdar discipline me for the wrongdoing of others."

"I don't see anything wrong if an indentured labourer needs to visit the loo, asks about pay, speaks when they wish, wears what they want, arrives when they choose, and works at a pace that is reasonable for him or her."

Gurdayal finally broke into a smile. He respected the intense passion Shivaji had stored inside him. His passion could rattle the colonial system, plantation owners, and overseers. It could invoke the Indians to strive for independence, equality, and for change to take place, thought the loyal peasant.

As the men entered the eastern section of the estate, Shivaji directed an imperative question towards Gurdayal. "Does your hand not tremble when you strike a labourer?"

"Indeed, my hand trembles. Also, my heart aches, my eyes water, and my brain stops processing after the first lash."

Shivaji inhaled deeply. He felt the lesions on his back split. "I have to stop," he said in a guttural voice.

Gurdayal noticed the change in Shivaji's facial expressions and tone. "It must be your wounds. We need to get to the hut as soon as possible. You should not be moving about.

The more you move, the more pain you will suffer," said Gurdayal as he endeavored to comfort his roommate.

Despite the soreness, Shivaji insisted on launching more questions at the loyal peasant. "Do you think God will forgive you, knowing that you are forced to commit these sins?"

"The Lord will not forgive me for my sins. I don't forgive myself for my barbarous acts. God will surely punish me. Be it in this life or the next, I will be punished. There were days when I returned to the hut after numerous flogging episodes wanting to sever my hands. Hidden in the hut, I would deliberately bash my hands against the walls. The same hurt I administered upon others, I inflicted upon myself. But the following day, when I returned to the sugarcane fields, the overseers were not pleased. Edward made sure that all the labourers of my band were thrashed, including the repentant slave driver whose hands were too disfigured to even hold the whip."

At last, Shivaji walked into the hut. Gurdayal helped the injured widower onto the ground. As Shivaji lay on his stomach, Gurdayal lightly dabbed at the bleeding lacerations with an unsoiled cloth. Within seconds, the cloth was covered in red. He then saturated the cloth in the pail of water nearby. With the wet material, he carefully dabbed Shivaji's blood-spattered feet. During the whipping, in the presence of overseers and labourers, Shivaji had not wanted his painful cries to be heard. He did not want to convey that he was vulnerable in any way. Inside the hut, however, Shivaji did let out his suppressed cries. After all, the only person to hear his outcries was a sufferer who once aspired to follow the path Shivaji had taken.

"Don't move from this position until I return," Gurdayal ordered Shivaji, like a father would order his son.

"When will you return?"

"I will return after sundown. Have you eaten?"

"Yes, I ate the khichdi which you left behind."

The loyal peasant started to chuckle. "That khichdi was not for you. I had stored it for myself. I was planning to eat it at night."

"What?" said Shivaji, astounded that his roommate did not care to share his food with him.

"Sorry, I presumed that you did not eat food made by others. I have had several roommates since I came to this estate, and all of them preferred to cook and eat their own food. I kept pestering them to taste my famous khichdi, but they refused," said Gurdayal as he got to his feet. "So, how was it?"

"It was delicious. After receiving watered-down rice and lentils on the Ship *Elbe* for over a month, I started to believe that khichdi was the most distasteful food on earth. But after tasting your khichdi this morning, I wouldn't mind eating the same dish for the entire year," replied Shivaji, before erupting into laughter. Unfortunately, his laughter led to anguish. The laughing caused slight movements which made the lesions on his back widen further.

"I think it's time for you to rest. And I must return to the sugarcane fields. Edward has me on a leash. If I don't report to the fields on time, I will be disciplined. It takes us Indians at least fifteen minutes to reach the fields. If we jog or run, perhaps ten minutes. But the unfair Edward has given me only fifteen minutes for this entire errand. Surely, Edward knows that no regular man or woman can walk from the fields to the coolie line and back in less than fifteen minutes. This provides him with the delightful opportunity to unleash his whip on my body. Some men desire to see others suffer. That is the kind of man Edward is—and will always be," said Gurdayal while he tossed the cloth, drenched in blood, into the pail of reddened water.

He then placed a tin cup of lukewarm water beside Shivaji. The insufficient space within the hut made it difficult for Gurdayal to move around. On his departure, he faced the challenge of not stepping on Shivaji. It took the loyal peasant only five strides to reach the door. As Gurdayal was about to shut it, the widower said, "I don't know who this coolie person is. I have no idea why I am called a firebrand. Neither of those is my name. My name is Shivaji Nair."

"Shivaji Nair, I hope that you are the one who will help the indentured labourers on this plantation understand the power and meaning of insurrection."

THE 46TH DAY

On the sugarcane fields, Ernest counted a total of fifty-two indentured labourers. The firebrand was nowhere to be seen. When the plantation owner asked Gurdayal where his roommate was, the loyal peasant explained that the punishment inflicted upon Shivaji had left him in a dreadful state. "Sirdar, the man is not able to move about. His wounds need time to heal. I promise that he will return as soon as his injuries settle."

Ernest did not like the idea of a coolie unable to work in the fields. In his view, production was of more importance than any trauma, mental or physical. If a coolie faced the loss of a family member, he or she was to report to work. If a coolie suffered from illness, he or she was to report to work. If a coolie was injured, he or she was to report to work. But there were exceptions when it came to injuries. If a coolie could not walk or stand properly, he or she was permitted to recover for the day.

"He must report to work tomorrow. The Indians from his recruit will be trained before he arrives in the fields. Gurdayal, you are to train him. As you know, he will be the upcoming slave driver of this plantation," said Ernest, patting his loyal peasant. He then marched over to his younger brothers. Edwin knew that his elder brother was not pleased. He stood idle, unable to meet his eyes. On the other hand, Edward, aware that he was about to receive an earful, stood in a carefree manner with his hands resting upon his hips.

"Edwin, how many lashes were administered upon the firebrand?" asked the irritated owner of the estate.

"As per your orders, ten lashes."

"Are you sure?" asked Ernest, sensing deceit in the answer.

"Yes, brother, the coolie received ten lashes."

"Hmm, ten is a small number. In the past, several coolies had received ten lashes and were able to return the following day. Then how is it that the firebrand is not able to function properly?"

"That is because your firebrand is a weakling. Like I have said before, he is useless. He will not be able to replace Gurdayal in his position as the slave driver," said Edward.

Ernest did not find it necessary to respond to his brother. He moved towards Gurdayal and asked, "What do you think? Is he suited for the position of a slave driver?"

Gurdayal was pleased that the owner of the estate did not question him about Edward or the ten lashes. Whenever the loyal peasant was forced to administer ten lashes or more, he would not apply much force. For others to believe that the lashes were executed with immense strength, Gurdayal would release an outcry with every whip. However, in the end, the whip was a fierce weapon. Once it abraded the skin, no matter how much force was behind the lash, it resulted in pain.

Gurdayal replied to the plantation owner, "Sirdar, I don't think the man knows that he is to work as a slave driver. I believe we must inform him. Once we do, perhaps then he will strive to perfect himself for the position."

"You're an Indian with a brain. That is the reason why you are my personal favorite. Unfortunately, you are ageing. Unfortunately, your progress in the fields has decelerated. Unfortunately, you don't have the same energy, endurance, and efficiency as you did five years ago. Your efforts of late have been damaging our production in the fields. You will soon be assigned to other duties in and around the estate," said Ernest before his brother interfered.

Edward did not want any of the labourers to be appreciated or complimented, especially not in his presence. "There is no need to praise Gurdayal. The less we see of him in the sugarcane fields, the better for our production. He will soon be demoted."

Ernest remained calm. He did not want to create a scene by overreacting to his brother's irrational remarks. "Edward, you have forgotten that he is the only peasant who understands and speaks English. If not for him, we'd never be able to get our messages across to the indentured labourers on this plantation. No matter what you say, Gurdayal is valuable to this estate."

Edward did not have much to say after receiving a potent knockback from his brother. He and Edwin returned to their duties of manning the labourers in the sugarcane fields. As for Ernest, he was not done with Gurdayal. He told Gurdayal to inform the firebrand of his appointed position.

The loyal peasant felt that his owner had placed a heavy burden on his chest. He did not want to be the one to provide the information to Shivaji. But it was something that needed to be done.

The long hours of the day reminded Shivaji of "the hole" on Ship *Elbe*. Enclosed in a small area which generated unbearable heat, Shivaji lay idle on his blanket. He was in a constant battle with the perspiration that developed on his body. The perspiration crossed boundaries with the lesions on his back. Perspiration contains salt; therefore, when the salt entered the wounds, Shivaji felt as if he had been bitten or stung by a harmful insect. To prevent the affliction, he struggled to remove the perspiration with a dry cloth. Shivaji wanted to recover quickly, but it seemed as if the wounds were healing at a sluggish pace. He did not want to be a burden on his roommate. He felt terrible that Gurdayal had food and water prepared for him before the break of dawn. Shivaji knew he had to repay the loyal peasant for his help.

There seemed to be no advancement in the day. Shivaji waited for darkness to prevail. And as he waited, his mind lingered on the reasons for setting forth on a path that had not been accepted by his wife. "If Vyjanti were alive, her request to abandon this path would have never been disregarded. But she is not here, and I have nobody to look after or live for," the widower said to himself.

Shivaji had once pondered the trigger behind his pursuit of challenging the colonial system and its enforcers. He finally received the answer to his question. Indeed, he believed that the British were responsible for his wife's death. But that was only part of the reason why he chose to struggle for his rights and freedoms. At that moment, the firebrand admitted to himself that he had been a rebel since his childhood. When he was a child, he rebelled against classmates and teachers. And when he became a teenager, he rebelled against his father. Whenever his peers resorted to cheating on tests, stealing from the canteen, or bullying the minors, Shivaji would raise his voice. And when his father dictated what he could or could not do, what he could or could not wear, what he could or could not eat, where he could or could not go, whom he could not befriend, and what he could or could not become, Shivaji was determined to neglect Muthuraman's orders.

His urge to challenge authority had been present since the tender age of seven. His automatic response to orders, demands, and commands expressed by those he felt were tyrants was to either reject or disrespect them. The widower did not accept that someone else had authority over what he said, what he ate, what he wore, where he lived, and so on. It infuriated him that he was repressed by his loved ones from acting or reacting to injustice. Reflecting on his disobedient acts of the past, Shivaji had unintentionally reinforced his determination to fight against the British and to set examples for the indentured labourers.

He was content that his mind was occupied with such matters. If that had not been the case, his thoughts would have wandered to his family members in the village or to Venkatesh and his family. But what surprised him most was that his mind was not captivated by the tragic incident that shattered his life. He instantly lifted his body from the ground, not wanting to lapse into a series of thoughts concerning the formidable voyage. Those thoughts and images were composed of remorse and despair. Shivaji decided not to dwell on remorse and despair as he stepped into a different chapter of his life.

To alleviate his mind, he staggered over to the pot which contained the famous khichdi made by Gurdayal.

From inside the hut, Shivaji looked forward to his roommate's arrival. While on the sugarcane fields, the indentured labourers breathlessly waited for the sun to disappear. There were days when the sun lowered its face behind the prodigious hills and other days when it hid beneath the vast ocean. The labourers admired nightfall because during those hours they were able to rest their aching bodies and stressful minds. Those were also the hours in which the Indians had the opportunity to converse with their family members, to reflect on memories of their loved ones back home, to properly treat themselves or another to food, to disinfect any injuries they sustained on the job, and to inhale and exhale the air of impunity.

When Gurdayal entered the hut that night, his roommate began praising the delicious khichdi. Shivaji thanked the loyal peasant from the bottom of his heart. "Generosity displayed by a stranger has more weight than generosity displayed by a relative," said Shivaji as he kept his roommate entertained with his conversations. The overworked Gurdayal first washed his hands, feet, and face. He then cleansed the nicks and pricks which he received in the sugarcane fields. Shivaji volunteered to assist him with the minor scratches and holes, but the loyal peasant kindly rejected his offer.

Before opening the lid to the pot of khichdi, Gurdayal asked the widower if he would like to eat some more. Mindful of the amount of rice and lentils left in the pot, Shivaji knew that it was best for Gurdayal to eat on his own. He wanted Gurdayal to sleep with a full stomach after a laborious day in the fields.

As the loyal peasant consumed his food, Shivaji did not cease his questions. "Was the plantation owner upset with my absence?" he asked.

"Yes, he was. He is not pleased by the fact that others from your recruit will be trained in various duties before you."

"How does missing one day make anyone from the new batch more skilled or trained than I?"

"Have you any idea how much labour is required per day? From dusk till dawn, the indentured labourers are ordered to do this, do that, cut this, cut that, plant this, plant that, store this, store that. We are constantly learning something new every day. Therefore, missing a day in the fields is ruinous for both the coolies and the sirdar."

"The plantation owner has enough hands at work," said Shivaji, brushing off the explanation provided by his roommate.

Gurdayal took a sip of water from his tin cup without removing his eyes from Shivaji. "That is not what he believes. Sirdar believes that even if one labourer is absent from the fields, it will result in a loss of production. Loss of production means less income. If one labourer is absent for a day, other labourers have to suffer. Sirdar and his brothers will practically fling their whips around for the labourers to work faster. Every five minutes, their arms, legs, or back is slashed by the whip, demanding them to move with excessive speed. More speed usually results in less efficiency. So if the labourers are declared inefficient, leather continues brushing their skin. Basically, the active labourers are to work twice as much as they normally do to recover the loss suffered due to the absence of the inactive labourer."

"Today, I was the cause of the extreme pains inflicted upon my fellow Indians," said Shivaji as if he was talking to himself. He imagined Venaktesh and his family members flogged incessantly by the hands of the Stanfield brothers. Shivaji felt saddened by the surreal picture. "Whenever I set out to challenge the system, I am always disrupted by an obstacle. But I will discover other methods of defying the oppressors. Shivaji Nair will report to work in the morning."

"What about your wounds?" Gurdayal asked with concern in his voice.

"They are not fully healed. But that does not matter. Tomorrow, I will reimburse the drudgery that the indentured labourers were forced to perform in the sugarcane fields."

The loyal peasant felt that this was the perfect opportunity to inform Shivaji of his appointed position. "Shivaji, I must tell you—" Before Gurdayal was able to complete his sentence, the widower intervened.

"I will arrive at the sugarcane fields. But it will be according to my time. So that means, I will rouse when I want to rouse, then get dressed when I want to get dressed, then eat when I want to eat, and then arrive when I want to arrive."

Gurdayal shook his head. "Why must you do that? That will result in another severe flogging. Once the punishment is delivered, you will be sent back home. And that means you will be absent for the remainder of the day."

Shivaji caught on to what the loyal peasant was referring to. This time, he did not intervene in the conversation.

"If the beating is more severe than the last, you will probably need more than a day to recover. Again, the indentured labourers will suffer from cruel treatment because of your selfishness. Or should I call it stubbornness?"

Shivaji was not bothered that Gurdayal voiced his words in such a curt manner. What bothered him was that he had been unable to think of this circumstance beforehand. "Is the obsession to revolt hampering my decisions? Shouldn't I be able to foresee what may or may not happen?" he asked himself.

Gurdayal sensed the tension swarming inside Shivaji. After all, he was still an adolescent confused about where he stood and what he stood for, thought the loyal peasant. He devoured the last morsel left on his tin plate. Before Gurdayal attended to the pail of water to cleanse his hands, he encouraged himself to deliver the truth. The loyal peasant was ready to break his silence about the role Shivaji had to enact on the plantation, but again the widower did not allow him to do so. Shivaji asked his roommate three essential questions that could reveal much about someone's personal life if answered: "Who are you? Where are you from? Why are you here?"

The loyal peasant, who had not revealed his past life to anyone on the plantation, did not resist telling Shivaji. The lengthy night had become lengthier as the peasant unfolded what he had kept hidden in the corner of his heart for more than five years. Gurdayal Singh came from a poverty-stricken family of Sikhs who lived in the Northern state of India. It was then when he first set foot on a sugar plantation. Along with his father, Gurdayal planted and harvested sugarcane on a farm owned by an Englishman. During this period, not once did he complain to his father that his small hands and feet hurt because of the demanding labour.

To better their lives, the family migrated to Kovai when Gurdayal was in his teenage years. Gurcharan Singh, the head of the family, was promised employment in the cotton cleaning and pressing factory upon arrival. The promise was made by a devoted servant who then worked for one of the English managers running the factory. The servant was from the same village as Gurcharan and shared a close bond with the Singh family. Within a few days of arrival, Gurcharan started to work in the factory, and from there on the family rose in status.

To work for a British company, to be managed by the British, and to be supervised by the British was considered a privilege. But the English held comfortable positions, mostly seated behind desks, while the Indians were appointed to the laborious positions where they were required to work prolonged hours. Working as an assistant to the managers and supervisors of the factory, Gurcharan was to handle menial duties such as polishing shoes, disinfecting the offices, preparing tea and biscuits, providing escorts within the facility, and racing to complete errands.

It was not until five years of working in the factory that Gurcharan was regarded as useful rather than useless by the English. By spending close to ten hours each day in an office environment with men who were fluent in English, Gurcharan was bound to learn the foreign language. The managers, supervisors, and the remaining office workers were all pleased that Gurcharan could translate their words to the Indian employees. But if an Indian employee desired their words to be translated to the English, the English instantly became deaf.

With days turning into years, the Singh family prospered. There was no need for Gurdayal to attend school because his father was his educator. Gurcharan taught his child everything he had learned from the British, including the foreign language, which was not effortlessly mastered by Indians. It took a lot of patience and effort for Gurdayal to attain the title of bilingual.

When Gurdayal entered his twenty-first year, his father was prepared to retire from his post. Fortunately, his position at the factory was reserved for his son to obtain. After much pestering and nonstop praising, Gurcharan was able to convince the managers and supervisors of the factory that his son was the perfect candidate for the job. Several weeks later, the management team was pleased to see that Gurdayal had picked up where his father had left off.

With years passing by and his daughters married, Gurcharan decided that the proper time had arrived for him to seek a bride for his son. A fine woman with traditional and cultural values was selected for Gurdayal. Soon, he was married. Then, there were children. Gurdayal and his wife became proud parents of three boys and one daughter, all of whom were born within seven years. With his father retired, mother satisfied, wife in good health, and children well-fed and clothed, Gurdayal felt blessed to live a life without dilemmas.

Nevertheless, there is no living soul on this planet that can evade trials and tribulations. In the nine years spent working at the factory, never did Gurdayal imagine a day where the Indian employees would challenge the management team. The Indian employees wanted to use Gurdayal as their ladder to reach the managers and supervisors who ran the factory. They wanted their words to be translated into English. They needed Gurdayal's voice to be their voice, his words to be their words.

After hearing their complaints and concerns regarding the workplace, Gurdayal felt that he needed to discuss the matter with the bosses. When talking to his superiors, Gurdayal felt dominated. He was outnumbered five to one. During the discussion, he learned that Indian employees were to receive a pay deduction. The assistant pleaded for the management team not to reduce the monthly pay for the Indians. But the headstrong team of managers and supervisors would not succumb.

Since the Englishmen were fond of the assistant, Gurdayal was spared from any kind of pay reduction. However, the decision made on behalf of the management team irritated Gurdayal. He was devastated by the fact that it was only the Indians who were wronged. The assistant felt that if a pay cut was to be implemented, then it should affect everyone working in the factory, including the English managers and supervisors.

Gurdayal informed his fellow employees that the management team was unwilling to budge. He also informed them that the employees who did not have white skin were the ones to receive a pay cut. This information made the Indians furious. From then on, their main priority was to deliver a message to the English. The Indians demanded equality. Questions were raised on why the English employees were not receiving a cut in their pay. The Indian employees starved for justice. For days, they withstood a hunger strike to prevent the management team from implementing the pay reduction. The Indians promised the management team that if they were to receive less pay at the end of the month, there would be a labour strike. So instead of working ten-hour shifts, the Indians planned to not work at all. On top of that, they were to spend the entire ten hours within the facility, protesting against the managers and supervisors of the factory.

So when the day arrived that the Indians were paid less, they did what they had to do. "We ask for respect, we ask for equality, we ask for justice," was the phrase repeated simultaneously throughout the factory. The powerful voices bounced from one wall to another. There was no escape from these loud cries.

"These Indians have never asked for a raise, and here you are reducing their pay. How is that fair?" asked the leader of the ensemble. Once the voice of their leader was heard, the group of employees on strike burst forth with cheers and chants. Yet there was no sympathy in the hearts of the management team members for the employees who had dedicated their lives to the cotton industry, employees who had never dared to speak against their managers and supervisors, and employees who relied on respectable earnings to shelter, feed, and clothe their families.

"Why are we not provided with the reasons behind the pay cut? What are the reasons? We want reasons," said Gurdayal in a demanding voice. From assistant to the management team to leader of the employees, Gurdayal had discovered his true identity once he decided to join the struggle to achieve respect, equality, and justice. He did not experience any disrespect or unfairness himself, but his fellow workers did. After all, he was one of them, an Indian. Just because he knew how to speak English did not mean that the color of his skin was white. Just because he served and befriended the English did not mean that he belonged to their society. Gurdayal believed that he was destined to guide the Indian employees to impartiality.

"I want the management team of this factory to reduce my income as well," Gurdayal said to the Englishmen gathered in the office, who remained deadpan as the protests intensified. "Yes, I say lower my pay as well. We shall all be equally paid." Gurdayal was a natural. No person would be able to tell that this was his very first protest. Anger was present in his voice. His expressions and words were domineering. He could captivate the audience. Not once did the crowd of employees take their eyes off him. The English management was perplexed. It was hard for them to believe that an assistant who never disregarded orders, who never protested against duties, who never retaliated against insults and threats, and who never challenged wrongful assumptions and decisions, was now the head of the protest demanding changes.

"We employees of the cotton factory report to duty on time. We employees of the cotton factory work lengthy and exhaustive hours. We employees of the cotton factory work diligently and efficiently. We employees of the cotton factory never give the managers and supervisors a chance to whine and moan. We employees of the cotton factory never ask for raises and promotions. Then why is it that we are to be deprived of our normal pay? Do we deserve this? I think not," stated Gurdayal as he gestured for his band to raise their voices.

"We ask for respect, we ask for equality, we ask for justice..."

The protests continued for several weeks. The machines in the factory remained untouched. The loss of production and profit was severe, compelling the management team to make a decision. A decision had to be made, and it had to be made fast. Gurdayal and his fellow employees believed that there was only one choice available: the Englishmen had to pay the Indians the normal rate for which they had worked before. But in reality, the management team had several options. Indeed, they could provide the Indians with the regular monthly payments, or they could select a different path.

There were discussions among the Englishmen that it would be beneficial to hire new workers—Indians willing to work for less pay, perhaps even less than what the current batch of Indians was receiving. The Englishmen viewed this as a slap in the face of the noncompliant Indians. And so, in the third week of the month, Gurdayal and his team of protesters were replaced by Indians desperate for work. Some of these newly recruited workers were so poor that they were willing to perform any duty, no matter how difficult or degrading, to receive the small amount of income offered.

Gurdayal left the factory with his head held high, but he was unable to foresee what the future had in store for him. Losing the position at the factory instantly led to disputes within the household. As the protests were happening, nobody in the Singh family was notified. Gurdayal did not tell his father, mother, or wife. He found it pointless to keep his family members tense about the outcome. Somewhere within, Gurdayal felt that the results from the protest were unlikely to be advantageous. Yet that did not change his mind about protesting against the Englishmen. There was no point in working for a company where Indians were treated unethically, thought Gurdayal.

But a man without employment was a man without earnings. To attain employment in a country where the British were the rulers and the Indians the servants was not difficult. But to expect Indians to be treated fairly was beyond the bounds of possibility. Over the next ten years, Gurdayal was not stable in his employment. He was often hired and then released due to his rancorous attitude and contentious behavior. Everywhere he went, he noticed that the Indians were considered inferior to the British. Wherever he landed, Gurdayal challenged the management for their discriminatory practices. He lodged complaints, uttered threats, initiated protests, and organized strikes. But not once did he or his group of protesters emerge victorious. Instead, they were released and replaced by other Indians.

Soon, word spread that Gurdayal was known to be a threat to any English manager or supervisor. As a result, he was arrested on several occasions. Several complaints about his disobedient acts were reported to the British enforcement, which resulted in days when Gurdayal returned home bruised and battered. His family members were planning to leave the state and return to their village. Gurdayal was so involved in his conflicts that he had forgotten he was the only breadwinner in the family. His children were coming of age, soon ready for marriage. His wife became restless since her husband was never there to spend time with her and the family. His mother and father were aging and longed for attention from their son. Not a single member of his household was content with him and his radical beliefs.

When Gurdayal turned forty-three, he had lost both his parents within the same year. The year was inauspicious and full of hardships. Leaving his family behind, he was forced to return to his village to sell a large portion of his property. After selling the property, which his father had placed under his name, he returned with the sufficient funds needed to get his children married. Like his father had done for him, Gurdayal found nubile brides for his sons. Once all three boys were married, the leftover wealth he received from his property was distributed among them. He did save a lesser amount for his only daughter. But the decent act was soon rejected.

At a tender age of fifteen, his daughter abandoned the family by disappearing with her secretive partner. She believed that her father would never approve of their marriage because her partner was not of the same caste. Gurdayal was embarrassed by his daughter's selfish act. His heart had shattered into little pieces. He had once believed that his daughter was the closest to him of all his children. "If she was that close to her father, then why did she not tell me about her feelings for this nameless person?" Gurdayal asked his wife as tears formed in his eyes.

With age, the confrontations, altercations, disputes, protests, and strikes that were once part of Gurdayal's life had eventually dissipated. He had paid his price for challenging the English. Unable to earn shillings, unable to pay his rent, unable to eat proper three meals a day, and unable to purchase decent clothes, Gurdayal regretted walking the path of an insurgent. He used to spend most of his days out and about confronting the system and the people enforcing it, disregarding the people who needed him the most. Gurdayal felt remorseful that he was not there to be a loving husband and father. But what disturbed him the most was that he was not there to take care of his parents. In the final years of their lives, both his father and mother insisted that Gurdayal share a few everlasting moments with them. But Gurdayal was too involved with his protests and strikes, so he did not even find time to touch their feet for a blessing.

As for his children, none of them found it essential to visit him. Once in a while, the eldest son came by, presuming that Gurdayal was not home, so he could meet his mother.

It was not as if Gurdayal had banned his children from meeting him or his wife. The truth was that his children did not prefer to see him. Gurdayal understood why he was ill-treated by his offspring. When his children were blossoming, Gurdayal was not there to care for them. What he did not do for his children, his children did not do for him. If Gurdayal had the opportunity to go back in time, he would do it in a heartbeat. He kept speculating on how life would have been if he had lived it differently. But he understood that there was no possible way to correct the mistakes he had already made.

Years had passed, and still there was no sign of his daughter. Gurdayal and his wife desperately struggled to locate her. At times, the father felt as if his daughter had vanished from this earth. "Perhaps death has claimed her," Gurdayal said under his breath. Once the line was said, Gurdayal realized how low his thoughts had sunk. He would then spend days not forgiving himself for the repulsive thought.

When his wife reached her mid-forties, her health began to deteriorate. She was unable to keep warm and often battled pneumonia. She was unable to eat properly, and therefore, she was forced to endure hunger. Gurdayal did not have the earnings to purchase his wife new clothes, so she had to wear outfits with holes in them. Despite such hardships, she never felt the urge to leave her husband. Everyone had abandoned Gurdayal—his parents, his children, and his friends—but his wife never dreamed of abandoning him.

Yet the man who was once self-seeking had decided to free his life partner from all burden and despair. The lowly jobs, such as boot polishing, sidewalk sweeping, and bullock cart driving, which Gurdayal was engaged in, did not promise a satisfying future. He was planning to send his wife to live with her eldest son, who was flourishing in all aspects of life. Whenever he visited, the son pleaded for his mother to move to his household to live a comfortable life. Her mother knew that his son proposed the kind offer for her alone. She responded to her son, "If you have room in your heart and your house for my husband only, then I will agree to live with you."

What Gurdayal was searching for was a route to absolute seclusion. First, he wanted to free his wife from a life full of miseries. Then, he wanted to set himself apart from his children, friends, and the environment in which he lived. Lastly, he wanted to detach himself from a past that forced him to believe he was a sinner for not performing his role as father, husband, and son. But Gurdayal had to wait several years before he encountered the route to absolute seclusion.

The path to isolation came in the form of a translator position on a vessel sailing from India to Fiji. British agents, who patrolled towns and villages day and night, were not only searching for peasants but also for translators who understood and spoke both Hindi and English. The position required Gurdayal to temporarily part from his wife and children. It demanded that he travel on a cargo ship for nearly three months. He was to go to Fiji with a ship full of indentured labourers and then return to India with a ship consisting only of Englishmen.

When Gurdayal informed his wife that the British required his services on a cargo ship sailing across the Pacific Ocean, she was quick to disapprove.

"I have not asked you. I am telling you that I must board this ship. The British will pay a fortune for this three-month position. I will not be performing backbreaking duties. I am to translate the words of the British to the Indians and vice versa. You should not be concerned; I will return," Gurdayal said to his wife as she ogled him with a blank face. At first, she did not consider her husband serious. But when Gurdayal revealed the advance payment offered to him for the position, his wife sobbed like never before. She pleaded for her husband not to venture into the sea, into foreign lands, into the hands of the British. But the resolute husband did not capitulate.

At that stage in his life, Gurdayal knew what was best for him. And he also knew what was best for his wife. He had difficulty clarifying to his wife that three months were not three decades. "Three months is small compared to the uncountable number of days and hours I left you to survive on your own. There were days when I'd leave home before you rose and return after you had fallen asleep. Do you not remember that?"

The wife did not have any words to say to her husband. Her unceasing tears had spoken enough. She was concerned that her disobedient husband might get into trouble with the Englishmen on the vessel. "The decision you have made is not proper. You don't see eye to eye with the British. You don't accept their system. Then how can you work for them? How will you act under their rule?" What his wife said was true. Gurdayal did not object, nor did he feel it necessary to answer the questions. His decision may not have been proper, though it was indispensable. Gurdayal did not want to see his wife suffer along with him. He regretted not being able to purchase her new clothing for the past five years. Whenever he saw his wife sweeping the floors of the compound, her sari revealing patches of skin through holes, Gurdayal's heart ached. At times, he was unable to afford fresh fruits and vegetables. The little amount of shillings he obtained was only good for rotting and overripe products. There were days when Gurdayal and his wife forced themselves to sleep without devouring even a small morsel of food. The couple endured sleepless nights due to the cries of their empty stomachs. Misery was endured, but it eroded the spirit. Gurdayal also felt that because of him, besides his eldest son, his other children did not visit their mother. The offense of separating a mother from her children paralyzed Gurdayal with disgrace. He and his wife shared the same dream of talking and laughing with their children and grandchildren. "These dreams will probably never come true for me, but I will make sure they come true for you," Gurdayal solemnly promised his wife.

The day his wife was received by their eldest son, Gurdayal struggled to control his tears. Deep inside, he sensed that he was betraying his wife. Husband and wife are to be together—through thick and thin, through ups and downs, through the good and the bad. His wife begged to accompany him on the expedition, but Gurdayal stood firm. He forbade an Indian woman to fulfill her role as a noble wife. By this, he felt that he had committed one more sinful act. Gurdayal believed it was time for his wife to forget him and focus on the children, who had become motherless due to his past decisions and actions. There was a whisper in Gurdayal's ear as his wife departed, tears cascading from her eyes. Whether it was a soft voice or a natural feeling, there was an indication that perhaps this was the last chance for Gurdayal to see his wife. She waved farewell to her husband, who stood on the front porch, motionless and emotionless, not lifting his hand in response. As she turned the corner with her son, Gurdayal finally lifted his numbed hand—but he then realized it was too late. She was no longer there.

The next morning, Gurdayal was collected by the British agents and transferred to the cargo ship. When he arrived, he was left astounded by the sea of Indians in queue to board the vessel. Never before had Gurdayal seen so many Indians gathered in one place. From the start, Gurdayal was handled differently than the rest. As the translator, a servant for the British, he did not have to wait in the long line to board. He was escorted by the British agents to the cargo ship and directly introduced to the captain. During his opening speech, the captain ensured that the translator was presented as an important member of the British team and sea voyage.

Right away, the labourers treated Gurdayal as if he were less of a translator and more of a traitor. How the Indians viewed Gurdayal tormented his soul. The coolies despised him because he did not sleep on the wooden floors as they did, he did not clean the lower deck as they did, he did not eat the same rice and lentils as they did, he did not have restrictions on water usage as they did, he did not have to use the same latrine, and he did not endure whips and beatings as they did. When an indentured labourer was punished by the whip or baton, Gurdayal felt the urge to rebel. He noticed that after taking a couple of steps forward, his feet seemed cemented to the floor. His clenched fists gradually hardened. He noticed his voice was eager to free itself, but trapped behind sealed lips. Even though the impulse to challenge authority gnawed at him, Gurdayal did not act or react to the injustice delivered by the Englishmen on board. He wanted to flee as far as possible from his past habits. Unlike before, Gurdayal was unable to feel the pain inflicted on the oppressed labourers. He could not place himself in their shoes. Besides remorse, nothing else was felt by Gurdayal until he faced treachery.

Upon arrival at the islands, the English seafarers unloaded the hundreds of coolies onto shore. At that moment, a deal was struck between the captain of the ship and the British commander in charge of the depot, who needed a capable translator. Without his consent, Gurdayal was forcefully escorted off the vessel. He was restrained by chains and led to the depot. Once there, he was informed of his duties, which he initially refused to perform. The translator was then abused like the other coolies. Whips, batons, and boots were used on his body until he was forced to undertake the role of translator on campus. Only then did Gurdayal feel the exact amount of pain that the indentured labourers on the vessel had endured. That night in the depot, Gurdayal accepted his fate. He knew the cargo ship on which he traveled had departed. "The ship is probably in the middle of the vast ocean, advancing towards India," he murmured under his breath. Gurdayal pondered if he would ever meet his wife again. He did not know what the British had in store for him. What if his ability to translate words turned out to be his worst enemy? What if his services were required for years? What if he was to spend the rest of his life on the islands? These questions circulated in his mind, not allowing Gurdayal to sleep the entire night.

Gurdayal spent nearly three months at the depot under the control of the British enforcers. Every month, a cargo ship with hundreds of indentured labourers arrived near the shore. As the coolies were transferred to the depot, it was Gurdayal's responsibility to translate the directions and commands voiced by the Englishmen to the uneducated Indians. At the depot, Gurdayal did not receive privileged treatment. He ate the same rice and lentils, rested on the same hard floor, and used the same latrine as the other coolies. But these losses were inconsequential to Gurdayal. The loss he brooded over was the abduction of his freedom. After four months of separation from his wife, children, and motherland, Gurdayal felt it was time to return. He knew that back in India his wife must be concerned for his welfare and eagerly awaiting his arrival. But he did not know how long the British enforcement would require him to remain on the islands. Payments in full were given to Gurdayal every month for his commitment as a translator. His savings were ample for him to provide for decades.

Finally, Gurdayal felt he had what was needed to provide his wife with a comfortable life. One day, he gathered the courage to approach the British commander. He did not declare that he planned to board the next vessel to his homeland. Instead, he politely asked if he was permitted to board the next ship to India. All the Englishmen on campus had egos as large as elephants. No Indian was to look them in the eye or voice a directive or request. As Gurdayal waited for an answer, he kept his eyes lowered.

"I will see what I can do. I know you were not to set foot on this island. But we required your assistance. The truth is, we still need your assistance. Though I understand you have a family waiting for you back in India, I will see what I can do," said the Englishman, lifting the translator's spirits.

So the countdown began for the arrival of the next cargo ship to the Fiji Islands. Gurdayal knew that the commander had not promised to send him back to his country. Nevertheless, the response had been positive, and from that, Gurdayal firmly believed he could return to his wife. At the depot, the enforcers were negative, the coolies were negative, the discussions were negative, the plans were negative, and the atmosphere was negative. Overall, the entire system was negative. Thus, when a British enforcer voiced a statement positively, it was something for the oppressed to embrace.

A few days before the arrival of the cargo ship carrying indentured labourers, an auction was held without the knowledge of the coolies at the depot. Usually, the Indians were cleansed and dressed suitably to look presentable in front of the buyers. Coolies were informed of such preparations at least a day before. But that was unnecessary for this auction. The indentured labourers who had not been purchased at the start of the month during the initial auction were gathered to be sold. On that day, not only was the remaining band of thirteen coolies sold, but the translator was bargained for as well. At first, Gurdayal was ordered to attend the event to fulfill his role as translator. He matched the commander word for word, translating English to Hindi so the coolies could understand which plantation owner had claimed their fate.

"Gurdayal Singh, please step forward. Buyers, let's start bidding," shouted the British commander before winking at the translator.

The Indian, promised the role of translator on the cargo ship, was now being sold to a planter who intended to use him as both an interpreter and a labourer. As Gurdayal began translating the commander's words, his voice cracked. He instantly realized he was saying his own name. "How can that be? I am not an indentured labourer. I did not sign any contract stating that I would work as an indentured labourer for five or ten years. There has to be some kind of misunderstanding," he said in a frantic voice.

During the public sale, the British commander was approached by Ernest Stanfield, who said he needed an English-speaking Indian. The commander informed the planter that the only Indian with that ability was the depot's translator, who was not to be sold under any circumstances. He mentioned that Gurdayal Singh was not an indentured labourer but a servant assigned by the British enforcement to perform specific duties. However, Ernest ignored this information. To rise to the top, outperform his competition, and be the best in the business, Ernest was determined to acquire the translator. For Gurdayal, the plantation owner was willing to pay any cost.

The British commander remained inflexible. Over and over again, he told Ernest that there was no way he would let the translator take part in the auction.

"In that case, I will have to use my last resort," said Ernest with a smirk.

Disconcerted by the plantation owner's ingenuity, the British commander did not know whether to view Ernest's words as a grave threat or frivolous boasting. The planter secretly informed the man in charge of the depot that, if allowed to purchase the translator, the commander would receive a large sum of money. Furthermore, the wealth could be shared with the full team of enforcers at the depot.

"That is for you to decide," said the resolute plantation owner.

At first, the commander did not believe that Ernest had such wealth on him. But when the renowned planter showed the commander what he had stored in his bag, greed overpowered all rules and regulations.

"This is between you and me. No one else needs to know," Ernest whispered into the commander's ear.

The bribe was accepted, and the deal was made to place the translator in the auction with seven hungry buyers waiting to claim any coolie who walked the platform. The fact that Gurdayal was not under an indenture contract no longer mattered to the British commander. Once again, Gurdayal experienced betrayal. He immediately began to panic. But with a quick signal from the commander to his guards, Gurdayal was forced to stand idle on the platform until the bidding ended. Unlike the coolies at the auction, Gurdayal fully understood his surroundings. He knew the purpose of the event, how it worked, and what it would result in.

"Sold to Ernest Stanfield," said the British commander, before ushering the guards to deliver Gurdayal to his new "owner."

Within minutes, Gurdayal was fastened in shackles. At that moment, his freedom, which had been already compromised, was permanently hijacked. Never did he expect a translator to be sold as an indentured labourer. "Why did I not foresee this? How could I not expect the British to deceive? I knew very well that the British have never lived up to their promises. Then why did I consent to the offer in the first place?" Gurdayal asked himself as he was dragged by the Stanfield brothers to the plantation where he would labour for years. He had no one to blame but himself.

Ernest and his brothers informed Gurdayal of his duties as soon as he arrived on the plantation. He was to translate between Hindi and English when required. He was also to follow the guidelines obeyed by all labourers on the estate. At the sugar plantation, Gurdayal was to cultivate, plant, nurture, and harvest—duties that required onerous manual labour, unlike the depot where he only interpreted words.

During his first month, Gurdayal challenged the Englishmen. Whatever was ordered, he defied. Whatever he was asked to translate, he ignored. Whatever evil he was instructed to administer, he bypassed. Whatever rule or regulation was implemented, he violated. Soon, he became a menace in the eyes of the Stanfield brothers. On the plantation, becoming a menace usually resulted in severe beatings. Whips, shovels, and batons were used on Gurdayal, but still, he frustrated his owners.

When Gurdayal demanded to be sent back to his motherland, Ernest pretended not to hear. When Gurdayal pleaded instead, Ernest said in his rigid voice, "You will not be sent home unless you start performing the duties I have set forth. I need you to translate my words, labour in the fields, and become an overseer."

Somewhere along the line, the Stanfield brothers had planned to use Gurdayal as a slave driver. It was his pugnacious behaviour and multilingual abilities that impelled Ernest and his brothers to make this permanent decision. After four weeks of defying orders and enduring brutal penalties, Gurdayal began translating dialogues and reporting to the sugarcane fields. He made this compromise only because he believed that sooner or later Ernest would send him back to India.

Months passed. Gurdayal proved to be a loyal peasant who did not challenge his owner's instructions. His childhood experience in the fields had molded him into a proficient labourer with immense speed and stamina. He was a fast learner, paid close attention to detail, and was not prone to blunders. His popularity among the Stanfield brothers grew steadily.

More months passed. Hoping Ernest would approve his return to India, Gurdayal strived to be the best day in and day out. Among the labourers, Gurdayal was least likely to be flogged by Edward. Though at least three licks per day were expected for an indentured labourer, almost every day, the loyal peasant escaped punishment. Gurdayal patiently waited for the green light to depart.

But instead, the loyal peasant was handed the responsibility of inflicting agony. As an overseer, Gurdayal was practically ordered to become an Englishman. He was to demand results from the coolies under his charge, monitor every labourer, and punish anyone who slowed down, conversed in the fields, or failed to meet expectations. Whenever he was required to wield the whip, his hands trembled with nervousness. He did not want to beat his Indian brothers and sisters, but he was compelled. Gurdayal had no choice but to scream, threaten, curse, and push the labourers to perform.

For him to return to his native land, Gurdayal had to become selfish once again. He developed an obsession—an obsession that demanded selfishness. Among the Indians, Gurdayal was seen as a defector, but to the Stanfield brothers, he was loyal. The man, whose path had been dictated by his captors, could not escape the guilt of betraying the indentured labourers, betraying his own kind.

As the year drew to a close, Gurdayal began to grow impatient. He felt as if the Stanfield brothers were leading him into an inescapable trap. Whenever he spoke to Ernest about his land, wife, and children, head bowed and eyes lowered, the planter made the loyal peasant feel invisible. When asked if he could return to his family, Ernest curtly replied, "Sooner than later."

Gurdayal was not satisfied with such an enigmatic response. His frustration with the Stanfield brothers had reached its peak. The anger inside him threatened to burst through the tamper-proof cage of his self-restraint. What disturbed him most was the belief that he had committed a far greater sin than any of his past transgressions. In the past, he had temporarily abandoned his family—sometimes leaving home before dawn and returning only at night, other times not returning at all. He considered these absences transgressions.

Now, with his life seized by the Stanfield brothers, Gurdayal felt he had permanently abandoned his wife and children, though this time the separation was beyond his control. "Will I ever see the faces of my wife and children again?" he asked himself daily. He dreamed of beginning a renewed life with his wife—a life full of promise and comfort. His savings from his work as a translator and labourer were intended to build a home in the heart of a lively town. But day by day, those dreams shattered, worn away by the endless labor on the plantation.

Eventually, Gurdayal resolved to take matters into his own hands. One morning, he refused to rise to attend the sugar fields. He would not leave the hut, would not eat, would not perform duties, and, above all, would not obey orders until he was officially approved to return to India. When Ernest and his brothers discovered his absence, Edward was sent to the eastern section of the plantation to find him. Armed and aggressive, Edward pounded on the front door of Gurdayal's hut.

"Open the door! I know you're in there!" yelled Edward, blood boiling with rage.

Gurdayal did not move.

"If you don't open this door, I will skin you alive with my razor-sharp blade!"

Gurdayal remained squatting in the corner, unmoving. "I will not open the door. I will not report to the fields. I will not labour for anyone. I must speak to sirdar. He is the one who will send me home."

"Brother Ernest is not here. I am. I am your master. You will obey my commands. Now, open the door," the aggravated Englishman shouted.

"I was told I'd be sent home soon. But that was long ago. I have waited far too long. Please send me home. I am no indentured labourer who has signed a five- or ten-year contract," Gurdayal explained, striving to make Edward understand.

Edward understood that Gurdayal was being held illegally. Yet he also knew that the loyal peasant was the most educated, skilled, and hardworking Indian on the plantation. Releasing him would devastate production in the sugarcane fields. Ernest and his brothers could not afford such a loss.

Edward did not wait for Gurdayal to open the door. Using his forearm and shoulder, he crashed through the barrier separating them. Seconds later, the door lay on the floor. Edward rushed toward the unarmed Gurdayal. The peasant knew he was about to be struck by the whip. But Edward wielded something else—a baton he had never faced before. Gurdayal winced, unable to imagine the pain that was about to be inflicted. His bones pleaded for mercy and his muscles begged for leniency even before the punishment began.

"All I want is to be sent home to my wife and children. I should never have been forced onto this island. Still, I have worked diligently for this plantation. Please understand..." Gurdayal began, but before he could finish, a sharp pain erupted near his abdomen. The words caught in his throat. Edward did not hesitate. He attacked Gurdayal like a wolf on a sheep, swinging the baton indiscriminately. Each strike connected with bone and muscle, but Gurdayal refused to yield. Over and over, he pleaded to return home. His cries, however, only provoked further punishment. Limbs discolored and muscles bruised, he endured relentless blows.

Edward, so engrossed in the punishment, lost track of time. Ernest had instructed him to return within thirty minutes so Gurdayal could lead his team in the sugarcane fields. Though enraged, Ernest remained calm. His elder brother advised Edward not to lay a finger on Gurdayal—presence in the fields was more important than a lesson in defiance.

After thirty-five minutes, with no sign of Edward or Gurdayal, Ernest mounted a horse and rode toward the eastern section to investigate. High-pitched screams echoed from the hut. Gurdayal, battered and swollen, could no longer lift his hands or feet to resist. His only method of resistance was to continue shouting, "Send me home!" His defiance deeply unsettled Edward, who finally paused his blows.

Edward then drew a more deadly weapon from his pocket. "You will not go to India. You will work on this plantation until your hands fall off. Do you understand?"

Disoriented, Gurdayal could not comprehend the command. "Please send me home... I want to return... She is waiting for me... You must send me home," he gasped.

"Earlier I said I would skin you alive if you didn't open the door. Did you open it? No, Gurdayal, you did not," Edward said, waving the dagger. His maniacal eyes promised death. As he advanced, Gurdayal shrieked for help. Blood spurted from the line Edward carved from his temple to his jaw. Limbs shook, voice fading, agony unbearable.

Luckily, Ernest arrived. He had anticipated his brother's punishment and intervened. Not pleased with Edward's cruelty, Ernest ordered him to leave immediately. Edward departed with a sinister grin.

"I will clean your wound. It must not get infected," Ernest said, taking on the calm authority of a medic. "I am sorry you were viciously beaten. This was not my order. My brother acts as he pleases. Heal quickly, Gurdayal. You may rest for the day, but at dawn, you return to the sugarcane fields," he added, the merciful doctor transforming once again into the demanding plantation owner.

"I will return, but not to the fields. I will return to my motherland," said Gurdayal, his voice jittery.

"At this time, that is impossible. You are too valuable for us to lose. Perhaps five to ten years from now, I will grant you freedom. The day I see that you can no longer endure the sugarcane fields, I will escort you to the coastline so you can depart from this island.

Do not lose hope—you will see your wife and children again. But first, you must help me turn this plantation into a goldmine."

"I have laboured in the sugar fields for six and a half years since my arrival on the islands. I have been enslaved here longer than many Indians bound by a five-year indenture contract. I have seen countless Indians come and go, yet I remain a captive who does not know if I will ever board a vessel back to India," said Gurdayal, his roommate's eyes brimming with tears.

Shivaji concealed his face with his sleeve, unwilling to show the water that streamed from his eyes. Shedding tears in front of another man embarrassed him. Listening to Gurdayal's story, Shivaji felt a kinship with the loyal peasant. Both were rebels in their own right: Gurdayal against the unjust colonial system, Shivaji against the British enforcers, seafarers, and overseers—but for deeply personal reasons. Shivaji longed to be free from slavery, to be treated as human, not animal. He wanted justice and retribution, most of all for his wife's death.

A taut string connected Shivaji's heart to his mind, yanked repeatedly by memories of Vyjanti's demise. Each tug reminded him of revenge. He waited for the moment that would ignite uncontrollable wrath. When that moment would come, he did not know.

After sharing his story, Gurdayal expected Shivaji to reciprocate. But Shivaji was not that kind of man. He rarely shared personal details, even with close friends or family. Observing his roommate's silence for several minutes, Gurdayal felt compelled to ask a question.

"Which state or district are you from?"

Shivaji, though not in the mood for questions, replied, "Red Lilies District."

Encouraged, Gurdayal continued. "How long is your indentured contract?"

"Five years."

"Were you a farmer in India?"

"No. I was a fisherman, selling fish at the local market."

"And your father?"

"I come from a family of potters. Both my father and grandfather were in the pottery business."

"Where are your family members?" Gurdayal asked, unaware that the questions were becoming personal.

"My family is back in India."

"So you traveled to the islands alone?"

"No, I was on a cargo ship with hundreds of other Indians from Southern India."

"Sorry, I wasn't clear. I meant, did you sail with anyone you share a personal relationship with?"

Shivaji narrowed his eyes, finding Gurdayal's line of questioning odd. "Are you an investigator?"

"No, no. Please don't say that. If I have offended you, I apologize," said Gurdayal, ashamed.

"I am not upset. I traveled with my childhood friend, his wife, and child."

"You haven't been separated from them?"

"No," Shivaji answered curtly.

"Shivaji, are you married?"

The question closed the night's session. Shivaji had already resolved not to discuss his deceased wife or personal grief. "It is late. We can continue this conversation another time. I should close my eyes now, as I am not used to rising early," he said, hoping Gurdayal would not press further.

Gurdayal understood his friend's subtle deflection. "Yes, we must rest. Don't worry—you will not oversleep. I will make sure you rise on time."

"Thank you," Shivaji said, surrendering quickly to sleep.

THE 47TH DAY

No signs of shock were revealed on the faces of the Stanfield brothers when Shivaji arrived on the sugarcane field minutes before the reporting time. Ernest was pleased to see the widower standing beside the other indentured labourers, properly dressed in a long-sleeved, tattered shirt and cotton pants that ended at least five inches above his ankles.

"So the firebrand has arrived. If it were not for the severe punishment, this coolie would have arrived late again," boasted Edward.

"Do you expect me to admire or congratulate you for the brutal whippings?" Ernest asked his brother, wanting to deflate his ego.

"Brother, the whipping has made your firebrand afraid. He will not dare to neglect the rules and regulations on this plantation again."

Ernest called for his loyal peasant and informed Gurdayal that the firebrand would have to labour the most today. "Since he was absent from the fields the last couple of days, I want the coolie fully trained by the end of the day. I assign this responsibility to you. Please, don't fail."

"Not to worry, sirdar. I will turn him into a skilled farmer," replied Gurdayal.

"Not only a skilled farmer. He is to relieve you from the overseer position. Have you not told him about his future position yet?"

"I am very sorry. He does not know yet. I will talk to him tonight."

Ernest did not seem pleased with Gurdayal's response but was in no mood to scold. "Talk to him tonight. He must be aware of his position. Gurdayal, his arrival can be your departure," said the owner of the estate.

Shivaji, who had not conversed with Venkatesh and his family members for days, eventually reunited with them during the gathering. Venkatesh tightly consoled his friend as Lachmaiya and Karthik looked on. Excited to meet his friend again, Venkatesh forgot that the lacerations on Shivaji's back were not fully healed. Shivaji tried to hide the discomfort, but it was visible on his face. It was the small child who first detected the pain his mama was bearing.

"Appa, you are hurting mama. Please let go," shouted Karthik. The child's voice rang like bells in his father's ears. Immediately, Venkatesh let go of his friend and expressed regret. Shivaji laughed hysterically.

"Venkatesh, this is only the beginning."

"What do you mean by that?" asked Venkatesh.

Before Shivaji could reply, Ernest called for the attention of every coolie on site. While Gurdayal pondered how to inform his roommate that he was mainly purchased to handle the role of a slave driver, he failed to translate the words spoken by his sirdar in Hindi.

"Gurdayal," roared the planter, "I want you to translate."

For many years on the plantation, Gurdayal knew that inaccuracies in translation were unacceptable. Thus, he ensured his ears were wide open and his mouth ready to interpret the words voiced by Ernest, Edward, and Edwin. But on this occasion, the loyal peasant was sidetracked by the gravity of the task before him.

As Ernest spoke and Gurdayal translated, the fifty-three indentured labourers listened carefully to their briefing.

"Today, you will follow the traditional method of ploughing and hoeing. Expect this day to be tedious. You are scheduled for two breaks, one at noon and one in the afternoon. All coolies must report to the fields on time after their fifteen-minute breaks. If you don't return on time—" Ernest hesitated mid-sentence.

Edward intervened, "If you don't return on time, expect to be physically abused."

The plantation owner was infuriated with his brother leaping in. "Edward, please don't interfere. How can you be so impolite? I am aware of the punishment you want to inflict. Yes, there will be consequences for tardiness, but not by whipping. Coolies, listen carefully: if you report late after your fifteen-minute break, you will have to work in the sugarcane fields for an extra hour. When the other labourers return to their huts, you will remain in the fields under my command."

Many of the indentured labourers groaned silently. Those who had been on the estate for years knew that an extra five to ten minutes of rest was not worth an additional sixty minutes of grueling labour.

"You," Ernest pointed directly at the widower, "what is your name?"

The question did not need translation for Shivaji. He knew the common English phrases. He did not wait for Gurdayal to translate and instantly replied, "My name is Shivaji Nair."

The planter was impressed. Until that day, he had believed Gurdayal was the only Indian on the plantation who spoke English. Shivaji was not as educated, but he knew enough to handle the basics.

"Yes, firebrand. Sorry, I mean Shivaji. You will shadow Gurdayal Singh for the entire day. Learn everything that needs to be learned. Though this is your first day in the fields, I will not treat you differently from the other coolies. Keep up with their pace. If not, Edward, Edwin, and Gurdayal are there to use the whip," said the plantation owner, with the loyal peasant fulfilling his duty as translator.

Without delay, Edward, Edwin, and Gurdayal led their bands of fifteen or more labourers to various areas of the Northern section. Once on scene, the women and children carried empty pails to the nearest well, filled them with water until they overflowed, and transported them to the male labourers, who collected hoes.

The newly recruited labourers struggling to adapt were paired with veteran peasants. With the veterans by their side, the newcomers felt less apprehensive even under the watchful eyes of overseer Edward. Most trusted the experienced to coach them. Nonetheless, most of the Indians who boarded Ship Elbe were seasoned farmers capable of learning and performing the tasks assigned by their sirdar.

From the eleven Indians Ernest had purchased, Shivaji was the only one with no experience in planting, nurturing, or harvesting. When Venkatesh and his family members were allocated to Edwin's band, the widower experienced mixed emotions. He was heartbroken that his childhood friend was not in the same group, but relieved that Venkatesh, Lachmaiya, and Karthik were not overseen by the savage Edward. Shivaji could not imagine the scrawny, tight-lipped, poker-faced Edwin wielding a whip or baton against the coolies. To him, Edwin seemed like an ignorant adolescent compelled to follow his brothers' orders.

For the Stanfield brothers, Gurdayal was a loyal peasant, but for the indentured labourers, he was an overseer. Gurdayal, born a natural leader, demanded that the men in his team follow his lead as he strolled over to Ernest to fetch a horse for the ploughing. He advised Shivaji to stay near him at all times. He wanted Shivaji to learn everything there was about cultivating sugarcane. Once the brunette-colored stallion was in hand, Gurdayal, his trainee, and the plough horse strutted back to their work area in a flash.

While the women and children were equipped with pails of water, the men waited for the overseer to begin ploughing. Every man had a hoe in hand except Shivaji. Without the tool, Shivaji felt useless. He was unsure of what Gurdayal had planned for him.

"My brothers and sisters, I need you to keep some distance behind the plough. For this assignment, I am not in command. The horse is in command. We are to follow its lead. Only when the horse moves forward do we move forward," said Gurdayal as the band of coolies watched him connect the straps from the horse to the plough. The antiquated mouldboard plough, made of timber, had been left uncared for on the soil for days. Shivaji had seen ploughs and horses in his village, but he had never witnessed how creature and tool worked together. When his trainer advised the other peasants on what to do and what not to do, Shivaji knew that those instructions did not apply to him. Gurdayal did not even make eye contact with his roommate when addressing the coolies.

"If I am not needed in the fields, I shall return to the hut," said Shivaji, hoping to make his trainer realize that he was upset.

"Shivaji, this is no time to rebel. I need you to follow my every step. I will be driving the plough to create a furrow. The next furrow must be created by you. That is why I need you to be attentive. Do you understand?" asked Gurdayal.

The widower did not understand. He did not know what furrows were, how to drive the plough, why the Indian men had hoes, or why the Indian women and children had collected pails of water. At that moment, nothing made much sense. Still, Shivaji was determined to learn. Though he despised being an indentured labourer, he wanted to excel at any task he undertook. In Red Lilies district, he had been the leading fisherman. If he had to be a farmer, he would strive to be the best on the plantation.

Shivaji understood that the task ahead was not simple. What made it worse was that he knew nothing about the components of the mouldboard plough. "If I do not know the parts of the machine, how will I operate it?" Shivaji whispered to himself.

"Let's begin," yelled Gurdayal, urging his team members to be alert. He gestured for Shivaji to hold the whip provided by the Stanfield brothers whenever he entered the sugarcane fields. To steer the plough comfortably, the Indian overseer needed to hand the weapon to his trainee. Gurdayal was never keen on carrying a weapon in the fields, but he had been instructed to do so. Nor was he only instructed to hold it; he was ordered to use it. Gurdayal never disciplined on his own will. Only when Ernest or Edward commanded did he wield the whip. But whenever Edward stumbled upon a labourer from Gurdayal's band who was chatting or sluggish, it left the overseer no choice but to strike forcefully. In such situations, if Gurdayal did not use the whip, Edward would, in a barbarous manner. To protect his team from life-threatening punishment, Gurdayal burdened himself with the task, using his own hands to administer the whip. He was careful not to inflict excessive pain, but no matter how delicately he wielded it, the shrill cries of the victims grew louder with each lash. In his swings, Gurdayal had to maintain realism. If the beats looked unnatural, the team of coolies was in trouble. Whenever delicacy tried to imitate realism, conflict was inevitable.

"Shivaji, you are required to assist the horse in moving forward. Most importantly, don't let it turn to either side. Keep it progressing in a straight line. Sometimes, she gets stubborn. That is when you need to use the whip," said the trainer.

"I will not use this weapon on any human or animal," declared the widower as he extended his hand to take it. "Nevertheless, I will keep it aside until you complete the duty."

"There is a need for you to use it. I don't want this horse wandering in the opposite direction. If you don't take responsibility, our furrows will not align. Shivaji, you need to understand: I can maneuver the plough. It is you who will maneuver the horse."

Shivaji did not reply. Instead, he caressed the braided leather with his thumb. It was his first time holding the lethal weapon that had once abraded his skin. "How can this tool, which looks so flimsy and rickety, inflict such damage?" Shivaji asked himself.

The bullwhip only appeared flimsy, but when used, the whooshing and cracking sounds, along with the lesions and scars, told a very different story.

To advance, Gurdayal signaled for the firebrand to crack the whip. At first, Shivaji thought he was to strike the horse. After a few seconds, he realized he was not to lash the animal but to create a booming sound to encourage it forward. Never taught how to use a whip, Shivaji tried his best to swing it above his head and strike the ground. The sound was not very effective but managed to awaken the stallion.

While both animal and machine proceeded, Gurdayal noticed the soil was dry, slightly impeding the plough's gradual movement. The plough had difficulty penetrating deep into the earth and left behind cloddy soil that the men with hoes were ready to tackle. As for the creature, its legs moved, but at this pace, it would take at least an hour to complete a single furrow. The labourers were not at fault; the intense sun was. For the past several days, the heat had drenched the indentured labourers with sweat and drained moisture from the land. If the hot temperatures persisted all week, it would be disastrous for both the coolies and the landscape. Usually, winter brought light showers to the islands, but this year Fiji did not see even a speck of rain.

"Shivaji, I need you to use the whip. I order you to strike that horse," cried Gurdayal, annoyed that the stallion had become lethargic.

The widower responded, but not by applying force. Instead, he created clicking and clacking noises with his tongue to get the horse moving. It did not take long for Shivaji to capture the animal's attention, though it remained reluctant to move.

"Do you want me to step off this machine? Because if I do, that whip will be exercised with force," threatened Gurdayal, the Indian overseer.

"No, that is not necessary," replied Shivaji. He then slapped the horse on its hindquarters. The clever move did not help, as the creature remained idle. Shivaji could not think of any other solution but to use the whip. The inexperience in his swing was immediately noticed by Gurdayal. Shivaji administered a blow on the upper portion of the horse's body. The animal neighed fiercely and then started to advance in a straight line. Constantly, the horse snorted and nickered as it struggled to haul the plough forward. The animal was in a fierce battle with the stubborn land.

Shivaji only used the whip on the horse when it came to a halt. What troubled him was that he did not know if his licks, which he considered light taps, were harming the animal. His brain did not want to accept that he was forced to harm a living creature. "Why must I sink this low?" he asked himself.

The landscape on which the sugarcane was to be planted seemed never-ending. While ploughing a single furrow, time seemed to have stopped. For the peasants, the straight line in which the plough was dragged appeared to have no end. Shivaji could not imagine the misery the horse endured. He felt as if the animal laboured more than the humans. By the time the animal and peasants had finished half the line, Shivaji noticed a change in the stallion's behaviour. Its body language, once expressing hardiness, now showed feebleness. The strength and energy displayed by the horse had suddenly evaporated. As its legs began to falter, the plough became impossible for Gurdayal to steer. He prayed that the machine would not change direction. Under no circumstances was the straight route to be abandoned. Shivaji was afraid the horse might collapse. He then did what no other peasant had witnessed on the sugarcane fields before.

At full speed, Shivaji rushed towards the four-legged creature. Without considering the outcome, the firebrand gripped the harness in which the animal was entangled. Shivaji jerked the horse's neck. "Instead of beating you, I will assist you," Shivaji muttered to the voiceless animal, as if it could understand. Using every last drop of strength, the widower heaved the slouched animal. Perhaps, Shivaji lifted not only the body but the spirit of the horse. It was as if the horse had been reborn. The firebrand and plough horse both forged ahead with unseen bursts of energy. Where that energy came from, no one knew.

"Keep moving. Let's keep the feet moving. There is no need to stop now," said Shivaji, trying to boost his own confidence while his team members believed he was once again talking to the horse. The widower was so engaged in guiding the horse that he did not notice when or how both his slippers had slipped off his feet. With his bare feet on the scorching stones and heated soil, the heroic Shivaji still managed to increase the horse's power and speed. Whether it was pure magic or a miracle, Shivaji was pleased that the once-submissive creature was now marching heavily toward the completion of the first drill.

As for Gurdayal, he understood immediately that his roommate was special. There was something in him that others on the plantation did not have: intrepidity. The Indian overseer was impressed with how Shivaji handled the chaotic situation in a humane manner. Now that the plough advanced steadily, no labourer from the group remained inactive. Shoulders, backs, legs, arms, feet, and hooves were all engaged. While Gurdayal and Shivaji handled the plough and horse, the Indian men diced the clods with hoes, and the women and children watered the furrows. The lumps of dirt, formed whenever the soil was turned, were hacked into small cubes as the plough moved forward.

Whenever the Indian overseer felt one of his team members was too close to the plough, he shouted at the top of his lungs to maintain a safe distance. The last thing he wanted was a peasant with a severed arm or leg. When the horse plough arrived at the end of the line, Gurdayal ordered his band of coolies to stop. He inspected the furrow they had created. To an extent, Gurdayal was a perfectionist. He wanted his lines as straight as a pencil. It did not take long to recognize that the furrow was a bit crooked, which happened because the stallion was uncooperative at the beginning. But from the middle onwards, the formation improved. If not for the widower, Gurdayal and his team would have still been struggling with the first drill.

Not even a full day spent in the sugarcane fields, and Shivaji began to introduce innovative methods. Where others would have lashed the horse with a whip or baton, the open-minded Shivaji chose unselfish solutions. He deliberately ignored the fact that he could have been punished for not punishing the animal. The labourers in Shivaji's group were fascinated to see an Indian daring to think outside the box. Peasants who had worked on the plantation for months and years were so brainwashed that they no longer exercised their minds. Instead of searching for other methods, they blindly followed the Stanfield brothers' orders. Seeing Shivaji's actions lifted their spirits. Once again, the firebrand was confirmed to be dangerous to oppressors and an inspiration to the oppressed.

After completing the first drill, Gurdayal and his trainee switched positions. Now, the tool of punishment was in the hands of the Indian overseer, while the ploughing machine was in Shivaji's hands. The firebrand became skittish when first placing his hands on the plough. Besides a small craft he occasionally sailed, he had never steered anything in his life. He had seen bull carts and motorized vehicles in his district often, but never operated one. Shivaji had no interest in machines or gadgets meant for transporting individuals. He believed God had given him two feet, which should be used to move from place to place. The stubborn chap wanted to rely on his feet rather than devices trying to replace human limbs.

At the sound of the whip, the horse began to move, with Shivaji directing the plough. Within minutes, the trainee felt comfortable as the operator. But he did not feel as if he was labouring as hard as the other team members, and that frustrated him. He sensed the machine controlled him, and the trainer controlled the animal. "So what is my role? What am I contributing?" Shivaji questioned. He was not the type to shy away from hard labour. If he was to be paid, he wanted to be worthy of it, no matter who he worked for or where.

While keeping his hands steady on the plough, Shivaji's trainer used the whip whenever the horse stopped or slowed. When Shivaji saw the weapon strike the animal's hide, he was immediately reminded of the agony he had suffered upon first entering the sugarcane fields. The sound of the snake-like whip still rang in his ears; the feeling of rips and tears on his flesh made him grimace. Occasionally, Shivaji glanced at the Indian men smashing clods and the women and children watering the furrows. Otherwise, his eyes were fixed on the various parts of the mouldboard plough. With no one explaining, and without asking, Shivaji decided to learn the functions on his own.

He first examined the mouldboard, placed below the soil. When the machine advanced, the curved blade turned the furrow over. He then shifted his eyes to the coulter, a knife-like blade mounted vertically on the plough, which cut vertically into the soil as the machine progressed. Understanding what turned the furrows, Shivaji then focused on what maneuvered the plough. To steer the horse, he grasped handles located on the rear of the machine. At the front was a small wheel that helped balance the plough. Shivaji used these components to the best of his ability to reach the end of the furrow.

At times, when the horse stopped due to exhaustion or the rigid soil, Shivaji felt the urge to abandon his post and help the creature forward. But his position did not permit it. He had to endure the horse's cries as it was lashed. As the team neared the end of the drill, the horse refused to move. The disobedience angered Gurdayal. To make matters worse, Edward was seen approaching. The Englishman was far in the distance, but close enough to be visible to the naked eye. Something had to be done, and it had to be done fast.

"Move... I said move! Why have you stopped?" shouted the Indian overseer at the horse.

The horse did not budge. Shivaji knew it was his turn to produce sounds. Unfortunately, his tongue failed to coax the animal. Gurdayal became panicky. He did not want Edward to declare that his group was lagging. In the back of his mind, Gurdayal knew that, with the amount of time passed, completing even one drill was a letdown. He did not want to imagine how Edward would react, so he decided to take full control. One after another, blows were delivered upon the creature's flesh in a brutal fashion. The miserable horse wailed. Its blatant cries echoed across the sugarcane fields, heard by every labourer. At that moment, Shivaji experienced the unexpected.

Fallen into a hallucinatory trance, he was relocated to a scene unknown. The landscape was no longer filled with furrows and labourers; it was littered with lifeless bodies stacked upon one another. The heavens were deserted as unnerving nightfall devoured the glistening stars that once illuminated the earth. The chill in the air brushed against unprotected skin. Small rivers of blood formed on the hardened soil. Footwear was smeared with red body fluid. The stench of blood was overpowering. The hundreds of departed martyrs had created a labyrinth for the living. With every nerve-racking movement, one was bound to step on or trip over a corpse.

Not far in the distance, voices rang out. Orders, threats, curses, insults, and advice were shouted into the ears. Explosions soon destroyed the ground and decorated the skies. The surrounding darkness was now embroidered with conflagration. The surface trembled with menacing force. Spirited bodies flew like figurines into the air. Death had conquered the soul even before the scorched bodies crashed onto the earth. Gunshots were fired relentlessly. Abandoned leaves were crumpled by panicked feet. The chest of a fallen tree was used as protection from the life-threatening musket balls. Deaths were confirmed by high-pitched screams. Endless firing and explosions resonated insanely in the ears.

Startlingly, a ball penetrated the dense body of the tree. It entered and exited within a fraction of a second. The sound of fatality triggered panic. The musket ball perhaps was destined for human flesh. Diminutive pieces of bark splintered onto faces. With a swipe of the hand, both timber and sweat were removed. Dismembered arms and legs littered the ground. Headless bodies evoked nausea. Quivering fingers indicated that life within the motionless bodies had not yet departed. Mayhem reigned. Unsafe and unharmed, there seemed to be no path to immunity. Death had to be accepted. Eyes were shut to embrace heaven or hell.

Then, a wondrous miracle occurred. Peace swept across the halcyon landscape. Outcries, explosions, and gunshots ceased. The land stopped trembling. Hearts began to settle. Fretfulness vanished from the faces of survivors. The suffering of others no longer assaulted the ears. At last, the eyes opened. The living roamed the earth in search of movement. Despite the winged insects swarming the cold bodies, the vast land remained still. With a sudden burst of energy, a single human dashed into the cemetery of martyrs. Leaping over corpses was necessary for progress. Placing the feet on a dead body was considered transgression. Still, the feet advanced without hesitation. No trail was etched to pursue. Smog in the air became an obstacle for the eyes. The palpitating heart felt ready to leap from the chest. Constant inhaling and exhaling tormented the lungs. Still, the feet advanced without hesitation.

Then, a high-pitched noise resonated across the landscape. With each step, the noise became louder. The feet hesitated. Cautionary steps were taken. The ears strained to identify the source. Close attention was paid to the cries of a creature. The excruciating wails increased in volume. The sounds of the whinnying beast indicated its species. Its suffering was hard to bear. Certainly, death loomed. But it decided to torment the animal first. The four-legged creature pleaded for someone to end its misery. It remained unseen. Therefore, the volume escalated. The helpless feet did not know whether to move forward or backward. The head spun. Tears formed in the eyes. The ears began to ache. A trickle of blood ran from the ear. Instinctively, the hand was placed on it. The hand was covered in blots of red. Blood cascaded like a waterfall. The eardrum had been punctured by the unbearable sound. There was no escape from the cries of the wounded horse.

The serpent had bitten the flesh of its enemy. Edward unleashed his whip upon the forearm of an inactive labourer, who seemed unaware of his surroundings. "What are you doing? I need you to move the horse. You were not hired to fantasize on this plantation," Edward shouted, swinging his whip viciously again. Shivaji eventually felt his skin burn as the leather grazed the inner portion of his thigh. The hissing sound of the leather, the stinging pain, and the raucous voice of the overseer helped the widower return to the present. He was unsure of how far his mind had wandered. The vision left him confounded. He did not know where to start. Was he to investigate the memory? Or interpret the significance behind the dolorous sequence?

"This is not the time, this is not the time," Shivaji repeated to himself.

Edward inspected the band of coolies who lagged behind in completing their furrows. He asked the man in charge, "Gurdayal, why are your coolies so far behind?"

The loyal peasant lowered his gaze in shame. "The land is rigid. The horse is not cooperating. Some of my team members are untrained," replied Gurdayal, intimidated both by the question and the man asking it.

"Those are excuses. This is unlike you and your coolies. Is this firebrand a hindrance? Is he the reason for the small quantity of furrows?" Edward demanded, wagging his finger at Shivaji.

Out of anger, the widower was struck again by Edward's whip. This time, Shivaji was lashed across the chest. His long-sleeved top was instantly torn, revealing the gash he had suffered. No matter how forceful the blow, Shivaji made sure not to show pain in his face or voice. He felt that if he expressed anguish, the battle would surely be claimed by the oppressor. Often, when he did not express pain, the oppressors increased the punishment. Gurdayal bit his lip. He resisted speaking his mind. Instead, he muttered, "Not to worry, sirdar. My team will recover. We need to regroup and execute."

As usual, Shivaji felt the urge to interfere. He wanted to tell Edward to move back to his section of the field. *"He has no business telling us where we stand or what we need to do. He should focus less on our team and more on his. Our lackluster results are not his problem. He is not the owner of this estate—Ernest is,"* Shivaji wanted to voice to the meddler.

The widower reminded himself not to react, not to act in any way that could put the other indentured labourers in danger. He was forbidden from being selfish under any circumstances. Swaggering near the line of coolies, Edward created a feared sound as his weapon dragged across the parched earth. The whip slithered like a venomous serpent, zigzagging across the land, eager to sink its fangs into human flesh. The coolies braced themselves for maltreatment.

While Edward marched back and forth, rousing suspense, Gurdayal felt the urgency to advise his labourers. He wanted to tell them to resume work on the unfinished second furrow. But before he could issue his order, Edward announced his ruthless scheme for Shivaji to execute:

"Now listen—the firebrand will have to move the animal. The plough needs to advance; the furrow must be completed. All this must be done as fast as possible," Edward explained to the Indians. *"In my hand lies the fatal weapon. One by one, it will strike the coolies until the firebrand completes this drill."*

The announcement left the Indians horrified. Gurdayal grew frustrated. He knew convincing Edward to revoke his order was impossible. Instead, the loyal peasant begged to assist his trainee in this critical task. Immediately, his request was denied. Both trainer and trainee knew that, no matter what transpired, one or two labourers were bound to endure pain. A miracle would be needed for none to be wounded. But this was not the time for miracles—it was time to be serious.

Shivaji understood the order. Like the other labourers, he did not want to participate in this duty. Edward required no approval; he demanded compliance. *"If you refuse, step forward. Those who advance will endure a ten-minute session of intense flogging,"* Edward told the indentured labourers. *"In ten minutes, I will administer fifty lashes. So what will it be? Trust the firebrand, or endure fifty lashes?"*

Gurdayal translated Edward's words with regret. No one in the line stepped forward. The horse was ten feet—or ten strides—away from finishing the drill. But the labourers did not know if Shivaji could maneuver the plough horse once more. They were willing to endure a few licks so long as the children remained untouched. Edward did not clarify whether children would be punished. Shivaji assumed the savage overseer had no empathy, so he believed Edward would not make an exception. The parents stationed their children behind them, standing wordless. No parent wanted their child introduced to flogging. They prayed to their Gods to shield their children. At that moment, Shivaji turned inward and prayed, *"Please, I beg of you, no child shall be punished if I fail to control this hapless creature."*

"Shall we begin?" Edward asked the firebrand.

Gurdayal translated for Edward. Shivaji felt the weight of the task pressing down on him. He did not want to be the cause of extreme punishment. But this world was not his; it belonged to the Stanfield brothers. Whatever they wanted was law. Having consulted his conscience, Shivaji decided to proceed.

As soon as Edward saw the firebrand move his scabbed feet, he cracked the whip, ready to let his arms go wild. All eyes were on Shivaji. Gurdayal and his team did not watch Edward or his weapon—they focused entirely on the saviour's movements. Shivaji placed two fingers between his parched lips and created a shrill sound. The horse, however, ignored him.

Edward struck the first coolie in line across the chest. The man plummeted to the earth, hands caked in dirt, pleading for mercy. The firebrand watched his teammate beg. The sight of an Indian folding his hands before an Englishman stirred resentment within him. Shivaji then made sounds with his tongue to coax the stallion forward. The unusual act succeeded in forming the drills but failed to prevent harm from Edward's whip. A whooshing strike followed by a vociferous cry echoed in Shivaji's ears.

This time, he did not dare to look at the line of coolies or the slayer hunting them one by one. The second victim was an Indian female, struck directly on her neck. She did not wince as she fell face-first. Blood gushed like water from a pipe. The force left her unmoving. The leather seemed more terrifying than before.

The other coolies, paralyzed by fear, did not help her. Their brains clouded by apprehension, no one offered water or assistance. They knew that intervening would provoke Edward's whip. So the sari-clad woman lay helpless, like a severed animal, until her blood drained.

At last, Shivaji felt compelled to act. What he did not want to do, he had to do. He slapped the horse on its behind, urging its legs to move. Still, there was no motion. His blood fuming, he slapped it again.

"Move... I need you to move. Please, move your legs. If you don't, others will be punished," he pleaded. *"I don't want to hurt you, but disobedience brings pain to others. Without your compliance, I cannot stop the punishment. I beg you... please listen. This is my last request."*

The horse, treated like a human with reason, remained placid. Encouraged, Shivaji tugged at the harness and pulled with all his strength. Blisters formed on his hands from the tight leather. Slowly, the horse moved. Even hesitant steps felt like relief.

Not far away, Edward forced the elderly peasant to the ground, lashes raining down upon him. The old man cried for assistance as his wife and bystanders powerlessly watched the immoral act. Pangs of remorse stirred in the hearts of the indentured labourers. Satisfied that his victim knelt, pleading for respite, Edward asked, *"So, whose next?"*

As Shivaji hauled the stallion to finish the drill, he wondered how many labourers had already been thrashed by the meddler. The count was at three, soon to be four. With the firebrand pushing and pulling the horse collar, there was nobody to man the mouldboard plough. The horse was not being steered properly, resulting in an uneven furrow. Shivaji assumed that if he had remained behind the plough, the animal would not have moved an inch.

He was convinced that combining his vigor with the horse was the fastest way to drag the plough to the end of the line. The faster he moved the animal and machine, the fewer coolies would be lashed. Gurdayal watched his trainee's inexhaustible exertion, a display meant solely for the coolies—Indians with whom Shivaji shared no bloodline, whose names he did not know, whose lives he had never learned about.

The trainer pondered Shivaji's reasoning. Why would he bear such hardship for strangers? Whatever the reason, his selfless actions compelled Gurdayal to assist him. The loyal peasant took a single step forward—a step heavy with thoughts of his wife and children in India. Helping Shivaji might jeopardize his hope of returning home, but for Gurdayal, selfishness was a sin—a sin he was willing to commit. At that moment, he accepted that his trainee's loyalty far surpassed his own. Shivaji's devotion to the people around him knew no bounds; it was pure, unlinked to greed or reward. In contrast, Gurdayal's loyalty to the Stanfield brothers was rooted in self-interest, a ticket to return to his beloved homeland.

Even as he remained idle, the Indian overseer prayed for the saviour and those he sought to save. Before Edward could strike the fourth victim—the wife of the aged man—her wails pierced the field. She begged the meddler to spare her. Her husband, desperate and powerless, grabbed Edward's legs.

"Sirdar, please don't beat my wife. Strike me instead. Do whatever you want to me, but spare her," the old peasant pleaded, feeling both useless and lost.

Edward was displeased by the interference. The elderly man nearly caused him to lose balance. To remove the obstacle, Edward performed a heinous act: he jammed the short handle of his whip into the old man's left eye. Agonized cries erupted across the sugarcane fields, so loud that even Ernest, in the northeast corner of the plantation, could hear them. The owner of the estate immediately mounted his stallion and darted northwest to witness the situation.

Meanwhile, Shivaji noticed a change in the plough horse's behavior. Its ears were pinned against its head, tail swished incessantly, and nostrils flared as it snorted and grunted. Most critical, its pace was slowing. The legs that had moved so powerfully minutes ago now faltered.

Gurdayal saw the shift in the animal's demeanor. At first, he flung his arms in the air to catch Shivaji's attention, but it proved futile. He then clapped his hands, hoping the firebrand would look his way—again, nothing. Finally, he chose to ignore Edward's presence, knowing the risk.

"Shivaji, watch out! The horse is entering its defensive state!"

The firebrand, absorbed in completing the line, did not hear the warning. Luckily, Edward did not either. Gurdayal forced himself to repeat the warning, his voice strained with urgency:

"Shivaji...listen. Be careful! The horse will rear. Shivaji...The horse will rear."

Shivaji finally caught the meaning. Though unfamiliar with the term *rearing*, he quickly removed his abraded hand from beneath the collar—just in time. Seconds later, the mammal stood on its hind legs. Its front legs rose violently, striking Shivaji in the back and throwing him onto the ground. Hooves crashed near him, the impact reverberating across the earth.

"Watch out, Shivaji!" Gurdayal yelled. *"It's trying to stomp on you!"*

The horse became uncontrollable. It neighed indignantly, lifting its forelegs up and down, while Shivaji rolled in the dirt to escape disaster. He knew well that if the stallion landed its full weight on his slender body, death would be inevitable. He also feared damage to the plough if the horse reared further.

The chaos drew every eye. Edward's victims, the irrational animal, Gurdayal's warnings, and Shivaji's desperate movements—all demanded attention. The indentured labourers could not treat the scene as trivial. It was impossible to tell who was controlling whom—the horse or the firebrand—and that left them mentally disoriented.

Edward began to chuckle as he watched Shivaji retreat from the scene.
"The firebrand has surrendered. The animal was too much for him to handle. So what will happen to you now?" he sneered at the female victim he had tormented for several minutes.

The wife of the old peasant could not respond. She did not understand English, and even if she had, the sobs choking her voice made any reply impossible.

"Why am I even asking you a question? You illiterate coolies don't even understand English," Edward spat, intentionally degrading the woman and the other Indians present. He brandished his mighty weapon, signaling the woman to prepare for another strike.

Shivaji did not dare glance back at the scene he had momentarily abandoned. He moved quickly toward Gurdayal, his trainer. As he approached, he saw Edward deliver a brutal blow that sent the woman crashing to the ground. Her husband, covered in streaks of blood, cried out for help—but no one dared intervene. Fear paralyzed the bystanders.

Shivaji's focus shifted to Gurdayal. He needed the whip. The Indian overseer hesitated, concealing his own weapon behind him. Shivaji's urgency was clear: Edward would strike again if the tool was not in his hands.

"I need the whip. Hand it over," Shivaji demanded.

"I will not. First, tell me what it will be used for," Gurdayal replied, slowly stepping backward.

"Please, hand it over. I don't have time to explain. I cannot watch Edward strike another labourer," Shivaji insisted, his voice weakening from the exhaustion of handling the stallion and witnessing the violence. He had decided to take a path of transgression—to act beyond the bounds of obedience to save lives.

"I will not let you lash him," Gurdayal said firmly.

Shivaji understood his trainer's concern: if he struck Edward, the entire team might be flogged without mercy. He calmed himself, clarifying, *"I will not lash him. I need to lash... the horse. Just a few taps to maneuver it."*

With no further delay, Shivaji snatched the whip from Gurdayal and raced toward the stubborn animal. Without the heavy plough strapped to its body, the horse might have fled the scene entirely. It reared on its hind legs, attempting to intimidate him—but Shivaji stood his ground. Seven feet separated man and animal, yet Shivaji met the stallion's gaze. An unusual certainty told him the horse understood what was about to happen.

He wrapped a few inches of the whip around his right hand for a firm grip and prayed for the horse to charge. A forward motion would mean progress for both the animal and the labourers. He cracked the whip in the dirt, calling out with every ounce of energy—but the horse refused to move. Its hooves dug into the soil, it neighed like a lion warning an intruder. Shivaji struck again and again. When the animal still refused, the firebrand had no choice but to land a measured blow.

Meanwhile, Edward eyed a small child hidden behind its father. The trembling father whispered prayers to his God. Edward sneered.

"If you want to get God's attention, I suggest you stop. Your God hasn't helped you before—why now?"

Through Gurdayal's translation, the message reached the father, but the sights and sounds of the whip, the wailing horse, and Shivaji directing the plough overpowered every other thought. With repeated strikes, the horse finally advanced. Shivaji had committed the transgression of hitting the animal, but he reasoned that the suffering of humans outweighed that of the horse. He knew he might later regret this act, yet at that moment, human life was paramount.

The horse completed the final stride of the drill. The line was imperfect, but it was finished. The remaining indentured labourers were spared from Edward's lash. The Indians could finally breathe. Edward, frustrated at only four victims, seethed silently. The labourers dared not show relief; any hint of satisfaction could provoke him anew.

Gurdayal assembled his team and informed them it was time for a fifteen-minute break. The coolies began moving toward the shaded areas under the massive pine trees—until Edward's voice cut across the field.

"Shut your mouth, Gurdayal. Your worthless team does not deserve a break. No one from your team will rest. Do I make myself clear?" he barked, spittle flying.

"Sirdar, it is noon. All the coolies start their breaks at this time," Gurdayal replied humbly, masking both defiance and fear.

"The other coolies have completed around five to seven drills. Your team has completed two. And, look at your lines. Both of your lines are not straight. No breaks for you and your team members until you complete five drills."

The firebrand had sprinted over to join his group, leaving the horse to recover from its exhaustion and injuries. He overheard some of the conversation between Gurdayal and the meddler and assumed that Edward had another hateful act planned, despite the challenge already overcome.

"Order your team to return to the fields immediately," Edward commanded the loyal peasant.

Returning to the fields to drudge under the sun was far better than enduring endless flogging sessions, thought Gurdayal. With that in mind, he prepared to dispatch his team back to the hoes, water pails, horse, plough, and uncultivated soil.

As Gurdayal was about to comply with Edward's intimidating instructions, the firebrand intervened with his viewpoint. He asked his trainer why the peasants had been stopped. While Gurdayal explained the situation in his native tongue, Edward grew visibly uncomfortable. He believed the Indians were mocking him behind his back.

"Stop talking that rubbish language. I know you both are talking ill. And I know you are talking about me," Edward accused, feeling betrayed by the people he sought to dominate.

He shoved Gurdayal aside and advanced toward the child he had previously targeted. The desperate father, sensing Edward's approach, grabbed his son's hand and tried to pull him close. But both Edward and the peasant struggled over the child like a fish on a hook.

In the end, Edward released the child momentarily to strike the father, who fell to the earth, before dragging the boy by his hair to an open area.

The screams of the child disturbed Shivaji. Unlike the other Indians, the firebrand could not remain silent. He did not want to stand idle while an innocent child suffered. He did not shed tears or shake his head in passive sorrow. He was prepared to revolt against injustice. Edward had crossed all limits by shoving the child onto the dirt. The force scraped the child's hands and chest, and Edward prepared to lash him with no pity.

Shivaji bumped his teammates aside, clearing a path to the sobbing child. *"Move out of the way! There is no point in your cowardice!"* he bellowed, reaching the boy. His legs were tucked to his chest, his face buried in his arms—a scene that etched itself into Shivaji's mind.

"Why is the child crying? At such a tender age... does he know leather will cut his skin?" Shivaji asked himself, as he listened to the whip cracking in the air. Edward was swinging indiscriminately, intimidating bystanders with every crack.

The moment Edward's whip descended toward the child, Shivaji acted without hesitation. He sacrificed his body to shield the boy. The whip struck Shivaji's left shoulder with full force. The pain provoked his resolve, and he muttered in anger, *"How can he strike a defenseless child?"*

The child was completely shielded, and Edward's fury erupted in verbal abuse and violent threats toward Shivaji. Yet the firebrand remained steadfast, comforting the child as if he were his own.

"Never again will I be blessed to hold a child so near my heart. That is why I must cherish this moment. His face resting on my chest, his small fingers clinging to my long-sleeved top, his feather-like hair brushing my chin... all inspire indescribable feelings. It inspires me to become a..." Shivaji whispered—interrupted by a fierce strike to his backside.

He suppressed his thoughts, refusing to complete the sentence. The pain did not stem from the whipping itself, but from the shattering of dreams once shared with Vyjanti. To escape the torment, Shivaji deserted the child, yet he felt no resentment toward Edward. He accepted the pain—from both the weapon and his own incurable thoughts.

As Edward prepared for another lash, a booming shot erupted into the sky, diverting his attention. The peasants and overseers were startled by the rare use of a firearm. Relief washed over them, for they knew the owner of the estate had arrived to intervene. Edward's mind raced with fear of his elder brother's disapproval.

Ernest leapt from his stallion, instructing Gurdayal to manage the stallion, the very same one Shivaji had struggled with. Calm and controlled, Ernest approached his brother, his face unreadable, neither frowning nor smiling. His gestures alone signaled Shivaji and the child to leave the scene.

Shivaji complied, prioritizing the child's safety. He reunited father and son, while his team stood vigilant, ready to observe the consequences Edward would face.

"Edward, why are you punishing the coolies? Today is critical. I don't want injuries. I don't want any peasants sent to the coolie line as a result of flogging. By day's end, I need at least fifteen drills completed with cane stems planted and covered in each one. You are interfering with Gurdayal and his peasants. How will they perform if you continue to lash them?"

Edward had a reply on the tip of his tongue for the owner of the estate, "Brother, I am not the hindrance. Your firebrand, Shivaji, is the hindrance. What he learns, he rejects. He does not comply with what is followed by other coolies on this plantation. It is because of him that Gurdayal and his team members are so far behind. Bloody hell, they have finished only two drills."

"And how many drills have your team of coolies finished?" A wily smirk formed on the face of the elder brother. The area fell silent. Edward did not have an answer.

"Well, well, well... Edward, your team is labouring in a different section. We both know your assistance is not required here. Gurdayal is the overseer of this band, not you. I suggest you move to a team that actually needs guidance," said Ernest.

Edward was flustered by his brother's harsh words.

"What overseer abandons his post and team members to inspect other areas and groups not under his supervision? You were nowhere near your section to see how your team performed. That is why you do not know how many furrows your team completed," continued Ernest, his lecture surpassing five minutes.

While the elder brother scolded, Edward intentionally ignored him. The words went in one ear and out the other. The plantation owner warned his brother not to intervene where he was not assigned, yet Shivaji and the other peasants could not comprehend the complicated language. However, the intense lip movement, finger-wagging, and stubborn tones hinted at a clash between the Englishmen.

As Edward returned to his forsaken band of coolies, Gurdayal was ordered to translate the plantation owner's words:

"Coolies, I apologize for what has happened. Edward will no longer meddle. But I am highly disappointed with your progress. I do not care for excuses—at least five drills were expected by this hour. Fifteen-minute breaks are not granted. Gurdayal, lead your team back into the sugarcane fields. I want fifteen drills completed before sundown."

After completing his first day in the sugarcane fields with twelve furrows accomplished, Shivaji was exhausted. Both fifteen-minute breaks had been revoked. Without a moment to breathe, the indentured labourers battled hunger, thirst, and physical pain.

As darkness descended, Ernest finally called it a day. Though twelve drills were completed, Gurdayal had expected fifteen. Yet, deep within, Ernest felt compassion for the labourers. He knew it was unfair to assign most of the newly recruited Indians to Gurdayal.

As the labourers left the fields, faces momentarily brightened with joy, though they knew the next day would extinguish it. They hated the sugarcane fields, calling them purgatory. Shivaji struggled to walk straight, dizzy and sore, with aching muscles and joints and stomach pangs from hunger.

He longed for his hut, water, food, and rest. Once there, the roommates cleaned and fed themselves. Gurdayal heated leftover khichdi, while Shivaji used a rag dipped in water to disinfect his wounds.

The hut reeked of sweat and dirt, though the men were accustomed to the stench. To an Englishman, however, the smell would cause gagging. Despite their efforts to bathe, lingering odor persisted. Shivaji felt his clothes cling to his body, longing for a proper bath but lacking the energy to fetch water.

After disinfecting wounds and heating food, they sat against the hut walls, legs stretched, savoring a rare moment of comfort.

"It has been only a day, and I feel like I've laboured for a week," said Shivaji.
"I felt the same at first. With time, you'll become accustomed. There is no day in the fields where labour subsides. We endure the sun, strict overseers, extreme punishments, and backbreaking work. Turn your flesh into armour capable of withstanding it all," replied Gurdayal.

Shivaji nodded, mouth full of khichdi.

Gurdayal continued, "Your actions today have earned respect from the coolies. Everyone praised your handling of the stallion and how you saved the child. Many were surprised at your courage."

Shivaji, frowning, replied, "I am surprised none of our team intervened. I don't care for praise, especially from cowards. How could they stand idle while an innocent child was being lashed? What if it had been their son?"

Gurdayal bit his lip, reminded of his own selfishness.

"We need unity and audacity to challenge oppressors. If we all rise against Edward, show him the fire in our hearts, and prove despair cannot constrain us, perhaps he would reconsider exposing us to harm," Shivaji said.

But Gurdayal remained pragmatic:

"Not everyone is an insurgent. Not everyone shares your views. The English carry the weapons: whips, batons, pistols. It is dangerous to act without caution."

Shivaji snickered.

"Then we take their weapons, or we use the tools they place in our hands. A hoe can crush a skull if used for self-defense. Have you never considered that?"

"That is nonsense. Do you not think of the consequences? There is no escaping this brutal plantation of traps and hounds. We are destined to remain slaves under British control," said Gurdayal.

Shivaji acknowledged the point, muttering, "No one can swim back to India," accepting the reality of his situation.

Once the khichdi was digested, the roommates covered themselves with ragged blankets. Gurdayal considered how to reveal the horrors of the plantation.

"Shivaji, you are a beginner. You do not know the misfortunes of this plantation. What I have seen and heard, you have not. Edward has done things my eyes and ears could not bear," Gurdayal began.

Shivaji interrupted, "We are cramped in our huts, living on rice and lentils, labouring with drowsy eyes, obeying all orders regardless of ethics, humiliated, threatened, beaten. What else have you seen that I haven't?"

Reluctant at first, Gurdayal finally confessed:

"Edward is devil incarnate. Whenever he leaves, he hands power to his brother. Under Edward, labourers fear for their lives. They pray for Ernest's return because dominance drives Edward insane."

Shivaji, bewildered, asked:

"How does Edward become a maniac?"

"There were incidents where Edward misled young women to desolate parts of the sugarcane fields. The women thought they were performing duties, but they were selected victims. Some were under thirteen, some were married. It did not matter to Edward. He has no conscience," Gurdayal explained.

Shivaji paused, unable to finish his question, horrified by the revelation.

"In between the innumerable rows of sugarcane, desperate voices were released. Some cried for their husbands. Some cried for their fathers and mothers. Others cried to God to save them from forced sexual assault. However, no one was there to listen or respond. Eventually, the desperate voices faded. The unfortunate women were defeated. In most cases, fathers, husbands, and brothers had been so absorbed in hacking or planting sugarcane that the disappearance of their loved ones went unnoticed."

As he listened to Gurdayal, the firebrand recalled the events that occurred on the Ship Elbe. Shivaji had drifted onto the scene where British seafarers abducted Vyjanti while he was unconscious. It seemed impossible to suppress the poignant incident, but he had to redirect his attention to his roommate.

"Edward was devious. Most women were effortlessly convinced to accompany him to different areas in the fields. These women, deceived, knew that refusal would bring severe punishment. They could not withstand the dread of flagellation. No woman wanted her bare back scourged. It is a woman's fate that is tested when she follows Edward to a private area where no one else can see her. Shivaji, I once saw the devil lead a girl, probably your age, into a secluded part of the fields. Soon after, I heard loud shrieks—sounds of struggle that still reverberate in my ears. I know I should have reacted, but the faces of my wife and children kept appearing in my mind. It was one of the hardest decisions I have ever made, a decision I am not proud of," said Gurdayal, remorse bleeding from his veins.

"I fled the scene, letting Edward devour the adolescent woman. I am certain that had I intervened, Edward would have lynched or lashed me to death."

Shivaji did not hesitate to condemn his roommate.

"I know you want to return to India. I am sure every labourer on this plantation wants to return home. Does that mean everyone should be selfish? Does everyone only think of themselves? If so, we Indians will never rise against injustice. We will remain enslaved forever."

"Shivaji, do you not yearn to return to your friends and family? Your heart must long to see your loved ones," asked Gurdayal.

"No! All those faces are from the past," replied Shivaji crudely.

"So, is your past no longer important to you?"

"The past is the past; no matter how pleasant or unpleasant, one must detach from it."

Gurdayal sensed that the firebrand was upset. Shivaji's anger was not directed at him, but at himself. To detach from his village, his house, his mother, father, sisters, friends, market stall, fishing, marriage, and wife was nearly impossible.

"I believe that to escape from the past and the memories it holds, death is necessary," Shivaji said in a hushed tone.

Sleep was on the verge of overpowering Gurdayal, so he believed the moment had arrived for Shivaji to understand his predetermined fate.

"The Stanfield brothers will not let you perish. Your presence is mandatory," said Gurdayal.

"Why is that?" Shivaji instantly replied.

"Sirdar purchased you to be an overseer on his plantation. He wants you to supervise the indentured labourers in the sugarcane fields. You are to step into my shoes, which is why I was ordered to prepare you for this role."

Shivaji became silent for a moment, unsure how to respond. The first realization that struck him burst into his mind:

"I understand. You are preparing me to be a slave driver so that you can leave this plantation as a free man."

Gurdayal did not lie to ease the situation. What Shivaji said was partially true. In a way, the trainer was using his trainee to secure his own freedom, placing his desire above everyone, including Shivaji. Whenever Gurdayal felt like a conniver or betrayer, his heart sank.

When he finally revealed the hidden information, Gurdayal felt his heart descend once more. Silence fell over the room. Shivaji lacked the energy to grieve his destined position, so he closed his eyes, resigned.

THE 51ST DAY

The first rays of sunlight peeped from the whistling skies onto the gruelling landscape where the indentured labourers mourned. Shivaji had risen from his sleep. Every inch of his body ached with discomfort. The past several days had been excruciating for all the coolies on the plantation. Along with steering the horse and plough to develop furrows, Shivaji had to dice the clods, generate drainage channels in case it showered, obtain cane from the large piles constructed on site, properly slice the cane, place the stems side by side inside the furrows, and cover the stems with three inches of soil. While most of the labourers were assigned to hoeing the soil and planting the stems in the drills, Shivaji was tasked with assisting in all duties. Since the firebrand was to replace Gurdayal as an overseer, it was required for him to learn all the assigned responsibilities in explicit detail. When his teammates were resting their tiresome limbs in a shaded area for fifteen minutes, Shivaji was still on the field receiving an earful from his trainer. Immense pressure weighed upon his burdensome shoulders. What worsened his situation was the lurking Edward. Not a day had passed with the meddler not meddling. Instead of two, four eyes were inspecting the firebrand. Shivaji was aware that his overseer was keeping an eye on him to see if he was performing his duties adequately. On top of that, he also noticed Edward inspecting him from a distance. If Shivaji faltered, the meddler was quick to raise his voice. Even before Gurdayal had the chance to explain where his trainee was at fault, Edward dashed towards them with a whip in his hand. The exhaustion from the fiery sun and intense labour clouded the brain and body, preventing it from performing duties in a timely and proper manner. Strikes were administered when Edward felt that the firebrand was behind in the number of drills completed and stems planted. His accidental mistakes, such as not placing the stems horizontally inside the furrows or not appropriately removing the flags from the cane, led to multiple lashes. At times, Edward would ride in on a horse and fling his whip, not caring where on the body it landed, as long as it landed on the firebrand. Various parts of his body felt his flesh tear. Nonetheless, most of the lacerations marred his back. That is the kind of person Edward was. By assaulting his victims from behind, he proved himself a man without dignity.

With the many laborious duties and wrongful penalties lived Shivaji Nair. Slaving on the plantation, he endured the fire that had been set upon him to cremate his body, bore the massive stone that had been placed upon his chest, and withstood the scarcity of air that made it difficult for him to breathe. When it was approved for the peasants to vacate the fields, Shivaji staggered to his hut, bringing with him his open cuts, profound scratches, vexatious rashes, hurting limbs, drowsy eyes, empty stomach, parched throat, and stained clothes, all of which needed to be attended to. Since the despicable information was voiced into his ears by his roommate, the firebrand chose to maintain only a professional relationship with Gurdayal. A personal relationship held no importance to Shivaji. Once both trainer and trainee had entered the hut, very little was asked and answered. But that did not stop Shivaji and his roommate from fulfilling their household duties. Water was still fetched from the well by Shivaji, while heating and cooking was still performed by Gurdayal. Nothing regarding the assigned role of a slave driver was discussed between the roommates. Since the initial conversation, not once did Shivaji accuse his trainer of deception. Words such as "traitor" or "hypocrite" were not voiced by him. Oddly, the firebrand kept his temper in check. He did not blast his roommate with accusations and disdain. Shivaji had accepted his fate. He welcomed the position of an overseer as long as he was not ordered to inflict pain upon any of his fellow labourers. Shivaji understood that lashing peasants was a necessary component of the role he was to undertake. What circled in his brain was the idea of self-sacrifice. He presumed that if he did not abide by the command to dispense pain upon another, then surely, the pain would be delivered upon his own flesh.

"So if Edward orders me to lash the body of a peasant, I must refuse. Challenging his authority will bruise his ego and incite an outrage. Only then will the whip be released upon my flesh," Shivaji said under his breath. "I would rather coax the tyrant into ripping the flesh off my body with his lashes. No overseer, no plantation owner, and no God will compel me to release a weapon in the direction of an Indian labourer. I will not engage in sin, but I will let sin be committed upon me."

It was unknown to Shivaji and the other peasants what exact course of action Edward would pursue. It was not as if the firebrand overlooked the fact that his refusal to lash the peasants might force Edward to lash not only him but also the peasant who was to be lashed. There was also the possibility that the abuse could be delivered upon the entire team of labourers. But these were risks that the firebrand was willing to take. He did not want to be a saviour. Nor did he want to play God. Shivaji wanted to lead by example. He believed it was necessary for Indians on the plantation to take a step forward in understanding the nature of altruism. To the indentured labourers, Shivaji desired to propose a simple question: if a person who was not a family member or friend sacrificed his body to rescue labourers from punishment, then why could the labourers not do the same for him or others on the plantation? His theory was that if the peasants took notice of, or simply observed, how Shivaji chose to suffer the punishment that was initially meant for them, then perhaps the decision to challenge and overthrow the Stanfield brothers would come forth. Aware that he was not able to single-handedly renounce the inequitable system, the firebrand was in desperate need to form a brigade of rebels. Time had come for alterations and amendments to be made. After all, a colonel without his battalion, a captain without his seafarers, and a leader without his supporters is a man with no authority.

A week had elapsed, and Shivaji felt as if he'd been living on the plantation for years. The amount of work done in a week as a peasant was far more than the years of work Shivaji had done as a fisherman in India. Most weeks, indentured labourers were given the privilege to rest their weary bodies and distressed souls on a Sunday. On that day, Indians had the liberty to do whatever they pleased as long as it was done within the premises. No labourer was to leave the coolie line located on the Eastern section unless ordered to do so by one of the Stanfield brothers. Within the small area allotted to them, the labourers rested their eyes, relaxed their bodies, recovered from their wounds, washed and dried their clothes, gathered exotic fruits from the trees, visited their companions, and spiritually communicated with God. Sundays were a blessing for the peasants.

On the Western section, Ernest and his brothers roused in the morning to be present at the religious function held five miles away from their plantation. Every Sunday, the British men, women, and children came together at a selected area within the district where the Bible was read, the pastor discoursed, conversations ensued, food was devoured, and God was found. After attending the church-like function, sometimes, the Stanfield brothers would return to the estate to prepare for the feast and dance to be held in the evening for the English invitees. Most of the invitees were English women. The invites were voiced by Edward and Edwin at the gathering without the consent of the estate owner. Ernest was never pleased with his brothers for inviting English men and women for parties and celebrations. He was not the kind of person fond of company. For that reason, he remained solitary in his cottage, infatuated with prosperity, while his brothers feasted on both the savory food and summoned women.

To prepare for the social gathering, hands from the coolie line were needed. Edward would then ride his stallion into the Eastern section to fetch Indians who were able to perform specific duties for the scheduled function. Not that he cared for or sympathized with the labourers, Edward remained fair by not choosing the same peasant every Sunday to help with collecting wood and preparing food. Men were selected to disappear into the forest area to compile firewood, while the women were selected as help in the kitchen and to serve at the function. These unfortunate men and women were commanded to travel to the Western section by foot. So, while the oppressor rode on the horse, the oppressed paced near the animal, struggling not to fall behind.

The day that promised relaxation had unexpectedly been snatched from the labourers who had been selected. They couldn't protest. A protest from the Indians to not labour for the evening function would have led to nothing less than twenty lashes. On the present Sunday, Edward was aware of who he wanted to select. As soon as he arrived at the coolie line, he called for the loyal peasant. Not a bit surprised by the oppressor's presence, Gurdayal began assembling the indentured labourers.

"Sirdar is here, I repeat, sirdar is here. Stop whatever you are doing. I want everyone to gather near him," said the translator in Hindi for the coolies to understand.

Shivaji, who had been busy washing his clothes by the well, was the last person to report to the assemblage. He purposely sauntered in a carefree manner, wanting to show that the presence of the tyrant was of little importance to him. His act was noticed by Edward, whose face instantly flushed with anger. The newly recruited labourers were not familiar with the proceedings. What Shivaji and others believed to be a formal announcement was, in reality for the unfortunate, the termination of the one day a week when the Indians had the pleasure of doing as they pleased. Shivaji placed his eyes on Karthik, whom he had not properly seen or spoken to for days. The child was held in the arms of his father and pressed against his chest. He turned his eyes aimlessly, probing for a familiar face. It seemed to Shivaji that Karthik was in search of the children he had recently befriended on the plantation. But when the wide-eyed child saw his mama, he leapt from his father's arms.

"Appa, I want to meet mama. He's over there—please take me to him," said Karthik as he lurched forward. Hands were waved, smiles were shared, and steps were taken for the childhood friends to unite. The feeling of euphoria was soon shattered by an order from Edward. "I choose the firebrand. Gurdayal, tell him that he must assist with the gathering of firewood. I will guide him and a few other coolies to the Southern section of the plantation. Once the bags are filled with timber, the coolies must then head to the cottages." Edward had selected a total of eight peasants. Three men, including the firebrand, were to follow him to the forest; the five women were to be led by Gurdayal to the Western section to prepare meals and scrub the floors.

When Lachmaiya was told by the translator that she had been chosen by the Englishman, her husband protested. He did not understand the need for his wife to be separated from him. The loyal peasant tried to explain the duties required of Lachmaiya, but Venkatesh did not want to hear any of it. "I will not permit her to leave. If you want her to attend to the Western section, then I will have to go as well."

With the ears of a predator, Edward overheard Venkatesh arguing with the loyal peasant. The husband was concerned for the safety of his wife. He did not know what evil awaited her at the Englishman's cottage.

"What is the matter, Gurdayal?" asked Edward.
"All is under control. I am speaking with the husband of the woman you have chosen."
"Why does it seem as if the bastard is not pleased with the selection of his wife?" Edward asked as he removed the leather whip from his waist.

Gurdayal assured the concerned husband that his wife would not be harmed. "She will be there to cook and clean. That is it; nothing more will be required from her. I advise you to drop this matter before trouble arrives for you and your family."

Meanwhile, Shivaji had assessed the situation. He did not expect his childhood friend to escalate the matter, but if he did, Shivaji was prepared to pounce. The teary-eyed wife of Venkatesh watched the tyrant close in on the scene. The weapon in Edward's hand was visible. She pleaded with her husband to stop arguing. Deep within, Lachmaiya felt anxious. She did not know what to expect. Was she to return or not? Was she to perform her duties in the kitchen and patio or be forced into the bedroom? After witnessing the Vyjanti incident, her heart palpitated whenever an Englishman set his eyes on her. But to save her husband from a severe thrashing, she suppressed the nervousness apparent on her face, in her voice, and in her body language. "I will have to go. I promise that I will be back soon. Take care of Karthik."

Venkatesh replied, his voice becoming emotional, "I cannot let you leave with these animals. You must understand, Lachmaiya."
"Trust me, I will be fine. By my side I have four other women who are heading to the

Western section. I am certain that we sisters will protect one another. Please, don't worry," said Lachmaiya in a serene manner. The ongoing tension was eased by the calmness of her voice. Venkatesh stepped back. The father did not want his son to witness how flesh is shredded by the whip. Nor did he want his son to be the victim of that fierce weapon. The possibility of Karthik and Lachmaiya suffering lashes never left his mind. In truth, Edward was merciless. He was not a man easy to fathom. A man who had the nerve to raise his whip upon an innocent child was capable of committing all kinds of sin, minor and major. It was for this reason that Venkatesh brooded for his wife. There was no way for him to stop Lachmaiya from leaving his side. He had to leave her in the hands of God. So when his wife departed from the coolie line, guided by the loyal peasant, Venkatesh extended his hands to the Lord and prayed.

Edward galloped into the Southern section of the plantation with the chosen peasants struggling to keep pace with the horse. When he looked back to see his selected coolies lagging behind, Edward finally instructed the stallion to stop. Once the coolies had caught up, Edward insulted and cursed them for their failure to run beside the animal. Shivaji had many words to utter to the oppressor, but he wisely chose not to squabble, for his protest might have led to violent punishment not only for him but for the other two Indians as well. En route to the forest, the coolies were forced to run between prickly bushes, leap across narrow streams, and avoid falling over stones and vines. While the other two coolies had sandals to protect them from the boiling earth, sharp rocks, and penetrating thorns, Shivaji had to bear the torture that Mother Earth and her allies laid upon him. With one of his sandals damaged from the plough-horse incident, Shivaji was compelled to discard the intact sandal as well. Whenever a thorn pierced his skin, the firebrand did not halt despite the sharp pain. Shivaji pressed on, not wanting to hear the abusive language and derogatory insults. Further offensive remarks might have provoked a violent response from the firebrand—one he certainly needed to avoid.

When Edward and his selected hands arrived at the destination—a stand of large evergreen trees numbering in the thousands—the freshness of the air invaded their nostrils. Shivaji breathed in the scent. He had never encountered such a fragrance in his life before. Before he was carried towards the everlasting scent of jasmine and its memory of Vyjanti, the tyrant handed him an oversized bag that held a wooden axe. The same items were provided to the other labourers on scene. Without orders or instructions, Edward set his coolies loose to wander into the forest. He demanded that wood be collected and hauled to the Western section for the organized bash.

Shivaji, not knowing where to begin, followed the Indian men whom he had not spoken to since leaving the coolie line. To him it seemed as if the men had been selected for this task before. Not the slightest indication of tension showed on their faces or in their body language. Immediately, the firebrand could tell that both men had known one another for a while. As the man with the domineering voice spoke with his companion, whom he addressed as Hunga, it did not take long for Shivaji to discover that the Indian with the bedraggled hair was mute. His replies to questions were made with hand signs, facial reactions, and head movements. To familiarise himself, Shivaji broke his silence.

"Instead of chopping wood into pieces, we should have chopped Edward into pieces." The unexpected humour left them astonished. The men turned to face Shivaji and looked directly into the firebrand's eyes. Then there were smiles—unprepared, sudden. In that moment, for the first time, Shivaji felt a connection with his workmates. All it took was a frivolous quip. The vocal man then shared his name with Shivaji. Bagiya explained in Tamil that it isn't wise to chop a standing tree. "Hunga and I have been sent into the forest on multiple occasions. We felled smaller trees to the ground. Once we locate a smaller tree that has fallen, we begin to hack at its trunk. The hacking produces chunks of wood that we must store in our bags. If we return with a bag not filled to the top, sirdar will be delighted to lash us in front of his guests."

During the search for a fallen tree, the men remained silent, not wanting to alarm any of the sleeping carnivores within the forest. It was expected that several man-eating beasts roamed the unforeseen wilderness.

"I would rather have a wild animal ingest my body than be subjected to bondage on this plantation for the next five years," said Shivaji.

This time, Hunga and Bagiya did not look amused. There was no reply to Shivaji's humour.

After every fifth step, Shivaji was met with a stout trunk. Dakua trees were covered with green leaves that shimmered whenever sunlight touched them. The firebrand tilted his chin toward the heavens. He examined the dense branches of the dakua tree, which sought to mask the undisturbed skies. What he perceived was an ongoing war between darkness and brightness. The sunlight felt challenged. It eventually created holes in the mask to distribute illumination upon the land. While the plants and animals dwelled in the light, the indentured labourers cherished the shaded areas where the rays of the sun were deferred.

Instead of a heat wave slapping his face, Shivaji felt a delicate breeze caress his skin. He no longer needed to remove perspiration from his forehead. His throat did not parch, his eyes did not burn, and his limbs did not tire. Shivaji realized that moments of aloneness spent in the forest were perhaps the only kind of freedom he would attain during his five-year lockdown. During these moments, Shivaji felt as if he were in India. He reflected on how he used to walk freely along the coastline, through the town and market areas, near the outskirts of the village, and along the trails and roads that led to his dwelling. When stumbling upon a stone or vine, Shivaji would snap back to reality.

"God, is it possible to live solo in this forest with my personal beliefs and memories?" asked Shivaji. To not be near the coolie line or sugarcane fields was indeed pleasurable for him. To not rise at the rooster's crow, to not dress in orderly fashion, to not listen to the sounds of the whip, to not hear the cries of an Indian, to not witness the scourging of flesh, to not comfort the body of a victim, to not toil in the fields, to not follow the directions of an overseer, and to not obey the commands of an Englishman—these were the privileges Shivaji and his workmates longed for daily. But the labourers knew that those desires could not be fulfilled regularly.

Carelessly, the men roamed deeper into the woodlands in search of a fallen dakua tree. With each step, the forest darkened more. The shaded areas that once allowed multiple rays of light to peep between the tree limbs had suddenly become ghoulish.

"Finally!" said Bagiya with excitement. "Look over there... It's a fallen tree."

Hunga immediately removed the sharp axe from his shoulder and prepared to slice wood until his arms surrendered from exhaustion. As for Shivaji, he was disheartened that a dakua tree, severed from below the waist, had finally been found. In fact, the firebrand was so content with the small but meaningful taste of liberty that he did not want himself or the others to come across a butchered tree. But he had forgotten that the impatient Edward was keen to inflict lashes upon the labourers who did not arrive on time with the required collection.

Then, insignificant sounds emerged. Shivaji glanced toward the earth, presuming one of his workmates had stepped on the withered leaves falling from the dakua trees. But neither had moved an inch. Once again, Shivaji's ears captured the subtle sound. His eyes immediately scanned the nearby area. Other than plants, trees, shrubs, and bushes, there was no human or animal movement perceived.

"I can hear them," said Shivaji, startling his workmates. "I sense that there are creatures among us. I don't know whether they are humans or animals."

"Either I am deaf or it's your imagination playing tricks. Anyways, what is it that you are hearing?" asked Bagiya as he investigated the proximate shrubbery.

"It is as if a tribe of humans or animals is loitering here. The crackling of the decayed leaves indicates that we are not alone. This may seem odd, but I can sense their eyes upon us."

Hunga nervously stepped backward. The axe he grasped tightly now dangled near his right leg. He kept his eyes fixed on Shivaji and Bagiya. Whatever his workmates decided, he was ready to follow. If they fled, he would flee; if they stayed, he would stay. Since childhood, Hunga had been a man heavily dependent on others for instructions, judgment, and guidance. It was not in his character to act first in crucial situations.

"Hunga, we'll chop and gather the wood as fast as possible. Once the bags are full, we shall depart. We don't need to be afraid. Your hideous appearance will chase them away," said Bagiya jokingly.

Shivaji tried, but he could not hold back the laughter that leapt from his belly. Without entirely disregarding the unknown and unseen, the men hustled to the fallen dakua and commenced axing its trunk. Repeatedly, they hacked the body of the tree, which was at least three meters in diameter. Instead of taking turns, the labourers chose to utilize their axes simultaneously. Soon, they developed a rhythm, which helped avoid mishaps between tools.

As they severed the dakua tree, none wanted their axe damaged or to damage another's. That is why the chemistry among them was crucial. Once a large portion of the tree was severed, the labourers reduced the wood to the width and length of a human forearm. Previously strangers, these men now laboured as a team. They did not labour only for themselves but for each other. Shivaji did not consider his bag the only one to be filled. The men assisted each other, filling all three bags with wood.

While Hunga cringed at the thought of death, Bagiya was the complete opposite. To him, death was a mere fragment of life. He who had no parents, who was not loved by a wife, and who was not respected by siblings, did not have much to live for. Death was not feared by the lonesome peasant. He shrugged off the troublesome situation. Meanwhile, Shivaji lowered the axe with immense force, driving it deep into the timber. With every hit, mottled bark propelled into the air. Perspiration could not be contained. Even with the coolness in the air, salty fluid appeared on the men's faces.

As they neared completion of their duty, Shivaji's senses became alert to obscure sounds. But this time, it was not footsteps—he heard whispering voices, in a language he did not recognize. Soon, Bagiya and Hunga could hear the intimate murmuring. Hunga held his breath. His eyes shifted frantically as he tried to discover the source. While the mute labourer fretted, Bagiya remained composed. Never before had the seasoned labourers encountered human voices in the forest.

The voices grew louder. Once Shivaji detected that the situation was escalating, he called out: "Whoever or whatever you are, please show your faces. We don't wish to harm you, nor to be harmed. Come forth and identify yourselves. I repeat, please show your faces," he said authoritatively.

Again and again, the firebrand proved himself a ringleader, prepared to rise when needed. From behind the trees and bushes emerged human forms and faces previously unseen by the labourers. Shivaji and his fellow labourers could not tell the race or religion of the tribe. Comprising six fearless and fearsome males, the tribe advanced.

The tribal warriors had such distinctive presence and appearance that anyone on earth would reconsider interaction. Along with their distinctive appearance, these humans, whom the Indians doubted were human at first, were frightening. Their bulging limbs, chiseled torsos, heavy shoulders, massive chests, flat stomachs, and staunch hands revealed their power. In comparison, Shivaji and the peasants seemed small. The tribal warriors were twice as large in width and height compared to the labourers.

Most warriors wore minimal clothing. Other than banana leaves covering their private areas, the rest of the body was exposed. The tribal chief, whose identity was immediately apparent, displayed fearlessness, standing like a brick wall in front of his men. He was the first to interact, the first to reply, and the first to come face to face with the enemy. He was the first to strike and the first to receive a blow. The tribal chief had the body of a rhino, the strength of a bull, the speed of a horse, and the courage of a lion.

Unlike his tribe, the chief's weaponry and attire were exceptional. Instead of banana leaves, he wore a grass skirt extending from waist to ankles. While the other warriors carried striking and crushing clubs, the chief held a bladed club, axe-like, capable of separating flesh from bone. Clubs were crafted from the butts of uprooted trees, suited to each warrior's build, status, and preference.

Additionally, from the six warriors, one had a richly carved spear thirteen feet long. Another carried a bow with an arrow aimed directly at Shivaji's heart. With such weapons, the tribal warriors advanced. Soon, Shivaji distinguished their skin color—it resembled the tone he had painted on his own flesh. These men were not entirely black or white but somewhere in between.

Hunga believed that if he remained idle for five more seconds, the tribal warriors would surely butcher him. He began to retreat. Bagiya noticed the movement beside him. "Hunga, do not move. Plant your feet firmly into the soil."

Gently, with his left hand, Shivaji signalled for silence. "These people are neither English nor Indian."

"Then who or what are they?" asked Bagiya, concern etched on his face.

At last, the tribe halted. The warriors and peasants stood seven feet apart.

Not an inch of Shivaji's body wanted to flee the scene. Once he saw the clubs, spears, bows, and arrows, the idea of turning his back on the tribal warriors seemed reckless. If he were to turn, it was likely a spear or arrow would be launched. The confidence with which the warriors clutched their handmade tools suggested that no weapon would miss its mark. Should one pierce flesh, Shivaji's life would be in extreme danger.

Not wanting the tribe to detect any sign of trepidation, Shivaji put on a brave façade. He locked eyes with the tribal chief, unaware of the consequences this boldness might bring. The peasant and the warrior studied one another. While Shivaji had to lift his eyes to assess the towering man, the tribal chief let his eyes descend to inspect what seemed a puny, fragile human.

The tribe's men did not resemble Indians. Their hair, eyes, noses, and lips were unlike those of most Indians. Their eyes were fiery red and barely open, indicating that they had not slept for days. Their noses and lips were dense, flat, and far larger than any Englishman or Indian man Shivaji had ever encountered. Instead of the fine, straight hair common among the English and Indians, the tribal warriors had wavy, curly hair intertwined into a massive fro. A mere glance at their hairstyles convinced Shivaji they were indeed barbaric. He knew pre-judging was inappropriate, but he could not suppress his assumptions.

Shivaji believed the armed tribe was preparing to attack him and his workmates. The tribal chief bellowed words in an obscure language to his warriors. Slowly, he moved forward, drilling his bare feet into the soil and leaving deep footprints. Immediately, Hunga's arm was clutched by Bagiya.

"Whatever happens, do not flee. We have a better chance if we remain together. Do you understand?" Bagiya asked the voiceless peasant.

Hunga nodded. His feet wavered from apprehension, yet he did not step forward or backward as the chief advanced. At the same time, Shivaji noticed a lavaliere dangling from the chief's massive neck. The necklace bore a curved whale tooth pendant, shaped in a circle. None of the other warriors wore such a pendant. The rest of the tribe's necklaces were made from shells, corals, feathers, threads, and strings. Shivaji suspected the whale tooth marked the chief as a valued member.

While he observed, Bagiya lifted his axe onto his shoulder, signaling readiness.

"Place the axe on the ground. We don't want him to think we are ready to fight. Let us show them we are peace-makers, not trouble-makers," Shivaji said.

Bagiya did not comply. His fear-clouded judgment forced erratic decisions. As Shivaji watched the chief close in, he diverted his eyes from the tribal leader to the reckless labourer.

"Bagiya, the tool must not appear as a weapon. Drop the axe. If you don't, we will be slaughtered. Listen to me," Shivaji urged calmly.

"Life isn't guaranteed by discarding our weapon. I believe we must defend ourselves. Before they attack, we should strike first," Bagiya replied.

Shivaji felt the urge to shout but restrained himself. Calmly, he said, "As long as they don't feel threatened, we will not be harmed."

Before he could elaborate, Hunga used facial expressions and hand signals to tell Bagiya to drop the axe. He slapped Bagiya's arm lightly. Realizing he was outnumbered, Bagiya felt defeated. Both Shivaji and Hunga frowned at his impulsiveness. Finally, Bagiya let go of the axe and watched it fall heavily to the earth.

"I hope you know we won't live to see another day," Bagiya muttered, regretting relinquishing the weapon.

Shivaji expected a spear or arrow to pierce his flesh, but none came. As the chief approached, Shivaji's sensitive nose detected a pungent odour—familiar from the decks of the Ship Elbe, where indentured labourers had been confined without bathing for days.

Shivaji's gaze swept the ground. He was directly beneath the chief, whose towering frame made eye contact impossible. At five feet seven inches, Shivaji could only look up to the chief's lower chest. Then he realized the odour emanated from the chief.

The behemoth circled the peasants like a predator selecting its prey, closing in on the smallest, Hunga. The mute peasant shut his eyes. Although his feet were planted, his mind urged flight. Shivaji and Bagiya glanced at him, silently praying he would not flee.

Despite the chief's proximity, Hunga was unharmed. The behemoth sniffed him, assessing whether he posed a threat. Losing interest, the chief advanced toward Bagiya, who struggled with his conscience to refrain from grabbing the axe. Shivaji repeated silently: "Be calm, be calm, be calm," careful not to speak aloud. To his relief, Bagiya removed his gaze from the axe. The chief sniffed Bagiya, then returned to his original position, standing directly opposite Shivaji.

Standing just a foot away, Shivaji noticed the chief's exposed body smothered in grime. "He must have rolled in mud with pigs. How else can someone be this dirty?" Shivaji wondered. It confused him that, even facing possible death, his mind wandered to irrelevant thoughts.

After a tense silence, the chief bellowed for his warriors: "Kanediya... Kanediya!"

Shivaji and his workmates did not understand the word. Was it one word or more? A sound or a command? As the chief repeated it, the tribe joined in. Were they extending hands in friendship or warning the peasants of danger? Shivaji's heart pounded as "Kanediya" echoed.

The chief retreated slowly, keeping the Indians in view. He vanished behind the trees silently, leaving no sound on the fallen leaves or twigs. The tribe relocated with stealth, and soon their voices faded into the distance. Shivaji and his workmates did not move until the last shadow disappeared into the dakua tree. Only then did they relax—minds composed, hearts steadied, bodies loosened.

Exhausted, the labourers raced against the descending sun. Determined to reach the Western section before darkness fell, they hauled the heavy bags of firewood. Unable to lift them fully, they dragged the bags along the ground. With forty minutes before sunset, Shivaji was not concerned about the dimness.

"Ernest must be waiting for the firewood. The encounter delayed us. I bet the short-tempered Englishman is already fuming," Bagiya said, letting his bag fall. Shivaji and Hunga permitted a brief rest for weary shoulders, arms, and legs.

"Honestly, my arms will fall off with all this hauling. Let's rest a minute," said Bagiya.

"There's no harm in resting. Let's take at least five minutes. Ernest is probably choosing a weapon for the anticipated flagellation, so we might as well give him time," Shivaji said wittily.

Bagiya and Hunga chuckled.

"Shivaji, do you think the Stanfield brothers will believe us if we tell them what happened in the forest?"

"I don't know. Perhaps they have encountered the tribe before, or perhaps not. Englishmen rarely share such adventures with us," Shivaji replied.

"What if we are the first to witness this tribe? Besides the English and Indians, I thought no other race lived here," Bagiya added.

"I hope we are the first. We must not tell the Stanfield brothers—or anyone—what we saw today," Shivaji said.

"Why not?"

"If we tell the English, they might capture, torture, and enslave the tribe, forcing them into the sugarcane fields with a cane knife and hoe. No one deserves that. So we must keep silent. Bagiya, not a word."

Bagiya understood. Keeping quiet was easy, as the tribe had proven unobtrusive and harmless.

Hunga, using hand signals, confirmed he could not reveal the encounter even if he wanted to.

"So, do you think the tribe members were brought here like us indentured labourers?" Bagiya asked, posing as a new recruit.

Shivaji had intended to ask Bagiya these questions himself. He never expected to be on the receiving end. Yet he noticed that both Bagiya and Hunga looked to him for answers, expecting guidance. A sense of responsibility washed over him—a mantle he did not hesitate to assume.

"Bagiya, if I had to guess," Shivaji said, "those men we saw in the forest are probably natives of Fiji. They seem to belong to this land. I feel their kind has been here for centuries."

Despite aching shoulders, stiff backs, and overworked limbs, the labourers quickened their pace. Yet their minds continually returned to the tribal warriors, and the sheer luck that had spared them from death. Advancing along the trail in pitch-black darkness could have led them astray. For an indentured labourer, missing a step while performing assigned tasks was harshly punished by the Stanfield brothers. Worse, stepping outside the estate at night risked encountering British patrols on horseback. Anyone caught was labeled a runaway, facing imprisonment, torture, or even hanging.

The heavy sac of firewood slowed Shivaji's return to the Western section. Bagiya and Hunga, seasoned labourers, were accustomed to hauling such loads; at least once a month, they were assigned this strenuous task. Unlike them, Shivaji did not know what awaited at the Western section.

When the labourers arrived, Shivaji was stunned by the scene. Voices clamoured from every direction—English men and women competing for auditory dominance, their tones sharp and piercing, vying for attention. Fair-skinned men and women held proper glassware, not tin cups. They were dressed not in ragged slave clothing but in waistcoats, pantaloons, cravats, top hats, boots, gloves, gowns, shawls, bonnets, armlets, and slippers. Their garments—linen, silk, velvet, fur, and leather—stood in stark contrast to the hemp attire of the peasants.

Shivaji observed the Englishmen and women engrossed in their conversations, too oblivious to notice the idle peasants waiting to place wood on the porch. He recognized the disparity—how differently his kind was treated.

Amid the chatter, the howling and barking of six bloodhounds filled the air. Fortunately, the hounds were chained to posts outside the vacant cottage belonging to the absent Ernest. The canines had sniffed the peasants upon arrival. With no freedom to charge, they could only intimidate with growls and yelps, vibrating in Shivaji's ears.

"Let's step forward. Maybe then Edward will notice us," Bagiya whispered.

Shivaji hesitated, his mind frozen by the vicious hounds. He cringed at the saliva dripping from their jaws.

"Don't look them in the eyes," Bagiya urged. "These hounds are murders."

"What? You mean they kill?" Shivaji asked, diverting attention to the lonesome peasant.

"Yes. I've heard stories of them biting and chewing Indians to death."

Shivaji gulped. "Enough. I will not listen to this." Disgusted, he moved forward, dragging the bags with his workmates. As he walked, memories of his village surfaced—the barn, the roosters and hens, the pigs rolling in mud, horses seeking attention, and the familiar farm smells.

The reflections were interrupted when Lachmaiya appeared, carrying a silver tray of food for Edward's guests. She paced with a forced smile, unwillingly serving the honoured guests.

"An Indian's feelings are only understood by an Indian, not the English," Shivaji muttered under his breath. His heart pained as he saw the wife of his childhood friend eyeing the ground as Englishmen scrutinized her, being shooed or insulted by jealous women.

Then Edward appeared, radiating authority.

"Stop this instant! Remain still," he roared. "Do not set foot on this porch! I don't want my honoured guests to vomit from the intolerable odour you coolies bear."

Laughter, applause, and whistles followed from the visitors. Though the peasants did not understand the words, Edward's hand gestures signalled them to halt. Shivaji and his workmates lowered their bags. Observing the commotion, relentless stares, and finger-pointing, Shivaji sensed they were being slandered. Shame ignited a fire in his heart; he wished his eyes could permanently close.

Edward ordered the peasants to open their bags for inspection. One by one, he checked the load. Bagiya and Hunga's bags pleased him. Shivaji's, however, drew a frown. Though the contents matched the others, Edward sought to assert control, proving to his guests that it was he, not Ernest, who commanded the plantation.

"What is this? Why does your bag have less wood than the others? Were you sent to labour or sleep under a dakua tree?" Edward demanded.

Shivaji was confused, but he noted the strong scent of alcohol on the oppressor's breath. Edward glared, gesturing his displeasure at the timber collected. Shivaji struggled to explain in broken English:

"No less, Bagiya. No less, Hunga. I same, Hunga same, Bagiya same."

The assembled men and women giggled, exactly what Edward had intended—public humiliation.

Edward commanded Shivaji to undress. Confused, Shivaji hesitated, while Bagiya and Hunga recognized the order from past experience. Edward lost patience, grabbing Shivaji's shirt and tearing it off. Exposed to countless eyes, Shivaji felt the hostility directed at him.

Edwin, Edward's brother, ran forward with a whip, but Edward ignored him. Shivaji fell face-down, back exposed to the whip. Thoughts raced: ten blows, thirty, fifty, a hundred? Each strike had the potential to force screams of agony from every man or woman struck.

The whooshing sounds of the leather indicated that the flogging was to be administered with immense force. Edward flaunted his weapon to the gathered crowd on the porch. Then, he unleashed blow after blow without hesitation. Usually, when Edward used the whip on a coolie, he delayed to evoke further consternation within the victim's brain. At times, he'd pause between the lashes to utter nonsensical accusations and threats. But this time, he chose not to waste any time. Within a dozen seconds, Shivaji's back was decorated with numerous lacerations. The blood dripping from the whip showed the severity of the punishment. Not a single English man or woman turned their faces, lowered their heads, or covered their eyes. Instead, the scene was relished with cheers. The British were neither surprised nor sickened by the detestable act. It seemed as if they were used to this kind of barbarity. It was a given that on the plantations within the island, indentured labourers were mistreated. Somewhere not far from the

Stanfield estate, coolies were overworked, flogged, and raped. Whenever the opportunity to humiliate or harass an Indian emerged, the English oppressors would never let it pass by. The indentured labourers were told that there was no justice or justice system in the islands of Fiji. Even if there was, it was not created to serve Indians. When Edward felt his arms give way after delivering exactly twenty-five lashes, he shifted his eyes to the porch. The invitees were rooting for Edward to continue.

"Go on, Edward, tear that coolie's skin apart," said an Englishman as he pounded his fist in the air.

An English woman with a high-pitched voice, which irritated several eardrums nearby, shouted at the top of her lungs, "We want to see more! Strike the Indian."

"You have not made him scream. Edward, make that bastard scream," said an intoxicated Englishman before sipping on his glass.

The last comment spurred Edward. It finally settled into his brain that Shivaji had not released a single cry from the whipping.

"Is he dead?" Edward asked himself. He booted the firebrand in the midsection to see if he reacted. Finally, Shivaji squirmed as he tried to lift himself off the earth. He believed that the punishment was done. However, he underestimated Edward. The oppressor still had more energy to release. The firebrand believed that twenty-five lashes had left Edward breathless, but that was not the case. Edward was not defeated; he was determined to defeat his adversary. He came down with all his strength on the next lash. The leather connected with Shivaji's raised back and sent him crashing face-first onto the ground. The encouragement from the guests powered Edward's arms to deliver further punishment. He did not find it necessary to consider what Ernest would say or do once he discovered how severely the firebrand had been abused. Blow after blow, the tears on Shivaji's back widened. He tightened his jaw and grated his teeth to prevent a piercing scream from being released. Shivaji did not want the oppressor and bystanders to feel that he was unable to endure the punishment. His workmates struggled to keep their eyes upon the brutal scene. If one was to interfere, he or she would have been ordered to strip, then lie down, and finally be slashed open by the whip. Bagiya and Hunga decided not to involve themselves for that precise reason.

Sounds of heavy breathing entered Shivaji's ears. He was able to tell that the oppressor was weakening. Edward's hands were filled with blisters, his arms were numb, and his knees had become feeble. Administering his final lash, he turned to his honorable guests and bowed. His performance was received with loud applause. He then shifted his hateful eyes to Bagiya and Hunga. Surprised that the peasants were not taking part in the applauding, Edward motioned for them to bring their hands together. With no uncertainty shown, Bagiya and Hunga both complied.

At that moment, Shivaji's soul was pierced by disgrace and his heart was punctured by anguish. He felt as if everyone in the entire world—Indians, English, and God—wanted to see him demoralized. With his back covered in open wounds, even the slightest movement resulted in unbearable pain. Soon, images of his wife floated into his mind. "If Vyjanti were still alive, she'd never be able to witness such nastiness imposed upon her husband. It is difficult to say this, but I am thankful to God that she is not here to see blood unceasingly dripping from the lacerations etched on my body. At least she has been rescued from a life of inevitable tragedies and miseries that our past sins have enforced upon us," Shivaji said under his breath. Then, his eyes began to shut without his consent. The firebrand battled against unconsciousness but did not have the power or energy to last. Shivaji sensed that his wife was transferring him to a universe in which peace prevailed. Despite the fact she was not living, Vyjanti did what no other person could do for Shivaji—she reduced his pain.

Shivaji fluttered his eyelids as he arose to the clatter of pots and pans. Inside the hut, Gurdayal was in the process of brewing his tempting dish of rice and lentils. The dwelling was filled with the aroma of the delicacy. Shivaji understood where he was. However, what left him baffled was how he had returned to his hut. As he struggled to manoeuvre his body, Shivaji felt the lacerations stretch on his back. The pain forced him to shut his eyes and clench his teeth. He inhaled the air thick with resentment, thinking of the degradation he had borne in front of the numerous faces that displayed antipathy instead of sympathy. He attempted to glance at the open wounds on the upper portion of his left shoulder, but the stiffness in his neck did not permit him to do so. Then, his eyes came to rest upon the pail and rag placed not too far from his body. The worthless piece of cloth, hanging loosely on the side of the pail, was saturated with blood.

In the past, whenever Shivaji saw loads of blood, he ended up feeling queasy. Now he was forced to see and smell blood often—be it his or that of others. So much blood of his and his fellow Indians had been spilt by the British that Shivaji had become accustomed to the sight and smell of it. The pail and rag indicated that his wounds had been cleansed by the wet cloth and dabbed with cotton. There was no one else in the hut besides Gurdayal, which meant it was he who had done the needed treatment. Although the firebrand was still upset with Gurdayal for past events, he knew that his roommate must be shown appreciation for the provided aid. Once again, Shivaji felt indebted to the loyal peasant for his benevolence. "Thank you for treating my wounds," he said in his subdued voice.

Astonished that his roommate had acknowledged him, Gurdayal responded, "You're welcome, Shivaji. Hopefully, you have come to understand that I am not always self-centered. Once in a while, even a narcissist extends his or her hand to assist others who are in trouble."

Those lines struck like a punch to the chest, thought Shivaji. Unable to reply to Gurdayal's truthful yet hurtful words, the firebrand decided to instantly change the subject. "The last time I was conscious, I was enduring an undeserved punishment in the Western section of the estate. Now, I am here inside the hut—but I don't know how I arrived here."

Gurdayal was quick to reply, "Remember the peasants you were sent to the forest with?"

"Yes, I do. Bagiya and Hunga are their names," answered Shivaji, wishing that no sinful act was performed upon them by the oppressor.

"Well, those sympathetic individuals were the ones who hoisted you in their arms and carried your body to the hut."

"I pray to God that there comes a day when I get the opportunity to repay them for their kindness."

Gurdayal felt reluctant to ask his roommate what led to the flagellation. He felt the question could irritate the firebrand, so he did not permit his sealed lips to move. Now that the roommates were on speaking terms, both were to be extra cautious with their questions and answers. The firebrand and the loyal peasant did not want to upset each other. Neither of them wanted their egos to force them into remaining silent in the hut for days. For all indentured labourers, silence led to loneliness. And for those who had no partner, parent, sibling, or child, loneliness became the enemy that tortured first and then slaughtered.

Without his roommate even asking, Shivaji revealed details of what had happened in the Western section. While the firebrand unraveled the reason for his flogging, Gurdayal lowered his face in shame. There was a part of Gurdayal that regretted being the loyal peasant who tolerated the commands hollered by his sirdars. Then, during the latter portion of the narrative, came a loud beating at the door of the hut.

"Who can this be?" asked the stunned Gurdayal.

Shivaji was clueless. "It is so late into the day. Who is it that travels in darkness?"

Rising to his feet, the loyal peasant sped to the door. "Who's at the door?" Gurdayal asked before placing his hands on it.

"Please open the door. It is I, Venkatesh. I am here to see my friend, Shivaji."

Shivaji wanted to burst with excitement when Venkatesh announced his name, but the condition he was in forbade him to move. The loyal peasant opened the door and asked Venkatesh to enter. When their eyes met, Gurdayal nodded at the visitor as a form of greeting. The kind gesture made Venkatesh feel comfortable in his surroundings. At first, he was skeptical about visiting his childhood friend. He did not know whether it was acceptable to visit someone else's hut during the night. With no torch in his possession, Venkatesh believed the darkness of the night might have directed him onto an erroneous path. Also, he did not know what resided inside the bushes and behind the trees. Regardless of all these fears, Venkatesh was determined to meet his friend when Lachmaiya informed him of the devastating incident that had occurred in the Western section.

Once he was let into the hut, Venkatesh struggled to kneel beside Shivaji. Water began to form in his eyes. On several occasions, he had seen his friend wounded. But never before had he seen Shivaji punished in such an extreme manner. There was not a trace of undamaged skin left on his back. It was a spectacle that became difficult to bear. As seconds turned into minutes, Venkatesh still did not utter a single word. Aware that his friend was distressed, Shivaji took the initiative to start the conversation. "It has been a while, Venkatesh. How is little Karthik?"

"He is fine," replied Venkatesh in a pithy manner.

"Did Lachmaiya return home safely from the Western section?"

Venkatesh's voice had risen, "Yes, she has returned. She was present during your beating. With tears in her eyes and a massive stone placed on her chest, Lachmaiya informed me of everything that happened between Edward and you."

Shivaji grunted as if the incident was of no importance to him.

"Why, Shivaji? Why did you not argue with Edward? I am sure that your bag contained a sufficient amount of wood. I know for a fact that Shivaji Nair is a perfectionist; he fulfills his duties to the fullest."

"Yes, my bag was filled to the top with wood."

"Why did you not escape from the whipping?"

"Where can I escape to? There is no salvation for an indentured labourer. We are to sustain the cruel treatment. That is what I did. Not once did I shriek or groan from the hurtful misery that was delivered upon my flesh. Those English men and women watching the punishment, rooting for the punishment, and laughing at the punishment were not the only people enjoying themselves. Even I was enjoying the incident."

Gurdayal, who was pouring the cooked rice and lentils onto tin plates, listened to Shivaji talk as if the injuries had affected his brain.

"What are you saying? How is it that you enjoyed the incident?" asked Venkatesh with confusion plastered on his face.

"These English men and women, including Edward, craved to witness an oppressed Indian squirm and squeal like a pig. Unfortunately for them, the Indian did not squirm or squeal despite the countless number of licks rendered on his back. Venkatesh, again I have defeated them. Again, we have defeated them."

"Nanban, this is no war. Why are you so focused on winning and losing? If this continues, these oppressors will end your life. Shivaji, you need to let go of defiance. You have to understand that we cannot reverse what we have sown."

When Venkatesh used the word nanban, it was music to Shivaji's ears. Finally, the firebrand felt like he had been reunited with his childhood friend. "Thank you, Venkatesh. It feels like years since you last addressed me as nanban. Nanban means friend. You are a friend indeed; the only friend who has not left my side." Shivaji and his lines had so deeply affected Venkatesh that he was unable to respond.

"You have a life that is worth living for. You have a wife and a son to look after, so I ask you not to be concerned for my health and safety. It is time for you to forget that you have a childhood friend," said Shivaji as he started to drift apart from the initial matter of conversation.

To Venkatesh, it seemed as if his friend was talking under the influence of alcohol. Although he was infuriated by the firebrand's comments, Venkatesh let him proceed on with his rambling.

"I need you to understand who I am. Today, I will tell you what I truly feel and think," said Shivaji as he gestured for his friend to inch over so he could see his face. As Venkatesh changed his position to suit his friend's needs, Gurdayal stationed two plates mounted with khichdi in front of the visitor and his roommate. "I apologize for not asking if you wanted a plate of khichdi or not. Now that the food has been served, please don't refuse to eat," Gurdayal said to Venkatesh with politeness in his voice.

As his friend was about to reply, Shivaji barged in, "You must taste the khichdi. I tell you, nanban, it is delicious. There is no doubt he is the best cook on this plantation," said

Shivaji, referring to his roommate.

"If that is so, please don't inform the Stanfield brothers. If this is reported to the sirdar, I will have to work my fingers to the bone inside their kitchens till God knows when," said Gurdayal, who had generated a smile upon the faces of the childhood friends.

Both visitor and roommate wished to assist Shivaji by feeding him the rice and lentils. But the firebrand bluntly refused the help. If that was to occur, Shivaji would have felt like a child being spoon-fed by his parents. Despite the numbness of his fingers, the firebrand battled his arm and hand to conquer stability. At times, he succeeded. Then, there were times he failed. When the spoon fell from his hands or when the khichdi was not able to reach his mouth, Shivaji maintained his composure, portraying to his friends that everything was normal. He then noticed that Venkatesh was not able to remain seated in one position for more than a minute. Venkatesh kept shifting his legs. He was surely uncomfortable.

"Nanban, is something troubling you?" asked Shivaji.

"No... Not at all. I am fine."

"How is the khichdi?"

"Spectacular! If I had not tasted the khichdi, I would have never come to know that a dish consisting of only rice and lentils can be so appetizing," replied Venkatesh. After finishing the khichdi, he thanked Gurdayal for satisfying his taste buds. Meanwhile, Shivaji devoured the food bit by bit, endeavoring not to accidentally drop more food on the ground. He was in no condition to clean his mess, nor did he want his roommate to clean it. When he outstretched his arm to feed himself, the lacerations on his back extended. The pain was excruciating. But no matter how excruciating the pain was, he did not let others see or feel that he was in discomfort.

As Venkatesh handed the empty plate over to the loyal peasant, he asked his childhood friend, "So, nanban, weren't you going to reveal what you truly feel and think?"

After collecting a mouthful of rice and lentils with his spoon, Shivaji paused. He then lowered the spoon, placing it on the edge of the plate. Aware that the upcoming conversation was of importance, Gurdayal leaned against the wall of the hut for support. Indeed, his eyes were drowsy and his limbs were exhausted, but his need to listen to Shivaji—who he assumed had a disorganized brain, a soul that was dispirited, and a heart that was defective—was undeniably resolute.

"What I want is to be free. I want to be free from the oppression, the inequality, the degradation, and the maltreatment that an indentured labourer experiences. And what I have learned is that my brain has selected the route of unfaithfulness," said Shivaji.

Paying close attention to his friend, Venkatesh asked, "How can one's brain be unfaithful? We all have control over our brains, Shivaji."

"I don't agree. A man whose soul has been incapacitated no longer has control over his brain. The day destiny stole Vyjanti from my arms was the day I lost control of my brain. My visions, reflections, perceptions, and judgements alter from day to day. Sometimes, I feel like rebelling against the British and their system. Then come days when I feel like forfeiting. I endure the punishment without a confrontation. At times, I can control my emotions. Then there are times when I lose control over them. No doubt, uncontrollable ego and anger do impair my judgements. Venkatesh, I believe that there is nothing for me to gain or achieve in life anymore. I also understand that one single labourer revolting against the oppressors on this plantation is futile. It is either that we Indians don't have the strength within us to challenge the British, or that we Indians are too hesitant to overthrow the colonial system."

Not able to resist, Venkatesh intervened, "You must understand the reasons behind the hesitation to overthrow the colonial system. Most of the indentured labourers who have travelled from India were accompanied by their family members. Shivaji, no father will choose to rebel against the British over the safety of his wife and children."

"Yes, I understand. It seems as if everyone is committed to someone, except for me. If Vyjanti was still alive, I would restrain myself or would be restrained from challenging the Stanfield brothers."

Gurdayal wanted to be included in the conversation. But for him to be included, he needed to interfere with the lines that were voiced. Feeling a bit hesitant, the loyal peasant dove into the conversation without looking back. "Sorry to intrude, but it seems to me as if Shivaji is unable to forget his past and move forward in life."

"Correct," yelled Shivaji, startling his friends. "That is correct. I am not able to forget or forgive. Even you are not able to forget and forgive. If you were able to let go of the past, you would not have been striving to return home to your family members."

An extensive silence permeated the hut. It was the firebrand's insolent yet candid words to Gurdayal that sealed the mouths of both visitor and roommate. The loyal peasant was not expecting Shivaji to respond in such a manner. His comment to the firebrand was not made to attack him, but he did feel that Shivaji delivered a counter-attack. Since he was older than his roommate, Gurdayal did not take offense to the rash words. Instead, he broke the silence by asking Venkatesh if he wanted a cup of water to drink. Venkatesh refused the offer but thanked him for his kindness.

"Shivaji, are you thirsty?" Gurdayal asked his roommate.

"No, thank you," replied Shivaji in a hushed voice. Feelings of shame and remorse overshadowed his soul. He eventually understood that what he had said should not have been said, especially in front of company.

"So, where were we?" asked Venkatesh, not wanting his night to end on a dull note. Gurdayal was peering at his roommate, who didn't even hear the question. Paying no attention to his friends, Shivaji kept his eyes fixed on the ground. He was lost in his trail of thought.

"Shivaji, what is the matter? What is meandering in that brain of yours?" asked Venkatesh, expecting his friend to grasp the question.

This time, Shivaji did not sidestep his company. He expressed in detail what was revolving in his mind.

"I was thinking about the scenario that occurred in the Western section today. Even before the oppressor raised his voice for me to lay flat on the ground, there I was, an obedient son embracing Mother Earth. As Edward whirled and swayed the whip to impress his honorable guests, I reflected upon the sayings of appa.

One fine day—as every day was fine for a thirteen-year-old—I was sweeping the porch when appa returned with damaged pots secured under his arms. The pots that he had crafted with his own hands were nicked and pricked by some flying animal with a bill. He ordered me to assist in shifting the items to the porch, where appa planned to repair the pots for the remainder of the day. Once the pots were shifted, appa sent me to collect several other damaged pots from his working station located behind the house.

Throughout the day, I walked onto the porch to see if appa had finished repairing the pots, which he desired to sell in the market the following morning. Honestly, I made at least ten visits—one every hour—and still the old man was not finished. With moonlight replacing sunlight, appa had trouble locating and patching the holes in the pots. On my last visit, before planning to rest my eyes, I dared to ask appa a question. I asked him, 'What is the use of labouring so hard on an item that breaks easily?'

My question went unanswered. Perhaps it was so foolish that it was not worth answering. So, being the pest I was, I asked him more questions. 'Is there not a possibility for these pots to be damaged again? What if a bird places its eyes on the pots overnight or early in the morning? How many pots still need fixing? Why not hire someone to assist you?'

After the mouthful of enquiries, I waited several minutes for him to answer. Still, appa did not find it necessary to reply to a single question. Only then did I decide to surrender to appa's unwillingness and muteness. As I began to enter our home, a strict tone called out my name. Appa asked me to sit on the floor beside him for reasons I did not know. I obeyed his request. He then voiced the most influential, significant, enlightening, and appropriate words that every father should disclose to his son.

'God has chosen a path for every man on earth; a path which must be accepted by the man. The man commences on this path full of hardships and obstacles. As the man walks, he leaves behind footprints—each footprint representing a moment from his life. And when his journey is about to end, the man looks back at the trail of footprints. Some of the footprints have vanished, some have faded, and some are still evident. Only the footprints that remain completely visible are the ones he takes with him to the next life.'

From where these words derived, I haven't a clue. What provoked him to utter them, I haven't a clue. Did his words reflect the situation he was in, I haven't a clue. Was the saying a response to my many questions, I haven't a clue. And what appa was feeling or thinking when he unraveled his theory on the pattern of life, I haven't a clue.

But what I do know is that I must abide by what he said. At last, I have accepted my fate. I shall live with everlasting memories. Eventually, I will incarnate again."

THE 53RD DAY

Shivaji rose to the scent of jasmine hovering in the air. After a full day of permitted inactivity, he shifted onto his knees without reopening or widening the lacerations on his body. Though the soreness had abated, Shivaji had to be careful not to crash into or brush against a person or object, since his contusions were still fresh and delicate. Once the potent aroma was detected, the widower frantically searched for his deceased wife. Jasmine was the flower that Vyjanti had cherished. She often decorated her hair with a strand of jasmine flowers. Usually, Shivaji was relaxed by the scent of jasmine. But at that moment, the scent circulated in the air with much affection. The smell was sweeter than ever.

The widower needed to place his eyes upon her elegant face, to lock his eager fingers between hers, to whisper words of love and devotion in her ears. He twisted his neck in all directions, desperate to locate an image of his wife. Vyjanti was nowhere to be seen. A painful sensation began to dominate his forehead. Shivaji felt that his brain was toying with his senses.

During that night, the widower had dreamt of Vyjanti. Hand in hand, husband and wife strolled near the banks of Kolavai Lake. With laughter piercing the silence, the married couple drowned their feet in the shallow waters of the exquisite lake. The passion within their hearts had escalated. Shivaji grasped his wife from behind. His face was buried in Vyjanti's hair, in which a strand of jasmine flowers was attached. His nose inhaled the exotic fragrance of jasmine. And then, it all diminished.

His brain was still in an unconscious state; however, no images of Vyjanti or Kolavai Lake lingered. As Shivaji reflected upon his dream, his pulsating heart began to settle. The perturbed behavior that he displayed was replaced with composure. He believed that his wife was there within the hut. He felt someone breathing on his neck. He heard someone murmur in his ears. He sensed the presence of a body close by.

"Vyjanti..." the widower called for his wife. "I know you are here. What is it that you want to say?"

Not a single word or slightest motion penetrated the dimness inside the hovel. Quietness prevailed until Shivaji's focus was disturbed by his roommate. Barging in with pails of water in each hand, Gurdayal was prepared to cook the everyday dish of rice and lentils.

"Shivaji, how do you feel?" asked the loyal peasant, setting the pails of water aside.

"I feel better than before. Once again, I thank you from the bottom of my heart. If it were not for your treatment, I'd probably still be lying flat on the ground."

To prepare breakfast, Gurdayal ignited the fire with the help of the collected wood. He was surprised to see that his roommate was on his feet despite the injuries he had sustained.

"If any other person were to face such brutality, he or she would not have risen for days. And here is the firebrand, prepared to encounter the burdens of the sugarcane fields after resting for a single day," Gurdayal murmured to himself.

Although the loyal peasant did not know it, behind the normal stance and movement exhibited by Shivaji, he deliberately concealed the intolerable pain he was enduring. The pain was excruciating, yet he knew that he needed to tolerate it.

"It is unfortunate that an injured peasant, no matter how severe his or her injuries, is given only a day to heal from lacerations. No wound can heal within a day. The Sirdar must understand this."

Shivaji breathed out heavily. "The oppressors will never understand. Our injuries are of no matter to them. These people want us to labor for hours and hours, from dusk till dawn. So that is what we indentured laborers will do—and will continue doing."

Staggered by the firebrand's passive comments, Gurdayal stirred the pot in a circular motion as the delectable aroma seeped into the air. The aroma made Shivaji's mouth water and his stomach grumble.

"So, what have I missed? Have our duties changed?"

Gurdayal was quick to reply. "Yes, we are now placing the stems into the furrows. Once the stems are positioned appropriately, we are to cover them with soil. The peasants are fortunate because the work is not as difficult as it was during the horse plowing. For the condition you are in, this task is manageable."

In response, Shivaji beamed at his roommate. "So, will the khichdi be done after I return from rinsing my mouth and washing my face?"

"Yes, it will be done," replied Gurdayal, unbothered that his roommate had changed the subject.

"I asked because my stomach is whining," said Shivaji. During that moment, his brain was forced to visit a past memory—a memory better left repressed or forgotten. "I remember how frustrated I used to become when my wife did not have food prepared on the table when I returned from my bath. I regret that I used to become so upset with her. She did not deserve that."

Once the stomachs were full and the empty plates cleaned, a deafening blast was released from the barrel of the weapon held by the owner of the estate. The landscape was unnerved by the roar of the Lee-Enfield. Before the indentured laborers rushed to the scene, they demanded that the children remain inside the huts until it was safe to appear. The children did not reject the order from their parents. Most of them huddled into a corner of the hut, consoling themselves or one another to help dispel their despair.

The bullet was set free in the direction of the heavens for the laborers to assemble in front of Ernest. A formal announcement was to be made by the plantation owner. Instantly, Gurdayal understood the situation. His talents were required by the planter. The loyal peasant did not waste time. Within seconds, he positioned himself near the stallion on which Ernest was seated.

All of the indentured laborers on the plantation, except for the children, were quick to gather among the Stanfield brothers. In the assemblage, Edward located Shivaji. He peered hatefully at his nemesis. No malicious stare ever went unnoticed by Shivaji. Instead of fixing his eyes firmly upon the oppressor, Shivaji searched the earth as if he had lost a personal item.

The resentment Edward had toward the firebrand had escalated since the moment he was disciplined by the owner of the estate. He was also disgruntled by his tattletale brother. When Edwin informed the plantation owner of the maltreatment that unfolded in the Western section, Edward was urged to choke the squealing rat. Ernest had punished his disobedient brother by forbidding him to step foot on the sugarcane fields for an entire day. For Edward, the punishment was a slap in the face. His ego was battered. He could not forget that someone who shared his blood—his very own brother—had disciplined him for thrashing a measly Indian.

Nonetheless, Ernest had warned his brother that if he were to lash a peasant without permission, there would be consequences to pay. To not have one or both of his brothers in the fields, despite them both maintaining the role of overseer, was acceptable. But to have one less peasant drudging in the sugarcane fields was nightmarish for Ernest. In fact, he was let down by the impulsive acts of his brother Edward.

Meanwhile, Edward felt as if he had been backstabbed by his once-reliable brother, Edwin. As for Edwin, he was upset with both of his oppressive brothers for mistreating and misusing the Indians. "The Indians are contracted laborers. Then why is it that we treat them as slaves?" he often asked himself.

As soon as eye contact was made between the plantation owner and his translator, Ernest began to address the crowd of laborers. "Coolies, I stand before you to announce that I will be gone from the plantation for the next forty-eight hours. I will be traveling a great distance to attend several meetings regarding the purchasing of the cane we dispense."

As Gurdayal translated the words into Hindi, most of the veteran laborers breathed in apprehension. The loyal peasant himself stumbled upon the lines he uttered. The indentured laborers knew that the plantation owner would select Edward as his temporary replacement. Whenever Edward was appointed to the position, the bodies of the laborers were bound to be disfigured.

Extended hours of toil, additional tasks, demeaning orders, and barbarous sessions of flagellation awaited them. There was not a single laborer in the sugarcane fields left untouched by the leather or unspoken to by the oppressor.

It was the adolescent Indian women—married and unmarried—who were most afraid. While Ernest talked, the women shivered with trepidation. It was only when the plantation owner was absent from the estate that Edward lured the Indian women into the isolated corners of the sugarcane fields, where he forced himself upon them. The helpless women screamed and screamed, but their voices were absorbed by the distant landscape before they reached the ears of a toiling laborer.

Ernest continued with his announcement, "Once I depart from the plantation, Edwin will be in charge."

The crowd of peasants was astonished. Smiles began to form on their faces. Sighs of relief were released. The news of Edwin as the lead planter instead of Edward filled the indentured laborers with contentment and amazement. Controlling their emotions, the focus of the laborers shifted to Edwin. The assemblage expected the face of the Stanfield brother to be lit with happiness. But that was not the case. Edwin was not pleased that he had been assigned such a dominant role. It was known that Edward desperately anticipated the day when he'd be the one running the plantation, but that opportunity was now seized by the less authoritative, less intimidating, and less merciless Edwin. The tyrant had something else planned in his mind. As soon as the owner of the estate departed, Edward was prepared to exchange roles with his younger brother.

"For the next forty-eight hours, Edwin will be your sirdar. You are to treat him as you treat me. Don't forget that no matter what, the labor in the fields must not abate. The same or better results are to be produced daily. On my return, I don't want to hear that my coolies have slackened. If that is the case, then I will be forced to unleash the whip," said Ernest, who did not often associate himself with weapons and punishments. He then ordered Gurdayal and several others to prepare the two-wheeled cart for the excursion he was keen to set forth on. Gurdayal and three other laborers rushed to collect the cart, which was regularly stored near the coolie line. It took the loyal peasant and his team exactly seven minutes to roll the cart to where everyone had gathered. Meanwhile, Ernest had a private conversation with his youngest brother. Words of advice were shared by the eldest to the youngest as Edward eyeballed his brothers with envy. After the brief conversation, Ernest leaped into his vehicle that was perfectly strapped onto the horse by the selected laborers. He did not find it in his heart to forgive Edward for the incident that occurred on the Western section. In his view, the disobedient act was still fresh and memorable. Without bidding farewell to his unmanageable brother, Ernest began to depart with the cart and stallion. Before he turned the corner, the planter shouted, "Colonial Sugar Refining Mill, here I come."

Edward did not wait for his eldest brother to vanish in the distance. He was quick to say, "Edwin, as long as I live, I will not give you the chance to single-handedly operate the estate."

The decisive words were heard but deliberately ignored. Edwin's eyes were still lost on the trail on which Ernest traveled. An unusual feeling overcame his soul. With his eldest brother not present, evil was bound to overshadow the plantation. Edwin began thinking about the indentured laborers and what suffering Edward was to enforce upon them. The assumptions, which caused distress within Edwin, were interrupted as the laborers received an order to attend to the sugarcane fields within the next fifteen minutes.

"If you're late, do expect the whip to be revealed," added Edward before bursting into laughter.

Not a second was wasted as the indentured laborers dashed into their huts to put on the clothes that were mandatory in the fields. Edward and Edwin, without discussing matters, advanced on two different paths. While Edward proceeded to the Western section to collect his various weapons, Edwin proceeded to the Northern section to investigate the sugarcane fields. Some peasants were in such a rush that when they exited their huts, they forgot to close the door behind them. Once they were on the route that led to the fields, some sprinted, some jogged, and some were forced to walk due to certain injuries. Shivaji carefully observed the laborers who dashed past him to save their bodies from the injurious weapon. His eyes were sharp enough to capture the faces of Bagiya and Hunga, with whom he had toiled in the forest. For Shivaji, the vision of the men was similar to the wild horses he had once seen galloping into the dawn's light. Feelings of regret poured over the firebrand as he was not able to express his gratitude to his co-workers for transporting him back to his dwelling after the heinous incident on the Western section.

Soon, he came to realize that many of the fifty-three laborers had proceeded ahead of him. But he did not feel as if this was a competition to see who could arrive at the Northern section first. Shivaji was confident that, at the pace he was moving, there was no doubt that he'd arrive at the sugarcane fields before the decided time. For the sake of curiosity, Shivaji looked behind him to see if he was the last peasant on the trail. To his surprise, with his very own eyes, he perceived Venkatesh, Lachmaiya, and Karthik. Approximately thirty feet from where Shivaji stood, Venkatesh and his family members advanced at a languid pace. As the image of Venkatesh became more visible, Shivaji was able to understand why his childhood friend did not advance energetically. Venkatesh was limping. Lachmaiya endeavored to assist by supporting her husband's upper body. Meanwhile, Karthik followed his mother with a concerned look etched on his face. The child's expression shattered Shivaji's heart into the tiniest pieces. No innocent child on the face of the earth deserved to see their father in misery. Shivaji took to his heels to help his friend. Swiftly, he slid his free limb under Venkatesh's armpit. With that maneuver, Shivaji bore half of Venkatesh's weight. As soon as Lachmaiya observed that Shivaji's arm was stabilizing and supporting her husband, she decided to relieve herself from the deed. Finally, her palpitating heart settled. She began to dry her tears. Lachmaiya knew that her husband was in good hands.

"Why are you limping? How did this happen? Who has done this to you?" bellowed Shivaji in a furious manner.

Venkatesh struggled to use his left foot, which was severely bloated. The foot was uncovered. It was not hidden by plaster or cloth, and no herbal medicine was applied to it.

"Shivaji, why are you here? I need you to leave. In fact, I need you all to leave. If you don't arrive in the fields on time, Edward will harm your bodies with countless lashes."

The firebrand intervened, "Shut up, Venkatesh! How can I and your family leave you behind? You must not talk such nonsense. Please, tell me what happened to your foot?"

Venkatesh kept mum. His obstinacy disturbed Shivaji. The firebrand then met eyes with Lachmaiya, wishing she'd unveil the mystery behind the injury. But even she did not open her mouth.

"Appa accidentally placed his foot on a sharp and slender object," said Karthik, revealing the truth.

"Once appa pulled the metal object from his foot, blood started to pour. There was so much blood, mama. Do you know what I did? I shut my eyes. It was too hard to watch."

Eager for information, Shivaji asked the child when the injury happened.

"It happened three days ago. At first, it seemed like the boo-boo was fine. But it worsened yesterday. It was swollen and bleeding for the entire day. Mama, can you please fix appa?"

Shivaji ceased his movement. He recalled last night when his childhood friend came to visit him. "Did I not see his foot? Did I not see how he walked? Did I not see him struggle to seat himself upon the earth?" Shivaji said under his breath. In his mind, Shivaji cursed himself for paying less attention to his friend.

"I beg you, Shivaji, let me be. Please, take Lachmaiya and Karthik and leave. Edward can unleash his whip upon my body, but I will not let him flog my wife and child," said Venkatesh.

"I will not abandon you, Venkatesh. No one here wants to abandon you. And we sure can't take you back to the hut. So you must not fret. And please don't fuss. I will not let Edward lay a finger on your wife and child. Not that he will, but if he does, Edward has to walk over my dead body in order to come near them."

Lachmaiya sobbed uncontrollably once Shivaji voiced his devotion. In her view, Shivaji was similar to the guardian Lakshmana, who will forever be remembered for his commitment and faithfulness towards his brother Rama.

With Shivaji's assistance, Venkatesh and his family members were able to reach the Northern section before Edward started the briefing. The strategy that Shivaji used to arrive on time was that he forced Venkatesh to talk less and walk more. Edward, who stood before the assembled laborers, had his eyes fixed on the firebrand as soon as he walked into view. The oppressor immediately called for Gurdayal. As the loyal peasant attended to the shouting of his name, like a pet attends to his or her owner, Edwin decided to interfere. "Gurdayal, as I talk, please be kind to translate in Hindi for our laborers."

For a second, Edward was bewildered. Never before had his brother taken the initiative to address the indentured laborers. He felt that Edwin wanted to overthrow him and seize the temporary position that he held. "I will never let Edwin evolve into a planter," he said under his breath.

Once the translator was positioned in front of the crowd, Edwin opened his mouth to speak. Before he was able to complete his first sentence, Edward shoved his brother aside with immense force. The shove sent Edwin stumbling onto the ground.

"What is the matter with you?" Edwin shouted at his brother.

"I have told you once—there is no need to tell you again—that I am in command," replied Edward with arrogance in his voice.

"Brother Ernest has appointed me as the owner of the estate."

"It does not matter what brother says. Whenever he departs from this plantation, I automatically become the man in charge."

When the younger brother retained his argument, the elder brother warned him to cease his voice. "Edwin, if you don't shut your mouth, I will shut it for you. The whip that I have in my hand is not only kept to be used on Indians. It can also be used on Englishmen."

Not willing to provoke a further confrontation, Edwin decided to submit to his elder brother. He then lowered his face in shame, concealing his eyes from the laborers who desired him to be their leader. As the brothers squabbled, Gurdayal knew not to translate for the laborers on the scene. He placed himself on standby until Edward regained his focus on the assemblage. So when the focus was regained and the voices began to diffuse amongst the crowd, the oppressed listened faithfully to what the oppressor had to disclose.

"First and foremost, coolies, I need you to forget what Ernest announced." Then Edward, with his index finger, guided the eyes of the peasants in the direction of his brother. "He is no plantation owner. I am the leader of this estate. A boy is not suitable for a position that requires a man. So, from this point onwards, you must listen to what I have to say."

Edwin bit his tongue, as he was aware that if he did not, curses and insults were bound to escape from his mouth.

Edward continued, "There will be two teams. The teams will be led by Edwin and Gurdayal. They will be overseeing you, and I will be overseeing them. Today, I want the remaining furrows to be planted with sugarcane stems. The women and children are to gather the cane from the piles situated nearby the furrows. Then, the leaves from the cane are to be separated from its body. Once the stem is chopped into foot-long pieces, it must be passed on to the men. The men are to place the stems into the furrows, side by side. Once again, I repeat—side by side. The stems are to be placed horizontally. If I find the stems placed upright or vertically, the men of the team will have to remove their clothes and prepare themselves for a severe flagellation."

The new recruits engraved the words *"side by side"* in their minds. Some of these laborers even chanted the words in a whisper, as if they were verses from the Bible, Quran, or Gita.

"Lastly, when the stems are properly laid into the furrows, the men are to use either their hands or hoes to cover the stems with soil," said Edward. After explaining the obligatory duties, he added, "Now, aren't these duties effortless?"

Most laborers were too focused on the dreadful images of the oppressor utilizing his whip to hear the question. So, Edward decided to answer it himself. "Well, the answer is no. As you know, these duties only appear to be easy. I promise that soon your arms and legs will be desperate for rest. So enjoy a day filled with extreme heat, blisters on hands and feet, indecent curse words, and leather slashing flesh."

As soon as the briefing was completed, the laborers were dispatched into the sugarcane fields with cane knives and hoes resting upon their shoulders. The overseers even placed knives into the hands of several children who were to separate the flags from the body of the cane. Destined to be in the fields and on the imperious plantation, a grin still formed on the faces of the children whenever a significant responsibility was assigned to them. If a knife or hoe was handed to them, the children felt as if they had taken one of the many steps that led to adulthood.

While the children were in high spirits when allowed to labor alongside their fathers and mothers, the parents were shedding tears. To have their sons and daughters toil in the fields was similar to having a parent shove his or her child down a well. By no means did the mothers and fathers want their children to encounter intense aversion from the whites. There wasn't a night that passed without a parent asking God to protect their child or children from the sinful eyes of an Englishman.

Shivaji was concerned for the minors when he observed the razor-sharp knives tightly gripped in their hands. He tried to repress the presumption that a fatal accident was bound to occur. However, that was not the only concern Shivaji had. He was distressed by the assumption that Edward would detect the injury that Venkatesh had suffered on his foot. "If that is so, Venkatesh will not be spared," Shivaji said to himself.

When Edward placed Venkatesh and his family members in the same team as the firebrand, the placement was quietly celebrated by the childhood friends. On top of that, both men were under the supervision of Gurdayal. These small factors did not abolish the continuation of malice, but to some extent, they did relieve distress.

On most plantations, if given the choice, an indentured laborer would choose to drudge for an Indian overseer over an English overseer. But the ability to choose was not given to them. On the estate controlled by the Stanfield brothers, not a single laborer desired for Edward to be his or her overseer. For the Indians to labor under the supervision of Edwin or Gurdayal was considered a privilege. Both overseers promised less physical and verbal abuse.

Five minutes into the shift, Shivaji heard both the swaying of the whip and the shrieks of a laborer. And yet not a muscle flinched. In his view, to live through the day, he needed to ignore the distracting surroundings in which he slaved. He was to neglect everyone except his loved ones. His eyes incessantly shifted onto Venkatesh, Lachmaiya, and Karthik. Once he witnessed the anguish on Venkatesh's face, he felt as if a dagger had been lodged into his heart.

After every step, Venkatesh was compelled to hide the pangs that dominated his foot. Not able to sit and not able to lean, he longed to rest his foot for at least fifteen minutes. Whenever the ears of a laborer caught a clip-clop, he or she was aware that the planter and horse were nearby. Immediately, the laborers were to increase the speed of their hands and feet before the planter had the chance to administer a lash.

When Edward rode into the section where the loyal peasant and his team labored, Gurdayal was fast to ignite speed within his team members by uttering a threat. "If you coolies don't move faster, I will scourge your backs with thirty lashes." The threat was an indicator Gurdayal regularly used to inform his laborers that an Englishman was closing in.

As Edward disembarked from the horse, Venkatesh felt his knees shudder with fear. Despite his nervousness, in a frantic attempt, Venkatesh strained his limbs to move faster to exhibit that he was on par with others. While lifting his feet to step forward, he sensed that fluid was seeping from his injured foot. But that did not stop him from covering the drill with his hands. All the laborers were provided with a hoe when topping a drill, but in some areas, the land became exceptionally stubborn. In those cases, hands functioned better than the hoe.

Close to fifteen feet apart from his childhood friend, Shivaji stole fast glances at Venkatesh. His eyes moved from the stem in his hands onto Venkatesh and then from the drill, in which he placed the stem, onto Edward. The routine that his eyes had formed was exploited by the firebrand until he was certain that Venkatesh had survived the unsafe situation he was in.

Meanwhile, to control her sobbing and hide her tears, Lachmaiya draped her face with a long scarf. Although she was an emotional mess, her hands did not halt once while separating the flags from the cane. She yelled at Karthik, not permitting him to deliver the stems to his father or the other peasants stationed beside the drills. No mother wanted her son or daughter to fall into the hands of an Englishman, especially if the Englishman was Edward Stanfield.

As she toiled, Lachmaiya whispered religious mantras to obtain God's attention. In such a critical situation, an Indian woman was limited to prayer. Her outcries, her efforts, her uprising were of no use. No laborer had the tenacity to assist the person in need, and no laborer dared to include themselves in the uprising—except for one, and he too was standing on the edge of defeatism.

With an unpleasant look displayed on his face, it seemed as if Edward had selected a target. As he walked past Venkatesh, Edward untangled the leather weapon that he normally kept wrapped around his waist. Since the oppressor had his back facing the men who laid the stems, Shivaji anticipated that a woman from the flag-removing and cane-slicing team was soon to be lashed. He wanted his presumption to be incorrect, but that was not the case. A vicious lash was released directly onto the hands of a middle-aged female. As the whip grazed her flesh, she yelped. The lash was unexpected by the woman, who began cursing in her native language. The act left Edward flabbergasted. Never before had he heard a female voluntarily interact with him. When an Indian female talked to him, it was because he demanded her to do so. He was aware that what had been spoken was in Tamil, but he did not know that the foul words were directed at him. "Do I look Indian to you?" Edward mockingly asked the woman.

As soon as his ears detected words in English, Gurdayal advanced towards the planter to fulfill his duty as the translator. The loyal peasant's fast response made Edward satisfied.

"Gurdayal, what did this coolie say?"

The laborers were afraid for the female. If the loyal peasant unveiled the truth to Edward, the female was likely to receive forty lashes. However, whenever Gurdayal had the opportunity to save or help a team member, he did so, as long as he knew that the act did not accompany pitfalls for him. His clever brain devised a lie seconds after the question was proposed. "Sirdar, the woman said that she will move her hands faster."

"Yes, I want everyone to work faster. Speed is what I want to see. If I see listless hands and feet, a lick will be administered upon the flesh. The lick is a reminder that I prefer activeness, not inactiveness," said Edward. As the oppressor talked, no laborer was to halt with the slicing, laying, and topping of the sugarcane. However, the laborers were to keep their ears wide open and mouths firmly shut.

"Soon the coolies will be awarded a fifteen-minute recess. Before recess, I want at least five drills completed. If the five drills are not complete, I will revoke the break," said the tyrant before he leaped onto the horse and galloped to where Edwin and his team drudged. Edward did not have faith in his brothers or the coolies. He had faith in no one except himself. He was a meddler that needed to meddle. What occurred on the estate—small or big, important or unimportant—he had to know of. He wanted to be the solution to all problems, unaware that on the plantation, his brothers and the laborers considered him to be the problem.

With Edward gone, the Indian overseer tried to lift the spirits of his team members. He kept reiterating to the laborers that the fourth and fifth drills would be completed in no time. On the spur of the moment, Shivaji intervened with words of encouragement. "Our fifteen-minute recess awaits us. A breather we shall not wait for, a breather we shall strive for. We shall fulfill these duties that seem infeasible, for it will shower us with pride. Let us hold our heads high, I say, let us hold our heads high." From where the urge came to enlighten the laborers, Shivaji did not recall. However, whatever he voiced had the Indians performing the duties at high speed.

With the escalation of speed came the diminishment of endurance. Exhaustion was flooding the lungs, pummeling the heart, impairing the eyes, and restraining the muscles. Perspiration was coursing down Shivaji's forehead as he used his bare hands to drive the soil into the furrow. Every inch of his body was dampened. Perspiration was hazardous for the lacerations he sustained. The meeting between perspiration and laceration caused a burning sensation. When the salty fluid trickled inside the open wounds, Shivaji felt as if hundreds of pesky red ants were nipping his back. Unable to remove the perspiration, the coolies drudged, letting the fluid travel across their faces. Their hands were so involved in the cane preparation and soil topping that they couldn't spare a mere second to wipe or dab the wetness.

Not far from where Shivaji toiled, a line of blood was visible on the earth. It extended along the side of the drill which the team was laboring in. At first, Shivaji believed that the lacerations on his back had widened; therefore, it was his blood that started to dribble onto the soil. But when he rose to collect the foot-long stems from the children, his eyes were able to locate Venkatesh standing ten feet apart from him. Before laying the stems, Shivaji stole a glance to see how his friend's foot was faring. "The foot is a bloody mess," he said under his breath. More and more, his heart wept. He was disappointed with himself for not attending to the injured foot. Venkatesh was in severe pain, and his dependable friend was not there to provide him aid. However, it was not that simple. If Shivaji was to assist his childhood friend, his hands and feet were to be absent from the sugarcane fields for at least ten minutes. Those ten minutes were crucial for Shivaji. As a matter of fact, on several occasions, he felt the urge to guide Venkatesh to a shaded area, possibly under a banyan tree, and start examining the foot injury. Nonetheless, he understood that a considerable amount of labor could be performed within that time frame. Since the team was under a time limit where the laborers were to complete five drills before the arrival of recess, Shivaji decided to overlook the blood which stained the earth and his soul.

"Hold on, Venkatesh. When recess arrives, I will attend to you. But for recess to arrive, we must first complete the drills. All the hands and all the feet in this section are required to be constantly active. Seconds are not to be wasted. For if we do fail this mission, our entire team will have to undergo punishment," Shivaji said to himself before he felt one of his many lacerations split. He did not wince; he endured, focusing not on his pain but the possibility of Edward inflicting pain upon his team members for the sole reason of not fulfilling his demand.

Once again, far in the distance, sounds of the galloping horse vibrated in the ears of the numerous laborers. Fortunately, the Indian overseer and his team members were on the verge of completing the fifth drill. To expedite the process, Gurdayal ordered the women and children to assist by topping the remaining portions of the drill with soil. Approximately seven yards of the drill were uncovered. Fearful that Edward was closing in with immense speed, the women and children united with the men to finish the task. Hoes were handed to the women to use, while the children used their hands and feet to direct the soil into the furrows. The men labored as they had never labored before. Their strength and speed had escalated to a level that was never witnessed before. It was as if God had instilled the power of a bull in their bodies. All of the indentured laborers had a message for the oppressor: not to underestimate the peasant, for the peasant can overcome devised hindrances and hardships.

Before Edward was able to descend from the horse, the laborers had the fifth drill completed. Rest was needed for the laborers. Perspiration was gushing, blisters started to erupt, lacerations began to expand, and limbs chose to forfeit. If the Indians were to push themselves further, they were likely to faint or vomit. Gurdayal was dumbfounded when he viewed the drained laborers staring at the oppressor. Before Edward had the chance to discover that the laborers were idle, the Indian overseer roared at his team members. "Let's go, let's go... Proceed onto the sixth furrow. I don't want to see a useless peasant. You are to keep your hands and feet moving. I repeat, you are to keep the hands and feet moving."

Immediately, Shivaji and the others understood that if the command was not followed, Edward's desire to lash the coolies would be fulfilled. To escape the miseries of a scourged body was the initial and ultimate reason why the laborers had raised their exertion to overthrow the planter. But Edward usually found reasons to punish the laborers. His reasons usually consisted of lies. And that is what Gurdayal and his team members dreaded.

Strutting in the direction of the loyal peasant, Edward inspected the laborers in the field. He was pleased to witness that they had their hands full with slicing, placing, and topping.

"Welcome, Sirdar! I am pleased to inform you that we have fulfilled your order. The five drills that were asked for are waiting to be reviewed," Gurdayal said to the oppressor.

Edward grunted. He practically ignored the statement. As soon as he strolled past the loyal peasant, Edward started to count the number of drills completed. When his count arrived at five, he forcefully cracked the whip to grasp the attention of the toiling laborers. The laborers acted as if their ears were not able to detect the whooshing sound. Once again, Edward let his whip do the talking. Still, the laborers did not react. The oppressor attempted to capture, at least, one of the laborers with their hands or feet idle. However, what he longed for was close to impossible. What the Indians longed for was to experience how it felt to confute an Englishman. Furious that he was unable to hoax the coolies into responding to the sound of the whip, Edward proceeded to the drills. Standing close to the drills, he examined if the stems were properly covered in soil. Edward was not able to locate imperfection. All he needed was a flaw, even if the flaw was preposterous, to send his weapon on a rampage. "What kind of plantation owner am I? I can't even find a defect in the labor presented by the coolies," Edward asked himself.

The truth was that there were no defects for the human eye to witness. The oppressor knew the truth, but he was not willing to accept it. Villainous schemes were forming in his mind. He ordered Gurdayal to assemble his team. Once the laborers were massed, Edward let his asperity do the talking.

"Coolies, you can go for your fifteen-minute recess," said the oppressor, biting his tongue. What he said was not what he wanted to say. Though, a destructive idea had been formulated in his mind before he permitted a temporary stoppage in labor.

"When you coolies return from your recess, I will be here. Yes, I will be here to oversee you. I will be keeping a close eye on each and every one of you. You will have to complete fifteen drills by the next recess, which is during the afternoon. So that gives you four hours. Fifteen drills in four hours—I believe that is fair."

High in spirits, at last, the laborers had the opportunity to rest their sore bodies and itinerant minds. But the pleasures of a fifteen-minute resting period were spoiled by the challenge delivered by the oppressor. The Indian overseer and his teammates were expecting Edward to retaliate. The laborers had bruised his ego and butchered his esteem. The completion of the drills was a slap on his face. This slap was no ordinary slap. It was so loud that it echoed in the ears of the oppressor until he decided to seek revenge. Now that Edward placed the task of completing fifteen drills on the burdensome chests of the laborers, once again, he felt victorious.

"It is not possible to complete fifteen drills in four hours. The most that can be finished is eight to ten, but not fifteen," Edward kept repeating to himself.

The whip controlled by the planter was starving for flesh. To feed the whip with human skin and blood, Edward had to oversee the coolies as they struggled to finish the assigned task, which seemed undoable. Gurdayal led the laborers, who followed with long faces and moist eyes, in the direction of the baka trees.

The baka trees blessed the indentured laborers with shade. As the laborers stretched their arms and legs to relieve their fatigued joints and tendons, a light breeze came whirling into the shaded area. During the four hours of laboring in the fields, the laborers never encountered such a swooshing breeze. So, for them to feel the coolness in the air was gratifying. Most of the laborers were seated with their family and friends. Many were consuming whatever food and water they had stored inside their bags or clothes. Others were too exhausted to lift their hands or feet. In that case, they slept on the earth until the overseer bellowed that the fifteen-minute recess was over.

Instead of eating, resting, or sleeping, Shivaji immediately provided his assistance to the injured Venkatesh. With both Karthik and Lachmaiya close by, the firebrand promised them that his childhood friend would be able to last the day.

"Karthik, please stop crying. Appa will be fine. If you want to, you can watch how I get rid of Appa's boo-boo."

Karthik rubbed his wet eyes. Indeed, he was a child; however, that did not mean he was unable to feel. He knew the condition his father was in and understood how his father felt. Whatever pain Venkatesh suffered, Karthik could detect in his father's expressions. Dressed in rags, Shivaji did not care for his uniform. He was quick to discover a tear on his sleeve. Using his thumb and index finger, Shivaji further tore his sleeve. Soon his entire left sleeve was removed, uncovering his blemished skin. He instructed Lachmaiya to wash the blood from Venkatesh's feet. Even the touch of water on an injured foot resulted in agony. As he listened to his father shriek, Karthik became numb. Shivaji called his name, but there was no response. Shivaji snapped his fingers. Still, there was no response. "Karthik!" shouted Shivaji.

First, the child blinked. Then he diverted his attention to Shivaji.

"Karthik, I want you to close your eyes, cover your ears, and look somewhere else."

"Why, mama? Is this some kind of game?"

"Yes, Karthik, it is a game. For at least a minute you must not listen or see. If you place your eyes on appa, amma, or even mama, you will lose the game. Do you understand?"

"I do understand, mama."

No child, regardless of their age, should listen to a parent noisily groan or see a parent severely bleed, thought Shivaji. Once Karthik placed his hands on his ears and turned his body in the opposite direction, the firebrand began wrapping the piece of cloth around Venkatesh's foot. The faster his hands moved, the more his lacerations stretched. Yet Shivaji aimed not to showcase his discomfort. To get Venkatesh and his family members to feel as if they were indestructible, he needed to convince them that he was indestructible. Even Venkatesh held back the cries of misery when the cloth, which acted as a bandage, touched his swollen foot. As soon as the foot was covered, Shivaji asked his childhood friend if the bandage was a nuisance.

"It is not loose, nor is it tight; it's perfect. I am indebted to you. How will I ever repay you, Shivaji?"

"You will not have to, Venkatesh," replied Shivaji. "Now listen, if your foot starts bleeding again, you will have to let it bleed until the next fifteen-minute recess. As you know, I will not be able to respond to the bleeding once we set foot onto the sugarcane fields."

"That is true," replied Venkatesh in a low tone.

To lift his spirits, Shivaji uttered, "Don't worry. You will be fine."

Venkatesh was afraid. He knew that sooner or later, Edward would come to know of his wound. Though the husband was not afraid for himself, he was afraid for his wife and son. Venkatesh knew that if he kept pace with others in the fields, he and his family were safe. He was prepared to struggle with the countless laborers who bore lesions, swellings, blisters, and infections.

After the foot was sealed in cloth, Shivaji tapped on the shoulder of the abiding child. Karthik uncovered his eyes and freed his eardrums. He then turned to face his mama. Without saying a word, Shivaji embraced the child. Emotions started to circulate, leading to the formation of water in his eyes. The firebrand behaved as if he had never embraced Karthik before. Several minutes later, the child whispered into Shivaji's ears, "Mama, you can let go now."

For the final three minutes of recess, Shivaji isolated himself from everyone. He chose to rest under a mango tree. This mango tree was distant from its parents, siblings, cousins, friends, aunts, and uncles. The tree was apart from the rest. It was situated where Shivaji could not hear the sounds of the laborers moaning, the children wailing, or the overseers roaring. He did not even hear the whistling breeze, rustling leaves, singing birds, or chirping insects. Although Shivaji was visible to others, he imagined that no one could see him.

For the first time since he had placed his foot on the estate, the firebrand was at peace. Undisturbed by his surroundings, Shivaji embraced the state of privacy. It was his chance to reflect on the past. He remembered the moment when he was eight years of age and his appa let him wedge clay to form a pot. The hard-headed Muthuraman incessantly scolded his son whenever he performed his tasks differently. "Appa never changed the instructions, nor did he want others to change them. His set instructions were to be followed," Shivaji explained to himself.

As images of Muthuraman seated on the front porch of their household flashed, Shivaji regretted shattering his appa's hopes and desires of molding him into a potter. Then, as his tears dribbled, Shivaji went from his appa to his amma. He was grateful to Lord Almighty for providing him with such a warm-hearted amma. Considerate and understanding, she stood beside her son at all times, even if it meant disagreeing with her husband.

Shivaji dwelled upon the moments when his amma reasoned and feuded with Muthuraman. Whatever Shivaji wanted to voice to his father, his amma voiced on his behalf. The memory of his amma clashing with her husband for Shivaji's desire to become a fisherman affected the heart of a son who secretly longed to meet his parents. He was not disowned as the son of the Nair family because of his amma's four-week battle. In those four weeks, his amma strived to convince her husband that Shivaji's decision to commit his life to fishing and selling had to be accepted.

Muthuraman was stubborn; however, after thirty days, he succumbed. He was forced to accept his son as a menial fisherman since his wife decided not to eat or drink for three consecutive days. The sacrifices that his amma had made were appreciated by Shivaji. But these sacrifices were at times hazardous for his amma's welfare. No son wanted his mother's stomach to wail for food or her relationship with her husband to be contaminated.

Before Shivaji lingered deeper into his memories of how selfless his amma was—a trait that had been passed from mother to son—he redirected his thoughts to his sisters, whom he seldom reflected upon since departing from his motherland. Shivaji cursed himself for never landing on the adolescent ladies who trusted and respected their anna. His spirits lifted as he recalled the moment when his sisters asked for a tour of the market.

Both had visited the market with appa on several occasions. But whenever they did, Muthuraman never asked if they wanted sugar treats. The truth was that sugar treats were cherished by Indian children and adolescents. The sisters had a sugar craving, but both were too reluctant to ask Muthuraman. With their anna, though, it was less stressful. So, one fine afternoon, when the brother led his sisters into the market, both quickly asked for sugar treats, knowing that Shivaji would never refuse. The instant memory of returning home that day with empty pockets compelled Shivaji to smile.

After relishing that tiny pinch of happiness, he was prepared to include the deceased Vyjanti in his emotional reverie. As soon as he began to receive an image of his wife dressed in a yellow sari, a familiar sound resonated in his ears. At first, Shivaji ignored it. The sound was of no importance to him. But seconds later, his ears detected vibration again. It was a voice—a voice that called for someone. Though, who was being called, Shivaji did not know. Shifting his attention from the past to the present, he carefully listened to the words and who they were for.

"Shivaji... Shivaji, where are you?"

At the sound of his name, Shivaji lifted himself from the earth. His heart pounded, and his nerves tensed. He did not want to accept the fact that someone was uttering his name. "Shivaji...You must return."

At last, Shivaji realized that his presence was required in the fields of enslavement. The fifteen-minute recess had ended.

Shivaji did not waste time. He dashed to the fields in search of Gurdayal, whom he believed had called him. As he sprinted toward the indentured laborers, he felt an ache in his heart for abandoning the recollections and imaginings of his beloved wife. Since his arrival on the islands, the widower had spent less time reflecting upon Vyjanti. Deep within, he began to believe that the oppressors were on a mission to separate his deceased wife from his attention and rumination. "How can I not think of Vyjanti? Should I not be thinking of her constantly? Instead of blaming the enemy, I should be blaming myself," murmured Shivaji as he chastised himself for the unforgivable sin.

When he arrived on the scene, Shivaji felt as if someone was carving his flesh with a keen blade. The lacerations were once again troubling the firebrand. While he tried to catch his breath, Shivaji noticed that his team members had not begun placing and covering the stems. Several of the indentured laborers were just arriving from their fifteen-minute recess. It seemed to Shivaji that recess had ended only moments ago.

"Who was the person that called my name?" Shivaji pondered. He did not know why someone had called for him when his presence was not required in the fields. Also, being called during recess was unlikely. It was during recess that laborers demanded to be undisturbed. These were the only moments that Indians had to themselves. Nevertheless, Shivaji was certain he had heard a voice calling his name. Was it male or female? Shivaji was not sure. Could it have been a child, perhaps Karthik? Or did the voice belong to Edward, who was likely in search of the firebrand to flog him? Again and again, Shivaji associated the voice with a person, without considering that it might have been his own conscience.

His eyes then fell upon Gurdayal. Instantly, he assumed the Indian overseer might have an answer. He was quick to ask, "Did you call for me?"

The question left Gurdayal puzzled. "What are you saying?"

"Earlier, during recess, did you call my name?"

"No, Shivaji, I did not."

"I was seated a bit far from the rest of the peasants. Do you know where the mango tree is?"

"Yes, I do. But I never go there."

"Well, that is where I was resting. Are you sure you did not call for me?"

"I did not. Nor did I send anyone to fetch you," replied Gurdayal.

The Indian overseer noticed how strained Shivaji had become. "Shivaji, what is the matter?"

"I was under the mango tree, adrift in past memories, and then I heard someone utter my name. At first, I thought it was you."

Gurdayal did not let the firebrand finish, "I am telling you, Shivaji, I did not call your name. This is the first time I have laid eyes on you since we left for the fifteen-minute recess."

"Then, who was it?"

"Please, don't tell me the sirdar was calling for you?"

"I am not sure. Though I doubt it was him. If it had been, he would have let his whip do the talking."

When the Indian overseer announced that his team members should resume their duties, Edward was present at the scene, his face radiating malevolence. He was to act as a judge, ready to punish any laborer for wrongdoing. No signs of tiredness or listlessness were to be detected by Edward, for if they were, the flesh of the laborer was sure to be torn by the whip. The indentured laborers knew what Edward demanded. Most of them felt anxious in their stomachs. The hands and feet of some began to quiver. Some were drenched in sweat and tears before the drudgery even commenced. The laborers were to perform without ceasing. They were to commit no mistakes.

Shivaji believed that as long as his limbs were mobile, there should be no reason for the oppressor to apply his weapon. "No matter what happens, I will not stop my hands from laying and covering the stems," Shivaji muttered.

As the laborers toiled, Shivaji risked eye contact with his childhood friend. His eyes met Venkatesh's. Not once did his hands stop moving. Believing the oppressor might discover Venkatesh's injured foot, Shivaji felt compelled to signal his friend to keep his hands and feet moving. He did not want to see Venkatesh lashed. He did not want Lachmaiya to see her husband beaten. And he certainly did not want Karthik to witness his father's suffering. Shivaji, ten feet apart from his friend, kept his glances consistent.

Meanwhile, Venkatesh shoveled dirt into the furrow. Then, without warning, Edward struck. His whip cut into Shivaji's flesh. Over and over, Edward hit the firebrand. The new lacerations mingled with old ones, forming a portrait of misfortune on Shivaji's body.

"Coolies, this is an example of what occurs under my rule. The firebrand is focusing on others instead of himself. He needs to concentrate on his duties, not the duties of others," said Edward, with the loyal peasant translating. "I will not strike once; I will strike five times, so the coolies understand. Focus on completing the drills. Don't forget, you have four hours to finish fifteen drills."

Looking at his childhood friend, Shivaji felt more wounded than by the five lashes he received. He did not want Edward to discover Venkatesh's injury. But his wandering eyes had unintentionally exposed his friend. From then on, Edward was determined to watch the childhood friends, desperate to find errors.

"God, what have I done? I have placed my friend in danger," whispered Shivaji. "I ask the creator, protector, and transformer of the world to shield Venkatesh and his family from harm."

Edward and his weapon were both merciless. If a laborer uttered a word, the whip was applied. It did not matter if the word related to work. The oppressor forbade Indian languages within his realm. If a laborer used even a second to wipe perspiration from the forehead, the whip was used. The oppressor wanted all hands and feet engaged only in labor. Removing sweat, stretching, veiling sensitive areas, or signaling teammates was prohibited. If a laborer looked at Edward, the whip was applied. Edward demanded that laborers lower their eyes and heads when addressed. This behavior fed his pride and confidence, making him feel like the prime example of how an Englishman should be treated by Indians.

If a laborer halted, the whip was applied. A full stop was the worst offense. Though uncommon, exhaustion sometimes forced a pause. When Edward noticed, the whip was used viciously. Despite toiling correctly, Shivaji endured the whip tearing his flesh. No matter how hard he worked, Edward identified errors, often unjustly. Edward despised Shivaji's vitality, audacity, and defiance. Deep down, Edward knew he could never match Shivaji's strength. He tried to annihilate that feeling, but failed. Whenever Edward set eyes on Shivaji, envy turned to exasperation.

Earlier, when Shivaji was unaccustomed to flogging, each hit increased the pain. Now, accustomed to punishment, each strike hurt less. So when the oppressor struck, Shivaji did not flinch. "I'd rather have my flesh torn than see Venkatesh and his family battered," Shivaji resolved.

When Edward ended the punishment, Shivaji stole another glance at his childhood friend. The glimpse lasted seconds, leaving him unable to interpret what he saw. When the whip landed on another peasant, a loud cry resonated, causing heads to tilt, eyes to wander, and ears to perk. While Edward lashed another, Shivaji saw that Venkatesh's foot was bleeding through the bandage. Uncontrollably, Shivaji envisioned horrendous outcomes. He wished he could take Venkatesh's place.

After several hours, the laborers completed seven drills—a respectable number to the Indians—but the Englishman remained displeased. "Don't be proud of what you have accomplished. By now, I expected ten drills," said Edward, crushing their confidence intentionally. "Seven drills? Shameful. I, Edward Stanfield, plantation owner, will not let this slide. To extract better performance, I will use the whip more frequently and severely."

The pace of the laborers intensified with the swish of leather and high-pitched cries. Never before had they labored so excessively, been lashed so relentlessly, or pressured so nervously. Despite loyal peasants and innocent children, Edward ensured everyone was whipped.

Because Edward shadowed the laborers, Gurdayal was demoted from overseer to field hand and translator. He did not let the change bruise his pride. Actually, had he overseen with Edward watching, Gurdayal would have been assaulting teammates. Taking the backseat was preferable.

As Shivaji passed the loyal peasant, he felt compelled to convey the urgency for Venkatesh. Seeing his friend hobbling, he knew something had to be done. Five Indian men used hoes for drills; the rest used hands and feet to move the soil. The bodies outnumbered the tools provided by the Stanfield brothers. Gurdayal, unaware of Venkatesh's injury, needed to be guided. Shivaji wanted him to hand a hoe to Venkatesh, the tool that relieved discomfort by reducing kneeling and the use of bare hands and feet.

Transferring the message was nearly impossible. At all times, Shivaji felt Edward breathing down his neck. Whipping no longer stung, but speaking risked Venkatesh's punishment. With an hour remaining until the next recess, the laborers completed twelve of fifteen drills. This time, Edward appeared pleased, but credited only himself.

"If I were not the planter, if I were not overseeing, you coolies would still be on the eighth drill. It was I who drove you to labor as if your life depended on it," said the oppressor, swaggering for inspection. "Well, three drills remain. Let's not waste time."

For the peasants to listen to his boastful dialogue, Edward allowed them to pause their work briefly. While Gurdayal translated, the laborers absorbed the heedlessness Edward had poured upon them. Among the twenty-five laborers on the scene, no one dared to raise a voice. In Shivaji's case, the words slipped in one ear and out the other. He was too concerned for Venkatesh to worry about the sayings of a pompous Englishman.

As the laborers resumed their duties, Venkatesh realized that his foot was starting to go numb. He felt as if the foot had been severed from his leg. Though, in reality, the foot was present—and above all, it needed to be hidden. To disguise the blood-covered foot, Venkatesh buried it in the piles of dirt near the furrows. Soon, the redness on the bandage blended with the color of the soil, dark brown.

When her husband was seen performing this desperate act, Lachmaiya was constrained to hold back her tears. Eventually, she could not contain them. Silent tears ran down her face. An impulse within pressed her to unleash a vociferous cry, but she suppressed it, and that is exactly what she did.

While assisting with the transferring of the stems, Karthik's course shifted between his amma and his appa. First, he collected the hacked stems from his amma. Then, he rushed over to his appa to deliver the cane. While fulfilling his duties as the child peon, Karthik never looked toward the injured foot. The child knew that his appa was injured, but Lachmaiya had instructed him to focus on his assigned duties.

As a wife, Lachmaiya feared her husband might faint or collapse from excessive blood loss. As a mother, she feared her son might commit a blunder and fall under the oppressor's scrutiny. Her back was coated with fresh welts from lashes she had received for monitoring her son and husband. She struggled to fix her eyes on the stems. Her apprehensions for Venkatesh and Karthik outweighed her pain from the whip and lacerations.

Whenever the whip scraped her flesh, Venkatesh felt a surge of rage. During those moments, he wanted to grab a handful of dirt and fling it at Edward, but he knew that if he acted on his anger, the situation could worsen for him, his wife, and his child. Venkatesh, who had several welts of his own, was surprised that, even with Edward nearby, his wound had not yet been discovered. His teammates, aware of his situation, remained silent. Awareness did not result in assistance. None dared endure lashes for someone not blood-related.

The one person who did not hesitate to act for others was Shivaji, silently praying for the expected moment not to arrive. A feeling stirred within him, signaling him to be prepared.

At last, the injured foot was spotted by Edward. The dirt on the bandage was disturbed by seeping blood. Lachmaiya's vigilant eyes noticed Edward probing Venkatesh. She trapped her voice, refusing to alert her husband that Edward was closing in. When her child returned to fetch the sliced cane, Lachmaiya seized his arm and whispered for him to stay still. Karthik obeyed, silent.

As Edward walked alongside the furrow, not a single laborer dared lift their head. All Indians pretended to be engrossed in their labor. Shivaji tracked Edward's footsteps with his ears. He sensed the oppressor's figure nearing. Soon, the intimidating shadow was visible. Shivaji expected the whip to bite into his flesh, but it did not. Gradually, Edward walked past Shivaji. A sigh of relief did not escape him. His heartbeat continued racing, and his perspiration continued dripping. Shivaji felt nervous as he watched Edward approach his childhood friend.

From the corner of his eye, Venkatesh saw the oppressor and worked faster, placing stems into the furrow to divert Edward's attention. Though he worked swiftly, Venkatesh did not realize that the bandage on his foot had turned from brown to red. Edward's footsteps halted once he arrived next to Venkatesh. Not once did the Indian lift his face. Venkatesh kept toiling as if Edward did not exist.

Edward scratched his bristled chin, feigning casualness. Several times, his eyes locked on the wound. Venkatesh was squatting, his left foot fully exposed. Abruptly, a boisterous cry erupted across the sugarcane fields. Edward brought his leathered boot down on Venkatesh's foot. The pain was excruciating. Venkatesh wept silently, refusing to call for aid. He did not want Shivaji or his family intervening.

Seconds later, Edward stomped again, this time shifting his entire weight onto Venkatesh's foot. "Oh, have I stepped on your foot? Well, if I have, I am sorry," said Edward mockingly. The shrieks grew louder, the torment escalated. Still, Venkatesh did not ask for help. Lachmaiya and Karthik wept silently, glancing at Shivaji, who forcefully swatted at a pile of dirt to shove into the furrow, dominated by indignation.

Meanwhile, Edward repeatedly trampled the wound. The laborers could no longer maintain focus. Venkatesh's high-pitched screams distracted everyone, and the pace of their work slowed until all attention was on the oppressor and his victim. Lachmaiya fell to her knees, shins against the ground, hopelessly folding her hands, begging for help. The Indian men and women pretended not to notice. Deep inside, they felt pity, guilt, rage, and worthlessness—the last because they could not aid Venkatesh. No one was willing to risk punishment for helping a fellow laborer.

With the laborers frozen in place, including Shivaji, Lachmaiya was immensely disturbed. "Is there not a single man on this team with the fortitude to stop the Englishman?" she shouted. She looked at her workmates. The gathered women avoided her gaze, ashamed. "Sisters, what has happened to the men? Do all the men wear bangles now?" Lachmaiya's words bit like venom, instantly affecting the men.

Gurdayal, who had remained inconspicuous, felt humiliated. He wanted to tap Edward's shoulder, telling him to end the cruelty, but his selfish personality restrained him. With Gurdayal and his team idle, Lachmaiya decided to act alone. Before moving, she gave Shivaji an angry, disappointed stare, then turned to her child. "Karthik, I want you to sit down."

The child obeyed immediately.

"Now I want you to cover your eyes."

"Why?"

"Karthik, cover your eyes. This is not the time or place for questions," Lachmaiya's voice rose.

The child obeyed.

"You must not move from where you are seated. Do you understand?"

"Yes, amma," replied Karthik.

"Listen carefully. If you hear amma or appa scream, do not open your eyes or move an inch."

Karthik absorbed her instructions silently.

"God, please rescue your devotee from the hands of this sinner," cried Venkatesh. When Edward heard him speak in Tamil, his mind raced. He quickly believed that Venkatesh was uttering swearwords—or perhaps begging for help. To respond, Edward rammed his boot deeper into the soil, crushing Venkatesh's foot beneath it. The victim's shrieks turned wild, no longer human but like an animal on the verge of slaughter. All the tendons and bones in the foot were pulverized. He felt as if his foot had been dismembered. In reality, it was deformed. Venkatesh hovered between consciousness and unconsciousness.

As his eyelids flickered, he saw flashes of Lachmaiya advancing closer. With ineffectual hands, he tried to motion her to turn back. He did not want her to fall into Edward's hands. But with the indentured laborers frozen, Lachmaiya became desperate. She had one option: snatch a hoe from one of the Indians and charge toward Edward.

Shivaji could hardly believe his eyes. Never before had he seen such ferocity and courage in Lachmaiya. A thrill surged through him, and his feet tensed for action. This was it. This was his call. All eyes watched Lachmaiya as she approached the oppressor.

Edward kept his eyes fixed on her from the moment she left the line of women cane slicers. He released the pressure on Venkatesh's foot, shifting focus to the armed woman.

I'd rather watch Lachmaiya than the unarmed Venkatesh, thought Edward. In his eyes, she was a threat because she possessed a weapon.

"Gurdayal, you foolish Indian, where are you?" bellowed Edward, eyes never leaving Lachmaiya. He did not want to risk being struck by the hoe. Within seconds, Gurdayal arrived, jittery. In his years on the plantation, he had never seen an Indian wield a weapon at an Englishman.

"Sirdar, how may I assist you?"

"Tell this shrew to lower the weapon, or else..." Edward's words faltered. Though he did not admit it, he was nervous. Being struck on the head by a ten-pound hoe was frightening.

Gurdayal warned Lachmaiya that the oppressor wanted her to abandon the hoe, explaining that her boldness would have severe consequences. "Stop. This is insanity. If the situation worsens, these Englishmen will not spare you, Venkatesh, or Karthik," he said.

Even after the warning, Lachmaiya refused to yield. "I will not abandon the weapon until my husband is freed," she declared hoarsely, circling Edward like a vulture eyeing a corpse.

Soon, Edward anticipated her attacking with the hoe. He knew his whip was no match, but also knew he was faster, stronger, and cleverer. With the leathered weapon ready, Edward waited for a chance to flay her.

"Gurdayal, what is she saying? Why does she still hold the weapon? Has she not obeyed me?" Edward's nervousness pushed him to bombard Gurdayal with questions.

Gurdayal replied as best he could, "Sirdar, she is unwilling to comply. She wants her husband freed."

"Gurdayal, if I had a rifle, I would have freed him immediately."

The loyal peasant flinched at the menacing words.

While this unfolded, Shivaji tiptoed within eight feet of Edward and Lachmaiya. He moved silently, unsure whether his mission was to reason with Lachmaiya or attack Edward physically. Before he could decide, the unexpected occurred.

"Let go of the hoe," Venkatesh said to his wife. With the limited power he possessed, Venkatesh signaled his wife to return to her field position. Since Venkatesh could not rise from the ground due to his incapacitated foot, his hand motions became an indicator for Lachmaiya to retreat from the danger she had placed herself in.

Lachmaiya understood that she could not withdraw. She had come too far, fallen too deep into the pit, to rescue her husband. Her aggressive movements, hateful expressions, insolent tone, and decision to intimidate with the hoe were, in Edward's view, unforgivable. Lachmaiya gripped the hoe firmly, looking directly into the eyes of the oppressor. Edward reviled the act.

"No Indian is to look me in the eyes with despise," he whispered as the troubled Lachmaiya retreated out of his view. Anxiety besieged the oppressor as he watched Lachmaiya inch toward his rear. Edward believed she intended to knock him senseless from behind. Before she vanished from sight, he felt compelled to act. Nervous tension forced him to release his hand, and he swung his whip with immense force in Lachmaiya's direction. Without aiming, he struck her unmercifully.

When the leather chafed her face, Lachmaiya lost her grip on the hoe, and both she and the disloyal weapon collapsed onto the soil, with no intent to rise. Discovering her face slit and bloodied, she wailed, pressing it into the dirt to hide it from her husband. Meanwhile, Venkatesh had no choice but to shout at the top of his lungs, pleading for someone to intervene, to rescue him, to end the misery.

His prayers were answered. Prepared to strike again, Edward did not expect any laborers to intercede. He did not imagine that a firebrand still lingered in the sugarcane fields. With no time to plan, Shivaji raced toward the oppressor, shoulders bent forward, and drove them into Edward's ribcage. Both men crashed heavily to the ground.

For Edward, the sudden impact knocked the wind out of him. Panic set in. For a moment, he did not know what had happened or where he was. He felt his life being drawn out. Then, severe pangs of pain struck—sharpest around his ribs. The suffering forced him to spew abusive words and vicious threats, but they did not disturb the firebrand, who did not comprehend them.

Shivaji stood, shoulders erect, as if the collision had never occurred. Not a scratch marred his body. The indentured laborers watched in disbelief, mouths open, eyelids stretched, goosebumps raised. Most had halted their work to witness the extraordinary scene. Hesitantly, some advanced slowly for a better view. Gurdayal bit his tongue, struggling to believe the scene was real. He felt pleased that the Englishman who had tormented Indians was now suffering at the hands of one of their own. But he also recognized the potential cost—perhaps death. With that realization, Gurdayal approached Shivaji.

"Shivaji, what have you done? You have to leave. Leave this instant."

With eyes burning with vengeance and nostrils flared, Shivaji glared at the loyal peasant, choking him with the intensity of his stare. Gurdayal retracted his steps. He decided not to mediate. Shivaji then rested his gaze on Edward, who searched the ground for his whip. Each time he tried to lift himself, the pangs forced him back. He did not anticipate the whip was now in Shivaji's possession. When he saw it moving before his expressionless face, he was dumbfounded.

"No...Firebrand...You cannot...You must not...Please," muttered Edward, squirming in desperation.

The first lash delivered by Shivaji was the justice the Indians needed, a therapy to lessen their suffering. The shriek released by Edward served as relief for the oppressed.

"This single lash does not atone for the sins you committed against my fathers, mothers, brothers, sisters, and children," said Shivaji, raising the whip for another strike. "God will not punish me for lacerating a demon. You are a demon, and to punish a demon is just."

As Shivaji lashed persistently, the indentured laborers felt born for this day, born to witness a repressed Indian overpowering an English oppressor. The scene instilled a new perception in their lives: to no longer be abused, deceived, reformed, or exploited. Whether the Indians would act on this perception remained in the hands of destiny.

The sugarcane field resounded with Edward's ear-piercing cries. Shivaji did not relent, again and again striking through clothing into flesh. The pain Edward had inflicted on the Indians was now reciprocated. Shivaji recalled past struggles and tragedies: the investigation aboard the vessel, the forced consumption of meager meals, the whips and batons, the abduction of women, the storm at sea, the unity of Indians from different castes, the dog biscuits incident, Vyjanti climbing the railing, and her plunge into the ocean.

As the images flooded his mind, Shivaji paused, lowering the whip. His hand descended to his side. Emotionless, he ruminated on the absence of his wife to prevent this precipitous act.

"Shivaji...Shivaji...Shivaji!" Gurdayal called. With a snap of his fingers, he gained Shivaji's attention.

Disoriented, Shivaji took in the scene: Venkatesh drenched in blood, sweat and tears inching toward Lachmaiya, who made effort to conceal the scar on her face, and Venkatesh, drenched in blood, sweat, and tears. He glanced at Karthik, who was still obeying the blind-and-deaf game.

Gurdayal seized Shivaji and moved him away from Edward, who remained moaning on the ground.

"I will not ask why you did what you did. I will not lecture or criticize. All I want is for you to leave. Shivaji, you must return to the hut."

"Why shall I run? Why shall I hide? I am prepared to face the consequences."

"Shivaji, understand. You have placed yourself in a hostile situation. You must leave before Edward rises."

"I do not fear the outcome. The fifteen lashes I administered are insufficient. Edward deserves more. All abused laborers should participate in this necessary act."

Gurdayal, exasperated, tugged at Shivaji's shirt, propelling him toward the Eastern section. "Son, I am your father's age. I know what is best. Leave now."

Shivaji understood the paternal concern. Though Gurdayal and Muthuraman differed in personality, Shivaji felt the roommate's concern as a father's concern—like his father back in India when he and Vyjanti departed.

Walking toward the huts, Shivaji did not look back. He did not observe Edward attended by Edwin, or Gurdayal ordering the laborers back to work, or Venkatesh and Lachmaiya concealing their injuries for Karthik's sake. He felt no need to hurry and no fear of Edward's retaliation. Shivaji continued until the sounds of commands, cries, and frantic movement faded.

"Vyjanti once said the hardest feeling to attain is peace," Shivaji whispered to himself. "But why do I feel at peace with myself, my surroundings, and the situation?"

As he neared the Eastern section, memories surged: boarding the vessel, British inspections, meager meals, labor, lashings, abductions, storms, unity among Indians, dog biscuits, and Vyjanti's plunge into the ocean. He reflected on the hole, the dungeon, and the auction. He relived the oppressor's cruelty, the plow horse's stubbornness, saving a child, encounters with warriors, humiliation before English invitees, laborers' teamwork, and finally, Edward's thrashing by Shivaji.

The trance ended. Shivaji returned to the present, arriving in front of his hut. He stood in the doorway, tears streaming down his face. The past fifty-three days felt like a dream, though in reality, it was not a dream: deprived of freedom, justice, rest, caste, religion, motherland, a guru, a wife, and life itself.

Helpless and hopeless, Shivaji closed the door behind him.

"I will kill that bloody Indian. How dare he...How dare he!" shouted Edward, assisted to his feet by Edwin.

"Brother, he is not here. Please, calm down."

"Where is he? That arsehole? No Indian has ever used a whip on me. He will not live to see tomorrow. I will fill his chest with bullets."

"Do not let rage control you. He will be punished. We can sell him to another planter or at auction," said Edwin.

Edward ignored Edwin, examining his bloodied clothes. "I just purchased this shirt and pants. Look what that bastard did. Fifteen lashes—where is he hiding? He is a coward."

"Brother, head to the cottage. The laborers will finish the work. Before sunset, I will join you in the Western section," Edwin advised.

But Edward wanted conflict, not peace. "Yes, I will go to the Western section. Then I will enter Ernest's cottage."

Edwin intervened. "Brother Ernest is not present. You have no right to enter."

"I have no right, but I have a reason," Edward said, followed by a harsh laugh.

In the distance, Gurdayal acted as if nothing occurred, avoiding eye contact with the Stanfield brothers. Repeatedly ordering his team, the Indian overseer needed to show Edward he was uninvolved.

"Gurdayal, bring your arse over here," said Edward with a loutish attitude in his voice.

The Indian overseer's heart leaped into his throat. He understood that a sirdar's command was not to be disregarded. At his frail age, Gurdayal knew better than to get himself into trouble, so he responded to the call instantly. "Yes, sirdar — how may I assist you?"

"Where were you when that swine went on a rampage? Why did you not intervene? How come you did not stop him? Did you not hear the whooshing of the whip?" Edward bombarded the loyal peasant with questions.

Gurdayal felt the urge to cover his ears. He could hear the oppressor. In fact, he understood the questions. But he was stunned that Edward did not know his whereabouts during the entire incident. So he did what most people in his situation would do — Gurdayal played dumb. "Sirdar, I was far in the distance when it happened. Once I heard the cries —" Gurdayal paused to look at the oppressor, to see if he would be offended by the mention of his squealing in pain.

"Why have you stopped? Continue," Edward urged the loyal peasant.

Feeling relieved, Gurdayal answered, "As I was saying, once I heard the cries I rushed to the scene. When I arrived I pushed and pulled, I shouted and rebuked, but still I could not stop him from lashing you. I must apologize, sirdar. I am not as robust as before. My strength does not match that of an adolescent."

Edward scratched the bristles on his face. With a befuddled expression he said, "As far as I can recall, I did not see or hear you."

"But I was there, sirdar."

"Anyways, where is the firebrand? Where has he fled?"

Gurdayal swallowed. He was reluctant to tell Edward of his roommate's whereabouts. When Edward noticed the delay in the reply, he landed a violent blow on the loyal peasant's temple. The forceful collision left Gurdayal's brain ringing.

"You bastard — you know where he is. Where have you sent him?" The oppressor seized the loyal peasant's neck. The vicious action prompted Edwin's involvement. "Brother, leave Gurdayal. You must not treat him as the culprit. He is not the one that harmed you." The words slid off Edward as he stared directly into the loyal peasant's eyes. "Tell me where he is, or else…"

Gurdayal could not withhold the truth: the clasp on his neck tightened until he spoke. "I have ordered him to return to his hut."

"How sure are you he will return? What if he is on the run? What if he has left the plantation?" once again Edward tossed questions at the loyal peasant.

"No, sirdar. He will not run or hide. Believe me: the firebrand is on the Eastern section of the plantation." Gurdayal's words were accepted. Finally, the oppressor removed his hands from the loyal peasant's marred neck.

"Now listen to what I have to say. I want you to handle the coolies till Edwin and I return. All field hands are to work till sundown. Do you understand?"

Gurdayal felt an urge to slap himself. Once again remorse mixed into his system. He knew he should not have provided Edward with that information, but he also knew that if he had not disclosed Shivaji's location the oppressor would have strangled him. "Yes — I understand, sirdar. There is no need for you to leave the sugarcane fields. I promise he will be disciplined for what he has done. I will discipline him. If you want him flogged, I will flog him — thirty lashes, fifty lashes, one hundred lashes, whatever you prefer. But please, sirdar, I beg you — let him live."

The desperation in the loyal peasant's voice was ignored. "Gurdayal, you handle the coolies; I will handle the firebrand." Edward bit off the last words as an order, then climbed onto his stallion. Mounted on separate horses, the Stanfield brothers bolted westward. Gurdayal watched them go with a faint heart. "Why are they heading west?" he asked himself. "The hovels are in the Eastern section."

There were no footsteps to grace the surface of the eight-by-eight huts. There was no clinking or clattering of pots, plates and cups. No breeze stirred the branches of the stock-still trees. No crickets chirped. There was no child by the well splashing water; no adults sat by a doorstep engaged in conversation. To Shivaji, everything seemed inanimate. At first he felt the urge to speak to himself, but that recalled the frightful memories of "the hole" on Ship Elbe. He even entertained the idea of escaping the hut, the coolie line, the plantation and the island. After a careful assessment of the pros and cons, the firebrand abandoned the idea. He realized the cons far outweighed the pros. "I am confident I will not be seen departing the hut, the coolie line, or the estate; however, beyond the plantation are unknown routes, unknown animals, and unknown humans. To cross paths with a bloodhound or an English patroller is probable. And even if I run faster than the hounds and outwit the patrols, can I swim back to India?" Stressed by these floating notions, Shivaji tried to focus on his wife, parents, sisters and guru. But his mind kept reversing: images of the weapon landing on and scraping white skin kept returning.

Then unexpectedly Shivaji detected the hooves of trotting stallions. He rose from the earth where he had been settled and dashed to the hut door. Opening it from inside, he saw Edward and Edwin closing in. The distance between the Stanfield brothers and the hut was minimal. Shivaji had nowhere to flee. He knew that if he ran he would be captured in an instant. "Wait — why should I run?" he asked himself. He left the door open. The hut allowed only eight steps back. On his ninth backward step he collided with the wall. He felt his heart racing, though he did not know why. He felt wetness on his brow, though he did not know why. He felt his stomach flutter, though he did not know why. Should he escape, remain still, or defend himself? He did not know. Unaware of his forthcoming action, Shivaji impatiently awaited Edward and Edwin's arrival.

"Edwin, I need you to hitch the stallions," the tyrant said as he dismounted.

Edwin obeyed and led the horses to a nearby coconut tree. Edward eyed the open door for an ambush. He ushered Edwin to stand behind him. "The bloody Indian wants us to fall into his trap. He does not know who he's dealing with. A bullet from this barrel will obliterate him in seconds," Edward said as he unstrapped the Lee-Mitford rifle from his shoulder. Caressing the rifle as if it were a divine hand, he continued: "So Edwin, here's the plan: I will fire bullets inside the hut before we enter. The roaring shots will have the firebrand urinating in his pants. If we're lucky, one may strike him in the chest. If we hit him, any ambush will fall apart."

Unable to hold back, Edwin said, "Brother, I will take no part in this. I think I should leave."

"If I see you tiptoeing to the stallions, I will shoot you in the leg. I mean it; I am not fibbing. I don't care if you are my blood — you will bleed if you do not follow orders," Edward snapped.

Taken aback by his elder brother's heartless words, Edwin replied, "Brother, if you want to whip this firebrand then do so. If you want to boot him in the face, do so. If you want to force him to labour day and night, do so. There are many things besides shooting him."

"He deserves to be shot. We don't need his kind in the fields or on this plantation. We don't need a coolie who raises a whip on his planter or overseer. By flogging an Englishman he sets a bad example for the other fifty-two indentured labourers."

"Brother Ernest will ban you from the fields if you shoot this labourer. Did you not think of that?"

Edward erupted, "To hell with Brother Ernest — I am the planter now. What I say and do matters. I will send this firebrand to his grave. Never again will a coolie raise his hand on a Stanfield."

In the end Edwin lost the battle of reason with his brother. He did not want to join Edward in annihilating the firebrand, but he complied: he did not hold the fatal weapon.

A hush descended upon the coolie line. Not a word was uttered; not a footstep heard. Edward whispered to his brother, "Let's do this fast. We don't have much time — the light will fade." Edward nodded, secretly wishing the firebrand not to be inside. Then he aimed and fired. One shot after another echoed inside the hut, deafening across the plantation. The shots startled Gurdayal and the labourers in the Northern section. The loyal peasant felt his knees weaken and stumbled on the drill he was topping. Meanwhile, inside the hut, Shivaji lay face-down on the earth — no bullet had pierced his flesh. His head spun, his ears rang, and his hands trembled as he rose. Seconds mattered, but he still examined the ruin of his dwelling. Deformed pots, plates, cups and utensils lay scattered. The floor was littered with grass, hay, leaves and twigs where the walls had been punctured. Shivaji drew a finger along one of the many bullet holes, but that focus shattered when Edward barged inside, rifle in hand. Edwin, unarmed, was told to stay behind his brother at all times. Shivaji had seen a rifle before; he knew the death it could deliver. This was not a whip, club, dagger, spear or arrow — this weapon could kill.

"Now, what do we have here? The firebrand survived the hail of bullets. Isn't that a miracle?" Edward asked while he pointed the rifle at Shivaji. Before the oppressor could fire again, Shivaji charged. Three feet from Edward, the firebrand leapt. In a flash Shivaji was on top of him. Instead of punching Edward in the face or kneeing him in the ribs, he focused on seizing the rifle. The takedown freed Edward's finger from the trigger. As they tussled on the ground, Edwin panicked. Though his eyes watched, he was too afraid to act; he distanced himself from the trouble. Just as Edwin placed his feet outside the hut, Edward called, "Edwin! Help! For God's sake — get this Indian off me!"

Nervous and unsure where to place his hands, Edwin muttered, "Perhaps I should grab his arms. Or maybe push his chest." He had never intervened in a physical fight before, despite witnessing his elder brother lash labourers.

"Edwin, what are you waiting for? Kick him, punch him, choke him — do whatever you can!" Edward yelled as he struggled for the rifle.

With no time to deliberate, Edwin rushed the firebrand and seized him from behind. His arms wound like chains around Shivaji's torso. Once Edwin had him fastened, he lifted Shivaji off and away from Edward. Relief crossed Edward's face — one hundred and thirty pounds of weight were gone — but Edward didn't notice the rifle was no longer in his hands. While Edwin removed Shivaji, the firebrand tugged until the rifle was secure. Edward realized the weapon was gone and bellowed in outrage. Shivaji twisted, freed himself, and the flailing Edwin tumbled backward. With no obstacle, Shivaji slid his forefinger onto the trigger.

Once the finger rested, the rifle aligned with his shoulder, his head pressed to the stock, the barrel pointed at the oppressor, his left eye squinted for aim, Shivaji saw flashes. These were not visions of his life — not Vyjanti, not his parents or sisters. He saw an unfamiliar man running through a desolate forest with a firearm: running as if life depended on it, dodging trunks and stumps under a moonless sky, perspiration on his brow, anxious eyes, ragged breaths. The man stopped, muzzle to the ground; around him lay the unforgettable sight of dead bodies — stabbed flesh, pale faces, still eyes, dried blood and ravenous flies. Shivaji returned from the vision and met Edward's gaze — an act reviled by the oppressor, especially if done by an Indian. Yet even after the defiance, Edward did not immediately respond. For the first time Shivaji did not see outright hostility in the oppressor's eyes. "Perhaps Edward has accepted his defeat," Shivaji whispered.

Edwin, grasping at the moment, rose to prevent the shot. "Don't fire!" he shouted.

The phrase went unheard by Shivaji. He closed his eyes. "Pardon my sin," he whispered, then opened his eyes and pulled the trigger. The boom echoed; his eardrums felt as if they had exploded. Still holding the rifle, he lifted his eyes. Five feet away, Edward stood with a bullet lodged in the left portion of his chest. The firebrand had struck the centre of the heart. It was a shot meant to kill. How, when and where he had learned to hold, aim and fire — he could not recall. He was certain it was not learned in this life. How was I able to fire the bullet? he wondered. Simultaneously, both rifle and oppressor collapsed. Edwin darted past Shivaji to his brother with speed and strength, his knees scraping the ground. He felt no pain there — only for Edward, now inactive and bathed in blood. He seized his brother's hand, searched for a pulse. Nothing. He placed his fingers on Edward's neck — still nothing. Breathless, he rested trembling hands over the puncture on his brother's chest. Tears dribbled as he forced back a grievous wail. With no sign of movement, Edwin believed his brother was gone. "You have killed him. You bloody Indian — my brother is dead," he cried with a tone he had never used before.

Shivaji examined his hands in a daze. It seemed his mind had slipped. Though there was no blood on his palms, he believed there was. In a panic he wiped his hands on his tattered clothing. The blood seemed to remain. He was flustered; his senses tricked him. "This blood is not mine — it belongs to the devil I executed. It is the mark of the sin I have committed. I cannot remove it," he said aloud.

Without the rifle, Shivaji decided to leave the hut. He did not know where he was going nor whom he sought. All he desired was for his mind to stop racing, his heart to stop pounding, his eyes to stop watering, and his limbs to stop aching. He wanted to be saved. As he stepped outside, Edwin, who had lost control of his emotions, searched for the weapon. His hand found the stock and he lifted himself to his feet, face flushed with rage. Not in his senses, Edwin stormed after Shivaji. The sound of his footsteps warned the firebrand that danger approached. Shivaji deliberately neglected the threat; he chose to discard his life. His final wish was to be reunited with Vyjanti — wherever she might be: heaven, hell, or another life. As he held a memory of his wife's face, the rifle was aimed and the trigger was pulled.

BLAST!

PART 3

My Dear Suzy

Part 3- My Dear Suzy...

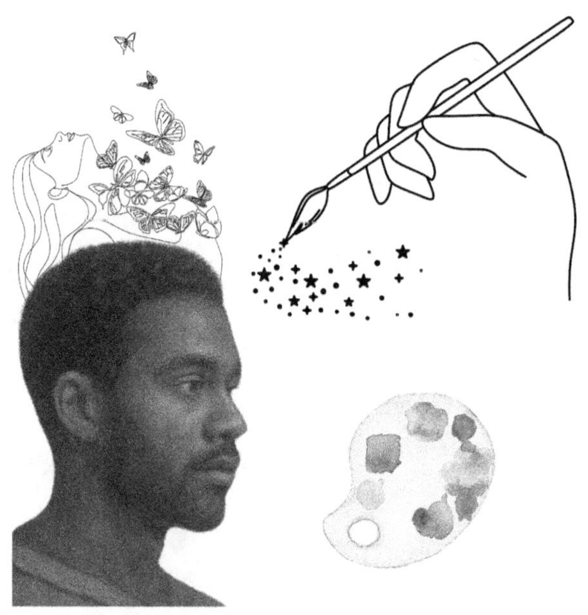

INTRODUCTION

Suzy! Hmm, that is perfect. Where this name came from, I have no clue. Perhaps, I saw it on a poster or heard it in an advertisement. Maybe, I came across it in a motion picture or read it in a novel. I apologize for not remembering where I saw, heard, or read your name. I am not the kind of person to name my personal belongings. It is not as if I name my ivy hat, polo t-shirts, cargo pants, casual slip-on shoes, or Fruit of the Loom underwear. Suzy, you are special. I will hold you close to my heart. I will share with you my innermost feelings. I will treat you as my dearest secret, never to be shared with others. Your status is that of a partner, my companion. If it were not for the respected Miss Yang, I doubt that you and I would have met. It was she who selected and presented you. Before I left to enter the world of university—teachers, students, classrooms, dormitories, roommates, exams, oral presentations, and visual arts—Miss Yang placed you in my hands. She told me to express my repressed feelings in the form of writing. In the numerous years that I have known Miss Yang, I have never ignored a single request she has made. So, I will write. I will write when the heart urges me to do so. Whenever I feel lonesome, I will come to you. Whenever I feel disheartened, I will come to you. Whenever I feel frustrated, I will come to you. And whenever I feel like venting, I will come to you. Wow! I have mentioned all the undesirable feelings. That is unfair. Don't worry, Suzy; I will also come to you whenever I feel content. It is not often that I feel content, but if that feeling does arise, I will ensure that you are the first to know. I am not like others who run to churches, temples, and mosques in search of God when life becomes miserable and then forget the path that leads to them once life returns to its normal state. I believe that God should never be forgotten but worshipped in both good and bad times. It is He who resides in our hearts; therefore, for a person to overlook God is surely egocentric and ungrateful. Suzy, you will not be forgotten. I will decorate you with ink, both when I am happy and unhappy. That's a promise.

By now, I am sure you must be wondering who Miss Yang is and what role she plays in my life. Well, she is my adoptive parent. At the age of fifteen, I was rescued by Miss Yang from the ruthless foster care system. That was when I first experienced how it feels to live in a home and to have a family. When I say family, I mean Miss Yang and Miss Yang only. Before I was adopted by this empathetic woman, she lived without a pet, without a child, without a husband. Miss Yang did not have a family of her own. Her husband departed from her life years ago. How he died, I never asked. Did I want to ask? Indeed, I did. However, whenever she talked about him, I sensed trauma in her voice. The water in her eyes instantly suppressed the questions I had. From within, she was devastated. And I believe she still is. Miss Yang does not have children of her own, which explains why she became an adoptive parent. As they say, it is primarily due to infertility that adults seek to embrace children who are not related to them. Miss Yang had no relation to my biological parents. She is not my aunt or grandmother, nor is she a distant relative. Despite all this, she still chose me to be a part of her life. Miss Yang, in my view, is an angel. She has fulfilled her role as a parent. If it were not for her, I would still be shifting from foster home to foster home. If it were not for her, I would never be properly fed or clothed. If it were not for her, I would have no education. It was because of her that I started attending classes instead of ditching them. She injected confidence into my system. The doubts and fears that I had amassed since childhood started to diminish. I realized that there was so much out there in the world to feel, learn, and experience. I am grateful that I have a roof over my head. I am grateful that I have clothes on my back. I am grateful that I am fed breakfast, lunch, and dinner. What no one else provided, Miss Yang did—and that was comfort. After sitting with numerous caseworkers, meeting numerous foster parents, living in numerous homes, and sharing beds with numerous homeless children, I forgot what comfort meant. But there is a God. And God has been favorable. Comfort was there—between the bedroom and me, between the television and me, between the house temperature and me, between the showers and me, between the refreshments and me. But the level of comfort I shared with Miss Yang was upsetting. I was her culprit. I was not able to fulfill my role as her son. There was very little interaction between us. As a mother, she wanted to share her thoughts and feelings. And whatever thoughts and feelings I had, she wanted them to be shared with her. When a conversation became personal, in a split second, I tuned out, paid no attention, and brushed off Miss Yang. I literally tried to keep the conversations as ordinary as possible. "Hi, hello, good morning, good afternoon, good evening, good night, how are you, how was your day, how was school, what do you want to eat, what would you like to drink, have you done your homework, have you cleaned your room, have you taken out the garbage," were the phrases that Miss Yang was limited to. I didn't want to treat Miss Yang with such a lack of respect. After all that she had done, poor Miss Yang is left with an unsociable son. But I feel as if my hands are chained to the walls of a dungeon. I am unable to heal the wounds and erase the scars that life has inflicted. It is because of these wounds and scars that I have been forced to place restrictions on my adoptive mother.

Without knowing them or seeing them, I still allow myself to be oppressed by disturbing thoughts. Questions such as who they are, where they live, what they do, and how they look are left hidden in the corner of my brain. But it is the question of why these parents abandoned, renounced, rejected, deserted, discarded, disowned, and ditched their son that forced him into isolation. I ask, how can a mother birth a child and dump him into the gutter, or leave him on the front porch of a house, or place him on the steps of a hospital, or toss him near a police station? I ask, how can a father not want to provide his child with the basic needs of life—shelter, food, and clothes? Suzy, the inability to understand at such a tender age eliminates any knowing of what situation the biological parents and forlorn child were in. Still, I want to know if those renouncers ever think about their child. Do they ever wonder if he is still alive—and if he is alive, where is he and how is he doing? Perhaps he was disowned because the mother was not supported by the father. Perhaps he was disowned because the mother was a teenager afraid of parenthood. Perhaps he was disowned because the parents were unable to financially support him. Perhaps he was disowned because they were overwhelmed with too many children. Or perhaps he was disowned because he was too ugly for this world to bear. Perhaps... Perhaps... Perhaps Malcolm was disowned because he was a mistake. Yes, I feel as if I was a mistake. My birth into this world was a big, fat mistake. Every time I write this, every time I say this, every time I think this, it destroys my soul. It urges me to believe that I am not wanted, that the life I live is unnecessary and unimportant. But then all I have to do is peek into the living room or dining room to secretly observe the angel, Miss Yang, whom God sent into my life. A glance at her and I feel as if I am wanted, I am needed, I am someone. There are times when I discreetly observe her for several minutes, which is plenty of time for my destroyed soul to rehabilitate. But now that I have left my house, neighborhood, and city to attend university, Miss Yang is not there to erase the anguish and frustrations that I encounter daily. So instead of relying on Miss Yang, I had to discover other solutions to cure the feeling of not being wanted. Suzy, you will not believe the things I did. Well, first and foremost, I wrote letters to Miss Yang. These letters were plain and simple, explaining how I fared in my classes and in the dormitory. Odd, isn't it? Even with the help of words and sentences, I was unable to express to Miss Yang what resided deep within my heart. In my spare time, I read biographies, wrote diary entries, and painted dreams. What I found truly surprising was that I befriended my roommates and classmates. Since I was never interested in forming relationships, I felt proud that I had friends. In group homes and high school, I was reluctant to communicate with others. In fact, in group homes, I did not even want to share a bed with another child. And in classrooms, I disliked sitting next to or across from a student. The problem I faced was that I did not want others to know that I was parentless. I felt as if I was not worthy of their friendship. In comparison to them, I was undesirable. Therefore, I neglected them, and in return, they neglected me. In all honesty, that is what I preferred. All that neglect discouraged my ability to interact. However, it encouraged my ability to concentrate. From high school onwards, I was able to focus on my studies. I was not out there experimenting with drugs and alcohol, flirting with blondes and brunettes, stealing soft drinks and chocolate bars, or partying at nightclubs and pubs. My focus was on the teachings and readings. I was not a topper, but I was sure to receive a minimum of three A's on my report cards. Suzy, I bet you will not be able to tell which subjects I received those A's in: English, History, and Art. I excelled in reading and writing, but I had this fear that one day sentences, commas, and periods would drag my life into the realms of apathy. My writings are restricted to only personal letters and journal entries. And my readings are restricted to memoirs and biographies. Honestly, I am not sure how I aced history class. I don't even know my own history—who my ancestors were, where they came from, and how they lived. Wait a minute! Let's not even go that far. I don't even know my own great-grandparents, grandparents, and parents. I ask myself: if I had a caste, what caste am I? If I belong to a religion, then what religion am I? Since I did not know my own history, it was intriguing to discover and learn about other people's caste, religion, and history. But it was not history that I chose to expand my knowledge in. My soul longed for art, my heart ached for art, my eyes searched for art, and my hands itched for art. It explains why I am a third-year student in the Fine Arts Diploma Program. Does it not?

Suzy, there is an unusual story behind how I was drawn into the world of art. It involves pastel paintings, a homeless person, and a withdrawn twelve-year-old. But first, let me properly introduce myself. With you as my companion, I don't feel hesitant about unveiling my name, gender, age, and status. Well, my name is Malcolm. Yes, it is Malcolm only, only Malcolm. I don't have a last name. I don't even know if I am legally a Yang. I remember the days when teachers used to ask students to print their full names on tests and assignments. Except for me, all the other students printed their first and last names on the front page. Some teachers were aware of my situation, while others were not. The ones that did not know requested that I print my last name on the top right-hand corner. I was pestered until my hand began to move. "Malcolm Only" is what I printed on the front page. Anyways, as my name hints, I am a male. My age is twenty-three. I am single, always prepared to mingle, but never desperate to mingle. I am slim-built and weigh one hundred and forty pounds. At five feet and seven inches, I like to believe that I am of average height. I have a straight, pointed nose, which is not common in my race. And I have curly black hair, which is definitely common in my race. The sideburns I flaunt descend to my earlobes. When I keep facial hair, it takes more than a couple of weeks for others to notice that I have a beard. And Suzy, it's not much of a beard; it grows in patches. I have a pair of eyes that my girlfriends say belong to a Shakespearean Romantic, whatever that means. To be clear, by girlfriends, I mean girls who are only friends. Lastly, I have a birthmark located in the middle of my hairless chest. Sometimes, I examine the birthmark in front of a mirror. It's shaped like a hoe—yes, the hand tool used for gardening. Well, there you go. I have given you plenty of information about who I am and how I look. Now let's begin the story of how paintings fascinated the twelve-year-old Malcolm.

From the day I was born to the day a caseworker told me that I had been adopted by Miss Yang, I was tossed from foster parent to foster parent. Even as a child, I felt unwanted. For most foster parents, I was a temporary plaything. When a plaything became tedious, he or she was returned to the foster care agency. The most I stayed at the various foster homes ranged from a week to six months. I remember once I was passed over to a destructive married couple who humiliated, cursed, and abused me. Day and night, both husband and wife were at war. Most of their battles were verbal, while some led to physical altercations. At the age of seven, I did not understand what the fights were about. Though amid the crying and shouting, I did hear my name uttered. As a kid, I had witnessed a considerable number of fights, I was exposed to the dirtiest and filthiest curse words, but I never imagined becoming a victim of cruelty. Then came the day when I was attacked with an unexpected blow to the face. The blow was so forceful that it left me unconscious. The mistake I committed was peeking inside the kitchen when I overheard the miserable wife shouting for help. The husband was not pleased with the act, therefore, in a fit of rage, he stormed toward me with his fist. The swollen eye was proof to my caseworkers that I was assaulted in that household. I was set free from that fighting cage and the animals it sheltered. I lived with those savages for a week, but the scar they engraved on my soul will last a lifetime.

Please forgive me, Suzy. On the verge of sharing how I was introduced to art, I steered the vessel onto a completely different path. I never thought I'd have so much to express, so much to share. I wish I had the time to reveal all my stories, but I don't. Still, I must disclose this story to you. I was in primary school when, for the first and last time, I met a hobo who did not beg or steal. Walking back from school to the temporary foster home I was placed in, I felt as if my feet were directed to his location by an unknown force. The man was indeed homeless. But unlike other homeless people, he did not seem to be addicted to drugs. He was no crackhead. His hands were stable, not tremulous, his face did not have cuts or scratches, his arms did not have holes or scabs, and his mouth contained front and rear teeth. He was seated on the walkway next to his pastel paintings. Each painting, distinctive and exquisite in its own way, had a two-digit number attached to it on the top right-hand corner. The two-digit number was the price of the artwork. On display were four paintings. The prices ranged from twenty-five to fifty-five dollars.

At first, I felt nervous to stand and observe the paintings. What if the hobo attacked? What if he was a kidnapper in disguise? What if he stole and sold children? What if he cast an evil spell on me? My brain was spinning with laughable notions. But I was not able to resist the vibrant colors, shades, and the perceptible lines and forms that leaped out from the paintings. I stepped into the uncrowded area for a closer look, removing the pointless fears that lingered. It was then that I was forced to take a whiff of the air. There was a smell in the area I had never encountered before. Whatever it was, it was malodorous.

"Sorry that you have to bear with my odor. I have not taken a shower for weeks," said the hobo as he rose from the unclean sidewalk. His attire, old and torn, was covered in grime. His hands were decorated with smudged colors. His hair was matted and fell to his abdomen. When the hobo rose to his feet, it was then that I realized how tall he was. I seemed like a midget in front of him. And he seemed like a giant in front of me. Judging by his kind voice and easygoing body language, he seemed like a friendly giant. When he came near, I did not flinch or flee. The foul odor that escaped from his body and clothes became stronger. I endeavored not to inhale with my nose. I was better off inhaling and exhaling from my mouth.

"So kid, which one is your favorite?" asked the hobo.
Not saying a word, I sauntered past him. I was moving toward the painting of an old fella

sitting under a tree. The old fella was dressed in Indian clothes. These clothes were not those of a prince, but of a beggar dressed in rags. Similar to the hobo, the old fella had matted hair, stretched limbs, and a haggard face. At the age of twelve, I did not care for trees. I did not know the name of the tree that was in the painting. During that age, the only trees I knew were the ones I saw on my walks to and from school. It was later in high school that I discovered the name of the tree. Fortunately, I came across the image in a history textbook under a section dedicated to India. So I did what everyone else does. I searched for its name on the internet. Merging the words *tree* and *India* in the search column, I was provided with sites listing the different kinds of trees in India. Under the names of the various trees were images of how they looked in reality. I was quick to recognize the tree. But the credit does not belong to my sharp eyes; it belongs to the hobo for painting the tree so lifelike. In fact, the old fella, the tamarind tree, the beaming sun, and the parched soil all seemed lifelike.

It has been over ten years since I have seen the painting. And still, the painting of the old fella under the tamarind tree appears in front of my eyes. I felt a connection with the painting, a connection that I am unable to explain. It seemed as if my eyes recognized the old fella. It seemed as if my mouth had tasted the tamarind that was suspended from the tree. It seemed as if my feet had landed on the parched soil. It seemed as if my skin had been charred by the fiery heat of the sun. As I was engaged by the painting, the hobo bent his knees and positioned himself to the side of my face. He whispered into my ear, "It's my favorite as well."

For close to thirty minutes, I studied the four paintings on display. I studied them hard. I did not know the craft and I did not understand the profession. But right there and then, I knew that painting was what I needed in my life. I felt the urge to ask the hobo which product he used to embellish the paper. I wanted to know and I wanted to know badly. So I turned to face the hobo. To my surprise, as I was studying the paintings, the hobo kept his eyes fixated on me. His stare was not of uncertainty but incredulity. It was difficult for him to believe that a boy of my age displayed such keen interest in his artwork. He saw in me what I did not see in myself. What he discovered was an artist, an artist that dwelled inside my heart and soul.

"Sir, did you use paint and brushes?" I asked the hobo with my eyes focused on the pavement.
He burst into a laugh which hurt his stomach. Holding onto his stomach, he replied, "No kid. I don't use paint or paintbrushes. And I don't use crayons or felt pens."

"Then, what do you use?"

The hobo extended his arm to collect an item from the pavement. The item was a tattered sack from which he extracted a handful of pastel sticks. These sticks were the size of an index finger. Their texture was similar to a crayon, and their form was similar to chalk. The hobo talked with his eyes, indicating for me to hold out my hands. As I did that, he dropped the pastel sticks into a nest which I created with my hands. I held the sticks as if I was holding a chick or duckling. Over and over again, under my breath, I counted the sticks. "One, two, three, four, five, six, seven, eight, nine, ten, eleven, twelve..."

"Can you tell me what this is?" asked the hobo.

"Is this chalk?" I replied with confusion plastered on my face.

"No, it's not chalk. It's pastel. And it's yours."

I looked directly into his eyes. I was unable to find deception in them.

"It's for you to keep," he said once again.

"Are you sure?" I asked, not convinced that he was positive about his decision.

"Yes, I am sure. It is a gift from a former artist to a forthcoming artist."

"Thank you, sir," I replied, without understanding his last phrase.

"Remember, when painting, you are to use not only your wrist but your whole arm."

"Sir, I promise..."

"What do you promise?"

"I promise that I will use my whole arm."

I felt blessed that a homeless person who lived on the streets, who needed the pastel sticks more than I did, whose life depended on his paintings, had donated his valuables to a child whose name he did not know, who he had never met before, and who he was not related to. From that day onwards, whenever I felt the urge to paint, I remembered what the hobo said—to use my whole arm. Filled with passion, I set forth on the trail of painting. The first lesson I discovered was to use the end of the pastel sticks to draw lines, shapes, and figures. I realized that the harder I pressed, the more pastel was planted on the sheet of paper. Even the smallest fragment of pastel was still usable.

Suzy, I can never forget how careful I used to be. Literally, there were moments when my hands were trembling. I was scared to make a blunder. If I did make one, there was no recovery. The lead was erasable, but pastel was not. After all, I was not using a pencil with an eraser. But months later, I reiterated to myself, "There is no right or wrong in painting." To be an excellent painter, I had to let loose, I had to be free. Painting should not be a stress giver but a stress reliever. It was my remedy, my treatment, my cure for loneliness.

As I became older, I became smarter. I learned more, understood more. I studied different techniques used to enhance the quality of a painting. The most crucial lesson I absorbed was that pastel can only be mixed on paper, not on a palette. So to mix pastel, to merge colors, I had to use my hand and fingers. To blend or smudge colors in a small area, I used my index finger. To blend or smudge colors in a large area, I used the side of my hand. During these years, in a black-and-white life, colors like red, blue, and yellow started to appear. With each day, life became more colorful.

With age, I stumbled upon masking, shading, hatching, crosshatching, stippling, feathering, and fixating. I was even able to differentiate between the various pastels: soft pastel, hard pastel, and oil pastel. I knew that pastels were supposed to be used on fine sandpaper, watercolor paper, velvet paper, and pastel paper. I understood that hard pastels were to be used when sketching the composition or image. I was aware that when oil pastels were used, a fixative was not required. I learned that a glossy finish is the best finish to a painting; therefore, fixating was mandatory.

Suzy, every time I made the connection between a pastel stick and the grain of the paper, I felt relieved from the pains and strains of life. Though, the obstacle between painting and me was affording the supplies. A set of soft, hard, and oil pastels, pastel paper, an h-frame easel, and a fixative spray were the required materials. Unfortunately, such items cannot be purchased at low cost. I knew that if I asked Miss Yang to purchase these items, she'd deliver in a heartbeat. In fact, Miss Yang would be on cloud nine for weeks. By asking her, the end result for both of us would have been pleasurable. But I never asked Miss Yang for things. Whatever I received, I received without asking. It is not that I am ungrateful. I am very grateful for what Miss Yang has done. Never before have I rejected her offerings. Underwear, socks, pants, shirts, hats, shoes, books, puzzles, toys, a desktop computer, a camera, a cellphone, an mp3 player—all that she has gifted, I have accepted. Perhaps, these items were necessary for a regular person's life. Honestly, I did not care for them. Not even the clothing. All I needed were art supplies.

So, what do you think I did? I did not ask Miss Yang for the supplies. Instead, I asked her if she'd let me apply for a job. To convince her, I informed her that ninety percent of the students my age in school had a part-time job. Actually, I did not have to put in much effort to convince Miss Yang. Her approval opened the doors to hostile guests, congested kitchens, and unclean washrooms. Suzy, trust me, I am not complaining. A job is a job, no matter how inglorious it is. I felt proud that I was working. And I felt even prouder when I eventually purchased the art supplies with my very own, self-earned cash. The one month, two days a week, and eight-hour shifts were considered a measly exertion when I laid eyes on the colors, paper, easel, and fixative. At first, I believed that once the items were purchased, I would quit the job. But I was no quitter. I kept the job until the next chapter of my life unfolded. I believe that, at least once in life, everyone is given the opportunity to reveal his or her brilliance. And thanks to a high school art competition, I was given that opportunity.

In my final year of high school, I was invited by the principal to partake in an art competition. Never before had the school board hosted such a competition. There were debate rivalries, math competitions, spelling bees, and sports-related tournaments. But no painter in our school district had ever had the chance to display his or her artistic works.

Involved in the competition were ten schools, and from these schools, two students were selected to participate. Suzy, when the art teacher revealed in front of the entire class that I was one of the chosen students, I was unable to control my emotions. Without delay, I wanted to paint my feelings of exuberance and gratification onto the canvas.

The other chosen student, who I did not hesitate to consider an opponent, was the queen of paper mâché. Paper mâché is a form of art that I never mastered. I was untroubled by her mastery, but at the same time, I understood that she, like the other eighteen artists, was competing for the same prize. And the prize was earth-shattering. It was a scholarship for a high-end university that paid for the Fine Arts Diploma Program.

Can you believe it? At first, I couldn't. Three years of schooling covered by the university, school board, the president, the government — whatever or whoever it was. Honestly, I didn't want to think about post-secondary education.

Often Miss Yang questioned me about what I wanted to become in life, what I wanted to do with my life, and where I wanted to be in life. She behaved like a mother — concerned for her son. But I never had the answers to her questions. Do you know why, Suzy? I didn't want to be a burden on her or for her.

All that Miss Yang had done for me, those good-for-nothing biological parents of mine would have never been able to do. In my view, requesting Miss Yang to pay for college or university would be an act of selfishness. If she did pay, I would live the remainder of my life in shame.

So to be victorious in this competition was important — very important. This was no mere competition; it was for a promised and secured future.

With this scholarship, I would be able to polish my skills and abilities in visual arts. With this scholarship, I would be able to see beyond pastels and paintings. With this scholarship, I would be able to dismiss Miss Yang's personal queries regarding a stable career. With this scholarship, I would be able to provide Miss Yang with contentment and reassurance. With this scholarship, I would be able to defend myself from isolation.

The school board gave us three weeks to develop our artwork for the competition. A painting, drawing, ceramic, sculpture — basically whatever seemed like art — was to be submitted.

The pastels resting in the jar at the foot of my bed were keenly waiting to be tested by my inventive fingers. My fingers were all set, but my brain was unresponsive. Ideas were not formulating. I didn't know where to start. I didn't know what to paint. There was nothing I perceived in reality that intrigued my senses. I was nowhere, not even all over the place.

I needed my brain to roam, but it seemed imprisoned. Now the question was — if my brain was imprisoned, how long would it remain there? Well, it escaped five days before the competition. And it was a nightmare that helped this painter to escape. Yes, a nightmare.

What I had seen — I felt as if I had seen before. Though, I can't truly recall if I did. There must have been truth behind the images shown in the nightmare. Why did I feel like the soldier in the nightmare was me — that his mournful eyes were mine, that his palpitating heart was mine, that the remorse displayed on his face was mine?

Unable to forget the nightmare, within five days I rendered it onto a pastel canvas. Suzy, to complete the painting on time, I even abandoned a full day of school. I did what I had to do. I lied. I was not proud of it, and I did not hurt Miss Yang or anyone else.

"I don't feel well. I might be sick," is what I said.
"No school for you today. I need you to rest, drink lots of water, and eat lots of fruits. I want you to recover before the competition," was what Miss Yang said.

So then arrived the day of the competition, in which the panel of judges was presented with different kinds of artwork. I felt relieved to see that I was the only one to submit a pastel painting.

As the various artworks were examined by the judges and studied by the contestants, I was focused on the proud family members — especially the mothers and fathers. Most of the siblings of these contestants were making comical facial expressions or happily waving at their brother or sister from the stands.

As for the emotional mothers and overconfident fathers, they stood beside their son or daughter's inspiring artwork. Suzy, I had never felt lonelier than I did in that moment when there was no parent by my side. Unexpectedly, Ben E. King's classic tune, *Stand By Me*, kept playing inside my head.

Since Miss Yang informed me that she'd be arriving late to the event, I had to stand alone. Her reason for the late entry was pardonable, so I did not protest or complain. Nevertheless, before the panel of judges placed their eyes on my artwork, Miss Yang arrived on the scene.

During the five days that I painted, I did not let Miss Yang have a glimpse of the painting. I wanted to surprise her. And from her reaction at the competition, I knew that she was surprised. It looked as if she was not content with the painting. Her non-existent words and deadpan facial expressions trampled my spirits.

"If Miss Yang did not appreciate the painting, then how will the judges appreciate it?" I asked myself.

In her view, the painting was less of a surprise and more of a disturbance. She was not disturbed by the colors, shapes, and forms in the painting — she was disturbed by my decision to paint a living soldier surrounded by lifeless soldiers.

Perhaps she thought her son was troubled. Or probably, she thought I was suicidal. Whatever she thought, I didn't exactly know. But I was neither troubled nor suicidal.

Fortunately, the reaction from the panel of judges was not one of disturbance. They came with scrutinizing eyes and left with a mouthful of compliments. One of the judges even took the initiative to shake my hand. I was respected, I was praised, and I felt as if I was on top of the world.

"And the winner of our first-ever art competition is Malcolm...umm...Malcolm Only," announced the head judge of the panel.

By painting the remorseful soldier, I won the art competition. But to acquire the scholarship, I was required to write an eight-hundred-word essay describing the reasons for pursuing the Fine Arts Diploma Program. On top of that, I was to hand in a sketchbook of paintings or five canvas pieces that I believed in.

Now, if the Diploma Program Coordinator appreciated what I had to say in my essay and appreciated the five canvas paintings selected to be entered, only then would I receive the scholarship.

Since I excelled in English and writing, I didn't have any problems with the essay. As for the paintings, I had to show the coordinator that, with time, I matured as a painter. So for that, I decided on a chronological format.

I entered a painting of the real-life hobo seated on the pavement with his hands decorated in various pastel colors. I was fifteen years of age when I completed that painting. The other painting I entered was from the benefit of a recurring dream.

The images that flashed in my brain were that of a horse and a slave toiling in the plantation fields. In the past twenty-three years, I have never seen a plantation. As a matter of fact, I have never faced a horse. I've seen horses in Clint Eastwood's western films but never in reality.

When it comes to slavery, I have learned about it in history class, read about it in books, and seen it in documentaries. But the slavery that I learned, read, and saw was purely American slavery. The dreams that I experienced revealed an Indian slave helping a fatigued horse to plow a drill.

I ask you, Suzy — what connection do I have with Indians, with India, with slavery, with plantations, with horses?

The dream stood idle in front of my eyes for days, weeks, and then months. For the dream to rest in peace, I had to lay it on a canvas. So that is what I did. The cuts and bruises, tattered attire, unkempt facial hair, wearisome eyes, perspiring forehead, disciplined horse, bullwhip, lines of blood, dehydrated soil, and roasting sun were the details that I focused on when painting this illusion.

I ended that consistent illusion by finishing the painting.

A month after I sent the essay and artwork, a response arrived at the door of Miss Yang's house. The letter confirmed that I was to receive a three-year scholarship for the Fine Arts Diploma Program. The scholarship also included boarding fees. In other words, I was to live in a dorm located on campus without paying a single cent.

As expected, there were expectations and restrictions that accompanied the scholarship. To be a student at this university, I was to achieve a C+ or higher in all my courses. Also, a ninety percent attendance was required for each course. And if I arrived more than ten minutes late for a class, I'd be recorded as absent.

But these hurdles were not difficult to surpass. Confidence was seeping from my head, eyes, arms, hands, and fingers. I knew that I was far more passionate than the rest when it came to education and visual arts.

Now isn't that a fierce combination — education and visual arts? I was prepared and motivated to ace those courses. But at the same time, I was a bit distressed that I had to leave Miss Yang behind.

Since the day the letter pertaining to the scholarship arrived, Miss Yang performed her role as the encouraging mother fairly well. Even if I did not behave like a son, I was still her son. And it is a son who knows exactly how his mother feels.

From the outside, Miss Yang was jovial, expressing how pleased she was that I was chosen to attend such a reputable university. But from the inside, surely Miss Yang was heartbroken. After all, it was not three weeks or three months — it was three years that I'd be missing from her life.

She loved her son, and I loved her. But the separation was indispensable. To elevate her spirit, I promised Miss Yang that I would visit during the intervals between each semester. These intervals lasted for only nine days.

"Nine days are better than no days," I explained to Miss Yang after she criticized the school board and its system. She then demanded that I write letters and place calls to her at least once a month. To watch her smile, I agreed to her favorable order.

Now that I think of it, if it was not for the foster agency, I'd never have been introduced to Miss Yang. If it was not for Miss Yang, I'd never have been introduced to you. If it was not for you, I'd never have been introduced to my inner thoughts and feelings.

Why is it that in life everything is connected? Why do I believe that my present is connected to my past? Why are my paintings connected to my dreams? Why do I believe that everything happens for a reason?

Does a soul transfer from one body to another? Have I been reincarnated? Who am I? Who was I?

Suzy, like every other person in this world, I don't understand life and its workings.

SATURDAY, SEPTEMBER 17

The importance of a person is truly understood when he or she is not there. When that person is with you, his or her importance is often overlooked. Why is that, Suzy? Well, I believe that we take advantage of the people who love us, who care for us, who help us. It has been a week since I returned to university, and I have to admit that I miss her. I can almost picture Miss Yang seated in the living room with her eyes fixed on the mounted portrait of her son in his graduation outfit. Since I am fond of skipping breakfast, she must be wondering if I ate this morning or not.

"Breakfast is necessary for your brain and body to function, Malcolm," she'd say almost every morning.

At times, I was forced to eat toast, cereal, eggs, waffles, or pancakes before leaving for school. Then, there were days when I had to turn down the food, tolerating the sour look on Miss Yang's face that clearly conveyed the effort she had put into preparing breakfast for her one and only son. This occurred when I rose late from bed or when I lost track of time in the shower. But whenever I returned from school in the afternoon, I was eager to devour the morning breakfast that was prepared with so much love and care.

The nine-day interval from university gave my brain the opportunity to rest. It wasn't that I preferred to flush out teachings, readings, crafts, and art from my system. But I needed a break—a break to regenerate. For the past several months, I had discovered that my paintings lacked innovation. I was desperate for new ideas, new styles, new techniques, new visuals, and most importantly, new dreams. I felt that nine days in my hometown, neighborhood, house, and bedroom might evoke what I needed. Actually, what I felt was indeed true.

In the form of dreams, I received images that soon began to take control. For three consecutive days, I dreamt of pigeons. Yes, six passenger pigeons resting on a steel gate. The dream kept returning, night after night. It wasn't until I painted the images onto a pastel canvas that the passenger pigeons stopped hovering in my brain and in front of my eyes. Isn't it unusual that the treatment and remedy for my dreams is simply to paint them?

I have seen, held, and fed pigeons before. Suzy, I am sure you know which pigeons I am referring to. The pigeons I see on a daily basis are grey with black stripes and spots, act as if humans don't intimidate them, and go coo-coo and poo-poo all over the place. The passenger pigeons that I have seen in my dreams were the opposite of domestic pigeons in terms of existence and appearance. I am one hundred percent sure that I have never encountered a passenger pigeon. I say this with confidence because passenger pigeons are extinct and have been for the last hundred years. These birds were last seen in the early nineteen-hundreds. So if I have never seen, held, or fed this bird, then why has it appeared in my dream? I did not let my brain tangle itself in that question. Instead, I embraced the dream and let my whole arm and pastel sticks take control.

Only a week into my final year of studies, and the teachers had already flooded students with projects, assignments, exams, and presentations. Suzy, if this is what it's like in the first week, then imagine how it will be in the weeks to come. Honestly, I was expecting the final year of the Fine Arts Diploma Program to be less demanding compared to the first and second years. However, school is school, studies are studies, art is art, and Malcolm is Malcolm. I am obsessed with art and want to be occupied with art, so I was not troubled by the heavy workload.

You see, I felt that to leave the brain idle was perilous. If my brain was left unoccupied for more than fifteen seconds, it led to unpleasant thoughts—thoughts of abandonment, the abandoners, the foster care agency, the foster homes, the foster parents, the foster children, the group homes, the caseworkers, and the feeling of being unwanted. That is the reason why I strived to keep my brain engaged in what I preferred: visual arts.

If I was not at the university or dormitory talking, reading, writing, typing, researching, or painting, then to keep my brain occupied, I was elsewhere—immersed in something or someone. Sometimes, I visited the pond nearby the campus. At the pond, I was distracted by the wonders of beauty. The sights, sounds, and scents there were enough to captivate my brain. Occasionally, I'd seat myself in a movie theatre to watch a film. When I felt like watching a film, I wanted to watch it alone. I did not want others in the cinema hall. If there were more than five moviegoers, I returned the ticket for a different showtime or a different day.

Odd...Perhaps! It was not that I disliked humans. It was not that I disliked company. I was against distractions while viewing a film. In order to watch a film, I needed complete silence. Any chitter-chatter inside the cinema hall was a definite no-no.

I also have a part-time job on the weekends that keeps my mind from wandering. Hired by an elderly lady of Indian descent to work as a clerk at her corner store, I took the position and its duties seriously. Every Saturday and Sunday, I worked from eight to four, which included a thirty-minute paid break, covered by the owner, Mrs. Krishnaswami. The customers poured in by the hour; therefore, my hands and feet were in full action. While my hands operated the cash register, my feet assisted with directing guests to certain items. I did not have a co-worker because Mrs. Krishnaswami felt that I did not require assistance. In all honesty, she did not want to confess that it was not in her budget to pay for another employee.

Suzy, one day I will take you to this corner store. It is a tiny store but filled with all sorts of items and all sorts of deals. You name it, we have it: chocolates, candy, gum, chips, ice cream, dried meat snacks, soft drinks, hot drinks, energy drinks, aspirin, cough syrup, sinus medication, lip balm, tobacco, lighters, flashlights, batteries, umbrellas, tooth-brushes, toothpaste, air fresheners, incense sticks, newspapers, magazines, lottery tickets, and more. Besides the numerous items, the corner store has the friendliest and sweetest little lady.

Mrs. Krishnaswami was the owner of the store, but she never enforced dominance as the manager. She treated me as her own—as a son. I recall the first time I met her. Luckily, I had seen the listing for the store clerk position in the local newspaper. Although the job required forty minutes of travel time, the part-time weekend schedule was perfect because it did not interfere with my school or studies. So I walked from the dorm to the nearest train station, which took ten minutes. Then, I rode the train for twenty minutes until I reached the correct stop. Once I disembarked, I walked for another ten minutes until I reached the corner store. There you are, Suzy—forty minutes in total from the dorm to the store.

As I arrived, an elderly lady in her late fifties greeted me with her hands folded. "Vanakkam, welcome," she said.

I was astounded. My voice sought to utter words, but my lips were tightly sealed. Honestly, I did not know how to respond, but I wanted to—I had to respond to the motherly lady who stood at the front door.
"Vanaaa...Vana," I stammered.

Once her laughter subsided, she responded to my foolishness, "Welcome, son! I am so glad that you came." Her voice sounded familiar. It was light as paper and soft as wool.
"Miss, were you not expecting my arrival?"
"It is not Miss, it is Mrs.," said the elderly lady, not in an impolite but polite manner. "You can address me as Mrs. Krishnaswami."
"Mrs. Krish...ish...ish...na."
"No, son, it is Krishna...Swami."

I tried to carefully pronounce her name in my head. Failing and faltering, I tried again and again. "Mrs. Krishnaaa...Swamiii...I talked to you on the phone in regards to the store clerk position."
"Yes, I remember. So tell me, what is your name, what is your age, and where are you from?"

It did not surprise me that Mrs. Krishnaswami started an interview inside the corner store, in the presence of the soon-to-resign clerk and a customer who kept looking over his shoulder. Let's face it; I was not expecting a panel interview at some law or brokerage firm with a spectacular view of downtown.

"My name is Malcolm."
Before I had the opportunity to answer her remaining questions, she interrupted, "Malcolm, what is your last name?"
"My name is Malcolm...Malcolm Only," I replied as brusquely as possible.

Suzy, I was sick and tired of people asking for my last name. What is there in a last name? Does my last name tell people who I am, how I am, and why I am?
"Hmm...How old are you?"
"I am of legal age to work in this country."

Her face lit with a smile. Perhaps she appreciated my clever response.
"Where are you from?"
"Well, I am not from this city. But I do live in this city. I am a university student living in a dorm located on campus."
"That does not answer my question," she replied in a serious tone.
"I don't know. Ask the woman who gave birth to me. I am certain she knows where I am from."

Mrs. Krishnaswami's face revealed an expression of disbelief. My answer was unforeseen and unforgettable. There I was, in need of a job, yet behaving like a world-class asshole. Right then and there, I knew that the store clerk position had slipped out of my hands. However, Mrs. Krishnaswami did not take offense to my last response. Instead, she asked if I kept in touch with the woman who had given birth to me.

"No, I am not in touch with her. I don't even know who or where she is," I replied, without noticing how personal the conversation was becoming.

For some time—possibly seconds or minutes—the elderly lady was silent. The silence grew increasingly awkward. At that moment, I felt like stepping outside. I was disturbed by her questions, which did not relate to the position she offered or the qualities I possessed. And if she voiced another question that was not job-related, then I would certainly step outside the door without replying. I examined her while she stood idle with her arms crossed, back straightened, and eyes on the floor. Her skin tone was the color of chestnut. The wrinkles and spots on her skin were visible, and the color of her hair was the blackest of blacks with snowy lines descending to her waist. When I looked at the black and grey hair, she reminded me of a zebra. She didn't need a cane for support or a wheelchair to move from one place to another. These facts proved that she had robust limbs. Since the ninth month of the year brought heavy rains and strong winds, Mrs. Krishnaswami was dressed in a warm sweater, baggy trousers, and a comfy scarf. Her eyes, shielded by prescription eyeglasses, often glistened without the assistance of the sun and its sunshine. Others will say that it was the lenses on her eyeglasses that shone, but I am positive that it was her eyes that shone, not the lenses. Her silence was broken as soon as she extended her arm for a handshake.

"Malcolm, the job is yours. You start next Saturday, eight o'clock in the morning."

It took Mrs. Krishnaswami only sixteen hours to accept me as her son. I felt privileged. Most of us come into this world knowing, loving, and caring for one mother. Well, Suzy, I have two. I must have been a good son to a content mother in a past life; that is why God has awarded me the love of not one but two mothers. The surprising part is that neither of them is my biological mother. These divine souls don't belong to ordinary humans. Surely, they are angels who have descended upon earth to look after the unfortunate. I am the unfortunate who, by the love and affection of these ladies, has become fortunate.

Mrs. Krishnaswami, who I view as mother number two, used food to win my heart. You will not believe it, Suzy; I don't have to purchase lunch on the weekends. Every Saturday and Sunday, I am fed by Mrs. Krishnaswami at noon. The food she prepares at home in the morning for her husband and children is the same food I eat with her at the corner store. It was she who relieved me during lunch hour. And it was she who I purchased the chocolate bars, potato chips, and soft drinks from. Mrs. Krishnaswami did not prefer that

I eat what she called "junk pa tunk." What that phrase meant, I did not know, and I did not ask. Her tone was too serious for me to barge in with a question.

"What is this? Is this what you call proper food? From now on, you are not to purchase snacks from here. I, your mother, will bring you food. Is that understood, Malcolm?"

"You sound more like my boss and less like my mother," I replied wittily.

At first, I didn't feel comfortable with her benevolent act. I didn't want her to cook extra food for me—and for me only. And what if her children and husband didn't want her to feed an outsider? I was a bit taken aback by her kindness. To have a person display such a high degree of love and concern for a stranger was hard to accept. It was hard—very hard—to accept that people like Mrs. Krishnaswami and Miss Yang existed in this world. Suzy, I have seen, met, and interacted with all kinds of people. I'd say that one out of five people in this world is compassionate. As for the other four, they are lowdown, selfish, and harmful. Unfortunately, in my life, I have encountered fewer people who are sympathetic and more who are inconsiderate.

Suzy, I don't want others to believe that I deserve pity. Nobody should feel sorry for Malcolm. I want people to accept me for who I am, not for what I have done or what has happened in the past. But with Miss Yang and Mrs. Krishnaswami, I was convinced that both mothers needed me in their lives as much as I needed them. Because of that, I have never encountered unnecessary sympathy in their words or actions.

"Son, you are overthinking. This is no serious issue, no serious matter. My husband and children know of you. They know who you are and what you do. And they know that you are my son. I see no difference between you and my children at home. So if I can cook for them, why can't I cook for you?" asked Mrs. Krishnaswami on the day I refused to accept the Indian dish she prepared.

"Mrs. Krishnaswami, I believe that you and I have been destined to meet life after life after life. Maybe in a past life, you were my own, my kin, my blood, my mother. How else do I explain this bond we share?"

Mrs. Krishnaswami snickered as if the comment I made was absolute nonsense. But that was not the reason behind the half-suppressed laugh. She placed the dish of rice and lentils on the counter. The smell of the dish was pure Indian. The flavors were so tempting that I was able to taste them even before lifting the spoonful of rice and lentils into my mouth. Chili, cumin, clove, turmeric, onion, and garlic equaled tastiness. One bite and I was sent directly to India. I felt as if I had tasted the rice and lentils before.

"God is God, the past is the past, the present is the present, and the future is the future.

Whatever, whatever, whatever... All I know is that we share a bona fide relationship. And I feel blessed to have a son like you. Now, eat, my boy, eat," said Mrs. Krishnaswami.

"This is delicious. What is it called?"

"Khichdi..."

I was so occupied with my writings about my angel-like mothers that I forgot to mention the incident that happened on the train ride. Suzy, let me tell you, this incident sent my brain into overdrive. There I was on the train, delighted that I had finished an eight-hour shift and was returning to campus, when I noticed that most travelers nearby decided to stand instead of sitting. I examined my surroundings and discovered that the only vacant seat was located next to mine.

Five minutes on the train, three stops had passed by, close to a dozen passengers entered and exited at every stop, and still, nobody wished to take a seat beside me. I don't know if I am becoming overly emotional, but why is it that not a single person rested their bottom on the empty seat? Was it the color of my skin that screamed DANGER? If that is so, then I must ask: how long will my kind be treated as lowlifes, scoundrels, or miscreants? Suzy, I am no thug or hoodlum. I am no pimp or hustler. I am no gangster or mobster. Do I carry a scent that is intolerable? Maybe that is why no one preferred to occupy the vacant seat. But how can that be? I don't wear perfume. The closest item I have to perfume is underarm deodorant, which I apply daily.

Also, it is not as if I perspire on the job. I don't pump iron. I don't lift heavy materials. I don't cook over a heated stove. I don't scrub pungent washrooms. And I don't roll around on the grimy floors of the corner store. I surely have no odor issues. There were no personal items of mine on the seat, and I ensured that no part of my body or clothing was obstructing it. For God's sake, I even checked for a piece of gum that may have been stuck to the seat.

As my eyes meandered from one face to another, I noticed that whites were seated with whites, blacks with blacks, elders with elders, and teenagers with teenagers. The pattern was not vague, but it did trouble my brain. Are we humans not able to blend with contrast and deviation? Once again, I felt unwanted... until the next stop.

At the next stop entered a vagrant. The foul odor that accompanied him forced the passengers to cover their noses with hands and handkerchiefs. In fact, the odor was familiar—it was the very same stench that accompanied every vagrant I had faced in life. A combination of not bathing for weeks or months, wearing the same attire for weeks or months, tasting and handling all kinds of drugs and alcohol, pissing, and shitting in pants were the reasons behind such a foul odor. Suzy, the most awful reek is the reek of dried urine. Its smell overpowers all the other smells in the world.

Believe it or not, the empty seat was filled instantly. The vagrant plunged into it, unaware that a person was seated beside him. I had a feeling that he did not know where he was or where he was going. Despite the fact that his unwashed body was pressed against mine, I did not leave my seat. Despite the fact that his pants were covered in urine stains, I did not leave my seat. Despite the fact that he had alcohol on his breath, I did not leave my seat. Despite the fact that he was perspiring relentlessly, I did not leave my seat. And despite the fact that he was mumbling to himself, I did not leave my seat.

Was I intimidated by his presence? Not even for a second. Instead of covering my nostrils, evading the area, or requesting transit security, I was in search of his eyes. "To meet eyes with a person who didn't have to ruminate before occupying the empty seat will be my pleasure," I said to myself.

The vagrant was dressed in clothes that had tears and holes in them. His shoes were layered with filth. His hands were shriveled and shaky. The nails on his fingers were blackened from the muck of the streets. Like other vagrants in the city, he had matted hair and a scruffy beard. He wore an oversized jacket that protected his chest and arms from the cold weather. With his face in his hands, the vagrant rocked back and forth in his seat. The words that he uttered to himself were unclear. For a moment, I was unable to tell if he was talking to himself or to me. I had difficulty seeing his face, looking into his eyes, and voicing my concern. If it were someone else, most likely, he or she would have disregarded the elderly fella who seemed to be in his late fifties. But I had to know—I had to know whether or not he was fine. So I carefully rested my hand on his shoulder, not wanting to frighten or provoke him.
"Sir, are you ok?" I asked the vagrant.

During the same moment, the train came to a stop for the passengers to disembark. The present station was not where I had to disembark, so I turned my concentration back onto the vagrant.
"Sir, can I help you?"

The numerous doors of the train started to open. At every stop, the doors were left open for ten to fifteen seconds for the passengers to enter and exit the train. And then, in a flash, the vagrant rose to his feet and headed into the crowd of impatient passengers. Each and every one of the passengers seemed to be in a rush. Surely, they were in a hurry to be somewhere. As the vagrant maneuvered his body through the passengers, I noticed that an item from the pocket of his jacket descended to the floor. Eventually, I had to leave my seat. I leapt into the midst of the crowd to recover the item. Whatever the item was, valuable or invaluable, I did not want it to be trampled upon. Suzy, I had a set of eyes that belonged to an eagle. That is why I was able to spot and retrieve the item within seconds. With no time to even glance at the item recovered, I darted in the direction of the vagrant. It was then that I discovered how tall the vagrant was. I was taken aback by the vagrant's towering presence. When seated, he did not look more than five feet ten inches. But when he stood tall, he was more like six feet.

"Sir, please wait! You have dropped..." Before I was able to complete the line, he exited the train and the doors were shut. I peered through the window in search of the vagrant. Where was he? Why did he not respond to my calls? Why did he not look back? Was he hiding his face? Did I know him? Did he know me? I felt obliged to deliver the item to its rightful owner, though he was nowhere to be seen. Unfortunately, the vagrant was devoured by the immense crowd on the platform. I then placed my eyes on the item. It was trapped inside a small-sized Ziploc bag. The texture was soft and the color was black. Suzy, the person who I idolize, whose style and form I replicate, and who to this day inspires and encourages me to paint, had given me another one of his pastel sticks. The giving was unintentional, but I felt lucky to have one of his artistic tools in my hand. At that very moment, I decided to never use the black pastel stick. I didn't want it to perish, nor did I want his teachings and memories to ever fade. I still can't believe it was him. I can't believe that I wasn't able to recognize him. But it was him. And he was the one and only father figure I had in my life.

SATURDAY, OCTOBER 08

For the past several weeks, I had expected to come across the vagrant on the train, on the platform, or on the streets, but as usual, my luck proved disloyal. Unlike others, I believe in this lucky and unlucky business. I often display superstitious behavior, embrace superstitious beliefs, and conform to superstitious practices. Actually, I feel no shame in declaring that I am a superstitious person. But to what extent, I have never mentioned to anyone before. Since you are my favorite, I will unveil these secrets that I have kept to myself.

Suzy, if I noticed a black feline crossing my path, I would come to a full stop, turn entirely around, and then look for a different path to continue on. At times, I would be late for school, work, or dinner because I was left with no other decision but to take an extensive route to my preferred location. People say that if a black feline crosses one's path, that person faces seven years of misfortune. So I ask you, would a sane person not retreat if he or she saw a black feline?

Once in a while, we encounter the day of bad luck, Friday the 13th. On this day, my feet turn from mobile to immobile. I endeavor to spend the day painting and sketching in my bedroom. As a matter of fact, I avoid looking at others, talking to others, and responding to others. It is a day on which I am extra cautious. I don't want to say or do things that I would later regret, so I keep to myself and respond only if necessary. I don't want to put my life or any other person's life in danger by walking the streets, riding the train, or attending functions. Now I know that all this may sound ridiculous, but this is how I am. Even if I tried, I can't alter this.

Suzy, let's make this clear: I am not frightened by how spiders look or move. Rather, I am scared of accidentally flattening one of them. I believe that by killing a spider, we bring upon ourselves an evil omen. So whenever I see an itsy-bitsy spider, I ensure to keep myself at least ten feet apart from the insect. I recall Mrs. Krishnaswami once saying that people from her culture believe that if one kills a spider, intentionally or unintentionally,

God will let it rain. On that day or the next day, people of that locality will have to endure a torrential downpour. Now, if I were living in a parched desert where it had not rained for weeks, months, or years, then I would probably disregard the superstition and set out in search of a spider.

Indeed, there is a mystery behind Mrs. Krishnaswami's belief. Some humans in this world are in desperate need of rainfall. So do these humans welcome misfortune by killing a spider? I predict that thousands of spiders are killed every day. So does it rain in these places where a spider is killed? Well, myth arouses while fact pacifies. And we humans succumb to whatever arouses, engages, and captivates our brain.

These superstitions that I mentioned are believed by people from different countries, cultures, races, and religions. But there is a superstition I like to believe I invented. It's not that I want others to believe in this superstition. In fact, nobody knows what I consider to be good luck and bad luck. When I was in grade school, I noticed that people in this world have no respect for coins. Everyone was after the paper bills: tens, twenties, fifties, and hundreds. One-cent, five-cent, ten-cent, and twenty-five-cent coins were found on the grounds in and around my school. When a student found a twenty-five-cent coin on the ground, it meant that he or she was born under a lucky star. If a ten- or five-cent coin was spotted on the ground, it was sometimes pocketed, sometimes booted, sometimes mistaken for a twenty-five-cent coin, and sometimes ignored by the eyes and fingers. And when a nonessential one-cent coin was spotted, it was definitely ignored. The one-cent coin meant diddly-squat to people.

But that was not how I perceived it. When I faced a coin on the ground, I bent low to study it. I did not want to know whether it was five cents or twenty-five cents. The amount did not fascinate me. I needed to see which side the coin was lying on. Now, if the tails side was up and the heads side was down, that meant if one were to pocket the coin, he or she would be shadowed by misfortune. I never pocketed this kind of coin to sacrifice myself for others. Instead, I flipped the coin for the heads side to remain up. With that move, I felt as if I was saving others from misfortune.

I am no hero, and I don't want to be one. But I like to believe that if you do good things for others, others will do good things for you. Whenever I faced a coin with its heads side up and tails side down, I did not hesitate to collect it. I believed that to pocket a coin found with its heads side up resulted in good fortune. In the years that I have lived with various foster parents, life became so miserable that I literally searched the grounds for coins. I believed that the more coins I had, the less depressed I would be. There were actually days when I would return home with dozens of one-cent coins jingling in my pockets.

Suzy, I don't know what greed is. If one tells me to define or explain greed, I'd provide them with the meaning of generosity. Several times, I have found a two-dollar or one-dollar coin lying on the ground with its tails side up. But never have I let greed overpower my beliefs. I had no regret flipping that two-dollar or one-dollar coin to its heads side up. No regrets whatsoever. I must admit there is a lot that I don't know. We can only understand ourselves to an extent. There is no person in this world who fully understands him or herself.

Why I believe in and how I came to believe in superstitions are questions that I will not be able to answer. Superstitions that involve the black feline, the spiders, and the bad luck day were either mentioned by someone, somewhere in the past. But the theory behind the coins, the heads-and-tails superstition, and the belief of good and bad fortune was my own creation. And I believed in what I had created.

Suzy, I apologize for not letting you enter into my dorm life. It is important for you to know that I don't live alone but share a room with others. The suite that I have been given includes three bedrooms, one washroom, and one kitchen. The bedroom consists of a single bed, desk, chair, study lamp, bookshelf, built-in closet, and wall-mounted mirror. What the bedroom did not include was pillows, sheets, blankets, towels, and a television set. So, when I first arrived at the dorm, I made sure to bring these items with me, with the exception of a television set. And what Miss Yang does not know is that I borrowed a framed picture of hers to decorate my new bedroom. Hmm...She probably knows by now.

Overall, the dormitory was homelike. It was far better than all the foster homes and group homes I had lived in. The best part was that students didn't have to leave the dorm or campus to do the necessary. We had a lounge in the dorm where students made phone calls, organized meetings, formed study groups, enjoyed potlucks, and watched television. On Sundays, during the evening, most students attended the lounge for movie night. If I was not occupied with pastels and paintings, or if I was not exhausted by working at the corner store, then I was certainly at the lounge viewing a film.

The dorm also has a laundry room with coin-operated washers and dryers, a laundry sink, folding counters, irons, and ironing boards. I have to say this: I hate washing, drying, folding, and ironing my clothes. With so much happening in life, with the overload of assignments and exams, with the weekend shifts at the corner store, with the additional painting and writing, I don't want to create time for the laundry room, even if time can be created. Then again, I can't walk around the halls or sit in the classroom dressed in soiled attire. So, once a week, I am in the laundry room with my shirts, pants, underwear, socks, towels, and bed sheets.

When it comes to receiving mail, I am required to visit the housing office located on the bottom floor of the dorm. All incoming mail is delivered to the office and stored behind the counter. Suzy, I don't visit the office frequently. I write and send a letter to Miss Yang on the first week of every month. Thus, I assume I will receive a letter in return by the end of the month. So at the end of every month, I visit the housing office to be greeted by the ever so attractive service representative. As a matter of fact, I know male students who visit the office every day for the sake of leering at and conversing with this fine lady behind the desk. Was I one of them? Absolutely not!

Now, coming to my roommates, I'd like to say that Sundar Trivedi and Herbert Chang are peculiar characters. The word Sundar meant beautiful in Hindi; however, Trivedi was the total opposite of beautiful. Students on campus who knew him referred to Sundar by his last name. Trivedi this, Trivedi that, Trivedi yes, Trivedi no, Trivedi please! Everyone used Trivedi so often that even the professors on campus started addressing him by his last name rather than his first.

Trivedi is of average height, slim-built, greasy-haired, and spectacle-donning, with a personality that was difficult to comprehend. He is in the final year of the Business Administration Degree Program. And he is by far the most unpredictable student and roommate that I have met. There is a reason why I say that Trivedi is enigmatic. I know this is hard to believe, but Trivedi is a student who receives an A in one course and a D in another. The hardest courses he passes with flying colors, but the easiest courses he fails miserably. There are times when Trivedi never studies for a test or a quiz, yet he still receives a high grade. And then, there are times when Trivedi studies for hours, yet he still receives a low grade.

As a roommate, he is not the nosy or bossy type. In fact, he keeps to himself on weekdays. He remains silent and idle in his bedroom. He is so reticent that sometimes I wonder if he is in the suite at all. I literally have to knock on his bedroom door to ask him if he is fine, or if he wants to eat, or if he wants to visit the lounge, or if he can lend an item or tool that I require.

Then, as the weekend lands, Trivedi is not the cool, calm, and collected Trivedi anymore. He changes from this reserved Indian male to this uncontrollable super freak.

Basically, he is Rick James incarnated. He believes that Saturdays and Sundays are for partying and drinking. Trivedi made sure that on weekends he was at some nightclub or house party. He knew that I was not fond of parties held within our suite, so that idea had never arisen in his mind. And if that idea did arise, he did not have the balls to share it with his roommate.

Even if he was forbidden to change our suite into a nightclub, every weekend Trivedi had a party to attend. These parties were often held outside the campus. But every now and then, I'd come to know about parties taking place in one of the suites in the dorm. Not a single weekend has elapsed where Trivedi did not pester me to accompany him to some nightclub or house party. And my response was a permanent NO. I did not even need to make excuses. A flat no was all that was required to get Trivedi off my case.

All these places that Trivedi visited consisted of drugs and alcohol. Well, I don't drink. Nor do I use drugs. To enjoy myself, I don't need gin or vodka. For a high, I don't need marijuana or cocaine. As a matter of fact, there is no high more intense than the high I receive from painting. So when other students partied until late hours, I was in my bedroom, usually painting or writing. And when loneliness confined my body and depression tortured my spirit, I was left with nothing but tears.

For most students on campus, weekdays involved studies and studying, while weekends involved parties and partying. As for me, I remained focused all the time. There is a flaming desire within me to become a professional artist, a famed painter. And I will not let anyone or anything extinguish these flames. With the help of my paintings, I want people to understand who I am and who I was. What I can't understand, perhaps others can.

Suzy, I don't want you to misunderstand me. I am not saying that others are not passionate, or that others lack the desire to attain success. Nor am I saying that I am the only person focused on his career and future. As a matter of fact, Herbert Chang, the other student I live with, is a striver. He strives to become successful in life—or rather, let's forget the word *successful*. Basically, he aims to be a millionaire. While others doubt him, I feel that Herbert has a real chance to become a prosperous businessman.

Herbert, who is referred to as Herb, comes from an extremely rich family. His father owns a chain of Hakka restaurants earning him plenty of money, while his mother is a full-time registered nurse, laboring day and night in the local hospital. Since he comes from wealth, Herb's Business Administration Degree Program, as well as his room and board at the dormitory, were all paid for. His bedroom is filled with expensive outfits, fashion accessories, hair and body products, electronic devices, and stashes of *herb*.

Now, you may be thinking, Herbert... Herb... the connection is there—and yes, it relates to marijuana. Herb has been nicknamed for his habit of smoking a joint to ease his brain, relax his body, and settle his nerves before an exam. For the past several years, Herb believed that his "medicine" was the vital reason behind the A's he received. On days when he could not obtain it before an exam, he went berserk. Without marijuana, his body and brain were in disorder, and his turbulent nerves forced him to disremember all he had learned.

Herb's pockets are filled with bundles of cash, so buying the substance was never a problem. The problem was that, on campus, so many students depended on the popular marijuana that sometimes the stock ran out. In that case, Herb was informed that he would have to wait seven to ten business days for the next batch. To me, this method seemed preposterous. But I have to admit—the method worked for him. And it was not as if Herb overused or misused the substance; he only used it hours before an exam.

Herb is a gentle soul, the cool, calm, and collected type. He is completely unlike most Asians on campus. I don't want to sound stereotypical, but Herb did not have straight, fine hair. His hair is thick and wavy—a feature I did not see in other Asians. Herb is five feet eleven inches tall and weighs around 170 pounds. With long arms and legs, prescription eyewear, and relaxed attire, he reminded everyone of Waldo from the children's book. In the book, readers had to search for Waldo hidden in a crowd. Luckily, that was not the case for Herb. He was easy to find: his bedroom, the lounge, and dorm parties were the only three places to look.

Through Herb, I met Eliza and Hayley. Since Eliza is my age and race, both Herb and Trivedi preferred that I ask her out on a date. But I was not attracted to her. I could not see Eliza as my girlfriend. On top of that, I had no time for commitment or relationships. Indeed, Eliza is attractive, but I have no regrets. The men on campus, with their high testosterone levels, dreamed of scoring her number, flirting with her, dating her, and getting her into bed. When I said I was not attracted to her, I meant her personality. I felt no connection between us when we looked at each other or talked. Her eyes often scrutinized, her voice commanded, her words humiliated, and her intelligence intimidated. Within a week, I knew she and I were worlds apart. But Suzy, I did not hate her. She is different—different from me—and different is not bad.

In fact, the connection I desire with another woman, I have not yet felt with anyone. Well, if I have not felt it before, how do I know such a connection exists? Suzy, believe me—it does exist. The connection I long for will be full of bliss. It will allow me to reveal my deepest and darkest secrets. She will know who I am, where I came from, what I do, what I need, and where I am headed.

As for Hayley, I respect her rebellious attitude. She often criticizes the system, the government, the media, the school board, the professors, the university, and the students. From top to bottom, she is dynamic. At first, I could not believe that a tiny lady with an unblemished face, blue eyes, and blonde hair could roar like a lion. As a matter of fact, Hayley is the captain of the debate team. Her team, her coach, and her colleagues rely on her to prevail at district competitions. I have not yet witnessed a debate competition, but I heard that Hayley can silence anyone with her two-fisted arguments.

Since Hayley is a philosophy student, I welcomed her views on science and religion, humans and animals, the heart and the brain, life and death, art and beauty. I do not have the voice to debate her, but still, there is a rebel inside me that wants to compete. And so we battle. I must say—I have a blast disagreeing with her opinions on subjects that persuade or provoke me. I do not compete with Hayley to prove she is wrong or to outdo her with facts. It is purely defiance. You see, defiance is an intoxicating thrill. And from time to time, I am in desperate need of this intoxication. To refuse, to disobey, and to challenge—this is necessary in life. Don't you agree?

SUNDAY, OCTOBER 23

I have never loved a person who didn't love me. I don't believe in unconditional love. In fact, I blame my dreadful past for not letting me believe in it. In my view, it is necessary for love to be returned. If love is not returned, then it is of no use to me. I am no fool to love first. Instead, I wait for others to love me first. I love Miss Yang. I love Mrs. Krishnaswami. But I have never loved my temporary friends. Yes, I call them temporary because I know that the women I find attractive, converse with, date, or bed don't want to spend their entire lives with me. These women don't love me, which is fair because I don't love them. I use them for my needs, they use me for theirs, and after that, we part. In a way, it is a mutual agreement between two people who consent to a no-strings-attached policy. I don't feel proud of having non-serious relationships. But I do feel proud that I have not broken hearts or hurt feelings through these flings and one-night stands. It is not often that I entangle myself in these frivolous alliances. Honestly, with school and work, there is no time for love and relationships. The only relationships that matter are the ones I share with my angel-like mothers. Actually, there is one more relationship that matters. It is a relationship that I secretly long for. It is a relationship that is unattainable. And this relationship was with a loving father. I searched for him in classes, on campus, on the streets, on the train, at the corner shop, and at the pond, but I was unable to find him.

Suzy, I feel ashamed to say that when an unknown man, between forty and fifty years old, extends his hand, initiates a conversation, smiles gleefully, and rests his hand on my back, I tend to view him as a fatherly figure. Even if I had never seen that man before, even if that interaction lasted for seconds or minutes, I forced myself to believe that a father had connected with his son. Why do I behave like this? I had Miss Yang and Mrs. Krishnaswami, so why was I in need of a father? The truth is that since birth I have lived without a father. What fathers teach their sons, I learned by myself. Suzy, a male teen without a father's guidance is ill-equipped for the adult world. I know it, which is why I say it.

When I entered puberty, I did not have a father explaining why I had developed hair in certain parts of my body, or why I noticed a change in my voice, or why acne began to erupt on my face, or why I started increasing in height and weight. When I first shaved, I did not have a father to explain that I should go with the grain, not against it. If he had been there, I would have avoided those razor burns, bumps, and cuts that I suffered back in the day. When I had my first crush on a schoolmate, I did not have a father to explain why I developed those feelings or what I needed to do with them. I did not have a father to show me how to kick a soccer ball, shoot a hockey puck, dribble a basketball, or throw a baseball. I did not have a father to show me how to tie my laces, ride a two-wheeler, or drive a vehicle. When I most needed a father, I did not have one. Well, I still don't have a father. And that is why I feel ecstatic when an unknown man refers to me as "son." However, no one has addressed me as "my son." After all, these strangers, these acquaintances, these men who may have been extra courteous or generous, probably have children of their own, and I am sure they refer to their children as "my son" or "my daughter." Blessed are the children who have a father and mother that help them surpass obstacles, pass tests, figure puzzles, and overcome the battles that life throws at them.

Isn't it strange that in the past I have met dozens of foster parents, yet there was not a single person who acted or behaved like a parent? No one treated Malcolm as their son, as their own, until Miss Yang entered his life. I know you must be saying, "Poor little Malcolm, lived with many but still lived alone." Please, don't feel sorry, especially not for me. Even I don't feel sorry for myself. I say grieve for those who don't have an angel, who don't have a Miss Yang in their miserable lives. The children who live in third-world countries, who have no food to eat or water to drink, who suffer from life-threatening diseases, who labor day and night in factories so we can dress in fancy clothes and shoes, who are forced to live in the slums and on the streets begging for alms, and who are misguided into the path of destruction and a life of detestation, are the ones I weep for.

There were indicators in the sky, in the air, in the trees, and on the ground that autumn had come. The leaves on the trees began to change. The usual color green was replaced with the unusual reds, oranges, yellows, and browns. While most of the trees were garbed in vibrant colors, others were deprived of a garment. These deprived trees stood erect, firm, proud, and naked, with no hints of shame revealed. As I walked the streets, I felt the moisture in the air land on my face. It was the haze that drifted above the landscape. With my artistic brain, I formulated the existing spectacle as the colorless phantom trying to vanquish the colorful season of autumn by obscuring its beauty. Though, no matter how dominant the haze, there is beauty—plenty of beauty—within the city to be seen by the human eyes.

In fact, there is a place that stays beautiful even on the rainiest and muddiest days. It's a pond that I discovered en route to Miss Krishnaswami's corner store. The pond is a gem; a gem that I cherish. The rounded pond is surrounded by a cemented path on which old-timers sit on benches, children ride tricycles, and adolescents walk their dogs. Basically, the pond is the finger, while the path is the ring. Both are wedded. One without the other is incomplete. Most of the people who visit this place come for both the pond and the path. I often visited on weekends. But if I felt distressed, lonesome, or abandoned, I did not hesitate to visit on a school day. Rain or shine, if I felt an urge or a push to visit the pond, I would be there. I understood that this wondrous location was quite a distance from campus, but if artwork or schoolwork was not capable of distracting my thoughts and feelings, then the pond was the last resort to ease the pain and sadness I bore.

Suzy, you won't believe it, but I have visited the pond during mornings, afternoons, evenings, and nights. There are more visitors at the pond on weekends than on weekdays. But I enjoyed visiting on weekdays during sundown. During those hours, there are fewer people at the pond. And if fortunate, there is no one present. Suzy, it is not that I dislike humans or humankind. It is not that I am afraid of humans or shy to interact with them. But when I am not distracted by conversations and interruptions, I have the chance to discard negativity and replace it with positivity. The pond gives me the opportunity to liberate myself from the pressures of school, the responsibilities of work, and the misfortunes of the past. The pains I have in my heart and the stressors I have in my brain are temporarily forgotten when I visit the pond. I say temporarily because there is no permanent removal of our miseries. After all, we are to suffer, in this life and in the next life.

Today, I left campus an hour earlier than usual to attend work. I was not asked why or how come by Trivedi or Herb. My roommates were too busy quarreling over which party to attend that they did not even notice me as I sauntered past them. On weekends, my presence did not matter to them. It was as if I did not exist. But I am not complaining. That was what I needed. Fewer disturbances equaled more quietness. So, the hour-early departure from campus was for visiting the pond.

Suzy, I have never told anyone that I visit the pond. No one has ever asked, and I am sure no one wants to know. But I do want to share this magical place with you. The pond, to me, is what Disneyland is to children or what Las Vegas is to adults. The pond welcomes people of all ages and ethnicities. People come there to chit-chat, snap photos, exercise, and picnic. Though on rainy days, people abandon the pond. A place visited for pleasure daily is left deserted during an excessive downpour. Yes, I know that places don't have feelings. But this truly shows how ungrateful people are.

Seated on a bench facing the pond, I paid no attention to the people in the vicinity. The children shouting and whining, the elders incessantly conversing, the birds fluttering and chirping, the rabbits hopping, the ducks quacking, the dogs breathing heavily, the bicycles whooshing, the roller-skates dancing, and leaves trampled by human feet were the sounds that disturbed me on a regular day at the pond. But today, I turned a deaf ear. During that moment, I tried to discard all the information that I learned and studied in the past week. Everything school-related was to be tossed. I ensured that my brain did not drift to Miss Yang or Mrs. Krishnaswami. Even thoughts of pastels and paintings were to be removed. There was a desperate need—a need to rest my brain. I remember that one foster parent I lived with often said, "In life, peace is the hardest thing to attain." As a child, I perceived the line as insignificant. But as I matured, I realized he was correct. Peace is hard to attain. And I believe it can only be attained in heaven, not in hell.

Once the brain was emptied, I closed my lids, absorbing the darkness. For some odd reason, a reason that was inexplicable, I enjoyed living in darkness. In my bedroom, the lights are turned on if I am reading, studying, or painting. The rest of the time, my bedroom is ruled by darkness. Even if I am pondering, sobbing, resting, or praying, my bedroom is unlit. The absorption of darkness lasted nearly ten seconds. It was the ears—the sense of sound—that surrendered. I was interrupted by the voices of a father and daughter, voices so endearing that I was unable to resist. Instantly, I was on the prowl to overhear their conversation. Eavesdropping is no crime. First the ears, then the eyes—I dedicated my entire attention to both father and daughter.

""Daddy!"

"What is it, dear?"

"Look... look over there, daddy."

"What is it that you are pointing at?"

"Daddy, do your eyes not work? Do you want to borrow mine?"

"Hmm... watch your tongue."

"Sorry, but you have to see it. Look harder, look stronger, look better."

"I am looking the best I can."

"Look at the rock in the middle of the pond."

"Yes, I am looking at the rock. It's in the middle of the pond, it's surrounded by water, and it's circular in shape."

"Oh... my... goodness... can't you see what is sitting on top of the rock?"

Although there was minimal sunlight, the father still shaded his eyes with his hand. He then squinted for a better look at what his daughter seemed interested in. Finally, he was able to catch a glimpse of movement on the rock. "Hey, it's moving. It's a... it's a... it's a..."

"It's a turtle, a tiny wimpy turtle. I want it. Can I please have it?" said the five-year-old daughter.

"Umm... I don't think so," replied the father, expecting his daughter to continue badgering him.

"Daddy, please? Please, pretty please, pretty please with a cherry on top," said the daughter in a whining tone.

"There is no possible way for me to capture the turtle."

The daughter became teary-eyed. "Daddy, can't you swim there?"

"I am sorry, but I don't know how to swim."

"But I have seen you swimming in the backyard pool."

"Oh... so you have... umm..." the father was left tongue-tied. He felt more ashamed for lying to his daughter than for being caught. "Well, do you want daddy to get his clothes wet? What if the water is freezing and daddy catches pneumonia? And what if the turtle bites daddy's finger?"

"Your clothes will dry. The water is not too cold. And turtles don't bite," replied the daughter, providing a gleeful smile at the end of her sentence.

The father was stunned by his daughter's witty response.

"Daddy, I think you forgot that I am only in kindergarten. Children in kindergarten don't know what pneumonia is. Now, can you please get the turtle? I want to take it home."

The father knelt down to his knees to face his daughter. He softly brought her close to him. "Ok, suppose a person you did not know took you away from me, how would you feel?"

"Daddy, I'd feel sad. I can't live without you."

"Well then, the turtle will not be able to live without its parents too. What I am trying to say is that we can't separate the turtle from its family and home. You don't want to see the turtle cry, now do you?"

"No, daddy," replied the daughter. "I want the turtle to be happy. I want the turtle to be with its parents. Daddy, I understand that humans are not the only beings with feelings. Animals have feelings too."

"Wow... did I ever mention how wise you are?"

"Daddy, remember... I am only in kindergarten. Children in kindergarten don't know the meaning of wise."

The father embraced his daughter. He then swirled her in the air as if he were the wind and she was the revolving turbine. It was an image of pure bliss; an image that I was encouraged to paint. Though, both father and daughter produced a cascade of emotions within my heart. The chemistry between them, the innocence in their conversation, the respect and understanding they shared, stirred jealousy in my veins, bloodstream, and heart. At last, for once in this life, I felt envious.

Envy is a feeling with two layers. The first layer is fulfilling, while the second layer is full of remorse. At first, I asked myself, "Why can't I have a father like him? Why is it that he has a daughter and I don't? Why is it that she has a father and I don't? Why can't I smile and laugh as they do?" Then as seconds elapsed, I began to regret that I asked myself such questions. I regretted envying an ideal relationship—a devoted father and a treasurable daughter.

Truth is that deep inside, I wanted to feel what they felt. I wanted to feel their bliss. Yes, I do want to have a father like him. But what I want more is to be a father like him. I believe the reason why we envy someone is because we secretly desire to act like the one envied. The sight of the father and his daughter pinched my longing to become a father, to have a daughter, and to relish parenthood.

Once again, I am sharing one of my innermost, deepest feelings with you. Suzy, I dream to fall in love, to be wedded, to have a daughter, and to be there for her till my heart ceases. This is a dream I wish to dream about each and every day. I don't want to be like the father I never had. What my father hasn't done for his child, I want to do for mine. Unlike my father, I will be there for the child when she takes her first step, when she utters her first word, when she learns to sing her ABCs, when she learns to count one-two-three, when she learns to ride a bicycle, when she discovers lipstick, when she goes on her first date, when she graduates from high school, when she sets out into the real world, when she starts working and earning for herself, when she pursues further education, when she brings home an academic degree, when she truly falls in love, when she gets married, and when she has children of her own.

I am opposed to such words as abandoner, betrayer, and deserter. Never will I let those words be associated with who I am. For God, I want to remain devoted. For my wife, I want to remain faithful. For my daughter, I want to remain permanent.

Suzy, I know you must be saying, "How in the world does Malcolm know that he will have a daughter, let alone, how does he know that he will fall in love and marry?" Well, you can blame instincts, intuition, impulses, or imagination. All I know is that it will happen. But how and when—that is what I don't know.

TUESDAY, NOVEMBER 8

With the stars lit, to some extent, the upper air seemed lustrous. As I walked the placid streets in the late afternoon, my eyes were captivated by the stillness of the trees. Surprisingly, there was no cool breeze in the air, which seemed rare in the evenings of autumn. I often did not leave campus on weekdays because I was buried in textbooks, readings, and notes. Projects and assignments took several weeks to complete. Soon, I was to study—not cram, but study—for the final exams held in winter. I did have school and schoolwork in mind, but that did not bind my hands and feet. I was free. I was to reach the corner store. I was to meet Mrs. Krishnaswami. I was to wish her a happy birthday. I was to gift her flowers that I had purchased.

Suzy, let me tell you, no one knows flowers like Asians do. At the end of the block, at the public malls, at the marketplace, it was the Chinese, Japanese, and Koreans who owned flower shops. Roses, tulips, carnations, daisies, daffodils, orchids, and lilies—these Asians had them watered, priced, and bundled. God knows from where they import such beauty. It was definitely not the land I came from.

The arrangement I purchased for Mrs. Krishnaswami was a representation of who she is as a person. The vibrant colors and prominent form of the bouquet matched her personality. When I first looked at the colorful bouquet of flowers, I instantly pictured Mrs. Krishnaswami's exuberant face.

As I entered the corner store, I found Mrs. Krishnaswami positioned behind the counter. Placed on top of the counter was a slice of black forest cake that looked tempting. I literally heard my stomach grumble. But first I had to wish the angel who had personally requested her non-blooded son to meet her at the corner store. That certain act of Mrs. Krishnaswami wishing for me to visit her, instead of spending the entire day with her husband and children, revealed the kind of person she is. Unique, rare, one of a kind—that's Mrs. Krishnaswami.

"Happy Birthday!"

"Thank you, Malcolm. Are these for me?" she asked, her eyes glistening.

"Yes, these are for you. It is your birthday, isn't it?"

Mrs. Krishnaswami tittered before receiving the bouquet. I watched her lips part as they formed a radiant smile. "Once again, thank you. You shouldn't have..."

Before she concluded, I pounced, "Don't say that. It is your birthday. I hope you like them."

"I do, I do. The bouquet is lovely," replied Mrs. Krishnaswami, as she cradled the bundle of flowers in her arms like it was an infant.

"So, why did you ask me if the flowers were for you?"

"Hmm... it could have been for someone else."

"Someone else..."

"Perhaps this someone else is attractive, your age, and in university. Maybe someone you have a crush on, like, or even love."

The drift she was on, I picked up immediately. I knew what she was talking about. "Mrs. Krishnaswami, I don't have anyone else to give flowers to."

"Are you serious? No dating, no girlfriend?" she uttered, astonishment revealing itself in her voice.

"What are you saying?"

"Malcolm, don't act surprised. I want to know if you have a special lady in your life."

"Yes, I do. I have not one but two."

For at least five seconds, Mrs. Krishnaswami focused disapproval into my eyes. "So, you have two. Hmm, where is my broom?"

"It's in the storage area. Why do you need a broom?"

"I need to hit your bum-bum with a broom—that is what I need to do."

Her last comment had me in splits. I laughed so hard that my stomach hurt. In computer terms, LOL—laugh out loud.

"Why... why do you want to... what did I say wrong?" I faltered, words failing me because of the incessant laughter.

"I am your mother, and no mother wants her son to hurt other people's feelings. Two women in your life... you will have to hurt one of them. Why are you playing such foolish games?"

The controllable laughter had now become uncontrollable.

"I am serious, Malcolm," she said in a berating tone, as a rightful mother should.

Immediately, I put a stop to the fun and jokes. "The two women that I have in my life are you and Mrs. Yang. Other than you two, I have no one else."

Mrs. Krishnaswami wagged her finger. "You naughty shotty boy. You are a splendid actor. We need people like you in our Indian film industry."

Within fifteen minutes, not a single customer walked through the front door. No customer visiting the store was bad for business, but at that moment, it was good for Mrs. Krishnaswami and me. We talked without interruption. Actually, she did most of the talking, while I did most of the listening. Since I was passionately involved with the black forest cake, I preferred to listen rather than talk. Whenever I spoke with a mouthful of cake, Mrs. Krishnaswami did not hesitate to rebuke me. I loved it when she ordered me to do or not to do certain things. I never took offense. Never did I respond with hate, dislike, or frustration. I responded with compliance.

"Malcolm, why is it that you don't want to meet my husband and children?"

"I never said that I don't want to meet them. Umm... I think it's too soon... I don't think I am comfortable," I replied, unable to express how I truly felt.

"I can see it in the avoidance in your eyes. I can hear it in your hesitant voice. You are not being honest. Why are you hiding the truth?"

I succumbed to Mrs. Krishnaswami, and there was no regret that I did. She deserved to know how I felt, what I felt. "I am afraid. I am afraid of losing you. I have this feeling that your family members will not be fond of me."

"Why?" she asked firmly.

"I am a hard person to like and connect with. I see myself as the unwanted person."

"Why do you say such things?" she asked, a hint of crossness in her voice.

"It's simple. I was unwanted from the day I came into this world, unwanted by parents, by foster parents, by schoolmates, and by teachers. I felt it, I feel it. If these people, who I have mentioned, do not prefer to see my face, then what impels you to think that your family does?"

"Hmm... I sense aggression in your voice. But let me tell you, not everyone in this world despises you. I surely don't. Want is nothing compared to need. And you are needed. I need you in my life. I need you to be my son. And I need you to meet my family," said Mrs. Krishnaswami, before she placed her hand on mine.

"One day, someday, I will," I replied, providing her with assurance.

We both talked about her birthday celebrations, the gifts she received from her husband and children, my latest paintings, and work-related matters. And then, I expressed that her special day belonged to her children, and not her weekend employee. She replied with an intense lecture on how she treats me the same as her children and how fortunate she is to have me in her life. On top of that, she praised me left, right, and center.

Suzy, every person in this world loves to be praised. And when humans are praised, some remain modest and brush it aside, while others ingest it and let it conquer the brain. It was not often that I was praised, but still, I was not the type of person who'd let it tinker with my brain.

"Anyways, back to the girlfriend shirlfrend?" said Mrs. Krishnaswami, who resurrected a subject that I wanted buried.

"I don't have a girlfriend. So let's change the topic."

"No, no, no... I want to know."

I did not expect it, but my voice became hostile. "What do you want to know?"

"Be calm, Malcolm. I am your mother; you will have to answer my questions." Her equable tone melted the hostility in my voice.

"You don't go dating, shating?" she asked.

"I don't have time for dates and girlfriends."

"What a bore you are. Everyone your age is dating. Almost everyone has a boyfriend or girlfriend. Have you never fallen in love, Malcolm?"

"Umm... this is kind of awkward... no, no I haven't."

With her index finger, Mrs. Krishnaswami tapped her chin. "Hmm," she murmured. "So, no lovey-dovey? Well, not to worry. All relationships are made from beforehand. She will enter into your life. You have known her, maybe in a past life or the life before that."

Intrigued by her last sentence, I had no choice but to intervene. "Wait a minute! Past life or the life before that... what do you mean?"

"Malcolm, if you are Christian or Muslim, then please ignore what I said."

I sensed that Mrs. Krishnaswami was retreating from the words she voiced. But I did not want her to. She probably thought I was harmed by her words, but there was no harm intended and no harm done. "I am neither Christian nor Muslim."

"Then, what religion do you follow?"

"I follow God. I believe in karma. I believe in good deeds and bad deeds."

"Malcolm, do you believe in reincarnation?"

"Well, I have my own philosophy of life. And reincarnation does play a crucial role in my philosophies. So yes, I do believe in reincarnation."

"Reincarnation is indispensable."

Understanding her statement, I replied, "So that means life is indispensable. Living humans and animals are indispensable. Moral and immoral acts are indispensable."

"Slow down, slow down! How can immoral acts be indispensable?" she asked.

"It is the people who sin that are incarnated. No sinners, no incarnation. No incarnation, no living souls on earth."

The words, "You have known her, maybe in a past life or the life before that," kept repeating themselves in my ears. For once, I was not distracted by the bizarre conversations, the foolish arguments, the loud music, the foul smells, the overpaid and underworked train attendants, the opening and closing of doors, or the obnoxious intercom voice. Usually, when I ride the train, I see and hear all sorts of things. Most of the people on the train behave as if they are at home or in a lounge. When these people talk, they ensure that others within earshot can distinctly hear the conversation. Calls from bosses, parents, partners, children, friends, and enemies—personal or not—are broadcast live by the call-takers.

Then we have the train riders who are intoxicated dimwits with no respect for themselves or others. With their breaths reeking of alcohol, these drunks went from person to person hoping to initiate small talk. Some cursed without reason, and some argued for the sake of arguing. And every single one of them did not have a clue how dumb they looked or how stupid they acted. From time to time, we had the homeless who smelled like excrement and urine. These deprived men and women scoured for loose cans and bottles. When in the mood, they panhandled for coins. I say coins because coins were all they received. I regularly witnessed passengers on the train cover their noses when a vagrant passed by. I had a soft spot for the vagrants, so I was not disturbed by their presence, no matter how smelly or dirty they were. I felt for them because, in a way, I was sort of like them once: unwanted, unneeded, and unfortunate.

So, there I was, returning to campus, and I was not distracted by the usual factors. Instead, the conversation that Mrs. Krishnaswami and I had at the corner store lingered in my mind. Suzy, you must be wondering why I am so interested in the cycle of life, karma, and reincarnation. I believe that everyone has their own perspective on life. Everyone tries to define or describe it. However, what the true meaning of life is, no one knows—and no one will ever know. The explanation I have is no better than his or hers or yours. I am not Aristotle. I am not Plato. I am Malcolm, and I say that heaven is at the feet of God, and hell is the earth we live on.

To attain heaven, to attain God, we have to break the cycle of life. Basically, we have to terminate the process of reincarnation. Life after life, we are reborn in a different body. That body can be human or animal. That is for God to decide. It is the sins we commit that drive us into the formidable cycle. To be reborn into the world is not a privilege. In reality, the world—planet Earth—is hell. I am here, living and breathing, because in my past life I indulged in bad deeds and committed awful sins. To set me free from the prisons, walls, and chains of rebirth and hell, I have to walk on the path of virtue. I have to prove to God that I am no sinner; I am no committer of bad deeds. I have to let my soul rest in peace. The soul needs to arrive at the gates of heaven to be welcomed by God.

I know, Suzy, that my beliefs are similar to Hindus and Sikhs. Why is that? Perhaps I was a Hindu or Sikh in my past life. It is possible, is it not?

With one stop left to disembark the train, my brain was still at the corner store, hung on the words uttered by Mrs. Krishnaswami. Then, unexpectedly, I was introduced to a rich scent that entered the holes of my nose. It was a floral smell—sugary and exotic. The smell was familiar. I had come across it before. When and where—that is what I attempted to recollect. The smell rose from strong to stronger, from powerful to most powerful.

So, what did I do? Well, Suzy, I tilted my head back, shut my eyes, relaxed my brain, and inhaled the scent of jasmine. Jasmine on the train! I was intoxicated by the sweetness. I was also showered with tranquility. The kind of peace I received from that scent on the train, I had not received in a lifetime. I wished that I could sit there in a state of relaxation, forever and ever, but my stop had come. I was to disembark the train.

Stepping onto the platform, I realized that not once did I look to the front, back, or side to see who or what carried that scent. Maybe, I should have.

MONDAY, DECEMBER 05

Next week, I will be answering questions, writing formal essays, and uncovering my paintings for the five classes I have been enrolled in this semester. Once the finals are done, the semester will end, and I will shift over to Miss Yang's home for a week. I received her letter at the housing office today. It plainly said, "I am expecting you to visit for Christmas," in bold letters. Suzy, Miss Yang knows that her son will never hurt her feelings by not visiting for the holidays. I would rather spend Christmas in a homely place with a real-life angel who showers me with love, care, and presents—a whole lot of presents. During the holidays, Miss Yang ensures that her Christmas tree is filled with gifts. Out of ten attractively wrapped presents, nine are mine, and one is hers. That's my angel—self-sacrificing and big-hearted. That single present belonging to Miss Yang comes from her one and only son.

During high school, I gave her handmade cards, photo collages, and paintings for Christmas. Then, when I started earning, I gifted her perfumes, body lotions, mittens, scarves, and sweaters. But this year, I want to gift her something momentous. She deserves better than materialistic items. I have to think of a gift that is not sold at a boutique or placed on a counter for sale.

Before I let my brain continue with this mission, I have to tell you about a discussion that took place inside the dorm room. The discussion involved topics such as life, death, heaven, and hell. It was between Trivedi, Herb, Eliza, Hayley, and me. From it, I learned alternative perspectives on the cycle of life. There are so many different views on how God and His creation operate, so many opinions on what life stands for and what life means. I will admit that I am more of a listener than a talker. Suzy, some people are better at expressing themselves in public conversations and speeches. I have words, but they are not often expressed aloud; they are expressed on paper. So today, for more than half of the discussion, I listened to my friends share their perspectives on what had become the latest hot topic in my life.

"Hey Malcolm, give it a rest. Come sit with us," said Trivedi.

He was right. I needed a breather from the continuous studying. From eight in the morning until one in the afternoon, I had been trapped in my bedroom. The forceful drive to ace the exams would not let my brain or eyes rest. Five straight hours, eyes fixated on readings and paintings, and not once did water emerge in my eyes. I wonder if I even blinked since opening the textbooks.

"So what's up?" I asked my friends seated in the living room area.

Herb was fast to reply, "Trivedi was telling us that he talks to the mirror in his bedroom."

"What...Wait a minute?" I replied, unsure if the comment was true or false. "Are you serious?" I looked at Trivedi for confirmation. Herb and Eliza soon became victims of a belly laugh. Hayley, the most solemn of the lot, seemed disinterested.

Using his famous white-toothed smile, Trivedi replied, "Let me tell you that I don't talk to the mirror. I am saying this clearly and loudly: I don't talk to the mirror. I talk to myself in front of it."

The laughter in the room escalated. Herb, seated on the edge of the couch, fell to his knees. Both he and Eliza could not control themselves. Before I could ask Trivedi why he talked to himself, Hayley intervened. Her voice revealed annoyance:

"Malcolm, let it be. Trivedi must be high or drunk. What he does in his personal time and personal space is none of our business."

"Aye, I am talking to Malcolm. If you don't want to listen to me, cover your ears," replied Trivedi.

I sensed Hayley breathing heavily. She was about to erupt. To prevent a squabble, I asked Trivedi to reveal what exactly he talks about in front of the mirror.

"Oh yes, back to me, myself, and the mirror. At times, I stand in front of the mirror and ask myself simple questions. The simple questions are: Who am I? Why am I here? Where did I come from?"

At first, I thought Hayley would pounce on Trivedi like a tigress, but she displayed hints of interest. "Those are not simple questions," she uttered with composure.

"She is right, Trivedi," I replied.

Trivedi stalled for a moment, avoiding eye contact. I felt as if he wanted to express himself but feared ridicule. I knew that feeling very well. To assist him, I raised the conversation. "Trivedi, you are not the only person."

Instantly, his eyes lit with reassurance. He asked, "Do you also talk to yourself?"

The discourteous Eliza interjected, "Who doesn't?"

"Yes, Trivedi. I talk to myself. I ask myself certain questions. But I don't talk to the mirror."

"Malcolm don't talk to no mirror. He talks to his paintings," said Eliza, diving nose-first into the conversation.

I did not care for her witty remarks. I knew she was upset—upset because I never stared at her assets. To be precise, I did not stare at her massive cleavage or curvaceous hips. What bothered her was that I, Malcolm Only, never paid attention to her and did not want to be her boy-toy. I was unlike other men on campus, and for reasons best known to her, she detested that.

"Phew...I am not alone. Honestly, I feel relieved," said Trivedi.

"So life...what about life?" asked Herb, eventually overcoming the laughter.

"We control our lives. We choose our paths. We create our destiny," said Trivedi, before he was booed and hissed at.

"If that is so, then what role does God play in our lives?" Hayley asked.

"God is God, humans are humans. Basically, God is the creator. Once created, humans are left on their own. Humans live for themselves. Humans fend for themselves. There are so many paths to choose from. Some paths lead to happiness. Some paths lead to sadness. God does not lead us on the path of right or wrong; we choose it on our own."

"Hey, aren't your parents religious?" asked Herb.

"Yes, they are. But that does not mean I am religious. Look," said Trivedi, stressed that his friends were having difficulty understanding his perspective, "I believe in God, but I don't believe that He is in charge of our destiny."

"You're not a true Hindu, Trivedi," said Eliza.

"I don't need to be. At least I am true to myself."

Before Eliza could unleash curse words, Hayley gestured to stop. Hayley was not pleased with Trivedi's perspective. The intelligent blonde had words of her own.

"I have to disagree with Trivedi. I believe that God does play a role in our lives. God is our guardian. He creates and nurtures. God is no abandoner. He's not like those mothers who give birth and then abandon or betray their child."

Hayley's comment pierced my heart. For a moment, I ventured into my forbidden past.

"God directs His children onto the righteous path. We are all directed by God, every single one of us," said Hayley.

"If God directs us onto the righteous path, then why do some of His children become evil?" asked Trivedi, proud of his counter-attack.

"Not bad, Trivedi. You have a point there," said Herb, patting his Indian friend on the back. He then shifted focus to Hayley. As a matter of fact, everyone did.

"It is because some humans reject the path that God has chosen for them. The human who rejects is destined for the path of thorns," said Hayley, greeting my eyes with a ravishing beam. Then she added, "Guess what? Even the path of thorns is chosen by God."

"Aye, that doesn't make sense," said Trivedi.

"Yes, it does. The world consists of good and bad people. The people who listen for the cues and recognize the signs are the moral ones. And the ones who purposely ignore or reject God's cues and signs are the immoral ones. We are all children of God. Even if a person is a criminal, a killer, a thief, or a hooker, God will accept him or her as His child."

Even if Hayley's perspective was a bit confounded, I was impressed. I was impressed by her words and the aplomb in which they were uttered. Hayley was a rising philosopher and captain of the debate team; Trivedi had no chance in a one-on-one discussion with her. He'd be bitten, chewed, and spat out if he continued the dispute. Perhaps he did not understand her standpoint, or maybe he did but knew it was useless to challenge her. Whatever the reason, Trivedi remained silent. Eliza and Herb were also hushed.

With nobody talking, the moment came for me to ask Hayley a question.

"Hayley, with all that you have said, what is your take on sinners? Are they welcomed in heaven?"

"Well, God forgives everyone. So, there is no hell. There is only heaven. After death, God leads us to heaven."

Ten minutes into the discussion, Hayley had us captivated by her words. She was, as I often believed, the one with the most impactful voice and notable sayings. Now isn't that a lethal combination? She had a mind of her own. Her feelings and beliefs were not the same as the rest. In appearance, she was like every other blonde in university, though not every blonde was intelligent like her. Hmm, that was rude. I apologize, Suzy. But it is not my fault that an execrable stigma is attached to blonde women. I cannot overlook the fact that Hayley is easy on the eyes, easy to spend time with, and easy to listen to.

"Malcolm, sinners are forgiven by God. Every one of us attains heaven. You, I, and even Trivedi will one day be in heaven," said Hayley.

Surprisingly, Trivedi did not attack in response. Instead, he flashed his prominent white-toothed smile, a sign of reluctant acceptance.

"Girl, are you serious? Hell does exist," said Eliza. "Hell and heaven go hand in hand. Heaven cannot function without hell. Babe, don't you think it's unfair if everyone goes to heaven?"

Perplexed, Hayley asked her to elaborate.

"Well, after death, if murderers, terrorists, serial killers, and child molesters enter heaven, how is that fair to people like us? We ain't no sinners. Every day, we fight to remain moral human beings. But these killers and rapists don't."

"I agree with Eliza," said Trivedi, content that one friend was on the same page.

"To tell you the truth, I don't want to share heaven with offenders. We spend our lives praying not to be harmed by offenders and not to become one. The least God can do is let us breathe without fear in heaven," added Eliza.

Her words made us chortle, though I don't think she intended humor. Three of my friends had shared their perspectives. Herb and I remained. I was in no mood to share my own thoughts on this particular topic. It was not fear of Eliza, Hayley, or Trivedi. You see, Suzy, my perspective is based on reincarnation. And what I found peculiar was that nobody had once mentioned rebirth. It forced me to ponder: Do people still believe in reincarnation? Do Hindus still believe in it? Has time and society changed how people look at rebirth?

So there I was, feeling the need to ask Trivedi about his views on rebirth, when Herb finally took center stage.

"You know what I believe?" said Herb.

"What do you believe?" replied Trivedi and Eliza simultaneously.

"There is no heaven, no hell, and no life after death. You crazies are talking about good people, bad people, heaven, and hell. What for? Once we take our last breath, life is over. Pitch black. You will be left in darkness with a non-functional brain and non-beating heart."

Everyone looked at Herb with their mouths open. What he had voiced made absolute sense. His perspective on life after death was grounded. Yet, none of us wanted to believe it. Everyone wants there to be more associated with death than just blankness and black-ness. I know I sure did.

Despite the shocked faces, Herb continued, "I believe we live one life, and one life only. So make the best of it: live life to its fullest, live like there is no tomorrow." Since Herb was not a believer in past lives, past relations, and past incidents, his perspective abolished the concept of reincarnation. A believer in reincarnation must believe in heaven, hell, good deeds, bad deeds, and karma. Without these additional tools, there is no logic behind reincarnation.

"Herb, you are so blunt," said Haylee.

"Yes, Herb, I did not expect this from a Buddhist," said Trivedi, playfully shoving his friend.

"I am not a Buddhist," replied Herb.

"Then, what are you? You an atheist?" asked Eliza, her voice revealing its usual obnoxiousness.

Honestly, I felt like strangling her. She was constantly on the hunt to either mortify or infuriate others. Since the first day I met her, Eliza had not changed a bit. The more I understood her, the more I disliked her. The fact is, she is the total opposite of how I behave.

Herb did not take offense to Eliza's question. "It depends... Now, if I say God has no form, no substance, and no appearance, but still exists here, there, and everywhere, does that make me an atheist?"

"And this is coming from the dude who smokes a joint before writing an exam," Haylee mocked.

Herb dropped onto the carpeted floor. He crossed his legs, placed both hands on his kneecaps, shut his lids, and fell silent. All eyes were on him. No one understood what he was doing or why.

"I think the Chinaman has gone mad," said Trivedi.

"Hush!" shouted Herb, startling everyone except me. "Do not insult my wisdom. The existence of a human being terminates with death. And once dead, there is no returning. So, live a content life. Experiment with drugs, party till early in the morning, have lots and lots of sex, consume all kinds of food and beverages, travel to different countries and cities, fall in love over and over again, make an impact in other people's lives, bring a child into the world. Do anything and everything to contribute to life—your life. One life, one chance..."

"Herb, get your ass up off the floor. You ain't no guru. You ain't no Buddha," Eliza intervened, not letting Herb complete his speech.

When Herb climbed back into his seat, Trivedi stopped giggling like a little schoolgirl, Eliza rested her explosive mouth, and the courteous Haylee said, "Malcolm, it is your turn. What do you believe?"

Finally, I had the chance to talk. The time had come. I had to explain my theory. I had to inform them about the cycle of life. I had to prove that this world cannot function without reincarnation. I had to...I had to...I had to. But in the end, I left the discussion with a vague explanation—an explanation my friends would probably never understand. "We humans need to liberate ourselves from the cycle of life."

The seventeen-minute discussion on life and life after death came to a stop when I delivered my line. I had more to say than just one line. But when I discovered the extent to which rebirth is overlooked, I withdrew from the perspective that defines why I am. Suzy, I am not a devotee of the Hindu faith. Then why do I believe in reincarnation? I am no expert in Hinduism, Sikhism, or Buddhism. I only know bits and pieces of these religions. I know there is a God, but I don't attend churches, temples, or shrines. Nobody has ever shown me how to pray, what time to pray, what day to pray, or even what to say in a prayer. Do I ever talk to God? Yes, I do. I let my heart and soul do the talking. Though I have to say, I have never asked God for materialistic items. When I need to talk to Him, all I ask is to keep Miss Yang and Mrs. Krishnaswami content.

I once viewed a group of men kneeling on the floor, folding their hands, bowing their heads, and uttering religious verses, and I wished—I secretly wished—I was that devoted to God. I respect the men and women who devote not just time, but their lives to God. Any person can devote time to God, but not everyone can dedicate their lives to Him. Thus, I salute the purified monks, nuns, priests, and people from the Hare Rama Hare Krishna movement. We need people like them in this world to remind us that God is to be worshipped, if not worshipped, at least considered, and never disregarded.

Suzy, I know this is out of the blue, but do you think I was an Indian in my past life? I don't know why, but I feel as if I was part of a historical occurrence. I feel as if I had been deprived and subjugated. I feel as if I committed sins—terrible sins. Well, that is why I am here, isn't it? I must have committed a sin—or multiple sins—to be cast into this world again, with the same soul, but in a different body. God, I hope I did not kill someone. Or worse, I hope I did not kill many. Indians, oppression, and sins... Why?

Suzy, once again, I was faced with unavoidable dreams. These dreams were not the ones that fade with time. These were here to remain. What I perceived were distinct images of tumultuous waves, a massive vessel, a pitch-black dungeon, a thrashing whip, and open wounds. Is this a cue or sign from God? Is He trying to tell me something? Are these images from a different life, my past life?

As a result of these questions, for the next few days, my brain will be working overtime. With final exams on the horizon, this is not the proper time to reflect on what may have been or may not have been. I am aware of this, but will I apply it? Anyways, wish me the best of luck with my exams. I sure need it.

SATURDAY, DECEMBER 31

I know, I know, it has been weeks since I talked to you. You must be thinking how inconsiderate I have been for not communicating with you during my Christmas holidays spent with Miss Yang. But you have to understand that a mother needed her son. From my first step into the house, I was not left alone by Miss Yang, unless I visited the washroom or went to sleep. The angel wanted to pour all of her love, care, and attention into her soon-to-be-graduated son. She was more excited than I was for the graduation. I tell you, Suzy, every day, every hour, she mentioned the graduation. I had four months left until graduation, and Miss Yang had a three-piece, double-breasted suit on hold at the most popular apparel store in town. Wow! Can you believe that? She had a suit chosen for Malcolm Only. I have never worn a suit before. It would be my first-ever, very own suit. And guess what, Suzy? It had no association with the nine gifts placed under the enchanting Christmas tree.

"Let's call the three-piece suit a pre-grad present," said Miss Yang, her smile radiant.

I tried; I seriously tried not to be a recluse this Christmas. I did not want to be the same Malcolm who talked less, asked less, responded less, and shared less. I am proud to say that for the holidays, I dedicated myself to Miss Yang. I did not avoid her. I did not leave the house at every given opportunity or spend half of the day inside my bedroom. I connected with her. For the first time, I expressed how I felt. Even the simplest comments like, "I feel a bit stressed. I hope I did fine on my exams," meant the world to her. I saw it on her face—she was on cloud nine. When I told her about my friends, my dorm room, my classes, my paintings, my job, and Mrs. Krishnaswami, she responded with happiness. I went so far as to tell her that her pancakes tasted delicious, that her choices of gifts were superb, that her letters were momentous, and that her love and support are the reason why I am breathing. It is true. Before I left, at the train station, I told Miss Yang, "If it were not for your love and support, who knows where I'd be—whether alive or dead, I don't know."

"Don't say that," she replied as tears rolled down her cheeks.

Once again, I left behind my angel, house, and town to attend university. But this time, I departed to attend the final semester. I had four months left until I received a degree in Fine Arts. Four months left until I was finished with exams and presentations. Four months left until I set forth into the real world. This is it, Suzy. I had my share of challenges, but I knew that my shoulders were strong enough to carry them with ease. Maintaining a 3.5 GPA was the biggest challenge, but I undertook it as a personal goal. I was not going to let the 3.5 decline. Besides preserving the GPA, I had to assemble a portfolio and prepare myself for the graduation exhibition. As for Miss Yang, she was prepared for both the graduation and exhibition. The suit she had kept on hold was perfect for both occasions.

Days before Christmas, I accompanied Miss Yang to the ever-so-popular apparel store. Suzy, can you imagine your friend in a light-grey suit? When I first tried the suit on, Miss Yang said that I resembled the good-looking homeboy from *Fresh Prince of Bel-Air*. Since when do elder ladies use the word "homeboy"? And how does Miss Yang know about a television show that aired in the early nineties? Well, at that moment, I was too dumbfounded to question her. On top of that, I was impressed by Miss Yang's selection. I loved the suit. Suzy, this was the best Christmas holiday of my life. I did not know I had it in myself to change—for the better. But when I did, I fueled both Miss Yang and myself with contentment. Finally, I became the son Miss Yang needed in her life.

Wait, wait, wait, I almost forgot. I gifted Miss Yang a pastel painting of her standing at the entrance of our home.

"It's beautiful. You are so talented, Malcolm."

"Thanks," I replied as I noticed her eyes welling up with tears.

"How do you—how is that...Umm...Are you a spy?"

"What?" I was puzzled by her question.

"Well, how do you know that every day I stand at the front door for several minutes?"

"I saw it in a dream—that you were standing by the entrance. It looked as if you were waiting for someone, perhaps your husband, Mr. Yang."

She lowered her eyes to hide the flowing tears. She then expressed, "I do wait for someone. But that someone is not Mr. Yang; it's you. I wait for my son to return. When you are not here, Malcolm, I don't feel like a mother. I feel like a nobody."

Suzy, I fulfill my promises. Be it small or big, unimportant or important, the promises I make, I ensure to keep. A promise was made to Mrs. Krishnaswami that I would work at the corner store on New Year's Eve. Since New Year's Eve was on the weekend this year, I had to limit my stay with Miss Yang. At first, she frowned and forbade it. But eventually, she succumbed to Malcolm's sweetly persuasive talk. I did not want to let down either of the angels. I wanted both of them to be content for the holidays. I understood that without her son, Miss Yang is alone. But if I chose not to work on New Year's Eve, Mrs. Krishnaswami would have been alone. She would not have the opportunity to be with her husband and children on a day full of colors, lights, music, and celebration. If it were an ordinary day, Mrs. Krishnaswami may have covered the shift herself. But since it was the one day every year that she and her family enjoy celebrating, Mrs. Krishnaswami needed a favor.

I recall our conversation before the holidays where she asked if I had plans for New Year's Eve.

"Please, let it not be an invitation to her place. I am still not ready to meet her husband and children," I said under my breath.

But there was no invitation. Instead, there was a request.

"Umm...Malcolm...Can you work on New Year's Eve?" she asked hesitantly.

Mrs. Krishnaswami viewed her request as selfish and uncaring, but I knew she was in need. She required a generous son, friend, and employee—all of which I am.

"I am sorry, Malcolm. I should not have asked you. I know that you are on holiday. I know that your mother wants to spend time with you. Please forgive me."

I could not believe my ears. Mrs. Krishnaswami was apologizing. A mother should not apologize to her son. I responded at once, "What time shall I work on the 31st of December?"

Her tightened face loosened. She was relieved. "You are a savior. This day is so important to my family. We spend New Year's Eve together every year, but this year it seemed impossible. Though I should have known, you, Malcolm, make nothing impossible."

I smiled. But behind the smile was a scowl. I was angry with myself. Not informing Miss Yang that I would be leaving her four days earlier than scheduled was improper and unfair.

"Will Miss Yang be upset?"

"Yes, I believe so."

Mrs. Krishnaswami's eyes were itching with regret. "Don't worry, Malcolm. It is best if you stay with Miss Yang in your hometown. I will cover the shift myself or hire someone for the day."

"I will man the counter on New Year's Eve. I will open the shop at eight in the morning and close it at eight at night. Mrs. Krishnaswami, you refer to me as your son. So, what use is it to be a son if a son cannot help his mother?"

Within a blink of an eye, I was embraced by Mrs. Krishnaswami. "Malcolm, I am so grateful to you. But I must ask—did you not have plans for New Year's Eve?"

"No," I replied flatly.

"Should you not be at those New Year's Eve parties or raves?"

"Parties and raves, I don't care for. I would rather stay home or work."

"But don't handsome men like you meet handsome women at parties, sharties, clubs, and subs?"

"Subs? Do you want a sub?" I teased her.

"No, I have eaten. Now listen, you need to attend outings. Who knows, you may connect with a sexy lady friend."

I laughed hard and wild. Her comment had me in splits. "Mrs. Krishnaswami, I don't think the ladies who visit raves, parties, clubs, and bars are my type."

"Then, what is your type?" she asked.

"Hmm," I drifted into the world of longing. "Someone I'd feel a connection with, despite voicing a single word."

"Good luck with that, ranjhanaa."

"Huh, what did you say?"

"Ranjhanaa—it means beloved one."

In the end, I explained Mrs. Krishnaswami's situation to my big-hearted parent. Miss Yang, on her own free will, sacrificed the four days that were intended for her and me. She did not want Mrs. Krishnaswami's children to be without their mother on New Year's Eve. And I agreed with her.

"Keep it up, Malcolm. Collect the good deeds," she said.

Suzy, on New Year's Eve, where do you think I should have been? Should I have been with Trivedi and Herb at the New Year's Eve rave held downtown? Perhaps with Eliza at the local dorm party on campus? If permitted, should I have been with Haylee at her parents' home for the Times Square countdown? As you know, I was at none of those places. I dedicated myself to the corner store.

For the entire twelve-hour shift, I encountered a total of fifteen customers. That was far less than the normal number of customers we receive daily. Seriously, do people need to visit the corner store on New Year's Eve? Everyone is out and about. Men are too excited to get drunk and laid. Women are too busy selecting which dress to wear. Parents are too busy stressing about their children's nocturnal ventures. And Malcolm is too busy manning his counter.

But like I said before, I preferred to work at the corner store instead of visiting a rave, party, or gathering. To escape boredom, I even brought my handy sketchbook. The sketches in this book served as the first step to developing a painting. So, to kill time, I sketched various representations until it was time to close the store. Once the till was emptied, the items were organized, and the doors were locked, I set forth into the streets of mayhem. The streets were crowded with throngs of people in full celebration. People were not alone but in groups of two or more. I felt a bit embarrassed. Tonight, I was the only person walking the streets alone. Unlike others, I had no parent, spouse, child, relative, or friend by my side.

As I walked to the train station, a mannish voice inside me crooned, "Lonely, I am so lonely, I have nobody of my own." I haven't a clue who sang this melody, but whoever he is, I wish I had a voice like his.

Suzy, I despise large gatherings, crowded areas, and loud noises. To reach the campus, I had to face these irritations with a calm demeanor. The train and crowds of people were unavoidable. But to flag down a taxi on New Year's Eve was almost impossible. On top of that, a taxi ride to the dorm was a bit too expensive.

So there I was, inside the train with more than thirty people jammed into a single train car. With so many bodies around, I still found an untaken seat. I was fast to capture the seat, unaware of who sat ahead, behind, or next to me. As the car twisted and turned from side to side, the people on board conversed, paced, screamed, whispered, sang, danced, and paid no attention to the train's movements. The men were dressed to impress, while the ladies were dressed to kill. People were dressed in flamboyant suits, exotic dresses, fancy heels, and suave hats. The skirts were the shortest and the ties the thinnest. Probably the latest style—I don't know.

For a moment, I closed my eyes. But still, I was disturbed by the commotion. I then breathed in deeply and exhaled heavily, yet the commotion remained. So I let my brain wander. I pictured Mrs. Krishnaswami, her husband, her children, downtown, the black skies, and the colorful fireworks.

Before I could continue, the flashing images were interrupted by a seductive voice. "Boy, you so fine. What's your name?" asked the sultry woman. She had fake nails, fake eyelashes, and fake breasts. The woman had heels as tall as the Eiffel Tower. Clack, clack,

clack went her heels as she walked. Despite the artificiality she possessed, the woman had a decent face. In fact, she was not bad-looking. But she was not highly attractive either.

"My name is Not Interested," I replied, avoiding eye contact.

"Well then, my name is Very Interested." The woman positioned her voluptuous body directly in front of me. As she came near, I detected the pungent scent emanating from her skin and clothes. "What say? I'm alone, you're alone, let's get together."

At that moment, I have to admit, I was a bit afraid. I did not know how to respond. "Umm... sorry... but I... I don't think so."

"I promise it will be a memorable night," she uttered with a straight face.

Suzy, I am not desperate like Trivedi or Herb. For God's sake, she was older—much older than I am. She was either drunk or high. I didn't know what she was attracted to. What did I have that the fifteen other males in the train car did not?

Before I could say a word, she burst into laughter. "Sorry... I apologize... I seriously do. It was a dare. I was dared to seduce you. I can't believe it; I can't believe you fell for it."

The blood flowing in my veins turned to indignation. "Let it go, Malcolm. Please, let it go. There is no use in counter-attacking," I said to myself. But I did not want to listen to my conscience. I wanted to rise. I observed her movements with vengeful eyes. She reunited with her gang of deceivers. They pointed, they laughed, and on the receiving end of the humiliation was Malcolm.

Suzy, on the train, I have encountered addicts, convicts, drunkards, beggars, former child soldiers, and the mentally insane. Some ask for change, while others ask for cigarettes. Some talk to themselves, while others talk to the vociferous intercom. Some tell you to come near, while others tell you to go away. But with all honesty, I have never been humiliated like I was on New Year's Eve by that deceiving woman.

I looked to the front, then to the left, and then to the right. Fortunately, nobody was snickering or whispering. Not a single pair of eyes was fixated on me. I was thankful, but the overflowing resentment remained. Then, I heard a giggle that may have been partially covered by a hand. It came not from beside me, but from behind me. I wanted to turn—I should have turned—but I didn't.

There was innocence in her laughter that I had never witnessed before. No one laughed in such a manner. She was laughing at me, at what had happened, but I did not mind. Instead of being furious, I felt relaxed. Who was she? How did I know that she was a she? And why did she have such a calming effect on me? I desired to see her face, to see what she looked like. But I just could not turn around to face her. It was too drastic a move. If I were to catch her red-handed, she would feel awkward.

Minutes passed. The next station was mine. I kept receiving impulses to turn around and face her, but I was unable to muster the courage. Then, in time, I had an idea. Situated in front of me was a fiber screen that provided a mirror-like reflection. With the help of this fiber screen, I had a fifty percent chance of seeing her. Hoping that I was not noticed by her or others, I focused my eyes on the fiber screen. I tried hard to shift and adjust, but the combination of my body and shadow covered her face.

The way I acted in the seat probably made others believe that I was a strange drug addict, a quivering vagrant, or that I had ants in my pants. As expected, the intercom voice obstructed the quest I was on.

Arriving too soon was my station. I had to disembark. While rising from my seat, I controlled the forceful urge to turn or look back. My feet were now on the platform. Gradually, I started to walk ahead. Then I heard the doors of the train close. This was my chance—the last chance to see her. I was in desperation mode. I had to turn around. "If not now, then when?" I asked myself.

At last, I turned. Thank God, I turned. Right then and there, my life changed forever. Suzy, she was my type. Despite not saying a word, I felt an instant connection with her.

WEDNESDAY, JANUARY 11

S uzy, I hope you don't feel jealous, but she is the one. You will always be my first and foremost, but she is the one. Unlike you, she may not listen to what I have to say, but she is the one. Unlike you, she may not be trustworthy, but she is the one. Unlike you, she may not be compassionate, but she is the one.

On New Year's Eve, when the train left the platform, I remained there, motionless and disoriented. I experienced the feeling of déjà vu. It seemed as if life had repeated itself. I believe it was an occurrence from a past life that repeated itself in the present. Someone, somewhere, in some way, was departing. It was someone I knew, someone I had feelings for. Perhaps she was from my past. Perhaps she was not. But when our eyes met, I felt strange—a feeling that cannot be described. I had never felt like that before.

How to explain it, Suzy? Ahhh, it was as if I had seen her before, or I had met her before. God, what a beautiful face! There was a connection, and that connection was indestructible. I looked at her with intense eyes—eyes that asked, *Where have you been all this time?* My heart pounded rapidly; a heart that recognized the love and compassion that were once shared. The insides of my stomach were in knots—knots formed by the tension of losing her once more. My brain was entangled between the past and present lives, different but similar, complete yet incomplete.

I wanted to press both lips against her delicate cheeks, run a finger down her tempting neck, and take hold of her cordial hands. I needed to whisper in her ears, *I am yours, and you are mine.* But that was impossible. She and I were not inseparable. We were separated by the closed doors, the fiberglass, and the moving train.

As I watched her, not once did I see her eyes blink. Her lids were still as rock. Her forehead was tense with lines of an enigma. Her lips did not exhibit signs of happiness or unhappiness. I was fixated on her; she was fixated on me. Second by second, the train carried her exquisitely beautiful appearance further away. An urge to launch my arms and legs in pursuit of the train was emerging. But that was pointless. There was nothing I could do. I had no chance of stopping the train with my bare hands, and even if I did stop the train, what next? How would I approach her, and what would I say?

Suzy, do you really think I would say, *"Whoever you are, whatever your name is, I know you. I have seen you before. I don't recall where or when, but I have seen you before. So, do you remember who I am?"* When talking to a lady, I know never to use the line, *"I have seen you before."* It is the oldest, lamest, and cheapest pick-up line invented to gain a woman's attention. However, considering the situation I was in, this was no pick-up line. Indeed, she and I had met. Certainly, we had interacted. And probably, we had fallen in love.

Those pouty lips, mesmerizing eyes, extensive lashes, taut jawline, sharp nose, and flawless chin were not only familiar but relished by my eyes. And the mole above her right lip was not a distraction but a worthy attraction. Even the mole swirled inside my brain, attempting to remind me of its significance.

In the end, the train vanished, but I did not. I stood on the platform with my brain conquered by the recollection of past events. Who was she, and who is she? These were the questions that needed answers. It wasn't until the next train arrived, with its ear-splitting loudness and wind-blowing speed, that I regained my senses. During that moment, I traveled from past life to present life. I returned to the real world—the darkness, the chill, the station, the platform, and the flocks of people.

It has been eleven days since New Year's Eve, and still, I am unable to discard her from my system. I am afraid to say this, but she has moved deep within my heart. Love, infatuation, or obsession—I will soon discover the truth. Honestly, I want it to be love. I could forgive myself if it turns out to be infatuation. But if I realize it is obsession, I would either hate myself or kill myself. Suzy, at times, love wears the mask of infatuation or obsession. And I don't want to be misled—not by humans or by emotions.

It is close to midnight, and here I am with you and in need of you. Seconds ago, I had risen from a nightmarish dream. Suzy, by now you know that I am the painter of dreams. I am the painter of my dreams. The series of images I encounter when unconscious are remembered or recorded. If the dream is transparent, it is likely to be remembered. I ensure I store that dream in my brain for future needs. If the dream is vague, what I saw, felt, and absorbed is easily forgotten. In cases like these, I share the dream with you.

So, when I need to paint the dream, I come to you for the description of what occurred. Sometimes, when I rise from a dream, it vacates my brain within minutes. I sit on the edge of my bed, striving to recollect the images and thoughts that disappear without a sound or trace. Dreams can be pleasant or unpleasant, but their peculiarity never fades. At times, you will not remember the entire dream, but you will remember bits and pieces of it. I spent hours, days, months attempting to sort those bits and pieces together to make sense of what I had seen. In the end, I concluded that dreams are related to our past and present lives.

Transparent dreams represent our present life. These dreams can be interpreted. They reflect what we do, what we think, and what we feel in our present life. On the contrary, vague dreams represent our past life or lives. These dreams are unexpected, unexplained, and unresolved.

Suzy, do you know who you were in your past life? Do you know whether you were black or white, tall or short, a Christian or a Jew, a Hindu or a Muslim, optimistic or pessimistic, a believer or a nonbeliever, rich or poor, intelligent or unintelligent, sane or insane, cool or uncool? Well, I don't. Perhaps, with these vague dreams, God is trying to provide us with clues that relate to our past lives and the people we were connected to in those lives. The main purpose of these clues is to help us understand the cycle of life.

Though I assume more than half the people in this world never think or talk about the cycle of life. So, what does that mean? Does it mean I'm abnormal? Suzy, there are dreams I want to reflect on, but then there are dreams I want to erase. The dream that occurred moments ago is the kind that needs to be erased. It was a series of flashing images, so bona fide, so evident, that it played inside my brain like a story. Each frame seemed to have its own story to tell.

The first set of images showed a body falling into the vast ocean, then crashing into the waters, then unwillingly resisting the murderous waves, then descending to the ocean floor, and finally into absolute blackness. There was a pause; my brain was empty. Then moments later, the brain was again occupied with flashing images.

The erratic waves of the ocean moved back and forth as they propelled a motionless body to the shore. It was the same body that had crashed into the embraceable arms of the vast ocean. She was dressed in wet Indian attire that clung to her body. Her face was partially hidden by her long black hair. The skin that was once light brown had turned pale white due to the cold waters. Her hands and fingers did not move. There were no signs of life. Wave by wave, she moved closer to the shore. Then, as her body collided with the inanimate sand, she came to a full stop.

The ocean had swallowed her and spat her out. When spat out, she landed on the coastline of an obscure place. She lay face down on the earth as the intense breeze rushed across the desolate landscape. The last moments of the dream showed the breeze sweep aside the damp hair that covered her face. Still, there was no way of recognizing her eyes, nose, or lips. The fine sand had veiled most of her face.

With all that said, I have to ask you—what in the world was that? Was the dream related to my past life? Who was that woman in the dream? Was she dead or alive? Had I ever seen her before? Did I share a relationship with her? Why such a traumatic dream? Suzy, I will have to repeat myself: the dream was one of God's clues or cautions.

That woman—she was Indian. Dressed from head to toe, light brown skin, extensive hair—I have no doubts she was Indian. In one of my past dreams, I had seen an Indian slave on a plantation. Indian and Indian. Two dreams related to Indians—there must be a connection. There has to be a reason I see Indians in my dreams. Was I an Indian in my past life? God's clues say I was.

Though, what if these dreams were not clues but cautions? What if God is attempting to warn me that evil or danger is upon the horizon? Suzy, who knows? I probably have to stay clear of the oceans. So many questions and practically no answers! But the most important question is what to believe and what not to believe.

SATURDAY, JANUARY 21

Suzy, I'm a person who dislikes more than he likes, hates more than he loves. Please don't judge. All this disliking and hating does not mean that I am a negative person. I am not a pessimist. I try to be as positive as I can be. There are certain people, actions, and sayings that drive me up the wall.

The difference between hate and dislike is clear in my books. I believe hate contains intense passion, and thus we use our heart to hate. Suzy, we cannot dislike someone with passion. But we can hate someone with passion. Instead of the heart, we use our brains to dislike. Suzy, it is harder to control the heart than the brain. It is harder to forgive people, actions, or sayings that are hated. Don't you agree?

So let's begin. I hate people who hate for no apparent reason. I dislike people who know they are doing wrong but do it anyway. I hate people who demand respect but show none. I dislike people who deceive, boast, gossip, and stereotype. I hate people who harm others for the sake of gratification. I dislike people who attempt to hog the spotlight. I hate clubs, bars, strip joints, parties, and raves. I dislike large crowds, noisy places, and lightless rooms. I hate alcohol, cigarettes, marijuana, heroin, cocaine, steroids, and crystal meth. I dislike soft drinks, fast food, overpriced items, and overly hyped things.

I hate it when people use *shit, ass,* and *fuck* after every fourth or fifth word spoken. I dislike it when people cough or sneeze without covering their mouths. I hate it when people fart and belch in public. I dislike the fact that politicians and journalists dupe civilians. I hate the fact we still deal with poverty, pollution, racism, and terrorism. I dislike the fact that numerous animals are endangered or close to endangerment. I hate the fact that we still don't have an explicit cure for cancer. I dislike the fact that there are only twenty-four hours in a day.

I hate the fact that, in spite of illustrious lives, celebrities destroy themselves through overdoses or divorces. I dislike the fact that excessively talented personalities die young—Reggae artist Bob Marley, King of Rock and Roll Elvis Presley, English musician

John Lennon, Prince of Motown Marvin Gaye, King of Soul Sam Cooke, instrumentalist Jimi Hendrix, Rock artist Jim Morrison, Princess of Wales Diana, writer Anne Frank, sex symbol Marilyn Monroe, martial artist Bruce Lee, American comedian Chris Farley, Saturday Night Live's Jim Belushi, Australian actor Heath Ledger, Godfather of Rap Eric Wright, American rapper Tupac Shakur, hit-maker Christopher Wallace, Queen of Urban Pop Aaliyah, human rights activist Malcolm X, former president John F. Kennedy, and the nonviolent Martin Luther King Jr. I believe that is enough to verify my point.

I hate and dislike all this and more—but I admire her. Yes, I think I am beginning to fall in love with that woman I encountered on the train. Wherever she is, I will find her. Whoever she is, I will get to know her. Today, my eyes predicted her arrival on the train ride to work, but she did not appear. It has been three consecutive weeks since I saw her on New Year's Eve. Is she from this city? If so, where does she live? Is she studying? If so, which school? Is she working? If so, which company? Is she single? If so, will she give me a chance?

I needed the answers to these questions—and I needed them fast. I was eager to know about her life, personality, childhood, family, friends, career, hobbies, goals, likes, and dislikes. But for that to happen, I first had to meet her and then talk to her.

"Did you see her today?" asked Mrs. Krishnaswami.

"No, I have not seen her for twenty-one days," I replied, feeling downhearted.

Mrs. Krishnaswami attempted to cover her smile but failed miserably. "Malcolm, you have counted the days? Wow, it does seem like you truly admire this lady."

"I do...Well...I think I do...Umm, I kind of..."

"Hmm, Malcolm has fallen in lovey-dovey." Perhaps Mrs. Krishnaswami was correct. At that moment, I did not care whether it was love, like, or lust. What mattered was that when imagining this woman's face, I felt at ease. When I recollected her attractive eyes and flawless lips, all my worries and tensions subsided. When I envisioned the mole above her lip, I received a sensation that life is worthy. Without even knowing her, I knew her. I knew that I'd have no regrets striving for this woman.

"So when you first met her, did you ask for her name?" asked Mrs. Krishnaswami.

"Well, I did not meet her. But I did see her. She was beautiful. So, so, so beautiful," I replied.

"Wait a minute! You saw her on the train...On New Year's Eve...Is that not meeting her?"

"Well, if I interacted with her, if I introduced myself, if she introduced herself, then I'd say we've met."

Mrs. Krishnaswami stared with a blank face. "So, no name, no number, no email address, no home address, no Facebook, no Twitter, no Skype...What is the matter with you?"

"I know, I know...But the train had departed... I had to disembark...She was too attractive...And I'm unattractive."

"Malcolm," she said in a rasping tone. Her tone indicated that she was not impressed with my excuse. "Who said you're not attractive? You are Mrs. Krishnaswami's son; all my children are attractive. Do you understand?"

"Yes, ma'am," I replied as if I were a soldier responding to his senior.

"You are a handsome man. Don't ever judge yourself or others on the basis of looks. You don't need to impress with looks to win her heart. Impress her with your personality. Personality is what matters in the end."

Her comment forced me to ponder. The question—did I only fall for this woman because she is good-looking—emerged in my brain. "She is the most beautiful woman I've seen, but there is more to it than beauty. There is a connection. And this connection, relation, sensation, and vibration are far more important than how pleasing she is to the eyes," I said to myself.

The pondering ended when Mrs. Krishnaswami snapped her fingers. "Malcolm, stop dreaming. Now answer my question. What is she? Is she Canadian, American, Chinese, Japanese, Indian?"

"You will not believe this, she's Indian."

Mrs. Krishnaswami covered her mouth, responding as if I had committed a blunder. "Are you serious? Is she Indian? Is she Indian from India? Did she look North Indian or South Indian?"

I grinned at her curiosity. "I don't know if she is North or South Indian. I don't know if she was born here or in India. But I do know that her face has not left my brain since New Year's Eve."

"As I said before, you must have been Indian in your past life. A person of your race who enjoys idli and dosa, rasam and sambar, makki di roti and saag, tandoori chicken, and mutton biryani is hard to find. And on top of that, now you select an Indian to fall in lovey-dovey with. You are one of a kind, Malcolm."

"Hmm, am I obsessed with Indians? I have an Indian friend. I have an Indian mother. I crave Indian food. I agree with Indian beliefs. I respect Indian culture. And now, I am head over heels in love with an Indian woman."

"So you do admit it—you are in lovey-dovey," said Mrs. Krishnaswami while pinching my cheek as if I were a little child. "Son, you have even fallen in lovey-dovey Indian style."

I was baffled by her statement. "What does that mean?"

"Well, the way you have fallen in lovey-dovey—that is entirely the Indian way." She explained, "You see, in the past, an Indian man needed one glance—that is all he needed—to fall in love with an Indian woman. A glance, then some eye contact, then a half-smile, and then a few words of love...That was enough to conquer a heart. And it even sealed the deal."

"Sealed the deal?"

"Yes, sealed the deal—marriage."

"I don't think a few words of love will seal the deal today. That was the past; this is the present. Women are harder to please and attract."

"I don't agree, Malcolm. Women are women. We don't change. It was not difficult to please us then, and it is not difficult to please us now. This formula of love worked thirty years ago when Mr. Krishnaswami, my husband, sealed the deal. All it took was—"

I had to; I wanted to, so I interrupted her, "All it took was a glance, then some eye contact, then a half-smile, and then a few words of love."

WEDNESDAY, FEBRUARY 15

For the past several weeks, there has been a tussle between my brain and heart. The brain says to concentrate on school, readings, drawings, and paintings. But it is the heart—the dimwit heart—which shifts my concentration to the woman from the train. Suzy, as you know, this is my final semester, and in this semester my goal is to top no one but myself. When I say top myself, that means I need to surpass my previous grades. I must turn the B's and B+'s into A's. I don't view the other students in my classes as rivals; the only competition I have is me—Malcolm Only. This is the viewpoint I stand by, and there is no person or thing that can alter it.

Lately, I have not been able to focus on my classes and studies. That unknown woman has captivated my heart. On top of that, she is on the verge of captivating my brain. "Stop, Malcolm!" That is what I say to myself, over and over again. But it never seems to stop images of her exquisite face. Sometimes, I even slap myself—not violently, but with enough force to bestir myself. Yet it never seems to eliminate the hope of bumping into her again.

Then one day, I ran to the bathroom, turned on the shower, and stood under the cold water. The cold shower was a penalty for spending an hour musing about her—her hair, her forehead, her eyebrows, her eyes, her nose, her mole, her lips, her chin, and her neck. Suzy, can you believe it? One whole hour! I should have dedicated that hour to my current projects and assignments. I had to let her slide—I had to, at least until my finals were completed. It took a whole lot of convincing, but eventually, my heart and brain understood that I had to entirely commit myself to schoolwork.

A few nights ago, I thought—and I thought hard. Next month was the final exam of my final term. A month after that was my graduation exhibition. I was in desperate need of finishing my portfolio, in desperate need of preparing for my exams, and in desperate need of creating a painting for the exhibition. So, it was best for her to leave. Well, for now.

There is a reason why I'm enrolled in the Fine Arts Degree Program—a reason why I attend university, a reason why I achieve high grades, and a reason why I have an extraordinary GPA. I'm an honors student who dreams of becoming an established painter. I want people to feel connected to my paintings. I want them to identify with them. I want them to see themselves—or a feature of their lives—in my art.

Besides, I had to show myself that despite facing abandonment, despite having no biological parents, I was somebody. Attaining a career, a name, and perhaps even fame was proof that someone with a past as dreadful as mine could lead a successful and meaningful life.

As for Miss Yang, she was the prime reason I endeavored to secure a career—a future. Ten years down the line, Miss Yang will be at the age when she'll need my care and support. And I am not a person who'd leave his adoptive mother in a care home. For years she was there by my side. When I most needed her, she was there. The day will arrive when I I'll have the opportunity to care for her—and when that day arrives, I will surely be there. I will never leave her, and I will never let her leave me.

The degree, that I promise to attain, belongs to Miss Yang. After all, she is the backbone, the driving force of my accomplishments.

In case you are wondering, it has been posted. Yes, the written letter was posted to Miss Yang in the first week of the month. And yes, I mustered enough courage to reveal my feelings about the nameless woman. Though I must admit, I did feel a bit timid. Expressing that you love someone whose name you don't know, whose voice you've never heard, whose house you've never seen, and whose family you've never met seems ridiculous. Also, for a son to express to his mother that he is in love with someone is definitely awkward. Thank God my voice was hidden behind ink, paper, letters, and words. If I were to voice my words to Miss Yang in person or over the phone, certainly I would not be able to open my mouth.

Once the letter was mailed, I started to overthink. "What if she feels disappointed? What if she feels that I am not dedicated to school? What if she feels that the unknown woman is a distraction? What if she feels threatened by this woman? What if she feels that this woman can destroy a mother-and-son relationship?" These were the absurd questions that revolved inside my brain. Suzy, I was overwhelmed by my inner thoughts and feelings until the 15th of February. Today, after forty-six days, eighteen hours, and ten minutes, I was blessed with her presence.

On Valentine's Day, I was imprisoned in my room. No one had placed me there—I chose to be there. Every second was dedicated to the handouts and notes that lay on the table. I reviewed the material that was significant. Even with my eyes becoming dog-tired, I pushed myself. Soon, there was a chant inside my head: "Ace the exams, ace the exams, ace the exams." Instead of having a supportive effect, the chant was stressful. I was too stubborn to realize that by pushing myself, I was pressuring myself.

Hours later, with my brain loaded with all kinds of material, I permitted my hands to take control. I drew in my sketchbook, capturing memorable images from my personal life and vivid dreams. One of these drawings was to be painted on a canvas and submitted for the graduation exhibition. But I was not sure if I had a creation that was praiseworthy. Suzy, when I painted, I ensured it was my best. Whatever the image contained, it had to be worthwhile—it had to be meaningful.

With a couple of months left until the exhibition, I was still unsure of what—or who—to place on the canvas. By the end of the day, the understanding, memorizing, note-taking, and drawing had numbed my brain. My muscles were cramped due to a lack of movement. My eyes were filled with unemotional tears due to excessive usage. My stomach was growling from skipping lunch and dinner. And my bottom was aching from sitting on a wooden chair for hours.

Today, I decided to rest my brain to some extent. I did attend classes at university, I did concentrate on the lectures, I did purchase food at the cafeteria, and I did study in the library—but I did not return to the dormitory. If I had, I know I'd be caged inside the room. Once caged, there was no escaping. I'd be entrapped with my focus on the sketchbook and textbooks, so involved that a knock on the door—or even someone calling my name—would not be detected.

So, the desire was to emancipate the brain. I needed to be free. I needed to feel peace within. In a situation like this, it is the pond I visit. The pond has the ability to ease my brain, settle my heart, and comfort my soul. Besides, it also provides the opportunity to come face to face with her—the woman from the train.

"Perhaps luck will be on my side today. Who knows, I may come across her on the train," I said to myself. Actually, I was beginning to lose hope. It felt like ages since I had seen her—but in reality, it had been only six weeks. Since I chose not to visit the dorm after the last class, I fastened the Swiss backpack over my shoulders and headed directly to the train station.

The journey from the campus to the train station was excruciating. Do I look like a soldier, Suzy? Do you think I'm a soldier capable of trekking through forests and mountains with a hulking backpack fastened to his shoulders? My Swiss backpack didn't contain food, water, ammunition, or weaponry—it contained a sketchbook, textbooks, binders, papers, pens, pencils, pastels, erasers, and a stainless steel water bottle. To you and others, these items may seem easy to lift and carry. Well, ask my shoulders how they felt. To haul these items for fifteen minutes was no easy task.

Eventually, I arrived at the train station. As I walked on the platform, my eyes captured a shining reflection—the sunlight glinting off a silver coin. Others noticed it but intentionally disregarded it. With people dashing past, beside, and even over the coin, I inched closer for a better look. Malcolm never disregarded or disrespected a coin on the ground. I was praying to see the head of a prominent figure. "Heads side up, please, heads side up," I said out loud.

Descending to the platform, I noticed the judging eyes of the bystanders. I positioned one knee on the ground for balance, scooped up the coin, and slipped it into the left pocket of my trousers. As I stood, I released a shout filled with excitement. Everyone on the platform was left dumbfounded. Some turned their heads. They probably believed I was under the influence of something—or simply intoxicated. I paid no attention. After all, these people were unaware of my beliefs.

At that moment, I was extremely satisfied. The dime that I collected rested on the platform with its heads side up, which meant it promised good fortune. Believe it or not, that coin provided inspiration. With this dime in my pocket, I felt lucky. My spirit was lifted. My soul came alive. Right then and there, I started to believe I was capable of acing my final exams. I started to believe I could paint a worthwhile creation for the exhibition. I started to believe that sooner or later, I'd spot that woman. Suzy, Malcolm is back. I think it's fair to say I have somewhat calmed my heart and brain.

An evening at the pond was the ideal place to unwind—the perfect spot to forget our troubles, concerns, pressures, responsibilities, commitments, and desires. I selfishly claimed a bench for myself. With my backpack slid to one corner, I parked my bottom and rested my limbs on the available space.

The unclouded skies on a winter evening were rare. Unlike most winter days and nights when rain poured or frost emerged, today was more cool than chilly. Despite the coolness, I was dressed as if the weather forecast predicted heavy snowfall. I wore a warm jacket, cotton sweater, khaki pants, and a wool toque. I also wore leather mittens to protect my fingers from going numb.

Suzy, I am not the kind of person who dresses to impress the ladies. I dress according to the weather. The clothes I wore today didn't match in style or color—but that was the least of my concerns. So what if I didn't look or dress like models from a fashion catalog? Even today, as I rode the train, no one preferred to sit in the empty seat beside me. Do you think it's the way I dress? Do people think I look like a clown or a hipster? Maybe these passengers feel too embarrassed to sit beside me. Whatever it may be, I had to release it from my system.

I was at the pond. I was to focus on my surroundings. Emptying the nonessential, I scanned the area. At first, my eyes beheld devastation. The trees that were once filled with red, orange, yellow, and brown leaves had changed. Not a single leaf was spotted on the branches of the naked trees. From dressed to undressed, healthy to unhealthy, colorful to colorless, the trees were on the verge of pushing me back into the dismal state from which I had escaped—until my ears caught the sound of ducks quacking nearby.

It was a sight to remember, a sight I was eager to render in my sketchbook. I viewed a clan of ducks paddling across the waters from one end to another. The ducks moved in a straight line. The family—mother, father, sons, and daughters—were at ease. Not once did these ducks expect to be harmed or harassed, not by humans and not by other animals. When humans came near them, they had the audacity not to flinch until the last second. There was no fear in the hearts of these birds. And the reason for this was the white goose.

The goose was their protector—a sentinel. Every moment, the ducks were guided and assisted by the waterbird. As the ducks swam, the goose led the way. When the ducks waddled on land, the goose kept a close eye on unfriendly or over-friendly humans. When the skies were intruded upon by predators, the goose honked to alert the ducks.

Suzy, why was a lone goose among a family of ducks? Did God send the goose to protect them—just as He sent Miss Yang to protect me? Honestly, isn't that a bit odd?

Relaxing on the bench, I focused on the exquisite birds of the pond. I noticed that the male and female ducks were different in appearance. The males had green-colored faces with black stripes on light greyish bodies. Their white tails shifted from side to side as they waddled past each other. The females also had white tails, but their bodies were covered in black and brown specks. Despite the somber colors, the females were far more attractive than the males.

Their femininity was displayed in and around their eyes—a black line extending from the corner of the eye to the side of the head, similar to mascara on a woman's eyelashes. The thought of mascara and eyelashes reminded me of the woman from the train. In those seconds when our eyes met, surprisingly, I did notice the enhancing mascara. The liquid invention complemented her eyes.

God, she was beautiful! I so wished—truly wished—that she was there at the pond. I wished for her to tiptoe behind me, place her hands over my eyes, then bring her lips close to my ear and whisper, "Guess who? Malcolm, do you know who I am?"

One more look at her beauty—and that would be plenty to heal and fulfill.

Leaving the pond, I was occupied with her thoughts. Ambling down the sidewalk, I was occupied by her thoughts. Nearing the train station, I was still lost in her thoughts. Entering the platform, I was revived by the loud commotion of human voices and moving trains. As soon as I returned to my senses, I noticed the train waiting at the station to board passengers. But what I did not see was when the train arrived at the station. Any other day, I would let the train proceed, unless I was in a rush to arrive someplace. Though I was in no rush today, my feet were at full speed. Bolting across the platform, I asked myself, "Why is it necessary to board this train?" I knew that the next train would arrive five minutes after the current one departed. I knew that there was no one waiting for my arrival at the dormitory. Yet I was bolting in the direction of the train as if my life depended on it. Who or what force was behind this action, I had no clue. I was still three to five steps away from the train when the automated sound indicated that the doors were about to close. So do you want to know how much time I had before the doors shut in my face? I am sure you do, Suzy. Well, I had one second. Call it a miracle, but I was able to use my left knee to force open the doors. As the doors closed inward, I succeeded in wedging my knee inside, not letting the doors connect until I entered. When the knee hindered the closing, I barged the doors open with my hands. The act instantly compelled other passengers on board to stare. A bit shame-faced for the disliked act, I nervously took an empty seat without meeting the alienating eyes of the passengers. I thought once, twice, and then thrice before scanning the train car. I was fortunate to reach the doors within a second. I was fortunate that the doors were obstructed by my timely knee. I was fortunate that no passenger on board confronted the act. And I was fortunate that I was not given the opportunity to retaliate with hostile words or expressions. Deep within, I knew that I had the ability to both attack and counterattack. I had the courage not to back down from a physical or verbal altercation. But never did I want this ability to surface. Never did I want this ability to be used. It was better to store this ability deep within the heart.

Suzy, I have seen numerous passengers do what I did today. Passengers forcefully hold the doors open for their friends and even strangers to gain entry. In fact, at times, these people hold the doors open for more than ten seconds. Sometimes, I feel as if everyone in the world is in a hurry. Life is fast, and for humans to survive, they have to be fast as well. It seems like most people don't have patience. But I do—I have patience. Suzy, I know you must be wondering, if Malcolm is patient, then why hadn't he waited to board the next train? But like I said before, I felt as if I was controlled by an unknown force. Who knows, it could have been God.

I scanned the train car and observed the passengers involved in conversations, engaged in cellphone talk, occupied with headphones and music players, absorbed in video games, and immersed in reading the latest bestseller. Instantly, these people had forgotten that I delayed them for a full second. Yes, one full second. With this fact in mind, I smiled to myself, for myself. To keep myself from drifting into a barrage of thoughts, I decided to view the city lights as the train progressed. However, before I could do that, my eyes landed upon her—the woman from the train, the woman that I love, and the woman that I need to connect with. She was there.

The vision I had of her was distinct. From where I was seated, I was able to see what she had been wearing. She wore black denim jeans with a plain white blouse. The blouse was partially covered by a not-so-flashy but classy long coat. Her hands were mittenless, her neck scarf-less, and her waist beltless. She had silver hoops dangling from her ears, and she wore leather boots that reached her knees. Simplicity did not minimize beauty; instead, it enhanced it. As for the woman on the train, her beauty was her simplicity. She did not seem like the women who dressed to impress men, nor did she seem like the woman who dressed to receive attention. Not an inch of her skin was revealed; no assets were flaunted. For a large number of men, no display of skin is a letdown. In my case, I began to respect and adore her even more. Her sense of fashion—practically her dressing style—hinted that she was a well-mannered, intelligent, hard-to-get woman.

Between her and me was a distance of ten steps, five seats, and seven people. At that moment, I felt like walking over to her and introducing myself. My eyes were on her, but her eyes were on the needle and yarn. She was hard at work. Not a hundred percent sure, but it looked as if she was knitting a toque. The beat of my heart resonated—thump-thump, thump-thump, thump-thump. It was hard to believe that the woman I dream of, daydream about, and dwell on was so close by. This was my chance. Who knows if this chance would reappear? I had to rise to my feet. I did rise—but then I sat back down. I noticed that the seat beside her was not empty but occupied by her backpack. If I were to stride over to her location, what then? Where would I sit? Her backpack looked overpacked. It must have contained textbooks, notebooks, pens, pencils, food containers, snacks, and drinks. I guessed that she attended a nearby college or university. Perhaps she was a Fashion Design or Visual Arts student.

These thoughts I was fiddling with were supposed to be turned into practical questions for her to answer. But the unavailable seat beside her clearly said, "She does not want to talk, therefore, please look for a different seat." I had a feeling that by placing her backpack on the seat beside her, she was purposely avoiding desperate men, obnoxious pickup lines, and intolerable sweet talk. But among all those men who desired her, I was the one who truly loved her. Hmm, that may not be true. What if she has a loving boyfriend? Or what if she is engaged? Or what if she is married and has children? The thought of her face to face, hand in hand, or lip to lip with someone else sent a harpoon straight into my wistful heart.

Suzy, I fell for her—and fell for her hard. She pulled at my heartstrings. This woman, whom I have not voiced a single word to, changed me. I had to talk to her. I had to ask her who she was, where she was from, and what she did. But first and foremost, I needed to ask for her name. There was a definite vibe in the air, a vibe that surrounded her. This vibe had an influence on my limbs. I was not able to lift myself off the seat, walk over to her, look her in the eyes, and ask if I could sit beside her. It seemed as if there was a protective shield revolving around her. It was her reclusive behavior that did not permit others to approach her. Suzy, I wonder if she is the "I'm too good for you" type. I'm not attracted to those kinds of women. But I had my fingers crossed.

While I literally intertwined my fingers, her fingers were operating nonstop. The reason she did not involve herself with others was that she was engaged in knitting. Honestly, seven out of ten people on the train kept to themselves. A train is a place of reclusiveness more than gregariousness. People have all kinds of excuses to be left alone. Some of these include covering their ears with headphones, listening to melodious tunes, talking to friends on their phones, studying for tests or exams, reading spellbinding novels, or looking at the scenery outside. What I usually did on the train was ruminate, ruminate, and ruminate. But right then, I didn't have the opportunity to ruminate. I was too focused on watching her.

She looked at ease while knitting the toque. The movement of her fingers showcased years of experience. I am certain that knitting for her is more than a hobby—it is a part of her life. It also has the power to illuminate her. Surely, it makes her feel lighthearted. When disturbed, lonely, or restless, she runs to her needles and yarn. There was no doubt that what painting meant to me, knitting meant to her.

The programmed announcement for the next stop echoed in the background. Since all my senses were concentrated on her, I did not know what the previous stop was or what the upcoming one would be. Instead, I was too busy adoring her beauty. At times, strands of hair fell in front of her eyes. Immediately, her expression altered. Her carefree state was overtaken by annoyance. She did not want to lift her hand to brush aside the strands. She was not willing to disrupt the perfect rhythm in which her fingers moved. If I were in her shoes, I would have done the same. I'd continue until my stop arrived. Unfortunately, the pestering strands of hair did not back down.

Her response to the annoyance carved a grin on my face. It was my first grin, courtesy of her. Not willing to use her hand, she used the air and her lips to blow upward. It was the comical expression she made that carved the grin on my face. The act did steer the loose hairs aside, but soon they fell back near her eyes again. Realizing that she had lost the battle, her fingers eventually came to a stop. She placed the tools and material beside her. Promptly, the loose hairs were collected and set into place. She then unzipped her backpack. After dropping her items inside, she rose to her feet.

When she rose, I was able to see her full body. She was not all skin and bones. She was not thick or plump. In fact, she was perfect. I stared at her figure, ensuring not to drool. She had the ideal body—the body of a curvy heroine. She probably visited the gym or attended yoga sessions. So if I ever feel the need to search for her, I'll go directly to a gym or yoga institute. She flung the backpack over her shoulder. She was prepared to disembark, as the next stop was hers.

I did not expect her to look here or there—and that is where I faltered. Not once during the train ride did she remove her eyes from the needle and yarn. She did not look up, left, right, or down. She did not even know who sat behind her or in front of her. But when the train was closing in on the platform, she lifted her eyes—and her eyes landed directly upon mine. With her eyes, she captured my eyes capturing her. As soon as her eyes met mine, I withdrew. My gaze dropped to the floor within a heartbeat.

I hoped she did not think I was stalking her. I hoped she did not think I was a pervert. I hoped she did not think I was high or drunk. Suzy, I was overreacting, but I was nervous.

I did not want her to view me as some loser. I am no loser. I need to remove the 's' from loser and replace it with a 'v.'

"Enough! I have to face her," I said to myself as the train halted. The station had arrived. The doors were about to open. People were eager to leave. This opportunity may have been my last. Perhaps, I would never see her again. It is not through silence that we express our feelings to the people we love; it is through words and actions.

So there I was, prepared to act and talk, but I had no idea what to do or say. In this case, I left it in the hands of God. I silently prayed for Him to provide the help and support I needed in dealing with her. Lifting my face and eyes, I rose from the seat. She observed the rise of Malcolm. While I searched for hope, desire, or love in her reddish-brown eyes, she remained still as passengers around her exited the train. Her face was unlit until she lit it with a beam. Her smile was so exhilarating that I unwittingly fell back into the seat.

That smile was for me—and only me. It was a smile that indicated she knew. Suzy, she knew how I felt. She knew who I was. She had not forgotten New Year's Eve, the encounter on the train, the feelings of déjà vu. Maybe this isn't one-sided love. Maybe our love is mutual.

It was after she disembarked that I realized, once again, not a single word had been voiced to her. But Suzy, without voicing a single word, I still felt that profound connection. After that heavenly smile, she walked onto the crowded platform. The ocean of people devoured her within seconds. At that moment, I was convinced that she and I would meet again. And the next time we meet, I will definitely talk to her.

THURSDAY, MARCH 1

Several days ago, I received a letter from Miss Yang. She had responded to my initial letter in which I disclosed that her son had fallen in love. I updated her on my school, classes, grades, exams, and Mrs. Krishnaswami. I even discussed my ideas for the painting that was to be submitted at the graduation exhibition. In response, Miss Yang had plenty to say.

Son, how are you? I hope you are fine. I miss you. I can't wait for you to return home. Home is not home without you. Apart from that, I am fine, my health is fine, and my work is fine. Malcolm, I hope you like surprises. The reason why I am asking is that I have so much planned for us. But I will not tell you about these plans. I will keep it a secret. Anyhow, it is wonderful to know that you're passing the exams and maintaining high grades. It has been a dream to see you walk on the podium, dressed in a black gown, to receive the degree you've strived for. And soon that dream will come true.

Malcolm, you will not believe it, I have already selected the dress, earrings, and heels that I'll wear to your graduation. Also, the light grey suit, in which you looked dashing, has been placed in your closet. It will be in your hands as soon as I meet you at the dormitory. You have no idea how excited I am. The countdown has begun. Only thirty-five days remain. Finally, I will have the opportunity to see my son achieve a degree with honors.

Malcolm, if I am not stopped, I can talk and write about the graduation for hours. But don't worry, I will not bore you. Your ideas for the painting, which need to be submitted, are unique. Though, I am not the right person to advise you on which sketch is best to move forward with. You are the painter, not your mother. Only you know what should be painted and what shouldn't. Believe in yourself, Malcolm. You have impressed before; you will impress again. All I know is that whatever the painting will be, it will be magnificent.

Sure, your paintings are not for everyone to understand. Even I don't understand them sometimes. Though, it is not the message but the elegance of the painting that counts.

And I will say this for the rest of my life — no one else paints like my son. You have your own style. So please don't ever change that style for others.

Okay, now let's dive into a serious matter. What is this I hear about you falling in love? This woman you have encountered on the train — do you truly love her? It is hard to love someone without fully knowing them. Love is serious, Malcolm. I know you are serious, but I also know that you don't have her name, age, occupation, home address, or contact number. Son, I don't want to hurt your feelings, but I have to reveal what I truly feel. I think you should fully concentrate on your exams and paintings. This is your last semester; this is worth all the marbles. Once the final exam period is done, you will be free.

When you're free, then divert your attention to the woman from the train. My advice to you is, don't search for her. If she is meant to be a part of your life, God will bring her to you. Have faith and patience. No more back-and-forth letters, Malcolm. In a month, I will be there for you at the graduation and exhibition. Have I told you how excited I am? I am sure I did, but I will say it once more — I am truly excited to attend your graduation. Malcolm, I have to say that it is a blessing to have you as my son. Words can't express how much I love you and how proud I am of you. Before this letter gets soaked with tears, I will take your leave.

Good luck with your exams.

Love you.

Suzy, I apologize. You and I will not meet for the next four weeks. I will be in full-time study mode for the entire month of March. It will be hard, and I will miss you. But you have to understand, these are my finals. Miss Yang is counting on her son. I am counting on myself. For most courses, these exams account for twenty-five to fifty percent of the final grade. At this moment, the final term exams are what separate me from the outside world.

Once the exams are finished, I will not be enslaved by the university, professors, studying, exams, presentations, and GPA. Instead, I will be enslaved by the real world — the companies, the bosses, the guidelines, the deadlines, the customers, and the money. I ask myself if we are born slaves. Do we come into this world as slaves? If I say that this life, this world, is hell, then I believe we are slaves. We come into this world as slaves and leave either to be reincarnated into the cycle or liberated from it.

Life can be blissful, however, only to an extent. In the end, sadness overpowers all kinds of happiness. Hmm, why am I talking so negatively? It is probably because I am in study mode. When studying, I act like some prisoner chained to the walls of a dungeon. From morning till night, I stay locked inside the bedroom. Trivedi and Herb both know not to disturb me, not to raise their voices, and not to knock on my door. In fact, both of them never did. They were aware of my unpleasantness when finals were around the corner.

During the exam period, I become extra serious and tense. I don't accept nonsense, and I don't accept wittiness. There was no chance for discussions unrelated to Fine Arts or final exams. The once easygoing Malcolm will soon be remembered as the man who often lost his cool. I pray to God that I don't say or do anything regretful. You see, the burden of acing the exams can force me to become enraged, inconsiderate, and disrespectful.

Actually, I'm a bit afraid. I don't want to hurt feelings, break hearts, or terminate relationships. I have a month left on campus and in university, so I want to leave on a good note and good terms.

"During this month, if I ever talk or act rudely, please let it slide. Sometimes, I will pay no attention to you because my attention will be devoted to textbooks. At times, I may respond in frustration because an unclear concept in the textbook has frustrated me. So please let it slide," I explained to Trivedi and Herb, who understood that I was requesting forgiveness before performing the wrongful deed.

I, Malcolm Only, who used to feel so dejected because of isolation, will now live in seclusion for a month. For God's sake, I even promised myself not to ruminate on her — the woman from the train. It will be difficult, but I have to ignore her for some time. The brain has to be restrained whenever her face appears.

Also, I have talked to Mrs. Krishnaswami about quitting my weekend shifts at the corner store. I informed her about the final term exams and that I decided to return to Miss Yang after graduation. It is painful to leave a mother behind, but I had to leave Mrs. Krishnaswami to reunite with Miss Yang.

If only both mothers lived in the same city, I'd be so fortunate. If only both mothers lived in the same household, I'd be extremely fortunate. But Mrs. Krishnaswami has a loving husband and children. She is also devoted to her convenience store. Her hands are full of responsibilities. As for Miss Yang, she has no one else besides me. I am needed in her life more than I am needed in Mrs. Krishnaswami's.

However, I have said it before and I will say it again — it is painful to leave a mother behind. Suzy, this is exactly how I felt when I left Miss Yang behind to start a new life on campus. During our heartfelt conversation, Mrs. Krishnaswami accepted my leave of absence from the corner store and her life.

With her troubled voice she said, "Malcolm, your decision to return home is acceptable. But I do expect you to keep in touch. Please don't forget your Indian mother."

As I spoke to her from the housing office, I felt tears roll down my cheeks. "I will never forget you. And God will never forgive me if I do."

"Malcolm, please do visit before you leave. I will be very upsetty wetty if you don't come by to see your mother."

"Upsetty wetty — is that a new one?" I asked her, desperate to lighten the mood.

She did not reply. Mrs. Krishnaswami became silent. It was not likely for her to stay mum.

"Hello, are you still there?"

"Yes, Malcolm, I am still here. I am waiting for your response. Will you visit me?"

"No, I will not visit you," I waited for a couple of seconds before uttering, "Because you will visit me. Mrs. Krishnaswami, I want you to attend my graduation exhibition. And I want you to bring your husband and children too. I am ready to meet your family. So, what say? Will you come?"

THURSDAY, APRIL 5

At last, the day had come for Malcolm Only to graduate. After extensive days and countless hours of studying, acknowledging, and remembering, I wrote my final exams. Suzy, God be praised, I am free. I feel like a slave who has been liberated after years of hardship. In the final week of March, the results for the exams were posted online. I logged into the university website to view the results. Suzy, guess what? I aced all five exams. In all the exams, I had a percentage of ninety or higher. Can you believe that? To my knowledge, I did study hard. I did feel confident before writing the exams. But to receive such high grades in my courses was a pleasant surprise. So the days, hours, minutes, and seconds locked inside my bedroom paid off in the end.

Miss Yang was proud when she heard that I finished with an overall 3.75 GPA. For the entire morning, I received warm hugs and soft handshakes. Miss Yang, Trivedi, Herb, Eliza, and Haylee were the first people to congratulate me. As I walked down the halls, I was commended by professors who did not endeavor to understand my paintings. These were professors who judged paintings based on art and craft. I praise them for not searching for a message behind every painting.

Talking of praise, my ears nearly drowned from all the praise Miss Yang showered upon me. She arrived in the city last night. Not wanting to be a disturbance, she preferred to occupy a hotel for a couple of nights. At first, I did not agree with her plans, but there was no other choice since she couldn't stay at the dormitory. Miss Yang's heart was made of gold. She did not mind resting in a three-star hotel. "Anything for you, Malcolm," she said in a poised manner.

Suzy, the extent to which a mother can bend for her child is admirable. After embracing her son, Miss Yang handed over the graduation present. It was the ever-so-popular, three-piece, light grey suit. Along with the suit came black dress shoes and a white dress shirt. Then unexpectedly, Miss Yang searched her purse as if she had misplaced an item.

Her hand scrambled inside the purse until she extracted a black tie. Now, this was no ordinary tie — it was a clip-on bow tie.

"Are you serious?" I asked her, with an unsmiling face.

"Isn't it adorable? I honestly think it will suit you. If it suits Fresh, it will suit you too," she replied, excitement in her voice.

"Fresh? Who or what is Fresh?"

"Fresh... Fresh Prince from television. Remember, I once said that you resemble him. He wears bow ties. Actually, he wears funky-colored bow ties like purple and yellow..."

Before Miss Yang could continue with her absurdness, I had to step in, "Thank God it is not purple or yellow. Black is normal. Whether it suits me or not, I will put the bow tie on. I have never said no to you, and I never will."

After delivering the graduation attire, Miss Yang took a cab back to the hotel. Fortunately, the hotel she booked was close to the university. Before leaving, she ordered that I was not to be late for my graduation. Her stern instructions were to be properly dressed and to be at the graduation hall thirty minutes before the ceremony. When I asked her why so early, she replied, "Malcolm, there is a reason I purchased a brand-new camera. The camera debuts at this event. Please, I need you to be there half an hour before the ceremony starts."

I was able to see jubilation in her eyes, hear the satisfaction in her voice, and notice pride in her body language. Miss Yang was proud — and she was proud of nobody else but her son. If one can give happiness to their parents by achieving and performing, only then is he or she a respectable son or daughter. Suzy, never have I considered myself a worthy son. But today I feel different. I feel worthy, I feel respected, I feel important — and it is entirely because of Miss Yang. I am very grateful to have a supportive mother like her, a mother who is happy only when her son is happy. So believe me, I am happy.

"There is nothing that can make this day better than it already is," I said to myself while dressing in black, grey, and white.

During my late teen years, when I somewhat explored different religions, Miss Yang said that instead of asking God for what you desire, thank Him for what you have. That advice has never left my brain. The days I separate myself and whisper to God, I make sure to thank Him for everything in my life. And today was the perfect day to repeat this act.

"God, wherever you are, whoever you may be, I thank you for this life. I thank you for all my five senses. I thank you for allowing me to breathe. I thank you for the abounding parents. If it was not for them, I would have never come across Miss Yang. I thank you for sending the angel, Miss Yang. If it was not for her, I would have never experienced the love of a mother. I thank you for a parent who is considerate and supportive. Without her support, I would have never been able to study Fine Arts. I thank you for introducing the hobo. If it was not for that homeless man, I would have never discovered art, paintings, and pastels. He is my idol, and it is because of him that I will strive to become a renowned painter in the near future. I thank you for the grade school teachers and university professors who shared knowledge and provided the assistance needed for students to progress in their lives and careers. I thank you for the friends I made in university. From them, I received different viewpoints. If it was not for them, I would have never figured out how different I am compared to others. I thank you for a second mother, Mrs. Krishnaswami. If it was not for her, I would have never discovered the Indian in me. From her, I learned the true meaning of unconditional love. She proved that in this world unconditional love still exists. Who am I to her? Who is she to me? Did I ever say that I love her like a mother? No, I have never said that. But I do, I do love her. Since the first day we met, I had sensed the love — the kind of love a mother hails upon her son. And last but not least, I thank my disturbing past. Despite my passion for art, it was my past that drove me to attend university, to pass my exams, to ace my courses, and to become an honored graduate. I wanted to prove to myself that I could eliminate my dreadful past and continue toward a hopeful future."

After this heart-to-heart with God, I studied myself in the mirror. Miss Yang was not kidding; I did look handsome in the light grey suit. To my surprise, the light grey complemented my ebony skin. I touched my cheeks to feel the smoothness left behind by the electric razor. At first, the clean-shaven face looked unusual, but I soon realized that I had become accustomed to my patchy stubble. I then used the Afro pick, which I had not touched since God knows when, to comb my hair. A decision for a haircut before graduation was made, but the exams had deprived my body of vitality.

The five days between the posting of results and the celebrated graduation were my resting period. During this period, I lounged while viewing overdone television sitcoms and listened to Trivedi and Herb's outrageous stories. Besides lounging, I worked on the painting that needed to be completed and submitted for the graduation exhibition.

You know, Suzy, from high school to university I had considered myself only average-looking. Striking, attractive, good-looking, drop-dead gorgeous — these words don't explain my appearance. Malcolm and handsome? I don't think so. But today was my day.

Believe me when I say this: "Malcolm Only will make heads turn, eyes wander, and mouths open at the graduation ceremony and exhibition."

Before heading for the door, I polished my shoes, tucked in my shirt, fixed my collar, and adjusted my bow tie. As my hand clutched the doorknob, I remembered the woman from the train. The brain formed an image of her. There she was, under a blossoming jasmine tree, dressed in a yellow-colored sari, impatiently waiting for someone. "God, I thank you for her," I said under my breath.

The graduation hall was located on the university campus. It took four minutes to walk from the dorm to the hall. Entering the doors to the lounge, within seconds my eyes rested upon the formally dressed Miss Yang. She wore a navy blue dress with black heels and earrings. Never before had I seen Miss Yang dressed so elegantly. She was not overdressed or underdressed for the occasion. She was not too showy or too simple. She was the best dressed among all the mothers in the sea of proud parents.

As soon as she located me, I did not have the chance to pose or smile for the pictures. Her finger needed to be removed from the button. Snap, snap, snap went her camera. Without expecting the act, I tightly embraced her. Eventually, her photo-snapping came to a halt.

"Words can't express how proud I am of you, Malcolm," she said, her voice quavering.

Before she became emotional with teardrops, I withdrew and started to pose. "It's photo-shoot time!" With that remark, I dried the imminent tears from her eyes. Miss Yang was so ecstatic that she almost blinded me with nonstop photo snapping.

Minutes later, I was rescued by my classmates from the Fine Arts Diploma Program. When these fine gentlemen arrived to congratulate and be congratulated, I introduced them to Miss Yang. These were the same classmates I had studied with for the last couple of years. And these were the same classmates whom I never viewed as competition. Suzy, I am sure you noticed that I referred to them as classmates, not friends. We were not friends, nor were we foes.

I asked one of them to snap a picture of Miss Yang and me together. Once we smiled at the camera, all eyes were on us. Everyone in the lounge gaped as if we were both aliens from outer space. Why? Was it because we are not the same color? Was it because we don't have the same features? In all honesty, I don't think Miss Yang even noticed. She was too involved with her soon-to-be diploma holder. On top of that, she was obsessed with her camera.

"You seriously have to give that camera a rest. What if the battery dies in the middle of the actual ceremony?" I asked her.

"Don't worry, I have the charger in my purse," she replied.

When the principals and professors announced for the graduates to collect behind the stage, Miss Yang applauded energetically. Her rapture was showcased via her facial expressions and body language. I believe she was the most excited of all the mothers and fathers attending. Miss Yang consistently expressed that I made her feel proud. Well, I feel proud of her. Embarrassment was not linked with her presence, appearance, support, or love. She publicly displayed that her love had no boundaries, and I did not have a problem with that.

On the verge of entering the backstage area, I advised Miss Yang to find a decent seat in the hall before it was too late. I told her that the first five rows were booked for principals, professors, graduates, and guest speakers. Despite these five rows, every other row and seat was for the graduates' family and friends.

"For sure, I will be in the sixth row," said Miss Yang confidently. Suzy, I don't think I have told you, but from my side, Miss Yang was the only person attending the graduation ceremony. It's not that others would not have come. It's that I did not invite others to come. No person in my life is more valued than Miss Yang. This is her moment. It is her dream to see her son graduate with a diploma. This event should be cherished by her and her alone. By not inviting others, I wanted Miss Yang to know she is the most important — more important than anyone else.

Even with the graduation hall located on campus, I had never visited it before. I did not expect the hall to be so massive. As the band of graduates from various programs walked in single file to their rows, I examined the hall. Its decor was similar to a monumental church. The podium had a long red carpet on which the graduates walked to receive their certificates. At the far corner of the podium was a mic and stand for the professors and guest speakers involved in the ceremony. Hundreds of lights on the walls and ceilings made the hall look energized and enthusiastic. Even if I were to spend the whole day inside the hall, I would not be able to count the number of seats it contained. The rows were filled with human bodies and faces. Most of the faces were hard to identify. Also, spotting an empty seat was impossible. It seemed to be a full house.

Families applauded continuously, waving their hands in the air, shouting on top of their lungs, and clicking photos like there was no tomorrow. The reception was grand for us graduates. Honestly, I received goosebumps from the flashing lights, clapping hands, and vociferous motivation. The noise level declined as soon as we graduates took our seats. Seated with close to a hundred graduates and three hundred guests, the temperature inside the hall became stifling. I was boiling inside my gown. Picture this, Suzy: I was dressed in a shirt, vest, blazer, and gown — that is four layers of clothing. To make things worse, the shirt was polyester. Yes, it clung to my skin.

Overlooking the heat and sweat, I rotated my neck in search of Miss Yang. At first, she was nowhere to be found. Then, before the opening speech, I looked behind and found my angel. Unexpectedly, I was blinded. It was a flash — a camera flash. After rubbing the shine from my eyes, I was greeted by Miss Yang. Who else clicked my photo other than Miss Yang? As promised, she was seated in the sixth row. I was a couple of rows below her. Her face glowed with a smile. In return, I did my best to match the loveliest smile in the world.

The ceremony lasted one hundred and forty minutes, which included the showing of pictures and videos, collecting awards and prizes, congratulatory speeches, and receiving our diplomas. When the principal of the university finished his uplifting speech, the graduates celebrated by tossing their academic caps in the air. Suzy, I was probably the only graduate who did not play toss-and-catch. I climbed over the seats to unite with Miss Yang. Arriving at her position, I removed the academic cap and placed it in her hands.

"This belongs to you, Mom."

The art exhibition began an hour after the graduation ceremony had finished. A total of forty-five graduates from the Fine Arts program were asked to proceed to the exhibition halls. An announcement was made for the parents and friends to gather around the front doors of the exhibition halls at four o'clock. At that time, the doors would be opened for the guests to view the creative paintings. As the professors from the Fine Arts unit led us to the exhibition halls, I waved to Miss Yang. It was visible in her eyes that she was excited to see what I had painted. No one knew what I had in store for them. The painting was not intended to surprise others, but I did believe that once the painting was viewed, there would be a lot of questions related to whom, when, and why.

Suzy, do you know what I mean by whom, when, and why? If not, then soon you will find out. Arriving at the exhibition halls, the team of professors asked the graduates to remove their gowns and caps. After sweating profusely inside the gown, I felt overjoyed to remove the extra piece of clothing. The graduates were then requested to stand near their paintings that were to be exhibited. Each painting had a title or name of its own, and these paintings were posted on the exhibition display boards in alphabetical order. To find my painting was not difficult.

As I sauntered in the direction of my painting, I examined the various styles, colors, lines, patterns, and formations on the display boards. Never once did I compare my artistic work with the other students' work. Instead, I ruminated on how different these paintings were from mine. There was so much to discover and learn. Some of the techniques used by the other painters were awe-inspiring. During that moment, I understood that creativity has no bounds. To be innovative, you have to be different from others. And I am different from others, just like they are different from me.

There was not a single person out of the forty-five graduates who submitted a pastel painting except for Malcolm Only. No other person's fingers were smudged with pastel except mine. That itself made me believe that I was different. The further I walked, the more I appraised the exhibition halls. Suzy, the place was similar to a set from a Hollywood film. Seriously, it was the ideal place to be for a painter. The only things decorated were the canvases pinned to the display boards. Despite the canvases, which held artistic talent, the entire space was not adorned. The walls, floors, and ceiling inside the exhibition halls were colorless. Even the constructed display boards were plain white.

You know, Suzy, it is a pleasure for us artists to see blankness. These halls were a painter's delight. I was craving to decorate the walls with mountains, rivers, trees, and flowers. I was longing to create various shapes and patterns on the floor and paint the moon and stars on the ceiling. While examining the uncolored halls and colored paintings, I didn't notice how fast time passed by. Stationed by what I felt was my all-time favorite creation, I ensured that the information written below the painting was correct. I read the title out loud, "She Awaits Your Presence." Then under the name of the painting, it said, "It was I who fell for you in the past. It was I who fell for you in the present. Today, in different bodies we may exist, but our souls are connected from one life to another." The title and information posted on the display board were accurate to what I had submitted. I had no complaints to report.

Suzy, this exhibition was not a competition. There were no first, second, or third prize winners. There were no grades or percentages involved. It was a function held to encourage parents, friends, and students. It was for everyone to appreciate and respect our talent. All the graduates, proud and positive, eyed the front doors, waiting for the guests to step into the halls. We all hoped to impress.

When the front doors opened, parents, friends, and university students poured in. Suzy, I don't think I have mentioned before that students from the university were also permitted to attend the graduation exhibition held on campus. Altogether, close to one hundred and fifty people walked into the halls. Satisfied parents, excited friends, and interested students crowded near the exhibition display boards. I searched high and low, far and wide for Miss Yang, but I was unable to see her in the abundant crowd. I was positive that the organizers had not anticipated such a vast turnout. It seemed like most of the people who attended the graduation ceremony were also present for the art exhibition.

Minute after minute, I was greeted by known and unknown faces. I was asked various questions, such as what kind of painting it was, what tools and materials I used for the painting, and what kind of pastels I used. Others even asked whether I knew the woman I painted, what kind of clothing she was wearing, and what tree she was holding onto. I received all kinds of questions and answered to the best of my ability. Then, I heard a familiar voice. It was the voice of my angel.

"Hmm, she is the one...The one that you are in love with."

"Yes, she is," I replied.

"Was she covered in a sari on the train?"

"No, she wasn't," I replied.

"Was this an image from your dream?"

"Yes, it was," I replied.

"Is she that beautiful in reality?"

"She certainly is," I replied.

Miss Yang moved closer to the display board. She examined the painting as if she had all the time in the world. Her hmm's indicated that she did not understand the creation. Then her aaah's indicated that she was impressed with the creation. Her overall reaction was impossible to predict, so I was left with no choice but to ask her, "So, what do you think?"

Miss Yang turned. She then concentrated on my face. As she talked, I was able to perceive the water in her eyes. "This is your best painting. There is a message in this painting, a message which is for you. Malcolm, it has a message that only you understand. We as viewers can only appreciate the excellence of this painting, but it is you who understands what it stands for."

I was awakened by her comment. You know why, Suzy? Simply because Miss Yang was correct. I did not expect others to understand my painting. I did not expect others to interpret what it stood for or what it meant. This was the first time I did not completely paint for others — for the professors, for the courses, and for the grades. Instead, I completely painted for myself, like I used to back in the day. I wanted others to notice its beauty, her beauty. And I do believe that my creation was noticed.

While Miss Yang and I conversed, guests passed by with sincere compliments and various questions. I responded to both compliments and questions with a beaming face. I was glad to have a constant flow of people nearby my area. Most of them were intrigued by the Indian wife waiting for her beloved husband's presence. In more detail, she was garbed in a yellow sari made of pure cotton. Her attire included gold earrings, gold bangles, and gold anklets. She held onto a blossoming jasmine tree while her teary eyes looked at the pathway. Her eyes desired to see the person she loved. Where was he? How was he? Will he ever return? These were the questions circulating in her brain.

After the first thirty minutes, the movement within the hall simmered down. Lots of people were discussing the painting and painters in small crowds. Some people were located at the snacks and beverages table. Others, who chose not to view all forty-five paintings, decided to exit the hall. At last, I received the opportunity to breathe in. Not that I am complaining, but I disliked overfilled areas. The halls were so congested that I had difficulty inhaling air. I needed to step outside for a breath of fresh air. Miss Yang agreed.

"Don't worry, Malcolm. I will stand here for you. And whenever someone passes by, I will let them know that it is my son who created this painting," she said, pride in her voice.

As soon as I inched towards the front doors, I felt a tap on my shoulder.

"Sorry for being latey waitey."

Suzy, I knew who tapped my shoulder. There is no one else in this world who utters phrases like latey waitey other than Mrs. Krishnaswami. At once, I turned around to embrace her. She was held for a dozen seconds before I said, "Thank you so much for coming."

"Thank you so much for the invitation. My family and I feel honored to be part of such a momentous day in your life."

I was introduced to Mr. Krishnaswami, Pallav, and Pallavi. Mrs. Krishnaswami sounded lively when introducing her husband, son, and daughter. The angel behaved like she was introducing royalty to her family. Suzy, I was no person of royal blood or status, but at that moment, I did not mind the feeling of importance. After the handshakes were executed and the warm smiles faded, I signaled for Miss Yang to come near. Once she did, I introduced my one and only family member.

"Everyone, I would like you to meet the person behind my achievements in life. I am who I am only because of her. She is my mother, father, and friend."

Intervening between the emotional words, Mrs. Krishnaswami said, "This must be the ever-so-famous Miss Yang. It is a pleasure to finally meet you."

Both angels embraced one another. Both mothers uniting was a dream come true. I secretly wished for them to meet, and finally, they did.

As the women conversed, I scrutinized Mr. Krishnaswami. He is a tall, lean, and well-dressed man. His complexion is brown. His nose is sharp. His chin is round. His eyes are protected by spectacles. Suzy, I do not like judging others without knowing them, but my first reaction to Mr. Krishnaswami was that he is a stern, silent type of person. I was not keen to start a conversation with him.

My eyes then fell upon Pallav, who is not Mrs. Krishnaswami's only son. I am sorry, Pallav, but your mother has another son. And that son is Malcolm. Pallav resembles his father in terms of appearance. He is also tall and lean. Even Pallav has a sharp nose and round chin. The immature acne on his face specified that he is a teenager. For some odd reason, I felt that he was a bit timid. After the handshake, he did not say a word. He did not say a word to me, his father, his mother, or his sister. Perhaps he did not want to be present at the exhibition. He may have been forced to attend the event.

After some time, I lifted my eyes from the boring Pallav and shifted them onto his sister, Pallavi. First and foremost, I have to say that Pallavi is an unusual name. I still don't know what it means. I will have to look it up in my Hindi dictionary. She is older than I am. She is between twenty-five to thirty years of age. In terms of appearance, she was a mixture of both her father and mother. It seemed as if both children inherited their father's sharp nose. Pallavi's nose was sharper than sharp. It was definitely noticeable. But what captured my sight were her extensive locks. Like her mother, she also had hair descending to her waist. Unlike her father and brother, she unveiled her personality. She kept a permanent grin on her face that was not once removed. She made sure to involve herself in the conversations. On top of that, she did not let the massive crowd and nonstop commotion inside the halls faze her.

When the angels finished conversing, I felt the urge to present my creation to Mrs. Krishnaswami and her family. I wanted to see her reaction to my painting. Since the painting was all India and all Indian, there was no disappointing Mrs. Krishnaswami.

As I elaborated on the painted woman and tree, Mr. Krishnaswami paid close attention. However, Pallav was in another hemisphere. He did not listen to a word I said or was saying.

As for Pallavi, she looked intrigued. I felt that she had plenty of questions to ask, but since I was talking, she decided not to interfere. Well, the daughter did not interfere, but her mother did. At first, I thought Mrs. Krishnaswami had a silly-willy type of question or comment on her mind. But when I observed her facial expressions, it distinctly expressed that I was in for a surprise.

"Hmm...I have seen her. Yes, the woman in the painting, I have seen her," she said while tapping her lips with the index finger.
"What?" I burst in elation. "When and where? Do you know her? Is she related to you?"
"No, no, no...Not every Indian is related to me," she replied in a humorous tone. "I can't recall, but I have seen her. Wait, a second...I bumped into her minutes ago."

I was about to lose my head. I was overwhelmed by all sorts of feelings. I was a bit shocked. I was a bit confused. I was a bit nervous. And I was a bit excited. "Was Mrs. Krishnaswami saying what I wanted her to say? Was I about to hear what I wanted to hear? The woman from the train...Was she actually here? Was she here at the exhibition, inside the halls, looking at different paintings?" I asked myself.

"Malcolm...Malcolm...Are you okay?" Miss Yang snapped her fingers.
Returning to my senses, I answered her question, "Yes, I am fine."
"Malcolm, is she the one? Is she the woman you encountered on the train?" asked Mrs. Krishnaswami while gazing at my painting.
I responded with a nod. Along with Mrs. Krishnaswami and Miss Yang, I too searched the halls for her ravishing face. It was hard to believe that the woman of my dreams, the woman with whom I feel a connection, the woman who I love wholeheartedly, was located somewhere inside the halls.

"Malcolm, your **lovey-dovey** is here somewhere. I have seen her with my own eyes. By God, she is a **beauty-sheuty**. You must find her," said Mrs. Krishnaswami.
"Or you can stand here and let her come to you," added Miss Yang.

At that moment, never before **had** I felt my heart pump so fast, never before **had** I listened to my heartbeat so loud. I asked myself, "Am I suffering from heart palpitations?" Obviously, I was. Nervous and excited, I stood by my painting as the faithful painter. Ruminating on what Miss Yang had said, I decided to let fate take charge. Besides, whatever is destined to happen **will** surely happen. Will it not, Suzy?

An hour **into** the event, Miss Yang, Mrs. Krishnaswami, and her family members set forth into the crowd to behold other paintings. Suzy, I did not feel envious that my invitees went to explore and examine other paintings. I was the one who encouraged them. Since the event ran for three hours, I advised them to view every painting. After all, these various creations were a delight for the eyes. With no company, I was left to meditate on her. I paced back and forth near my painting. I needed to see her. I needed to talk to her. I needed her to witness my creation. I had a tempting impulse to leave my post, but that was not possible. To neglect the guests who attended the event was discourteous. What if someone had a question about my painting and I was not there? That was not acceptable.

Despite my feet insisting **on beginning** a search for the woman on the train, I remained idle. To keep busy, I reflected **on** her face when she first made eye contact. Her eyes had plenty to say. **They asked** questions such as, "Have I seen you before? Did we meet sometime in this lifetime? Why do I feel as if we are connected?" Perhaps **these questions were not hers but mine**. Who knows? She may not have thought or felt anything. "She probably does not remember the encounter. She probably does not remember my face. She probably did not even feel a connection between us," I said to myself. Back and forth I went, from hope to hopelessness, endeavoring to understand her. And then I fell silent. My brain had ceased and my lips were sealed. Her presence **was discerned**.

As she gracefully walked in the midst of hundreds of unclear faces, my eyes **welled up**. Though I did not let the water descend onto my skin. It was restrained, prevented from independence. In my direction, she came with the halting of time and movement. Placing my eyes upon her, I did not consider time. Time had become a mere factor. Everything was **at a standstill**. There was no movement from others. And even if there was movement, my senses were too **focused** on her to notice. At that moment, I considered a motion to be a distraction. I did not want others to block her path as she came near. Every couple of seconds our eyes interacted. It was as if our eyes were flirting with one another. Indeed, my eyes flirted more than hers.

When she was not **making eye contact**, I let my eyes absorb the stylish garb on her body. Her outfit was fetching. The woman from the train was not dressed in a traditional sari or casual jeans and top. For this event, she was dressed in formal attire. It was a gown, not too fancy and not too flashy. The elegantly demure gown had a wide neckline that ran horizontally. It revealed her perfectly shaped collarbone. Other than her collarbone, the sleeveless gown exposed her partially toned arms. The royal blue gown, which descended to her toes, was made of fine polyester. In my **point of view**, the gown and its color were ideal for the private event.

I was surprised by the number of adolescent guests and students who **were dressed** in loud colors, precisely because the event involved artistry and creativity. It is not that only bright colors define art and everything related to it. Bold and dull colors matter too. The only bright colors associated with her were the noticeable lipstick and impactful mascara on her face. Unlike other women, she was not caked with makeup. The beauty that I perceived was more **natural than artificial**.

I was inches away from her when she positioned herself beside me, shoulder to shoulder. I capitalized **on** the moment by inhaling the fragrance she wore. The fragrance **was** a combination of jasmine and lavender. Surely an odd combination, but the scent itself made her exotic. She faced the picture, which contained no one else but her. Well, Suzy, do you think she recognized herself in the painting? She did not move an inch or say a word. I expected a reaction—some kind of reaction, any kind of reaction. Situated behind her as she embraced the painting, I waited for praise or insult. Either **would** do, as long as she did not inform the police that some creeper had painted an image of her and was exhibiting it to others without her approval. At that moment, I was a bit concerned. "I might be in trouble," I said under my breath.

It seemed like I **had waited** for this moment my entire life. This was the moment—the moment to talk to her, the moment to express how I truly felt. But my heart and brain were not supportive. My heart kept pumping the lines, "Talk to her, introduce yourself, ask for her name," while my brain kept reiterating the phrase, "She will sue, she will sue, she will sue." Will she sue? Can she sue? On what grounds **could** she sue? I let my brain take control with questions that disturbed me until she voiced a word.

"Exquisite..."

"Pardon?" I said intentionally, wishing for her to elaborate.

"If I had one word to describe the painting, I'd choose exquisite." Her voice was pleasant and relaxing. There was no hint of an Indian accent in her words. When she turned, I was unable to remove my stare. Never before **had** she been this close. The moment felt unreal. I had an urge to pinch myself. But this was reality; she was real, and she really was in front of me. I searched for her lips—not for a kiss, but for more words. Though I must admit, her lips on mine would **not** be a bad idea.

"Have we met before?" she asked.

"Perhaps, in another place, another time, another life," I replied. My answer confused her.

But it also confused me. Why and how that saying emerged, I have no idea. Suzy, it was as if someone else was talking in my place. Strange!

"Is this...Ahhh...Is that supposed to be...Umm...This woman in the painting, is that me?" she said, stumbling over her words.

I was forced to smile after viewing her nervousness. "That is you. It's you in India, under a jasmine tree, dressed in a sari."

"What?" she exclaimed. "I have never been to India. My parents are from South India, but I have never visited Chennai. Wait, wait, wait...Have you ever seen me in traditional Indian clothing?"

"No, I haven't! But I did see you on the train. Don't you remember that?" I winced before and after proposing the question.

"I...I do...Yes, I remember New Year's Eve. But, you know what? I don't understand the painting."

"Well, I am glad you remember the encounter on New Year's Eve. As for the painting, it's entirely visionary. One day, I was thinking about you, and I was led to an image of you standing under the jasmine tree, dressed in a sari with earrings, bangles, and whatnot."

It was not until I looked at her face that I noticed she **had turned** blushing red. With a slight grin on her face, she lowered her eyes. "So, for the art exhibition, you decided to submit a painting of me?"

My heart sank. I hesitated before replying, "I understand that your permission was necessary. But I don't know your name. I don't know where you live. I don't know where you work. And I don't know your phone number. It was impossible to meet or contact you. I know that my reasons may sound like excuses...I'm sorry."

"Don't worry, I will not sue you," she said before tittering. "Instead, I thank you. The painting is magnificent. I am not saying that I am exquisite or magnificent. It is the painting and the hands of the painter that deserve the credit."

"Well, thank you. Whatever I paint comes from the real world and my dreams. Basically, whatever I find attractive in the real world and whatever I find significantly influential in my dreams is what I paint on the canvas."

"Hmm...The real world...So that means you find me attractive."

"Yes, I do."

Her comments lifted my spirit. The **inoffensive** manner in which she talked encouraged me to communicate freely and openly. Never did I imagine the conversation between us would be so effortless. I fretted, fretted, and fretted. I thought this and I thought that.

How to approach her, how not to approach her, what to say to her, what not to say to her—these questions were eating my brain consistently. In the end, there I was, conversing naturally and fluently with the woman who tiptoed into my heart. And when I talked to her, I felt as if we had talked for years, centuries, or even lifetimes.

To progress the conversation, I tried my **best** to initiate small talk. "So...I have never seen you on campus. Does that mean you are a guest at the exhibition?"

"Yes, my cousin is the one who graduated. She and her painting are both located near the entrance of the halls. I am so fortunate to attend this event. If it **were not** for the exhibition, I'd never come across a talented person like you."

I wanted to ask for her cousin's name but thankfully restrained myself. Suzy, I did not even ask for her name, and there I was, prepared to ask for her cousin's name. At times, I can be so dumb.

"Umm...I'm sorry for not asking before...What is your name?"

"My name is Vyjanti," she replied.

"It is a pleasure to meet you, Vyjanti. My name is Malcolm," I stalled for a moment until I met eyes with Miss Yang, "Malcolm Yang." It was the first time I called myself a Yang. And I was proud—very proud that I did. I was no longer an Only.

Vyjanti looked at me in disbelief. "Are you serious?"

"Yes, that's my name. And that lady over there," I pointed to Miss Yang, "she is my mother."

I wanted to ask for her cousin's name but thankfully restrained myself. Suzy, I did not even ask for her name, and there I was, prepared to ask for her cousin's name. At times, I can be so dumb.

"Umm...I'm sorry for not asking before...What is your name?"

"My name is Vyjanti," she replied.

"It is a pleasure to meet you, Vyjanti. My name is Malcolm," I stalled for a moment until I met eyes with Miss Yang, "Malcolm Yang." It was the first time I called myself a Yang. And I was proud—very proud that I did. I was no longer an Only.

Vyjanti looked at me in disbelief. "Are you serious?"

"Yes, that's my name. And that lady over there," I pointed to Miss Yang, "she is my mother."

9 781069 227287